# IRWIN SHAW
# SHORT STORIES:
# FIVE DECADES

Published by
Dell Publishing Co., Inc.
1 Dag Hammarskjold Plaza
New York, New York 10017

Some of the stories in this volume have appeared in *Accent, Collier's Weekly, Esquire, Harper's, Harper's Bazaar, McCall's, Mademoiselle, The New Republic, The New Yorker, New York Herald Tribune, Playboy, Redbook, The Saturday Evening Post, Story Magazine,* and *This Week.*

Laurel ® TM 674623, Dell Publishing Co., Inc.

ISBN: 0-440-34075-6

Reprinted by arrangement with Delacorte Press
Printed in the United States of America
First Laurel printing—January 1983

LAUREL

# Irwin Shaw Short Stories:
# Five Decades

"A rich feast of a book. . . . [Shaw is] a master craftsman of the short story . . . a shrewd and intelligent observer in perfect step with his times. . . . His stories move and inform, and, God forbid, they entertain."

—BRUCE JAY FRIEDMAN, *Esquire*

"There is never a wrong word, a phrase that makes you stop, reread, make sure you've gotten the sense right. . . . Coupled with the narrative gift is the ability to write with an ease and a clarity that only Fitzgerald had."

—*The New York Times Book Review*

"There is something in this collection for everyone."

—*The Wall Street Journal*

"Stories which, once read . . . [stay] with you the rest of your life. . . . [Shaw] put in five decades . . . turning out the kind of good hard declarative sentences that are about as easy to accomplish as a triple play on every play of every game every day in the year."

—JERRY TALLMER, *New York Post*

"A record of Shaw's durability as a storyteller, this collection demonstrates his persistent interest in the private truths that underlie social facades, and the lost opportunities that bedevil us all."

—*The Washington Post Book World*

"Shaw obviously revels in storytelling for its own sake and easily communicates his pleasure in man's quirky and ironic progress . . . his moral insights rarely overburden the humanity of his characters. . . . Many pieces capture perfectly the modulations of mood and event in experience. . . . A fine and varied collection."

—*Library Journal*

"He is a genuine professional. . . . He has a sharp and penetrating eye for social nuance and he is unfailingly entertaining. . . . He sees clearly, he understands what he sees, and he describes it pointedly. [These stories] are the work of a writer who knows what he is doing and . . . does it very well indeed."

—JONATHAN YARDLEY, *Book World*

*To Arthur Stanton*

# Contents

# Introduction

I am a product of my times. I remember the end of World War I, the bells and whistles and cheering, and as an adolescent I profited briefly from the boom years. I suffered the Depression; exulted at the election of Franklin D. Roosevelt; drank my first glass of legal 3.2 beer the day Prohibition ended; mourned over Spain; listened to the Communist sirens; sensed the coming of World War II; went to that war; was shamed by the McCarthy era; saw the rebirth of Europe; marveled at the new generations of students; admired Kennedy; mourned over Vietnam. I have been both praised and blamed, all the while living my private life the best way I could.

I have written stories in Brooklyn, Greenwich Village, on Fifth Avenue, in the *New Yorker* office on 43rd Street, in Connecticut, Cairo, Algiers, London, Paris, Rome, the Basque country, on ships, in the Alps, in the Mojave Desert, and bits and pieces on transcontinental trains.

All these things, in one way or another, are reflected in my stories, which I now see as a record of the events of almost sixty years, all coming together in the imagination of one American. Of course there are gaps. Other writers have filled many of these but some remain and will never be filled.

Why does a man spend fifty years of his life in an occupation that is often painful? I once told a class I was teaching that writing is an intellectual contact sport, similar in some respects to football. The effort required can be exhausting, the goal unreached, and you are hurt on almost every play; but that doesn't deprive a man or a boy from getting peculiar pleasures from the game.

In a preface to an earlier collection I described some of those pleasures. Among them, I wrote, there is the reward of the storyteller, sitting cross-legged in the bazaar, filling the need of humanity in the humdrum course of the ordinary day for magic and distant wonders, for disguised moralizing that will set everyday transactions into larger perspectives, for the compression of great matters into digestible portions, for the shaping of mysteries into sharply edged and comprehensible symbols.

Then there is the private and exquisite reward of escaping from the laws of consistency. Today you are sad and you tell a sad story. Tomorrow you are happy and your tale is a joyful one. You remember a woman whom you loved wholeheartedly and you celebrate her memory. You suffer from the wound of a woman who treated you badly and you denigrate womanhood. A saint has touched you and you are a priest. God has neglected you and you preach atheism.

In a novel or a play you must be a whole man. In a collection of stories you can be all the men or fragments of men, worthy and unworthy, who in different seasons abound in you. It is a luxury not to be scorned.

Originally this book was intended to contain all of my stories, but when the count was made the total came to eighty-four, and to include them all would have meant a formidably bulky and outrageously expensive book. Since my publishers and I agreed that we did not wish to produce a volume that the reader could neither carry nor afford, we fixed on sixty-three stories as a reasonable number and began the sad process of winnowing out the ones we would leave behind. It was a little like being the commander of a besieged town who knows he cannot evacuate all his troops and is forced to decide who shall go and who shall stay to be overrun by the enemy. And the enemy in this case might be oblivion.

The experience of going through the stories was also something like what is supposed to happen when a man is drowning, as scene after scene of his life passes before his eyes. If the drowning man is devout, it can be imagined that in those final moments he examines the scenes to determine the balance between his sins and his virtues with a view toward eventual salvation. Since I am not particularly devout, my chances for salvation lie in a place sometime in the future on a library shelf. These stories were selected, often with doubts and misgivings, with the hope that a spot on that distant shelf is waiting for them.

—IRWIN SHAW

1978

# The Eighty-Yard Run

The pass was high and wide and he jumped for it, feeling it slap flatly against his hands, as he shook his hips to throw off the halfback who was diving at him. The center floated by, his hands desperately brushing Darling's knee as Darling picked his feet up high and delicately ran over a blocker and an opposing linesman in a jumble on the ground near the scrimmage line. He had ten yards in the clear and picked up speed, breathing easily, feeling his thigh pads rising and falling against his legs, listening to the sound of cleats behind him, pulling away from them, watching the other backs heading him off toward the sideline, the whole picture, the men closing in on him, the blockers fighting for position, the ground he had to cross, all suddenly clear in his head, for the first time in his life not a meaningless confusion of men, sounds, speed. He smiled a little to himself as he ran, holding the ball lightly in front of him with his two hands, his knees pumping high, his hips twisting in the almost girlish run of a back in a broken field. The first halfback came at him and he fed him his leg, then swung at the last moment, took the shock of the man's shoulder without breaking stride, ran right through him, his cleats biting securely into the turf. There was only the safety man now, coming warily at him, his arms crooked, hands spread. Darling tucked the ball in, spurted at him, driving hard, hurling himself along, his legs pounding, knees high, all two hundred pounds bunched into controlled attack. He was sure he was going to get past the safety man. Without thought, his arms and legs working beautifully together, he headed right for the safety man, stiff-armed him, feeling blood spurt instantaneously from the man's nose onto his hand, seeing his face go awry, head turned, mouth pulled to one side. He pivoted away, keeping the arm locked, dropping the safety man as he ran easily toward the goal line, with the drumming of cleats diminishing behind him.

How long ago? It was autumn then, and the ground was getting hard because the nights were cold and leaves from the maples around the stadium blew across the practice fields in gusts of wind, and the girls were beginning to put polo coats over their sweaters when they came to watch practice in the afternoons. . . . Fifteen years. Darling walked slowly over the same ground in the spring twilight, in his neat shoes, a man of thirty-five dressed in a double-breasted suit, ten pounds heavier in the fifteen years, but not fat, with the years between 1925 and 1940 showing in his face.

The coach was smiling quietly to himself and the assistant coaches were looking at each other with pleasure the way they always did when one of the second stringers suddenly did something fine, bringing credit to them, making their $2,000 a year a tiny bit more secure.

Darling trotted back, smiling, breathing deeply but easily, feeling wonderful, not tired, though this was the tail end of practice and he'd run eighty yards. The sweat poured off his face and soaked his jersey and he liked the feeling, the warm moistness lubricating his skin like oil. Off in a corner of the field some players were punting and the smack of leather against the ball came pleasantly through the afternoon air. The freshmen were running signals on the next field and the quarterback's sharp voice, the pound of the eleven pairs of cleats, the ''Dig, now *dig!*'' of the coaches, the laughter of the players all somehow made him feel happy as he trotted back to midfield, listening to the applause and shouts of the students along the sidelines, knowing that after that run the coach would have to start him Saturday against Illinois.

Fifteen years, Darling thought, remembering the shower after the workout, the hot water steaming off his skin and the deep soapsuds and all the young voices singing with the water streaming down and towels going and managers running in and out and the sharp sweet smell of oil of wintergreen and everybody clapping him on the back as he dressed and Packard, the captain, who took being captain very seriously, coming over to him and shaking his hand and saying, ''Darling, you're going to go places in the next two years.''

The assistant manager fussed over him, wiping a cut on his leg with alcohol and iodine, the little sting making him realize suddenly how fresh and whole and solid his body felt. The manager slapped a piece of adhesive tape over the cut, and Darling noticed the sharp clean white of the tape against the ruddiness of the skin, fresh from the shower.

He dressed slowly, the softness of his shirt and the soft warmth of his wool socks and his flannel trousers a reward against his skin after the harsh pressure of the shoulder harness and thigh and hip pads. He drank three glasses of cold water, the liquid reaching down coldly inside of him, soothing the harsh dry places in his throat and belly left by the sweat and running and shouting of practice.

Fifteen years.

The sun had gone down and the sky was green behind the stadium and he laughed quietly to himself as he looked at the stadium, rearing above the trees, and knew that on Saturday when the 70,000 voices roared as the team came running out onto the field, part of that enormous salute would be for him. He walked slowly, listening to the gravel crunch satisfactorily under his shoes in the still twilight, feeling his clothes swing lightly against his skin, breathing the thin evening air, feeling the wind move softly in his damp hair, wonderfully cool behind his ears and at the nape of his neck.

Louise was waiting for him at the road, in her car. The top was down and he noticed all over again, as he always did when he saw her, how pretty she was, the rough blonde hair and the large, inquiring eyes and the bright mouth, smiling now.

She threw the door open. "Were you good today?" she asked.

"Pretty good," he said. He climbed in, sank luxuriously into the soft leather, stretched his legs far out. He smiled, thinking of the eighty yards. "Pretty damn good."

She looked at him seriously for a moment, then scrambled around, like a little girl, kneeling on the seat next to him, grabbed him, her hands along his ears, and kissed him as he sprawled, head back, on the seat cushion. She let go of him, but kept her head close to his, over his. Darling reached up slowly and rubbed the back of his hand against her cheek, lit softly by a street lamp a hundred feet away. They looked at each other, smiling.

Louise drove down to the lake and they sat there silently, watching the moon rise behind the hills on the other side. Finally he reached over, pulled her gently to him, kissed her. Her lips grew soft, her body sank into his, tears formed slowly in her eyes. He knew, for the first time, that he could do whatever he wanted with her.

"Tonight," he said. "I'll call for you at seven-thirty. Can you get out?"

She looked at him. She was smiling, but the tears were still full in her eyes. "All right," she said. "I'll get out. How about you? Won't the coach raise hell?"

Darling grinned. "I got the coach in the palm of my hand," he said. "Can you wait till seven-thirty?"

She grinned back at him. "No," she said.

They kissed and she started the car and they went back to town for dinner. He sang on the way home.

Christian Darling, thirty-five years old, sat on the frail spring grass, greener now than it ever would be again on the practice field, looked thoughtfully up at the stadium, a deserted ruin in the twilight. He had started on the first team that Saturday and every Saturday after that for the next two years, but it had never been as satisfactory as it should have been. He never had broken away, the longest run he'd ever made was thirty-five yards, and that in a game that was already won, and then that kid had come up from the third team, Diederich, a blank-faced German kid from Wisconsin, who ran like a bull, ripping lines to pieces Saturday after Saturday, plowing through, never getting hurt, never changing his expression, scoring more points, gaining more ground than all the rest of the team put together, making everybody's All-American, carrying the ball three times out of four, keeping everybody else out of the headlines. Darling was a good blocker and he spent his Saturday afternoons working on the big Swedes and Polacks who played tackle and end for Michigan, Illinois, Purdue, hurling into huge pile-ups, bobbing his head wildly to elude the great raw hands swinging like meat-cleavers at him as he went charging in to open up holes for Diederich coming through like a locomotive behind him. Still, it wasn't so bad. Everybody liked him and he did his job and he was pointed out on the campus and boys always felt important when they introduced their girls to him at their proms, and Louise loved him and watched him faithfully in the games, even in the mud, when your own mother wouldn't know you, and drove him around in her car keeping the top down because she was proud of him and wanted to show everybody that she was Christian Darling's girl. She bought him crazy presents because her father was rich, watches, pipes, humidors, an icebox for beer for his room, curtains, wallets, a fifty-dollar dictionary.

"You'll spend every cent your old man owns," Darling protested once when she showed up at his rooms with seven different packages in her arms and tossed them onto the couch.

"Kiss me," Louise said, "and shut up."

"Do you want to break your poor old man?"

"I don't mind. I want to buy you presents."

"Why?"

"It makes me feel good. Kiss me. I don't know why. Did you know that you're an important figure?"

"Yes," Darling said gravely.

"When I was waiting for you at the library yesterday two girls saw you coming and one of them said to the other, 'That's Christian Darling. He's an important figure.' "

"You're a liar."

"I'm in love with an important figure."

"Still, why the hell did you have to give me a forty-pound dictionary?"

"I wanted to make sure," Louise said, "that you had a token of my esteem. I want to smother you in tokens of my esteem."

Fifteen years ago.

They'd married when they got out of college. There'd been other women for him, but all casual and secret, more for curiosity's sake, and vanity, women who'd thrown themselves at him and flattered him, a pretty mother at a summer camp for boys, an old girl from his home town who'd suddenly blossomed into a coquette, a friend of Louise's who had dogged him grimly for six months and had taken advantage of the two weeks that Louise went home when her mother died. Perhaps Louise had known, but she'd kept quiet, loving him completely, filling his rooms with presents, religiously watching him battling with the big Swedes and Polacks on the line of scrimmage on Saturday afternoons, making plans for marrying him and living with him in New York and going with him there to the night clubs, the theaters, the good restaurants, being proud of him in advance, tall, white-teethed, smiling, large, yet moving lightly, with an athlete's grace, dressed in evening clothes, approvingly eyed by magnificently dressed and famous women in theater lobbies, with Louise adoringly at his side.

Her father, who manufactured inks, set up a New York office for Darling to manage and presented him with three hundred accounts, and they lived on Beekman Place with a view of the river with fifteen thousand dollars a year between them, because everybody was buying everything in those days, including ink. They saw all the shows and went to all the speakeasies and spent their fifteen thousand dollars a year and in the afternoons Louise went to the art galleries and the matinees of the more serious plays that Darling didn't like to sit through and Darling slept with a girl who danced in the chorus of *Rosalie* and with the wife of a man who owned three copper mines. Darling played squash three times a week and remained as solid as a stone barn and Louise never took her eyes off him when they were in the same room together, watching him with a secret, miser's smile, with a trick of coming over to him in the middle of a crowded room and saying gravely, in a low

17

voice, "You're the handsomest man I've ever seen in my whole life. Want a drink?"

Nineteen twenty-nine came to Darling and to his wife and father-in-law, the maker of inks, just as it came to everyone else. The father-in-law waited until 1933 and then blew his brains out and when Darling went to Chicago to see what the books of the firm looked like he found out all that was left were debts and three or four gallons of unbought ink.

"Please, Christian," Louise said, sitting in their neat Beekman Place apartment, with a view of the river and prints of paintings by Dufy and Braque and Picasso on the wall, "please, why do you want to start drinking at two o'clock in the afternoon?"

"I have nothing else to do," Darling said, putting down his glass, emptied of its fourth drink. "Please pass the whisky."

Louise filled his glass. "Come take a walk with me," she said. "We'll walk along the river."

"I don't want to walk along the river," Darling said, squinting intensely at the prints of paintings by Dufy, Braque and Picasso.

"We'll walk along Fifth Avenue."

"I don't want to walk along Fifth Avenue."

"Maybe," Louise said gently, "you'd like to come with me to some art galleries. There's an exhibition by a man named Klee. . . ."

"I don't want to go to any art galleries. I want to sit here and drink Scotch whisky," Darling said. "Who the hell hung those goddam pictures up on the wall?"

"I did," Louise said.

"I hate them."

"I'll take them down," Louise said.

"Leave them there. It gives me something to do in the afternoon. I can hate them." Darling took a long swallow. "Is that the way people paint these days?"

"Yes, Christian. Please don't drink any more."

"Do you like painting like that?"

"Yes, dear."

"Really?"

"Really."

Darling looked carefully at the prints once more. "Little Louise Tucker. The middle-western beauty. I like pictures with horses in them. Why should you like pictures like that?"

"I just happen to have gone to a lot of galleries in the last few years . . ."

"Is that what you do in the afternoon?"

"That's what I do in the afternoon," Louise said.

"I drink in the afternoon."

Louise kissed him lightly on the top of his head as he sat there squinting at the pictures on the wall, the glass of whisky held firmly in his hand. She put on her coat and went out without saying another word. When she came back in the early evening, she had a job on a woman's fashion magazine.

They moved downtown and Louise went out to work every morning and Darling sat home and drank and Louise paid the bills as they came up. She made believe she was going to quit work as soon as Darling found a job, even though she was taking over more responsibility day by day at the magazine, interviewing authors, picking painters for the illustrations and covers, getting actresses to pose for pictures, going out for drinks with the right people, making a thousand new friends whom she loyally introduced to Darling.

"I don't like your hat," Darling said, once, when she came in in the evening and kissed him, her breath rich with Martinis.

"What's the matter with my hat, Baby?" she asked, running her fingers through his hair. "Everybody says it's very smart."

"It's too damned smart," he said. "It's not for you. It's for a rich, sophisticated woman of thirty-five with admirers."

Louise laughed. "I'm practicing to be a rich, sophisticated woman of thirty-five with admirers," she said. He stared soberly at her. "Now, don't look so grim, Baby. It's still the same simple little wife under the hat." She took the hat off, threw it into a corner, sat on his lap. "See? Homebody Number One."

"Your breath could run a train," Darling said, not wanting to be mean, but talking out of boredom, and sudden shock at seeing his wife curiously a stranger in a new hat, with a new expression in her eyes under the little brim, secret, confident, knowing.

Louise tucked her head under his chin so he couldn't smell her breath. "I had to take an author out for cocktails," she said. "He's a boy from the Ozark Mountains and he drinks like a fish. He's a Communist."

"What the hell is a Communist from the Ozarks doing writing for a woman's fashion magazine?"

Louise chuckled. "The magazine business is getting all mixed up these days. The publishers want to have a foot in every camp. And anyway, you can't find an author under seventy these days who isn't a Communist."

"I don't think I like you to associate with all those people, Louise," Darling said. "Drinking with them."

"He's a very nice, gentle boy," Louise said. "He reads Ernest Dowson."

"Who's Ernest Dowson?"

Louise patted his arm, stood up, fixed her hair. "He's an English poet."

Darling felt that somehow he had disappointed her. "Am I supposed to know who Ernest Dowson is?"

"No, dear. I'd better go in and take a bath."

After she had gone, Darling went over to the corner where the hat was lying and picked it up. It was nothing, a scrap of straw, a red flower, a veil, meaningless on his big hand, but on his wife's head a signal of something . . . big city, smart and knowing women drinking and dining with men other than their husbands, conversation about things a normal man wouldn't know much about, Frenchmen who painted as though they used their elbows instead of brushes, composers who wrote whole symphonies without a single melody in them, writers who knew all about politics and women who knew all about writers, the movement of the proletariat, Marx, somehow mixed up with five-dollar dinners and the best-looking women in America and fairies who made them laugh and half-sentences immediately understood and secretly hilarious and wives who called their husbands "Baby." He put the hat down, a scrap of straw and a red flower, and a little veil. He drank some whisky straight and went into the bathroom where his wife was lying deep in her bath, singing to herself and smiling from time to time like a little girl, paddling the water gently with her hands, sending up a slight spicy fragrance from the bath salts she used.

He stood over her, looking down at her. She smiled up at him, her eyes half closed, her body pink and shimmering in the warm, scented water. All over again, with all the old suddenness, he was hit deep inside him with the knowledge of how beautiful she was, how much he needed her.

"I came in here," he said, "to tell you I wish you wouldn't call me 'Baby.' "

She looked up at him from the bath, her eyes quickly full of sorrow, half-understanding what he meant. He knelt and put his arms around her, his sleeves plunged heedlessly in the water, his shirt and jacket soaking wet as he clutched her wordlessly, holding her crazily tight, crushing her breath from her, kissing her desperately, searchingly, regretfully.

He got jobs after that, selling real estate and automobiles, but somehow, although he had a desk with his name on a wooden wedge on it, and he went to the office religiously at nine each morning, he never managed to sell anything and he never made any money.

Louise was made assistant editor, and the house was always full of strange men and women who talked fast and got angry on abstract subjects like mural painting, novelists, labor unions. Negro short-story writers drank Louise's liquor, and a lot of Jews, and big solemn men with scarred faces and knotted hands who talked slowly but clearly about picket lines and battles with guns and leadpipe at mine-shaft-heads and in front of factory gates. And Louise moved among them all, confidently, knowing what they were talking about, with opinions that they listened to and argued about just as though she were a man. She knew everybody, condescended to no one, devoured books that Darling had never heard of, walked along the streets of the city, excited, at home, soaking in all the million tides of New York without fear, with constant wonder.

Her friends liked Darling and sometimes he found a man who wanted to get off in the corner and talk about the new boy who played fullback for Princeton, and the decline of the double wing-back, or even the state of the stock market, but for the most part he sat on the edge of things, solid and quiet in the high storm of words. "The dialectics of the situation . . . The theater has been given over to expert jugglers . . . Picasso? What man has a right to paint old bones and collect ten thousand dollars for them? . . . I stand firmly behind Trotsky . . . Poe was the last American critic. When he died they put lilies on the grave of American criticism. I don't say this because they panned my last book, but . . . ."

Once in a while he caught Louise looking soberly and consideringly at him through the cigarette smoke and the noise and he avoided her eyes and found an excuse to get up and go into the kitchen for more ice or to open another bottle.

"Come on," Cathal Flaherty was saying, standing at the door with a girl, "you've got to come down and see this. It's down on Fourteenth Street, in the old Civic Repertory, and you can only see it on Sunday nights and I guarantee you'll come out of the theater singing." Flaherty was a big young Irishman with a broken nose who was the lawyer for a longshoreman's union, and he had been hanging around the house for six months on and off, roaring and shutting everybody else up when he got in an argument. "It's a new play, *Waiting for Lefty;* it's about taxi-drivers."

"Odets," the girl with Flaherty said. "It's by a guy named Odets."

"I never heard of him," Darling said.

"He's a new one," the girl said.

"It's like watching a bombardment," Flaherty said. "I saw it last Sunday night. You've got to see it."

"Come on, Baby," Louise said to Darling, excitement in her eyes already. "We've been sitting in the Sunday *Times* all day, this'll be a great change."

"I see enough taxi-drivers every day," Darling said, not because he meant that, but because he didn't like to be around Flaherty, who said things that made Louise laugh a lot and whose judgment she accepted on almost every subject. "Let's go to the movies."

"You've never seen anything like this before," Flaherty said. "He wrote this play with a baseball bat."

"Come on," Louise coaxed, "I bet it's wonderful."

"He has long hair," the girl with Flaherty said. "Odets. I met him at a party. He's an actor. He didn't say a goddam thing all night."

"I don't feel like going down to Fourteenth Street," Darling said, wishing Flaherty and his girl would get out. "It's gloomy."

"Oh, hell!" Louise said loudly. She looked coolly at Darling, as though she'd just been introduced to him and was making up her mind about him, and not very favorably. He saw her looking at him, knowing there was something new and dangerous in her face and he wanted to say something, but Flaherty was there and his damned girl, and anyway, he didn't know what to say.

"I'm going," Louise said, getting her coat. "I don't think Fourteenth Street is gloomy."

"I'm telling you," Flaherty was saying, helping her on with her coat, "it's the Battle of Gettysburg, in Brooklynese."

"Nobody could get a word out of him," Flaherty's girl was saying as they went through the door. "He just sat there all night."

The door closed. Louise hadn't said good night to him. Darling walked around the room four times, then sprawled out on the sofa, on top of the Sunday *Times*. He lay there for five minutes looking at the ceiling, thinking of Flaherty walking down the street talking in that booming voice, between the girls, holding their arms.

Louise had looked wonderful. She'd washed her hair in the afternoon and it had been very soft and light and clung close to her head as she stood there angrily putting her coat on. Louise was getting prettier every year, partly because she knew by now how pretty she was, and made the most of it.

"Nuts," Darling said, standing up. "Oh, nuts."

He put on his coat and went down to the nearest bar and had five drinks off by himself in a corner before his money ran out.

The years since then had been foggy and downhill, Louise had been nice to him, and in a way, loving and kind, and they'd fought only once, when he said he was going to vote for Landon. ("Oh, Christ," she'd said, "doesn't *anything* happen inside your head? Don't you read the papers? The penniless Republican!") She'd been sorry later and apologized for hurting him, but apologized as she might to a child. He'd tried hard, had gone grimly to the art galleries, the concert halls, the bookshops, trying to gain on the trail of his wife, but it was no use. He was bored, and none of what he saw or heard or dutifully read made much sense to him and finally he gave it up. He had thought, many nights as he ate dinner alone, knowing that Louise would come home late and drop silently into bed without explanation, of getting a divorce, but he knew the loneliness, the hopelessness, of not seeing her again would be too much to take. So he was good, completely devoted, ready at all times to go any place with her, do anything she wanted. He even got a small job, in a broker's office and paid his own way, bought his own liquor.

Then he'd been offered the job of going from college to college as a tailor's representative. "We want a man," Mr. Rosenberg had said, "who as soon as you look at him, you say, 'There's a university man.'" Rosenberg had looked approvingly at Darling's broad shoulders and well-kept waist, at his carefully brushed hair and his honest, wrinkle-less face. "Frankly, Mr. Darling, I am willing to make you a proposition. I have inquired about you, you are favorably known on your old campus, I understand you were in the backfield with Alfred Diederich."

Darling nodded. "Whatever happened to him?"

"He is walking around in a cast for seven years now. An iron brace. He played professional football and they broke his neck for him."

Darling smiled. That, at least, had turned out well.

"Our suits are an easy product to sell, Mr. Darling," Rosenberg said. "We have a handsome, custom-made garment. What has Brooks Brothers got that we haven't got? A name. No more."

"I can make fifty, sixty dollars a week," Darling said to Louise that night. "And expenses. I can save some money and then come back to New York and really get started here."

"Yes, Baby," Louise said.

"As it is," Darling said carefully, "I can make it back here once a month, and holidays and the summer. We can see each other often."

"Yes, Baby." He looked at her face, lovelier now at thirty-five than it had ever been before, but fogged over now as it had been for five years with a kind of patient, kindly, remote boredom.

"What do you say?" he asked. "Should I take it?" Deep within him he hoped fiercely, longingly, for her to say, "No, Baby, you stay right here," but she said, as he knew she'd say, "I think you'd better take it."

He nodded. He had to get up and stand with his back to her, looking out the window, because there were things plain on his face that she had never seen in the fifteen years she'd known him. "Fifty dollars is a lot of money," he said. "I never thought I'd ever see fifty dollars again." He laughed. Louise laughed, too.

Christian Darling sat on the frail green grass of the practice field. The shadow of the stadium had reached out and covered him. In the distance the lights of the university shone a little mistily in the light haze of evening. Fifteen years. Flaherty even now was calling for his wife, buying her a drink, filling whatever bar they were in with that voice of his and that easy laugh. Darling half-closed his eyes, almost saw the boy fifteen years ago reach for the pass, slip the halfback, go skittering lightly down the field, his knees high and fast and graceful, smiling to himself because he knew he was going to get past the safety man. That was the high point, Darling thought, fifteen years ago, on an autumn afternoon, twenty years old and far from death, with the air coming easily into his lungs, and a deep feeling inside him that he could do anything, knock over anybody, outrun whatever had to be outrun. And the shower after and the three glasses of water and the cool night air on his damp head and Louise sitting hatless in the open car with a smile and the first kiss she ever really meant. The high point, an eighty-yard run in the practice, and a girl's kiss and everything after that a decline. Darling laughed. He had practiced the wrong thing, perhaps. He hadn't practiced for 1929 and New York City and a girl who would turn into a woman. Somewhere, he thought, there must have been a point where she moved up to me, was even with me for a moment, when I could have held her hand, if I'd known, held tight, gone with her. Well, he'd never known. Here he was on a playing field that was fifteen years away and his wife was in another city having dinner with another and better man, speaking with him a different, new language, a language nobody had ever taught him.

Darling stood up, smiled a little, because if he didn't smile he knew the tears would come. He looked around him. This was the spot. O'Connor's pass had come sliding out just to here . . . the high point. Darling put up his hands, felt all over again the flat slap of the ball. He shook his hips to throw off the halfback, cut back inside the center, picked his knees high as he ran gracefully over two men jumbled on the ground at the line of scrimmage, ran easily, gaining speed, for ten yards, holding the ball lightly in his two hands, swung away from the halfback diving at him, ran, swinging his hips in the almost girlish manner of a back in a broken field, tore into the safety man, his shoes drumming heavily on the turf, stiff-armed, elbow locked, pivoted, raced lightly and exultantly for the goal line.

It was only after he had sped over the goal line and slowed to a trot that he saw the boy and girl sitting together on the turf, looking at him wonderingly.

He stopped short, dropping his arms. "I . . ." he said, gasping a little, though his condition was fine and the run hadn't winded him. "I—once I played here."

The boy and the girl said nothing. Darling laughed embarrassedly, looked hard at them sitting there, close to each other, shrugged, turned and went toward his hotel, the sweat breaking out on his face and running down into his collar.

# Borough of Cemeteries

During the cocktail hour, in Brownsville, the cab drivers gather in Lammanawitz's Bar and Grill and drink beer and talk about the world and watch the sun set slowly over the elevated tracks in the direction of Prospect Park.

"Mungo?" they say. "Mungo? He got a fish for a arm. A mackerel. He will pitch Brooklyn right into the first division of the International League."

"I saw the Mayor today, His Honor, himself. The Little Flower. What this country needs . . ."

"Pinky, I want that you should trust me for a glass of beer."

Pinky wiped the wet dull expanse of the bar. "Look, Elias. It is against the law of the State of New York," he said, nervously, "to sell intoxicating liquors on credit."

"One glass of beer. Intoxicatin'!" Elias's lips curled. "Who yuh think I am, Snow White?"

"Do you want me to lose my license?" Pinky asked plaintively.

"I stay up nights worryin' Pinky might lose his license. My wife hears me cryin' in my sleep," Elias said. "One beer, J. P. Morgan."

Regretfully, Pinky drew the beer, with a big head, and sighed as he marked it down in the book. "The last one," he said, "positively the last one. As God is my witness."

"Yeah," Elias said. "Keep yer mouth closed." He drank the beer in one gulp, with his eyes shut. "My God," he said quietly, his eyes still shut, as he put the glass down. "Fer a lousy dime," he said to the room in general, "yuh get somethin' like that! Fer a lousy dime! Brooklyn is a wonderful place."

"Brooklyn stinks," said another driver, down the bar. "The borough of cemeteries. This is a first class place for graveyards."

"My friend Palangio," Elias said, "Il Doochay Palangio. Yuh don't like Brooklyn, go back to Italy. They give yuh a gun, yuh

26

get shot in the behind in Africa." The rest of the drivers laughed and Elias grinned at his own wit. "I seen in the movies. Go back t' Italy, wit' the fat girls. Who'll buy me a beer?"

Complete silence fell over the bar, like taps over an army camp.

"My friends," Elias said bitterly.

"Brooklyn is a wonderful place," Palangio said.

"All day long," Elias said, reflectively rubbing his broken nose, "I push a hack. Eleven hours on the street. I now have the sum of three dollars and fifty cents in my pocket."

Pinky came right over. "Now, Elias," he said, "there is the small matter of one beer. If I'd knew you had the money . . ."

Elias impatiently brushed Pinky's hand off the bar. "There is somebody callin' for a beer down there, Pinky," he said. "Attend yer business."

"I think," Pinky grumbled, retreating, "that a man oughta pay his rightful debts."

"He thinks. Pinky thinks," Elias announced. But his heart was not with Pinky. He turned his back to the bar and leaned on his frayed elbows and looked sadly up at the tin ceiling. "Three dollars and fifty cents," he said softly. "An' I can't buy a beer."

"Whatsamatta?" Palangio asked. "Yuh got a lock on yuh pocket?"

"Two dollars an' seventy-fi' cents to the Company," Elias said. "An' seventy-fi' cents to my lousy wife so she don't make me sleep in the park. The lousy Company. Every day for a year I give 'em two dollars an' seventy-fi' cents an' then I own the hack. After a year yuh might as well sell that crate to Japan to put in bombs. Th' only way yuh can get it to move is t' drop it. I signed a contract. I need a nurse. Who wants t' buy me a beer?"

"I signed th' same contract," Palangio said. A look of pain came over his dark face. "It got seven months more to go. Nobody shoulda learned me how to write my name."

"If you slobs would only join th' union," said a little Irishman across from the beer spigots.

"Geary," Elias said. "The Irish hero. Tell us how you fought th' English in th' battle of Belfast."

"O.K., O.K.," Geary said, pushing his cap back excitably from his red hair. "You guys wanna push a hack sixteen hours a day for beans, don' let me stop yuh."

"Join a union, get yer hair parted down the middle by the cops," Elias said, "That is my experience."

"O.K., boys." Geary pushed his beer a little to make it foam.

27

"Property-owners, Can't pay for a glass a beer at five o'clock in th' afternoon. What's the use a' talkin' t' yuh? Lemme have a beer, Pinky."

"Geary, you're a red," Elias said. "A red bastidd."

"A Communist," Palangio said.

"I want a beer," Geary said loudly.

"Times're bad," Elias said. "That's what's th' trouble."

"Sure." Geary drained half his new glass. "Sure."

"Back in 1928," Elias said, "I averaged sixty bucks a week."

"On New Year's Eve, 1927," Palangio murmured, "I made thirty-six dollars and forty cents."

"Money was flowin'," Elias remembered.

Palangio sighed, rubbing his beard bristles with the back of his hand. "I wore silk shirts. With stripes. They cost five bucks a piece. I had four girls in 1928. My God!"

"This ain't 1928," Geary said.

"Th' smart guy," Elias said. "He's tellin' us somethin'. This ain't 1928, he says. Join th' union, we get 1928 back."

"Why the hell should I waste my time?" Geary asked himself in disgust. He drank in silence.

"Pinky!" Palangio called. "Pinky! Two beers for me and my friend Elias."

Elias moved, with a wide smile, up the bar, next to Palangio. "We are brothers in misery, Angelo," he said. "Me and th' Wop. We both signed th' contract."

They drank together and sighed together.

"I had th' biggest pigeon flight in Brownsville," Elias said softly. "One hundred and twelve pairs of pedigreed pigeons. I'd send 'em up like fireworks, every afternoon. You oughta've seen 'em wheelin' aroun' an' aroun' over th' roofs. I'm a pigeon fancier." He finished his glass. "I got fifteen pigeons left. Every time I bring home less than seventy-five cents, my wife cooks one for supper. A pedigreed pigeon. My lousy wife."

"Two beers," Palangio said. He and Elias drank with grave satisfaction.

"Now," Elias said, "if only I didn't have to go home to my lousy wife. I married her in 1929. A lot of things've changed since 1929." He sighed. "What's a woman?" he asked. "A woman is a trap."

"You shoulda seen what I seen today," Palangio said. "My third fare. On Eastern Parkway. I watched her walk all th' way acrost Nostrand Avenue, while I was waitin' on the light. A hundred-

and-thirty-pound girl. Blonde. Swingin' her hips like orchester music. With one of those little straw hats on top of her head, with the vegetables on it. You never saw nothin' like it. I held onto the wheel like I was drownin'. Talkin' about traps! She went to the St. George Hotel.''

Elias shook his head. ''The tragedy of my life,'' he said, ''is I was married young.''

''Two beers,'' Palangio said.

''Angelo Palangio,'' Elias said, ''yer name reminds me of music.''

''A guy met her in front of the St. George. A big fat guy. Smilin' like he just seen Santa Claus. A big fat guy. Some guys . . .

''Some guys . . .'' Elias mourned. ''*I* gotta go home to Annie. She yells at me from six to twelve, regular. Who's goin' to pay the grocer? Who's goin' to pay the gas company?'' He looked steadily at his beer for a moment and downed it. ''I'm a man who married at the age a' eighteen.''

''We need somethin' to drink,'' Palangio said.

''Buy us two whiskies,'' Elias said. ''What the hell good is beer?''

''Two Calverts,'' Palangio called. ''The best for me and my friend Elias Pinsker.''

''Two gentlemen,'' Elias said, ''who both signed th' contract.''

''Two dumb slobs,'' said Geary.

''Th' union man,'' Elias lifted his glass. ''To th' union!'' He downed the whisky straight. ''Th' hero of th' Irish Army.''

''Pinky,'' Palangio shouted. ''Fill 'em up to the top.''

''Angelo Palangio,'' Elias murmured gratefully.

Palangio soberly counted the money out for the drinks. ''Now,'' he said, ''the Company can jump in Flushing Bay. I am down to two bucks even.''

''Nice,'' Geary said sarcastically. ''Smart. You don't pay 'em one day, they take yer cab. After payin' them regular for five months. Buy another drink.''

Palangio slowly picked up his glass and let the whisky slide down his throat in a smooth amber stream. ''Don't talk like that, Geary,'' he said. ''I don't want to hear nothin' about taxicabs. I am busy drinkin' with friends.''

''You dumb Wop,'' Geary said.

''That is no way to talk,'' Elias said, going over to Geary purposefully. He cocked his right hand and squinted at Geary. Geary backed off, his hands up. ''I don't like to hear people call my friend a dumb Wop,'' Elias said.

29

"Get back," Geary shouted, "before I brain yuh."

Pinky ran up excitably. "Lissen, boys," he screamed, "do you want I should lose my license?"

"We are all friends," Palangio said. "Shake hands. Everybody shake hands. Everybody have a drink. I hereby treat everybody to a drink."

Elias lumbered back to Palangio's side. "I am sorry if I made a commotion. Some people can't talk like gentlemen."

"Everybody have a drink," Palangio insisted.

Elias took out three dollar bills and laid them deliberately on the bar. "Pass the bottle around. This is on Elias Pinsker."

"Put yer money away, Elias." Geary pushed his cap around on his head with anger. "Who yuh think yuh are? Walter Chrysler?"

"The entertainment this afternoon is on me," Elias said inexorably. "There was a time I would stand drinks for twenty-five men. With a laugh, an' pass cigars out after it. Pass the bottle around, Pinky!"

The whisky flowed.

"Elias and me," Palangio said. "We are high class spenders."

"You guys oughta be fed by hand," Geary said. "Wards of the guvment."

"A man is entitled to some relaxation," Elias said. "Where's that bottle?"

"This is nice," Palangio said. "This is very nice."

"This is like the good old days," Elias said.

"I hate to go home." Palangio sighed. "I ain't even got a radio home."

"Pinky!" Elias called. "Turn on the radio for Angelo Palangio."

"One room," Palangio said. "As big as a toilet. That is where I live."

The radio played. It was soft and sweet and a rich male voice sang "I Married an Angel."

"When I get home," Elias remembered, "Annie will kill a pedigreed pigeon for supper. My lousy wife. An' after supper I push the hack five more hours and I go home and Annie yells some more and I get up tomorrow and push the hack some more." He poured himself another drink. "That is a life for a dog," he said. "For a Airedale."

"In Italy," Palangio said, "they got donkeys don't work as hard as us."

"If the donkeys were as bad off as you," Geary yelled, "they'd have sense enough to organize."

"I want to be a executive at a desk." Elias leaned both elbows on the bar and held his chin in his huge gnarled hands. "A long

30

distance away from Brownsville. Wit' two thousand pigeons. In California. An' I should be a bachelor. Geary, can yuh organize *that*? Hey, Geary?"

"You're a workin' man," Geary said, "an' you're goin' to be a workin' man all yer life."

"Geary," Elias said. "You red bastidd, Geary."

"All my life," Palangio wept, "I am goin' to push a hack up an' down Brooklyn, fifteen, sixteen hours a day an' pay th' Company forever an' go home and sleep in a room no bigger'n a toilet. Without a radio. Jesus!"

"We are victims of circumstance," Elias said.

"All my life," Palangio cried, "tied to that crate!"

Elias pounded the bar once with his fist. "Th' hell with it! Palangio!" he said. "Get into that goddamn wagon of yours."

"What do yuh want me to do?" Palangio asked in wonder.

"We'll fix 'em," Elias shouted. "We'll fix those hacks. We'll fix that Company! Get into yer cab, Angelo. I'll drive mine, we'll have a chicken fight."

"You drunken slobs!" Geary yelled. "Yuh can't do that!"

"Yeah," Palangio said eagerly, thinking it over. "Yeah. We'll show 'em. Two dollars and seventy-fi' cents a day for life. Yeah. We'll fix 'em. Come on, Elias!"

Elias and Palangio walked gravely out to their cars. Everybody else followed them.

"Look what they're doin'!" Geary screamed. "Not a brain between the both of them! What good'll it do to ruin the cabs?"

"Shut up," Elias said, getting into his cab. "We oughta done this five months ago. Hey, Angelo," he called, leaning out of his cab. "Are yuh ready? Hey, Il Doochay!"

"Contact!" Angelo shouted, starting his motor. "Boom! Boom!"

The two cars spurted at each other, in second, head-on. As they hit, glass broke and a fender flew off and the cars skidded wildly and the metal noise echoed and re-echoed like artillery fire off the buildings.

Elias stuck his head out of his cab. "Are yuh hurt?" he called. "Hey, Il Doochay!"

"Contact!" Palangio called from behind his broken windshield. "The Dawn Patrol!"

"I can't watch this," Geary moaned, "Two workin' men." He went back into Lammanawitz's Bar and Grill.

The two cabs slammed together again and people came running from all directions.

"How're yuh?" Elias asked, wiping the blood off his face.

31

"Onward!" Palangio stuck his hand out in salute. "Sons of Italy!"

Again and again the cabs tore into each other.

"Knights of the Round Table," Palangio announced.

"Knights of Lammanawitz's Round Table," Elias agreed, pulling at the choke to get the wheezing motor to turn over once more.

For the last time they came together. Both cars flew off the ground at the impact and Elias's toppled on its side and slid with a harsh grating noise to the curb. One of the front wheels from Palangio's cab rolled calmly and decisively toward Pitkin Avenue. Elias crawled out of his cab before anyone could reach him. He stood up, swaying, covered with blood, pulling at loose ends of his torn sweater. He shook hands soberly with Palangio and looked around him with satisfaction at the torn fenders and broken glass and scattered headlights and twisted steel. "Th' lousy Company," he said. "That does it. I am now goin' to inform 'em of th' accident."

He and Palangio entered the Bar and Grill, followed by a hundred men, women, and children. Elias dialed the number deliberately.

"Hullo," he said, "hullo, Charlie? Lissen, Charlie, if yuh send a wreckin' car down to Lammanawitz's Bar and Grill, yuh will find two of yer automobiles. Yuh lousy Charlie." He hung up carefully.

"All right, Palangio," he said.

"Yuh bet," Palangio answered.

"Now we oughta go to the movies," Elias said.

"That's right," Palangio nodded seriously.

"Yuh oughta be shot," Geary shouted.

"They're playin' Simone Simon," Elias announced to the crowd. "Let's go see Simone Simon."

Walking steadily, arm in arm, like two gentlemen, Elias and Angelo Palangio went down the street, through the lengthening shadows, toward Simone Simon.

# Main Currents of American Thought

"Flacker: all right now, Kid, now you'd better talk," Andrew dictated. "Business: Sound of the door closing, the slow turning of the key in the lock. Buddy: You're never going to get me to talk, Flacker. Business: Sound of a slap. Flacker: Maybe that'll make you think different, Kid. Where is Jerry Carmichael? Buddy: (Laughing) Wouldn't you like to know, Flacker? Flacker: Yeah. (Slowly, with great threat in his voice) And I'm going to find out. One way or another. See? Business: Siren fades in, louder, fades out. Announcer: Will Buddy talk? Will Flacker force him to disclose the whereabouts of the rescued son of the railroad king? Will Dusty Blades reach him in time? Tune in Monday at the same time, etcetera, etcetera . . .''

Andrew dropped onto the couch and put his feet up. He stretched and sighed as he watched Lenore finish scratching his dictation down in the shorthand notebook. "Thirty bucks," he said. "There's another thirty bucks. Is it the right length?"

"Uhuh," Lenore said. "Eleven and a half pages. This is a very good one, Andy."

"Yeah," Andrew said, closing his eyes. "Put it next to Moby Dick on your library shelf."

"It's very exciting," Lenore said, standing up. "I don't know what they're complaining about."

"You're a lovely girl." Andrew put his hands over his eyes and rubbed around and around. "I have wooden hinges on my eyelids. Do you sleep at night?"

"Don't do that to your eyes." Lenore started to put on her coat. "You only aggravate them."

"You're right." Andrew dug his fists into his eyes and rotated them slowly. "You don't know how right you are."

"Tomorrow. At ten o'clock?" Lenore asked.

"At ten o'clock. Dig me out of the arms of sleep. We shall leave Dusty Blades to his fate for this week and go on with the

33

further adventures of Ronnie Cook and His Friends, forty dollars a script. I always enjoy writing Ronnie Cook much better than Dusty Blades. See what ten dollars does to a man." He opened his eyes and watched Lenore putting her hat on in front of the mirror. When he squinted, she was not so plain-looking. He felt very sorry for Lenore, plain as sand, with her flat-colored face and her hair pulled down like rope, and never a man to her name. She was putting on a red hat with a kind of ladder arrangement going up one side. It looked very funny and sad on her. Andrew realized that it was a new hat. "That's a mighty fine hat," he said.

"I thought a long time before I bought this hat," Lenore said, flushing because he'd noticed it.

"Har-*riet!*" The governess next door screamed in the alley to the next-door neighbor's little girl. "Harriet, get away from there this minute!"

Andrew turned over on his stomach on the couch and put a pillow over his head. "Have you got any ideas for Ronnie Cook and His Friends for tomorrow?" he asked Lenore.

"No. Have you?"

"No." He pulled the pillow tight around his head.

"You'll get them by tomorrow," Lenore said. "You always do."

"Yeah," said Andrew.

"You need a vacation," Lenore said.

"Get out of here."

"Good-bye," Lenore started out. "Get a good night's sleep."

"Anything you say."

Andrew watched her with one eye as she went off the porch on which he worked and through the living room and dining room, toward the stairs. She had nice legs. You were always surprised when a girl with a face like that had nice legs. But she had hair on her legs. She was not a lucky girl. "Oh, no," Andrew said as the door closed behind her, "you are not a lucky girl."

He closed his eyes and tried to sleep. The sun came in through the open windows and the curtains blew softly over his head and the sun was warm and comforting on his closed eyes. Across the street, on the public athletic field, four boys were shagging flies. There would be the neat pleasant crack of the bat and a long time later the smack of the ball in the fielder's glove. The tall trees outside, as old as Brooklyn, rustled a little from time to time as little spurts of wind swept across the baseball field.

"Harr*iet!*" the governess called. "Stop that or I will make you stand by yourself in the corner all afternoon! Harriet! I demand you to stop it!'' The governess was French. She had the only unpleasant French accent Andrew had ever heard.

The little girl started to cry, ''Mamma! Mamma! Mamma, she's going to hit me!'' The little girl hated the governess and the governess hated the little girl, and they continually reported each other to the little girl's mother. ''Mamma!''

''You are a little liar,'' the governess screamed. ''You will grow up, and you will be a liar all your life. There will be no hope for you.''

''Mamma!'' wailed the little girl.

They went inside the house and it was quiet again.

''Charlie,'' one of the boys on the baseball field yelled, ''hit it to me, Charlie!''

The telephone rang, four times, and then Andrew heard his mother talking into it. She came onto the porch.

''It's a man from the bank,'' she said. ''He wants to talk to you.''

''You should've told him I wasn't home,'' Andrew said.

''But you are home,'' his mother said. ''How was I to know that . . . ?''

''You're right.'' Andrew swung his legs over and sat up. ''You're perfectly right.''

He went into the dining room, to the telephone, and talked to the man at the bank.

''You're a hundred and eleven dollars overdrawn,'' said the man at the bank.

Andrew squinted at his mother, sitting across the room, on a straight chair, with her arms folded in her lap, her head turned just a little, so as not to miss anything.

''I thought I had about four hundred dollars in the bank,'' Andrew said into the phone.

''You are a hundred and eleven dollars overdrawn,'' said the man at the bank.

Andrew sighed. ''I'll check it.'' He put the phone down.

''What's the matter?'' his mother asked.

''I'm a hundred and eleven dollars overdrawn,'' he said.

''That's shameful,'' his mother said. ''You ought to be more methodical.''

''Yes.'' Andrew started back to the porch.

''You're awfully careless.'' His mother followed him, ''You really ought to keep track of your money.''

''Yes.'' Andrew sat down on the couch.

"Give me a kiss," his mother said.

"Why?"

"No particular reason." She laughed.

"O.K." He kissed her and she held him for a moment. He dropped down on the couch. She ran her finger under his eye.

"You've got rings under your eyes," she said.

"That's right."

She kissed him again and went to the rear of the house. He closed his eyes. From the rear of the house came the sound of the vacuum cleaner. Andrew felt his muscles getting stiff in protest against the vacuum cleaner. He got up and went to her bedroom, where she was running the machine back and forth under the bed. She was down on one knee and was bent over, looking under the bed.

"Hey!" Andrew yelled. "Hey, Mom!"

She turned off the machine and looked up at him. "What's the matter?"

"I'm trying to sleep," he said.

"Well, why don't you sleep?"

"The vacuum cleaner. It's shaking the house."

His mother stood up, her face setting into stern lines. "I've got to clean the house, don't I?"

"Why do you have to clean the house while I'm trying to sleep?"

His mother bent down again. "I can't use it while you're working. I can't use it while you're reading. I can't use it until ten o'clock in the morning because you're sleeping." She started the machine. "When am I supposed to clean the house?" she called over the noise of the cleaner. "Why don't you sleep at night like everybody else?" And she put her head down low and vigorously ran the machine back and forth.

Andrew watched her for a moment. No arguments came to him. The sound of the cleaner so close to him made his nerves jump. He went out of the room, closing the door behind him.

The telephone was ringing and he picked it up and said, "Hello."

"Ahndrew?" his agent's voice asked. His agent was from Brooklyn, too, but he had a very broad A, with which he impressed actors and sponsors.

"Yes, this is Ahndrew." Andrew always made this straight-faced joke with his agent, but the agent never seemed to catch on. "You didn't have to call. The Dusty Blades scripts are all through. You'll get them tomorrow."

"I called about something else, Ahndrew," his agent said, his voice very smooth and influential on the phone. "The complaints're piling up on the Blades scripts. They're as slow as gum. Nothing ever happens. Ahndrew, you're not writing for the *Atlantic Monthly*."

"I know I'm not writing for the *Atlantic Monthly*."

"I think you've rather run out of material," his agent said lightly, soothingly. "I think perhaps you ought to take a little vacation from the Blades scripts."

"Go to hell, Herman," Andrew said, knowing that Herman had found somebody to do the scripts more cheaply for him.

"That's hardly the way to talk, Ahndrew," Herman said, his voice still smooth, but hurt. "After all, I have to stand in the studio and listen to the complaints."

"Sad, Herman," Andrew said. "That's a sad picture," and hung up.

He rubbed the back of his neck reflectively, feeling again the little lump behind his ear.

He went into his own room and sat at his desk looking blankly at the notes for his play that lay, neatly piled, growing older, on one side. He took out his checkbook and his last month's vouchers and arranged them in front of him.

"One hundred and eleven dollars," he murmured, as he checked back and added and subtracted, his eyes smarting from the strain, his hands shaking a little because the vacuum cleaner was still going in his mother's room. Out on the athletic field more boys had arrived and formed an infield and were throwing the ball around the bases and yelling at each other.

Dr. Chalmers, seventy-five dollars. That was for his mother and her stomach.

Eighty dollars rent. The roof over his head equaled two Ronnie Cook's and His Friends. Five thousand words for rent.

Buddy was in the hands of Flacker. Flacker could torture him for six pages. Then you could have Dusty Blades speeding to the rescue with Sam, by boat, and the boat could spring a leak because the driver was in Flacker's pay, and there could be a fight for the next six pages. The driver could have a gun. You could use it, but it wouldn't be liked, because you'd done at least four like it already.

Furniture, and a hundred and thirty-seven dollars. His mother had always wanted a good dining-room table. She didn't have a maid, she said, so he ought to get her a dining-room table. How many words for a dining-room table?

"Come on, Baby, make it two," the second baseman out on the field was yelling. "Double 'em up!"

Andrew felt like picking up his old glove and going out there and joining them. When he was still in college he used to go out on a Saturday at ten o'clock in the morning and shag flies and jump around the infield and run and run all day, playing in pickup games until it got too dark to see. He was always tired now and even when he played tennis he didn't move his feet right, because he was tired, and hit flat-footed and wild.

Spain, one hundred dollars. Oh, Lord.

A hundred and fifty to his father, to meet his father's payroll. His father had nine people on his payroll, making little tin gadgets that his father tried to sell to the dime stores, and at the end of every month Andrew had to meet the payroll. His father always gravely made out a note to him.

Flacker is about to kill Buddy out of anger and desperation. In bursts Dusty, alone. Sam is hurt. On the way to the hospital. Buddy is spirited away a moment before Dusty arrives. Flacker, very smooth and oily. Confrontation. "Where is Buddy, Flacker?" "You mean the little lad?" "I mean the little lad, Flacker!"

Fifty dollars to Dorothy's piano teacher. His sister. Another plain girl. She might as well learn how to play the piano. Then one day they'd come to him and say, "Dorothy is ready for her debut. All we're asking you to do is rent Town Hall for a Wednesday evening. Just advance the money." She'd never get married. She was too smart for the men who would want her and too plain for the men she'd want herself. She bought her dresses in Saks. He would have to support, for life, a sister who would only buy her dresses in Saks and pay her piano teacher fifty dollars a month every month. She was only twenty-four, she would have a normal life expectancy of at least forty years, twelve times forty, plus dresses at Saks and Town Hall from time to time . . .

His father's teeth—ninety dollars. The money it cost to keep a man going in his losing fight against age.

The automobile. Nine hundred dollars. A nine-hundred-dollar check looked very austere and impressive, like a penal institution. He was going to go off in the automobile, find a place in the mountains, write a play. Only he could never get himself far enough ahead on Dusty Blades and Ronnie Cook and His Friends. Twenty thousand words a week, each week, recurring like Sunday on the calendar. How many words was *Hamlet?* Thirty, thirty-five thousand?

Twenty-three dollars to Best's. That was Martha's sweater for her birthday. "Either you say yes or no," Martha said Saturday night. "I want to get married and I've waited long enough." If you married you paid rent in two places, light, gas, telephone twice, and you bought stockings, dresses, toothpaste, medical attention, for your wife.

Flacker plays with something in his pocket. Dusty's hand shoots out, grabs his wrist, pulls his hand out. Buddy's little penknife, which Dusty had given him for a birthday present, is in Flacker's hand. "Flacker, tell me where Buddy Jones is, or I'll kill you with my bare hands." A gong rings. Flacker has stepped on an alarm. Doors open and the room fills with his henchmen.

Twenty dollars to Macy's for books. Parrington, *Main Currents in American Thought*. How does Dusty Blades fit into the *Main Currents of American Thought?*

Ten dollars to Dr. Farber. "I don't sleep at night. Can you help me?"

"Do you drink coffee?"

"I drink one cup of coffee in the morning. That's all."

Pills, to be taken before retiring. Ten dollars. We ransom our lives from doctors' hands.

If you marry, you take an apartment downtown because it's silly to live in Brooklyn this way; and you buy furniture, four rooms full of furniture, beds, chairs, dishrags, relatives. Martha's family was poor and getting no younger and finally there would be three families, with rent and clothes and doctors and funerals.

Andrew got up and opened the closet door. In it, stacked in files, were the scripts he had written in the last four years. They stretched from one end of a wide closet across to another, bridge from one wall to another of a million words. Four years' work.

Next script. The henchmen close in on Dusty. He hears the sounds of Buddy screaming in the next room . . .

How many years more?

The vacuum cleaner roared.

Martha was Jewish. That meant you'd have to lie your way into some hotels, if you went at all, and you never could escape from one particular meanness of the world around you; and when the bad time came there you'd be, adrift on that dangerous sea.

He sat down at his desk. One hundred dollars again to Spain. Barcelona had fallen and the long dusty lines were beating their way to the French border with the planes over them, and out of a sense of guilt at not being on a dusty road, yourself, bloody-footed and in fear of death, you gave a hundred dollars, feeling at the same time that it was too much and nothing you ever gave could be enough. Three-and-a-third The Adventures of Dusty Blades to the dead and dying of Spain.

The world loads you day by day with new burdens that increase on your shoulders. Lift a pound and you find you're carrying a ton. "Marry me," she says, "marry me." Then what does Dusty do? What the hell can he do that he hasn't done before? For five afternoons a week now, for a year, Dusty has been in Flacker's hands, or the hands of somebody else who is Flacker but has another name, and each time he has escaped. How now?

The vacuum roared in the hallway outside his room.

"Mom!" he yelled. "Please turn that thing off!"

"What did you say?" his mother called.

"Nothing."

He added up the bank balances. His figures showed that he was four hundred and twelve dollars overdrawn instead of one hundred and eleven dollars, as the bank said. He didn't feel like adding the figures over. He put the vouchers and the bank's sheet into an envelope for his income-tax returns.

"Hit it out, Charlie!" a boy called on the field. "Make it a fast one!"

Andrew felt like going out and playing with them. He changed his clothes and put on a pair of old spikes that were lying in the back of the closet. His old pants were tight on him, Fat. If he ever let go, if anything happened and he couldn't exercise, he'd blow up like a house, if he got sick and had to lie in bed and convalesce . . . Maybe Dusty has a knife in a holster up his sleeve . . . How to plant that? The rent, the food, the piano teacher, the people at Saks who sold his sister dresses, the nimble girls who painted the tin gadgets in his father's shop, the teeth in his father's mouth, the doctors, the doctors, all living on the words that would have to come out of his head. See here, Flacker, I know what you're up to. Business: Sound of a shot. A groan. Hurry, before the train gets to the crossing! Look! He's gaining on us! Hurry! Will he make it? Will Dusty Blades head off the desperate gang of counterfeiters and murderers in the race for the yacht? Will I be able to keep it up? The years, the years ahead . . . You grow fat and the lines become permanent under your eyes and you drink too much and you pay more to the doctors because death is nearer and there is no stop, no vacation from life, in no year can you say, "I want to sit this one out, kindly excuse me."

His mother opened the door, "Martha's on the phone."

Andrew clattered out in his spiked shoes, holding the old, torn fielder's glove. He closed the door to the dining room to show his mother this was going to be a private conversation.

"Hello," he said. "Yes." He listened gravely. "No," he said. "I guess not. Good-bye. Good luck, Martha."

40

He stood looking at the phone. His mother came in and he raised his head and started down the steps.

"Andrew," she said, "I want to ask you something."

"What?"

"Could you spare fifty dollars, Andrew?"

"Oh, God!"

"It's important. You know I wouldn't ask you if it wasn't important. It's for Dorothy."

"What does she need it for?"

"She's going to a party, a very important party, a lot of very big people're going to be there and she's sure they'll ask her to play. . . ."

"Do the invitations cost fifty dollars apiece?" Andrew kicked the top step and a little piece of dried mud fell off the spiked shoes.

"No, Andrew." His mother was talking in her asking-for-money voice. "It's for a dress. She can't go without a new dress, she says. There's a man there she's after."

"She won't get him, dress or no dress," Andrew said. "Your daughter's a very plain girl."

"I know," his mother's hands waved a little, helpless and sad. "But it's better if she at least does the best she can. I feel sorry for her, Andrew . . ."

"Everybody comes to me!" Andrew yelled, his voice suddenly high. "Nobody leaves me alone! Not for a minute!"

He was crying now and he turned to hide it from his mother. She looked at him, surprised, shaking her head. She put her arms around him. "Just do what you want to, Andrew, that's all. Don't do anything you don't want to do."

"Yeah," Andrew said. "Yeah. I'm sorry. I'll give you the money. I'm sorry I yelled at you."

"Don't give it to me if you don't want to, Andrew." His mother was saying this honestly, believing it.

He laughed a little. "I want to, Mom, I want to."

He patted her shoulder and went down toward the baseball field, leaving her standing there puzzled at the top of the steps.

The sun and the breeze felt good on the baseball field, and he forgot for an hour, but he moved slowly. His arm hurt at the shoulder when he threw, and the boy playing second base called him Mister, which he wouldn't have done even last year, when Andrew was twenty-four.

# Second Mortgage

The bell rang and I went to the window to see who it was.

"Don't answer it," my father called. "It may be a summons."

"They can't serve summonses on Sunday," I said, parting the curtains cautiously.

"Don't answer it, anyway." My father came into the living room. He didn't know how to handle bill-collectors. They bullied him and he made wild promises, very seriously, to pay, and never did and they'd come and hound him terribly. When he was home alone he never answered the doorbell. He never even went to see who it was. He just sat in the kitchen reading the paper while the bell clanged over his head. Even the postman couldn't get the front door opened when my father was home alone.

The bell rang again. "What the hell," I said, "it's only a little old lady. She's probably selling something. We can open the door."

"What for?" my father asked. "We can't buy anything."

I opened the door anyway. The little old lady jumped when the door swung back. Her hands fluttered. They were plump little hands, swollen, without gloves. "I'm Mrs. Shapiro," she said, waiting.

I waited. She tried a smile. I waited sternly. Strangers are never friends at the doors of the poor. I was only seventeen but I had learned that anyone who rang our doorbell might turn out to be the Edison Electric Company or the Brooklyn Borough Gas Company, intent on shutting off the electricity or the gas.

Mrs. Shapiro hunched inside her shapeless little coat. "I own the second mortgage," she said.

Still I waited, sternly. Another enemy.

Her hand came out, cold, plump, and pleading. "I want to speak to your father, maybe," she said.

My father had retreated to the kitchen and the Sunday *Times*, hoping that nothing would happen at the front door that would require his tearing himself out of that peaceful welter of journalism.

"Pop!" I called. I heard him sigh and the rustle of the Sunday *Times* as he put down the editorial page. Mrs. Shapiro came in and I closed the door. My father came in, wiping his glasses, longing for the kitchen.

"This is Mrs. Shapiro, Pop," I said. "She owns the second mortgage . . ."

"Yes." Mrs. Shapiro was eager and bright and apologetic for a moment. She moved into the middle of the room. There were runs in her fat little stockings and her shoes were shapeless. "I came because . . ."

"Yes," my father said, with his imitation of a businesslike attitude, that he always tried on bill-collectors and which he lost as soon as they started to bully him. "Yes. Of course. Just wait a moment . . . My wife . . . my wife knows more about this than . . . Oh . . . Helen! Helen!"

My mother came down from upstairs, fixing her hair.

"Mrs. Shapiro," my father said. "The second mortgage . . ."

"It's this way," Mrs. Shapiro said, moving toward my mother. "In 1929, I . . ."

"Won't you sit down?" My mother pointed to a chair. She glanced at my father, tightening her mouth. My mother was always contemptuous of my father at those times when my father proved unequal to the task of beating off the representatives of our poverty.

Mrs. Shapiro sat on the very edge of the chair, leaning forward, her knees together. "The second mortgage is eight hundred dollars," Mrs. Shapiro said. We all sat silent. Mrs. Shapiro was disheartened by the silence, but she went on, her fat gray cheeks moving anxiously over her words. "Eight hundred dollars is a lot of money," she said.

We didn't contradict her.

"In 1929," Mrs. Shapiro said, "I had eight thousand dollars." She looked to our faces for pity, envy, anything. We sat there expressionless, with the faces of people who have become used to owing money. "Eight thousand dollars, I worked all my life for it. I had a vegetable store. It's hard to make money in vegetables nowadays. Vegetables are expensive and they spoil and there is always somebody else who sells them cheaper than you can . . ."

"Yes," my mother said, "vegetables are very expensive. I paid twenty cents for a head of cauliflower yesterday . . ."

"It wasn't any good, either," my father said, "I don't like cauliflower. It reminds me of cabbage, somehow."

"When Mr. Shapiro died of cancer, it took him two years to

43

die,'' Mrs. Shapiro went on, trying to please us. ''I had eight thousand dollars. I had rheumatism and high blood pressure and I couldn't take care of the store any more.'' Once more she begged our faces for that crumb of pity. ''I took the eight thousand dollars out of the bank and I went to Mr. Mayer and I said, 'Mr. Mayer, you're a big man, you have a fine reputation, I am giving you a widow's life's savings, invest it for me so that I have enough to live on. I don't need much, Mr. Mayer,' I told him, 'just a few dollars a week until I die, that's all,' I said, 'just a few dollars.' ''

''I know Mayer,'' my father said. ''He's not doing so well now. The Trust Company's in receivership now.''

''Mr. Mayer,'' Mrs. Shapiro said with passion, her fists quivering on her little thighs, ''is a crook! He took my money and he put it out in second mortgages. Eight thousand dollars' worth of second mortgages!''

She stopped. For the moment she could not say another word.

''Today,'' my father said, ''even first mortgages are no good. Nothing's any good any more.''

''In the last two years,'' Mrs. Shapiro said, her eyes filling with tears, ''I haven't got a penny out of them . . . out of eight thousand dollars' worth of second mortgages, not a penny . . .'' A little rag of a handkerchief came out and wiped at her eyes. ''I used to go to Mr. Mayer and he'd tell me I'd have to wait. How long can I wait? I don't have with what to eat now, as it is! Can I wait longer than that?'' Triumphantly she wept. ''Now Mr. Mayer won't see me any more. They tell me he's out when I go there. It doesn't do any good to go there.'' She stopped, wiping her eyes. We sat, uncomfortable and still.

''I'm going to the houses where I have the second mortgages,'' Mrs. Shapiro said. ''Nice houses, they are . . . like this. With rugs and curtains and steam heat and something cooking on the stove that you can smell inside. I have the second mortgage on houses like that, and I don't have enough to eat . . .'' Her tears soaked through the rag of a handkerchief. ''Please,'' she cried, ''please . . . give me something. I don't want the eight hundred dollars, but something. It's my money . . . I have nobody. I have rheumatism and there's no heat in my room and there're holes in my shoes. I walk on my bare feet . . . Please . . . please . . .''

We tried to stop her but she kept on, crying, ''Please . . . please . . . just a little bit. A hundred dollars. Fifty. My money . . .''

''All right, Mrs. Shapiro,'' my father said. ''Come back next Sunday. I'll have it for you then . . .''

The tears stopped. "Oh, God bless you," Mrs. Shapiro said. Before we knew what she was about she flung herself across the room and was on her hands and knees in front of my father and was kissing his hand wildly, "God bless you, God bless you," she cried over and over again. My father sat through it nervously, trying to pick her up with his free hand, looking pleadingly at my mother.

Finally my mother could bear it no longer. "Mrs. Shapiro," she said, breaking in over the "God bless you"'s, "listen to me! Stop that! Please stop it! We can't give you anything! Next Sunday or any Sunday! We haven't got a cent."

Mrs. Shapiro dropped my father's hand. She stayed on her knees in front of him, though, looking strange there in the middle of our living room. "But Mr. Ross said . . ."

"Mr. Ross is talking nonsense!" my mother said. "We have no money and we're not going to have any! We expect to be thrown out of this house any day now! We can't give you a penny, Mrs. Shapiro."

"But next Sunday . . ." Mrs. Shapiro tried to make my mother understand that she didn't expect it now, not for another week . . .

"We won't have any more next Sunday than we have today. And we have eighty-five cents in the house right now, Mrs. Shapiro!" My mother stood up, went over to Mrs. Shapiro, where she was kneeling on the floor. Before my mother could touch her, Mrs. Shapiro keeled over onto the floor, hitting it heavily, like a packed handbag that's been dropped.

It took us ten minutes to pull her out of her faint. My mother gave her tea, which she drank silently. She didn't seem to recognize us as she drank her tea and made ready to go off. She told us that this was the fifth time in two months that she had fainted like that. She seemed ashamed of herself, somehow. My mother gave her the address of a doctor who would wait for his money and Mrs. Shapiro went out, her fat, shabby stockings shaking as she went down the steps. My mother and I watched her as she shambled down the street and disappeared around the corner, but my father went into the kitchen and the New York *Times*.

She was back the next Sunday and two Sundays after that, ringing the bell, but we didn't open the door. She rang for almost a half-hour each time, but we all sat quietly in the kitchen, waiting for her to go away.

# Sailor off the Bremen

They sat in the small white kitchen, Ernest and Charley and Preminger and Dr. Stryker, all bunched around the porcelain-topped table, so that the kitchen seemed to be overflowing with men. Sally stood at the stove turning griddle-cakes over thoughtfully, listening intently to what Preminger was saying.

"So," Preminger said, carefully working his knife and fork, "everything was excellent. The comrades arrived, dressed like ladies and gentlemen at the opera, in evening gowns and what do you call them?"

"Tuxedoes," Charley said. "Black ties."

"Tuxedoes," Preminger nodded, speaking with his precise educated German accent. "Very handsome people, mixing with all the other handsome people who came to say good-bye to their friends on the boat; everybody very gay, everybody with a little whisky on the breath; nobody would suspect they were Party members, they were so clean and upper class." He laughed lightly at his own joke. He looked like a young boy from a nice Middle Western college, with crew-cut hair and a straight nose and blue eyes and an easy laugh. His laugh was a little high and short, and he talked fast, as though he wanted to get a great many words out to beat a certain deadline, but otherwise, being a Communist in Germany and a deck officer on the *Bremen* hadn't made any obvious changes in him. "It is a wonderful thing," he said, "how many pretty girls there are in the Party in the United States. Wonderful!"

They all laughed, even Ernest, who put his hand up to cover the empty spaces in the front row of his teeth every time he smiled. His hand covered his mouth and the fingers cupped around the neat black patch over his eye, and he smiled secretly and swiftly behind that concealment, getting his merriment over with swiftly, so he could take his hand down and compose his face into its usual unmoved, distant expression, cultivated from the time he got out

46

of the hospital. Sally watched him from the stove, knowing each step: the grudging smile, the hand, the consciousness and memory of deformity, the wrench to composure, the lie of peace when he took his hand down.

She shook her head, dumped three brown cakes onto a plate.

"Here," she said, putting them before Preminger. "Better than Childs restaurant."

"Wonderful," Preminger said, dousing them with syrup. "Each time I come to America I feast on these. There is nothing like it in the whole continent of Europe."

"All right," Charley said, leaning out across the kitchen table, practically covering it, because he was so big, "finish the story."

"So I gave the signal," Preminger said, waving his fork. "When everything was nice and ready, everybody having a good time, stewards running this way, that way, with champagne, a nice little signal and we had a very nice little demonstration. Nice signs, good loud yelling, the Nazi flag cut down, one, two, three, from the pole. The girls standing together singing like angels, everybody running there from all parts of the ship, everybody getting the idea very, very clear—a very nice little demonstration." He smeared butter methodically on the top cake. "So then, the rough business. Expected. Naturally. After all, we all know it is no cocktail party for Lady Astor." He pursed his lips and squinted at his plate, looking like a small boy making believe he's the head of a family. "A little pushing, expected, maybe a little crack over the head here and there, expected. Justice comes with a headache these days, we all know that. But my people, the Germans. You must always expect the worst from them. They organize like lightning. Method. How to treat a riot on a ship. Every steward, every oiler, every sailor, was there in a minute and a half. Two men would hold a comrade, the other would beat him. Nothing left to accident."

"The hell with it," Ernest said. "What's the sense in going through the whole thing again? It's all over."

"Shut up," Charley said.

"Two stewards got hold of Ernest," Preminger said softly. "And another one did the beating. Stewards are worse than sailors. All day long they take orders, they hate the world. Ernest was unlucky. All the others did their jobs, but they were human beings. The steward is a member of the Nazi party. He is an Austrian; he is not a normal man."

"Sally," Ernest said, "give Mr. Preminger some more milk."

"He kept hitting Ernest," Preminger tapped absently on the porcelain top with his fork, "and he kept laughing and laughing."

"You know who he is?" Charley asked. "You're sure you know who he is?"

"I know who he is. He is twenty-five years old, very dark and good-looking, and he sleeps with at least two ladies a voyage." Preminger slopped his milk around in the bottom of his glass. "His name is Lueger. He spies on the crew for the Nazis. He has sent two men already to concentration camps. He is a very serious character. He knew what he was doing," Preminger said clearly, "when he kept hitting Ernest in the eye. I tried to get to him, but I was in the middle of a thousand people, screaming and running. If something happens to that Lueger that will be a very good thing."

"Have a cigar," Ernest said, pulling two out of his pocket.

"Something will happen to him," Charley said, taking a deep breath, and leaning back from the table. "Something will damn sure happen to him."

"You're a dumb kid," Ernest said, in the weary tone he used now in all serious discussions. "What do you prove if you beat up one stupid sailor?"

"I don't prove anything," Charley said. "I don't prove a goddamn thing. I am just going to have a good time with the boy that knocked my brother's eye out. That's all."

"It is not a personal thing," Ernest said, in the tired voice. "It is the movement of Fascism. You don't stop Fascism with a personal crusade against one German. If I thought it would do some good, I'd say, sure, go ahead . . ."

"My brother, the Communist," Charley said bitterly. "He goes out and he gets ruined and still he talks dialectics. The Red Saint with the long view. The long view gives me a pain in the ass. I am taking a very short view of Mr. Lueger. I am going to kick the living guts out of his belly. Preminger, what do you say?"

"Speaking as a Party member," Preminger said, "I approve of your brother's attitude, Charley."

"Nuts," Charley said.

"Speaking as a man, Charley," Preminger went on, "please put Lueger on his back for at least six months. Where is that cigar, Ernest?"

Dr. Stryker spoke up in his dry, polite, dentist's voice. "As you know," he said. "I am not the type for violence." Dr. Stryker weighed a hundred and thirty-three pounds and it was almost possible to see through his wrists, he was so frail. "But as Ernest's

48

friends, I think there would be a definite satisfaction for all of us, including Ernest, if this Lueger was taken care of. You may count on me for anything within my powers." He was very scared, Dr. Stryker, and his voice was even drier than usual, but he spoke up after reasoning the whole thing out slowly and carefully, disregarding the fear, the worry, the possible great damage. "That is my opinion," he said.

"Sally," Ernest said, "talk to these damn fools."

"I think," Sally said slowly, looking steadily at her husband's face, always stiffly composed now, like a corpse's face, "I think they know what they're talking about."

Ernest shrugged. "Emotionalism. A large useless gesture. You're all tainted by Charley's philosophy. He's a football player. He has a football player's philosophy. Somebody knocks you down, you knock him down, everything is fine."

"I want a glass of milk, too," Charley said. "Please, Sally."

"Whom're you playing this week?" Ernest said.

"Georgetown."

"Won't that be enough violence for one week?" Ernest asked.

"Nope," Charley said. "I'll take care of Georgetown first, then Lueger."

"Anything I can do," Dr. Stryker said. "Remember, anything I can do. I am at your service."

"The coach'll be sore," Ernest said, "if you get banged up, Charley."

"The hell with the coach. Please shut up, Ernest. I have got my stomachful of Communist tactics. No more. Get this in your head, Ernest." Charley stood up and banged the table. "I am disregarding the class struggle, I am disregarding the education of the proletariat, I am disregarding the fact that you are a good Communist. I am acting strictly in the capacity of your brother. If you'd had any brains you would have stayed away from that lousy boat. You're a painter, an artist, you make water colors, what the hell is it your business if lunatics're running Germany? But all right. You've got no brains. You go and get your eye beat out. O.K. Now I step in. Purely personal. None of your business. Shut your trap. I will fix everything to my own satisfaction. Please go and lie down in the bedroom. We have arrangements to make here."

Ernest stood up, hiding his mouth, which was twitching, and walked into the bedroom and closed the door and lay down on the bed, in the dark, with his eye open.

The next day, an hour before sailing time, Charley and Dr. Stryker and Sally went down to the *Bremen*, and boarded the ship on different gangplanks. They stood separately on the A Deck, up forward, waiting for Preminger. Preminger came, very boyish and crisp in his blue uniform, looked coldly past them, touched a steward on the arm, a dark, good-looking young steward, said something to him, and went aft. Charley and Dr. Stryker examined the steward closely, so that two weeks later, on a dark street, there would be no mistake, and left, leaving Sally there, smiling at Lueger.

"Yes," Sally said two weeks later, "it is very clear. I'll have dinner with him, and I'll go to a movie with him, and I'll get him to take at least two drinks, and I'll tell him I live on West Twelfth Street, near West Street. There is a whole block of apartment houses there, and I'll get him down to West Twelfth Street between a quarter to one and one in the morning, and you'll be waiting there, you and Stryker, under the Ninth Avenue L, and you'll say, 'Pardon me, can you direct me to Sheridan Square?' and I'll start running."

"That's right," Charley said, "that's fine." He blew reflectively on his huge hands, knotted and cleat-marked from last Saturday's game. "That is the whole story for Mr. Lueger. You'll go through with it now?" he asked. "You're sure you can manage it?"

"I'll go through with it," Sally said. "I had a long talk with him today when the boat came in. He is very . . . anxious. He likes small girls like me, he says, with black hair. I told him I lived alone, downtown. He looked at me very significantly. I know why he manages to sleep with two ladies a voyage, like Preminger says. I'll manage it."

"What is Ernest going to do tonight?" Dr. Stryker asked. In the two weeks of waiting his voice had become so dry he had to swallow desperately every five words. "Somebody ought to take care of Ernest tonight."

"He's going to Carnegie Hall tonight," Sally said. "They're playing Brahms and Debussy."

"That's a good way to spend an evening," Charley said. He opened his collar absently, and pulled down his tie. "The only place I can go with Ernest these days is the movies. It's dark, so I don't have to look at him."

"He'll pull through," Dr. Stryker said professionally. "I'm making him new teeth; he won't be so self-conscious, he'll adjust himself."

"He hardly paints any more," Sally said. "He just sits around the house and looks at his old pictures."

"Mr. Lueger," Charley said. "Our pal, Mr. Lueger."

"He carries a picture of Hitler," Sally said. "In his watch. He showed me. He says he's lonely."

"How big is he?" Stryker asked nervously.

"He's a large, strong man," Sally said.

"I think you ought to have an instrument of some kind, Charley," Stryker said dryly. "Really, I do."

Charley laughed. He extended his two hands, palms up, the broken fingers curled a little, broad and muscular. "I want to do this with my own hands," he said. "I want to take care of Mr. Lueger with my bare fists. I want it to be a very personal affair."

"There is no telling what . . ." Stryker said.

"Don't worry, Stryker," Charley said. "Don't worry one bit."

At twelve that night Sally and Lueger walked down Eighth Avenue from the Fourteenth Street subway station. Lueger held Sally's arm as they walked, his fingers moving gently up and down, occasionally grasping tightly the loose cloth of her coat and the firm flesh of her arm just above the elbow.

"Oh," Sally said. "Don't. That hurts."

Lueger laughed. "It does not hurt much," he said. He pinched her playfully. "You don't mind if it hurt, nevertheless," he said. His English was very complicated, with a thick accent.

"I mind," Sally said. "Honest, I mind."

"I like you," he said, walking very close to her. "You are a good girl. You are made excellent. I am happy to accompany you home. You are sure you live alone?"

"I'm sure," Sally said. "Don't worry. I would like a drink."

"Aaah," Lueger said. "Waste time."

"I'll pay for it," Sally said. She had learned a lot about him in one evening. "My own money. Drinks for you and me."

"If you say so," Lueger said, steering her into a bar. "One drink, because we have something to do tonight." He pinched her hard and laughed, looking obliquely into her eyes with a kind of technical suggestiveness he used on the two ladies a voyage on the *Bremen*.

Under the Ninth Avenue L on Twelfth Street, Charley and Dr. Stryker leaned against an elevated post, in deep shadow.

"I . . . I . . ." Stryker said. Then he had to swallow to wet

51

his throat so that the words would come out. "I wonder if they're coming," he said finally in a flat, high whisper.

"They'll come," Charley said, keeping his eyes on the little triangular park up Twelfth Street where it joins Eighth Avenue. "That Sally has guts. That Sally loves my dumb brother like he was the President of the United States. As if he was a combination of Lenin and Michelangelo. And he had to go and get his eye batted out."

"He's a very fine man," Stryker said. "Your brother Ernest. A man with true ideals. I am very sorry to see what has happened to his character since . . . Is that them?"

"No," Charley said. "It's two girls from the YWCA on the corner."

"He used to be a very merry man," Stryker said, swallowing rapidly. "Always laughing. Always sure of what he was saying. Before he was married we used to go out together all the time and all the time the girls, my girl and his girl, no matter who they were, would give all their attention to him. All the time. I didn't mind. I love your brother Ernest as if he was my young brother. I could cry when I see him sitting now, covering his eye and his teeth, not saying anything, just listening to what other people have to say."

"Yeah," Charley said. "Yeah. Why don't you keep quiet, Stryker?"

"Excuse me," Stryker said, talking fast and dry. "I don't like to bother you. But I must talk. Otherwise, if I just stand here keeping still, I will suddenly start running and I'll run right up to Forty-second Street. I can't keep quiet at the moment, excuse me."

"Go ahead and talk, Stryker," Charley said gently, patting him on the shoulder. "Shoot your mouth right off, all you want."

"I am only doing this because I think it will help Ernest," Stryker said, leaning hard against the post, in the shadow, to keep his knees straight. "I have a theory. My theory is that when Ernest finds out what happens to this Lueger, he will pick up. It will be a kind of springboard to him. It is my private notion of the psychology of the situation. We should have brought an instrument with us, though. A club, a knife, brass knuckles." Stryker put his hands in his pockets, holding them tight against the cloth to keep them from trembling. "It will be very bad if we mess this up. Won't it be very bad, Charley? Say, Charley . . ."

"Shhh," said Charley.

Stryker looked up the street. "That's them. That's Sally, that's her coat. That's the bastard. The lousy German bastard."

"Shhh, Stryker. Shhh."

"I feel very cold, Charley. Do you feel cold? It's a warm night but I . . ."

"For Christ's sake, shut up!"

"We'll fix him," Stryker whispered. "Yes, Charley, I'll shut up, sure, I'll shut up, depend on me, Charley . . ."

Sally and Lueger walked slowly down Twelfth Street. Lueger had his arm around Sally's waist and their hips rubbed as they walked.

"That was a very fine film tonight," Lueger was saying. "I enjoy Deanna Durbin. Very young, fresh, sweet. Like you." He grinned at Sally in the dark and held tighter to her waist. "A small young maid. You are just the kind I like." He tried to kiss her. Sally turned her head away.

"Listen, Mr. Lueger," she said, not because she liked him, but because he was a human being and thoughtless and unsuspecting and because her heart was softer than she had thought. "Listen, I think you'd better leave me here."

"I do not understand English," Lueger said, enjoying this last coyness.

"Thank you very much for a pleasant evening," Sally said desperately, stopping in her tracks. "Thank you for taking me home. You can't come up. I was lying to you. I don't live alone . . ."

Lueger laughed. "Little frightened girl. That's nice. I love you for it."

"My brother," Sally said. "I swear to God I live with my brother."

Lueger grabbed her and kissed her, hard, bruising her lips against her teeth, his hands pressing harshly into the flesh of her back. She sobbed into his mouth with the pain, helpless. He released her. He was laughing.

"Come," he said, holding her close. "I am anxious to meet your brother. Little liar."

"All right," she said, watching Charley and Stryker move out from the L shadow. "All right. Let's not wait. Let's walk fast. Very fast. Let's not waste time."

Lueger laughed happily. "That's it. That's the way a girl should talk."

They walked swiftly toward the elevated ramp, Lueger laughing, his hand on her hip in certainty and possession.

"Pardon me," Stryker said. "Could you direct me to Sheridan Square?"

"Well," said Sally, stopping, "it's . . ."

53

Charley swung and Sally started running as soon as she heard the wooden little noise a fist makes on a man's face. Charley held Lueger up with one hand and chopped the lolling head with the other. He carried Lueger back into the shadows against a high iron railing. He hung Lueger by his overcoat against one of the iron points, so he could use both hands on him. Stryker watched for a moment, then turned and looked toward Eighth Avenue.

Charley worked very methodically, getting his two hundred pounds behind short, accurate, smashing blows that made Lueger's head jump and loll and roll against the iron pikes. Charley hit him in the nose three times, squarely, using his fist the way a carpenter uses a hammer. Each time Charley heard the sound of bone breaking, cartilage tearing. When he got through with the nose, Charley went after the mouth, hooking along the side of the jaws with both hands, until teeth fell out and the jaw hung open, smashed, loose with the queer looseness of flesh that is no longer moored to solid bone. Charley started crying, the tears running down into his mouth, the sobs shaking him as he swung his fists. Even then Stryker didn't turn around. He just put his hands to his ears and looked steadfastly at Eighth Avenue.

When he started on Lueger's eye, Charley talked. "You bastard. Oh, you lousy goddamn bastard," came out with the sobs and the tears as he hit at the eye with his right hand, cutting it, smashing it, tearing it again and again, his hand coming away splattered with blood each time. "Oh, you dumb, mean, skirt-chasing son-ofabitch, bastard." And he kept hitting with fury and deliberation at the shattered eye. . . .

A car came up Twelfth Street from the waterfront and slowed down at the corner. Stryker jumped on the running board. "Keep moving," he said, very tough, "if you know what's good for you."

He jumped off the running board and watched the car speed away.

Charley, still sobbing, pounded Lueger in the chest and belly. With each blow Lueger slammed against the iron fence with a noise like a carpet being beaten, until his coat ripped off the pike and he slid to the sidewalk.

Charley stood back, his fists swaying, the tears still coming, the sweat running down his face inside his collar, his clothes stained with blood.

"O.K.," he said, "O.K., you bastard."

He walked swiftly up under the L in the shadows, and Stryker hurried after him.

Much later, in the hospital, Preminger stood over the bed in which Lueger lay, unconscious, in splints and bandages.

"Yes," he said to the detective and the doctor. "That's our man. Lueger. A steward. The papers on him are correct."

"Who do you think done it?" the detective asked in a routine voice. "Did he have any enemies?"

"Not that I know of," Preminger said. "He was a very popular boy. Especially with the ladies."

The detective started out of the ward. "Well," he said, "he won't be a very popular boy when he gets out of here."

Preminger shook his head. "You must be very careful in a strange city," he said to the interne, and went back to the ship.

# Strawberry Ice Cream Soda

Eddie Barnes looked at the huge Adirondack hills, browning in the strong summer afternoon sun. He listened to his brother Lawrence practice finger-exercises on the piano inside the house, onetwo threefour*five*, onetwothreefour*five*, and longed for New York. He lay on his stomach in the long grass of the front lawn and delicately peeled his sunburned nose. Morosely he regarded a grasshopper, stupid with sun, wavering on a bleached blade of grass in front of his nose. Without interest he put out his hand and captured it.

"Give honey," he said, listlessly. "Give honey or I'll kill yuh . . ."

But the grasshopper crouched unmoving, unresponsive, oblivious to Life or Death.

Disgusted, Eddie tossed the grasshopper away. It flew uncertainly, wheeled, darted back to its blade of grass, alighted and hung there dreamily, shaking a little in the breeze in front of Eddie's nose. Eddie turned over on his back and looked at the high blue sky.

The country! Why anybody ever went to the country . . . What things must be doing in New York now, what rash, beautiful deeds on the steaming, rich streets, what expeditions, what joy, what daring sweaty adventure among the trucks, the trolley cars, the baby carriages! What cries, hoarse and humorous, what light laughter outside the red-painted shop where lemon ice was sold at three cents the double scoop, true nourishment for a man at fifteen.

Eddie looked around him, at the silent, eternal, granite-streaked hills. Trees and birds, that's all. He sighed, torn with thoughts of distant pleasure, stood up, went over to the window behind which Lawrence seriously hammered at the piano, onetwothreefour*five*.

"Lawrrrence," Eddie called, the rrr's lolling with horrible gentility in his nose, "Lawrrrence, you stink."

Lawrence didn't even look up. His thirteen-year-old fingers, still pudgy and babyish, went onetwothreefour*five*, with unswerving precision. He was talented and he was dedicated to his talent and

56

some day they would wheel a huge piano out onto the stage of Carnegie Hall and he would come out and bow politely to the thunder of applause and sit down, flipping his coat-tails back, and play, and men and women would laugh and cry and remember their first loves as they listened to him. So now his fingers went up and down, up and down, taking strength against the great day.

Eddie looked through the window a moment more, watching his brother, sighed and walked around to the side of the house, where a crow was sleepily eating the radish seeds that Eddie had planted three days ago in a fit of boredom. Eddie threw a stone at the crow and the crow silently flew up to the branch of an oak and waited for Eddie to go away. Eddie threw another stone at the crow. The crow moved to another branch. Eddie wound up and threw a curve, but the crow disdained it. Eddie picked his foot up the way he'd seen Carl Hubbell do and sizzled one across not more than three feet from the crow. Without nervousness the crow walked six inches up the branch. In the style now of Dizzy Dean, with terrifying speed, Eddie delivered his fast one. It was wild and the crow didn't even cock his head. You had to expect to be a little wild with such speed. Eddie found a good round stone and rubbed it professionally on his back pocket. He looked over his shoulder to hold the runner close to the bag, watched for the signal. Eddie Hubbell Dean Mungo Feller Ferrell Warnecke Gomez Barnes picked up his foot and let go his high hard one. The crow slowly got off his branch and regretfully sailed away.

Eddie went over, kicked away the loose dirt, and looked at his radish seeds. Nothing was happening to them. They just lay there, baked and inactive, just as he had placed them. No green, no roots, no radishes, no anything. He was sorry he'd ever gone in for farming. The package of seeds had cost him a dime, and the only thing that happened to them was that they were eaten by crows. And now he could use that dime. Tonight he had a date.

"I got a date," he said aloud, savoring the words. He went to the shade of the grape arbor to think about it. He sat down on the bench under the cool flat leaves, and thought about it. He'd never had a date before in his life. He had thirty-five cents. Thirty-five cents ought to be enough for any girl, but if he hadn't bought the radish seeds, he'd have had forty-five cents, really prepared for any eventuality. "Damn crow," he said, thinking of the evil black head feeding on his dime.

Many times he'd wondered how you managed to get a date. Now he knew. It happened all of a sudden. You went up to a girl where she was lying on the raft in a lake and you looked at her, chubby in a blue bathing suit, and she looked seriously at you out of serious blue eyes where you stood dripping with lake water, with no hair on your chest, and suddenly you said, "I don't s'pose yuh're not doing anything t'morra night, are yuh?" You didn't know quite what you meant, but she did, and she said, "Why, no, Eddie. Say about eight o'clock?" And you nodded and dived back into the lake and there you were.

Still, those radish seeds, that crow-food, that extra dime. . . .

Lawrence came out, flexing his fingers, very neat in clean khaki shorts and a white blouse. He sat down next to Eddie in the grape arbor.

"I would like a strawberry ice cream soda," he said.

"Got any money?" Eddie asked, hopefully.

Lawrence shook his head.

"No strawberry ice cream soda," Eddie said.

Lawrence nodded seriously. "You got any money?" he asked.

"Some," Eddie said carefully. He pulled down a grape leaf and cracked it between his hands, held up the two parts and looked at them critically.

Lawrence didn't say anything, but Eddie sensed a feeling developing in the grape arbor, like a growth. "I gotta save my money," Eddie said harshly. "I got a date. I got thirty-five cents. How do I know she won't want a banana-split tonight?"

Lawrence nodded again, indicating that he understood, but sorrow washed up in his face like a high tide.

They sat in silence, uncomfortably, listening to the rustle of the grape leaves.

"All the time I was practicing," Lawrence said, finally, "I kept thinking, 'I would like a strawberry ice cream soda, I would like a strawberry ice cream soda . . .' "

Eddie stood up abruptly. "Aaah, let's get outa here. Let's go down to the lake. Maybe something's doing down the lake."

They walked together through the fields to the lake, not saying anything, Lawrence flexing his fingers mechanically.

"Why don't yuh stop that fer once?" Eddie asked, with distaste. "Just fer once?"

"This is good for my fingers. It keeps them loose."

"Yuh give me a pain."

"All right," Lawrence said, "I won't do it now."

They walked on again, Lawrence barely up to Eddie's chin, frailer, cleaner, his hair mahogany dark and smooth on his high, pink, baby brow. Lawrence whistled. Eddie listened with disguised respect.

"That's not so bad," Eddie said. "You don't whistle half bad."

"That's from the Brahms second piano concerto." Lawrence stopped whistling for a moment. "It's easy to whistle."

"Yuh give me a pain," Eddie said, mechanically, "a real pain."

When they got to the lake, there was nobody there. Flat and unruffled it stretched across, like a filled blue cup, to the woods on the other side.

"Nobody here," Eddie said, staring at the raft, unmoving and dry in the still water. "That's good. Too many people here all the time." His eyes roamed the lake, to the farthest corner, to the deepest cove.

"How would yuh like to go rowing in a boat out in that old lake?" Eddie asked.

"We haven't got a boat," Lawrence answered reasonably.

"I didn't ask yuh that. I asked, 'How'd yuh like to go rowing?' "

"I'd like to go rowing if we had a . . . ."

"Shut up!" Eddie took Lawrence's arm, led him through tall grass to the water's edge, where a flat-bottomed old boat was drawn up, the water just lapping at the stern, high, an old red color, faded by sun and storm. A pair of heavy oars lay along the bottom of the boat.

"Jump in," Eddie said, "when I tell yuh to."

"But it doesn't belong to us."

"Yuh want to go rowing, don't yuh?"

"Yes, but . . ."

"Then jump in when I give yuh the word."

Lawrence neatly took off his shoes and socks while Eddie hauled the boat into the water.

"Jump in!" Eddie called.

Lawrence jumped. The boat glided out across the still lake. Eddie rowed industriously once they got out of the marsh grass.

"This isn't half bad, is it?" He leaned back on his oars for a moment.

"It's nice," Lawrence said. "It's very peaceful."

"Aaah," said Eddie, "yuh even talk like a pianist." And he rowed. After a while he got tired and let the boat go with the wind. He lay back and thought of the night to come, dabbling his fingers in the water, happy. "They oughta see me now, back on a Hunnerd and Seventy-third Street," he said. "They oughta see me handle this old boat."

"Everything would be perfect," Lawrence agreed, picking his feet up out of the puddle that was collecting on the bottom of the boat, "if we only knew that when we got out of this boat, we were going to get a strawberry ice cream soda."

"Why don't yuh think of somethin' else? Always thinkin' of one thing! Don't yuh get tired?"

"No," Lawrence said, after thinking it over.

"Here!" Eddie pushed the oars toward his brother. "Row! That'll give yuh somethin' else t' think about."

Lawrence took the oars gingerly. "This is bad for my hands," he explained as he pulled dutifully on the oars. "It stiffens the fingers."

"Look where yuh're goin'!" Eddie cried impatiently. "In circles! What the hell's the sense in goin' in circles?"

"That's the way the boat goes," Lawrence said, pulling hard. "I can't help it if that's the way the boat goes."

"A pianist. A regular pianist. That's all yuh are. Gimme those oars."

Gratefully Lawrence yielded the oars up.

"It's not my fault if the boat goes in circles. That's the way it's made," he persisted quietly.

"Aaah, shut up!" Eddie pulled savagely on the oars. The boat surged forward, foam at the prow.

"Hey, out there in the boat! Hey!" A man's voice called over the water.

"Eddie," Lawrence said, "there's a man yelling at us."

"Come on in here, before I beat your pants off!" the man called. "Get out of my boat!"

"He wants us to get out of his boat," Lawrence interpreted. "This must be his boat."

"You don't mean it," Eddie snorted with deep sarcasm. He turned around to shout at the man on the shore, who was waving his arms now. "All right," Eddie called. "All right. We'll give yuh yer old boat. Keep your shirt on."

The man jumped up and down. "I'll beat yer heads off," he shouted.

Lawrence wiped his nose nervously. "Eddie," he said, "why don't we row over to the other side and walk home from there?"

Eddie looked at his brother contemptuously. "What're yuh—afraid?"

"No," Lawrence said, after a pause. "But why should we get into an argument?"

For answer Eddie pulled all the harder on the oars. The boat flew through the water. Lawrence squinted to look at the rapidly nearing figure of the man on the bank.

"He's a great big man, Eddie," Lawrence reported. "You never saw such a big man. And he looks awfully sore. Maybe we shouldn't've gone out in this boat. Maybe he doesn't like people to go out in his boat. Eddie, are you listening to me?"

With a final heroic pull, Eddie drove the boat into the shore. It grated with a horrible noise on the pebbles of the lake bottom.

"Oh, my God," the man said, "that's the end of that boat."

"That doesn't really hurt it, mister," Lawrence said. "It makes a lot of noise, but it doesn't do any damage."

The man reached over and grabbed Lawrence by the back of his neck with one hand and placed him on solid ground. He was a very big man, with tough bristles that grew all over his double chin and farmer's muscles in his arms that were quivering with passion now under a mat of hair. There was a boy of about thirteen with him, obviously, from his look, his son, and the son was angry, too.

"Hit 'im, Pop," the son kept calling. "Wallop 'im!"

The man shook Lawrence again and again. He was almost too overcome with anger to speak. "No damage, eh? Only noise, eh!" he shouted into Lawrence's paling face. "I'll show you damage. I'll show you noise."

Eddie spoke up. Eddie was out of the boat now, an oar gripped in his hand, ready for the worst. "That's not fair," he said. "Look how much bigger yuh are than him. Why'n't yuh pick on somebody yuh size?"

The farmer's boy jumped up and down in passion, exactly as his father had done. "I'll fight him, Pop. I'll fight 'im! I'm his size! Come on, kid, put yer hands up!"

The farmer looked at his son, looked at Lawrence. Slowly he released Lawrence. "O.K.," he said. "Show him, Nathan."

Nathan pushed Lawrence. "Come into the woods, kid," he said belligerently. "We kin settle it there."

"One in the eye," Eddie whispered out of the corner of his mouth, "Give 'im one in the eye, Larry!"

But Lawrence stood with eyes lowered, regarding his hands.

"Well?" the farmer asked.

Lawrence still looked at his hands, opening and closing them slowly.

"He don't wanna fight," Nathan taunted Eddie. "He just wants t' row in our boat, he don't wanna fight."

"He wants to fight, all right," Eddie said staunchly, and under his breath, "Come on, Larry, in the kisser, a fast one in the puss . . ."

But Larry stood still, calmly, seeming to be thinking of Brahms and Beethoven, of distant concert halls.

"He's yella, that's what's the matter with him!" Nathan roared. "He's a coward, all city kids're cowards!"

"He's no coward," Eddie insisted, knowing in his deepest heart that his brother was a coward. With his knees he nudged Lawrence. "Bring up yuh left! Please, Larry, bring up yuh left!"

Deaf to all pleas, Lawrence kept his hands at his sides.

"Yella! Yella! Yella!" Nathan screamed loudly.

"Well," the farmer wanted to know, "is he goin' to fight or not?"

"Larry!" Fifteen years of desperation was in Eddie's voice, but it made no mark on Lawrence. Eddie turned slowly toward home. "He's not goin' to fight," he said flatly. And then, as one throws a bone to a neighbor's noisy dog, "Come on, you . . ."

Slowly Lawrence bent over, picked up his shoes and socks, took a step after his brother.

"Wait a minute, you!" the farmer called. He went after Eddie, turned him around. "I want to talk to ye."

"Yeah?" Eddie said sadly, with little defiance. "What do yuh wanna say?"

"See that house over there?" the farmer asked, pointing.

"Yeah," Eddie said. "What about it?"

"That's my house," the farmer said. "You stay away from it. See?"

"O.K. O.K.," Eddie said wearily, all pride gone.

"See that boat there?" the farmer asked, pointing at the source of all the trouble.

"I see it," Eddie said.

"That's my boat. Stay away from it or I'll beat hell outa ye. See?"

"Yeah, yeah, I see," Eddie said. "I won't touch yer lousy boat." And once more, to Lawrence, "Come On, *you* . . . ."

"Yella! Yella! Yella!" Nathan kept roaring, jumping up and down, until they passed out of earshot, across the pleasant fields, ripe with the soft sweet smell of clover in the late summer afternoon. Eddie walked before Lawrence, his face grimly contracted, his mouth curled in shame and bitterness. He stepped on the clover blossoms fiercely, as though he hated them, wanted to destroy them, the roots under them, the very ground they grew in.

Holding his shoes in his hands, his head bent on his chest, his hair still mahogany smooth and mahogany dark, Lawrence followed ten feet back in the footsteps, plainly marked in the clover, of his brother.

"Yella," Eddie was muttering, loud enough for the villain behind him to hear clearly. "Yella! Yella as a flower. My own brother," he marveled. "If it was me I'd'a been glad to get killed before I let anybody call me that. I would let 'em cut my heart out first. My own brother. Yella as a flower. Just one in the eye! Just *one*! Just to show 'im . . . But he stands there, takin' guff from a kid with holes in his pants. A pianist. Lawrrrrence! They knew what they were doin' when they called yuh Lawrrrrence! Don't talk to me! I don't want yuh ever to talk to me again as long as yuh live! Lawrrrrence!"

In sorrow too deep for tears, the two brothers reached home, ten feet, ten million miles apart.

Without looking around, Eddie went to the grape arbor, stretched out on the bench. Lawrence looked after him, his face pale and still, then went into the house.

Face downward on the bench, close to the rich black earth of the arbor, Eddie bit his fingers to keep the tears back. But he could not bite hard enough, and the tears came, a bitter tide, running down his face, dropping on the black soft earth in which the grapes were rooted.

"Eddie!"

Eddie scrambled around, pushing the tears away with iron hands. Lawrence was standing there, carefully pulling on doeskin gloves over his small hands. "Eddie," Lawrence was saying, stonily disregarding the tears. "I want you to come with me."

Silently, but with singing in his heart so deep it called new tears to his wet eyes, Eddie got up, blew his nose, and followed after his brother, caught up with him, walked side by side with him across the field of clover, so lightly that the red and purple blossoms barely bent in their path.

Eddie knocked sternly at the door of the farmhouse, three knocks, solid, vigorous, the song of trumpets caught in them.

Nathan opened the door. "What do ye want?" he asked suspiciously.

"A little while ago," Eddie said formally, "yuh offered to fight my brother. He's ready now."

Nathan looked at Lawrence, standing there, straight, his head up, his baby lips compressed into a thin tight line, his gloved hands creased in solid fists. He started to close the door. "He had his chance," Nathan said.

63

Eddie kept the door open firmly. "Yuh offered, remember that," he reminded Nathan politely.

"He shoulda fought then," Nathan said stubbornly. "He had his chance."

"Come on," Eddie almost begged. "Yuh wanted to fight before."

"That was before. Lemme close the door."

"Yuh can't do this!" Eddie was shouting desperately. "Yuh offered!"

Nathan's father, the farmer, appeared in the doorway. He looked bleakly out. "What's goin' on here?" he asked.

"A little while ago," Eddie spoke very fast, "this man here offered to fight this man here." His eloquent hand indicated first Nathan, then Lawrence. "Now we've come to take the offer."

The farmer looked at his son. "Well?"

"He had his chance," Nathan grumbled sullenly.

"Nathan don't want t' fight," the farmer said to Eddie. "Get outa here."

Lawrence stepped up, over to Nathan. He looked Nathan squarely in the eye. "Yella," he said to Nathan.

The farmer pushed his son outside the door. "Go fight him," he ordered.

"We can settle it in the woods," Lawrence said.

"Wipe him up, Larry!" Eddie called as Lawrence and Nathan set out for the woods, abreast, but a polite five yards apart. Eddie watched them disappear behind trees, in silence.

The farmer sat down heavily on the porch, took out a package of cigarettes, offered them to Eddie. "Want one?"

Eddie looked at the cigarettes, suddenly took one. "Thanks," he said.

The farmer struck a match for the cigarettes, leaned back against a pillar, stretched comfortably, in silence. Eddie licked the tobacco of his first cigarette nervously off his lips.

"Sit down," the farmer said, "ye kin never tell how long kids'll fight."

"Thanks," Eddie said, sitting, pulling daringly at the cigarette, exhaling slowly, with natural talent.

In silence they both looked across the field to the woods that shielded the battlefield. The tops of the trees waved a little in the wind and the afternoon was collecting in deep blue shadows among the thick brown tree-trunks where they gripped the ground. A chicken hawk floated lazily over the field, banking and slipping with the wind. The farmer regarded the chicken hawk without malice.

"Some day," the farmer said, "I'm going to get that son of a gun."

"What is it?" Eddie asked, carefully holding the cigarette out so he could talk.

"Chicken hawk. You're from the city, ain't ye?"

"Yeah."

"Like it in the city?"

"Nothing like it."

The farmer puffed reflectively. "Some day I'm goin' to live in the city. No sense in livin' in the country these days."

"Oh, I don't know," Eddie said. "The country's very nice. There's a lot to be said for the country."

The farmer nodded, weighing the matter in his own mind. He put out his cigarette. "Another cigarette?" he asked Eddie.

"No, thanks," Eddie said, "I'm still working on this."

"Say," said the farmer, "do you think your brother'll damage my kid?"

"It's possible," Eddie said. "He's very tough, my brother. He has dozens a' fights, every month. Every kid back home's scared stiff a' him. Why," said Eddie, sailing full into fancy, "I remember one day, Larry fought three kids all in a row. In a half a hour. He busted all their noses. In a half-hour! He's got a terrific left jab—one, two, bang! like this—and it gets 'em in the nose."

"Well, he can't do Nathan's nose any harm." The farmer laughed. "No matter what you did to a nose like that it'd be a improvement."

"He's got a lot of talent, my brother," Eddie said, proud of the warrior in the woods. "He plays the piano. He's a very good pianoplayer. You ought to hear him."

"A little kid like that," the farmer marveled. "Nathan can't do nothing."

Off in the distance, in the gloom under the trees, two figures appeared, close together, walked slowly out into the sunlight of the field. Eddie and the farmer stood up. Wearily the two fighters approached, together, their arms dangling at their sides.

Eddie looked first at Nathan. Nathan's mouth had been bleeding and there was a lump on his forehead and his ear was red. Eddie smiled with satisfaction. Nathan had been in a fight. Eddie walked slowly toward Lawrence. Lawrence approached with head high. But it was a sadly battered head. The hair was tangled, an eye was closed, the nose was bruised and still bled. Lawrence sucked in the blood from his nose from time to time with his tongue. His collar was torn, his pants covered with forest loam, with his bare knees skinned and raw. But in the one eye that still could be seen shone a clear light, honorable, indomitable.

"Ready to go home now, Eddie?" Lawrence asked.

"Sure." Eddie started to pat Lawrence on the back, pulled his hand back. He turned and waved at the farmer. "So long."

"So long," the farmer called. "Any time you want to use the boat, just step into it."

"Thanks." Eddie waited while Lawrence shook hands gravely with Nathan.

"Good night," Lawrence said. "It was a good fight."

"Yeah," Nathan said.

The two brothers walked away, close together, across the field of clover, fragrant in the long shadows. Half the way they walked in silence, the silence of equals, strong men communicating in a language more eloquent than words, the only sound the thin jingle of the thirty-five cents in Eddie's pocket.

Suddenly Eddie stopped Lawrence. "Let's go this way," he said, pointing off to the right.

"But home's this way, Eddie."

"I know. Let's go into town. Let's get ice cream sodas," Eddie said; "let's get strawberry ice cream sodas."

# Welcome to the City

As he drew nearer to it, Enders looked up at his hotel through the black drizzle of the city that filled the streets with rain and soot and despair. A small red neon sign bloomed over the hotel entrance, spelling out CIRCUS HOTEL, REASONABLE, turning the drizzle falling profoundly around it into blood.

Enders sighed, shivered inside his raincoat, and walked slowly up the five steps to the entrance and went in. His nostrils curled, as they did each time he opened the door of the hotel, and his nose was hit by the ancient odor of ammonia and Lysol and old linoleum and old beds and people who must depend on two bathrooms to the floor, and over the other odors the odor of age and sin, all at reasonable rates.

Wysocki was at the desk, in his gray suit with the markings of all the cafeteria soup in the city on it, and the pale face shaven down to a point where at any moment you half-expected to see the bone exposed, gleaming and green. Wysocki stood against the desk with the thirty-watt bulb shining down on his thinning hair and his navy-blue shirt and the solid orange tie, bright as hope in the dark hotel lobby, gravely reading the next morning's *Mirror*, his pale, hairy hands spread importantly, with delicate possessiveness, on the desk in front of him.

Josephine was sitting in one of the three lobby chairs, facing Wysocki. She wore a purple tailored suit with a ruffled waist, and open-toed red shoes, even though the streets outside were as damp and penetratingly cold as any marsh, and Enders could see the high red polish under her stockings, on her toenails. She sat there, not reading, not talking, her face carved out of powder and rouge under the blonde hair whose last surge of life had been strangled from it a dozen years before by peroxide and small-town hairdressers and curling irons that could have been used to primp the hair of General Sherman's granite horse.

"The English," Wysocki was saying, without looking up from

his paper. "I wouldn't let them conduct a war for me for one million dollars in gilt-edged securities. Debaters and herring-fishermen," he said. "That's what they are."

"I thought Jews ate herring," Josephine said. Her voice scraped in the lobby, as though the Circus Hotel itself had suddenly broken into speech in its own voice, Lysol and ammonia and rotting ancient wood finally put into sound.

"Jews eat herring," Wysocki said. "And the English eat herring."

Enders sighed again and walked up to the desk. In the chair near the stairway, he noticed, a girl was sitting, a pretty girl in a handsome green coat trimmed with lynx. He watched her obliquely as he talked to Wysocki, noticed that her legs were good and the expression cool, dignified, somehow hauntingly familiar.

"Hello, Wysocki," Enders said.

"Mr. Enders." Wysocki looked up pleasantly from the newspaper. "So you decided to come in out of the rain to your cozy little nest."

"Yes," said Enders, watching the girl.

"Did you know," Josephine asked, "that the English eat herring?"

"Yes," Enders said, digging into his mind for the face the girl reminded him of.

"That's what Wysocki said." Josephine shrugged. "I was living in happy ignorance."

Enders leaned over so that he could whisper into Wysocki's ear. "Who is she?" Enders asked.

Wysocki peered at the girl in the green coat, his eyes sly and guilty, as a thief might peer at a window at Tiffany's through which he intended to heave a brick later in the evening. "Zelinka," Wysocki whispered. "Her name's Bertha Zelinka. She checked in this afternoon. You could do worse, couldn't you?" He chuckled soundlessly, his bone-shaven face creasing without mirth, green and gleaming under the thirty-watt bulb.

"I've seen her some place," Enders whispered, looking at the girl over his shoulder. She sat remote, cold, her legs crossed beautifully under the green coat, looking under heavy lids at the scarred and battered clock over Wysocki's head. "I know that face," Enders said. "But from where?"

"She looks like Greta Garbo," Wysocki said. "That's where you know her from."

Enders stared at the girl in the green coat. She did look like Greta Garbo, the long pale face, the long eyes, the wide, firm mouth, the whole thing a mirror of passion and pain and deep Northern melancholy and bony, stubborn beauty. Suddenly Enders realized that he was a stranger in a strange city, a thousand miles from home, that it was raining out, that he had no girl, and that no one in this huge and wrangling seven-million town had ever said anything more tender to him than "Pass the mustard." And here, before him, solid as his hand, in a green coat with a lynx collar, sat a tall, melancholy girl who looked enough like Greta Garbo, pain and passion and beauty and understanding all mixed on the bony, pale face, to be her twin sister. His voice charged at his throat, leaping to say the first tender word in this rat-eaten, roach-claimed hotel lobby.

"Enders!" His name was spoken gaily, warmly. He turned from looking at Bertha Zelinka, wrenching his soul. "Mr. Enders, I was waiting for your appearance." It was Bishop, the owner of the hotel, a little fat, gray-faced man with wet mustaches. He was rubbing his hands jovially now. "You were just the person I wanted to see tonight," he said.

"Thanks," said Enders.

"Wait!" Bishop's voice trilled. "Don't move an inch from the spot! I have a treat in store for you."

He darted back of the desk through the door into his office. Enders turned and looked at Bertha Zelinka, sitting there as calmly, as remotely, as Garbo herself.

"Observe!" Bishop darted out again from his office. "Look!" He held his hand high above his head. From it dangled a dead, wet chicken. "See what I've saved for you. I am willing to give you this chicken for sixty cents, Mr. Enders."

Enders looked politely at the chicken, hanging sadly in death from Bishop's proud hand.

"Thanks, Mr. Bishop," Enders said. "But I have no place to cook a chicken."

"Take it to your home." Bishop whirled the chicken lovingly, giving it a spruce and electric appearance of life, the wings spreading, the feathers ruffling, "Your mother would be delighted with this bird."

"My mother's in Davenport, Iowa," Enders said.

"You must have some relatives in the city." Bishop pushed it lovingly under his nose, spreading the limp wings for inspection. "They'll receive you with open arms with this chicken. This is a guaranteed Plymouth Rock chicken, Birds like this are exhibited in poultry shows from coast to coast. Sixty cents, Mr. Enders," Bishop said winningly. "Can you go wrong for sixty cents?"

Enders shook his head. "I have no relatives in the city," he said. "Thanks a lot, but I can't use it."

Bishop looked at him coldly. He shrugged. "I could've sold this chicken five times already," he said, "but I was saving it for you because you looked so pale. You gained my sympathy." He shrugged again, and holding the Plymouth Rock by the neck, he went into his office.

"Well," said Enders loudly, looking squarely at Bertha Zelinka, "I guess I'll turn in for the night."

"Want some company, Baby?" Josephine asked, in her voice the first note of hope she had allowed to sound there all evening.

"No, thank you," Enders said, embarrassedly, glad that Miss Zelinka wasn't looking at him at the moment.

"You certainly are a great ladies' man," Josephine said, her voice rasping through the lobby. "Don't you know you'll go crazy, you go so long without a woman? You been here two weeks, you haven't had a woman all that time. They face that problem in Sing Sing, the convicts climb on the walls."

Enders looked uneasily at Miss Zelinka. He didn't want a girl who looked like Greta Garbo to hear him mixed up in that kind of a conversation. "Good night," he said and walked past Miss Zelinka down the hallway to his own room, which was on the ground floor, at the bottom of an airwell, three dollars a week. He looked back regretfully. Miss Zelinka's legs were visible, jutting out, like a promise of poetry and flowers, past the grime and gloom of the hallway. Sadly he opened the door and went into his room, took off his hat and coat and fell on the bed. He could hear Josephine talking, as though the walls, the vermin, the old and wailing plumbing, the very rats hurrying on their gloomy errands between the floors, had at last found a voice.

"The papers are full of boys like him," Josephine was saying. "Turning the gas on and stuffing their heads into the oven. What a night! What a stinking whore of a night! They'll find plenty of bodies in the river tomorrow morning."

"Josephine," Wysocki's voice floated down the hallway. "You ought to learn to talk with more cheerfulness. You're ruining your business, Josephine. The wholesale butchers from Tenth Avenue, the slaughterhouse workers, your whole regular clientele, they're all avoiding you. Should I tell you why?"

"Tell me why," Josephine said.

"Because you're gloomy!" Wysocki said. "Because you depress them with your talk. People like a woman to be cheerful. You can't expect to succeed in your line if you walk around like the last day of the world is beginning in two and three-quarter hours, Bulova watch time."

70

"The butchers from Tenth Avenue!" Josephine snarled. "Who wants them? I give them to you as a gift."

Enders lay on the bed, regretting that a proud and beautiful woman like Bertha Zelinka had to sit in one of the three chairs of the lobby of the Circus Hotel on a rainy night and listen to a conversation like that. He put on the light and picked up the book he was reading.

> *I was neither at the hot gates*
> *Nor fought in the warm rain*
> *Nor knee deep in the salt marsh, heaving a cutlass,*
> *Bitten by flies, fought . . .*

"What a night!" Josephine's voice scraped down the hallway. "The river will be stuffed with bodies in the morning."

Enders put down T. S. Eliot. It was hard to read T. S. Eliot in the Circus Hotel without a deep feeling of irony. Enders got up and looked around the doorpost, down the hall. The proud, poetic legs were still there, lean, muscular, beautifully shaped, aristocratic, stemming down into slim ankles and narrow feet. Enders leaned dreamily against the doorpost, regarding Miss Zelinka's legs. Music played from a well-known orchestra in a night club lit by orange lamps, where no dish cost less than a dollar seventy-five, even tomato juice, and he danced with Bertha Zelinka, both of them dressed beautifully, shiningly, and he made those deep, long eyes, charged with Northern melancholy, crinkle with laughter, and later grow sober and reflective as he talked swiftly of culture, of art, of poetry. " 'Nor fought in the warm rain,' in the phrase of T. S. Eliot, a favorite of mine, 'nor knee deep in the salt marsh . . .' "

He walked quickly down the hallway, looking neither to right nor left until he stopped at the desk. "Have there been any telephone calls for me today?" he asked Wysocki, carefully avoiding looking at Miss Zelinka.

"No," said Wysocki. "Not a thing."

Enders turned and stared full at Miss Zelinka, trying, with the deep intensity of his glance, to get her to look at him, smile at him . . .

"Heads like yours, my friend," Josephine said, "they find in ovens."

Miss Zelinka sat passionless, expressionless, heedless, looking at a point twenty-five feet over Wysocki's shoulder, patiently, but coolly, in the attitude of a woman who is expecting a Lincoln to drive up at any moment and a uniformed chauffeur to spring from

71

it and lead her fastidiously to the heavy, upholstered door, rich with heavy hardware.

Enders walked slowly back to his room. He tried to read some more. "April is the cruellest month . . ." He thumbed through the book. "Here, said she, is your card, the drowned Phoenician Sailor . . ." Enders put the book down. He couldn't read tonight. He went to the door and looked out. The legs, silk and skin and firm muscle, were still there. Enders took a deep breath and walked back toward the desk.

"Look," said Josephine, "the shuttle's back."

"I forgot to ask." He looked straight at Wysocki. "Is there any mail for me?"

"No mail," said Wysocki.

"I'll tell you frankly, friend," Josephine said. "You should've stayed in Davenport, Iowa. That's my honest opinion. New York City will break you like a peanut shell."

"Nobody asked for your opinion," Wysocki said, noticing Enders peering uneasily at Miss Zelinka to see what impression Josephine's advice had made on her. "He's a nice boy, he's educated, he's going to go a long way. Leave him alone."

"I'm only giving him my honest opinion," Josephine said. "I've been in New York a dozen years. I see them begin and I see them wind up in the river."

"Will you, for Christ's sake, stop talking about the river?" Wysocki slammed his hand on the desk.

Gratefully, Enders noticed that Miss Zelinka was listening to the conversation, that her head tilted just a little, a shade went across her disdainful, beautiful eyes.

"I come from Fall River," Josephine said. "I should've stayed there. At least when you're dead in Fall River they bury you. Here they leave you walk around until your friends notice it. Why did I ever leave Fall River? I was attracted by the glamor of the Great White Way." She waved her red and white umbrella ironically, in salute to the city.

Enders noticed that a hint, a twitch of a smile, played at the corner of Miss Zelinka's mouth. He was glad that she'd heard Wysocki say he was educated, he was going to go a long way.

"If you'd like," he heard his voice boom out suddenly in the direction of Miss Zelinka, "if you'd like, if you're waiting for someone, you can wait in my room. It's not so noisy there."

"No, thank you," Miss Zelinka said, speaking curiously, her lips together, not showing her teeth. Her voice, behind the closed, beautiful lips, was deep and hoarse and moving, and Enders felt it grip at his throat like a cool, firm hand. He turned to Wysocki, determined now that he was not going back to his room.

"I was curious," he said. "Where did Bishop get that chicken he wants to sell me?"

Wysocki looked behind him carefully, "Don't buy those chickens, Enders," he said in a low voice. "I advise you as a good friend. Bishop picks them up on Tenth Avenue, alongside the railroad tracks."

"What're they doing there?" Enders asked.

"The trains bring them in from the farms, from the country," Wysocki said. "The ones that died on the trip for one reason or another, the trainmen throw them off the cars and they're piled up alongside the tracks and Bishop picks out the ones that look as though they died most peaceful and he tries to sell them." Wysocki slid back to the office door, listened guiltily for a moment for Bishop, like a spy in the movies. "I advise you not to buy them. They're not the most nourishing articles of food in the world."

Enders smiled. "Bishop ought to be in Wall Street," he said. "With talent like that."

Miss Zelinka laughed. Feeling twice as tall as he had felt a moment before, Enders noticed that Miss Zelinka was laughing, quietly, and without opening her mouth, but true laughter. He laughed with her and their eyes met in friendly, understanding amusement.

"May I buy you a cup of coffee?" hurled out of his throat, at Miss Zelinka's head, like a hand grenade.

The light of thought, consideration, appeared in the large gray eyes, while Enders waited. Then Miss Zelinka smiled. "All right," she said. She stood up, five feet six inches tall, graceful as a duchess.

"I'll be right back," Enders said, quickly. "Just have to get my coat."

He fled lightly down the hall toward his room.

"That's what keeps me poor," Josephine said. "Girls like that. What a night, what a dirty whore of a night!"

"I'm a dancer," Bertha Zelinka was saying two hours later, her coat off, in Enders' room, as she drank the whisky straight in one of the two water tumblers the room boasted. "Specialty dancing." She put the whisky down, suddenly sank beautifully to the floor in a split. "I'm as supple as a cat."

"I see," Enders said, his eyes furious with admiration for Miss Zelinka, full-breasted, flat-bellied, steel-thighed, supple as a cat,

73

spread magnificently on the dirty carpet. It was more pleasant to look at her body, now that he had seen her eating, mouth opened to reveal the poor, poverty-stricken, ruined teeth jagged and sorrowful in her mouth. "That looks very hard to do."

"My name's been in lights," Miss Zelinka said, from the floor. "Please pass the whisky. From one end of the country to another. I've stopped show after show. I've got an uncanny sense of timing." She stood up, after taking another draught of her whisky, closing her eyes with a kind of harsh rapture as the Four Roses went down past the miserable teeth, down inside the powerful, long white throat. "I'm an actress, too, you know, Mr. Enders."

"I'm an actor," Enders said shyly, feeling the whisky beat in his blood, keeping his eyes fiercely and wonderingly on Miss Zelinka. "That's why I'm in New York. I'm an actor."

"You ought to be a good actor," Miss Zelinka said. "You got the face for it. It's refined." She poured herself another drink, watching the amber liquor pour into her glass with a brooding, intense expression in her face, "I had my name in lights from coast to coast. Don't you believe it?"

"I believe it," Enders said sincerely, noting that half the bottle was already gone.

"That's why I'm here now," she said. She walked beautifully around the small, flaky-walled room, her hands running sorrowfully over the warped bureau, the painted bedstead. "That's why I'm here now." Her voice was faraway and echoing, hoarse with whisky and regret. "I'm very much in demand, you know. I've stopped shows for ten minutes at a time. They wouldn't let me get off the stage. Musicals that cost one hundred and fifty thousand to ring the curtain up. That's why I'm here now," she said mysteriously, and drained her glass. She threw herself on the bed next to Enders, stared moodily through almost closed eyes, at the stained and beaten ceiling, "The Shuberts're putting on a musical. They want me for it. Rehearsals are on Fifty-second Street, so I thought I'd move close by for the time being." She sat up, silently reached for the bottle, poured with the fixed expression, brooding and infatuate, which she reserved for the distillers' product. Enders, too full for words, sitting on the same bed with a woman who looked like Greta Garbo, who had stopped musical shows with specialty dancing from coast to coast, who got drunk with the assured yet ferocious grace of a young society matron, watched her every move, with hope, admiration, growing passion.

"You might ask," Miss Zelinka said, "what is a person like myself doing in a rat-hole like this." She waited, but Enders merely gulped silently at his whisky. She chuckled and patted his hand. "You're a nice boy. Iowa, you said? You come from Iowa?"

"Iowa."

"Corn," Miss Zelinka said. "That's what they grow in Iowa." She nodded, having placed Iowa and Enders firmly in her mind. "I passed through Iowa on my way to Hollywood." Half the whisky in her glass disappeared.

"Have you acted in pictures?" Enders asked, impressed, sitting on the same bed with a woman who had been in Hollywood.

Miss Zelinka laughed moodily. "Hollywood!" She finished her drink. "Don't look for my footprints in front of Grauman's Chinese." She reached fluently for the bottle.

"It seems to me," Enders said seriously, breathing deeply because Miss Zelinka was leaning across him for the moment. "It seems to me you'd do very well. You're beautiful and you've got a wonderful voice."

Miss Zelinka laughed again. "Look at me," she said.

Enders looked at her.

"Do I remind you of anybody?" Miss Zelinka asked.

Enders nodded.

Miss Zelinka drank moodily. "I look like Greta Garbo," she said. "Nobody could deny that. I'm not being vain when I tell you when I photograph you couldn't tell me apart from the Swede." She sipped her whisky, ran it lovingly around in her mouth, swallowed slowly, "A woman who looks like Greta Garbo in Hollywood is like the fifth leg on a race horse. Do you understand what I mean?"

Enders nodded sympathetically.

"It's my private curse," Miss Zelinka said, tears looming in her eyes like mist over the ocean. She jumped up, shaking her head, walked lightly and dramatically around the room. "I have no complaints," she said. "I've done very well. I live in a two-room suite on the twentieth floor of a hotel on Seventy-fifth Street. Overlooking the park. All my trunks and bags are up there. I just took a few things with me, until the rehearsals are over. Seventy-fifth Street, on the East Side, is too far away; when you're rehearsing a musical comedy, you've got to be on tap twenty-four hours a day for the Shuberts. A very luxurious two-room suite in the Hotel Chalmers. It's very exclusive, but it's too far from Fifty-second Street." She poured some more whisky for herself, and Enders noticed that the bottle was almost empty. "Oh, yes," she said, crooning to the glass in her hand, "I've done very well. I've danced all over the country. In the most exclusive nightspots, I was the featured entertainment. I'm very greatly in demand." She sat down, close to him, her body moving gently and rhythmically as she spoke. "Seattle, Chicago, Los Angeles, Detroit." She gulped her whisky and her eyes clouded with a final, deep, vague mist and her voice suddenly got very throaty and hoarse. "Miami, Florida." She sat absolutely still and the cloud dissolved into tears and the tears coursed slowly down her face.

"What's the matter?" Enders asked anxiously. "Did I do something?"

Miss Zelinka threw the empty tumbler against the opposite wall. It broke heavily and sullenly, scattered over the carpet. She threw herself back on the bed, wept. "Miami, Florida," she sobbed. "Miami, Florida . . ."

Enders patted her shoulder consolingly.

"I danced in The Golden Horn in Miami, Florida," she cried. "It was a Turkish night club. Very exclusive."

"Why're you crying, darling?" Enders asked, feeling sorry for her, but elated, too, because he had said "darling."

"Every time I think of Miami, Florida," Miss Zelinka said, "I cry."

"Can I do anything to help?" Enders held her hand softly.

"It was January, 1936." Miss Zelinka's voice throbbed with old, hopeless, broken tragedy, forlorn as the story of a siege of a lost and ruined village. "I was dressed in Turkish garments: a brassiere, and veils around my legs and nothing around the middle. At the end of the dance I had to do a back-bend. I leaned back and touched the floor with my hands, with my hair falling down to the floor. There was a bald man. There was a convention of the Metal-Trades Union in Miami, Florida. He had on a badge. The whole night club was full of them." The tears and the anguish pulled at her face. "I'll remember that bald son of a bitch until the day I die. There was no music at that part of the dance. Drums and tambourines. He leaned over and put an olive in my navel and sprinkled it with salt." Miss Zelinka rolled suddenly over on her face and, clutching the bedspread, her shoulders heaving, burrowed into the grayish cotton. "It was a cartoon. He saw it in a cartoon in a magazine. It's funny in a magazine, but wait until it happens to you! The humiliation," she wept. "Every time I think of the humiliation I want to die. Miami, Florida."

Enders watched the bedspread stain with tears, mascara and rouge. With genuine sympathy, he put his arm around her. "I want to be treated with respect," Miss Zelinka wailed. "I was brought up in a good family, why shouldn't I be treated with

76

respect? That fat, bald man, with the badge from the Metal-Trades Union Convention. He leaned over and put the olive in my navel like an egg in an egg cup and sprinkled salt like he was starting breakfast and everybody laughed and laughed, including the orchestra . . . ." Her voice went wailing up the air well, lost, despairing, full of an ancient and irreparable sorrow.

She sat up and threw her arms around Enders, digging her grief-torn head into his shoulder clutching him with strong hands, both of them rocking back and forth like Jews praying, on the enameled bed that squeaked and wailed in the little room.

"Hold me tight," she wept, "hold me tight. I haven't got a two-room suite on East Seventy-fifth Street. I got no trunks in the Hotel Chalmers, hold me tight." Her hands dug into him and her tears and rouge and mascara stained his coat. "The Shuberts aren't giving me a job. Why do I lie, why do I always lie?" She lifted her head, kissed his throat fiercely. He shook at the soft, violent pressure, at the wetness of her lips and the tragic and exhilarating trickle of her tears under his chin, knowing that he was going to have this woman, this Bertha Zelinka. Lonely, far from home, on a rainy night, the city was pulling him in, making a place in its wild and ludicrous life for him. As he kissed her, this woman who looked like Greta Garbo, the century's dream of passion and tragedy and beauty, this woman whom he had met in a rat-tenanted lobby off Columbus Circle, among whores thinking of death and a Pole in an orange tie checking in each night's transients, age and sin, at reasonable rates, Enders felt suddenly at home, accounted for. The city had produced for him a great beauty, supple as a cat, full of lies and whisky and ancient, shadowy victories, a woman with magnificent, proud legs and deep, stormy eyes who wept bitterly behind the frail, warped door because once, in 1936, a bald man from a Metal-Trades Union had put an olive in her navel. Enders held Bertha Zelinka's head in his two hands, looked intently at the bony, drunken, beautiful, tear-stained face. Bertha Zelinka peered longingly and sadly at him through half-closed classic lids, her mouth hanging softly open in passion and promise, her poor jagged teeth showing behind the long, heart-breaking lips. He kissed her, feeling deep within him, that in its own way, on this rainy night, the city had put out its hand in greeting, had called, in its own voice, wry and ironic, "Welcome, Citizen."

Gratefully, near tears, hating himself, his hands shaking exultantly, Enders bent to his knees and took the scraped, year-worn shoes, swollen with the streets' rain, from the long and handsome feet of Bertha Zelinka.

77

# The Girls in Their Summer Dresses

Fifth Avenue was shining in the sun when they left the Brevoort and started walking toward Washington Square. The sun was warm, even though it was November and everything looked like Sunday morning—the buses, and the well-dressed people walking slowly in couples and the quiet buildings with the windows closed.

Michael held Frances' arm tightly as they walked downtown in the sunlight, They walked lightly, almost smiling, because they had slept late and had a good breakfast and it was Sunday. Michael unbuttoned his coat and let it flap around him in the mild wind. They walked, without saying anything, among the young and pleasant-looking people who somehow seem to make up most of the population of that section of New York City.

"Look out," Frances said, as they crossed Eighth Street, "You'll break your neck."

Michael laughed and Frances laughed with him.

"She's not so pretty, anyway," Frances said. "Anyway, not pretty enough to take a chance breaking your neck looking at her."

Michael laughed again. He laughed louder this time, but not as solidly. "She wasn't a bad-looking girl. She had a nice complexion. Country-girl complexion. How did you know I was looking at her?"

Frances cocked her head to one side and smiled at her husband under the tip-tilted brim of her hat. "Mike, darling . . ." she said.

Michael laughed, just a little laugh this time. "O.K.," he said. "The evidence is in. Excuse me. It was the complexion. It's not the sort of complexion you see much in New York. Excuse me."

Frances patted his arm lightly and pulled him along a little faster toward Washington Square.

"This is a nice morning," she said. "This is a wonderful morning. When I have breakfast with you it makes me feel good all day."

"Tonic," Michael said. "Morning pick-up. Rolls and coffee with Mike and you're on the alkali side, guaranteed."

"That's the story. Also I slept all night wound around you like a rope."

"Saturday night," he said. "I permit such liberties only when the week's work is done."

"You're getting fat," she said.

"Isn't it the truth? The lean man from Ohio."

"I love it," she said, "an extra five pounds of husband."

"I love it, too," Michael said gravely.

"I have an idea," Frances said.

"My wife has an idea. That pretty girl."

"Let's not see anybody all day," Frances said. "Let's just hang around with each other. You and me. We're always up to our neck in people, drinking their Scotch, or drinking our Scotch, we only see each other in bed . . ."

"The Great Meeting Place," Michael said. "Stay in bed long enough and everybody you ever knew will show up there."

"Wise guy," Frances said. "I'm talking serious."

"O.K., I'm listening serious."

"I want to go out with my husband all day long. I want him to talk only to me and listen only to me."

"What's to stop us?" Michael asked. "What party intends to prevent me from seeing my wife alone on Sunday? What party?"

"The Stevensons. They want to drop by around one o'clock and they'll drive us into the country."

"The lousy Stevensons," Mike said. "Transparent. They can whistle. They can go driving in the country by themselves. My wife and I have to stay in New York and bore each other tête-à-tête."

"Is it a date?"

"It's a date."

Frances leaned over and kissed him on the tip of the ear.

"Darling," Michael said. "This is Fifth Avenue."

"Let me arrange a program," Frances said. "A planned Sunday in New York for a young couple with money to throw away."

"Go easy."

"First let's go see a football game. A professional football game," Frances said, because she knew Michael loved to watch them. "The Giants are playing. And it'll be nice to be outside all day today and get hungry and later we'll go down to Cavanagh's and get a steak as big as a blacksmith's apron, with a bottle of wine, and after that, there's a new French picture at the Filmarte that everybody says . . . Say, are you listening to me?"

"Sure," he said. He took his eyes off the hatless girl with the

79

dark hair, cut dancer-style, like a helmet, who was walking past him with the self-conscious strength and grace dancers have. She was walking without a coat and she looked very solid and strong and her belly was flat, like a boy's, under her skirt, and her hips swung boldly because she was a dancer and also because she knew Michael was looking at her. She smiled a little to herself as she went past and Michael noticed all these things before he looked back at his wife. "Sure," he said, "we're going to watch the Giants and we're going to eat steak and we're going to see a French picture. How do you like that?"

"That's it," Frances said flatly. "That's the program for the day. Or maybe you'd just rather walk up and down Fifth Avenue."

"No," Michael said carefully. "Not at all."

"You always look at other women," Frances said. "At every damn woman in the City of New York."

"Oh, come now," Michael said, pretending to joke. "Only pretty ones. And, after all, how many pretty women *are* there in New York? Seventeen?"

"More. At least you seem to think so. Wherever you go."

"Not the truth. Occasionally, maybe, I look at a woman as she passes. In the street. I admit, perhaps in the street I look at a woman once in a while . . ."

"Everywhere," Frances said. "Every damned place we go. Restaurants, subways, theaters, lectures, concerts."

"Now, darling," Michael said, "I look at everything. God gave me eyes and I look at women and men and subway excavations and moving pictures and the little flowers of the field. I casually inspect the universe."

"You ought to see the look in your eye," Frances said, "as you casually inspect the universe on Fifth Avenue."

"I'm a happily married man." Michael pressed her elbow tenderly, knowing what he was doing. "Example for the whole twentieth century, Mr. and Mrs. Mike Loomis."

"You mean it?"

"Frances, baby . . ."

"Are you *really* happily married?"

"Sure," Michael said, feeling the whole Sunday morning sinking like lead inside him. "Now what the hell is the sense in talking like that?"

"I would like to know." Frances walked faster now, looking straight ahead, her face showing nothing, which was the way she always managed it when she was arguing or feeling bad.

"I'm wonderfully happily married," Michael said patiently. "I am the envy of all men between the ages of fifteen and sixty in the State of New York.''

"Stop kidding," Frances said.

"I have a fine home," Michael said. "I got nice books and a phonograph and nice friends. I live in a town I like the way I like and I do the work I like and I live with the woman I like. Whenever something good happens, don't I run to you? When something bad happens, don't I cry on your shoulder?''

"Yes" Frances said. "You look at every woman that passes.''

"That's an exaggeration.''

"Every woman." Frances took her hand off Michael's arm. "If she's not pretty you turn away fairly quickly. If she's halfway pretty you watch her for about seven steps . . .''

"My lord, Frances!''

"If she's pretty you practically break your neck . . .''

"Hey, let's have a drink," Michael said, stopping.

"We just had breakfast.''

"Now, listen, darling," Mike said, choosing his words with care, "it's a nice day and we both feel good and there's no reason why we have to break it up. Let's have a nice Sunday.''

"I could have a fine Sunday if you didn't look as though you were dying to run after every skirt on Fifth Avenue.''

"Let's have a drink," Michael said.

"I don't want a drink.''

"What do you want, a fight?''

"No," Frances said so unhappily that Michael felt terribly sorry for her. "I don't want a fight. I don't know why I started this. All right, let's drop it. Let's have a good time.''

They joined hands consciously and walked without talking among the baby carriages and the old Italian men in their Sunday clothes and the young women with Scotties in Washington Square Park.

"I hope it's a good game today," Frances said after a while, her tone a good imitation of the tone she had used at breakfast and at the beginning of their walk. "I like professional football games. They hit each other as though they're made out of concrete. When they tackle each other," she said, trying to make Michael laugh, "they make divots. It's very exciting.''

"I want to tell you something," Michael said very seriously. "I have not touched another woman. Not once. In all the five years.''

"All right," Frances said.

"You believe that, don't you?''

"All right.''

They walked between the crowded benches, under the scrubby city park trees.

"I try not to notice it," Frances said, as though she were talking to herself. "I try to make believe it doesn't mean anything. Some men're like that, I tell myself, they have to see what they're missing."

"Some women're like that, too," Michael said. "In my time I've seen a couple of ladies."

"I haven't even looked at another man," Frances said, walking straight ahead, "since the second time I went out with you."

"There's no law," Michael said.

"I feel rotten inside, in my stomach, when we pass a woman and you look at her and I see that look in your eye and that's the way you looked at me the first time, in Alice Maxwell's house. Standing there in the living room, next to the radio with a green hat on and all those people."

"I remember the hat," Michael said.

"The same look," Frances said. "And it makes me feel bad. It makes me feel terrible."

"Shhh, please, darling, shhh . . ."

"I think I would like a drink now," Frances said.

They walked over to a bar on Eighth Street, not saying anything, Michael automatically helping her over curbstones, and guiding her past automobiles. He walked, buttoning his coat, looking thoughtfully at his neatly shined heavy brown shoes as they made the steps toward the bar. They sat near a window in the bar and the sun streamed in, and there was a small cheerful fire in the fireplace. A little Japanese waiter came over and put down some pretzels and smiled happily at them.

"What do you order after breakfast?" Michael asked.

"Brandy, I suppose," Frances said.

"Courvoisier," Michael told the waiter. "Two Courvoisier."

The waiter came with the glasses and they sat drinking the brandy, in the sunlight. Michael finished half his and drank a little water.

"I look at women," he said. "Correct. I don't say it's wrong or right, I look at them. If I pass them on the street and I don't look at them, I'm fooling you, I'm fooling myself."

"You look at them as though you want them," Frances said, playing with her brandy glass. "Every one of them."

"In a way," Michael said, speaking softly and not to his wife, "in a way that's true. I don't do anything about it, but it's true."

"I know it. That's why I feel bad."

82

"Another brandy," Michael called. "Waiter, two more brandies."

"Why do you hurt me?" Frances asked. "What're you doing?"

Michael sighed and closed his eyes and rubbed them gently with his fingertips. "I love the way women look. One of the things I like best about New York is the battalions of women. When I first came to New York from Ohio that was the first thing I noticed, the million wonderful women, all over the city. I walked around with my heart in my throat."

"A kid," Frances said. "That's a kid's feeling."

"Guess again," Michael said. "Guess again. I'm older now, I'm a man getting near middle age, putting on a little fat and I still love to walk along Fifth Avenue at three o'clock on the east side of the street between Fiftieth and Fifty-seventh Streets, they're all out then, making believe they're shopping, in their furs and their crazy hats, everything all concentrated from all over the world into eight blocks, the best furs, the best clothes, the handsomest women, out to spend money and feeling good about it, looking coldly at you, making believe they're not looking at you as you go past."

The Japanese waiter put the two drinks down, smiling with great happiness.

"Everything is all right?" he asked.

"Everything is wonderful," Michael said.

"If it's just a couple of fur coats," Frances said, "and forty-five-dollar hats . . ."

"It's not the fur coats. Or the hats. That's just the scenery for that particular kind of woman. Understand," he said, "you don't have to listen to this."

"I want to listen."

"I like the girls in the offices. Neat, with their eyeglasses, smart, chipper, knowing what everything is about, taking care of themselves all the time." He kept his eye on the people going slowly past outside the window. "I like the girls on Forty-fourth Street at lunch time, the actresses, all dressed up on nothing a week, talking to the good-looking boys, wearing themselves out being young and vivacious outside Sardi's, waiting for producers to look at them. I like the salesgirls in Macy's, paying attention to you first because you're a man, leaving lady customers waiting, flirting with you over socks and books and phonograph needles. I got all this stuff accumulated in me because I've been thinking about it for ten years and now you've asked for it and here it is."

"Go ahead," Frances said.

"When I think of New York City, I think of all the girls, the

Jewish girls, the Italian girls, the Irish, Polack, Chinese, German, Negro, Spanish, Russian girls, all on parade in the city. I don't know whether it's something special with me or whether every man in the city walks around with the same feeling inside him, but I feel as though I'm at a picnic in this city. I like to sit near the women in the theaters, the famous beauties who've taken six hours to get ready and look it. And the young girls at the football games, with the red cheeks, and when the warm weather comes, the girls in their summer dresses . . .'' He finished his drink. "That's the story. You asked for it, remember. I can't help but look at them. I can't help but want them.''

"You want them,'' Frances repeated without expression. "You said that.''

"Right,'' Michael said, being cruel now and not caring, because she had made him expose himself. "You brought this subject up for discussion, we will discuss it fully.''

Frances finished her drink and swallowed two or three times extra. "You say you love me?''

"I love you, but I also want them. O.K.''

"I'm pretty, too,'' Frances said. "As pretty as any of them.''

"You're beautiful,'' Michael said, meaning it.

"I'm good for you,'' Frances said, pleading. "I've made a good wife, a good housekeeper, a good friend. I'd do any damn thing for you.''

"I know,'' Michael said. He put his hand out and grasped hers.

"You'd like to be free to . . .'' Frances said.

"Shhh.''

"Tell the truth.'' She took her hand away from under his.

Michael flicked the edge of his glass with his finger. "O.K.,'' he said gently. "Sometimes I feel I would like to be free.''

"Well,'' Frances said defiantly, drumming on the table, "anytime you say . . .''

"Don't be foolish.'' Michael swung his chair around to her side of the table and patted her thigh.

She began to cry, silently, into her handkerchief, bent over just enough so that nobody else in the bar would notice. "Some day,'' she said, crying, "you're going to make a move . . .''

Michael didn't say anything. He sat watching the bartender slowly peel a lemon.

"Aren't you?'' Frances asked harshly. "Come on, tell me. Talk, Aren't you?''

"Maybe,'' Michael said. He moved his chair back again. "How the hell do I know?''

"You know," Frances persisted. "Don't you know?"

"Yes," Michael said after a while, "I know."

Frances stopped crying then. Two or three snuffles into the handkerchief and she put it away and her face didn't tell anything to anybody. "At least do me one favor," she said.

"Sure."

"Stop talking about how pretty this woman is, or that one. Nice eyes, nice breasts, a pretty figure, good voice," she mimicked his voice. "Keep it to yourself. I'm not interested."

"Excuse me." Michael waved to the waiter. "I'll keep it to myself."

Frances flicked the corner of her eyes "Another brandy," she told the waiter.

"Two," Michael said.

"Yes, ma'am, yes, sir," said the waiter, backing away.

Frances regarded him coolly across the table. "Do you want me to call the Stevensons?" she asked. "It'll be nice in the country."

"Sure," Michael said. "Call them up."

She got up from the table and walked across the room toward the telephone. Michael watched her walk, thinking, what a pretty girl, what nice legs.

# Search Through the Streets of the City

When he finally saw her, he nearly failed to recognize her. He walked behind her for a half block, vaguely noticing that the woman in front of him had long legs and was wearing a loose, college-girl polo coat and a plain brown felt hat.

Suddenly something about the way she walked made him remember—the almost affected rigidity of her back and straightness of throat and head, with all the movement of walking, flowing up to the hips and stopping there, like Negro women in the South and Mexican and Spanish women carrying baskets on their heads.

For a moment, silently, he watched her walk down Twelfth Street, on the sunny side of the street, in front of the little tired gardens behind which lay the quiet, pleasantly run-down old houses. Then he walked up to her and touched her arm.

"Low heels," he said. "I never thought I'd live to see the day."

She looked around in surprise, then smiled widely, took his arm. "Hello, Paul," she said. "I've gone in for health."

"Whenever I think of you," he said, "I think of the highest heels in New York City."

"The old days," Harriet said. They walked slowly down the sunny street, arm in arm, toward Sixth Avenue. "I was a frivolous creature."

"You still walk the same way. As though you ought to have a basket of laundry on your head."

"I practiced walking like that for six months. You'd be surprised how much attention I get walking into a room that way."

"I wouldn't be surprised," Paul said, looking at her. She had black hair and pale, clear skin and a long, full body, and her eyes were deep gray and always brilliant, even after she'd been drinking for three days in a row.

Harriet closed her coat quickly and walked a little faster. "I'm

86

going to Wanamaker's," she said. "There're a couple of things I have to buy. Where are you going?"

"Wanamaker's," Paul said. "I've been dying to go to Wanamaker's for three years."

They walked slowly, in silence, Harriet's arm in his.

"Casual," Paul said. "I bet to the naked eye we look casual as hell. How do you feel?"

Harriet took her arm away. "Casual."

"O.K. Then that's how I feel, too." Paul whistled coldly to himself. He stopped and looked critically at her and she stopped, too, and turned toward him, a slight puzzled smile on her face. "What makes you dress that way?" he asked. "You look like Monday morning in Northampton."

"I just threw on whatever was nearest," Harriet said. "I'm just going to be out about an hour."

"You used to look like a nice big box of candy in your clothes." Paul took her arm again and they started off. "Viennese bonbons. Every indentation carefully exploited in silk and satin. Even if you were just going down to the corner for a pint of gin, you'd look like something that ought to be eaten for dessert. This is no improvement."

"A girl has different periods in clothes. Like Picasso," Harriet said. "And if I'd known I was going to meet you, I'd've dressed differently."

Paul patted her arm. "That's better."

Paul eyed her obliquely as they walked: the familiar, long face, the well-known wide mouth with always a little too much lipstick on it, the little teeth that made her face, when she smiled, look suddenly like a little girl's in Sunday school.

"You're getting skinny, Paul," Harriet said.

Paul nodded. "I'm as lean as a herring. I've been leading a fevered and ascetic life. What sort of life have you been leading?"

"I got married." Harriet paused a moment. "Did you hear I got married?"

"I heard," Paul said. "The last time we crossed Sixth Avenue together the L was still up. I feel a nostalgic twinge for the Sixth Avenue L." They hurried as the light changed. "On the night of January ninth, 1940," Paul said, holding her elbow, "you were not home."

"Possible," Harriet said. "I'm a big girl now; I go out at night."

"I happened to pass your house, and I noticed that the light wasn't on." They turned down toward Ninth Street. "I remembered how hot you kept that apartment—like the dahlia greenhouse in the Botanical Gardens.''

"I have thin blood," Harriet said gravely. "Long years of inbreeding in Massachusetts."

"The nicest thing about you," Paul said, "was you never went to sleep,"

"Every lady to her own virtue," Harriet said. "Some women're beautiful, some're smart—me—I never went to sleep. The secret of my great popularity . . . ."

Paul grinned. "Shut up."

Harriet smiled back at him and they chuckled together. "You know what I mean," he said. "Any time I called you up, two, three in the morning, you'd come right over, lively and bright-eyed, all the rouge and mascara in the right places. . . ."

"In my youth," said Harriet, "I had great powers of resistance."

"In the morning we'd eat breakfast to Beethoven. The Masterwork Hour. WNYC. Beethoven, by special permission of His Honor, the Mayor, from nine to ten." Paul closed his eyes for a moment. "The Little Flower, Mayor for Lovers."

Paul opened his eyes and looked at the half-strange, half-familiar woman walking lightly at his side. He remembered lying close to her, dreamily watching the few lights of the towers of the night-time city, framed by the big window of his bedroom against the black sky, and one night when she moved sleepily against him and rubbed the back of his neck where the hair was sticking up in sharp little bristles because he had had his hair cut that afternoon. Harriet had rubbed them the wrong way, smiling, dreamily, without opening her eyes. "What a delicious thing a man is . . ." she'd murmured. And she'd sighed, then chuckled a little and fallen asleep, her hand still on the shaven back of his neck.

Paul smiled, remembering.

"You still laughing at my clothes?" Harriet asked.

"I remembered something I heard some place . . ." Paul said. " 'What a delicious thing a man is . . .' "

Harriet looked at him coldly. "Who said that?"

Paul squinted suspiciously at her. "Oswald Spengler."

"Uhuh," Harriet said soberly. "It's a famous quotation."

"It's a well-turned phrase," said Paul.

"That's what I think, too." Harriet nodded agreeably and walked a little faster.

They passed the little run-down bar where they'd sat afternoons all winter drinking martinis and talking and talking, and laughing so loud the people at the other tables would turn and smile. Paul waited for Harriet to say something about the bar, but she didn't even seem to notice it. "There's Eddie's Bar," Paul said.

"Uhuh." Harriet nodded briskly.

"He's going to start making his martinis with sherry when all the French vermouth runs out," Paul said.

"It sounds horrible." Harriet made a face.

"Is that all you have to say?" Paul said loudly, remembering all the times he'd looked in to see if she was there.

"What do you want me to say?" Harriet looked honestly puzzled, but Paul had never known when she was lying to him or telling the truth, anyway, and he hadn't improved in the two years, he discovered.

"I don't want you to say anything. I'll take you in and buy you a drink."

"No, thanks. I've really got to get to Wanamaker's and back home in a hurry. Give me a raincheck."

"Yeah," Paul said sourly.

They turned up Ninth Street toward Fifth Avenue.

"I knew I'd meet you some place, finally," Paul said. "I was curious to see what would happen."

Harriet didn't say anything. She was looking absently at the buildings across the street.

"Don't you ever talk any more?" Paul asked.

"What *did* happen?"

"Every once in a while," he started, "I meet some girl I used to know . . ."

"I bet the country's full of them," Harriet said.

"The country's full of everybody's ex-girls."

Harriet nodded. "I never thought of it that way, but you're right."

"Most of the time I think, isn't she a nice, decent person? Isn't it wonderful I'm no longer attached to her? The first girl I ever had," Paul said, "is a policewoman now. She subdued a gangster single-handed in Coney Island last summer. Her mother won't let her go out of the house in her uniform. She's ashamed for the neighbors."

"Naturally," Harriet said.

"Another girl I used to know changed her name and dances in the Russian Ballet. I went to see her dance the other night. She has legs like a Fordham tackle. I used to think she was beautiful. I used to think you were beautiful, too."

"We were a handsome couple," Harriet said. "Except you always needed a shave. That electric razor . . ."

"I've given it up."

They were passing his old house now and he looked at the doorway and remembered all the times he and Harriet had gone in and come out, the rainy days and the early snowy mornings with the milkman's horse silent on the white street behind them. They stopped and looked at the old red house with the shabby shutters and the window on the fourth floor they had both looked out of time and time again to see what the weather was and Paul remembered the first time, on a winter's night, when he and Harriet had gone through that door together.

"I was so damn polite," Paul said softly.

Harriet smiled, knowing what he was talking about. "You kept dropping the key and saying, 'Lord, Lord,' under your breath while you were looking for it."

"I was nervous. I wanted to make sure you knew exactly how matters stood—no illusions. Good friends, everybody understanding everybody else, another girl coming in from Detroit in six weeks, no claims on me, no claims on you . . ." Paul looked at the window on the fourth floor and smiled. "What a fool!"

"It's a nice, quiet street," Harriet said, looking up at the window on the fourth floor, too. She shook her head, took Paul's arm again. "I've got to get to Wanamaker's."

They started off.

"What're you buying at Wanamaker's?" Paul asked.

Harriet hesitated for a moment. "Nothing much. I'm looking at some baby clothes. I'm going to have a baby." They crowded over to one side to let a little woman with four dachshunds pass them in a busy tangle. "Isn't it funny—me with a baby?" Harriet smiled. "I lie around all day and try to imagine what it's going to be like. In between, I sleep and drink beer to nourish us. I've never had such a good time in all my life."

"Well," said Paul, "at least it'll keep your husband out of the army."

"Maybe. He's a raging patriot."

"Good. When he's at Fort Dix I'll meet you in Washington Square Park when you take the baby out for an airing in its perambulator. I'll put on a policeman's uniform to make it proper. I'm not such a raging patriot."

"They'll get you anyway, won't they?"

"Sure. I'll send you my picture in a lieutenant's suit. From Bulgaria. I have a premonition I'm going to be called on to defend a strategic point in Bulgaria."

90

"How do you feel about it?" For the first time Harriet looked squarely and searchingly at him.

Paul shrugged. "It's going to happen. It's all damned silly, but it isn't as silly now as it was ten years ago."

Suddenly Harriet laughed.

"What's so funny?" Paul demanded.

"My asking you how you felt about something. I never used to have a chance . . . You'd let me know how you felt about everything. Roosevelt, James Joyce, Jesus Christ, Gypsy Rose Lee, Matisse, Yogi, liquor, sex, architecture . . ."

"I was full of opinions in those days." Paul smiled a little regretfully. "Lust and conversation. The firm foundations of civilized relations between the sexes."

He turned and looked back at the window on the fourth floor. "That was a nice apartment," he said softly. "Lust and conversation . . ."

"Come on, Paul," Harriet said. "Wanamaker's isn't going to stay open all night."

Paul turned up his collar because the wind was getting stronger as they neared Fifth Avenue. "You were the only girl I ever knew I could sleep in the same bed with."

"That's a hell of a thing to say to a girl." Harriet laughed. "Is that your notion of a compliment?"

Paul shrugged. "It's an irrelevant fact. Or a relevant fact. Is it polite to talk to a married lady this way?"

"No."

Paul walked along with her, "What do you think of when you look at me?" he asked.

"Nothing much," Harriet said carefully.

"What're you lying about?"

"Nothing much," Harriet said flatly.

"Don't you even think, 'What in the name of God did I ever see in him?' "

"No." Harriet put her hands deep in her pockets and walked quickly along the railings.

"Should I tell you what I think of when I look at you?"

"No."

"I've been looking for you for two years," Paul said.

"My name's been in the telephone book." Harriet hurried even more, wrapping her coat tightly around her.

"I didn't realize I was looking for you until I saw you."

"Please, Paul . . ."

"I would walk along the street and I'd pass a bar we'd been in

91

together and I'd go in and sit there, even though I didn't want a drink, not knowing why I was sitting there. Now I know. I was waiting for you to come in. I didn't pass your house by accident.''

"Look, Paul," Harriet pleaded. "It was a long time ago and it was fine and it ended. . . .''

"I was wrong," Paul said. "Do you like hearing that? I was wrong. You know, I never did get married, after all.''

"I know," Harriet said. "Please shut up.''

"I walk along Fifth Avenue and every time I pass St. Patrick's I half look up to see if you're passing, because I met you that day right after you'd had a tooth pulled, and it was cold; you were walking along with the tears streaming from your eyes and your eyes red and that was the only time I ever met you by accident any place. . . .''

Harriet smiled. "That certainly sounds like a beautiful memory.''

"Two years . . .'' Paul said. "I've gone out with a lot of girls in the last two years." He shrugged. "They've bored me and I've bored them. I keep looking at every woman who passes to see if it's you. All the girls I go out with bawl the hell out of me for it. I've been walking around, following girls with dark hair to see if it'll turn out to be you, and girls with a fur jacket like that old one you had and girls that walk in that silly, beautiful way you walk. . . . I've been searching the streets of the city for you for two years and this is the first time I've admitted it even to myself. That little Spanish joint we went the first time. Every time I pass it I remember everything—how many drinks we had and what the band played and what we said and the fat Cuban who kept winking at you from the bar and the very delicate way we landed up in my apartment. . . .''

They were both walking swiftly now, Harriet holding her hands stiffly down at her sides.

"There is a particular wonderful way you are joined together . . .''

"Paul, stop it." Harriet's voice was flat but loud.

"Two years. In two years the edge should be dulled off things like that. Instead . . ." How can you make a mistake as big as that? Paul thought, how can you deliberately be as wrong as that? And no remedy. So long as you live, no remedy. He looked harshly at Harriet. Her face was set, as though she weren't listening to him and only intent on getting across the street as quickly as possible. "How about you?" he asked. "Don't you remember . . . ?''

"I don't remember anything," she said. And then, suddenly, the tears sprang up in her eyes and streamed down the tight, distorted cheeks. "I don't remember a goddamn thing!" she wept. "I'm not going to Wanamaker's. I'm going home! Good-bye!" She ran over to a cab that was parked at the corner and opened the door and sprang in. The cab spurted past Paul and he had a glimpse of Harriet sitting stiffly upright, the tears bitter and unheeded in her eyes.

He watched the cab go down Fifth Avenue until it turned. Then he turned the other way and started walking, thinking, I must move away from this neighborhood. I've lived here long enough.

# The Monument

"I do not want any of his private stock," McMahon said firmly. He blew on a glass and wiped it carefully. "I have my own opinion of his private stock."

Mr. Grimmet looked sad, sitting across the bar on a high stool, and Thesing shrugged like a salesman, not giving up the fight, but moving to a new position to continue the attack. McMahon picked up another glass in his clean, soft bartender's hands. He wiped it, his face serious and determined and flushed right up to the bald spot that his plastered-down hair couldn't cover. There was nobody else in the bar at the front part of the restaurant.

It was three o'clock in the afternoon. In the rear three waiters stood arguing. Every day at three o'clock the three waiters gathered in the back and argued.

"Fascism," one waiter said, "is a rehearsal for the cemetery."

"You read that some place," another waiter said.

"All right," said the first waiter, "I read it some place."

"An Italian," the third waiter said to the first waiter. "You are one lousy Italian."

Mr. Grimmet turned around and called to the waiters, "Please reserve discussions of that character for when you go home. This is a restaurant, not Madison Square Garden."

He turned back to watching McMahon wiping the glasses. The three waiters looked at him with equal hate.

"Many of the best bars in the city," Thesing said in his musical salesman's voice, "use our private stock."

"Many of the best bars in the city," McMahon said, using the towel very hard, "ought to be turned into riding academies."

"That's funny," Thesing said, laughing almost naturally. "He's very funny, isn't he, Mr, Grimmet?"

"Listen, Billy," Mr. Grimmet said, leaning forward, disregarding Thesing, "listen to reason. In a mixed drink nobody can tell how much you paid for the rye that goes into it. That is the supreme beauty of cocktails.''

McMahon didn't say anything. The red got a little deeper on his cheeks and on his bald spot and he put the clean glasses down with a sharp tinkle and the tinkle went through the shining lines of the other glasses on the shelves and sounded thinly through the empty restaurant. He was a little fat man, very compact. He moved with great precision and style behind a bar and you could tell by watching him whether he was merry or sad or perturbed, just from the way he mixed a drink or put down a glass. Just now he was angry and Mr. Grimmet knew it. Mr. Grimmet didn't want a fight, but there was money to be saved. He put out his hand appealingly to Thesing.

''Tell me the truth, Thesing,'' he said. ''Is your private stock bad?''

''Well,'' Thesing said slowly, ''a lot of people like it. It is very superior for a blended product.''

''Blended varnish,'' McMahon said, facing the shelves. ''Carefully matched developing fluid.''

Thesing laughed, the laugh he used from nine to six. ''Witty,'' he said, ''the sparkling bartender.'' McMahon wheeled and looked at him, head down a little on his chest. ''I meant it,'' Thesing protested. ''I sincerely meant it.''

''I want to tell you,'' Mr. Grimmet said to McMahon, fixing him with his eye, ''that we can save seven dollars a case on the private stock.''

McMahon started whistling the tenor aria from *Pagliacci*. He looked up at the ceiling and wiped a glass and whistled. Mr. Grimmet felt like firing him and remembered that at least twice a month he felt like firing McMahon.

''Please stop whistling,'' he said politely. ''We have a matter to discuss.''

McMahon stopped whistling and Mr. Grimmet still felt like firing him.

''Times're not so good,'' Mr. Grimmet said in a cajoling tone of voice, hating himself for descending to such tactics before an employee of his. ''Remember, McMahon, Coolidge is no longer in the White House. I am the last one in the world to compromise with quality, but we must remember, we are in business and it is 1938.''

''Thesing's private stock,'' McMahon said, ''would destroy the stomach of a healthy horse.''

"Mussolini!" the first waiter's voice came out from the back of the restaurant. "Every day on Broadway I pass forty-five actors who could do his act better."

"I am going to tell you one thing," Mr. Grimmet said with obvious calmness to McMahon. "I am the owner of this restaurant."

McMahon whistled some more from *Pagliacci*. Thesing moved wisely down the bar a bit.

"I am interested in making money," Mr. Grimmet said. "What would you say, Mr. McMahon, if I ordered you to use the private stock?"

"I would say, 'I'm through, Mr. Grimmet.' Once and for all."

Mr. Grimmet rubbed his face unhappily and stared coldly at the waiters in the back of the restaurant. The waiters remained silent and stared coldly back at him. "What's it to you?" Mr. Grimmet asked McMahon angrily. "What do you care if we use another whisky. Do you have to drink it?"

"In my bar, Mr. Grimmet," McMahon said, putting down his towel and the glasses and facing his employer squarely, "in my bar, good drinks are served."

"Nobody will know the difference!" Mr. Grimmet got off his stool and jumped up and down gently. "What do Americans know about liquor? Nothing! Read any book on the subject!"

"True," Thesing said judiciously. "The general consensus of opinion is that Americans do not know the difference between red wine and a chocolate malted milk."

"In my bar," McMahon repeated, his face very red, his wide hands spread on the bar, "I serve the best drinks I know how to serve."

"Stubborn!" Mr. Grimmet yelled. "You are a stubborn Irishman! You do this out of malice! You are anxious to see me lose seven dollars on every case of liquor because you dislike me. Let us get down to the bedrock of truth!"

"Keep your voice down," McMahon said, speaking with great control. "I want to remind you of one or two things. I have worked for you since Repeal, Mr. Grimmet. In that time, how many times did we have to enlarge the bar?"

"I am not in the mood for history, McMahon!" Mr. Grimmet shouted. "What good is a bar as long as the *Normandie* if it is not run on a businesslike basis?"

"Answer my question," McMahon said. "How many times?"

"Three," Mr. Grimmet said, "all right, three."

"We are three times as big now as we were six years ago,"

McMahon said in a professor's tone, explaining proposition one, going on to proposition two. "Why do you think that is?"

"Accident!" Mr. Grimmet looked ironically up to the ceiling. "Fate! Roosevelt! The hand of God! How do I know?"

"I will tell you," McMahon said, continuing in the professorial vein. "People who come into this bar get the best Manhattans, the best Martinis, the best Daiquiris that are made on the face of the earth. They are made out of the finest ingredients, with great care, Mr. Grimmet."

"One cocktail tastes like another," Mr. Grimmet said. "People make a big fuss and they don't know anything."

"Mr. Grimmet," McMahon said with open contempt, "it is easy to see that you are not a drinking man."

Mr. Grimmet's face reflected his desperate search for a new line of defense. His eyebrows went up with pleasure as he found it. He sat down and spoke softly across the bar to McMahon. "Did it ever occur to you," he asked, "that people come into this place because of the food that is served here?"

"I will give you my final opinion of Greta Garbo," the first waiter's voice sounded out defiantly. "There is nobody like her."

For a moment McMahon looked straight into Mr. Grimmet's eyes. A slight, bitter smile played at one corner of his mouth. He breathed deeply, like a man who has just decided to bet on a horse that has not won in fourteen races. "Shall I tell you what I think of the food that is served in your restaurant, Mr. Grimmet?" McMahon asked flatly.

"The best chefs," Mr. Grimmet said quickly, "the best chefs in the City of New York."

McMahon nodded slowly. "The best chefs," he said, "and the worst food."

"Consider," Mr. Grimmet called. "Consider what you're saying."

"Anything a cook can disguise," McMahon said, talking now to Thesing, disregarding Mr. Grimmet, "is wonderful here. Anything with a sauce. Once I ate a sirloin steak in this restaurant . . ."

"Careful, McMahon." Mr. Grimmet jumped off his stool and ran around to face McMahon.

"What can be done to disguise a sirloin steak?" McMahon asked reasonably. "Nothing. You broil it. Simply that. If it was good when it was cut off the steer, it's good on your plate. If it was bad . . ."

"I pay good prices!" Mr. Grimmet yelled. "I'll have no allusions . . ."

"I would not bring a dog into this restaurant to eat sirloin steak," McMahon said. "Not a young dog with the teeth of a lion."

"You're fired!" Mr. Grimmet pounded on the bar. "This restaurant will now do without your services."

McMahon bowed. "That is satisfactory to me," he said. "Perfectly satisfactory."

"Well, now, everybody. Boys!" Thesing said pacifically. "Over a little thing like private stock rye . . ."

McMahon began taking off his apron. "This bar has a reputation. It is my reputation. I am proud of it. I am not interested in remaining at a place in which my reputation will be damaged."

McMahon threw his apron, neatly folded, over a towel rack and picked up the little wooden wedge on which was printed, in gold letters, "William McMahon, *In Charge*." Mr. Grimmet watched him with trouble in his eyes as McMahon lifted the hinged piece of the bar that permitted the bartenders to get out into the restaurant proper.

"What is the sense," Mr. Grimmet asked as the hinges creaked, "of taking a rash step, Billy?" Once more Mr. Grimmet hated himself for his dulcet tone of voice, but William McMahon was one of the five finest bartenders in the City of New York.

McMahon stood there, pushing the hinged piece of the bar a little, back and forth. "Once and for all," he said. He let the hinged piece fall behind him,

"I'll tell you what I'll do, Billy," Mr. Grimmet went on swiftly, hating himself more and more, "I'll make a compromise. I will give you five dollars more per week." He sighed to himself and then looked brightly at McMahon.

McMahon knocked his shingle thoughtfully against the bar. "I will try to make you understand something, Mr. Grimmet," he said, gently. "I am not as fundamentally interested in money as I am fundamentally interested in other things."

"You are not so different from the rest of the world," Mr. Grimmet said with dignity.

"I have been working for twenty-five years," McMahon said, knocking the shingle that said, "William McMahon, *In Charge*," "and I have constantly been able to make a living. I do not work only to make a living. I am more interested in making something else. For the last six years I have worked here night and day. A lot of nice people come in here and drink like ladies and gentlemen. They all like this place. They all like me."

"Nobody is saying anything about anybody not liking you,"

Mr. Grimmet said impatiently. "I am discussing a matter of business principle."

"I like this place." McMahon looked down at the shingle in his hand. "I think this is a very nice bar. I planned it. Right?" He looked up at Mr. Grimmet.

"You planned it. I will sign an affidavit to the effect that you planned it," Mr. Grimmet said ironically. "What has that got to do with Thesing's private stock?"

"If something is right here," McMahon went on, without raising his voice, "people can say it's William McMahon's doing. If something is wrong here they can say it's William McMahon's fault. I like that, Mr. Grimmet. When I die people can say, 'William McMahon left a monument, the bar at Grimmet's Restaurant. He never served a bad drink in his whole life.' " McMahon took his coat out of the closet next to the bar and put it on. "A monument. I will not have a monument made out of Thesing's private stock. Mr. Grimmet, I think you are a dumb bastard."

McMahon bowed a little to the two men and started out. Mr. Grimmet gulped, then called, his words hard and dry in the empty restaurant. "McMahon!" The bartender turned around. "All right," Mr. Grimmet said. "Come back."

McMahon gestured toward Thesing.

"Any liquor you say," Mr. Grimmet said in a choked voice. "Any goddamn whisky you want!"

McMahon smiled and went back to the closet and took his coat off and took the shingle out of his pocket. He went back of the bar and slipped on his apron, as Thesing and Grimmet watched.

"One thing," Mr. Grimmet said, his eyes twitching from the strain, "one thing I want you to know."

"Yes, sir," said McMahon.

"I don't want you to talk to me," Mr. Grimmet said, "and I don't want to talk to you. Ever."

Thesing quietly picked up his hat and stole out the door.

"Yes, sir," said McMahon.

Mr. Grimmet walked swiftly into the kitchen.

"I will tell you something about debutantes," the first waiter was saying in the rear of the restaurant, "they are overrated."

McMahon tied the bow in his apron strings and, neatly, in the center of the whisky shelves above the bar, placed the shingle, "William McMahon, *In Charge*."

# I Stand by Dempsey

The crowd came out of Madison Square Garden with the sorrowful, meditative air that hangs over it when the fights have been bad. Flanagan pushed Gurske and Flora quickly through the frustrated fans and into a cab. Gurske sat on the folding seat, Flanagan with Flora in the back.

"I want a drink," he said to her as the cab started. "I want to forget what I saw tonight."

"They were not so bad," Gurske said. "They were scientific."

"Not a bloody nose," Flanagan said. "Not a single drop of blood. Heavyweights! Heavyweight pansies!"

"As an exhibition of skill," Gurske said, "I found it interesting."

"Joe Louis could've wiped them all up in the short space of two minutes," Flanagan said.

"Joe Louis is overrated," Gurske said, leaning across from the little folding seat and tapping Flanagan on the knee. "He is highly overrated."

"Yeah," Flanagan said. "He is overrated like the S. S. *Texas* is overrated. I saw the Schmeling fight."

"That German is a old man," Gurske said.

"When Louis hit him in the belly," Flora said, "he cried. Like a baby. Louis' hand went in up to the wrist. I saw with my own eyes."

"He left his legs in Hamburg," Gurske said. "A slight wind woulda knocked him over."

"That is some slight wind," said Flanagan, "that Louis."

"He's built like a brick privy," Flora remarked.

"I woulda liked to see Dempsey in there with him." Gurske rolled his eyes at the thought. "Dempsey. In his prime. The blood would flow."

"Louis would make chopmeat outa Dempsey. Who did Dempsey ever beat?" Flanagan wanted to know.

"Listen to that!" Gurske pushed Flora's knee in amazement. "Dempsey! The Manassa Mauler!"

"Louis is a master boxer," Flanagan said. "Also, he punches like he had a baseball bat in his both hands. Dempsey! Eugene, you are a goddamn fool."

"Boys!" Flora said.

"Dempsey was a panther in action. Bobbing and weaving." Gurske bobbed and weaved and knocked his derby off his small, neat head. "He carried destruction in either fist." Gurske bent over for his hat. "He had the heart of a wounded lion."

"He certainly would be wounded if he stepped into the ring with Joe Louis." Flanagan thought this was funny and roared with laughter. He slapped Gurske's face playfully with his huge hand and Gurske's hat fell off.

"You're very funny," Gurske said, bending over for his hat again. "You're a very funny man."

"The trouble with you, Eugene," Flanagan said, "is you don't have no sense of humor."

"I laugh when something's funny." Gurske brushed his hat off.

"Am I right?" Flanagan asked Flora. "Has Eugene got a sense of humor?"

"He is a very serious character, Eugene," Flora said.

"Go to hell," Gurske said.

"Hey, you." Flanagan tapped him on the shoulder. "Don't you talk like that."

"Aaah," Gurske said. "Aaah——"

"You don't know how to argue like a gentleman," Flanagan said. "That's what's the matter with you. All little guys're like that."

"Aaah!"

"A guy is under five foot six, every time he gets in a argument he gets excited. Ain't that so, Flora?"

"Who's excited?" Gurske yelled. "I am merely stating a fact. Dempsey would lay Louis out like a carpet. That is all I'm saying."

"You are making too much noise," Flanagan said. "Lower your voice."

"I seen 'em both. With my own eyes!"

"What the hell do you know about fighting, anyway?" Flanagan asked.

"Fighting!" Gurske trembled on his seat. "The only kind of fighting *you* know about is waiting at the end of a alley with a gun for drunks."

Flanagan put his hand over Gurske's mouth. With his other hand he held the back of Gurske's neck. "Shut up, Eugene," he said. "I am asking you to shut up."

Gurske's eyes rolled for a moment behind the huge hand. Then he relaxed.

Flanagan sighed and released him. "You are my best friend, Eugene," he said, "but sometimes you gotta shut up."

"A party," Flora said. "We go out on a party. Two gorillas. A little gorilla and a big gorilla."

They rolled downtown in silence. They brightened, however, when they got to Savage's Café and had two Old-Fashioneds each. The five-piece college-boy band played fast numbers and the Old-Fashioneds warmed the blood and friends gathered around the table. Flanagan stretched out his hand and patted Gurske amiably on the head.

"All right," he said. "All right, Eugene. We're friends. You and me, we are lifelong comrades."

"All right," Gurske said reluctantly. "This is a party."

Everybody drank because it was a party, and Flora said, "Now, boys, you see how foolish it was—over two guys you never even met to talk to?"

"It was a question of attitude," Gurske said. "Just because he's a big slob with meat axes for hands he takes a superior attitude."

"All I said was Louis was a master boxer." Flanagan opened his collar.

"That's all he said!"

"Dempsey was a slugger. That's all—a slugger. Look what that big ox from South America did to him. That Firpo. Dempsey had to be put on his feet by newspapermen. No newspaperman has to stand Joe Louis on his feet."

"That's all he said," Gurske repeated. "That's all he said. My God!"

"Boys," Flora pleaded, "it's history. Have a good time."

Flanagan toyed with his glass. "That Eugene," he said. "You say one thing, he says another. Automatic. The whole world agrees there never was nothing like Joe Louis, he brings up Dempsey."

"The whole world!" Gurske said. "Flanagan, the whole world!"

"I want to dance," Flora said.

"Sit down," Flanagan said. "I want to talk with my friend, Eugene Gurske."

"Stick to the facts," Gurske said. "That's all I ask, stick to the facts."

"A small man can't get along in human society," Flanagan said to the company at the table. "He can't agree with no one. He should live in a cage."

"That's right," Gurske said. "Make it personal. You can't win by reason, use insults. Typical."

"I would give Dempsey two rounds. Two," Flanagan said. "There! As far as I am concerned the argument is over. I want a drink."

"Let me tell you something," Gurske said loudly. "Louis wouldn't—"

"The discussion is closed."

"Who says it's closed? In Shelby, Montana, when Dempsey—"

"I ain't interested."

"He met 'em all and he beat 'em all—"

"Listen, Eugene," Flanagan said seriously. "I don't want to hear no more. I want to listen to the music."

Gurske jumped up from his chair in a rage. "I'm goin' to talk, see, and you're not going to stop me, see, and—"

"Eugene," Flanagan said. Slowly he lifted his hand, palm open.

"I—" Gurske watched the big red hand, with the heavy gold rings on the fingers, waggle back and forth. His lips quivered. He stooped suddenly and picked up his derby and rushed out of the room, the laughter of the guests at the table ringing in his ears.

"He'll be back," Flanagan said. "He's excitable, Eugene. Like a little rooster. He has got to be toned down now and then. Now, Flora. Let's dance."

They danced pleasantly for a half-hour, taking time out for another Old-Fashioned between numbers. They were on the dance floor when Gurske appeared in the doorway with a large soda bottle in each hand.

"Flanagan!" Gurske shouted from the doorway. "I'm looking for Vincent Flanagan!"

"My God!" Flora shrieked. "He'll kill somebody!"

"Flanagan," Gurske repeated. "Come on out of that crowd. Step out here."

Flora pulled at Flanagan as the dancers melted to both sides. "Vinnie," she cried, "there's a back door."

"Give me a ginger-ale bottle," Flanagan said, taking a step toward Gurske. "Somebody put a ginger-ale bottle in my hand."

"Don't come no nearer, Flanagan! This is one argument you won't win with yer lousy big hands."

"Where is that ginger-ale bottle?" Flanagan asked, advancing on Gurske step by step, keeping Gurske's eyes fixed with his.

"I warn you, Flanagan!"

Gurske threw one of the bottles. Flanagan ducked and it smashed against the back wall.

"You are going to regret this," Flanagan said.

Gurske lifted the other bottle nervously. Flanagan took another step, and then another.

"Oh, my God!" Gurske cried, and threw the bottle at Flanagan's head and turned tail and ran.

Flanagan caught the bottle in mid-flight, took careful aim with it, and let it go across the dance floor. It hit Gurske at the ankle and he went sailing over a table like a duckpin caught all alone on a bowling alley. Flanagan was on him and had him by the collar immediately. He lifted Gurske into the air with one hand and held him there.

"Gurske," he said. "You cockeyed Gurske. The hundred-and-thirty-pound Napoleon."

"Don't kill him!" Flora came running over to them distractedly. "For God's sake, don't kill him, Vinnie!"

For a moment Flanagan looked at Gurske hanging limply from his hand. Then he turned to the other guests. "Ladies and gentlemen," he said, "no damage has occurred."

"I missed," Gurske said bitterly. "I ought to wear glasses."

"Let everybody dance," Flanagan announced. "I apologize for my friend. I guarantee he won't cause no more trouble."


The orchestra struck up "The Dipsy Doodle" and the guests swung back with animation into their dancing.

Flanagan carried Gurske to their table and set him down. "All right," he said. "We will finish our discussion. Once and for all."

"Aaah!" Gurske said, but without spirit.

"Eugene," Flanagan said, "come here."

Gurske sidled up toward Flanagan, who was sitting with his feet out from the table, his legs spread comfortably apart.

"What about those prizefighters we mentioned some time ago?"

"Dempsey," Gurske said hoarsely. "I stand by Dempsey."

Flanagan laid his hand on Gurske's arm and pulled. Gurske fell face downward, seat up, over Flanagan's knees.

"The old woodshed," Flanagan said. He began to spank Gurske

with wide, deliberate strokes. The orchestra stopped playing after a moment and the smacks resounded in the silent room.

"Oh!" Gurske said at the seventh stroke.

"Oh!" the roomful of people answered in a single hushed tone.

At the ninth stroke the drummer of the band took up the beat and from then on the bass drum sounded simultaneously with the hard, unrelenting hand.

"Well," Flanagan said on the twenty-fifth stroke. "Well, Mr. Gurske?"

"I stand by Dempsey!"

"O.K.," Flanagan said, and continued with the spanking.

After stroke thirty-two Gurske called tearfully, "All right. That's all, Flanagan."

Flanagan lifted Eugene to his feet. "I am glad that matter is settled. Now sit down and have a drink."

The guests applauded and the orchestra struck up and the dancing began again. Flanagan and Flora and Gurske sat at their table drinking Old-Fashioneds.

"The drinks are on me," Flanagan said. "Drink hearty. Who do you stand by, Eugene?"

"I stand by Louis," Gurske said.

"What round would he win in?"

"In the second round," Gurske said. The tears streamed down his face, and he sipped his Old-Fashioned. "He would win in the second round."

"My friend Eugene," Flanagan said.

# God on Friday Night

Sol let himself quietly into the house and walked softly down the long hall toward the kitchen, the only sound the fashionable creaking of his pale tan shoes. He saw his mother bending over the stove, red-faced, peering into the roaster, basting a chicken.

"Ma," he said softly.

Ma grunted, busily pushing the potatoes.

"It's me, Ma. It's Sol."

Ma closed the oven and stood up wearily, her hand pushing helpfully at the hip.

"Kiss Mama," she said.

Sol kissed her and she sat down and looked at him. "You don't look so good, Sol. You don't look the way you looked when you were a young boy."

Every time she saw him she told him the same thing.

"What do you want, Ma?" Sol sighed, voicing the hopeless argument. "I'm not a young boy any more. I'm a man thirty-three years old."

"Even so." Ma wiped her forehead and looked anxiously at him. "The life you lead."

"A man who makes his living entertaining in night clubs can't live like a prize horse," Sol said. He sat down across the table and stretched his hand out tenderly to cover hers. "How're yuh, Ma?"

Ma sighed. "What do you expect? My kidneys. Always my kidneys. A woman with a family gets old like an express train." She looked closely at her son. "Sol, darling," she said, "you wear the worst clothes I've ever seen on a man's back. You belong on a merry-go-round."

"In my profession," Sol said with sober pride, "this is the way they dress."

"They should not be allowed out in the daytime." She shook

her head. "That tie. That material would be good to line closets with."

"Violet picked out this tie."

"How is Violet? Why can't she come visit her mother-in-law once in a while? Is the Bronx another world?"

"Violet's all right," Sol said flatly, looking at the glitter on his shoe tips. "Only . . ."

Ma sighed, her large, fashionably supported bosom heaving under the black net. "O.K., Baby, tell Mama."

Sol leaned over anxiously. "I must talk to you, private."

Ma looked around the kitchen. "Are we in Grand Central Station?"

"Real private, Ma. I don't want *nobody* to hear this. *Nobody.* Not even Pop."

"What've you done, Sol?" There was a note of stern alarm in Ma's voice, and she grabbed Sol's arm tightly. "Tell Mama the truth."

"I ain't done nothing. Honest. At least nothing bad. Don't worry, Ma."

"Nobody's sick?"

"Nobody's sick."

"All right." Ma sat back in her chair, holding her feet off the floor to take the weight off them. "Do you want to stay to dinner? You can always cut an extra portion out of a chicken."

"Lissen, Ma," Sol said intensely, "you got to lissen to me and you got to promise you won't tell nobody."

"I promise. All right, I promise. Will you stay to dinner?"

"Yeah," Sol said. "Well . . ." He hesitated. "This is complicated."

Lawrence came into the kitchen, throwing his books on the floor. "Hiya, Sol. Hello, Mom. Am I hungry, oh, Momma, am I hungry . . . Mom, whatta ye got to eat? Oh, am I hungry!"

"I'm talkin' to Ma, private," Sol said.

"I'm hungry," Lawrence said, looking in the icebox. "Go ahead and talk. I'll forget it anyway."

"I want to talk to Ma private," Sol said in measured tones.

"What the hell's so private?" Lawrence asked, gesturing with a bottle of milk. "What're you, a German spy? Boy, am I hungry!"

"Don't say 'hell,' Larry," Ma said. "And get out of here."

"I'm taking the bottle with me," Lawrence announced, marching toward the door. He patted his mother on the head. "Mata Hari." He went out.

"A brilliant boy," Ma said. "He leads his class."

Sol cleared his throat.

"Yes, Sol," Ma said. "I'm listening."

"I been thinking, Ma," he began in a low thoughtful voice, twisting his heavy gold ring slowly around on his finger. "I ain't a good boy."

"That's not such private news." Ma laughed at the expression on Sol's face. She pinched his arm. "You got a good heart, Sol," she said. "My baby Sol, with a heart like a house."

"I have done things, Ma," Sol said slowly, choosing his words with great care, "that were not so good."

"If we were all angels, we wouldn't need airplanes," Ma said with finality. "Let me look at the chicken."

She went over and looked at the chicken. "That butcher!" she said. "He is selling me eagles." She closed the oven door and sat down again.

"I have done things," Sol said quietly, "that God wouldn't like."

"I think God has other things on His mind, these days, Sol."

"Ma," Sol said, not looking at his mother, "Ma, would you light candles on Friday night and make the prayer?"

There was silence in the kitchen, broken only by the small crackle from the oven, where the chicken was browning.

"I haven't lighted candles for a long time, Sol," Ma said gently. "Ever since the day I married your father. He was a Socialist, your father."

"Would yuh light 'em now, Ma?" Sol pleaded. "Every Friday night?"

"What is it, Sol? Why should I light candles?"

Sol took a deep breath and stood up and walked back and forth in the kitchen. "Violet," he said, "Violet's goin' to have a baby."

"Oh!" Ma gasped, fanning herself. "Oh! Well! That blonde girl! Oh! A grandchild! Oh! Sol, Baby!" She grabbed Sol and kissed him. "My Sol!"

"Don't cry, Ma. Ma, please . . . ." Sol patted her solid wide back. "It's all right."

"It's about time, Sol. I thought you'd never . . . ." She kissed him on the forehead and smiled widely. "I thought Violet was beginning to look very good in the breasts. Congratulations from the bottom of my heart. We'll name him after my father."

"Yeah," Sol said. "Thanks. How about the candles now, Ma?"

"What do you need candles for? I had five children without burning a single candle."

"Violet's different," Sol said uneasily. "She's not like you."

"She is just built for children," Ma declared. "She is built like a horse. When I had you I weighed ninety-five pounds. Including you. She doesn't need candles."

"You don't know, Ma." Sol looked intently into his mother's eyes. "Today Violet slipped in the bathtub."

"Well?"

"She coulda killed herself. As it is, she fainted."

"So you want me to pray because your wife doesn't know how to take a bath. Sol!" Ma waved him away. "Every day millions of people fall down in bathtubs."

"Lissen, Ma," Sol said, holding both her hands. "Nuthin' can't happen to Violet. And nuthin' can happen to the kid. See, Ma? We been tryin' to have a kid for five years now and . . ." He stopped.

Ma shook her head in wonderment. "That big blonde horse."

"We want that kid, Ma. We gotta have that kid. Everybody should have a kid. What've I got if I haven't got a son?"

"Shhh, Baby," Ma said. "Sure, you're right. Only don't yell. You're too nervous to yell."

"All right, I won't yell." Sol wiped the sweat off his forehead with a blue silk handkerchief with a green monogram. "All right. What I want to say is, Violet's dumpin' herself in the bathtub was a omen."

"A what?"

"A omen. It's a . . ."

"I know."

"It shows us we can't take any chances, Ma."

"Loose in the head, my baby Sol," Ma said. "Too much night life."

"We got to pray to God, Ma," Sol said, "that nuthin' happens to that baby."

"If you want to pray to God, go ahead and pray. Did *I* make the baby?" Ma asked. "Let Violet pray."

Sol swallowed. "Violet's not fit to pray," he said gently. "She's a first-class girl and I would lay down on railroad tracks for her, but she ain't fit to pray to God."

"That's no way to talk about your own wife, Solly," Ma said. "Shame on you."

"I love her like she was my right arm," Sol said. "But she's not a very good woman, Ma. What's the sense in kiddin' ourselves? Violet has a weak character, Ma, and she has done two or three or five things. . . . Give Violet four drinks, Ma, and she says 'Yes' to the man from Macy's. She's young, she'll outgrow it an'

109

settle down, but right now . . ." Sol nervously lit a cigarette. "Right now, Ma, Violet's prayers'd carry top weight in the field."

"Sol, Sol," Ma said gravely, "why can't *you* pray?"

Sol sat quietly, observing his cigarette. The blush came up over his purple collar, like dye soaking in cloth. "I am not one hundred percent perfect in any respect, myself," he said. "First of all, Ma, in my business if yuh don't tell the customers dirty jokes, yuh might just as well apply to the WPA."

"You should've been a doctor, like I said."

"I know, Ma," Sol said patiently. "But I'm not. I'm a man who has to play in cheap night clubs in Philadelphia and Lowell, Massachusetts, and Boston, weeks at a time. Yuh don't know how lonely it can get at night in Lowell, Massachusetts."

"A lot, Sol?"

"A lot, Ma, a lot," Sol cast his eyes up at the kitchen ceiling.

"A boy with a face like yours." Ma shrugged. "Girls're funny."

"If I prayed, Ma, the words'd stick in my throat."

"So you want me. I don't even believe in God, Baby."

"That's all right, Ma," Sol said. "You're a good woman. Yuh never hurt anybody in all yer life."

Ma sighed hugely. "I'll have to go down to Mrs. Aaronson and get her to teach me the prayer. Sol, darling, you're a nuisance."

Sol kissed her, his eyes shining.

"I got to see what's happening to that bird," Ma said, bending over the chicken. "I'll pray that it's a boy," she said, "while I'm at it."

Every Friday night the candles were lighted and Ma steadfastly said the old words: *"Burach ee, burach shmoi, Burach ee, burach shmoi. Burach ee, burach shmoi. Burach ata adanoi eluchainu melach huoilom. Chaleck necht shil shabos."* And then she prayed for a boy.

It was on a Friday night that Sol and Violet brought the baby over to Ma's for the first time.

Sol held the smiling and pink and robust boy in his arms as if he were wood.

"See, Ma?" he said, holding the baby out.

Ma put her hand out slowly, and gently rubbed the little soft head. "Hair," she said. "He's got hair." She chuckled and took the baby's hand out and kissed it. "Take him into the bedroom, Violet," she said. "I'm busy here for a minute."

She turned and lighted the seven candles in the window, one by one.

"The last stronghold of religion," Lawrence said. "All of a sudden. This house."

"Shut up," Ma said. "City College philosopher."

And she said, *"Burach ee, burach shmoi. Burach ee . . ."* as the candles burned.

# Return to Kansas City

Arline opened the bedroom door and softly went over between the twin beds, the silk of her dress making a slight rustle in the quiet room. The dark shades were down and the late afternoon sun came in only in one or two places along the sides of the window frames, in sharp, thin rays.

Arline looked down at her husband, sleeping under the blankets. His fighter's face with the mashed nose was very peaceful on the pillow and his hair was curled like a baby's and he snored gently because he breathed through his mouth. A light sweat stood out on his face. Eddie always sweated, any season, any place. But now, when she saw Eddie begin to sweat, it made Arline a little angry.

She stood there, watching the serene, glove-marked face. She sat down on the other bed, still watching her husband. She took a lace-bordered handkerchief out of a pocket and dabbed at her eyes. They were dry. She sniffed a little and the tears started. For a moment she cried silently, then she sobbed aloud. In a minute the tears and the sobs were regular, loud in the still room.

Eddie stirred in his bed. He closed his mouth, turned over on his side.

"Oh, my," Arline sobbed, "oh, my God."

She saw, despite the fact that Eddie's back was toward her, that he had awakened.

"Oh," Arline wept, "sweet Mother of God."

She knew that Eddie was wide awake listening to her and he knew that she knew it, but he hopefully pretended he hadn't been roused. He even snored experimentally once or twice. Arline's sobs shook her and the mascara ran down her cheeks in straight black lines.

Eddie sighed and turned around and sat up, rubbing his hair with his hands.

"What's the matter?" he asked. "What's bothering you, Arline?"

"Nothing," Arline sobbed.

"If nothing's the matter," Eddie said mildly, "what're you crying for?"

Arline didn't say anything. She stopped sobbing aloud and turned the grief inward upon herself and wept all the more bitterly, in silence. Eddie wiped his eye with the heel of his hand, looked wearily at the dark shades that shut out the slanting rays of the sun.

"There are six rooms in this house, Arline darling," he said. "If you have to cry why is it necessary to pick the exact room where I am sleeping?"

Arline's head sank low on her breast, her beautiful beauty-shop straw-colored hair falling tragically over her face. "You don't care," she murmured, "you don't care one dime's worth if I break my heart."

She squeezed the handkerchief and the tears ran down her wrist.

"I care," Eddie said, throwing back the covers neatly and putting his stockinged feet onto the floor. He had been sleeping in his pants and shirt, which were very wrinkled now. He shook his head two or three times as he sat on the edge of the bed and hit himself smartly on the cheek with the back of his hand to awaken himself. He looked unhappily across at his wife, sitting on the other bed, her hands wrung in her lap, her face covered by her careless hair, sorrow and despair in every line of her. "Honest, Arline, I care." He went over and sat next to her on the bed and put his arm around her. "Baby," he said. "Now, baby."

She just sat there crying silently, her round, soft shoulders shaking now and then under his arm. Eddie began to feel more and more uncomfortable. He squeezed her shoulder two or three times, exhausting his methods of consolation. "Well," he said finally, "I think maybe I'll put the kid in the carriage and take him for a walk. A little air. Maybe when I come back you'll feel better."

"I won't feel better," Arline promised him, without moving. "I won't feel one ounce better."

"Arline," Eddie said.

"The kid." She sat up erect now and looked at him. "If you paid as much attention to me as to the kid."

"I pay equal attention. My wife and my kid." Eddie stood up and padded around the room uneasily in his socks.

Arline watched him intently, the creased flannel trousers and the wrinkled shirt not concealing the bulky muscles.

113

"The male sleeping beauty," she said. "The long-distance sleeping champion. My husband."

"I don't sleep so awful much," Eddie protested.

"Fifteen hours a day," Arline said. "Is it natural?"

"I had a hard workout this morning," Eddie said, standing at the window. "I went six fast rounds. I got to get rest. I got to store up my energy. I am not so young as some people any more. I got to take care of myself. Don't I have to store up energy?"

"Store up your energy!" Arline said loudly. "All day long you store up energy. What is your wife supposed to do when you are storing up energy?"

Eddie let the window shade fly up. The light shot into the room, making it harder for Arline to cry.

"You ought to have friends," Eddie suggested without hope.

"I have friends."

"Why don't you go out with them?"

"They're in Kansas City," Arline said.

There was silence in the room. Eddie sat down and began putting on his shoes.

"My mother's in Kansas City," Arline said. "My two sisters are in Kansas City. My two brothers. I went to high school in Kansas City. Here I am, in Brooklyn, New York."

"You were in Kansas City two and a half months ago," Eddie said, buttoning his collar and knotting his tie. "A mere two and a half months ago."

"Two and a half months are a long time," Arline said, clearing away the mascara lines from her cheeks, but still weeping. "A person can die in two and a half months."

"What person?" Eddie asked.

Arline ignored him. "Mama writes she wants to see the baby again. After all, that is not unnatural, a grandmother wants to see her grandchild. Tell me, is it unnatural?"

"No," said Eddie, "it is not unnatural." He combed his hair swiftly. "If Mama wants to see the baby," he said, "explain to me why she can't come here. Kindly explain to me."

"My husband is of the opinion that they are handing out gold pieces with movie tickets in Kansas City," Arline said with cold sarcasm.

"Huh?" Eddie asked, honestly puzzled. "What did you say?"

"How can Mama afford to come here?" Arline asked. "After all, you know, there are no great prizefighters in *our* family. I had to *marry* to bring one into the family. Oh, my God!" Once more she wept.

"Lissen, Arline." Eddie ran over to her and spoke pleadingly, his tough, battered face very gentle and sad. "I can't afford to have you go to Kansas City every time I take a nap in the afternoon. We have been married a year and a half and you have gone to Kansas City five times. I feel like I am fighting for the New York Central Railroad, Arline!"

Arline shook her head obstinately. "There is nothing to do in New York," she said.

"There is nothing to do in New York!" Eddie's mouth opened in surprise. "My God! There's something to do in Kansas City?" he cried. "What the hell is there to do in Kansas City? Remember, I have been in that town myself. I married you in that town."

"I didn't know how it was going to be," Arline said flatly. "It was nice in Kansas City. I was an innocent young girl."

"Please," said Eddie. "Let us not rake up the past."

"I was surrounded by my family," Arline went on shakily. "I went to high school there."

She bent over and grief took possession once more. Eddie licked his lips uncomfortably. They were dry from the morning's workout and the lower lip was split a little and smarted when he ran his tongue over it. He searched his brain for a helpful phrase.

"The kid," he ventured timidly, "why don't you play more with the kid?"

"The kid!" Arline cried defiantly. "I take very good care of the kid. I have to stay in every night minding the kid while you are busy storing up your energy." The phrase enraged her and she stood up, waving her arms. "What a business! You fight thirty minutes a month, you got to sleep three hundred and fifty hours. Why, it's laughable. It is very laughable! You are some fighter!" She shook her fist at him in derision. "With all the energy you store up you ought to be able to beat the German army!"

"That is the business I am in," Eddie tried to explain gently. "That is the nature of my profession."

"Don't tell me that!" Arline said. "I have gone out with other fighters. They don't sleep all the time."

"I am not interested," Eddie said. "I do not want to hear anything about your life before our marriage."

"They go to night clubs," Arline went on irresistibly, "and they dance and they take a drink once in a while and they take a girl to see a musical show!"

Eddie nodded. "They are after something," he said. "That is the whole story."

"I wish to God you were after something!"

"I meet the type of fighter you mention, too," Eddie said. "The night-club boys. They knock my head off for three rounds and then they start breathing through the mouth. By the time they reach the eighth round they wish they never saw a naked lady on a dance floor. And by the time I get through with them they are storing up energy, flat on their backs. With five thousand people watching them. You want me to be that kind of a fighter?"

"You're wonderful," Arline said, wrinkling her nose, sneering. "My Joe Louis. Big-Purse Eddie Megaffin. I don't notice you bringing back the million-dollar gate."

"I am progressing slowly," Eddie said, looking at the picture of Mary and Jesus over his bed. "I am planning for the future."

"I am linked for life to a goddamn health-enthusiast," Arline said despairingly.

"Why do you talk like that, Arline?"

"Because I want to be in Kansas City," she wailed.

"Explain to me," Eddie said, "why in the name of God you are so crazy for Kansas City?"

"I'm lonesome," Arline wept with true bitterness. "I'm awful lonesome. I'm only twenty-one years old, Eddie."

Eddie patted her gently on the shoulder. "Look, Arline." He tried to make his voice very warm and at the same time logical. "If you would only go easy. If you would go by coach and not buy presents for everybody, maybe I can borrow a coupla bucks and swing it."

"I would rather die," Arline said. "I would rather never see Kansas City again for the rest of my life than let them know my husband has to watch pennies like a streetcar conductor. A man with his name in the papers every week. It would be shameful!"

"But, Arline, darling"—Eddie's face was tortured—"you go four times a year, you spread presents like the WPA and you always buy new clothes . . ."

"I can't appear in Kansas City in rags!" Arline pulled at a stocking, righting it on her well-curved leg. "I would rather . . ."

"Some day, darling," Eddie interrupted. "We're working up. Right now I can't."

"You can!" Arline said. "You're lying to me, Eddie Megaffin. Jake Blucher called up this morning and he told me he offered you a thousand dollars to fight Joe Principe."

Eddie sat down in a chair. He looked down at the floor, understanding why Arline had picked this particular afternoon.

"You would come out of that fight with seven hundred and fifty

116

dollars.'' Arline's voice was soft and inviting. ''I could go to Kansas . . .''

''Joe Principe will knock my ears off.''

Arline sighed. ''I am so anxious to see my mother. She is an old woman and soon she will die.''

''At this stage,'' Eddie said slowly, ''I am not ready for Joe Principe. He is too strong and too smart for me.''

''Jake Blucher told me he thought you had a wonderful chance.''

''I have a wonderful chance to land in the hospital,'' Eddie said. ''That Joe Principe is made out of springs and cement. If you gave him a pair of horns it would be legal to kill him with a sword.''

''He is only a man with two fists just like you,'' Arline said.

''Yeah.''

''You're always telling me how good you are.''

''In two years,'' Eddie said, ''taking it very easy and careful, making sure I don't get knocked apart . . .''

''You could make the money easy!'' Arline pointed her finger dramatically at him. ''You just don't want to. You don't want me to be happy. I see through you, Eddie Megaffin!''

''I just don't want to get beaten up,'' Eddie said, shaking his head.

''A fine fighter!'' Arline laughed. ''What kind of fighter are you, anyhow? A fighter is supposed to get beaten up, isn't he? That's his business, isn't it? You don't care for me. All you wanted was somebody to give you a kid and cook your goddamn steaks and lamb chops. In Brooklyn! I got to stay in a lousy little house day in and . . .''

''I'll take you to the movies tonight,'' Eddie promised.

''I don't want to go to the movies. I want to go to Kansas City.'' Arline threw herself face down on the bed and sobbed. ''I'm caught. I'm caught! You don't love me! You won't let me go to people who love me! Mama! Mama!''

Eddie closed his eyes in pain. ''I love you,'' he said, meaning it. ''I swear to God.''

''You say it.'' Her voice was smothered in the pillow. ''But you don't prove it! Prove it! I never knew a young man could be so stingy. Prove it . . .'' The words trailed off in sorrow.

Eddie went over and bent down to kiss her. She shook her shoulders to send him away and cried like a heartbroken child. From the next room, where the baby had been sleeping, came the sound of his wailing.

Eddie walked over to the window and looked out at the peaceful Brooklyn street, at the trees and the little boys and girls skating.

"O.K.," he said, "I'll call Blucher."

Arline stopped crying. The baby still wailed in the next room.

"I'll try to raise him to twelve hundred," Eddie said. "You can go to Kansas City. You happy?"

Arline sat up and nodded. "I'll write Mama right away," she said.

"Take the kid out for a walk, will you?" Eddie said, as Arline started repairing her face before the mirror. "I want to take a little nap."

"Sure," Arline said, "sure, Eddie."

Eddie took off his shoes and lay down on the bed to start storing up his energy.

# Triumph of Justice

Mike Pilato purposefully threw open the door of Victor's shack. Above him the sign that said, "Lunch, Truckmen Welcome," shook a little, and the pale shadows its red bulbs threw in the twilight waved over the State Road.

"Victor," Mike said, in Italian.

Victor was leaning on the counter, reading Walter Winchell in a spread-out newspaper. He smiled amiably. "Mike," he said, "I am so glad to see you."

Mike slammed the door. "Three hundred dollars, Victor," he said, standing five feet tall, round and solid as a pumpkin against the door. "You owe me three hundred dollars, Victor, and I am here tonight to collect."

Victor shrugged slightly and closed the paper on Walter Winchell.

"As I've been telling you for the past six months," he said, "business is bad. Business is terrible. I work and I work and at the end . . ." He shrugged again. "Barely enough to feed myself."

Mike's cheeks, farmer-brown, and wrinkled deeply by wind and sun, grew dark with blood. "Victor, you are lying in my face," he said slowly, his voice desperately even. "For six months, each time it comes time to collect the rent you tell me, 'Business is bad.' What do I say? I say 'All right, Victor, don't worry, I know how it is.' "

"Frankly, Mike," Victor said sadly, "there has been no improvement this month."

Mike's face grew darker than ever. He pulled harshly at the ends of his iron-gray mustache, his great hands tense and swollen with anger, repressed but terrible. "For six months, Victor," Mike said, "I believed you. Now I no longer believe you."

"Mike," Victor said reproachfully.

"My friends, my relatives," Mike said, "they prove it to me. Your business is wonderful, ten cars an hour stop at your door; you sell cigarettes to every farmer between here and Chicago; on your slot machine alone . . ." Mike waved a short thick arm at the machine standing invitingly against a wall, its wheels stopped at two cherries and a lemon. Mike swallowed hard, stood breathing heavily, his deep chest rising and falling sharply against his sheepskin coat. "Three hundred dollars!" he shouted. "Six months at fifty dollars! I built this shack with my own hands for you, Victor. I didn't know what kind of a man you were. You were an Italian, I trusted you! Three hundred dollars or get out tomorrow! Finish! That's my last word."

Victor smoothed his newspaper down delicately on the counter, his hands making a dry brushing sound in the empty lunchroom. "You misunderstand," he said gently.

"I misunderstand nothing!" Mike yelled. "You are on my land in my shack and you owe me three hundred dollars . . ."

"I don't owe you anything," Victor said, looking coldly at Mike. "That is what you misunderstand. I have paid you every month, the first day of the month, fifty dollars."

"Victor!" Mike whispered, his hands dropping to his sides. "Victor, what are you saying . . . ? "

"I have paid the rent. Please do not bother me any more." Calmly Victor turned his back on Mike and turned two handles on the coffee urn. Steam, in a thin little plume, hissed up for a moment.

Mike looked at Victor's narrow back, with the shoulder blades jutting far out, making limp wings in the white shirt. There was finality in Victor's pose, boredom, easy certainty. Mike shook his head slowly, pulling hard at his mustache. "My wife," Mike said, to the disdainful back, "she told me not to trust you. My wife knew what she was talking about, Victor." Then, with a last flare of hope, "Victor, do you really mean it when you said you paid me?"

Victor didn't turn around. He flipped another knob on the coffee urn. "I mean it."

Mike lifted his arm, as though to say something, pronounce warning. Then he let it drop and walked out of the shack, leaving the door open. Victor came out from behind the counter, looked at Mike moving off with his little rolling limp down the road and across the cornfield. Victor smiled and closed the door and went back and opened the paper to Walter Winchell.

Mike walked slowly among the cornstalks, his feet crunching unevenly in the October earth. Absently he pulled at his mustache. Dolores, his wife, would have a thing or two to say. "No," she had warned him, "do not build a shack for him. Do not permit

120

him onto your land. He travels with bad men; it will turn out badly. I warn you!'' Mike was sure she would not forget this conversation and would repeat it to him word for word when he got home. He limped along unhappily. Farming was better than being a landlord. You put seed into the earth and you knew what was coming out. Corn grew from corn, and the duplicity of Nature was expected and natural. Also no documents were signed in the compact with Nature, no leases and agreements necessary, a man was not at a disadvantage if he couldn't read or write. Mike opened the door to his house and sat down heavily in the parlor, without taking his hat off. Rosa came and jumped on his lap, yelling, ''Poppa, Poppa, tonight I want to go to the movies, Poppa, take me to the movies!''

Mike pushed her off. ''No movies,'' he said harshly. Rosa stood in a corner and watched him reproachfully.

The door from the kitchen opened and Mike sighed as he saw his wife coming in, wiping her hands on her apron. She stood in front of Mike, round, short, solid as a plow horse, canny, difficult to deceive.

''Why're you sitting in the parlor?'' she asked.

''I feel like sitting in the parlor,'' Mike said.

''Every night you sit in the kitchen,'' Dolores said. ''Suddenly you change.''

''I've decided,'' Mike said loudly, ''that it's about time I made some use of this furniture. After all, I paid for it, I might as well sit in it before I die.''

''I know why you're sitting in the parlor,'' Dolores said.

''Good! You know!''

''You didn't get the money from Victor,'' Dolores wiped the last bit of batter from her hands. ''It's as plain as the shoes on your feet.''

''I smell something burning,'' Mike said.

''Nothing is burning. Am I right or wrong?'' Dolores sat in the upright chair opposite Mike. She sat straight, her hands neatly in her lap, her head forward and cocked a little to one side, her eyes staring directly and accusingly into his. ''Yes or no?''

''Please attend to your own department,'' Mike said miserably. ''I do the farming and attend to the business details.''

''Huh!'' Dolores said disdainfully.

''Are you starving?'' Mike shouted. ''Answer me, are you starving?''

Rosa started to cry because her father was shouting.

121

"Please, for the love of Jesus," Mike screamed at her, "don't cry!"

Dolores enfolded Rosa in her arms. . . . . "Baby, baby," she crooned, "I will not let him harm you."

"Who offered to harm her?" Mike screamed, banging on a table with his fist like a mallet. "Don't lie to her!"

Dolores kissed the top of Rosa's head soothingly. "There, there," she crooned. "There." She looked coldly at Mike. "Well. So he didn't pay."

"He . . ." Mike started loudly. Then he stopped, spoke in a low, reasonable voice. "So. To be frank with you, he didn't pay. That's the truth."

"What did I tell you?" Dolores said as Mike winced. "I repeat the words. 'Do not permit him onto your land. He travels with bad men; it will turn out badly. I warn you!' Did I tell you?"

"You told me," Mike said wearily.

"We will never see that money again," Dolores said, smoothing Rosa's hair. "I have kissed it good-bye."

"Please," said Mike. "Return to the kitchen. I am hungry for dinner. I have made plans already to recover the money."

Dolores eyed him suspiciously. "Be careful, Mike," she said. "His friends are gangsters and he plays poker every Saturday night with men who carry guns in their pockets."

"I am going to the law," Mike said. "I'm going to sue Victor for the three hundred dollars."

Dolores started to laugh. She pushed Rosa away and stood up and laughed.

"What's so funny?" Mike asked angrily. "I tell you I'm going to sue a man for money he owes me, you find it funny! Tell me the joke."

Dolores stopped laughing. "Have you got any papers? No! You trust him, he trusts you, no papers. Without papers you're lost in a court. You'll make a fool of yourself. They'll charge you for the lawyers. Please, Mike, go back to your farming."

Mike's face set sternly, his wrinkles harsh in his face with the gray stubble he never managed completely to shave. "I want my dinner, Dolores," he said coldly, and Dolores discreetly moved into the kitchen, saying, "It is not my business, my love; truly, I merely offer advice."

Mike walked back and forth in the parlor, limping, rolling a little from side to side, his eyes on the floor, his hands plunged into the pockets of his denims like holstered weapons, his mouth pursed with thought and determination. After a while he stopped and looked at Rosa, who prepared to weep once more.

"Rosa, baby," he said, sitting down and taking her gently on his lap. "Forgive me."

Rosa snuggled to him. They sat that way in the dimly lit parlor.

"Poppa," Rosa said finally.

"Yes," Mike said.

"Will you take me to the movies tonight, Poppa?"

"All right," Mike said. "I'll take you to the movies."

The next day Mike went into town, dressed in his neat black broadcloth suit and his black soft hat and his high brown shoes. He came back to the farm like a businessman in the movies, busily, preoccupied, sober, but satisfied.

"Well?" Dolores asked him, in the kitchen.

He kissed her briskly, kissed Rosa, sat down, took his shoes off, rubbed his feet luxuriously, said paternally to his son who was reading *Esquire* near the window, "That's right, Anthony, study."

"Well?" asked Dolores.

"I saw Dominic in town," Mike said, watching his toes wiggling. "They're having another baby."

"Well," asked Dolores. "The case? The action?"

"All right," Mike said. "What is there for dinner?"

"Veal," Dolores said. "What do you mean 'all right'?"

"I've spoken to Judge Collins. He is filling out the necessary papers for me and he will write me a letter when I am to appear in court. Rosa, have you been a good girl?"

Dolores threw up her hands. "Lawyers. We'll throw away a fortune on lawyers. Good money after bad. We could put in an electric pump with the money."

"Lawyers will cost us nothing." Mike stuffed his pipe elaborately. "I have different plans. Myself. I will take care of the case myself." He lit up, puffed deliberately.

Dolores sat down across the table from him, spoke slowly, carefully. "Remember, Mike," she said. "This is in English. They conduct the court in English."

"I know," said Mike. "I am right. Justice is on my side. Why should I pay a lawyer fifty, seventy-five dollars to collect my own money? There is one time you need lawyers—when you are wrong. I am not wrong. I will be my own lawyer."

"What do you know about the law?" Dolores challenged him.

"I know Victor owes me three hundred dollars." Mike puffed three times, quickly, on his pipe. "That's all I need to know."

"You can hardly speak English, you can't even read or write, nobody will be able to understand you. They'll all laugh at you, Mike."

"Nobody will laugh at me. I can speak English fine."

"When did you learn?" Dolores asked. "Today?"

"Dolores!" Mike shouted. "I tell you my English is all right."

"Say Thursday," Dolores said.

"I don't want to say it," Mike said, banging the table. "I have no interest in saying it."

"Aha," Dolores crowed. "See? He wants to be a lawyer in an American court, he can't even say Thursday."

"I can," Mike said. "Keep quiet, Dolores."

"Say Thursday." Dolores put her head to one side, spoke coquettishly, slyly, like a girl asking her lover to say he loved her.

"Stirday," Mike said, as he always said. "There!"

Dolores laughed, waving her hand. "And he wants to conduct a law case! Holy Mother! They will laugh at you!"

"Let them laugh!" Mike shouted. "I will conduct the case! Now I want to eat dinner! Anthony!" he yelled. "Throw away that trash and come to the table."

On the day of the trial, Mike shaved closely, dressed carefully in his black suit, put his black hat squarely on his head, and with Dolores seated grimly beside him drove early into town in the 1933 family Dodge.

Dolores said nothing all the way into town. Only after the car was parked and they were entering the courthouse, Mike's shoes clattering bravely on the legal marble, did Dolores speak. "Behave yourself," she said. Then she pinched his arm. Mike smiled at her, braced his yoke-like shoulders, took off his hat. His rough gray hair sprang up like steel wool when his hat was off, and Mike ran his hand through it as he opened the door to the courtroom. There was a proud, important smile on his face as he sat down next to his wife in the first row and patiently waited for his case to be called.

When Victor came, Mike glared at him, but Victor, after a quick look, riveted his attention on the American flag behind the Judge's head.

"See," Mike whispered to Dolores. "I have him frightened. He doesn't dare look at me. Here he will have to tell the truth."

"Shhh!" hissed Dolores. "This is a court of law."

"Michael Pilato," the clerk called, "versus Victor Fraschi."

"Me!" Mike said loudly, standing up.

"Shhh," said Dolores.

124

Mike put his hat in Dolores' lap, moved lightly to the little gate that separated the spectators from the principals in the proceedings. Politely, with a deep ironic smile, he held the gate open for Victor and his lawyer. Victor passed through without looking up.

"Who's representing you, Mr. Pilato?" the Judge asked when they were all seated. "Where's your lawyer?"

Mike stood up and spoke in a clear voice. "I represent myself. I am my lawyer."

"You ought to have a lawyer," the Judge said.

"I do not need a lawyer," Mike said loudly. "I am not trying to cheat anybody." There were about forty people in the courtroom and they all laughed. Mike turned and looked at them, puzzled. "What did I say?"

The Judge rapped with his gavel and the case was opened. Victor took the stand, while Mike stared, coldly accusing, at him. Victor's lawyer, a young man in a blue pinstripe suit and a starched tan shirt, questioned him. Yes, Victor said, he had paid each month. No, there were no receipts, Mr. Pilato could neither read nor write and they had dispensed with all formalities of that kind. No, he did not understand on what Mr. Pilato based his claim. Mike looked incredulously at Victor, lying under solemn oath, risking Hell for three hundred dollars.

Victor's lawyer stepped down and waved to Mike gracefully. "Your witness."

Mike walked dazedly past the lawyer and up to the witness stand, round, neat, his bull neck, deep red-brown and wrinkled, over his pure white collar, his large scrubbed hands politely but awkwardly held at his sides. He stood in front of Victor, leaning over a little toward him, his face close to Victor's.

"Victor," he said, his voice ringing through the courtroom, "tell the truth, did you pay me the money?"

"Yes," said Victor.

Mike leaned closer to him. "Look in my eye, Victor," Mike said, his voice clear and patient, "and answer me. Did you pay me the money?"

Victor lifted his head and looked unflinchingly into Mike's eyes. "I paid you the money."

Mike leaned even closer. His forehead almost touched Victor's now. "Look me *straight* in the eye, Victor."

Victor looked bravely into Mike's eyes, less than a foot away now.

"Now, Victor," Mike said, his eyes narrowed, cold, the light in them small and flashing and gray, "DID YOU PAY ME THE MONEY?"

Victor breathed deeply. "Yes," he said.

Mike took half a step back, almost staggering, as though he had been hit. He stared incredulously into the perjurer's eyes, as a man might stare at a son who has just admitted he has killed his mother, beyond pity, beyond understanding, outside all the known usage of human life. Mike's face worked harshly as the tides of anger and despair and vengeance rolled up in him.

"You're a goddam liar, Victor!" Mike shouted terribly. He leapt down from the witness platform, seized a heavy oak armchair, raised it murderously above Victor's head.

"Mike, oh, Mike!" Dolores' wail floated above the noise of the courtroom.

"Tell the truth, Victor!" Mike shouted, his face brick red, his teeth white behind his curled lips, almost senseless with rage, for the first time in his life threatening a fellow-creature with violence. "Tell it fast!"

He stood, the figure of Justice, armed with the chair, the veins pulsing in his huge wrists, the chair quivering high above Victor's head in his huge gnarled hands, his tremendous arms tight and bulging in their broadcloth sleeves. "Immediately, Victor!"

"Pilato!" shouted the Judge. "Put that chair down!"

Victor sat stonily, his eyes lifted in dumb horror to the chair above his head.

"Pilato," the Judge shouted, "you can be sent to jail for this!" He banged sternly but helplessly on his desk. "Remember, this is a court of law!"

"Victor?" Mike asked, unmoved, unmoving. "Victor? Immediately, please."

"No," Victor screamed, cringing in his seat, his hands now held in feeble defense before his eyes. "I didn't pay! I didn't!"

"Pilato," screamed the Judge, "this is not evidence!"

"You were lying?" Mike said inexorably, the chair still held, ax-like, above him.

"Mike, oh, Mike," wailed Dolores.

"It was not my idea," Victor babbled. "As God is my judge, I didn't think it up. Alfred Lotti, he suggested it, and Johnny Nolan. I am under the influence of corrupt men. Mike, for the love of God, please don't kill me, Mike, it would never have occurred to me myself, forgive me, forgive me . . ."

"Guiness!" the Judge called to the court policeman. "Are you going to stand there and let this go on? Why don't you do something?"

"I can shoot him," Guiness said. "Do you want me to shoot the plaintiff?"

"Shut up," the Judge said.

Guiness shrugged and turned his head toward the witness stand, smiling a little.

"You were lying?" Mike asked, his voice low, patient.

"I was lying," Victor cried.

Slowly, with magnificent calm, Mike put the chair down neatly in its place. With a wide smile he turned to the Judge. "There," he said.

"Do you know any good reason," the Judge shouted, "why I shouldn't have you locked up?"

Victor was crying with relief on the witness stand, wiping the tears away with his sleeve.

"There is no possible excuse," the Judge said, "for me to admit this confession as evidence. We are a court of law in the State of Illinois, in the United States. We are not conducting the Spanish Inquisition, Mr. Pilato."

"Huh?" Mike asked, cocking his head.

"There are certain rules," the Judge went on, quickly, his voice high, "which it is customary to observe. It is not the usual thing, Mr. Pilato," he said harshly, "to arrive at evidence by bodily threatening to brain witnesses with a chair."

"He wouldn't tell the truth," Mike said simply.

"At the very least, Mr. Pilato," the Judge said, "you should get thirty days."

"Oh, Mike," wept Dolores.

"Mr. Fraschi," the Judge said, "I promise you that you will be protected. That nobody will harm you."

"I did it," sobbed Victor, his hands shaking uncontrollably in a mixture of fear, repentance, religion, joy at delivery from death. "I did it. I will not tell a lie. I'm a weak man and influenced by loafers. I owe him three hundred dollars. Forgive me, Mike, forgive me . . ."

"He will not harm you," the Judge said patiently. "I guarantee it. You can tell the truth without any danger. Do you owe Mr. Pilato three hundred dollars?"

"I owe Mr. Pilato three hundred dollars," Victor said, swallowing four times in a row.

The young lawyer put three sheets of paper into his briefcase and snapped the lock.

The Judge sighed and wiped his brow with a handkerchief as he looked at Mike. "I don't approve of the way you conducted this trial, Mr. Pilato," he said. "It is only because you're a working man who has many duties to attend to on his land that I don't take you and put you away for a month to teach you more respect for the processes of law."

"Yes, sir," Mike said faintly.

"Hereafter," the Judge said, "kindly engage an attorney when you appear before me in this court."

"Yes, sir," Mike said.

"Mr. Pilato," the Judge said, "it is up to you to decide when and how he is to pay you."

Mike turned and walked back to Victor. Victor shrank into his chair. "Tomorrow morning, Victor," Mike said, waving his finger under Victor's nose, "at eight-thirty o'clock, I am coming into your store. The money will be there."

"Yes," said Victor.

"Is that all right?" Mike asked the Judge.

"Yes," said the Judge.

Mike strode over to the young lawyer. "And you," he said, standing with his hands on his hips in front of the young man with the pinstripe suit. "Mr. Lawyer. You knew he didn't pay me. A boy with an education. You should be ashamed of yourself." He turned to the Judge, smiled broadly, bowed. "Thank you," he said. "Good morning." Then, triumphantly, smiling broadly, rolling like a sea captain as he walked, he went through the little gate. Dolores was waiting with his hat. He took the hat, put Dolores' arm through his, marched down the aisle, nodding, beaming to the spectators. Someone applauded and by the time he and Dolores got to the door all the spectators were applauding.

He waited until he got outside, in the bright morning sunshine down the steps of the courthouse, before he said anything to Dolores. He put his hat on carefully, turned to her, grinning. "Well," he said, "did you observe what I did?"

"Yes," she said. "I was never so ashamed in my whole life!"

"Dolores!" Mike was shocked. "I got the money. I won the case."

"Acting like that in a court of law!" Dolores started bitterly toward the car. "What are you, a red Indian?"

Dolores got into the car and slammed the door and Mike limped slowly around and got into the other side. He started the car without a word and shaking his head from time to time, drove slowly toward home.

# No Jury Would Convict

"I come from Jersey City," the man in the green sweater was saying, "all the way from Jersey City, and I might of just as well stood home. You look at Brooklyn and you look at Jersey City and if you didn't look at the uniforms you'd never tell the difference."

Just then the Giants scored four runs and two men a few rows below stood up with grins on their faces and called to a friend behind us, "Johnny, Johnny! Did you see that, Johnny? You still here, Johnny? We thought you mighta left. What a team, Brooklyn!" They shook their heads in sardonic admiration. "What a team! You still here, Johnny?"

Johnny, wherever he was, didn't say anything. His two friends sat down, laughing.

The man in the green sweater took off his yellow straw hat and carefully wiped the sweatband with his handkerchief. "I been watching the Dodgers for twenty-three years," he said, "and I never seen anything like this." He put his hat on again, over his dark Greek face, the eyes deep and sad, never leaving the field where the Dodgers moved wearily in their green-trimmed uniforms. "Jersey City, Albany and Brooklyn, that would make a good league. One helluva league. I would give Brooklyn twenty-five games headstart and let them fight it out. They would have a hard fight stayin' in the New York-Penn League. They would have to get three new pitchers. They're worse than Jersey City, I swear, worse . . ."

"Ah, now, listen," the man beside him said, "if that's the case why isn't Brooklyn in Jersey City and Jersey City in Brooklyn?"

"I don't know," the man in the green sweater said. "I honestly couldn't tell ye."

"They haven't got such a bad team."

"They ought to move them into the New York-Penn League. A major league team . . ." He laughed sadly. "Look at that!" A man named Wilson was striking out for Brooklyn. "Look at Wilson.

Why, he's pitiful. They walk two men to get at him in the International League. I bet Newark could spot them five runs and beat them every day. I'd give odds."

"You can't make a supposition like that," the man beside him protested. "They never play each other. It's not a fair supposition."

"Five runs, every day. If they didn't have those green caps they could play in a twilight league in Connecticut and nobody'd ever tell the difference, not in ten years. Look at that!" The Brooklyn shortstop fell down leaping at a grounder to his right. "No guts," the man from Jersey City said, "a major league shortstop woulda had it and threw the man out. He fell to make a alibi."

"It was a hard-hit ball," his neighbor protested.

"Bartell woulda had it. He ain't no Bartell."

"He's got nine yards of tape on him," the man next to him said. "I saw with my own eyes in the dugout. He's a mass of cuts and bruises."

"That's Brooklyn. Always got tape all over them. They spend more money for tape than for players. Look at that."

One of the Giants hit a home run and three runs scored. The two men in front of us stood up with grins on their faces and called to their friend in back of us, "Still there, Johnny?" and sat down.

"For twenty-three years," the man in the green sweater said, "I been rootin' for this team. I'm gettin' tired of rootin' for a minor league team in a major league. I would hate to see what would happen to those guys in Jersey City."

"I come to see them every day," his neighbor said stubbornly, "and they're a major league team."

"Look at them," the man in the green sweater pointed his scorecard in accusation at the nine weary figures. "Take 'em one by one. Look at Wilson. Why, he's the worst ballplayer in the world. He's even worse than Smead Jolley."

He sat back triumphantly, having silenced his adversary for the moment.

He watched the play quietly for a few seconds, his Greek eyes bitter but resigned. "Why," he continued, "in Jersey City they put a catcher in to play center field instead of him. A catcher. I know Wilson."

"Wilson isn't the only one on the team," his neighbor said.

"All right. Cooney. What can Cooney do?"

"Cooney can field."

"All right, Cooney can field. But he has an air rifle for an arm. He can't reach second base in under seven bounces. Don't talk to me about Cooney."

"His arm's not so bad," the neighbor insisted.

"Not so bad? Why, Mac, if Cooney had an arm he'd be a pitcher."

"I never noticed anything wrong with his arm."

"Mac," the man in the green sweater said, "then you're the one man in the United States that don't know Cooney got a glass arm. The one man."

"How about Winsett?" his neighbor wanted to know.

Winsett was up at the plate by this time and the man in the green sweater watched him critically. "A cigar store Indian," he said finally. "Watch him swing."

"He hit sixty home runs the year before they brought him up," the Brooklyn fan said. "Cigar store Indians don't hit sixty home runs."

"I saw him," the man in the green sweater said, "when he was playin' in the International League. Do you know what he hit in the International League . . . 250 . . . You know why? It's an outcurve league. The National League is also an outcurve league. He ought to be out somewhere playin' night baseball." At the top of his voice he called, "Come on, you cigar store Indian!"

Winsett hit a home run.

"This is a fine time to hit it," the man from Jersey City said, "they're behind seven runs and there's nobody on base and he hits a home run."

In the next inning a pitcher named Cantwell took up the bitter burden of pitching for Brooklyn. The face of the man in the green sweater lightened. "There's a pitcher," he said. "One of the best. Out in Jersey City they were goin' to give him a new automobile but he went to the Giants. Watch him!" he said as Cantwell disposed of the first two batters. "A prince of a fellow. A prince. Everybody likes him."

"He's been pitching lousy," his neighbor said, as Cantwell suddenly filled the bases.

"What do you expect?" the man from Jersey City said, anxiously watching the misery below. "He don't look like the Cantwell of Jersey City. Terry double-crossed him, he wanted to stay in Jersey City, he woulda got an automobile, but Terry took him and double-crossed him and shipped him to Brooklyn. How do you expect him to pitch? He broke his heart."

Cantwell struck out the third batter. The man in the green sweater stood up and applauded as the pitcher trudged into the dugout. "You bet your life he can pitch, the poor son of a gun, he's

131

disgusted, the poor fella. That's it, Ben!'' He sat down. ''Wonderful pitcher, Ben, he's got a head.''

''I never saw him strike out a man before,'' the Brooklyn fan said.

''There's very few of them makes a living out of strikeouts. Now if they only give Ben something to work on . . .''

Brooklyn scored three runs. Two men died on base when Wilson popped out.

''That Wilson,'' the man in the green sweater said, ''they ought to trade him to the Salvation Army. He's the worst player in the world. Why, he's worse than Smead Jolley.''

But he cheered lustily when Cantwell came through another inning unscored upon. ''There's a pitcher,'' he said, ''if I had a team, I'd buy him.''

''You could buy him for the fare to Jersey City,'' a man in back said, ''eleven cents.''

''The only major leaguer on that ball club!'' the man in the green sweater said with finality. ''If only those cheap bastards would buy a couple more like him, they'd have something. I'm not saying Brooklyn's bad as a town, because it's not, but they got office boys running the ball club, office boys with snot in their ears. That cheap Grimes. I heard he used the groundkeeper's truck to move his furniture in.''

The Dodgers scored three more runs and the man in the green sweater was shouting triumphantly, the ancient Greek sorrow gone from his eyes for the first time in the entire afternoon. There was only one out and there was a man on third base and the Dodgers needed only one run to tie the score. Wilson was coming up to bat and the man in the green sweater groaned. ''That's what happens when you have somebody like that on a team. He comes up at a time like this. That's always the way it happens. He's pitiful. In the International League they walk two batters to get at him.''

But at the last moment somebody else batted for Wilson and struck out. ''On low ones,'' the man in the green sweater said in pain, ''a pinch hitter swinging at low ones.''

Cantwell was to bat next.

''Let him stay up there!'' the man from Jersey City shouted. ''Let him win his own game.'' He turned to his public. ''I would like to see old Ben smack one out and win the ball game,'' he said, ''and go right over to Terry and spit in his face.''

But old Ben didn't get a chance. Grimes put a man called Spence in to bat for him and Spence popped out.

In the next inning the Brooklyn second baseman juggled a ball and another run scored. All hope fled from the dark Greek face. "Why is it," he asked, "that other teams don't do it?" He got up, preparing to leave. "A man on third and one out," he said, "and no score. They ought to shoot Grimes for that. No jury would convict. Ah," he said, moving down toward the exit gate, "I'm going to root for a winning team from now on. I've been rooting for a losing team long enough. I'm going to root for the Giants. You don't know," he said to the Brooklyn fan moving along with him, "you don't know the pleasure you get out of rooting for a winning team."

And he went back to Jersey City, leaving his heart in Brooklyn.

# The Lament of Madam Rechevsky

The telephone rang and rang through the silken room, tumbled with sleep, lit here and there by the morning sunlight that broke through the hangings in little bright patches. Helen sighed and wriggled in the bed, and, still with her eyes closed, reached out and picked up the phone. The ringing stopped and Helen sighed in relief and wearily put the phone to her ear.

The sound of weeping, deep and bitter, welled along the wires.

"Hello, Momma," Helen said, still with her eyes closed.

"Helen," Madam Rechevsky said. "How are you, Helen?"

"Fine, Momma." Helen stretched desperately under the covers. "What time is it?"

"Nine o'clock." Helen winced, closed her eyes more tightly. "Momma, darling," she said gently, "why must you call so early?"

"When I was your age," Madam Rechevsky said, weeping, "I was up at six in the morning. Working my fingers to the bone. A woman thirty-eight shouldn't spend her whole life sleeping."

"Why do you always say thirty-eight?" Helen protested. "Thirty-six. Why can't you remember—thirty-six!"

"On this subject, Helen, darling," Madam Rechevsky said coldly, through her tears, "I am absolutely definite."

Helen finally opened her eyes, slowly, with effort, looked wearily up at the sun-streaked ceiling. "Why're you crying, Momma?"

There was a pause over the wires, then the weeping started afresh, on a new high pitch, deep, despairing, full of sorrow.

"Tell me, Momma," Helen said.

"I must go to Poppa's grave. You must come right downtown and take me to Poppa's grave."

Helen sighed. "Momma, I have three different places I have to be today."

"My own child!" Madam Rechevsky whispered. "My own

134

daughter! Refuses to take her mother to the grave of her own father.''

"Tomorrow," Helen pleaded. "Can't you make it tomorrow?"

"Today!" Madam Rechevsky's voice reached across Manhattan high and tragic, as in the old days, when she strode on the stage and discovered that her stepmother was wearing her dead mother's jewels. "I woke up this morning and a voice spoke to me. 'Go to Abraham's grave! Immediately! Go to the grave of your husband!' "

"Momma," Helen said gently. "Poppa's been dead fifteen years. How much difference can one day make to him?"

"Never mind," Madam Rechevsky said, with magnificent, resounding resignation. "Forgive me if I have troubled you on this trifling matter. Go. Go to your appointments. Go to the beauty parlor. Go to the cocktail parties. I will take the subway to your dead father's grave."

Helen closed her eyes. "I'll pick you up in an hour, Momma."

"Yes," said Madam Rechevsky decisively. "And please don't wear that red hat. For your father's sake."

"I won't wear the red hat." Helen lay back and wearily put the phone back on its pedestal.


"This is a fine car to be going to a cemetery in," Madam Rechevsky was saying as they drove out through Brooklyn. She sat up straight as a little girl in school, savagely denying her seventy-three years with every line of her smart seal coat, every expert touch of rouge, every move of her silken legs. She looked around her contemptuously at the red leather and chromium of Helen's roadster. "A sport model. A great man lies buried, his relatives come to visit him in a cream-colored convertible automobile."

"It's the only car I have, Momma." Helen delicately twisted the wheel in her eloquent, finely gloved hands. "And I'm lucky they haven't taken it away from me by now."

"I told you that was the wrong man for you, in the first place, didn't I?" Madam Rechevsky peered coldly at her daughter, her deep gray eyes flashing and brilliant, rimmed beautifully in mascara, with a touch of purple. "Many years ago I warned you against him, didn't I?"

"Yes, Momma."

"And now—now you are lucky when you collect alimony six

months out of twelve." Madam Rechevsky laughed bitterly. "Nobody ever listened to me, not my own children. Now they suffer."

"Yes, Momma."

"And the theater." Madam Rechevsky waved her hands fiercely. "Why aren't you on the stage this season?"

Helen shrugged. "The right part hasn't come along this season."

"The right part!" Madam Rechevsky laughed coldly. "In my day we did seven plays a year, right part or no right part."

"Momma, darling . . ." Helen shook her head. "It's different now. This isn't the Yiddish Theater and this isn't 1900."

"That was a better theater," Madam Rechevsky said loudly. "And that was a better time."

"Yes, Momma."

"Work!" Madam Rechevsky hit her thighs emphatically with her two hands. "We worked! The actor acted, the writer wrote, the audience came! Now—movies! Pah!"

"Yes, Momma."

"Even so, you're lazy." Madam Rechevsky looked at herself in her handbag mirror to make sure that the violence of her opinions had not disarranged her face. "You sit back and wait for alimony and even so it doesn't come. Also . . ." She examined her daughter critically. "The way you dress is very extreme." She squinted to sharpen the image. "But you make a striking impression. I won't deny that. Every one of my daughters makes a striking impression." Madam Rechevsky shook her head. "But nothing like me, when I was a little younger . . ." She sat back and rode in silence. "Nothing like me . . ." she murmured. "Nothing like me, at all. . . ."

Helen walked briskly beside her mother through the marble-crowded cemetery, their feet making a busy scuffle along the well-kept gravel walks. Madam Rechevsky clutched a dozen yellow chrysanthemums in her hands and on her face was a look of anticipation, almost pleasure, as they approached the grave.

"Perhaps . . ." A bearded old man in holy black, all very clean and pink-faced, came up to them and touched Madam Rechevsky's arm. "Perhaps you would like me to make a prayer for the dead, lady?"

"Go away!" Madam Rechevsky pulled her arm away impatiently. "Abraham Rechevsky does not need professional prayers!"

The old man bowed gently, spoke softly. "For Abraham Rechevsky I will pray for nothing."

Madam Rechevsky stopped, looked at the man for a moment.

Her cold gray eyes smiled a little. "Give the old man a dollar, Helen," she said and touched the man's arm with royal condescension.

Helen dug in her bag and produced a dollar and the old man bowed gravely again.

Helen hurried after her mother.

"See," Madam Rechevsky was muttering as she charged along. "See. Dead fifteen years and still he is famous, all over the world. I bet that old man hasn't offered to pray for anyone free for twenty-five years." She turned on Helen. "And yet you didn't want to come!" She strode on, muttering, "All over the world."

"Don't walk so fast, Momma," Helen protested. "Your heart . . . ."

"Don't worry about my heart." Madam Rechevsky stopped, put her arm out sharply to stop her daughter. "We are in sight. You stay here. I want to go to the grave alone." She spoke without looking at Helen, her eyes on the massive gray granite tombstone thirty yards away, with her husband's name on it and underneath his, space for her own. She spoke very softly. "Turn around, Helen, darling. I want this to be private. I'll call you when I'm ready for you."

She walked slowly toward the tombstone, holding the chrysanthemums before her like a gigantic bride's bouquet. Helen sat on a marble bench near the grave of a man named Axelrod, and turned her head.

Madam Rechevsky approached her husband's grave. Her face was composed, the lips set, the chin high, out of the smart seal collar. She knelt gracefully, placed the chrysanthemums in a compact spray of yellow on the cold earth against the granite. She patted the flowers lightly with one hand to make a pattern more pleasing to the eye, and stood up. She stood without speaking, looking at the even, dead, winter-brown grass that spread across the grave.

Slowly, still looking at the faded grass, she took off first one glove, then the other, and absently stuffed them into a pocket, leaving her white and brilliantly manicured hands bare.

Then she spoke.

"Abraham!" she cried, her voice ringing and imperious and fiercely intimate. "Abraham!" the proud, useful voice echoed and re-echoed among the marble on the small rolling hills of the cemetery. "Abraham, listen to me!"

She took a deep breath, and disregarding the formal stone, spoke directly to the earth beneath her. "You've got to help me, Abraham. Trouble, trouble . . . I'm old and I'm poor and you've left me alone for fifteen years.'' The resonance and volume had gone from her voice, and she spoke quietly, with the little touch of impatience that comes to women's voices when they are complaining to their husbands. ''Money, All your life you never made less than fifteen hundred dollars a week and now they bother me for rent.'' Her lips curled contemptuously as she thought of the miserable men who came to her door on the first of each month. ''You rode in carriages, Abraham. You always owned at least four horses. Wherever you went everybody always said, 'There goes Abraham Rechevsky!' When you sat down to eat, fifty people always sat down with you. You drank wine with breakfast, dinner and supper, and fifty people always drank it with you. You had five daughters by me and God knows how many by other women and every one of them was dressed from Paris from the day she could walk. You had six sons and each one of them had a private tutor from Harvard College. You ate in the best restaurants in New York, London, Paris, Budapest, Vienna, Berlin, Warsaw, Rio de Janeiro. You ate more good food than any other man that ever lived. You had two overcoats at one time lined with mink. You gave diamonds and rubies and strings of pearls to enough women to make up three ballet companies! Sometimes you were paying railroad fare for five women at one time crossing the country after you, on tour. You ate and you drank and you always had a baby daughter in your lap till the day you died, and you lived like a king of the earth, in all respects.'' Madam Rechevsky shook her head at the grave. ''And I? Your wife? Where is the rent?''

Madam Rechevsky paced deliberately to the foot of the grave and addressed herself even more directly to her husband. ''A king, to the day you died, with a specialist from Vienna and three trained nurses and four consulting doctors for an old man, seventy-seven, who had exhausted himself completely with eating and drinking and making love. Buried . . . buried like a king. Three blocks long. The line behind your coffin was three blocks long on Second Avenue at the funeral, thousands of grown men and women crying into their handkerchiefs in broad daylight. And I? Your wife? Forgotten! Money spent, theater gone, husband dead, no insurance . . . Only one thing left—children.''

Madam Rechevsky smiled coldly at her husband. ''And the children—like their father. Selfish. Thinking of themselves. Silly. Doing crazy things. Getting mixed up with ridiculous people. Disastrous. The whole world is disastrous, and your children have led disastrous lives. Alimony, movies, trouble with girls, never any money, never . . . Relatives are dying in Germany. Five hundred dollars would have saved them. No five hundred dollars. And I am getting older day by day and the ones that can help won't, and the ones that want to help can't. Three times a week the dressmaker calls me with old bills. Disastrous! Why should it happen to me?"

Once more, for a moment, Madam Rechevsky's voice went high and clear and echoed among the small graveyard hills. "Why should it happen to me? I worked for you like a slave. I got up at five o'clock in the morning. I sewed the costumes. I rented the theaters. I fought with the authors about the plays. I picked the parts for you. I taught you how to act, Abraham. The Great Actor, they said, the Hamlet of the Yiddish Theater, people knew your name from South Africa to San Francisco, the women tore off their gowns in your dressing room. You were an amateur before I taught you; on every line you tried to blow down the back of the theater. I worked on you like a sculptor on a statue. I made you an artist. And in between . . ." Madam Rechevsky shrugged ironically. "In between I took care of the books, I hired the ushers, I played opposite you better than any leading lady you ever had, I gave you a child every two years and fed all the others other women gave you the rest of the time. With my own hands I polished the apples they sold during intermission!"

Madam Rechevsky slumped a little inside her fashionable seal coat, her voice sank to a whisper. "I loved you better than you deserved and you left me alone for fifteen years and I'm getting older and now they bother me for rent. . . . " She sat down on the cold earth, on the dead winter grass covering the grave. "Abraham," she whispered, "you've got to help me. Please help me. One thing . . . One thing I can say for you—whenever I was in trouble, I could turn to you. Always. Help me, Abraham."

She was silent a moment, her bare hands outspread on the grass. Then she shrugged, stood up, her face more relaxed, confident, at peace, than it had been in months. She turned away from the grave and called.

"Helen, darling," she called. "You can come here now."

Helen left the marble bench on the plot of the man named Axelrod and walked slowly toward her father's grave.

# The Deputy Sheriff

Macomber sat in the sheriff's swivel chair, his feet in the waste-basket because he was too fat to lift them to the desk. He sat there looking across at the poster on the opposite wall that said, "Wanted, for Murder, Walter Cooper, Reward Four Hundred Dollars." He sometimes sat for seven days on end looking at the spot that said "Four Hundred Dollars," going out only for meals and ten hours' sleep a night.

Macomber was the third deputy sheriff and he took care of the office because he didn't like to go home to his wife. In the afternoon the second deputy sheriff came in, too, and sat tilted against the wall, also looking at the spot that said, "Four Hundred Dollars."

"I read in the newspapers," Macomber said, feeling the sweat roll deliberately down his neck into his shirt, "that New Mexico has the healthiest climate in the world. Look at me sweat. Do you call that healthy?"

"You're too goddamn fat," the second deputy sheriff said, never taking his eyes off the "Four Hundred Dollars." "What do you expect?"

"You could fry eggs," Macomber said, looking for an instant at the street blazing outside his window. "I need a vacation. You need a vacation. Everybody needs a vacation." He shifted his gun wearily, where it dug into the fat. "Why can't Walter Cooper walk in here this minute? Why can't he?" he asked.

The telephone rang. Macomber picked it up. He listened, said, "Yes, no, the sheriff's taking a nap. I'll tell him, good-bye."

He put the telephone down slowly, thought in his eyes. "That was Los Angeles," he said. "They caught Brisbane. They got him in the jail there."

"He'll get fifteen years," the second deputy said. "His accomplice got fifteen years. They can sing to each other."

"That's my case," Macomber said, slowly, putting on his hat. "I was the first one to look at the boxcar after they bust into it."

140

He turned at the door. "Somebody's got to go bring Brisbane back from Los Angeles. I'm the man, wouldn't you say?"

"You're the man," the second deputy said. "That's a nice trip. Hollywood. There is nothing wrong with the girls in Hollywood." He nodded his head dreamily. "I wouldn't mind shaking a hip in that city."

Macomber walked slowly toward the sheriff's house, smiling a little to himself, despite the heat, as he thought of Hollywood. He walked briskly, his two hundred and forty pounds purposeful and alert.

"Oh, for Christ's sake," the sheriff said when he told him about Brisbane, "what the hell turns up in Los Angeles." The sheriff was sleepy and annoyed, sitting on the edge of the sofa on which he'd been lying without shoes, his pants open for the first three buttons, after lunch. "We got a conviction out of that, already."

"Brisbane is a known criminal," Macomber said. "He committed entry."

"So he committed entry," the sheriff said. "Into a boxcar. He took two overcoats and a pair of socks and I have to send a man to Los Angeles for him! If you asked them for a murderer you'd never get him out of Los Angeles in twenty years! Why did you have to wake me up?" he asked Macomber testily.

"Los Angeles asked me to have you call back as soon as possible," Macomber said smoothly. "They want to know what to do with him. They want to get rid of him. He cries all day, they told me, at the top of his voice. He's got a whole cell-block yelling their heads off in Los Angeles, they told me."

"I need a man like that here," the sheriff said. "I need him very bad."

But he put his shoes on and buttoned his pants and started back to the office with Macomber.

"Do you mind going to Los Angeles?" the sheriff asked Macomber.

Macomber shrugged. "Somebody's got to do it."

"Good old Macomber," the sheriff said sarcastically. "The backbone of the force. Ever loyal."

"I know the case," Macomber said. "Inside out."

The sheriff looked at him over his shoulder. "There are so many girls there, I read, that even a fat man ought to be able to do business. Taking your wife, Macomber?" He jabbed with his thumb into the fat over the ribs, and laughed.

"Somebody's got to go. I admit," Macomber said earnestly, "it would be nice to see Hollywood. I've read about it."

When they got into the office the second deputy got up out of the swivel chair, and the sheriff dropped into it, unbuttoning the top three buttons of his pants. The sheriff opened a drawer and took out a ledger, panting from the heat. "Why is it," the sheriff wanted to know, "that anybody lives in a place like this?" He looked with annoyance at the opened ledger. "We have not got a penny," the sheriff said, "not a stinking penny. That trip to Needles after Bucher cleaned out the fund. We don't get another appropriation for two months. This is a beautiful county. Catch one crook and you got to go out of business for the season. So what are you looking at me like that for, Macomber?"

"It wouldn't cost more than ninety dollars to send a man to Los Angeles." Macomber sat down gently on a small chair.

"You got ninety dollars?" the sheriff asked.

"This got nothing to do with me," Macomber said. "Only it's a known criminal."

"Maybe," the second deputy said, "you could get Los Angeles to hold on to him for two months."

"I got brain workers in this office," the sheriff said. "Regular brain workers." But he turned to the phone and said, "Get me the police headquarters at Los Angeles."

"Swanson is the name of the man who is handling the matter," Macomber said. "He's waiting for your call."

"Ask them to catch a murderer in Los Angeles," the sheriff said bitterly, "and see what you get . . . They're wonderful on people who break into boxcars."

While the sheriff was waiting for the call to be put through, Macomber turned ponderously, the seat of his pants sticking to the yellow varnish of the chair, and looked out at the deserted street, white with sunlight, the tar boiling up in little black bubbles out in the road from the heat. For a moment, deep under the fat, he couldn't bear Gatlin, New Mexico. A suburb of the desert, a fine place for people with tuberculosis. For twelve years he'd been there, going to the movies twice a week, listening to his wife talk. The fat man. Before you died in Gatlin, New Mexico, you got fat. Twelve years, he thought, looking out on a street that was empty except on Saturday night. He could see himself stepping out of a barber shop in Hollywood, walking lightly to a bar with a blonde girl, thin in the waist, drinking a beer or two, talking and laughing in the middle of a million other people talking and laughing. Greta Garbo walked the streets there, and Carole Lombard, and Alice Faye. "Sarah," he would say to his wife, "I have got to go to Los Angeles. On State business. I will not be back for a week.''

"Well . . . ?'' the sheriff was calling into the phone. "*Well? Where is Los Angeles?*''

Ninety dollars, ninety lousy dollars . . . He turned away from looking at the street. He put his hands on his knees and was surprised to see them shake as he heard the sheriff say, "Hello, is this Swanson?''

He couldn't sit still and listen to the sheriff talk over the phone, so he got up and walked slowly through the back room to the lavatory. He went in, closed the door, and looked carefully at his face in the mirror. That's what his face looked like, that's what the twelve years, listening to his wife talk, had done. Without expression he went back to the office.

"All right,'' the sheriff was saying, "you don't have to keep him for two months. I know you're crowded. I know it's against the constitution. I know, I said, for Christ's sake. It was just a suggestion. I'm sorry he's crying. Is it my fault he's crying? Maybe you'd cry, too, if you were going to jail for fifteen years. Stop yelling, for Christ's sake, this call is costing the county of Gatlin a million dollars. I'll call you back. All right, by six o'clock. All right, I said. All right.''

The sheriff put the telephone down. For a moment he sat wearily, looking at the open top of his pants. He sighed, buttoned his pants. "That is some city,'' he said, "Los Angeles.'' He shook his head. "I got a good mind to say the hell with it. Why should I run myself into an early grave for a man who broke into a boxcar? Who can tell me?''

"He's a known criminal,'' Macomber said. "We got a whole case.'' His voice was smooth but he felt the eager tremor deep under it. "Justice is justice.''

The sheriff looked at him bitterly. "The voice of conscience. The sheriff's white light, Macomber.''

Macomber shrugged. "What's it to me? I just like to see a case closed.''

The sheriff turned back to the telephone. "Get me the county treasurer's office,'' he said. He sat there, waiting, looking at Macomber, with the receiver against his ear. Macomber walked over to the door and looked out across the street. He saw his wife sitting at the window of their house up the street, her fat elbows crossed, with the sweat dripping off them. He looked the other way.

He heard the sheriff's voice, as though distant and indistinct, talking to the county treasurer. He heard the county treasurer's voice rise in anger through the phone, mechanical and shrill. "Everybody spends money," the county treasurer screamed. "Nobody brings in money, but everybody spends money. I'll be lucky to have my own salary left over at the end of the month and you want ninety dollars to go joy-riding to Los Angeles to get a man who stole nine dollars' worth of second-hand goods. The hell with you! I said the hell with you!"

Macomber put his hands in his pockets so that nobody could see how tense they were as he heard the receiver slam on the other end of the wire. Coldly he watched the sheriff put the phone gently down.

"Macomber," the sheriff said, feeling his deputy's eyes on him, hard and accusing, "I'm afraid Joan Crawford will have to get along without you, this year."

"They will hang crepe on the studios when they hear about this," the second deputy said.

"I don't care for myself," Macomber said evenly, "but it will sound awfully funny to people if they find out that the sheriff's office let a known criminal go free after he was caught."

The sheriff stood up abruptly. "What do you want me to do?" he asked with violence. "Tell me what the hell more you want me to do? Can I create the ninety dollars? Talk to the State of New Mexico!"

Macomber shrugged. "It's not my business," he said. "Only I think we can't let criminals laugh at New Mexican justice."

"All right," the sheriff shouted. "Do something. Go do something! I don't have to call back until six o'clock! You got three hours to see justice done. My hands are washed." He sat down and opened the top three buttons of his pants and put his feet on the desk. "If it means so much to you," he said, as Macomber started through the door, "arrange it yourself."

Macomber passed his house on the way to the district attorney's office. His wife was still sitting at the window with the sweat dripping off her. She looked at her husband out of her dry eyes, and he looked at her as he walked thoughtfully past. No smile lit her face or his, no word was passed. For a moment they looked at each other with the arid recognition of twelve years. Then Macomber walked deliberately on, feeling the heat rising through his shoes, tiring his legs right up to his hips.

In Hollywood he would walk firmly and briskly, not like a fat man, over the clean pavements, ringing to the sharp attractive clicks of high heels all around him. For ten steps he closed his eyes as he turned into the main street of Gatlin, New Mexico.

He went into the huge Greek building that the WPA had built for the County of Gatlin. As he passed down the quiet halls, rich with marble, cool, even in the mid-afternoon, he said, looking harshly around him, "Ninety dollars—ninety lousy dollars."

In front of the door that said "Office of the District Attorney" he stopped. He stood there for a moment, feeling nervousness rise and fall in him like a wave. His hand sweated on the doorknob when he opened the door. He went in casually, carefully appearing like a man carrying out impersonal government business.

The door to the private office was open a little and he could see the district attorney's wife standing there and could hear the district attorney yelling, "For God's sake, Carol, have a heart! Do I look like a man who is made of money? Answer me, do I?"

"All I want," the district attorney's wife said stubbornly, "is a little vacation. Three weeks, that's all. I can't stand the heat here. I'll lie down and die if I have to stay here another week. Do you want me to lie down and die? You make me live in this oasis, do I have to die here, too?" She started to cry, shaking her careful blonde hair.

"All right," the district attorney said. "All right, Carol. Go ahead. Go home and pack. Stop crying. For the love of God, stop crying!"

She went over and kissed the district attorney and came out, past Macomber, drying the tip of her nose. The district attorney took her through the office and opened the door for her. She kissed him again and went down the hall. The district attorney closed the door and leaned against it wearily. "She's got to go to Wisconsin," he said to Macomber. "She knows people in Wisconsin. There are lakes there. What do you want?"

Macomber explained about Brisbane and Los Angeles and the sheriff's fund and what the county treasurer had said. The district attorney sat down on the bench against the wall and listened with his head down.

"What do you want me to do?" he asked when Macomber finished.

"That Brisbane is a man who should be behind bars for fifteen years. There wouldn't be any doubt about it, once we got him here. He's a known criminal. After all, it would only cost ninety dollars . . . If you said something, if you made a protest . . ."

The district attorney sat on the bench with his head down, his hands loose between his knees. "Everybody wants to spend money to go some place that isn't Gatlin, New Mexico. You know how much it's going to cost to send my wife to Wisconsin for three weeks? Three hundred dollars. Oh, my God!''

"This is another matter," Macomber said very softly and reasonably. "This is a matter of your record. A sure conviction."

"There's nothing wrong with my record." The district attorney stood up. "My record's fine. I got a conviction on that case already. What do you want me to do—spend my life getting convictions on a nine-dollar robbery?''

"If you only said one word to the county treasurer . . ." Macomber tagged after the district attorney as he started for his inner office.

"If the county treasurer wants to save money, I say, 'That's the sort of man we need.' Somebody has to save money. Somebody has got to do something else besides supporting the railroads."

"It's a bad precedent, a guilty man . . ." Macomber said a little louder than he wanted.

"Leave me alone," the district attorney said. "I'm tired." He went into the inner office and closed the door firmly.

Macomber said, "Son of a bitch, you bastard!" softly to the imitation oak door, and went out into the marble hall. He bent over and drank from the shining porcelain fountain that the WPA had put there. His mouth felt dry and sandy, with an old taste in it.

Outside he walked down the burning sidewalk, his feet dragging. His belly stretched against the top of his trousers uncomfortably, and he belched, remembering his wife's cooking. In Hollywood he would sit down in a restaurant where the stars ate, no matter what it cost, and have light French dishes, served with silver covers, and wine out of iced bottles. Ninety lousy dollars. He walked in the shade of store-awnings, sweating, wrenching his mind to thought. "Goddamn it, goddamn it!" he said to himself because he could think of nothing further to do. For the rest of his life in Gatlin, New Mexico, with never another chance to get even a short breath of joy . . . The back of his eyes ached from thinking. Suddenly he strode out from under the awning, walked up the steps that led to the office of the Gatlin *Herald*.

The city editor was sitting at a big desk covered with dust and tangled copy. He was wearily blue-penciling a long white sheet. He listened abstractedly as Macomber talked, using his pencil from time to time.

"You could show the voters of Gatlin," Macomber was leaning close over the desk, talking fast, "what sort of men they got serving them. You could show the property owners of this county what sort of protection they can expect to get from the sheriff, the district attorney, and the county treasurer they put into office. That would make interesting reading-matter, that would, letting men who committed crimes in this county go off thumbing their noses at law enforcement here. If I was you I would write one hell of an editorial, I would. For ninety lousy dollars. One expression of opinion like that in the paper and the sheriff's office would have a man in Los Angeles tomorrow. Are you listening to me?"

"Yeah," the city editor said, judiciously running his pencil in straight blue lines three times across the page. "Why don't you go back to being the third deputy sheriff, Macomber?"

"You're a party paper," Macomber said bitterly, "that's what's the matter with you. You're Democrats and you wouldn't say anything if a Democratic politician walked off with Main Street in a truck. You're a very corrupt organization."

"Yes," the city editor said. "You hit the nail on the head." He used the pencil again.

"Aaah!" Macomber said, turning away. "For Christ's sake."

"The trouble with you," the city editor said, "is you don't get enough nourishment. You need nourishment." He poised the pencil thoughtfully over a sentence as Macomber went out, slamming the door.

Macomber walked dully down the street, regardless of the heat beating solidly against him.

He passed his house on the way back to the office. His wife was still sitting there, looking out at the street that was always empty except on Saturday night. Macomber regarded her with his aching eyes, from the other side of the street. "Is that all you have to do," he called, "sit there?"

She didn't say anything, but looked at him for a moment, then calmly glanced up the street.

Macomber entered the sheriff's office and sat down heavily. The sheriff was still there, his feet on the desk.

"Well?" the sheriff said.

"The hell with it." Macomber dried the sweat off his face with a colored handkerchief. "It's no skin off my back." He loosened the laces of his shoes and sat back as the sheriff got Los Angeles on the phone. "Swanson?" the sheriff said into the phone. "This is Sheriff Hadley of Gatlin, New Mexico. You can go tell Brisbane he can stop crying. Turn him loose. We're not coming for him. We can't be bothered. Thanks." He hung up, sighed as a man

147

sighs at the end of a day's work. "I'm going home to dinner," he said, and went out.

"I'll stay here while you go home to eat," the second deputy said to Macomber.

"Never mind," Macomber said. "I'm not hungry."

"O.K." The second deputy stood up and went to the door. "So long, Barrymore." He departed, whistling.

Macomber hobbled over to the sheriff's swivel chair in his open shoes. He leaned back in the chair, looked up at the poster, "Wanted for Murder . . . Four Hundred Dollars," lit now by the lengthening rays of the sun. He put his feet into the wastebasket. "Goddamn Walter Cooper," he said.

# Stop Pushing, Rocky

Mr. Gensel carefully wrapped six feet of adhesive tape around Joey Garr's famous right hand. Joey sat on the edge of the rubbing table, swinging his legs, watching his manager moodily.

"Delicate," Mr. Gensel said, working thoughtfully. "Remember, delicate is the keyword."

"Yeah," Joey said. He belched.

Mr. Gensel frowned and stopped winding the tape. "Joey," he said, "how many times I got to tell you, please, for my sake, don't eat in diners."

"Yeah," Joey said.

"There is a limit to everything, Joey," Mr. Gensel said. "Thrift can be carried too far, Joey. You're not a poor man. You got as much money in the bank as a Hollywood actress, why do you have to eat thirty-five-cent blueplates?"

"Please do not talk so much." Joey stuck out his left hand.

Mr. Gensel turned his attention to the famous left hand. "Ulcers," he complained. "I will have a fighter with ulcers. A wonderful prospect. He has to eat garbage. Garbage and ketchup. The coming welterweight champion. Dynamite in either fist. But he belches forty times a day. My God, Joey."

Joey spat impassively on the floor and squinted at his neatly slicked hair in the mirror. Mr. Gensel sighed and moved his bridge restlessly around in his mouth and finished his job.

"Allow me, some day," he said, "to buy you a meal. A dollar-fifty meal. To give you the taste."

"Save yer money, Mr. Gensel," Joey said, "for your old age."

The door opened and McAlmon came in, flanked on either side by two tall, broad men with flat faces and scarred lips curled in amiable grins.

"I am glad to see you boys," McAlmon said, coming up and patting Joey on the back. "How is my little boy Joey tonight?"

"Yeah," Joey said, lying down on the rubbing table and closing his eyes.

"He belches," Mr. Gensel said. "I never saw a fighter belch so much as Joey in my whole life. Not in thirty-five years in the game. How is your boy?"

"Rocky is fine," McAlmon said. "He wanted to come in here with me. He wanted to make sure that Joey understood."

"I understand," Joey said irritably. "I understand fine. That Rocky. The one thing he is afraid of maybe some day somebody will hit him. A prizefighter."

"You can't blame him," McAlmon said reasonably. "After all, he knows, if Joey wants he can put him down until the day after Thanksgiving."

"With one hand," Joey said grimly. "That is some fighter, that Rocky."

"He got nothing to worry about," Mr. Gensel said smoothly. "Everything is absolutely clear in everybody's mind. Clear like crystal. We carry him the whole ten rounds."

"Lissen, Joey," McAlmon leaned on the rubbing table right over Joey's upturned face, "let him look good. He has a following in Philadelphia."

"I will make him look wonderful," Joey said wearily. "I will make him look like the British navy. The one thing that worries me all the time is maybe Rocky will lose his following in Philadelphia."

McAlmon spoke very coldly. "I don't like your tone of voice, Joey," he said.

"Yeah." Joey turned over on his belly.

"Just in case," McAlmon said in crisp tones, "just in case any party forgets their agreement, let me introduce you to Mr. Pike and Mr. Petroskas."

The two tall broad men smiled very widely.

Joey sat up slowly and looked at them.

"They will be sitting in the audience," McAlmon said. "Watching proceedings with interest."

The two men smiled from ear to ear, the flat noses flattening even deeper into their faces.

"They got guns, Mr. Gensel," Joey said. "Under their lousy armpits."

"It is just a precaution," McAlmon said. "I know everything will go along smooth. But we got money invested."

"Lissen, you dumb Philadelphia hick," Joey began.

"That isn't the way to talk, Joey," Mr. Gensel said nervously.

150

"I got money invested, too," Joey yelled. "I got one thousand dollars down even money that that lousy Rocky stays ten rounds with me. You don't need your gorillas. I am only hoping Rocky don't collapse from fright before the tenth round."

"Is that the truth?" McAlmon asked Mr. Gensel.

"I put the bet down through my own brother-in-law," Mr. Gensel said. "I swear to God."

"What do you think, McAlmon?" Joey shouted, "I throw away thousand-dollar bills? I'm a businessman."

"Take my word for it," Mr. Gensel said. "Joey is a businessman."

"All right, all right." McAlmon put out both his hands placatingly. "There is no harm done in straightening matters out complete beforehand, is there? Now nobody is in the dark about anything. That is the way I like to operate." He turned to Pike and Petroskas. "O.K., boys, just sit in your seats and have a good time."

"Why do those two bums have to be there?" Joey demanded.

"Do you mind if they enjoy themselves?" McAlmon asked with cold sarcasm. "It's going to damage you if they have a good time?"

"That's all right," Mr. Gensel said soothingly. "We don't object. Let the boys have a good time."

"Only get them out of here," Joey said loudly. "I don't like people with guns under their armpits in my room."

"Come on, boys," McAlmon said, opening the door. Both men smiled pleasantly and started out. Petroskas stopped and turned around. "May the best man win," he said, and nodded soberly twice and left, closing the door behind him.

Joey looked at Mr. Gensel and shook his head. "McAlmon's friends," he said. "Philadelphia boys."

The door swung open and an usher chanted "Joey Garr. Joey Garr is on next." Joey spat into his bandaged hands and started up the steps with Mr. Gensel.

When the fight started, Rocky dove immediately into a clinch. Under the thick bush of hair all over his chest and shoulders he was sweating profusely.

"Lissen, Joey," he whispered nervously into Joey's ear, hanging on tightly to his elbows, "you remember the agreement? You remember, don't yuh, Joey?"

"Yeah," Joey said. "Let go of my arm. What're you trying to do, pull it off?"

"Excuse me, Joey," Rocky said, breaking and giving Joey two to the ribs.

As the fight progressed, with the customers yelling loud approval of the footwork, the deft exchanges, the murderous finishers that missed by a hair, Rocky gained in confidence. By the fourth round he was standing up bravely, exposing his chin, moving in and out with his fists brisk and showy. His friends in the crowd screamed with pleasure and a loud voice called out, "Kill the big bum, Rocky! Oh, you Rocky!" Rocky breathed deeply and let a fast one go to Joey's ear. Joey's head shook a little and a look of mild surprise came over his face. "Wipe him out!" the voice thundered from among Rocky's following. Rocky set himself flat on his feet and whistled another across to Joey's ear as the bell rang. He strutted back to his corner smiling confidently at his friends in the arena.

Mr. Gensel bent and worked over Joey. "Lissen, Joey," he whispered, "he is pushing you. Tell him to stop pushing you. They will give him the fight if he don't stop pushing you."

"Aaah," Joey said, "it's nothing. For the crowd. His pals. A little excitement. Makes it look good. Don't worry, Mr. Gensel."

"Please tell him to stop pushing you," Mr. Gensel pleaded. "For my sake, Joey. He is supposed to go ten rounds with us but we are supposed to win. We can't afford to lose to Rocky Pidgeon, Joey."

In the fifth round Rocky kept up his charging attack, keeping both hands going, weaving, aggressive, shoving Joey back and forth across the ring, while the home-town crowd stood in its seats and shouted hoarse support. Joey kept him nicely bottled up, back-pedaling, catching punches on his gloves, sliding with the blows, occasionally jabbing sharply to Rocky's chest. In a corner, with Joey against the ropes, Rocky swung from behind his back with a right hand, grunting deeply as it landed on Joey's side.

Joey clinched, feeling the sting. "Say, Rocky," he whispered politely, "stop pushing."

"Oh," Rocky grunted, as though he'd just remembered, and backed off. They sparred delicately for thirty seconds, Joey still on the ropes.

"Come on, Rocky," the voice shouted. "Finish him. You got the bum going! Oh, you Rocky!"

A light came into Rocky's eyes and he wound up and let one go. It caught Joey on the side of the head as the bell rang. Joey leaned a little wearily against the ropes, scowling thoughtfully at

Rocky as Rocky strode lightly across to his corner amid wild applause. Joey went and sat down.

"How's it going?" he asked Mr. Gensel.

"You lost that round," Mr. Gensel said swiftly and nervously. "For God's sake, Joey, tell him to stop pushing. You'll lose the fight. If you lose to Rocky Pidgeon you will have to go fight on the team with the boys from the Hebrew Orphan Asylum. Why don't you tell him to stop pushing?"

"I did," Joey snapped. "He's all hopped up. His friends keep yelling what a great guy he is, so he believes it. He hits me in the ear once more I will take him out in the alley after the fight and I will beat the pants off him."

"Just tell him to take it easy," Mr. Gensel said, worriedly. "Remind him we are carrying him. Just remind him."

"That dumb Rocky," Joey said. "You got to reason with him, you got a job on your hands."

The gong rang and the two men sprang out at each other. The light of battle was still in Rocky's eye and he came out swinging violently. Joey tied him up tight and talked earnestly to him. "Lissen, Rocky, enough is enough. Stop being a hero, please. Everybody thinks you're wonderful. All right. Let it go at that. Stop pushing, Rocky. There is money invested here. What are you, crazy? Say, Rocky, do you know what I'm talking about?"

"Sure," Rocky grunted. "I'm just putting on a good show. You got to put on a good show, don't you?"

"Yeah," Joey said, as the referee finally pulled them apart.

They danced for two minutes after that, but right before the end of the round, from in close, Rocky unleashed a murderous uppercut that sent the blood squirting in all directions from Joey's nose. Rocky wheeled jauntily as the bell rang and shook his hands gaily at his screaming friends. Joey looked after him and spat a long stream of blood at his retreating, swaggering back.

Mr. Gensel rushed anxiously out and led Joey back to his corner.

"Why didn't you tell him to stop pushing, Joey?" he asked. "Why don't you do like I say?"

"I told him," Joey said, bitterly. "Look, I got a bloody nose. I got to come to Philadelphia to get a bloody nose. That bastid, Rocky."

"Make sure to tell him to stop pushing," Mr. Gensel said, working swiftly over the nose. "You got to win from here on, Joey. No mistake now."

"I got to come to Starlight Park, in the city of Philadelphia,"

Joey marveled, "to get a bloody nose from Rocky Pidgeon. Holy Jesus God!"

"Joey," Mr. Gensel implored, "will you remember what I told you? Tell him to stop . . ."

The bell rang and the two men leapt at each other as the crowd took up its roaring from where it had left off. The loud voice had settled into a constant, inspiriting chant of "Oh, Rocky, oh, you Rocky!" over and over again.

Joey grabbed Rocky grimly. "Lissen, you bum," he whispered harshly, "I ask you to stop pushing. I will take you out later and knock all your teeth out. I warn you."

And he rapped Rocky smartly twice across the ear to impress him.

For the next minute Rocky kept a respectful distance and Joey piled up points rapidly. Suddenly half the arena took up the chant, "Oh, Rocky, oh, you Rocky!" On fire with this admiration, Rocky took a deep breath and let sail a roundhouse right. It caught Joey squarely on the injured nose. Once more the blood spurted. Joey shook his head to clear it and took a step toward Rocky, who was charging in wildly. Coldly Joey hooked with his left, like a spring uncoiling, and crossed with his right as Rocky sagged with glass in his eyes. Rocky went fourteen feet across the ring and landed face down. For a split second a smile of satisfaction crossed Joey's face. Then he remembered. He swallowed drily as the roar of the crowd exploded in his ears. He looked at his corner. Mr. Gensel was just turning around to sit with his back to the ring and his head in his hands. He looked at Rocky's corner. McAlmon was jumping up and down, beating his hat with both fists in agony, screaming, "Rocky! Get up, Rocky! Get up or I'll fill you full of lead! Rocky, do you hear me?"

Behind McAlmon, Joey saw Pike and Petroskas, standing in their seats, amiable smiles on their faces, watching him interestedly, their hands under their armpits.

"Rocky!" Joey whispered hoarsely as the referee counted five, "good old Rocky. Get up, Rocky! For God's sake. Please get up! Please . . . please." He remembered the thousand dollars and tears filled his eyes. "Rocky," he sobbed, half-bending to his knees, in the corner of the ring, as the referee reached seven, "for the love of God . . ."

Rocky turned over, got to one knee.

Joey closed his eyes to spare himself. When he opened them again, there was Rocky, standing, weaving unsteadily, before him. A breath, a prayer, escaped Joey's lips as he jumped across the ring, swinging dramatically. He curled his arm viciously around the back of Rocky's neck. Even at that Rocky started to go again. Joey grabbed him under the armpits and made violent movements with his arms as though he were trying desperately to release them.

"Hold on, Rocky!" he whispered hoarsely, supporting the stricken fighter. "Just keep your knees stiff. You all right? Hey, Rocky, you all right? Hey, Rocky, answer me! Please, Rocky, say something!"

But Rocky said nothing. He just leaned against Joey with the glaze in his eyes, his arms hanging limply at his side, while Joey conducted the fight by himself.

When the bell rang, Joey held Rocky up until McAlmon could come out and drag him back to his corner. The referee eyed Joey narrowly as Joey went over to his own corner.

"A nice, interesting bout," the referee said. "Yes, siree."

"Yeah," Joey said, sinking onto his stool. "Hey, Mr. Gensel," he called. Mr. Gensel turned his face back to the ring for the first time since the middle of the round. Like an old man, he climbed the steps and haphazardly worked on his fighter.

"Explain to me," he said in a flat voice, "what you were thinking of."

"That Rocky," Joey said wearily. "He got the brains of a iceman's horse. He keeps pushing and pushing. I musta lost a quart of blood through the nose. I hit him to teach him a little respect."

"Yes," Mr. Gensel said. "That was fine. We were nearly buried in Philadelphia."

"I didn't hit him hard," Joey protested. "It was strictly a medium punch. He got a chin like a movie star. Like Myrna Loy. He shouldn't oughta be in this business. He should wait on customers in a store. In a dairy. Butter and eggs."

"Please do me a favor," Mr. Gensel said. "Kindly hold him up for the next three rounds. Treat him with care. I am going down to sit in the dressing room."

And Mr. Gensel left as Joey charged out and pounded Rocky's fluttering elbows severely.

Fifteen minutes later, Joey came down to him in the dressing room and lay wearily down on the rubbing table.

"So?" Mr. Gensel asked, not lifting his head.

"So we won," Joey said hoarsely. "I had to carry him like a baby for nine whole minutes. Like a eight-month-old baby girl. That Rocky. Hit him once, he is no good for three years. I never worked so hard in my whole life, not even when I poured rubber in Akron, Ohio.''

"Did anybody catch on?" Mr. Gensel asked.

"Thank God we're in Philadelphia," Joey said. "They ain't caught on the war's over yet. They are still standing up there yelling, 'Rocky! Oh, you Rocky!' because he was so goddamn brave and stood in there fighting. My God! Every ten seconds I had to kick him in the knee to straighten it out so he'd keep standing!"

Mr. Gensel sighed. "Well, we made a lot of money."

"Yeah," Joey said without joy.

"I'll treat you to a dollar-fifty dinner, Joey."

"Naah," Joey said, flattening out on the rubbing table. "I just want to stay here and rest. I want to lay here and rest for a long time."

# "March, March on Down the Field"

"For one dollar," Peppe said, "you could buy enough coal to keep this lousy locker room warm all week." He laced up his shoulder pads with numb fingers. "For one stinking dollar. We'll be stiff like concrete by the time we got to kick off. Somebody ought to tell that Scheepers something. For one dollar that Scheepers would freeze his grandmother. In sections. Yeah." He ducked his head into his jersey.

"We ought to get together," Ullman said. "We all ought to stick together and go to Scheepers and say, 'Scheepers,' we ought to say, 'you pay us to play football for you, *but*—'"

"Ullman," Peppe called from inside his jersey, "the City College Boy, Mr. Stalin's right-hand man. Fullbacks of the world, unite."

"Hey, shake your tails," Holstein said. "We want to go out and loosen up before the game starts."

"Loosen up!" Peppe finally got his head through the jersey. "They will have to broil me. On both sides. My God, I wish I was in the south of France. Along the Riviera. With the French girls."

"Put your pants on," Holstein said.

"Look!" Peppe pointed sadly to his naked legs. "I am turning blue. A dark shade of blue. From the ankle up. It's past my knees already. Look, boys. Another foot and that is the end of Peppe."

Klonsky, the right tackle, a tall, thick man, pushed Peppe to one side. "Excuse me," he said. "I want to look in the mirror."

"If I had a face like that—" Peppe began. Klonsky turned and looked at him.

"What did I say?" Peppe asked. "Did I say anything?"

Klonsky looked at himself in the mirror again, pulling down his lower lip. "It's my teeth," he explained without turning from the mirror. "I got three new teeth from the dentist this week."

"They'll sign you for the movies," Holstein said.

"Fifty bucks," Klonsky said. "The lousy dentist charged me

fifty bucks. In advance. He wouldn't put the teeth in until I put the money down. My wife, she insisted I got to have teeth in the front of my face. She said it was bad, a college graduate with teeth missing."

"Sure," Holstein said. "Listen to women in a case like that. They know what they're talking about."

"I lost them two years ago in the Manhattan game." Klonsky shook his head and turned from the mirror. "They are very rough— Manhattan. All they were interested in was hitting me in the teeth— they didn't give a damn who won the game."

"Watch out for Krakow," Peppe said. "He runs like a locomotive, that guy. You could chop off his leg, he would still run. He's got no sense. He played for Upsala for three years and he had to make every tackle in every game. It upset his brains. He plays like he don't get paid for it. He will break your back for three yards. Oh, my God, it's cold! That bastard Scheepers!"

The door opened and Scheepers came in, the collar of his pale camel's-hair coat up around his ears. "I heard somebody call me bastard," he said. "I don't like that, boys." He looked at them, his face set under the brim of his soft green hat.

"It's cold in here," Holstein said.

"There's ice in the East River," Ullman said.

"I am responsible," Scheepers said ironically, "I am responsible for the weather all of a sudden?"

"One dollar's worth of coal." Peppe blew on his hands. "That's all you need to keep this locker room warm. One lousy dollar's worth."

"Watch your language," Scheepers said. He turned to the rest of the team. "I ordered coal. I swear to God." He put his collar down and took off his pigskin gloves. "Anyway, it's not so cold. I don't know what you boys are complaining about."

"Some day," Peppe said, "you should get dressed here, Scheepers. That's all I ask. They would use you to freeze ice cubes."

"Lissen, boys!" Scheepers stood up on a bench and addressed the whole room. "I got a matter to discuss, a slight matter of money."

The locker room was silent.

"Call the pickpocket squad," Peppe said after a moment. "Scheepers is discussing money."

"I know you boys are joking." Scheepers smiled. "So I don't get sore."

"Get sore, Scheepers," Peppe said. "Get good and sore."

Scheepers hesitated and then spoke in a confidential voice. "Boys," he said, "it is not a warm day. This is not a pleasant Sunday afternoon, to be perfectly frank with you."

"Secrets," Holstein said. "Keep it to yourself, boys."

"It's cold. It's near the end of the season. It snowed this morning. The Dodgers are playing Pittsburgh at Ebbets Field. You fellers ain't put on such a good show for the last two weeks. In a word, there is not a large crowd today." He looked around him significantly. "I have made a deal with Krakow's All-Stars. I have reduced their guarantee fifty per cent because there is hardly anybody in the stands."

"That's nice," Holstein said. "That's a nice piece of business. You ought to be proud of yourself."

"What I am driving at—" Scheepers said.

"Don't tell us," Peppe said. "Let us guess. Ullman, you guess first."

"What I am driving at," Scheepers continued, "is that I expect you boys to take a small fifty-per-cent reduction for yourself."

"You know what you can do," Holstein said. "With my compliments."

"Scheepers!" Peppe said. "The Season's Leading Louse."

"It ain't hardly worth the risk," Klonsky said, feeling his teeth. "I borrowed that fifty bucks to pay the dentist. I gave a lien on my radio. If they take that radio, my wife is going to raise hell. Go ask somebody else, Scheepers."

"I am being fair," Scheepers said. "Absolutely fair. It is an impartial proposition. Everybody takes a small fifty-per—"

" 'The butcher, the baker, the candlestick-maker,' " sang Peppe, " 'were all in love with Marie.' "

"I am talking serious," Scheepers said. "And I want a serious answer."

"He wants a serious answer," Peppe said,

"I am trying to conduct business!" Scheepers screamed. "I got bills to pay, dammit!"

"Nuts," Peppe said mildly. "Nuts, Mr. Scheepers. That serious enough?"

"I am hereby telling you that I will go outside and pay back every admission ticket unless you boys do business," Scheepers said. "The game will be off. I got to protect myself."

The men looked at each other. Holstein scraped his cleats on the plank floor.

"I was thinking of buying a pair of shoes tomorrow," Ullman said. "I'm walking around in my bare feet."

"It's up to you, boys." Scheepers put his gloves on again.

"I got a date tonight," Peppe said bitterly. "A very fine girl. A girl from Greenwich Village. It will cost me six bucks sure. Scheepers, you're taking advantage."

"Profit and loss," Scheepers insisted. "I am merely trying to balance the books. Take it or leave it, boys."

"O.K.," Holstein said.

"It is strictly not a personal thing," Scheepers said. "I am in the red all season."

"Kindly leave the room, Scheepers," Peppe said, "while we feel sorry for you. The tears are blinding us."

"Wise guys," Scheepers said, sneering. "A collection of very wise guys. Remember, next season there will be games played too." He glanced at Peppe. "Football players are a drug on the market, remember. Every year five thousand boys come out of college who can block and tackle. I don't have to take insults from nobody."

"You stink," Peppe said. "That is my honest opinion. Oh, my God, it's cold!" He went to the first-aid kit and poured liniment over his hands to warm them.

"I got one or two more things to say." Scheepers spoke loudly to hold their attention. "I want you boys to open up today. A little zip. Some fancy stuff. Passes."

"Nobody can hold on to passes today," Holstein said. "It's cold. Your hands get stiff. Also, there's snow all over the field. The ball'll be sliding as though it had butter on it."

"What do you care?" Scheepers said. "They like passes—give them passes. And please, boys, play like you meant it. After all, we're in business, you know."

"On a day like this I got to play games." Peppe shivered. "I could be in Greenwich Village now, drinking beer in my girl's house. I hope Krakow falls and breaks his neck."

"I got a premonition," Klonsky said. "Something is definitely going to happen to my teeth."

"Also," Scheepers said, "there has been some slipup in the helmets. The amateur team that was supposed to play here this morning and leave the helmets didn't play on account of the snow, so you will have to play without helmets."

"Good old Scheepers," Holstein said. "He thinks of everything."

"It was an error," Scheepers said. "An unavoidable error. Lots of guys play without helmets."

"Lots of guys jump off bridges, too," Holstein said.

"What the hell good is a helmet anyway?" Scheepers demanded. "Every time you need it, it falls off."

"Any other little thing on your mind?" Holstein asked. "You're sure you didn't want us to play with only eight men because it's a small crowd?"

The men laughed, and then, one by one, they filed out onto the field, swinging their arms to keep warm in the freezing wind that swept down on them from the north. Scheepers watched them a moment and then he went into the field house and switched on the public-address system. " 'March, march on down the field,' " sang the public-address system as Scheepers' Red Devils lined up to receive the kick, without helmets.

# Free Conscience, Void of Offence

"To Chamberlain!" one of the women at the bar was saying, her glass held high, as Margaret Clay and her father came into the small, pleasant room, lit by candles, with a big oak fire burning steadily in the fireplace and the glassware and cutlery on the tables winking softly in the firelight. "He saved my son for me," the woman said loudly. She was a woman of nearly fifty who had obviously been pretty once. "To my good friend Neville Chamberlain!"

The other two women and the three men at the bar drank soberly as Margaret and her father sat down at a table.

"That Dorothy Thompson!" said the friend of Neville Chamberlain. "She makes me so mad! Did you see what she wrote about him? If I had her here!" She waved her fist and the wrinkles in her face suddenly bit deeper. "I won't read her any more. Not once more. You know what she is? She's a Red. She's rabid!"

"This is a nice place," Margaret's father said, looking around him with a happy expression. "It has a pleasant atmosphere. Do you come here often?"

"Boys take me here," Margaret said. "It's only about ten miles from school, and they like the candlelight and the open fire, even though it costs three bucks a dinner. Boys always think candlelight and an open fire act like heavy artillery on a girl's resistance. Two hours of that, they figure, and they can just walk in and mop up."

"Margaret," Mr. Clay said, like a father, "I don't like to hear you talk like that."

Margaret laughed, and leaned over and patted her father's hand. "What's the matter, Pop?" she asked. "Your long years at the Stork Club turn you tender?"

"You're too young to talk like that," Mr. Clay said, disliking the fact that she had called him Pop, disliking her thinking that he went often to the Stork Club. "A twenty-year-old girl should . . ."

The owner of the place, a beautifully dressed, pink-faced man of forty who looked like a boy, was standing beside their table. smiling, having come out from behind the bar, where at dinner-time he mixed the drinks scrupulously himself.

"Hello, Mr. Trent," Margaret said. "This is my father. He likes your place."

"Thank you," Trent said, bowing a little, smiling like a little boy. "I'm pleased."

"It has a very pleasant atmosphere," Mr. Clay said.

"Mr. Trent has a specialty," Margaret said. "He makes it with rum."

"Rum, lime juice, sugar, a little Cointreau in the bottom of the glass." Trent waved his hands delicately as he spoke.

"It comes out foamy," Margaret said. "It's nice on the teeth."

"I'm making it now with black Jamaica rum," Trent said. "Myers' rum, it's heavier, for the autumn. I make it on the electric mixer. It gives it a nice quality."

"Two," said Mr, Clay, wishing he had the courage to order a Martini.

The six people at the bar were singing now. "The old gray mare," they sang, loudly, consciously having a good time, con-sciously being gay and lively, and yet singing with a slight touch of burlesque, so that anybody could see these were no yokels. "The old gray mare," they sang, "she ain't what she used to be, oh, she ain't what she used to be . . ."

Margaret watched them, grouped at the bar, their heads together—a cluster of men's middle-aged sparse gray hair, neatly brushed; and carefully curled and elaborately arranged coiffures on the women that in this light, at least, had a last, desperate look of youth. The woman who had toasted Chamberlain had been here once before when Margaret had come for dinner. Mrs. Taylor, Trent had called her, and she'd been in with a man other than her husband, whose hand she was holding now. Margaret had noticed her quick look around the room before she seated herself, her tiny adjustment of her corset, betraying the fact that the achievement of that trim and almost elegant figure came only as a result of engineering and torture under the smart silk print dress. A man they called Oliver, who looked slightly older than the others, somehow more confident and breezy, as though he had more money in the bank than any of his friends, led the singing with elaborate gestures of his hands, like a burlesque of Stokowski. Mr. Taylor was the least noisy of the three men. He wheezed a little and drank sparingly. Margaret was sure he had a bad stomach and was already looking sorrowfully ahead to the aspirin and Alka-

Seltzer the next morning. The third man was fat, and his scalp bloomed through his hair and he had a piped vest, which made him look like a businessman in the movies, except that when he wasn't singing his face looked intelligent and very cold. The other two women were standard suburban mothers nearing fifty, forlornly carrying on their battle against age, loneliness, and death with powder, rouge, rejuvenating cream, accustomed now to neglect from their husbands and children, full of mild, half-formed regrets for their lives as they drove behind their middle-aged chauffeurs down to New York in the late mornings for lunch and shopping.

"What does that sign say?" Mr. Clay said loudly, over the noise of the singing. He was peering out the window at the large sign on the lawn with the name of the inn on it.

" 'Free conscience, void of offence, 1840,' " Margaret said.

"That's a queer thing to have on a sign advertising a restaurant," Mr. Clay said.

Trent had come to their table with the drinks. "It came with the place," he apologized. "I didn't have the heart to take it down."

"There's nothing wrong with it," Mr. Clay said quickly, hoping he hadn't hurt Trent's feelings. "It's an admirable sentiment." He tasted the drink. "Wonderful!" he said loudly, over the singing, to make Trent feel better. "Absolutely wonderful!"

Trent smiled and went back to the bar, where his six customers were calling for more drinks.

Mr. Clay settled back in his chair, savoring his drink, expecting a good dinner. "Now, tell me," he said, "why you dragged me up here."

Margaret played reflectively with her glass. "I wanted to ask your advice," she said.

Mr. Clay sat forward and stared intently at his daughter. Usually when girls that age asked advice in that sober, reflective tone, it was on only one subject. Margaret noticed him leaning forward, staring at her, his handsome gray eyes now full of worry and suspicion.

"What's the matter?" Margaret asked. "What're you looking so scared about?"

"You can tell me everything," Mr. Clay said, wishing she wouldn't.

"Oh!" Margaret said. "Please sit back. The patient isn't dying. All I brought you up here for was to tell you I wanted to quit school. Now, take that look out of your eyes." She laughed, but her laugh was nervous, and over her glass she eyed her father, who ran a great business and paid a huge income tax each year to the government.

"I didn't have any look in my eyes," Mr. Clay said, laughing, deciding instantly that that was the way to handle it—gently, with an easy laugh, pretending that it was all light and cheerful, that he was a good fellow, practically her own age, that he understood everything. "Who's the boy?"

"It isn't any boy."

"Now, Margaret," he said lightly, "your father's been around . . ."

"I know my father's been around," Margaret said. "The head-waiters' delight." Mr. Clay looked hurt, his eyes narrowing, his mouth falling into the straight line Margaret remembered, and she spoke hurriedly. "I don't mind it," she said. "In fact, I like it. It makes me feel I come from durable yet light-footed stock. Every time I see your picture with one of those girls in a mink coat, I feel proud. Honest."

"What I meant to say," Mr. Clay said coldly, "was that you could tell me the truth."

"There isn't any boy."

"To my daughter!" Mrs. Taylor said loudly, her glass held high. "This is an anniversary. A year ago I gave my pure and beautiful daughter away in marriage. Now I'm a grandmother. To my daughter!"

"To the grandmother!" said Oliver, the one who spoke the loudest and oftenest and with the most assurance. "To the poor, broken-down, pure, and beautiful old grandmother!"

All the people at the bar laughed, as though this was a wonderful joke, and Oliver slapped Mrs. Taylor heartily on the back. "Now, Oliver," she said mildly, wriggling her back.

"I just want to quit school," Margaret said, scowling a little at the people making so much noise at the bar. "It bores me."

"It's the best school for women in the country," Mr. Clay said. "And you've done very well. And you've only got two more years to go."

"It bores me."

"I've always thought," Mr. Clay said carefully, "that a good school was the best place for a young and unsettled girl to spend four very important years of her life."

"I'm in abeyance in school," Margaret said. "My whole life's in abeyance. Everything's happening outside and nothing's happening inside. A girls' school is a continual Junior League ball!"

"It seems to me there're a couple of classes to be attended," Mr. Clay said with heavy irony. "Or so I've heard."

"Remote, remote," Margaret said dreamily. "Anglo-Saxon literature. The development of the novel. The nervous system of the worm. You look at the front page of one newspaper, you listen to one conversation in the subway in New York, when you go in on a week-end, you see one play, and your mind begins to itch because you're stuck in that organdie-and-douche-bag nunnery."

"Margaret!" Mr. Clay said, honestly shocked.

"The French novel, Elizabethan poetry, *exclusive* of the drama—remote, remote, the world's racing by. Mr. Trent," Margaret called, "we want two more."

"A good college affords protection." Mr. Clay felt uneasy saying it, but felt he had to say it or something like it, play the father decently and in good form, although he had never played the father with Margaret, had always been friendly and easy with her until the past year, when she had suddenly changed. "It affords protection to a young girl at a time when she's unstable, easily swayed . . ."

"I don't want to be afforded protection," Margaret said. "I want to be easily swayed." She looked out at the sign, standing, lit, on the lawn, " 'Free conscience, void of offence, 1840.' That's the nicest thing about this whole place."

Trent came over with the drinks. Neatly and ceremoniously, he cleared away the old glasses, the wet paper napkins, flicked ashes, put down the fresh glasses, smiling admiringly at Mr. Clay, because his suit, shoes, wrist watch, the complexion of his skin were all handsome, expensive, rigorously correct.

Margaret watched the people at the bar while Trent fussed over the table. The men all had on dark-gray or blue double-breasted suits and starched white collars, as sharp and neat as knives, and ties, small, precise, of heavy silk, fitted into the collars so snugly that they seemed to spring from the throat itself. Cuff links, neat but expensive, gleamed at all their wrists, and their shoes, deeply shining and brought from England, made them look as though they were all equipped with exactly the same feet. Their faces, Margaret thought, were familiar, the faces of her friends' fathers, well barbered, controlled, with not too much fat on them; the lines not deep now but soon to be deep; the eyes, the mouths, assured, arrogant, superior, because the men had never found a place in the last forty years of their lives where they hadn't made themselves at home, felt themselves superior. They were the faces of businessmen ready to assume responsibility, give orders, watch machines run for them, money be counted for them. They had come from the same colleges, married the same girls, listened to the same sermons, were marked similarly, the way bullets fired from the same gun are similarly marked, can be identified when dug out of walls, picture frames, car moldings, victims.

"I'm going to get drunk tonight," Mrs. Taylor was saying. "I'm not going to church tomorrow. I prayed all week and I don't have to go to church tomorrow. I'm going to get drunk."

"Mrs. Chamberlain prayed every morning," one of the suburban mothers, a bright blonde, said. "She went in and prayed in Westminster Abbey while her husband was flying day after day to Germany."

"That's the sort of wife to have," Mr. Taylor said.

"It was the old man's first trip," the fattest man said. "He'd never been up in an airplane before. Sixty-nine years old. That's a hell of a first trip!"

" 'Out of this nettle, danger,' " the blonde said, " 'we pluck this flower, safety,' he said when he came back. It's from Shakespeare. He's a well-educated man."

"All those Englishmen are well educated," Mr. Taylor said. "The ruling class. They know how to run a country. Not like what we have here."

"The contacts you make at college," Mr. Clay said, "are the most important . . ."

"Sh-h-h." Margaret waved impatiently at him. "I'm listening."

"I'm going to get drunk tonight," Mrs. Taylor said. "I prayed for peace so my son wouldn't have to go to war, and I got peace. What do I have to go to church for any more? Let's have another round."

" 'Peace in our time,' " the blonde said. "That's what he said when he got off the plane. That old man with the umbrella."

"Do you want my advice?" Mr. Clay asked.

Margaret looked at him, at the face she remembered as the first thing in her life, deep down at the bottom of memory, the handsome, easy, cheerful face, now troubled, puzzled, in a funny way helpless, loaded tonight with this problem of a twenty-year-old daughter. "Sure," Margaret said softly, feeling suddenly sorry for her father. "I want your advice. That's why I asked you to come. You're dependable," she said, smiling. "After all, you were the one who advised me to cut my hair the first time."

Mr. Clay smiled happily. He sipped his drink, spread his beautiful, well-kept hands lightly on the table, talked gently to his daughter.

She watched the people at the bar as he talked about the friends you made at college, the people you could live with for the rest of your life, the memories you stored up, the important contacts.

A new party had come in, two men and two women, all of them with cold, red faces, as though they had been riding in an open car. One of the men was just like the other men at the bar—neat, double-breasted in blue, with English feet—and the women, though younger, lived on the same streets as the women already at the bar. The second man was a huge, fat man in a light tweed suit with a black slip-on sweater under it, and a white shirt, very white now under the heavy-hanging, deep-red jowls.

"Roar, Lion, Roar," the man in tweeds was singing. "Twenty-seven–fourteen."

"Who won?" asked Mr. Taylor.

"Columbia," the man in tweeds said. "Twenty-seven–fourteen. Hail Columbia! I'm a Columbia man."

"Who'd've thought that a team from New York City would ever beat Yale?" Mr. Taylor said.

"I don't believe it," Oliver said.

"Twenty-seven–fourteen," the man in tweeds said. "Luckman ran over them."

"We're from Yale," Mr. Taylor said. "All of us. Yale, 1912."

"Have a drink on a Columbia man," the man in tweeds said. "Everybody." He ordered the drinks and they sang "Roar, Lion, Roar," the two parties melting happily and naturally together.

Margaret heard her father going on seriously about your needing solid friends to depend on later on, and, by God, the place where you developed them, people of your own kind that you could cleave to through thick and thin. . . . She watched the huge man in tweeds as he drank, sang out "Roar, Lion, Roar," his behind quivering deeply under the expanse of heavy cloth.

"Can you sing 'Stand Columbia'?" Mrs. Taylor asked. "That's a Columbia song. You ought to be able to sing it."

"I would," said the fat man, "only my throat's too hoarse for a song like that."

They sang "Heigh-ho, Heigh-ho, It's Off to Work We Go," their voices hearty, full of whisky and pleasure and loud good-fellowship.

"I would like to hear 'Stand, Columbia,' " Mrs. Taylor said.

"Did you hear this one?" the fat man said. And he sang, "Heigh-ho, heigh-ho, I joined the C.I.O., I pay my dues to a bunch of Jews, heigh-ho, heigh-ho!"

Oliver, who had been slapping Mrs. Taylor on the back, slapped the fat man on the back in appreciation, and all the others laughed and beat on the bar approvingly, and Trent, who was standing behind the bar, looked out nervously across the room, scanning it for a Jewish face. Seeing none, he permitted himself to smile.

"Once again," the fat man said, beaming, standing up to lead with large gestures of his arms, "before we leave for Poughkeepsie."

All the voices, middle-aged, hoarse, joined happily in the chorus, the song more spontaneous, full of more joy and celebration and real pleasure, than any before that evening. "Heigh-ho," they sang joyously, "heigh-ho, we've joined the C.I.O., We've paid our dues to a bunch of Jews, heigh-ho, heigh-ho!"

They laughed and clapped each other on the back, the room echoing and re-echoing as they banged the bar and roared.

"Oh, I love it!" Mrs. Taylor gasped.

Margaret turned her back on them and looked at her father. He was laughing, too.

Margaret looked carefully at him, as though he were a man whom she had just met. Her father's face was not fat, Margaret noticed, but almost so. His gray suit was double-breasted and his collar was sharp, starched white. The heavy silk necktie flowed like a spring from his lined though ruddy throat, and his shoes looked as though they had been brought from England for carefully custom-built feet. She looked at his face, like the faces of the fathers of her friends, the men who had been graduated from the good colleges around 1910 and had gone on to stand at the head of businesses, committees, charity organizations, lodges, lobbies, political parties, who got brick red when they thought of the income tax, who said, "That lunatic in the White House." Her father was sitting across the table with that face, laughing.

"What're you laughing at?" Margaret asked. "What the hell are you laughing at?"

Mr. Clay stopped laughing, but a look of surprise seemed to hang over as a kind of transition expression on his face. Margaret stood up as the man in tweeds and his friends left to go to Poughkeepsie.

"Where're you going?" Mr. Clay asked.

"I don't feel like eating here," Margaret said, putting on her coat.

Mr. Clay left some bills for the check, and put his coat on. "I thought you wanted me to tell you what I thought," he said. "I thought you wanted me to advise . . ."

Margaret said nothing as they started out.

169

"I don't believe he was a Columbia man at all," Mrs. Taylor was saying as Margaret passed her. "He couldn't sing 'Stand, Columbia.'"

"That's right," said Mr. Taylor. "Too tweedy, too much sweater."

"To Neville Chamberlain!" Mrs. Taylor said, her thin, white fingers holding her cocktail glass high. "I'm going to get drunk tonight. I don't have to go to church tomorrow."

Margaret closed the door behind her and walked with her father toward their car, past the sign on the lawn, lit and shaking in the wind, with the dry leaves blowing against it.

This was in the autumn of 1938, the year Columbia beat Yale 27–14 in the first game of the season.

# Weep in Years to Come

They came out of the movie house and started slowly eastward in the direction of Fifth Avenue. "Hitler!" a newsboy called. "Hitler!"

"That Fletcher," Dora said, "the one that played her father. Remember him?"

"Uh huh," Paul said, holding her hand as they walked slowly up the dark street.

"He's got stones in his kidney."

"That's the way he acts," Paul said. "Now I know how to describe the way that man acts—he acts like a man who has stones in his kidney."

Dora laughed. "I X-rayed him last winter. He's one of Dr. Thayer's best patients. He's always got something wrong with him. He's going to try to pass the stones out of his kidney this summer."

"Good luck, Fletcher, old man," Paul said.

"I used to massage his shoulder. He had neuritis. He makes fifteen hundred dollars a week."

"No wonder he has neuritis."

"He asked me to come to his house for dinner." Dora pulled her hand out of Paul's and slipped it up to his elbow and held on, hard. "He likes me."

"I bet he does."

"What about you?"

"What about me what?" Paul asked.

"Do you like me?"

They stopped at Rockefeller Plaza and leaned over the marble wall and looked down at the fountain and the statue and the people sitting out at the tables, drinking, and the waiters standing around, listening to the sound of the fountain.

"I can't stand you," Paul said. He kissed her hair.

"That's what I thought," Dora said. They both laughed.

They looked down at the Plaza, at the thin trees with the light-green leaves rustling in the wind that came down between the buildings. There were pansies, yellow and tight, along the borders of the small pools with the bronze sea statues, and hydrangeas, and little full trees, all shaking in the wind and the diffuse, clear light of the flood lamps above. Couples strolled slowly down from Fifth Avenue, talking amiably in low, calm, week-end voices, appreciating the Rockefeller frivolity and extravagance which had carved a place for hydrangeas and water and saplings and spring and sea-gods riding bronze dolphins out of these austere buildings, out of the bleak side of Business.

Paul and Dora walked up the promenade, looking in the windows. They stopped at a window filled with men's sports clothes—gabardine slacks and bright-colored shirts with short sleeves and brilliant handkerchiefs to tie around the throat.

"I have visions," Paul said, "of sitting in my garden, with two Great Danes, dressed like that, like a Hollywood actor in the country."

"Have you got a garden?" Dora asked.

"No."

"Those're nice pants," Dora said.

They went on to the next window. "On the other hand," Paul said, "there are days when I want to look like that. A derby hat and a stiff blue shirt with a pleated bosom and a little starched white collar and a five-dollar neat little necktie and a Burberry overcoat. Leave the office at five o'clock every day to go to a cocktail party."

"You go to a cocktail party almost every afternoon anyway," Dora said. "Without a derby hat."

"A different kind of cocktail party," Paul said. He started her across Fifth Avenue. "The kind attended by men with starched blue pleated bosoms. Some day."

"Oh, Lord," Dora said as they ran to escape a bus, "look at those dresses."

They stood in front of Saks.

"Fifth Avenue," Paul said. "Street of dreams."

"It's nice to know things like that exist," Dora murmured, looking into the stage-lit window at the yellow dress and the sign that said "Tropical Nights in Manhattan" and the little carved-stone fish that for some reason was in the same window. "Even if you can't have them."

"Uptown?" Paul asked. "Or to my house?"

"I feel like walking." Dora looked up at Paul and grinned.

172

"For the moment." She squeezed his arm. "Only for the moment. Uptown."

They started uptown.

"I love those models," Paul said. "Each and every one of them. They're superior, yet warm; inviting, yet polite. Their breasts are always tipped at the correct angle for the season."

"Sure," Dora said, "papier-mâché. It's easy with papier-mâché. Look. Aluminum suitcases. Travel by air."

"They look like my mother's kitchen pots."

"Wouldn't you like to own a few of them?"

"Yes." Paul peered at them. "Fly away. Buy luggage and depart. Leave for the ends of the earth."

"They got a little case just for books. A whole separate little traveling bookcase."

"That's just what I need," Paul said, "for my trips on the Fifth Avenue bus every morning."

They passed St. Patrick's, dark and huge, with the moon sailing over it.

"Do you think God walks up Fifth Avenue?" Paul asked.

"Sure," said Dora. "Why not?"

"We are princes of the earth," Paul said. "All over the world men slave to bring riches to these few blocks for us to look at and say 'Yes, very nice' or 'Take it away, it stinks.' I feel very important when I walk up Fifth Avenue."

They stopped at the window of the Hamburg-American Line. Little dolls in native costumes danced endlessly around a pole while other dolls in native costume looked on. All the dolls had wide smiles on their faces. "Harvest Festival in Buckeburg, Germany," a small sign said.

A private policeman turned the corner and stood and watched them. They moved to the next window.

" 'A suggestion to passengers to promote carefree travel,' " Paul read off a booklet. "Also, Hapag-Lloyd announces a twenty-per-cent reduction for all educators on sabbatical leave. They are 'Masters in the Art of Travel,' they say."

"I used to want to go to see Germany," Dora said. "I know a lot of Germans and they're nice."

"I'll be there soon," Paul said as they passed the private policeman.

"You're going to visit it?"

"Uh huh. At the expense of the government. In a well-tailored khaki uniform. I'm going to see glamorous Europe, seat of culture, at last. From a bombing plane. To our left we have the Stork Club,

173

seat of culture for East Fifty-third Street. Look at the pretty girls. A lot of them have breasts at the correct angle, too. See how nature mimics art. New York is a wonderful city.''

Dora didn't say anything. She hung on to him tightly as they went down the street. They turned at the corner and walked down Madison Avenue. After a while they stopped at a shop that had phonographs and radios in the window. "That's what I want." Paul pointed at a machine. "A Capehart. It plays two symphonies at a time. You just lie on your back and out come Brahms and Beethoven and Prokofieff. That's the way life should be. Lie on your back and be surrounded by great music, automatically.''

Dora looked at the phonograph, all mahogany and doors and machinery. "Do you really think there's going to be a war?" she said.

"Sure. They're warming up the pitchers now. They're waiting to see if the other side has right-handed or left-handed batters before they nominate their starting pitchers.''

They continued walking uptown.

"But it's in Europe," Dora said. "Do you think we'll get into it?''

"Sure. Read the papers." He glanced at the window they were passing. "Look at those nice tables. Informal luncheons on your terrace. Metal and glass for outdoor feeding, That would be nice, eating out on a terrace off those wonderful colored plates, rich food with green salads. With a view of mountains and a lake, and inside, the phonograph.''

"That sounds good," Dora said quietly.

"I could get an extra speaker," Paul said, "and wire it out to the terrace, so we could listen as we ate. I like Mozart with dinner." He laughed and drew her to a bookstore window.

"I always get sad," Dora said, "when I look in a bookshop window and see all the books I'm never going to have time to read.''

Paul kissed her. "What did you think the first time you saw me?" he asked.

"What did *you* think?''

"I thought, 'I must get that girl!' ''

Dora laughed, close to him.

"What did you think?" Paul asked.

"I thought"—she giggled—"I thought, 'I must get that man!' ''

"Isn't New York marvelous?" Paul said. "Where did you say you come from?''

"Seattle," Dora said. "Seattle, Washington."

"Here we are on Madison Avenue, holding hands, shopping for the future. . . ."

"Even if there was a war," Dora said after a while, "why would you have to get mixed up in it? Why would the United States have to get mixed up in it?"

"They got into the last one, didn't they?" Paul said. "They'll get into this one."

"They were gypped the last time," Dora said. "The guys who were killed were gypped."

"That's right," said Paul. "They were killed for six-per-cent interest on bonds, for oil wells, for spheres of influence. I wish I had a sphere of influence."

"Still," said Dora, "you'd enlist this time?"

"Yop. The first day. I'd walk right up to the recruiting office and say, 'Paul Triplett, twenty-six years old, hard as nails, good eyes, good teeth, good feet; give me a gun. Put me in a plane, so I can do a lot of damage."

They walked a whole block in silence.

"Don't you think you'd be gypped this time, too?" Dora said. "Don't you think they'd have you fighting for bonds and oil wells all over again?"

"Uh huh."

"And even so, you'd sign up?"

"The first day."

Dora pulled her hand away from him. "Do you *like* the idea of killing people?"

"I hate the idea," Paul said slowly. "I don't want to hurt anybody. I think the idea of war is ridiculous. I want to live in a world in which everybody sits on a terrace and eats off a metal-and-glass table off colored plates and the phonograph inside turns Mozart over automatically and the music is piped out to an extra loud-speaker on the terrace. Only Hitler isn't interested in that kind of world. He's interested in another kind of world. I couldn't stand to live in his kind of world, German or homemade."

"You wouldn't kill Hitler," Dora said. "You'd just kill young boys like yourself."

"That's right."

"Do you like that?"

"I'm really not interested in killing Hitler, either," Paul said. "I want to kill the idea he represents for so many people. In years to come I'll cry over the young boys I've killed and maybe if they kill me, they'll cry over me."

175

"They're probably just like you." They were walking fast now.

"Sure," Paul said. "I'm sure they'd love to go to bed with you tonight. I bet they'd love to walk along the fountains with the bronze statues in Rockefeller Plaza, holding hands with you on a spring Saturday evening and looking at the sports clothes in the windows. I bet a lot of them like Mozart, too, but still I'll kill them. Gladly."

"Gladly?"

"Yes, gladly." Paul wiped his eyes with his hands, suddenly tired. "Gladly today. I'll weep for them in years to come. Today they're guns aimed at me and the world I want. Their bodies protect an idea I have to kill to live. Hey!" He stretched out his hands and caught hers. "What's the sense talking about things like this tonight?"

"But it's all a big fraud," Dora cried. "You're being used and you know it."

"That's right," Paul said. "It's all a big fraud, the whole business. Even so, I got to fight. I'll be gypped, but by a little bit I'll do something for my side, for Mozart on a terrace at dinner. What the hell, it's not even heroism. I'll be dragged in, whatever I say."

"That's too bad," Dora said softly, walking by herself. "It's too bad."

"Sure," Paul said. "Some day maybe it'll be better. Maybe some day the world'll be run for people who like Mozart. Not today."

They stopped. They were in front of a little art store. There was a reproduction of the Renoir painting of a boating party on the river. There was the woman kissing the Pekinese, and the man in his underwear with a straw hat and his red beard, solid as earth, and the wit with his cocked derby hat whispering to the woman with her hands to her ears, and there was the great still life in the foreground, of wine and bottles and glasses and grapes and food.

"I saw it in Washington," Paul said. "They had it in Washington. You can't tell why it's a great picture from the print. There's an air of pink immortality hanging over it. They got it in New York now and I go look at it three times a week. It's settled, happy, solid. It's a picture of a summertime that vanished a long time ago." Paul kissed her hand. "It's getting late, darling, the hours're dwindling. Let's go home."

They got into a cab and went downtown to his apartment.

# The City Was in Total Darkness

Dutcher stood at the bar, feeling clean after his shower and still thirsty, looking at the girls, glad that he was alone, listening with one ear to the conversation around him. "The British and French," a man in a hound's-tooth-check jacket was saying, "will shuttle back and forth over Germany from Paris to Warsaw. And besides, he has no oil. Everybody knows Hitler has no oil."

" 'Darling,' she says to me," a large blonde woman said loudly to another large blonde woman, " 'darling, I haven't seen you in for*ever*. Where've you been—in the summer theater?' She knows goddamn well I just finished two pictures for Fox!"

"It's a bluff," the man in the hound's-tooth-check said. "He's going to back down, Russia or no Russia. He has no oil. Where are you today without oil?"

"Mr. Dutcher." The barman brought over a phone and plugged it in. "For you."

It was Machamer on the phone. "What're you doing tonight, Ralph?" Machamer asked, his voice, as always, grating and noisy.

"I'm drinking tonight," Dutcher said. "I'm drinking and waiting for something good to happen to me."

"We're going to Mexico," Machamer said. "Want to come along?"

"Who's we?"

"Dolly and me. Want to come along?"

"What part of Mexico?" Dutcher asked. "What distant part of that verdant land? Vera Cruz, Mexico City . . . ?"

Machamer laughed. "Tia Juana. I got to be back on Tuesday to look for a job, Just overnight. For the races. Want to go?"

"Without oil," the man in the check was saying, "a war is absolutely impractical." Dutcher looked gravely at him, considering whether or not he wanted to go to Mexico. He had avoided people after playing tennis in the afternoon, because he'd wanted to be alone, by himself, with the decks clear for something special and significant to happen to him on this special and significant weekend.

"Have they got bullfights in Tia Juana?" he asked Machamer.

"Maybe," Machamer said. "They have them sometimes. Come on, this is Labor Day, there's nobody in Hollywood."

"I'm tired," Dutcher said. "I've been listening to the radio for seven nights and I played tennis and I'm thirsty."

"You can lie down in the back of the car, with a bottle," Machamer said. Machamer was a young writer and very impressed with Dutcher's two novels and constantly was after him. "I'll drive."

"I never saw a bullfight," Dutcher said. "Did you ever see one there?"

"Oh, nuts!" Machamer said. "Dolly and I'll be over in fifteen minutes to pick you up."

"Tonight," Dutcher said, "I would like to have a startling adventure."

"Oh, nuts," Machamer said. "Fifteen minutes."

Dutcher gravely put the phone back on its pedestal. "I've got to find another bar," he said to the barman. "Whenever people want to find me they call me here. It's bad for the reputation. In two years nobody'll give me a job." The barman grinned. "Another Rum Collins," Dutcher said, looking steadfastly at a slender girl down the bar who had long thick black hair and tremendous full breasts that jutted out like pennants in front of her. The barman looked too. "Doesn't it break your heart?" the barman said.

"California," Dutcher said. "Specialty of the country."

"That cameraman," one of the blonde ladies was saying, "he made me look like William S. Hart's mother. I told him, too, but *loud!*"

In Poland, now, the tanks were roaring over the dusty plains. German boys were climbing into bombers now, Dutcher thought, fiddling with the controls, peering at the instruments, thinking in this one minute when they were waiting and there was nothing to do, "Is this the last time?" and then getting the signal and sweeping off the field toward Warsaw. Cavalry, Dutcher remembered, the Poles had wonderful cavalry. He could just see a wonderful Polish cavalryman sitting heavily on his plodding mount, retreating, sleepless, from the border, stinking from the horse, listening to the bombers overhead, thinking of sleep and home and the English air force, kicking his horse wearily, saying, "Son of a bitch." And the rich and their women, like the rich and their women everywhere, leaving quietly out the back way, while the dawn broke and the light came up and the boy in the bomber could get a good clear view of the cavalryman on the long, open road below.

Dutcher looked at the girl with breasts like pennants. He sat at the bar, making believe he was staring blankly ahead, making believe nothing was happening inside him, feeling lust rise within him as definitely as water rising in a filling glass. General, non-particular lust, he thought, looking at the girl, pretty, with her black hair and long throat and bright print dress and that amazing bosom. I ought to be ashamed, Dutcher thought. The reader of Spinoza, the admirer of John Milton, the advocate of moral and economic reforms, a sufferer from general and indiscriminate lust ten times daily at the sight of a face, a ruffle, at the sound of a woman's laugh.

"We live on two planes," Dutcher said to the bartender. The bartender smiled weakly.

Hollywood, Dutcher thought, Hollywood had a great deal to do with it. It was the product of the neighborhood, and everywhere you went it was pushed in your face like cheese in Wisconsin, and you tried to keep yourself from thinking about *Murder at Midnight* and sex rushed in to fill the vacuum. *Murder at Midnight* was the picture he was writing. It had a long, complicated story about a night-club singer who got drunks to spend money on her but who was genuine, all the way through, as everyone always said in the conferences. She had a small son from whom she bravely tried to conceal the tawdriness of her profession, and she got mixed up in a murder and she fled town in the rain with the son and the cops picked up an innocent man. . . . Dutcher shook his head. He never could get the story straight. Anyway, this was the weekend. And he'd be through in two weeks and have enough money for eight months in New York. Why'm I kidding myself? he thought. I look at them in New York, too.

Hollywood, you could always blame everything on Hollywood. That was the nicest thing about Hollywood.

"Sacred and profane," he told the bartender. "That's the whole explanation."

Machamer came in with Dolly. "On to Mexico," Machamer said.

"Sit down," Dutcher said, "and give me some good arguments. Dolly, you look beautiful." Dolly looked as thin and as plain and nervous as ever, and Dutcher was always very careful, in this city of magnificent women, to be gallant and flattering to her. "Give me Dolly," he said to Machamer, "and I'll go to Mexico."

Dolly laughed. Her laugh was high and very nervous and always made Dutcher a little uncomfortable.

"Poor Dutcher," Dolly said. "Poor lonesome Dutcher."

"Get me a girl," Dutcher said, suddenly, not thinking about it or why he was saying it, "and I'll go with you."

"Now, Dutcher," Machamer protested. "Eight o'clock Saturday night, Labor Day weekend . . ."

"On a high moral plane," Dutcher said. "I just want to have somebody to talk to."

"You have plenty of girls," Machamer said.

"I'm tired of them," Dutcher said. "Tonight I'm tired of them. War, *Murder at Midnight*, the fickleness of the male character, I'm tired of them. Tonight I'm in the mood for a new face." Dutcher waved his hands elaborately, embroidering on the theme, although already half-sorry that he'd said anything about a girl. "A face moody, passionate, with the eyes cynical and despairing, the mouth lost and contemptuous and stormy, the hair tossed and black . . ."

"He wants a character out of Thomas Wolfe," Machamer said.

"A face for the weekend," Dutcher said, his tongue sliding joyfully in his mouth after the Rum Collins, "a face tragic and tortured by the guilt of a slaughtering and slaughtered world . . ."

Dolly jumped off her stool. "I'm going to call Maxine," she said.

"Who's Maxine?" Dutcher asked, warily.

"She's very pretty," Dolly said. "She's an actress at Republic."

"Oh, God," Dutcher said.

"Don't be such a snob," said Dolly. "Give me a nickel."

"What do you expect at eight o'clock Saturday night?" Machamer gave her a nickel. "Hedy Lamarr?"

"She's very pretty," Dolly repeated. "She just got in from New York and she may not be busy . . ." She started toward the phone.

"On a high moral plane!" Dutcher shouted after her. "Remember!"

Dolly strode out of sight toward the telephone booth. Dutcher watched her and then turned to Machamer. "When you read the papers," he said, "and you read about airplanes bombing people and then being shot down, do you ever think about what it's like up there, with the bullets coming at you and the plane bucking and all of a sudden just air below . . . ?"

"All the time," Machamer said soberly.

"During the Spanish War I used to dream about being machine-gunned by airplanes. I'd run and run along alleyways between garages and the planes would always come back and get me from an open side." Dutcher finished his drink. "I wonder what garages had to do with it. The trouble with the human race is it's too brave. You can get people to do anything—fly around and get shot at twenty thousand feet up, walk into hand grenades, fight naval battles. If the human race wasn't so damn courageous, this would be a much better world to live in. That's the sum total of my thinking in two months in Hollywood."

"Einstein is resting easy," Machamer said. "He's still got a good lead."

"I know," said Dutcher. "But he doesn't have to think in this climate."

Dolly slipped in between them. "It's all settled," she said. "Maxine is dying to go. She's heard about you."

"Good or bad?" Dutcher asked.

"She's just heard about you. She says you mustn't get fresh."

Dutcher wrinkled his nose. "Did she say 'fresh'?"

"Yes," Dolly said.

"I don't like Maxine."

"Nuts," Machamer said, and pulled him away from the bar and out to his car.

The big car sped toward Mexico. Dutcher sprawled luxuriously on the back seat with his head in Maxine's lap. Occasionally he moved his head lazily because Maxine was wearing a suit trimmed all the way down the front with red fox and the fur got into his nose and tickled him.

"He was an Italian," Maxine was saying. "He had large estates in Italy and he had a good job in New York, fifteen thousand a year, but he didn't like Mussolini."

"A character," Dutcher said softly. "A beautiful character."

"We were engaged to be married," Maxine said, speaking loudly, talking to Dolly, "but two weeks later he gave up his job. He relaxed; my little Wop relaxed." She laughed a little sadly, stroked Dutcher's head absently. "As soon as I meet a man he relaxes."

Machamer turned on the radio, and a man in London said that Hitler had not as yet answered Chamberlain's ultimatum and an orchestra played "I May Be Wrong, But I Think You're Wonderful."

Dutcher looked thoughtfully up at Maxine's face. It was a round, full face, with a little full mouth that looked as though it had been created in God's mind with a careful brilliant smear of lipstick already on it. "You're very pretty," he said seriously.

Maxine smiled. "I'm not so bad," she patted him in appreciation. "I'm a little fat at the moment. I drank too much wine in New York. Dolly, I heard that Gladys is marrying Eddie Lane. Is that true?"

"In October," Dolly said.

Maxine sighed. "That Gladys. Eddie Lane's old man is good for five hundred thousand a year. She was in my class at high school. Oil. Old man Lane is up to his navel in oil. Eddie Lane chased me for two years like a kid after a fire truck. What a goddamn fool I was to go to New York."

Dutcher laughed, looking up at her. "You have a nice, refreshing outlook on finance."

Maxine laughed with him. "Money is money," she said. "I'll get a little fatter and even Republic won't have me, and then where'll I be?"

"I'll write a play," Machamer said, at the wheel, "and you can act in it in New York. They like them fat in New York."

"I tried that, too," Maxine said grimly. "I thought of another way out. I had my step-father insured . . ."

"Holy God!" Dutcher said. "For how much?"

"Fifty thousand."

"We're in the dough," Dutcher said. "Stop and buy me a Lincoln."

"Hah," said Maxine. "I paid his insurance three years then he went and got married on me. A little Irish biddy he saw waiting on table in San Luis Obispo."

They all laughed. "You're wonderful," Dutcher said. He pulled her down and kissed her. She kissed politely, with reserve, carefully, yet with a hint of vulgar accomplishment.

Unsatisfactory, Dutcher thought, letting his head fall back, yet . . . Reader of Spinoza, admirer of John Milton . . .

"This is Berlin," a voice said on the radio. "The city is in total darkness. The Fuehrer has not replied as yet to the English ultimatum. There is constant troop movement at the Berlin railroad stations and trains are pouring toward the Polish frontier."

A band played "Begin the Beguine," and Maxine talked to Dolly about another friend of theirs who had married a seventy-year-old man with fourteen blocks of real estate in downtown Cleveland.

"The city is in total darkness," Dutcher murmured. He lay back comfortably. This wasn't so bad, racing through the night to a new country, with a new girl, even though it was only Tia Juana and only an ordinarily pretty girl, getting a little fat, and a little hard and not exactly the girl you'd pick to take with you on a visit to your old Professor of Ethics at Amherst. Still it was better than sitting at a bar all alone, thinking, "I'll wait another ten minutes and then go out and buy another paper, see what *they* have to say."

He turned and buried his face in the red fox. There was a heavy smell of perfume, which was pleasant over the old smell of leather and gasoline in the back of the car. "Prince Matchabelli," Dutcher said. "This fox fell into a well of Prince Matchabelli and drowned. A beautiful death. Machamer, did I ever tell you about Cynthia Messmore, who was a classmate of mine at PS 99 and Miss Finch's? She married old Shamus Goonan, from the eleventh assembly district . . ."

"No!" Machamer said, in tones of wonder.

"A brilliant match," Dutcher said. "He was on the WPA three days a week and he was good for seven hundred and sixty dollars a year, as long as he stayed sober. Sewer construction, he was a sewer construction magnate, he was up to his navel in . . ."

"Are you making fun of me?" Maxine's voice was hard, and Dutcher knew he ought to stop, but he couldn't. He sat up.

"I never should've left PS 99," he said sadly. "Sex is the opium of the people. Turn on the radio, Machamer."

Dolly was shaking her head at him, but Dutcher made believe he was looking out the window. Mean, he thought, I've been mean. And I liked it. Tonight I want to be everything . . . mean, angry, noble, gracious, lordly, docile, everything. I want my emotions to be engaged. I can't love her, I can't make her love me, but I can make her angry at me and then win her over, then . . .

"This is Paris," a voice said. "All the lights are out. The Cabinet has been in conference since seven o'clock this evening."

Machamer turned the radio off.

Dutcher felt Maxine eyeing him. He turned and looked pleasantly at her. After all, he thought, regarding her, she *is* a pretty girl, with a fine figure and we *are* going to be together until tomorrow night . . .

"Is that how you're going to the races tomorrow?" Maxine asked. "Without a tie?"

Dutcher felt at his collar. He was wearing a polo shirt, open at the throat. "I guess so," he said. "It's awfully hot."

"I won't go with you," Maxine said, "unless you wear a tie."

"I haven't got a tie."

"I won't go with you," Maxine said firmly.

"We live in a tropical climate," Dutcher said. "We mustn't ever forget that. I'm a Northern man, I sweat like . . ."

"I have an extra tie," Machamer said. "You can wear that."

Dutcher nodded. "If it'll make Maxine happy . . ." He smiled at her.

"I wouldn't be seen in front of all those people with a man who wasn't wearing a tie."

"You're right," Dutcher said, smiling pleasantly at her. "Now that I think of it, you're absolutely right."

Maxine smiled back at him. At least, he thought, I haven't thought of *Murder at Midnight* since the trip began. At least, she's done that.

They stopped in San Diego and drank at a bar among a lot of sailors from the naval base. Dolly took some of the pills she was always taking and for a moment gripped Machamer's arm and leaned over and kissed his neck. It was nearly two o'clock and the bar was closing and the sailors were drunk.

"The United States will not get into any war," a big blond farm boy jutting out of his flimsy blue uniform announced. "I have the guarantee of my congressman."

"Where you from?" Dutcher asked.

"Arkansas."

Dutcher nodded as though this convinced him. The sailor gulped down what was left of his beer.

"Let the Japs come over," he called. "We'll sweep 'em from the seas. I'd like to see the Japs just try and come over. I'd just like to see . . ."

Maxine was smiling at the sailor.

"I'm hungry," Dutcher said, herding Maxine and Dolly toward the door. "I hate discussions of relative naval strength."

"That was heartening," Machamer said, as they walked toward the bright lights of a waffle shop down the street. "An official representative of the United States armed forces says we won't get into a war."

"He was a nice-looking boy," Maxine said, as they entered the waffle shop. "If you took him out of that sailor suit."

The waffle shop was crowded, and they sat at a table that had not been cleared. Maxine and Dolly went to the ladies' room and Machamer and Dutcher were left at the table, looking at each other in the garish waffle-room light, across the dirty dishes and spilled coffee on the table.

"She's all right," Machamer said loudly, grinning at Dutcher.

"Dolly did all right for you, didn't she? She's got a wonderful figure."

"Machamer," Dutcher said, "if I had a cement mixer and I wanted somebody to make a speech while it was going, I would pick you."

Machamer looked around him apologetically. "Isn't it funny, how loud I talk?"

"Everybody in the Square Deal Waffle Shop now knows you think Maxine has a wonderful figure."

The waitress, very pale and harried-looking at two in the morning, rattled the dishes between them as she cleared the table.

"You're having a good time, aren't you?" Machamer asked. "She makes you laugh, doesn't she?"

"She makes me laugh," Dutcher said.

Dolly and Maxine came back. Dutcher watched Maxine walk down the aisle between the tables, her red fox shaking down the front of her suit and all the men in the place watching her. That suit, Dutcher thought, is one-half inch too tight, in all directions. Everything she wears, always, I bet, is one-half inch too tight. Even her nightgowns.

"You know what I'm thinking of?" Dutcher said to Maxine as she sat down.

"What?" Maxine asked, all newly powdered and rouged.

"Your nightgowns."

Maxine frowned. "That's not a nice thing to say."

"Dutcher's a very vulgar man," Machamer said. "You ought to read his books."

"The English," Maxine said, "just declared war on the Germans. The woman in the ladies' room told us."

That's how I found out, Dutcher thought. In the ladies' room in a waffle shop in San Diego, a woman told an actress from Republic, who drank too much wine in New York, that the English declared war on Germany, and that's how I found out.

"This fork is dirty," Maxine said loudly to the waitress, who was putting their waffles down on the table. "You have some nerve giving us dirty forks."

The waitress sighed and put down a clean fork.

"They'll get away with murder," Maxine said, "if you let them."

All through the room, people knifed slabs of butter and poured syrup and ate waffles, Dutcher noted, as he started on his. There was no change, just the usual restaurant noise of voices and plates.

"This waffle stinks," Maxine said. "That's my honest opinion. And they make a specialty of them! San Diego!"

Dutcher put his hand gently on hers to calm her.

"You got the hand of a day-laborer," Maxine said. "What do you do, hammer in nails with them at the studio?"

"It's the disgraceful heritage of my wasted youth," Dutcher said.

Maxine turned his hand over and carefully examined the palm. "You got a heart line that's branched many times," she said.

"Tell me more," said Dutcher.

"You're fickle, jealous, selfish." Maxine leaned over his hand very seriously. "And in the long run, you're not going to be very successful."

"What a catch!" Dolly said.

"Tell me more," said Dutcher.

"You're moody." Maxine ran her finger lightly over his palm. "You're a very moody man."

"They don't come any moodier," said Dutcher.

"Your life line is short."

Dutcher took his hand back gravely. "Thank you very much," he said, his hand still aware of the soft promising feel of Maxine's fingers. "Now I'm all cleared up about myself. I certainly am glad I brought you down to San Diego."

"It's all there in the palm," Maxine said defensively. "I didn't put it there." She drew her collar around her. "Let's get out of this joint." She walked toward the door, with all the men in the room watching her.

"You're not her type," Dolly whispered to Dutcher. "She told me in the ladies' room. She likes you, but you're not her type."

Dutcher shrugged. "Palmists don't like me. It's something I've always noticed."

He caught up with Maxine and held her elbow as they walked toward the car. "Now," he said, "we come to a most delicate point. We—uh . . . We have to go to a hotel—and—I . . ."

"I want my own room," Maxine said firmly.

"I just thought I'd ask." Dutcher shrugged.

"A gentleman doesn't ask," Maxine said.

"What does a gentleman do for girls?" Dutcher asked.

"He doesn't talk about it! It just happens."

"It never occurred to me before," Dutcher said as they got into the car. "But you're absolutely right."

They could only get a two-room suite at the hotel, because it was all filled up, and there were some other people from Hollywood

186

in the lobby and Dutcher tried to appear as though he were in no way connected with Maxine. If only she didn't have that red fox, he thought. And all day tomorrow, at the races, there would be people he knew, and he'd have to try to be eight paces in front of her or at the betting windows or at the bar . . .

Upstairs, Maxine primly put her bag down next to Dolly's in one of the two rooms. Machamer looked at Dutcher.

"We have the west wing," Dutcher said, and walked into the next room.

"Look." Machamer followed him. "This was supposed to be a holiday for Dolly and me. She lives at home and her mother prays to God every night to save her sinful daughter's soul." Dolly came in and looked at them. Then she giggled.

"Go in and talk to Maxine," Machamer shouted to Dutcher.

Dutcher shrugged. "I see my duty," he said.

He went into the next room. Maxine was sitting neatly on the bed, her hands folded, her eyes reflectively on the ceiling. "Maxine, old girl," Dutcher said.

"Don't make fun of me."

"I'm tired," Dutcher said wearily. "There's a war on. I give up. There're two beds inside. I promise not to touch you. For Machamer and Dolly . . ."

"Let Machamer be a gentleman!" Maxine said loudly. "For one night."

Dutcher went back into the other room. "She says let Machamer be a gentleman for one night," he said. He took off one shoe. "I'm going to sleep."

Dolly kissed Machamer. She hung on, her arms wound around his neck and Dutcher made a big business of carefully arranging his shoes neatly in line under a chair. Dolly came over and kissed Dutcher lightly. "You sure make a big hit with the girls," she said, and went in.

Machamer and Dutcher put on their pajamas and turned off the light and Machamer got into bed. Dutcher went to the door of the girls' room. "Latest bulletin," he announced. "Machamer has promised not to lay a hand on me. Good night."

The girls laughed and Machamer roared and Dutcher joined them, the two rooms resounding wildly with laughter, as Dutcher climbed into bed.

Outside, the newsboys, far off along the dark streets of San Diego, cried that England had declared war.

Dutcher lay in his bed and listened to the newsboys' cries, swelling and wailing in the streets, and looked up at the dark

187

ceiling; and the hour and the war, which had been kept off all night by drink and speed and laughter and lust, like lions warded off by a trainer's chair, now closed in on him. The cavalryman in Poland now lay across the dusty Polish road, his mouth open in surprise and death and his dead horse beside him and the boy in the German bomber flew back from Warsaw saying to himself, "One more time. I came back one more time."

"It's for Dolly's sake," Machamer's voice came across the small dark abyss between the beds, grating, but young and sorrowful. "It's nothing to me, but she's crazy to grab every hour. Do you want to go to sleep, Ralph?"

"No."

"She wants to grab everything. Everything. She hates to go to sleep. She always has her hands on me. She's going to die." Dutcher heard Machamer sigh and the bedsprings click gently and the newsboys coming nearer. "She's sick; the doctors can't cure her; she has Bright's disease. She gets numb, she feels as though an eye is falling out, an ear . . . That's why she takes those pills. She doesn't tell anybody except me. Her family doesn't know, and her boss . . ."

Dutcher lay rigid in his bed, looking up at the ceiling.

"I don't love her." Machamer's voice was harsh but small. "I tell her I do, but . . . I like other girls. . . . I tell her I do. She doesn't want to lose an hour."

"Shhh," Dutcher said gently. "Don't talk so loud."

"Even now," Machamer marveled. "Even now my voice would break down a wall. Are you sad, Dutcher?"

"Yes," said Dutcher.

"It came funny, didn't it?" Machamer asked.

"You hardly felt it." Dutcher talked with his eyes closed, his head straight back on the pillow. "You were waiting for it for six years and expecting it, and each time a shot was fired you'd say, 'Here it is,' but it wasn't, and you read the papers every day, and by the time it came you didn't feel it at all. We'll feel it later, we'll feel it later . . ."

"What're you going to do now?"

Dutcher laughed. "Go to sleep."

"Good night," Machamer said.

"Good night."

The bomber was coming down to a landing and the boy banked and looked down to see that the landing gear was out and he, Dutcher, was on his way with a fat citizen in a red fox-trimmed suit to a rat-eaten Mexican racetrack, where the youngest horse running was at least nine years old, where the Hollywood people in their scarves and dark glasses and buckskin shoes, with their agents and beauty-contest winners for the weekend gambled their crazy easy money in the dusty Mexican heat, talking of sex and dollars, saying over and over, "Colossal, terrific, he's hot this year, it lost Metro a million." The war was on, and it was on here, too, among these idle, unbombed, frivolous people. I'd stay here, in Hollywood, Dutcher thought, if I could bear *Murder at Midnight* and all the Murders at Midnight to come. I don't want to write any more books. An honest book is a criticism. Why should I torture myself into criticizing this poor, corrupt, frantic, tortured, agony-stricken world? Later, let the criticism come later. . . .

The newsboys wailed in the streets below.

Here I am, Dutcher thought, in a hotel room far from home, with a dying and unloved girl, cheated of an hour, and a movie writer who wanders like a refugee from studio to studio, week in, week out, beggary plain on his face, looking for a job, and a palm-reader who could have been bought for the night with three compliments and ten minutes of polite charade. Fickle, jealous, selfish, moody, not successful, short of life.

"England, England . . ." The boys' voices, wavering in the night wind, came faintly through the window. I'm ashamed of myself, Dutcher thought. I meet the tragic hour in a mournful and ludicrous costume.

Now is the time, Dutcher thought, for some noble and formidable act. Who will supply me with a noble and formidable act?

"I would like to speak to the continent of Europe," Dutcher said aloud.

"Huh?" Machamer murmured.

"Nothing." Dutcher pulled the covers up to his chin. "You know what I'm going to do?"

"Huh?"

"I'm going to get married. I'm going to have a wife and live on a farm and grow corn and wheat and grapes and watch the snow fall and slaughter pigs and become involved with the seasons. For a little while I want to become involved in an eternal motion."

"Sure," said Machamer. "I just dreamed Mervyn LeRoy was offering me a job. Isn't it too bad, isn't it too, too bad . . ." His voice trailed off.

"Involved with the seasons," Dutcher said, rolling it on his tongue. "Involved with the seasons." He closed his eyes.

Now the bomber stopped and the boy jumped out, feeling the ground solid under his feet and cold in the early morning. The boy grinned and the sweat of relief ran down under his arms and he said, "I made it, I made it again," as he went off across the field to report to his commanding officer.

# Night, Birth and Opinion

"Tents!" Lubbock was saying, gloomily swishing his beer around in his glass, his voice echoing hoarsely in the empty shadows of Cody's bar, dark and almost deserted now, deep in the heel of the winter night. "Yuh join the army, yuh sit in a tent and freeze yer tail all winter. I'm a civilized man, I'm used to living in steam-heated apartments."

He looked around him challengingly. He was a big man, with huge longshoreman's hands and a long neat scar down one side of his face. The other two men at the bar looked carefully into their beer.

"National defense," the bartender said. The bartender was a pale little man in a vest and apron, with pale, hairy arms and a long, nervous nose. "Everybody has to make certain sacrifices."

"The trouble with this country," Lubbock said loudly, "is there are too goddamn many patriots walking the streets."

"Don't say anything against patriotism," said the man nearest Lubbock. "Not in my presence."

Lubbock looked consideringly at him. "What's *your* name?" he asked.

"Dominic di Calco," the man said clearly, showing that he was not to be bullied. "I don't see anything wrong with being a patriot."

"He doesn't see anything wrong with being a patriot," Lubbock said. "An Italian patriot."

"They need you," said Sweeney, the man on the other side of Lubbock. "They need you bad—in Greece."

The others laughed. Sweeney looked around him proudly, his little creased red face beery and complacent.

"I'm an American citizen," Di Calco shouted. "After you boys get through laughing."

"You know what I'd like to see?" Sweeney waved his arms, laughing. "I'd like to see the Italian army try to invade Red Hook."

"I'm not in favor of Mussolini," Di Calco shouted. "But keep yer trap shut about the Italian army!"

"Three Irishmen," Sweeney said. "It would take three Irishmen about a half hour. The Italians're wonderful when they fight other Italians."

"Would you like to step outside, whatever yer name is?" Di Calco asked quietly.

"Boys!" The bartender spread his hands pacifically. "Remember, we're in America."

"Remember," Di Calco said, "I offered you satisfaction, whatever yer name is."

"My name is Sweeney!" Sweeney shouted. "I got two cousins in the Royal Air Force!"

"That's a hot one," Lubbock said. "A man by the name of Sweeney with two cousins in the English army. Yuh can just about imagine"—Lubbock spoke reasonably to the bartender—"what type of Irishman yuh could get to fight in the English army."

"What do you want?" the bartender asked. "You want to disagree with every patron of this saloon?"

"That must be some family, the Sweeneys." Lubbock went over and clapped Sweeney on the back.

"They're fightin' for you and me," Sweeney said coldly. "They're fightin' to preserve our way of life."

"I agree," said Di Calco.

"Yeah," said the bartender.

Lubbock turned on the bartender. "What's your name?"

"Cody," said the bartender. "William Cody."

Lubbock glared at him. "You kidding me?"

"I swear to God," said the bartender.

"They got a statue in Wyoming. Buffalo Bill. Any relation?" Lubbock asked.

"It's a pure coincidence," the bartender said.

"Beer, Buffalo Bill," Lubbock said. He watched the bartender draw the beer and place it before him. "From the very hand," Lubbock marveled. "A man with a statue in Wyoming. No wonder you're so patriotic. If I had a statue in Wyoming, I'd be patriotic too."

"Pure coincidence," protested the bartender.

Lubbock drank half his glass of beer, leaned back, spoke quietly and reflectively. "I just love to think of two Sweeneys in England protecting my way of life. I just love it. I feel safer already." He smacked the bar savagely. "Tents! We'll be sitting in tents in the middle of winter!"

"What do you want?" Di Calco said. "You want Hitler to come over here and clean up?"

"I hate him; I hate the bastard," Lubbock said. "I'm a Dutchman myself, but I hate the Germans."

"Give the Dutchman a beer," Sweeney said. "On me."

"I hate the Germans," Lubbock went on, "and I hate the English and I hate the French and I hate the Americans . . ."

"Who do you like?" the bartender asked.

"The Italians. You can't get them to fight. They're civilized human beings. A man comes up to them with a gun, they run like antelopes. I admire that."

Di Calco tapped warningly on the bar. "I'm not going to stand here and have the Italian army insulted."

Lubbock ignored him. "The whole world should be full of Italians. That's my program. My name is Lubbock, boys. I come from a long line of Dutchmen, but I hate them all. If the British're defending my way of life, they can stop right now. My way of life stinks."

"Boys," the bartender said. "Talk about something else, boys."

"The truth is," Sweeney said, "I wouldn't mind if there was a war. I make eleven dollars a week. Any change would be an improvement."

"This is the war of the Hotel Pee-yeah," Lubbock said.

"What do you mean by that?" Di Calco looked at him suspiciously, sensing a new insult to the Italian army.

"On Fifth Avenue and Sixtieth Street. They tea-dance." Lubbock scowled. "They tea-dance for the Empiuh."

"What's objectionable about *that?*" the bartender asked.

"Yuh ever see the people that go into the Hotel Pee-yeah?" Lubbock leaned over the bar and scowled at the bartender. "The little fat rabbits in the mink coats?"

"The best people," the bartender said defiantly.

"Yeah," Lubbock smiled mirthlessly. "If they're for anything, it must be wrong."

"I'm speaking carefully," Di Calco said in measured tones. "I don't want to be misconstrued, but to a neutral ear you sound like a Communist."

Lubbock laughed, drained his beer. "I hate the Communists," he said. "They are busy slitting their own throats seven days a week. Another beer, Buffalo Bill."

"I wish you wouldn't call me Buffalo Bill." The bartender filled Lubbock's glass. "You start something like that, you can wind up making life intolerable." He flipped the head off the glass and pushed it in front of Lubbock.

"A statue in Wyoming . . . ." Lubbock shook his head wonderingly. "Today they tea-dance for the Empiuh, tomorrow we get shot for the Empiuh."

"It don't necessarily follow." Sweeney moved closer, earnestly.

"Mr. Sweeney, of the flying Sweeneys." Lubbock patted him gently on the wrist. "The reader of the *New York Times*. I'll put a lily on yer grave in the Balkans."

"It may be necessary," Di Calco said. "It may be necessary to supply soldiers; it may be necessary for Sweeney to get shot."

"Don't make it so personal," Sweeney said angrily.

"Before we get through, Mr. Sweeney," Lubbock put his arm confidentially around him, "this war is going to be very personal to you and me. It will not be very personal to the rabbits from the Hotel Pee-yeah."

"Why can't you leave the Hotel Pierre out of this discussion?" the bartender complained.

"The snow will fall," Lubbock shouted, "and we'll be sitting in tents!" He turned on Di Calco. "The Italian patriot. I'd like to ask yuh a question."

"Always remember," Di Calco said coldly, "that I'm an American citizen."

"How will you feel, George Washington, sitting behind a machine gun with Wops running at you?"

"I'll do my duty," Di Calco said doggedly. "And don't use the term 'Wop.' "

"What do you mean running *at* him?" Sweeney roared. "The Italian army don't run at anything but the rear."

"Remember," Di Calco shouted at Sweeney, "I have a standing invitation to meet you outside."

"Boys," the bartender cried. "Talk about other matters. Please . . ."

"One war after another," Lubbock marveled. "One after another, and they get poor sons of bitches like you into tents in the wintertime, and yuh never catch on."

"I'm overlooking the language." Sweeney took a step back and spoke dispassionately, like a debater. "But I'd like to hear your solution. Since you're so clear on the subject."

"I don't want to overlook the language," Di Calco said hotly.

"Let him talk." Sweeney waved his hand majestically. "Let's hear everybody's point of view. Let the Dutchman talk."

"Well . . ." Lubbock started.

"Don't be insulting," the bartender said. "It's late and I'm ready to close up the bar anyway, so don't insult the patrons."

Lubbock rinsed his mouth with beer, let it slide slowly down his throat. "Don't yuh ever clean the pipes?" he asked the bartender. "Yuh know, that's the most important thing about beer—the pipes."

"He's got a comment on everything!" Di Calco said angrily. "This country's full of them!"

"They are dividing up the world," Lubbock said. "I got eighty-five cents to my name. No matter which way they finish dividing, I'll be lucky to still have eighty-five cents when it's all over."

"That's not the way to approach the problem," said Sweeney. "Your eighty-five cents."

"Will I get Greece?" Lubbock pointed his huge finger threateningly at Sweeney. "Will Di Calco get China?"

"Who wants China?" Di Calco asked triumphantly.

"We get one thing," Lubbock said soberly. "You and me and Sweeney and Buffalo Bill . . ."

"Please," said the bartender.

"We get trouble. The workingman gets trouble." Lubbock sighed and looked sadly up at the ceiling, and the other men silently drank their beer. "Military strategists agree," Lubbock said, his tongue going proudly over the phrase, "that it takes four men to attack a position defended by one man."

"What's that got to do with it?" Sweeney demanded.

"This war is going to be fought in Europe, in Africa, in Asia," Lubbock chanted. "It is not going to be fought in William Cody's Bar."

"Sorry I can't oblige you," the bartender said sarcastically.

"I've studied the situation," Lubbock said, "and I've decided that there's going to be four times as many Americans killed as anybody else. It stands to reason. They're not going to attack us here, are they? We're going to take the offensive. Four to one!" He banged the bar with savage certainty. "Us four poor dumb yokels'll get it just to put one lousy Dutchman out of the way. Military strategy guarantees!"

"Don't yell so loud," the bartender said nervously. "The people upstairs don't like me."

"The worst thing is," Lubbock shouted, glaring wildly around him, "the worst thing is I look around and I see the world full of poor dumb stupid bastards like Sweeney and Di Calco and William Cody!"

"The language," Di Calco snarled. "Watch the language."

"Hitler has to be beaten!" Sweeney yelled. "That's a fundamental fact."

"Hitler has to be beaten!" Lubbock's voice sank to a significant, harsh whisper. "Why does Hitler have to be beaten? Because poor ignorant bastards like you put him there in the first place and left him there in the second place and went out to shoot him down in the third place and in the meantime just drank yer beer and argued in bars!"

"Don't accuse me," said Sweeney. "I didn't put Hitler any place."

"Sweeneys all over the world!" Lubbock shouted. "And now I got to get shot for it. I got to sit in tents in the wintertime!" Suddenly he grabbed Sweeney by the collar with one hand. "Say . . ." Sweeney gasped. Lubbock's other hand shot out, grasped Di Calco by his collar. Lubbock drew the two men close to his face and stared with terrible loathing at them. "I would like to mash yer stupid thick heads," he whispered.

"Now, lissen," Di Calco gasped.

"Boys," said the bartender, reaching for the sawed-off baseball bat he kept under the counter.

"If I get shot it's your fault!" Lubbock shook the two men fiercely. "I oughta kill yuh. I feel like killin' every dumb slob walkin' the streets . . ."

Di Calco reached back for a beer bottle and Sweeney grabbed the big hand at his throat and the bartender lifted the sawed-off baseball bat. The door swung open and a girl stepped through it and looked blankly at them.

"Go right ahead," she said, the expression on her face not surprised or worried or amused. "Don't let me interrupt."

"Boys . . ." the bartender said and put the baseball bat away. Lubbock gave Sweeney and Di Calco a last little push and released them and turned back to his beer.

"People like you," Sweeney murmured, outraged, "people like you they ought to commit to asylums."

Di Calco straightened his tie and tried to smile gallantly through his rage at the girl, who was still standing by the open door, hatless, her dirty blonde hair falling straight down to her shoulders. She was a thin girl, with the bones showing plainly in her face, and her hands skinny and rough coming out of the sleeves of the light old gray coat she was wearing. Her face was very tired, as though she had been working too long, too many nights.

"Would you like to close the door, Miss?" the bartender asked. "It's getting awfully cold."

The girl wearily closed the door and stood against it for a moment, wearily surveying the four men.

"I need some help," she said.

"Now, Miss . . ." the bartender started.

"Oh, shut up!" she snapped at him. Her voice was flat and worn. "I'm not bumming anything. My sister's just had a kid and she's laying in a stinking little hospital and she was bleeding all day and they gave her two transfusions and that's all they got and they just told me maybe she's dyin'. I been walkin' past this saloon for the last half hour watchin' you four guys talkin', gettin' up nerve to come in. She needs blood. Any you guys got some blood you don't need?" The girl smiled a little.

The men carefully avoided looking at each other.

"We're busted," the girl said, her tone as flat as ever. "The kid came out seven months and her husband's a sailor; he's on his way to Portugal and there's nobody in this whole goddamned, freezin' town I can turn to." She shrugged. "My blood's the wrong type." She took a step nearer the bar. "She's only nineteen years old, my sister. She had to go marry a sailor . . ." Lubbock turned and looked at her.

"All right," Lubbock said. "I'll go with yuh."

"Me, too," said Di Calco.

Sweeney opened his mouth, closed it, opened it again. "I hate hospitals," he said. "But I'll come along."

Lubbock turned and looked slowly at the bartender.

"It's late anyway," the bartender said, nervously drying the bar with a towel. "I might as well come along, just in case. . . . My type blood might . . . Yes." He nodded vigorously, and started taking off his apron.

Lubbock reached over the bar and brought up a bottle of rye and a glass and silently poured it and pushed it in front of the girl. The girl took it without smiling and drained it in one gulp.

They all sat in the dreary hospital clinic room with the old dead light of the hospital on them and all the weary sorrowful smells of the hospital swelling around them. They sat without talking, waiting for the interne to come and tell them which one of them had the right type of blood for the transfusion. Lubbock sat with his hands between his knees, occasionally glancing sharply at Sweeney and Di Calco and Cody, all of them nervously squirming on their benches. Only the girl walked slowly back and forth down the middle of the room, smoking a cigarette, the smoke curling slowly over her lank, blonde hair.

The door opened and the interne came in and touched Lubbock on the arm. "You're elected," he said.

Lubbock took a deep breath and stood up. He looked around him, at Di Calco, at Sweeney, at Cody, triumphantly, smiled at the girl, and followed the interne out of the room.

When he was through, when the blood had poured out of his veins, slowly and delicately, into the veins of the pale, quiet girl on the table next to him, Lubbock got up and bent over her and whispered, "You're going to be all right," and she smiled weakly at him.

Then he put on his coat and went back into the clinic room. The others were still there. They stood there, scowling at him in the blue hospital light. He smiled widely at them.

"Everything all right?" Di Calco asked solemnly.

"Everything's fine," Lubbock said cheerfully. "My blood is singing in her system like whisky."

Di Calco looked at Sweeney, Sweeney at Cody, each with doubt and hesitancy in his eye.

"Say, Dutchman," Sweeney said loudly, "we'll buy you a drink. What d'yuh say?"

They waited, tense, almost ready for attack.

Lubbock looked consideringly at them. Cody put up the collar of his coat.

"Sure," Lubbock said, putting his arm around the girl. "It'll be an honor."

They walked out through the hospital doors together.

# Preach on the Dusty Roads

Nelson Weaver sat at his desk and wrote "Labor . . . Bridgeport plant . . . $1,435,639.77." Then he put his sharply pointed hard pencil down among the nine other sharply pointed hard pencils arrayed in severe line on the right side of the shining desk, below the silver-framed photograph of his dead wife.

He looked at the leather clock on the back edge of his desk. 10:35. Robert wouldn't be along for ten minutes yet.

Nelson Weaver picked up his pencil and looked at the long sheets of paper, closely covered with typewritten figures, to his right. "Depreciation . . . $3,100,456.25," he wrote.

The tax sheets for Marshall and Co., Valves and Turbines, were nearly done. He had sat at this desk for thirty-five days, working slowly and carefully, from time to time deliberately putting down a number on the page, like Cézanne with his six strokes a day on a water color, until the huge elaborate structure of Marshall and Co.'s finances, which reached from bank to bank and country to country, from Wilmington, Delaware, where it was incorporated, to Chungking, China, where it sold electrical equipment to Chiang Kai-shek; until all this sprawling, complex history of money paid and money gained and credit offered and rejected and profit and loss, palpable and impalpable, was laid bare and comprehensible on five short pages of his clean accountant's figures.

Nelson looked at the leather clock. 10:40. The train was leaving at 11:15. Robert had better hurry.

Nelson looked at the *$3,100,456.25* he had written. For the thousandth time he admired the delicate, tilted, bookkeeper's 2 he had early in his career learned to make. Somehow that 2 was to him a badge of his profession, a sign of his talents, an advertisement of the difficult rare world of figures in which he moved skillfully and at ease, turning sweat and clamor, heat and smoke, bonanza and disaster, into clear, rigid, immutable tables.

10:43. Where was Robert? Nelson got up and went to the window and looked out. He looked down the steel and granite fifty stories to the street. He laughed a little to himself when he realized he was trying to pick his son out of the hurry and confusion of Forty-ninth Street, five hundred feet below.

He went back to his desk and sat down and picked up the sheet of paper on which he had been working. Tax sheets represented a formal and intricate game in which the players solemnly and conventionally juggled abstractions, like Spinoza proving God, to bring about very real and tangible results, like the great man who, in 1932, proved that J. P. Morgan had no taxable income. Once, in 1936, Nelson, in a rare burst of capriciousness, had made up two tax sheets. One, that Marshall and Co. had actually submitted to the government. And the other, with a change here and there to conform more to the actual realities of iron and sweat rather than the formal accountant's symbolism of numbers and deductible percentages. There had been a difference of $700,962.12. Nelson had carried the second sheet around with him for his private amusement for a week and then burned it, wisely.

This year, with the blossoming expansion of Marshall and Co. for war orders and the jump in the surplus profits tax, the difference between the real and the formal would be immense, over a million dollars, Nelson figured. Marshall and Co. paid him $40,000 a year. He was quite a bargain, he told himself grimly.

10:47. No Robert yet. Nelson put down the paper because the figures were beginning to jump before his eyes. More and more frequently he found that happening to him. Well, along with the waistline that grew an inch a year and the tendency to wake at five in the morning and his lack of shock at overhearing people calling him a middle-aged gentleman, that had to be expected of a man who had led a quiet, rather unhealthy life at a desk and was now over fifty. . . .

The door opened and Robert came in in his new lieutenant's uniform, with the rawhide suitcase Nelson had given him in his hand.

"On our way, Pop," Robert said. "The U.S. Army is waiting on tiptoe."

They smiled at each other and Nelson took his beautiful gray Homburg out of the closet and put it carefully on before the mirror.

"I was afraid you wouldn't make it," he said, delicately fingering the brim of the hat.

Robert was over at the window, staring out at New York, shining all around in the early summer sun, with the Hudson a flat blue highway against the cliffs of New Jersey and the buildings piled against each other like stiff confectionery in the light morning air. "Lord, Lord . . ." Robert murmured. "What a place to work! You ought to be sitting here writing the Ninth Symphony, Pop."

Nelson smiled at him and took his arm. "I'm not writing the Ninth Symphony." He would have liked to carry Robert's bag for him to the elevator and even made a move for it, but Robert detected it and switched the bag without a word to the other hand.

There was a pretty, dark-haired woman in a fine, severe black dress that looked on her as black dresses are supposed to look on smart women who work in fashionable businesses, and rarely do. She had her hair swept up for the summer morning and she looked pert and sharp and pretty and grownup all at once, and she looked coolly and approvingly, Nelson noticed, at his tall son, standing beside him, very slender and straight and self-consciously handsome in his new dark-green lieutenant's blouse with the proud gold bar shining on each shoulder.

Robert smiled a little to himself, conscious of the cool approving stare, helplessly and a little ashamedly pleased with himself for provoking it.

"Sometimes," he said, as he and Nelson got out of the elevator and walked toward Fifth Avenue, with the woman lost behind them, "sometimes, Pop, they ought to be allowed to arrest a man for the thoughts that pass through his head."

They grinned at each other and Robert took a deep full breath, looking around him, the smile still on his lips, before he got into the taxicab and said, "Grand Central, please."

They sat quietly as the cab dodged through the streets. Nelson looked steadfastly at the shining rawhide bag. You saw bags like that, he thought, on Friday afternoons in the summertime, on station platforms where people in summer clothes gaily waited for trains going to New England, to the Adirondacks, to Cape Cod . . . Somehow, he felt, to make the picture complete, there should be a tennis racket lying beside it, in its bright rubber case, and a girl's voice, light and excited, dominating the scene, saying swiftly, laughing, "Olive oil and vinegar in equal parts and a few drops of glycerin and just smear yourself, darling, every hour. There was this lifeguard at Hobe Sound and he was out in the sun twelve hours a day and that was all he used and he was as brown as the outside of an old piece of roast beef. . . ."

But instead it was Robert's voice saying, "Five medium tanks . . ."

"What was that?" Nelson looked at his son, apologetically. "I'm sorry. I didn't quite . . ."

201

"When I get back," Robert said, "I'm put in command of five medium tanks. Twelve tons apiece, with a crew of four men. They represent an investment of about three hundred thousand bucks. And I've got to tell them, start, stop, go here, go there, kindly demolish that hot dog stand to the left, would you be so good as to put six shells into that corset and lingerie shop five blocks down the street." He grinned widely. "Me. I never even ran a set of electric trains before in my life. The faith that the U.S. Government has in me! I'm going to develop a beautiful case of stage fright when the time comes for me to look those five medium tanks in the eye."

"You'll do all right," Nelson said soberly.

Robert stared at him seriously for a moment, the smile gone. "I suppose so," he said.

The cab wheeled into Grand Central and they got out.

"We have fifteen minutes," Robert said, looking up at the clock. "How about one quick one, to oil the wheels?"

"Is anyone else seeing you off?" Nelson asked, as they walked through the dim, shuffling, echoing vault, toward the bar of the Commodore Hotel. "No girls?"

"Nope," said Robert, smiling. "Can't start that. If you invite one you've got to invite them all. It'd look like a reunion of Vassar graduates, classes of '38 to '41, inclusive." He laughed aloud. "I wouldn't like to make such a showy exit."

Nelson smiled at the joke, but was aware that the joke covered the fact that Robert had saved his final private good-bye before he went to war for his father. He wished there was some way to tell Robert he understood and was grateful, but whatever words he could think of would be clumsy and tragic, so he said nothing. They went into the Commodore and stood at the long bar, quiet now and cool and dim in the eleven o'clock pause before the day's drinking began.

"Two martinis," Robert said to the bartender.

"I haven't had a drink in the morning," Nelson said, "since Arthur Parker's wedding. 1936."

"What the hell," Robert said. "There's a war on."

There was the pleasant sound of the ice clinking in the mixer and the faint strange smell of the gin rising in the empty bar and the pungent tiny smell of the lemon peel that the bartender twisted delicately over the full cold glasses.

They lifted their drinks and Nelson looked past his son's lean, well-loved head, capped and young and martial, with the gold and leather of the United States Army shining on it. Nelson looked along the bar into the dim recesses of the low-ceilinged, long room, as neat and orderly and expectant with its empty and regular tables and chairs as only a bar or restaurant prepared for the day's eating and drinking can be. How many farewells had been said in this room, this drinking place next to the trains that spread out across the whole huge continent. How many final good-byes. How many last kisses between husband and wife. How many gulped and tasteless drinks, how much shock of alcohol to take the first terrible edge off the pain of loss and distance. How many farewelling ghosts sat at those regular tables, their endless irrevocable good-byes echoing among the frivolous glasses. How full the company of grieving leavetakers, each of them tasting death in this snatched last moment over whisky, before the train rolled out. . . .

Nelson looked squarely, steadily at his one child's military head. He raised his glass a little higher, touching his son's glass. "To a quick end of the business," he said.

They drank. The drink tasted powerful and rich and burning and immediately effective against his morning palate. Robert drank with zest, tasting the full savor of the drink happily, rolling it over his tongue. "You'd be surprised," he said, "how hard it is to get a good martini in the Tank Corps."

Nelson watched him drink and remembered a day in the country, three years ago, when Robert was twenty. It was summertime and they were both on vacation and had a house in Vermont and Robert had been out swimming all afternoon and had come in, wet-haired, tan, barefoot, wrapped in a huge white bathrobe, with a faded blue towel swung around his shoulders, summertime printed on his freckled nose and the tan backs of his lake-washed hands . . . He had swung through the screen door, singing loudly, "Stormy weather, since my gal and I ain't together. . . ." He had padded along barefoot, leaving high-arched stains of lakewater on the grass rugs directly to the kitchen. When Nelson had gone into the kitchen, he saw Robert sitting at the porcelain table, still humming "Stormy Weather," with an open bottle of cold beer in one hand, the moisture condensing coolly on the glass, and in the other hand a huge, ludicrous sandwich he had made for himself with two great jagged slices of rye bread and a quarter pound of Swiss cheese and two mountainous slices of cold baked ham and a tremendous cold beefsteak tomato cut in three fat, meaty slices. Robert was sitting there, tilted back in the flimsy kitchen chair, the late afternoon sun shining obliquely on him through the high old-fashioned window, slowly dripping lakewater, the giant of a sandwich and the bottle of beer happily in his hands, his mouth full of cheese and tomato and ham and bread and cold beer, the song somehow working out of his throat in a bumbling joyous monotone. He waved the sandwich airily at Nelson when Nelson appeared at the door.

"Starving," he mumbled. "Swam four miles. Got to keep my energy up."

"You've got to eat dinner in an hour," Nelson said.

Robert grinned through the food. "I'll eat dinner. Let nobody worry." And he took another fabulous bite from the monstrous sandwich.

Nelson watched him eat, smiling a little to himself.

"Want me to make you a sandwich?" Robert asked.

"No, thanks."

"Great maker of sandwiches . . ."

Nelson shook his head, smiling. "I'll wait for dinner." He watched his son eat. The full white teeth shining in the sunburned face, biting strongly and evenly into the food, the lean muscles of the strong throat, rising out of the white bathrobe, moving calmly as he tilted the bottle back and gulped the beer. . . .

"When I was your age," Nelson said, "I ate just like that. . . ."

And suddenly Robert had looked at him very soberly as though seeing his father twenty years old—and loving him——and seeing the long years that came after with pride and pity . . .

"Well . . ." Robert ate the olive at the bottom of his glass and put the glass down with a little flat tinkle that ran lightly through the quiet bar. "Well, the train's waiting. . . ."

Nelson looked around and shook his head and the Vermont kitchen and the sunburned boy and the bottle of beer beaded with icebox-cold all disappeared. He finished his drink and paid and together he and Robert hurried across the station to the gate where Robert's train was waiting. There was an air of bustle and impatience about the gate, and a soldier and his mother and two female relatives were weeping together in a sodden mass and somehow he and Robert shook hands and there was a last wave and no words because they each knew that any word through the tortured throat would bring with it sobs—and Robert went down the long incline to the dark station below. His rawhide bag gleamed among the descending passengers and he was gone. . . .

Nelson turned and walked slowly toward the street. As he walked he thought of the capped head and the rawhide bag going down the long incline to the waiting train, to the medium tanks, to the waiting guns, the waiting agony, going lightly and zealously and unquestioningly off to war. He remembered, although a little mistily, with the martini and the shuffling steps on the marble floor, and

204

the weeping at the gates of the soldier's women, all serving to blur and confuse and make remote, he remembered watching Robert playing tennis last summer. Robert played very smoothly and well, lanky and easy over the court, like those tall kids in California who play 365 days a year in a kind of lazy, expert boredom. Robert had a habit of talking jovially and half-irritably to himself when he missed a shot, looking up to heaven and muttering under his breath, "Weaver! *Weaver!* Why don't you just give up? Why don't you just go home?" He had seen his father looking down at him, smiling; and knew that his father understood the mumbled tirade he was delivering to himself. He had grinned and waved his racket and slammed the next three services so hard no returns were possible. . . .

Nelson walked up Madison Avenue toward the office of Marshall and Co., toward the formal and intricate sheets of figures waiting on his desk, toward the neat, professional, bookkeeper's 2 he was proud of. . . .

As he walked he wondered where his son would be sent to meet the enemy. Africa? Australia? India? England? Russia? Desert, plain, mountain, jungle, seacoast—and a twenty-three-year-old boy, ex-swimmer, ex-tennis-player, ex-eater of great sandwiches and drinker of cold beer, ex-lover of his father, hungry and full of jokes and ready for any climate, while his father, full of his slack fifty years, walked daily to his office. . . .

Nelson walked along Madison Avenue before the windows of the fine shops. Two women passed him and a high woman's voice said, "Taffeta. Baby-blue taffeta, shirred, with the back bare down to the hips. It has a startling effect."

It never occurred to me it could happen, Nelson thought, walking slowly and blindly away from the station where his son had set off to battle. There was one war and that was all. It's my fault. I had a son, but I didn't take my responsibility seriously enough. I worked and I dressed him and fed him and sent him to a good college and bought him books and gave him money to take out girls and took him with me on vacations to Vermont, but I didn't take my responsibility seriously enough. I worked, and it wasn't easy, and I was poor for a long time and only the poor know how hard it is to stop being poor. I worked, but for the wrong things. I've added millions of rows of figures, detailed the maneuverings of many corporations, year by year, and sometimes it was eighteen hours a day and no time for meals. . . . Nonsense! I'm guilty. I should've been out stopping this. . . . I am nearly the same age as Hitler. He could do something to kill my son. I should've been doing something to save him. I'm guilty. I should be ashamed to stand in the same room with my son in his lieutenant's green blouse. Money . . . I thought about the grocer, the insurance man, the electric light company . . . Nonsense, nonsense . . . I've wasted my life. I'm an old man and alone and my son has gone to war and all I did was pay rent and taxes. I was playing with toys. I was smoking opium. Me and millions like me. The war was being fought for twenty years and I didn't know it. I waited for my son to grow up and fight it for me. I should've been out screaming on street corners, I should've grabbed people by their lapels in trains, in libraries and restaurants and yelled at them. "Love, understand, put down your guns, forget your profit, remember God . . ." I should have walked on foot through Germany and France and England and America. I should've preached on the dusty roads and used a rifle when necessary. I stayed in the one city and paid the grocer. Versailles, Manchuria, Ethiopia, Warsaw, Madrid—battlefields, battlefields—and I thought there was one war and it was over.

He stopped and looked up. He was sweating now and the salt was in his eyes and he had to rub them to see that he was standing in front of the great monument of a building, serene and immutable, in which, in war and peace, Marshall and Co. conducted its business. His charts and figures were waiting for him, all the clever, legal, evasive, money-saving numbers that a global dealer in valves and turbines could assemble in this bloody and profitable year to turn over in its solemn annual report to the government of the republic. Depreciation . . . $3,100,456.25.

He looked up at the soaring shining building sharp against the soft summer sky.

He stood there, before the graven entrance, and people jostled him and came and went, but he didn't go in.

# Hamlets of the World

The captain was getting more and more remote every moment. He kept stuffing papers into a heavy saddle-leather bag, whistling tunelessly under his breath. From time to time he looked out over the windy plain, swirling with dust in the late afternoon sun. He would peer thoughtfully into the eye-burning distance, then shake himself a little and resume his packing, a little more quickly each time. He never looked at Lieutenant Dumestre.

Lieutenant Dumestre sat on the edge of the desk, very neat in his expensive uniform. He was a tall, fairish man, who looked too young to be in his lieutenant's uniform, too young to be so serious, too young to be in a war.

He never took his eyes off the Captain. The Captain was a round, solid man, who had been very jovial when they had met in Algiers and had paid for the wine and had sighed gallantly over all the pretty women in the café. There was nothing jovial or gallant about the Captain now, as he prepared in a businesslike way to disappear, each moment seeming more and more remote.

"Do you expect to come back, sir?" Lieutenant Dumestre finally asked, because the silence in the orderly room broken only by the low bumble of the Captain's humming was at last too much to bear.

The Captain stopped his packing and looked thoughtfully out over the plain again, as though there, in the dust and scrub, some answer to a profound although somewhat vague question was to be found. He stood silently, even forgetting to hum.

"Do you expect to come back, sir?" the Lieutenant asked loudly.

The Captain at last turned and looked at the Lieutenant. His eyes were very cool and you would never have thought from looking at him in this moment that he had ever bought a bottle of wine for a lieutenant in his life. "Come back?" the Captain said. He turned away and sturdily buckled his bag. "Who can tell?"

"What do I do with the Americans?" The Lieutenant's voice,

he noticed angrily, was much higher than it should have been. At Saint Cyr they had been after him all the time to pitch his voice lower. "An order given in the soprano register, Mister, is not calculated to drive troops to impossible glories." "What happens when the Americans arrive?"

The Captain was putting his helmet on very carefully in front of a mirror. "That is just what I hope to discover," he said.

"In the meantime?"

"In the meantime your orders are to resist. Naturally."

The Lieutenant peered out over the plain, hoping painfully that over the rim of the horizon the Americans would appear before the Captain could leave on his personal retreat. But the only movement to be seen was a corporal hurrying to the battery observation post.

"They'll arrive tomorrow morning, at the latest," the Lieutenant said.

"Quite possibly." The Captain picked up his bag decisively, marched out and into the command car. The Lieutenant followed him and saluted. The Captain saluted and the car started and the Captain drove down the road.

The Lieutenant plodded slowly up the road toward the forward gun, thinking of the Captain, in the command car, speeding over a macadam road to Algiers, where there would be other men to make the decisions, other men to say, "We will move to the left, we will move to the right . . ." and the Captain would have to make no decisions himself. No matter how things turned out, he would not be committed and would be a fine fellow with whichever side turned up on top, and would jovially buy wine for his new lieutenants at the second-best restaurant in town. . . .

The Lieutenant made his way to the aimless little mud house they used as an observation post and climbed the ladder and stood under the umbrella next to the red-eyed little corporal and peered through his glasses at the plain. He looked until his eyes ached, but aside from the blowing dust there was nothing.

The men who served the forward gun had rigged up a tarpaulin to one side and lay under it, out of the wind. Usually they slept all the afternoon, but today no one was sleeping.

Sergeant Fourier even went so far as to get up and look out across the plain.

"Anything?" Labat asked.

The Sergeant squinted anxiously. "Nothing."

"Waiting, everything is waiting," Labat said. He was a long, ugly man, with a big nose and large ears. He was from Paris and excitable and given to throwing his arms around in rage and was a great patriot of the French Republic. "In a war you wait for everything! Even the Americans! At last, I thought, things will finally move. The Americans are famous for their briskness. . . . We're still waiting. . . ."

"Only a day," said Boullard. Boullard was a big, quiet man, over forty, with a wrinkled, brown, farmer's face. "They'll be here soon enough."

"I can't wait," Labat said. He stood up and peered out. "For a year I sat in the Maginot Line. Now for two years I sit here. I am finally impatient. A day is too much."

"Shut up," Boullard said calmly. "You'll get us all nervous."

Labat lay down and put his hands behind his head and looked up at the tarpaulin angrily. Sergeant Fourier came back and sat down.

"More of the same," Sergeant Fourier said. "More nothing."

"It must be worse for Americans," Corporal Millet said. He was a man who, although he was nearly thirty-five, was still plagued by pimples. His face had raging red blots on it all the time and he suffered meanly under his affliction, taking his misfortune out on the work details in his charge. "It must be unbearable for Americans."

"Why?" Labat asked angrily. "What's wrong with the Americans?"

"They are not a military people," Corporal Millet said. He had a lawyer's voice, smooth and reasonable and superior, and on bad days it made men want to kill Corporal Millet. "They are used to sitting back and pushing buttons."

"Corporal," Labat said calmly, "you are perhaps the biggest idiot in the French Army of 1942."

"The jokes," Corporal Millet said. "We can do without the jokes. It is a fact that war is harder on some races than on others. The Americans must be suffering the tortures of the damned."

"I repeat," Labat said. "The biggest."

Corporal Millet was a devotee of Vichy, and Labat enjoyed making him angry.

"Push buttons," Boullard said reflectively. "I could use a few push buttons at the moment."

"See," Corporal Millet gestured to Boullard. "Boullard agrees."

"See," Boullard said. "Boullard does not agree."

There was silence for a moment, while the men thought of the

209

wind and the ugliness of the men around them and the possibility of dying tomorrow.

"Be more cheerful," Boullard said, "or kindly keep quiet."

The men sat silently for a moment, everyone heavy and gloomy because the word death had finally been mentioned.

"It will be a ridiculous thing," Labat said. "To be killed by an American." Labat had fought at Sedan and made his way bitterly down the length of France, cursing the politicians, cursing the officers, cursing the Germans and English and Italians and Americans. At last he had stowed away aboard a freighter to Algiers and without losing a day had joined up all over again and had since then sat, full of pent-up vengeance, in the gloom of Africa, waiting to fight the Germans once more.

"I refuse," Labat said. "I refuse to be killed by an American."

"You will be told what your orders are," Corporal Millet said, "and you will follow them."

Labat stared gloomily and dangerously at Corporal Millet. His face, which was ugly but usually pleasant enough, now was harsh and his eyes were squinted balefully. "Corporal," he said, "Corporal of the pimples, do you know what our orders are?"

"No."

"Does anybody know?" Labat looked around, his face still flushed and glowering, angry at Corporal Millet and the government of France and his position in the world that afternoon.

Sergeant Fourier cleared his throat professionally. "The Lieutenant. He must know. The Captain's gone . . ."

"What a wonderful thing," Boullard said, "to be a captain. . . ."

"Let us ask the Lieutenant," Labat said.

"Sergeant Fourier, we make you a committee of one."

Sergeant Fourier looked around him uneasily, pulling in his round little belly nervously, uncomfortable at the thought of any action that would make him conspicuous, endanger his pleasant anonymous future with the masseuse in Algiers. "Why me?" he asked.

"Highest non-commissioned officer present," Labat chanted. "Channels of communication with the commissioned personnel."

"I haven't said two words to him," Sergeant Fourier protested. "After all, he just got here five days ago. And he's reserved. . . . All he's said to me in five days is, 'Make sure the men do not smoke in the open at night.' "

"Enough," Labat said cheerfully. "It's obvious he likes you."

"Don't joke," Boullard said sharply. "We have no more time to joke."

"I'm only joking," Labat said soberly, "because I am willing to slit my throat."

He got up and went to the edge of the tarpaulin and stood there, his back to the men, watching across the enigmatic plain for the first fateful dust cloud.

"What sort of man is this Lieutenant Dumestre?" Boullard asked.

"It's hard to tell," Sergeant Fourier said, with the caution born of three years in an army where a hasty approval of a man, before all the facts of courage, sense and rectitude were in, might one day cause your death. "He's very quiet. Stiff . . ."

"A bad sign," said Boullard.

"Very rich in the uniform department."

"Another bad sign."

"It doesn't pay to be too hurried," Sergeant Fourier protested.

"It's the Americans," Boullard said. "They're in a hurry, not me. Well, there's only one thing to be done." He rubbed his cheek absently with the back of his hand, like a man determining whether or not he needs a shave. The other men watched him silently, anxious and curious about a definite plan that might have finally bloomed on this last nervous afternoon. "One thing," Boullard repeated. "We kill him."

Lieutenant Dumestre stood in the observation post and felt the headache coming on like an express train. Every afternoon the boredom and misery of the day accumulated in his brain pan and punished him for still living. He stared painfully over the darkening plain, which was silently enveloping itself in blue and purple folds, intangible and deceptive, in which the shapes of men and machines might be capriciously and dangerously lost. . . .

Lieutenant Dumestre shook his head and closed his eyes, measuring gloomily the exact extent of the pain in his skull.

How do you do it? he asked himself. How does a first lieutenant hand a battery over to an advancing army, without orders? How does a first lieutenant save his life in a situation like this? In the distance there is a puff of dust and soon the first shell dropping somewhere near you, and all around you doubtful and uncertain men whom you do not know but who, for the lack of a better word, are under your command. Why had he left his post in Algiers? In this one, crazy, fateful week, his transfer had to be granted, this transfer to dilemma, this transfer to death. . . . In the days of Napoleon it was said that every French private had a marshal's baton in his knapsack. Today every French soldier had in his knapsack a fatal and insoluble conundrum.

Lieutenant Dumestre had asked to be transferred from Algiers because he had been spending too much money there. It was as simple as that. The bills came in, the monthly reckonings were made, the deductions for the money sent home to his mother and father, who were lean and ailing in Paris, and it became clear that on a lieutenant's salary you could not save money in a gay town, especially if you had been rich all your life and your family rich before you and certain habits of eating and drinking and generosity ingrained in you, war or no war. . . .

So, it was too expensive, Algiers. So, the desert would prove to be even more expensive.

. . . . Back in Algiers he knew the men of his battery had mimicked him behind his back—his slow, painful way of delivering orders, full of agonized pauses, as he tried to remember to keep his voice down, tried not to sound like a young idiot imposing callously on these veterans of a war that had passed him by. . . . They had mimicked him, but he knew them and even felt they liked him, and if he were with them now in this tragedy of a situation he would be able to go to them, talk to them, draw strength and resolution, one way or another from the men who would have to bear the burden of living and dying with him.

But here he was, on the one important day of the last two years, with a group of sullen and bearded strangers, who regarded him only with steady and cool hostility, a newcomer and an officer in an army where newcomers were automatically suspect and officers automatically hated. . . .

Lieutenant Dumestre walked slowly out toward the west across the dusty scrub. The sun had set and the wind had died and the walking, he felt, might help somehow. Perhaps, he thought, smiling a little to himself, there will be an American patrol and I am unavoidably captured and there's an end to the problem. . . . It's like a child, he thought, hoping that by morning he will have a sore throat so he does not have to go to school and take his examination in arithmetic. What an arithmetic was being imposed upon him now! What a savage and pitiless calculation! He looked toward the last blur of the horizon beyond which the Americans were marching. How simple it was to be an American! In their arithmetic there was an answer to all problems. How merry and dashing a lieutenant in the artillery in the American army must feel tonight, marching beside men whom he could trust, who trusted him, who all believed the same thing, who knew an enemy

212

when they saw one, whose parents were well-fed and healthy, in no one's power, three thousand sweet miles from all battlefields. . . .

What a tragic thing to be a Frenchman this year! Hamlet, sword out, killing Polonius and uncle in blind unprofitable lunges. . . . Frenchmen, Hamlets of the world . . .

Lieutenant Dumestre stopped and sat down like a little boy on the dark earth and put his head in his hands and wept. He stopped suddenly and bit his lips and neglected to dry the tears from his cheeks. Nonsense, he thought, a grown man . . . There must be an answer to this, too. After all, I am not the only Frenchman afloat on this continent. The thing is, the men. If I knew what they wanted . . . If there was only some way to be present, without being seen. Armies have surrendered before. Detachments have surrendered before. Officers have appeared under a flag of truce and offered their services to their official enemies. The Captain was in Algiers, there was no one to stop him. "Dear sir, is there anyone here who speaks French? Dear sir, Lieutenant Dumestre, Battery C, wishes to state that he desires to join forces with the American Army in North Africa and put himself under the flag of the United States for the duration against the common enemy. . . ." There must be a technique to surrender, just the way there was a technique for everything else in the army. His mother and father would have to look out for themselves. Now, if only the men . . .

Lieutenant Dumestre slapped his thigh briskly as he stood up. At last he had reached a decision. He had faced the arithmetic and at least he knew what answer he wanted. There only remained going in frankly to the men and putting the situation up to them, in words of one syllable, simply. . . . He started back toward the forward gun, walking more swiftly than he had walked for a week.

"Men," he would say, remembering to keep his voice pitched low, "this is the way it is. You may or may not know it, but tomorrow an American army will appear." You never knew how much the men knew, what rumors had reached them, what facts confirmed, what punishments and discharges and prophecies and movements were peddled at the latrine or over a morning cigarette. "I am under orders to resist," he would say. "Personally, I do not believe we are bound by those orders, as I believe all Frenchmen to be on the side for which the Americans are now fighting." Perhaps that was too heroic, but it was impossible to fight a war without sounding from time to time a little heroic. "I intend to go out under a flag of truce and give over the guns of this battery." Now the question of dissenters. "Anyone who does not wish to join me in this action is free to leave toward the rear. . . ." No, they'd go back and talk and by morning a troop of cavalry would come up and Lieutenant Dumestre would be finished in thirty minutes. Keep them with him? How do that? Supposing they were all Vichy men? After all, they were being paid by Vichy and there were thousands of Frenchmen in Africa who had staked their lives on a German victory. They'd shoot him in cold blood.

Once more he cursed the trick that had landed him at this moment among two hundred strangers. In his old company he would have been able to take Sergeant Goubille aside and talk honestly and get an honest answer. Sergeant Goubille was forty-five years old and there was something fatherly and tolerant of young officers in his bearing, and a man like that would be worth a man's life on this harsh and doubtful plain tonight. Well, there was no Sergeant Goubille at hand. . . . Perhaps that Breton, that farmer, Boullard. He was an older man and he looked honest and pleasant.

He took a deep breath and walked swiftly, not knowing exactly what he would do but knowing he had to do something, toward the forward gun. . . .

Under the tarpaulin, Boullard was talking, his voice low and harsh, all the kindly, old countryman's lines somehow vanished from the set, desperate face. "There will be a token resistance," he was saying to the men, who were all sitting up, looking at the ground most of the time, looking up only occasionally at Boullard with a kind of deep embarrassment. "In a token resistance there are token deaths." He looked around him calmly from face to face, his thought plain in his eyes. "A token corpse feeds as many worms as any other. . . ."

Jouvet, the young one, was the only one who could not manage to sit still. He rubbed his heels back and forth, making marks in the sand, and studying them intensely.

"Kill the pretty Lieutenant," Boullard said, "and we have our own lives in our own hands. We dispose of them as we see fit."

"Let us look at it from the political angle," Labat said. "Politically, we are fried if the Germans win. . . ."

"Perhaps," Sergeant Fourier said uneasily, his voice full of the nagging pain of having to make a decision. "Perhaps we ought to wait and see what happens."

"We will wait and see ourselves buried," Boullard said.

"At least," said Labat, "we ought to talk to the Lieutenant. Sound him out."

"I was on the Meuse," said Boullard. "I know better than to talk to a lieutenant. I'll take the responsibility. If you're all afraid . . ." He looked around him with savage, peasant contempt.

"There're a lot of men still to be killed in this war. I don't mind making it one more or less, personally. . . ."

"We have to talk to him first," Labat said stubbornly.

"Why?" Boullard asked loudly.

"Maybe he's with us. Maybe he wants to fight with the Americans, too. . . ."

Boullard laughed harshly. Then he spat. "I'm surrounded by children," he said. "If he's still an officer in the French Army after two years, he is not fond of the Americans. I am. At this moment, I am crazy about Americans. If there is any hope for anybody in this stinking year, it is in the Americans. I'm forty-four years old and I've fought in two wars. The third one, I want to pick my own side . . . ."

"Still," Labat said, his voice low and persistent, "still, we ought to talk to him."

"For myself," Corporal Millet said briskly, standing up, "I am on duty at the observa—"

He let his hands fall gently to his sides as Boullard brought his rifle up and touched his chest lightly with the bayonet.

"You are on duty here, Corporal." Boullard moved the bayonet tenderly on a breast button. "There is a question before the house that must be decided by a full membership."

Corporal Millet sat down carefully.

"I don't care," Labat was saying, grinning at Corporal Millet, "what you do to the fighting Corporal, but nothing happens to the Lieutenant until we talk to him." He patted Boullard's shoulder, in a small, reassuring gesture. Boullard slowly took his eyes off Millet and the Corporal sighed.

Boullard looked around him searchingly at the men caught in this hour on this desert with him. Sergeant Fourier, haunted by dreams of a pension and his masseuse and still troubled by some obscure, painful sense of patriotism and honor, refused to look at him. Jouvet, faced at the age of twenty with the ancient, tangled threads of a bloody and complex century, looked ready to weep. Labat was smiling but stubborn. Corporal Millet was sweating, and was making a great effort to look like a man who did not intend to rush to the nearest officer and announce a mutiny.

"All right," Boullard said wearily, "if that's what you want. Although I tell you, two words too many and we are all against a wall, looking at a firing squad."

Jouvet fumbled with his handkerchief quickly and Boullard looked at him curiously and impersonally.

"It is not necessary to commit ourselves," said Labat. His long, workman's arms waved in argument. "We approach the subject, we skirt it, we take soundings like a boat coming into a harbor . . ."

"Better!" Sergeant Fourier said loudly, happy at all deferment. "Excellent! Much better!"

Boullard stared at him coldly and Sergeant Fourier became quiet and nervously took out a pack of cigarettes.

"It's possible," Labat was saying, convincing Boullard, "to judge a man without a direct question. . . ."

"Possibly," Boullard said with no enthusiasm. "Possibly."

"I'll do the talking," Labat said. "I'm used to things like this. I have talked at union meetings for seven years and nothing could be more delicate . . ." He looked around him anxiously, hoping for a little laughter to take some of the deadly tension away, but only little Jouvet, who was always polite, smiled nervously because he realized Labat had meant it as a little joke.

"All right," Boullard said. He fingered his rifle gently and let it dip almost imperceptibly toward Corporal Millet. "I will judge. And you . . ." The rifle dipped very clearly toward Corporal Millet. "You will not open your mouth. Is that clear?"

Corporal Millet sat up stiffly at attention, feeling sorrowfully within him that his honor demanded some show of resistance and that his life would not be worth a great deal if he was incorporated in the army of the United States. He looked at Boullard's huge crushing hands, calm on the rifle. "It is your affair," he said faintly. "I wash my hands of it."

Boullard laughed.

Sergeant Fourier lighted his cigarette, gift of his plump wife the masseuse, eating her dinner comfortably, all unknowing, in the curtainy little apartment in Algiers with three exposures. He sighed and stood up and walked between Boullard and the limp Corporal Millet and stood at the edge of the tarpaulin in the full darkness, pulling with small comfort at his cigarette, while behind him, under the tarpaulin, there was no sound from the waiting men.


Lieutenant Dumestre made his way slowly across the rough black ground toward the gun position, turning over in his mind his possible opening sentences to the gun crew. "Men," he could say, "I am going to be absolutely honest with you. I am putting a white flag up beside this gun and I am delivering this battery over to . . ." Or he could say, "There is a possibility that tomorrow morning American troops will appear. Hold your fire until I give the word . . ." while silently swearing to himself that the word would never be given. There was much to be said for this method,

as it was indefinite and seemed less dangerous and didn't tip his
hand until the last moment, when it would probably be too late
for anyone to do anything about it. Of course there was always
the possibility that he could stand up in front of the men and pour
his heart out to them, remind them in ringing words of their
country's shame, call upon them with blood and passion to forget
themselves, forget their families in France, remember only honor
and final victory. . . . He could see himself, pale and fluent, in
the dim light of the moon, roaring, whispering, his voice singing
in the quiet night air, the men listening entranced, the tears starting
down their cheeks. . . . He shook himself, smiled wryly at the
dream, remembering his harsh, slow way of speaking, plain, indefinite, without the power to move men to the nearest café, much
less throw themselves grandly and thoughtlessly upon a doubtful
and possibly fatal cause. . . .

Oh, Lord, he thought, I am the wrong man for this, the wrong
man, the wrong man. . . .

He turned the corner of the tarpaulin, seeing the watchful, hateful
shape of the gun outlined stubbornly against the starlit sky.

Sergeant Fourier was smoking pensively in the open and the
other men were sitting, strangely quiet, under cover. When Sergeant
Fourier saw him he started guiltily and threw his cigarette away
as unostentatiously as possible. He stood at attention and saluted
and with his right heel tried to douse the glowing speck in the
dirt. Somehow, the sight of the small man with the comfortable
little pot belly trying to pretend, like a vaudeville comedian, that
he hadn't been smoking, irritated Lieutenant Dumestre, who all
morning and all afternoon had been grappling bitterly with war
and fratricide and tragic, bloody policy. . . .

He returned the Sergeant's salute curtly. "What's wrong with
you?" he asked sharply, his high voice making all the men in the
tarpaulin turn their heads coldly and automatically to watch him.
"You know there's to be no smoking."

"Please, sir," Sergeant Fourier said stupidly, "I was not smoking."

"You were smoking," Lieutenant Dumestre said, weeping inside
because inside he knew how ridiculous this charge and countercharge
was.

"I was not smoking, sir." Sergeant Fourier stood very straight
and formal and stupid with the problem of the evening, almost
happy to have a simple little idiotic argument to worry about at
least for ten minutes. . . .

"You've been told, you've been told!" Lieutenant Dumestre

217

shrieked in his highest voice, mourning deep within himself for that womanly timbre, for his military insistence upon form and truth at this unmilitary hour, but somehow unable, with the Captain's departure and the imminence, potent and desperate, of the Americans over the horizon, to stop the high noise of his tongue. "At any moment we may be bombed. A cigarette glows like a lighthouse in a black desert at ten thousand feet! Why don't you draw a map of the gun position and publish it in the morning newspapers?" He saw Labat look at Boullard and shrug coldly and turn away with an air of dangerous significance and something within him clutched at his throat, but now there was no stopping that high, silly tongue, freed for a moment from the locked agony and doubt of the day's decision making. Here at least was familiar ground. Troops disobeying orders. Troops endangering security of the post or station. Troops slightly insubordinate, lying. . . . His weary, ragged mind, terribly grateful to be relieved of its unaccustomed task of painful exploration, relapsed into the formal, years-long grooves of Saint Cyr, of countless garrisons, countless lectures. . . . "There will be double security tonight, two-hour watches for everyone," the voice still high, but with the three-thousand-year-old bite of military command. "An extra half day's ammunition will be drawn up from the battery dump by three this morning." He saw the men's faces bleakly collapse and also something else in them, although he couldn't tell in the rush of his commands what it was. Even as he spoke he hated himself for what he was doing, knowing that a better man would have ignored the cigarette or joked about it. . . . .He hated Sergeant Fourier, standing there, pained and stupid and impassive, but in a way he was grateful to him, because he had given him the opportunity at this late hour once more for postponement.

He turned on his heel and strode away. Later, perhaps at midnight, he would come back, he told himself, and finally get this question of the Americans settled. He pulled his shoulders high in disgust as the sound of his own voice squalling about the cigarette sounded in his ears, but there was nothing to be done about it and he walked without looking back. Midnight, he thought, midnight is still time. . . .

Back under the tarpaulin, Boullard looked around him at the men. Their faces were grave, but except for Millet, there was consent in all of them.

Boullard walked out from under the tarpaulin with his rifle.

Midnight, Lieutenant Dumestre was thinking, when the bullet struck, midnight is still time. . . .

They buried him quickly without marking the grave and sat down in front of the gun to wait for the army of the Americans.

# Medal from Jerusalem

"The question that haunts me," Schneider was saying in his high, soft voice, "is, my jazz, is it real jazz or is it merely European jazz?" He was leaning against the bar of the Patio restaurant between Tel Aviv and Jaffa, which used to be the old German consulate, and speaking to Lieutenant Mitchell Gunnison in short, gaspy bursts of talk, smiling a little sadly and a little archly at Mitchell, and occasionally touching his sleeve lightly with the tips of his fingers. "I mean," he said, "I know it's good enough for Palestine, but in America what would they say about a pianist like me?"

"Well," said Gunnison gravely, "I'd say they'd think it was real jazz." He was young and he spoke slowly and he seemed to think very hard before he answered a question.

"You don't know," Schneider said, sighing, "how you've encouraged me. I listen to the records, of course, but they're old, and you never know what actually is going on in America and, after all, we all know there *is* no other jazz, no place, and with a war like this, and God knows how long it's going to last, a musician gets out of touch. And once you are out of touch, you might as well die. Just die."

"You have nothing to worry about," Mitchell said. "You'll be a sensation in America."

"If I ever get there." Schneider smiled sadly and shrugged a little. "Anyway, you must come tomorrow. I'm working on a new arrangement with the drummer. A rhumba, Viennese style. It's ridiculous, but I think you'll like it."

"I'm sorry," Mitchell said. "I won't be here tomorrow."

"Then next night," said Schneider.

"I won't be here then, either," Mitchell said. "I'm going tomorrow. Leave's up."

There was a little silence and Schneider looked down at the bar and flicked his beer glass with his fingernail, making a frail musical sound in the dark oak barroom. "Some more fighting?" Schneider asked.

"A little more fighting." Mitchell nodded soberly.

"You fly, no doubt," said Schneider. "I have no wish to intrude on military information, but the wings on the chest . . ."

"I'm a navigator." Mitchell smiled at him.

"It must be an interesting profession. Measuring the distance between one star and another star." Schneider finished his beer slowly. "Well, *sholom aleichem* . . . That's good luck. Or, to be more exact, peace be with you."

"Thank you," Mitchell said.

"Hebrew," said Schneider. "I'm ashamed to talk Hebrew to anybody who knows it. The accent, they tell me, is frightful. But you don't mind, do you?"

"No," said Mitchell. He turned to the bartender. "Mr. Abrams," he said, "another beer please, for Mr. Schneider."

"No, no." Schneider waved his hands in protest. "The artist should not drink before the performance. After . . . Another matter . . . Ah," he said, bowing elaborately, "*Fräulein*, we are enchanted."

Mitchell turned around. Ruth was standing there, looking a little hurried and out of breath, but smiling, and as pretty as ever in a light cotton dress, with her skin burned dark by the sun and her eyes full of welcome and pleasure at seeing him.

"I was afraid," she said, coming over to him and taking his hand, "I was afraid you were going to be angry and leave."

"I wasn't going to leave," Mitchell said. "Not until they closed the doors on me and threw me out."

"I am delighted." Ruth laughed and squeezed his arm. "I am so absolutely delighted."

"My presence," Schneider said, bowing, "I no longer consider necessary. A hundred thanks for the beer, Lieutenant. Now I play or Mr. Abrams will start complaining he is not getting his money's worth out of me. Listen, carefully, if it is not too much of a bore, to my version of 'Stardust.' "

"We'll listen very carefully," Mitchell said.

Schneider went outside to the patio, and a moment later preliminary erratic runs and fragments of melody came floating into the bar as he warmed up for the night's work.

"So." Ruth faced him, looking at him with an expression that was half ownership, half amusement. "So. What have we been doing all day?"

"Well," Mitchell started, "we . . ."

"You are the most beautiful lieutenant in the American Army," Ruth said, grinning.

"Well, we went swimming," Mitchell said, pleased and embarrassed, pretending she'd said nothing. "And we hung around on the beach. And we flew a couple of barroom missions. Gin and grapefruit juice."

"Isn't Palestinian grapefruit wonderful?" Ruth asked loyally.

"Sensational," Mitchell said. "Nothing like it in America."

"You're such a liar." Ruth leaned over and kissed him lightly.

"There was an Eighth Air Force pilot down from England," Mitchell said, "and he told us how tough it was over Wilhelmshaven and we told the lies about Ploesti and then it was time to shave and come to see you."

"What did you think while you were shaving? Were you sad because you had to leave your interesting friends and see me?"

"Broken-hearted," Mitchell said.

"You've got such a nice, skinny face." Ruth touched the line of his jaw. "You're as pretty as an English lieutenant. I'm not fond of the English, but they have the prettiest lieutenants of any army."

"We send our pretty ones to the Pacific," said Mitchell. "Guadalcanal. We preserve them for American womanhood."

Ruth signaled Mr. Abrams for a drink. "I was in Jerusalem today. I told my boss I was sick and went there. It's so bad—we never got to see Jerusalem together."

"Some other time," Mitchell said. "I'll come back and we'll see Jerusalem."

"Don't lie to me," Ruth said, seriously. "Please don't lie. You won't come back. You won't see me again. Absolutely no lies, please."

Mitchell felt very young. He felt there was something to be said, and an older man would know how to say it, but he felt dumb and bereaved and clumsy, and it must have showed on his face as he peered at his glass, because Ruth laughed and touched his lips with her fingers and said, "You have such a tragic face for an American. Where do you come from in America?"

"Vermont," Mitchell said.

"Has everybody got a face like yours in Vermont?"

"Everybody."

"I will visit there," Ruth drained her glass, "at some later date."

"I'll give you my address," Mitchell said.

"Of course," said Ruth politely. "You must write it down some time."

They went out into the patio and sat down at a table on the old flagstones under a palm tree, with the blue blackout lights shining dimly over the uniforms and pale dresses, and the moon riding over the Mediterranean and casting flickering shadows over the dancers who now claimed the spot where the German consul had lived well in days gone by. Mitchell ordered champagne because it was his last night. It was Syrian champagne, but not bad, and to both of them it gave an air of festivity and importance to the evening, as it rocked in its silver bucket of ice. Eric, the waiter with the limp, ceremoniously took Ruth's ration tickets, and Schneider, seated with the drummer across the patio, with the drum dimly lit from inside by an orange light of which Schneider was very proud, played "Summertime" because he had decided that was the song Mitchell liked best. The old song, played trickily and well in the soft, echoing patio, somehow sounded, by some ineradicable stamp in Schneider's blood, like Carolina and Vienna and the Balkans, with here and there chords of an old Hebrew chant, quite just and indigenous here between the heavy stone walls on the edge of the Sinai desert.

"I'm jealous of him," said Ruth, speaking over the edge of her glass.

"Who?"

"Schneider."

"Why?" Mitchell asked.

"Because of the way he looks at you. He's crazy about you. Has he asked you to come to tea with him and his mother?"

"Yes," said Mitchell, trying not to smile.

"I'll tear his eyes out," Ruth said. "I'm jealous of anybody who looks at you that way. The girls back in Vermont and those Red Cross girls."

"You have nothing to worry about," Mitchell said. "Nobody looks at me that way. Not even Schneider or you."

"That's the nicest thing about you," Ruth said. "You don't know anything. I'm so used to men who know just how many steps out of bed each look a woman gives them measures. I must visit America after the war. . . ."

"Where will you really go?" Mitchell asked. "Back to Berlin?"

"No." Ruth stared reflectively down at her plate. "No, not back to Berlin. Never back to Berlin. The Germans have made clear their feeling about me. A little thing like a war will not change them. The lamb does not go back to the slaughterhouse.

Anyway, I have nobody there. There was a young man . . . ." She leaned over and picked up the bottle and absently poured for Mitchell and herself. "I don't know what happened to him. Stalingrad, maybe, Alamein . . . who knows?"

Four men came into the patio and walked through the brief illumination of the blue lights. Three of them were Arabs in European dress, and the fourth was a man in the uniform of the American Army with the civilian technical adviser patch on his shoulder. They stopped at the table. The three Arabs bowed a little, ceremoniously, to Ruth, and the American said, "I thought you were sick."

"This is Mr. Carver," Ruth said to Mitchell, with a wave to the American. "He's my boss."

"Hi, Lieutenant," said Carver. He was a big, fat man, with a weary, puffy, intelligent face. He turned back to Ruth. "I thought you were sick," he repeated in a pleasant, loud, slightly drunken voice.

"I was sick," Ruth said, cheerfully. "I had a miraculous recovery."

"The American Army," Carver said, "expects every civilian worker to do her duty."

"Tomorrow," said Ruth. "Now please go away with your friends. The lieutenant and I are having an intimate talk."

"Lieutenant . . ." It was one of the Arabs, the shortest of the three, a slight, dark man, with a round face and liquid, veiled eyes. "My name is Ali Khazen. Permit me to introduce myself, as no one here seems to remember his manners well enough to do so."

Mitchell stood up. "Mitchell Gunnison," he said, putting out his hand.

"Forgive me," Carver said. "I'm suffering from drink. This is Sayed Taif . . ." He indicated the tallest of the Arabs, a middle-aged man with a severe, handsome, tight-lipped face. Mitchell shook hands with him.

"He doesn't like Americans," Carver said loudly. "He's the leading journalist of the local Arab world and he writes for thirty-five papers in the United States and he doesn't like Americans."

"What was that?" Taif asked politely, inclining his head in a reserved, small gesture.

"Also, he's deaf," said Carver. "Most useful equipment for any journalist."

Nobody bothered to introduce the third Arab, who stood a little to one side, watching Taif with a fierce, admiring stare, like a boxer dog at his master's feet.

"Why don't you all go away and eat your dinner?" Ruth said.

"Lieutenant," Carver said, ignoring her, "take the advice of a veteran of the Middle East. Do not become involved with Palestine."

"He's not becoming involved with Palestine," Ruth said. "He's becoming involved with me."

"Beware Palestine." Carver weaved a little as he spoke. "The human race is doomed in Palestine. For thousands of years. They chop down the forests, burn down the cities, wipe out the inhabitants. This is no place for an American."

"You drink too much, Mr. Carver," Ruth said.

"Nevertheless," Carver shook his big head heavily, "it is no accident that they picked this place to crucify Christ. You couldn't pick a better place to crucify Christ if you scoured the maps of the world for five hundred years. I'm a Quaker myself, from the city of Philadelphia, Pennsylvania, and all I see here is the blood of bleeding humanity. When this war is over I'm going back to Philadelphia and wait until I pick up the morning newspaper and read that everybody in Palestine has exterminated everybody else in Palestine the night before." He walked unsteadily over to Ruth's chair and bent over and peered intently into her face. "Beautiful girl," he said, "beautiful, forlorn girl." He straightened up. "Gunnison, I admonish you, as an officer and gentleman, do not harm one hair on this beautiful girl's head."

"Every hair," Mitchell said, gravely, "is safe with me."

"If you must drink," Ruth said to Carver sharply, "why don't you do it with Americans? Why do you have to go around with bandits and murderers like these?" She waved her hand toward the Arabs. The journalist smiled, his handsome face frosty and amused in the wavering light.

"Impartiality," Carver boomed. "American impartiality. We are famous for it. We are nobody's friend and nobody's enemy. We merely build airfields and pipelines. Impartially. Tomorrow I lunch with the President of the Jewish Agency."

Ruth turned to the journalist. "Taif," she said, loudly, "I read your last piece."

"Ah, yes," he said, his voice a little dead and without timbre. "Did you like it?"

"You'll be responsible for the death of thousands of Jews," said Ruth.

"Ah, thank you," he said. He smiled. "It is my fondest hope." He turned to Mitchell. "Naturally, Lieutenant," he said, "our

225

charming little Ruth is biased in the matter. It is necessary to give the Arab side of the proposition." He began to speak more seriously, with a severe, oratorical emphasis, like an evangelical preacher. "The world is dazzled by the Jewish accomplishment in Palestine. Fine, clean cities, with plumbing. Industries. Where once was desert, now the rose and the olive bloom. Et cetera."

"Taif, old boy," Carver pulled at his arm, "let's eat and you can lecture the lieutenant some other time."

"No, if you please." The journalist pulled his arm politely away from Carver's hand. "I welcome the opportunity to talk to our American friends. You see, my good Lieutenant, you may be very pleased with the factory and the plumbing, and perhaps, even, from one point of view, they may be good things. But they have nothing to do with the Arab. Perhaps the Arab prefers the desert as it was. The Arab has his own culture. . . ."

"When I hear the word 'culture,' " Carver said, "I reach for my pistol. What famous American said that?"

"To Americans and Europeans," the journalist went on, in his singsong, dead voice, "the culture of the Arab perhaps seems backward and dreadful. But, forgive us, the Arab prefers it. The virtues which are particularly Arab are kept alive by primitive living. They die among the plumbing."

"Now," said Ruth, "we have heard a new one. Kill the Jew because he brings the shower bath."

The journalist smiled indulgently at Ruth, as at a clever child. "Personally," he said, "I have nothing against the Jews. I swear that I do not wish to harm a single Jew living in Palestine today. But I will fight to the death to keep even one more Jew from entering the country. This is an Arab state, and it must remain an Arab state."

"Gunnison," Carver said, "aren't you glad you came?"

"Six million Jews have died in Europe," Ruth said, her voice harsh and passionate, and surprising to Mitchell. "Where do you want the survivors to go?" She and the journalist had forgotten the rest of them and were locked with each other across the table.

The journalist shrugged and looked for a moment up above the palm fronds at the dark sky. "That," he said, "is a question for the world to decide. Why must the poor Arab have the whole decision? We've taken in much more than our share. If the rest of the world really wants to see the Jewish race survive let them take them in. America, Britain, Russia . . . I do not notice those large countries taking in great masses of Jews."

"There are no great masses," Ruth said. "There is only a handful."

Taif shrugged. "Even so. The truth may be, perhaps," he paused, a little doubtfully, reminding Mitchell of an old Latin teacher in a class in Cicero, shrewdly hesitating for effect, before telling the class whether the word in question was in the ablative or dative absolute, "the truth may be that the rest of the world really wants to see the Jewish race die out." He turned and smiled warmly at Mitchell. "It is an interesting supposition, Lieutenant. It might be most interesting to examine it before talking any more about Palestine." He walked over to Ruth and leaned over and kissed her fleetingly on the forehead. "Good night, little Ruth," he said, and went to a table across the patio, with the silent, adoring Arab behind him.

"If I see you with that man once more," Ruth spoke to the man who had introduced himself to Mitchell, and who had remained standing at their table, "I'll never talk to you again."

The Arab looked swiftly at Mitchell, a veiled, probing flick of the eyes, and said something to Ruth in Arabic.

"No," said Ruth, her voice clipped and sharp. "Definitely no."

The Arab bowed slightly, put out his hand to Mitchell and, as they shook hands, said, "Very pleasant meeting you, Lieutenant," and went off to join his friends at their table.

"*Thé dansants* in old Tel Aviv," said Carver. "Bring the kiddies. Good night." He waddled over to the other table.

"Ruth," Mitchell started to talk.

"Lieutenant Gunnison . . ." It was the soft, apologetic voice of Schneider at his elbow. "I am so anxious for your opinion. What did you think of 'Stardust'?"

Mitchell turned slowly from staring at Ruth, who was sitting tense and upright in her chair. "Great, Schneider," Mitchell said. "I thought it was sensational."

Schneider beamed with pleasure. "You are too kind," he said. "I will play you 'Summertime' once more."

"Thanks a lot," said Mitchell. He put out his hand and covered Ruth's, lying on the table. "You all right?" he asked.

She smiled up at him. "Sure," she said. "I am an admirer of abstract political discussions." Her face grew serious. "Do you want to know what Khazen asked when he spoke to me in Arabic?"

"Not if you don't want to tell me."

"I want to tell you." Ruth absently caressed his fingers. "He asked me if I would meet him later."

"Yes," said Mitchell.

"I told him no."

"I heard you." Mitchell grinned at her. "They probably heard you in Cairo."

"I didn't want you to feel disturbed or doubtful," Ruth said, "your last night."

"I feel fine," Mitchell said.

"I've been going with him for four years." She played for a moment with the food on the plate that the waiter had put before her. "When I came here in the beginning I was frightened and lonely and he was very decent. He's a contractor for the Americans and British and he's made a fortune during the war. But when Rommel was outside Alexandria he and his friends used to celebrate in secret. I can't stand him any more. I tell him when I take up with other men. But he hangs on. Ah, finally, I suppose he'll get me to marry him. I'm not strong enough any more." She looked up at Mitchell and tried to smile. "Don't be shocked, darling," she said. "Americans can't understand how tired the human race can get." She stood up suddenly. "Let's dance."

They went onto the floor and Schneider broke into "Summertime" when he saw them and smiled fondly at them as they danced. She danced very well, lightly and passionately, and Mitchell knew as he danced that he was going to remember this for a long time, at odd moments, swinging away from targets with the flak falling off behind him, and later, if he made it, in the snowy hills of his home state, the light, soft pressure of the bright cotton dress, the dark, curved, delicate face below his, the hushed sound of their feet on the old floor under the palms, the clever, rich music of the piano under the small blue lights strung out from the stone building. There were a million things that crowded his throat that he wanted to tell her, and there was no way of saying them. He kissed her cheek as the music ended, and she glanced up at him, and smiled and said, "There, that's better," and they were laughing by the time they got back to their table.

He paid the bill and they went out, saying good night to Schneider, not looking back at the table where Carver and the three Arabs sat, but hearing Carver's deep voice rolling through the music and the darkness, calling, "Does anyone want an airfield? I'll build it for him. Does anyone want a crown of thorns? I'll build it for him."

There was an old carriage waiting outside the restaurant, its driver dozing and its lights dimmed, and they climbed in and sat close together as the driver clucked to the horse and they rattled slowly back toward town. The breeze had gone down as it did at

228

nine o'clock every night, and there was a small, warm breath of salt off the Mediterranean and every once in a while a jeep rushed past in a whistle of American wind, with its slits of cat's-eye lights cutting a darting, frail, skidding pattern in the darkness, making the creakings and rustlings of the old carriage older and dearer and more private as they sat there holding on to each other in silence.

They got off a block from where Ruth lived because the people from whom she rented her room were intensely moral and did not approve of their boarder going out with soldiers. They walked past the corner where the Italian bombers had killed a hundred and thirty people on a Friday morning the year before, and turned into Ruth's street. From a darkened window came the sound of someone practicing the third movement of the Brahms violin concerto, and Mitchell couldn't help smiling and realizing that one of his strongest memories of Tel Aviv would be the strains of Tchaikovsky and Brahms and Beethoven coming through the opened windows on every street of the town, as the furiously cultured inhabitants practiced runs and cadenzas with never-ending zeal,

All the houses were blacked out, but there was a tiny sliver of light along one of the windows in the third-floor apartment in which Ruth lived, and they stopped in dismay when they saw it.

"She's up," Ruth said.

"Doesn't she ever sleep?" Mitchell asked angrily.

Ruth giggled and kissed him. "She can't stay up forever," Ruth said. "We'll take a little walk and by the time we get back she'll be asleep."

Mitchell took her arm and they walked slowly down toward the sea. Soldiers and whores and fat, placid couples strolled on the concrete walk along the beach, and the Mediterranean heaved gently under the moon and broke in small white rolls of foam against the beach, with a steady, foreign grumble, not like the roar of the Atlantic on the cold northern beaches of home. From a café a hundred yards away came the sound of a string quartet playing a Strauss waltz as though Vienna had never been taken, the waltz never lost to the enemy.

Mitchell and Ruth went down the steps to the beach. A weaving British lance-corporal, coming up the steps with a girl, stiffened and saluted rigidly, his hand quivering with respect for authority, and Mitchell saluted back, and Ruth giggled.

"What're you laughing at?" Mitchell asked, when they had passed the lance-corporal.

"I laugh," Ruth said, "every time I see you salute."

"Why?"

"I don't know why. I just laugh. Forgive me." She took off her shoes and walked barefoot in the sand up to the water's edge. The sea swept softly in from Gibraltar and Tunis and Cyrene and Alexandria and lapped at her toes.

"The Mediterranean," Ruth said. "I hate the Mediterranean."

"What's the matter with it?" Mitchell stared out at the flickering silver path of the moon over the water.

"I was on it," Ruth said, "for thirty-three days. In the hold of a Greek steamer that used to carry cement. Maybe I oughtn't to tell you things like that. You're a tired boy who's been sent here to have a good time so he can go back and fight well. . . ."

"You tell me anything you want to tell me," Mitchell said. "I'll fight all right."

"Should I tell you about Berlin, too? Do you want to hear about Berlin?" Ruth's voice was hard and cold, and somehow a little sardonic, not at all like her voice as he had heard it in the whole week he had known her. The meeting with the journalist at the restaurant had started something stirring within her, something that he hadn't seen before, and he felt that before he left he should see that side of her too.

"Tell me about Berlin," Mitchell said.

"I worked for a newspaper," Ruth said, her toes digging lightly in the sand, "even after the Nazis came in, and I was in love with the man who wrote the Economics column and he was in love with me. . . ."

"Economics?" Mitchell was puzzled.

"The stock exchange. The prophecies and excuses."

"Oh," said Mitchell, trying to picture what a man who wrote stock-exchange tips in Berlin in 1934 would look like.

"He was very gay," Ruth said. "Very young, but elegant, with checkered vests, and he wore a monocle and he lost all his money at the races. His name was Joachim. He used to take me to the races and to the cafés and it used to drive my mother crazy, because if they ever found out I was a Jewish girl out with a Gentile man, they would have sentenced me to death for polluting the blood stream of the German nation, They'd have sent him to a concentration camp, too, but he was always easy and laughing, and he said, 'The important thing is to be brave,' and we were never questioned, and I went to every night club in Berlin, even nights that Goering and Goebbels were in the same room.

"My father was taken to a concentration camp and we decided it was time for me to leave, and Joachim got together all the money he could lay his hands on and gave it to me and I went to Vienna. I was supposed to go to Palestine, if I could, and send for my mother, and for my father, too, if he ever got out of the concentration camp. There was an office in Vienna, and it was filled with refugees from all over Germany, and we collected money to buy transportation and bribe the nations of the world to let some of us in. I slept in the bathtub and talked to sailors and thieves and murderers and crooked shipowners, and finally we got a Greek steamer that was supposed to put in at Genoa and pick us up if we managed to get there. We gave the man 75,000 dollars in cash in advance because that's the only way he would do it, and somehow we got the Austrian government and the Italian government to look the other way, at a price, and they piled us into freight cars, eight hundred of us, and locked us in, men, women and children, lying one on top of another, and the trip took a week and a day to Genoa, and when we got there the ship never arrived. The Greek took the 75,000 dollars and disappeared. There are all kinds of Greeks, and I have nothing against them, but this was a bad one. Then the Italian government sent us back to Vienna and six people committed suicide because they couldn't bear it, and we started in all over again."

Mitchell stared out at the dark line of the sea where it blended in the western distance with the purple of the sky. He tried to think of what it would have been like for his sister and mother if they had been locked into freight cars at Rutland and forced to travel for eight days up to Quebec, say, to wait for an illegal ship to an unknown country. His mother was tall and white-haired and unruffled and pleasant, and his sister was cool and pretty and had some irritating superior mannerisms that she had picked up when she had been foolishly sent for a year to a fancy girls' finishing school in Maryland.

"Let's start home," Ruth said. "If my landlady's still up, we'll shoot her."

They turned their backs on the quiet, white churn of the waves and walked, hand in hand, across the heavy sand of the beach toward the black pile of the buildings of the city.

"Well," Mitchell said, "I want to hear the rest of it."

"No, you don't," Ruth said. "Forgive me for telling you so much. It's too dreary."

"I want to hear," Mitchell said. In the week he had known Ruth, she had been gay and light-hearted, and had helped him to forget the planes spinning out of control and the dying men lying in their frozen blood on the tangled wires and broken aluminum of the Liberator floors, and now he felt as though he owed it to himself and to Ruth to take back with him some of her agony, too, not only the laughter and the tender jokes and the self-effacing merriment. Suddenly, tonight, she had become terribly dear to him, and he felt responsible to her in a way he had never felt responsible to a girl before.

"Tell me," he said.

Ruth shrugged. "Back in Vienna," she said, "we did it all over again. It took two months and the police caught a lot of us, and it meant hiding and running most of the time, but we collected the money again, and we found ourselves another Greek, and this time he turned out to be honest. Or at least as honest as people were to Jews without passports in those days in Europe. We got down to Genoa in only five days this time, and we boarded the steamer at night and they locked the hatch doors on us after we had paid every cent of the money in advance, and we set sail before dawn. The steamer had been built in 1887." They were at the edge of the beach now, and Ruth leaned on Mitchell's shoulder as she put on her shoes. "Nobody can have any idea," Ruth said, as they went up the steps to the concrete walk above, "of what dirt is like until he has been locked into the hold of a fifty-year-old Greek ship with 700 people for over a month. People died every day, and the ship captain would let a rabbi and three other people up on deck at night to perform the burial service and dump the body overboard. The only thing we got to eat was biscuit and canned beef, and there were always worms in everything, even the water we got to drink, and everybody got sores all over their bodies, and the old people got too weak to move and the children wept all day, and the relatives of the people who died screamed a good deal of the time, and it is impossible to tell anyone who was not on that boat what it smelled like, in the middle of the summer in the Mediterranean, with a ventilating system that had been installed in Salonika in 1903."

They turned off the beach walk and climbed slowly up the hill toward the center of the town, past the clean, white, very modernistic apartment houses with gardens and fountains and balconies that faced the sea.

"We were supposed to be let off in Turkey," Ruth went on, her voice almost without inflection and emotion, as though she were reciting from a ledger the business accounts of an importing firm for the year 1850. "And we had given the Greek money to pay off every officer of the port, but something went wrong and we had to put out to sea again, and we started toward Palestine, although the British had patrols along every mile of coastline. But there was no place else to go. People started to get hallucinations about food, and the sailors would sell a sandwich or a lemon for twenty dollars or a bowl of soup for a gold candlestick. And three of the girls couldn't stand it any more and allowed themselves to be taken up every night to be used by the sailors in exchange for regular meals. It was hard to blame them, but they were cursed by the older people as they walked through the crowd each night toward the ladder, and once a Polish woman with two small daughters knocked one of the girls down with an iron pin and tried to stab her with a kitchen knife she had in her bag.''

They turned into Ruth's street and looked up at the window just in time to see the thin edge of light under the blind disappear. They stopped and leaned against a stucco fence in front of a plain, shining white house with cactus plants and a fig tree in the front yard.

''We were on that ship for thirty-five days,'' Ruth said, ''and we came to the coast of Palestine between Haifa and Rehovoth, at night, and maybe someone had been bribed, and maybe it was just lucky, but people were waiting for us in rowboats and in eight hours we were all off. There was one woman, who looked as strong as anyone, a solid, sensible-looking woman, and she seemed cheerful and healthy when she got into the little boat with me, but she suddenly died ten feet off the coast, when the water was so shallow a child could have stepped out and walked ashore. Luckily, it was a dark night, and there were no patrols, and we were taken in cars to a movie theater in a little town near Haifa and put inside. The theater had been playing Betty Grable in 'Campus Confessions,' a musical picture, and there were signs with her in tights and ostrich plumes all over it, and the management had written all over the posters, 'Closed This Week for Repairs.' ''

''I saw the picture,'' Mitchell said. He had seen it one night in Cambridge, and he remembered how some of the boys in the audience had whistled when Miss Grable had kissed the leading man.

''We were all told to keep absolutely quiet,'' Ruth said, ''because the British had patrols going through every town. They must have known something, because that week three men high up in the police force were suspended and investigated. It wasn't so hard to keep the older people quiet, but it was awful with the children, and one man really proposed that a little girl who kept crying all day be strangled for the good of the others. We sat there for a week, whispering, making a noise like thousands of mice in a cupboard, and each night cars would come and some people would be taken away to a collective farm somewhere in the hills. Finally, my turn came and I stayed on that farm for two years, working in the fields and teaching children how to read and write German.

"After two years, the British gave you papers, if you managed to dodge them all that time, and I got my papers and started to work for a canning factory outside Tel Aviv. My father was let out of concentration camp in 1938, but his ship was turned back at Haifa, and he was put back in concentration camp in Germany, and for all I know he's still there now, although he's probably dead.

"Joachim wrote me, and my mother, from Berlin. They became good friends once I was gone, and he brought her food, and on Friday nights would come and watch her light the candles. My mother wrote me he told her he had a girl, but he was dissatisfied, he guessed he'd gotten the taste for Jewish girls." Ruth smiled slightly, thinking of the boy with the checkered vest and the monocle many years ago, and Mitchell wondered if he had dropped a bomb near the market-analyzer somewhere in Africa, or in Sicily or Italy.

"He helped my mother get out of Germany," Ruth went on, staring up at the window of her home, which was now secure and dark. "She came out in a Portuguese boat, and I heard she was coming and I was on the shore at Haifa Harbor when it came in. But the British wouldn't let it dock, and after six days they insisted that it turn back, and there were thousands of people on the shore, relatives and friends of the people on the boat, and the worst sound I've ever heard in the world was the sound those people on the shore made when the boat turned around and started to steam toward the Haifa breakwater. But the boat never got out of the harbor." Ruth paused and licked her lips, and spoke very matter-of-factly. "There was an explosion. We saw the puff of dirty black smoke first, then a long time later we heard the noise, and people on shore were screaming and laughing and crying. Then there was fire and the boat started to go down, and everybody grabbed at any kind of boat they could find and started out toward the steamer, and there were people who couldn't find boats who just jumped into the water, clothes and all, and started to swim, and nobody ever found out how many people drowned that way, because bodies were washed in to shore for three weeks afterward. My mother was drowned and five hundred other people on the boat, but seven hundred were saved, and then the British had to let them in, and I suppose that's what the people who set the bomb figured would happen. Some people would die, but some would be saved. If the boat went back to Europe, everybody would be killed. Of course, they bungled it somewhat, and they didn't figure on the fire, and they thought the boat would sink more slowly and only a few people would be killed, but even so it was a pretty fair bargain.'' Ruth lit a cigarette calmly and held the light for Mitchell. "My mother was washed up a week later, and at least her grave is in Palestine. I couldn't tell my father she was dead, so when I wrote to him in concentration camp, I forged letters from my mother, because I had a lot of her letters and I learned how to make good copies. Even now, through the Red Cross, I write him notes in my mother's handwriting, and if he's alive he thinks my mother is living on a farm with a family near Rehovoth.''

Ruth pulled at her cigarette and inhaled deeply and in the increased glow Mitchell looked at her and thought again, as he'd thought so many times before, that it was a wonderful and terrible thing that the human race covered its scars so completely, so that Ruth, standing there, with the torture and smuggling and burning and drowning and hiding and dying behind her, looked, with her lipstick and fluffy, cleverly combed hair, and her soft, fragile, print dress, like any one of a thousand girls at a dance in America, with nothing more behind them than a weekly allowance from father, and two proms a season at New Haven or Cambridge.

"Ah," Ruth said, throwing her cigarette away, "she must be asleep by now. Come." She smiled at him, dry-eyed and pleasant, and took his hand, and they walked quietly up through the dim hallways to the apartment in which she lived. She opened the door silently and waved him in, her finger to her lips, and when they were safely in her room, with the door locked behind them, she giggled like a child who has pulled some sly trick on the grown-up world, then kissed him hungrily in the dark room, and whispered, "Mitchell, Mitchell," making the name somehow foreign and tender by the way she said it.

He held her tight, but she pulled away. "Not yet, Lieutenant," she said, grinning, "not yet." She put on a light and went over to a chest of drawers in a corner and started to rummage under some scarves. "I have something for you. Sit down and wait, like a polite boy."

Mitchell sat on the low daybed, blinking in the light. The room was small and painted white and very clean. There was a large piece of Egyptian batik in red and dark green on the wall over the bed and there were three photographs on a dressing table. Mitchell looked at the photographs—a round, smiling woman, with a healthy, simple face, Ruth's mother, the picture taken long before the morning when the ship went down in Haifa Harbor. The other two photographs were of men. There was a man who looked like Ruth, obviously her father, a studious, humorous, rather weak face, with frail, delicate bones and shy, childish eyes. And there was the young man in the checkered vest, slender and laughing and proud of himself, with the monocle in his eye like a burlesque of a German general or a British actor.

"Here." Ruth came over to him and sat down beside him. She had a soft chamois bag, and there was a little rich clinking as she put it in his hand. "To take with you," she said.

Mitchell slowly opened the bag. A heavy silver medal on a chain, glittering dully in the lamplight, fell into his hand. Ruth was crouched on her knees on the couch beside him, looking anxiously at his face to see if her present would meet with favor. Mitchell turned it over. It was a Saint Christopher, old and irregular, of heavy silver, with the Saint awkward and angular and archaic and very religious in the loving workmanship of a silversmith who had died a long time before.

"It's for voyages," Ruth said, hurriedly. "For a navigator, I thought, it might be quite—quite useful. . . ." She smiled uncertainly at him. "Of course," she said, "it is not in my religion, but I don't think it would do any harm to give it to you. That's why I went to Jerusalem. Something like this, something holy, might have a tendency to be more effective if it comes from Jerusalem, don't you think?"

"Of course," Mitchell said. "It's bound to be."

"Will you wear it?" Ruth glanced quickly and shyly at him, sitting there, dangling the medal on its chain.

"All the time," Mitchell said. "Day and night, every mission, every jeep-ride, year in, year out."

"May I put it on for you?"

Mitchell opened his collar and gave the medal to Ruth. She stood up and he bowed his head and she slipped it on, then leaned over and kissed the back of his neck where the chain lay against the flesh.

She stepped back. "Now," she said matter-of-factly. "There we are." She went over to the lamp. "We don't need this any more." She put the light out and went over to the window and threw back the blackout blinds, and a faint breeze carrying salt and the scent of gardens came into the room. She stood at the window, looking out, and Mitchell got up and crossed over to her, feeling the unfamiliar cool jewelry of the medal dangling against his chest. He stood behind her, silently, holding her lightly, looking out over the city. The white buildings shone in the heavy moonlight machined and modern and Biblical all at once, and from the west came the faint sound of the sea. Mitchell wanted to tell her that he would remember her, remember everything about her, her drowned mother and imprisoned father, her old, courageous lover, drinking champagne with her at the Nazi cafés; he wanted to tell her that he would remember the dealings with the Greek sailor and the hold of the ship that had been built in 1887 and the dying Jews buying a lemon with a gold candlestick; he wanted to tell her that flying over the Germans in Europe or watching the first snow fall at Stowe he would remember the small boat grating on the sand in the darkness outside Rehovoth and the week in the closed movie theater with the British patrols outside; he wanted to tell her that the terror and courage would not be forgotten, but he didn't know how to say it, and besides, being honest with himself, he knew it would be difficult to remember, and finally, back in Vermont, it would blur and cloud over and seem unreal as a story in a child's book, read many years ago and now almost forgotten. He held her more tightly, but he said nothing.

"There he is," Ruth said, her voice casual and unimpressed. "See him standing down there next to the house with the picket gate. . . ."

Mitchell looked over Ruth's shoulder. Down on the street, thirty yards from the entrance of Ruth's house, was a small dark figure, almost completely lost in shadow.

"Ali Khazen," Ruth said. "He comes and waits outside my window. Ah . . ." she sighed, "I suppose finally he'll kill me."

She turned away from the window and led him back to the couch across the strip of moonlight that divided the room. She looked up at him gravely, then suddenly pushed him gently down to the couch and fell beside him, holding on to him. She held him and kissed his cheek and chuckled a little. "Now, Lieutenant," she said, "tell me about Vermont."

# Walking Wounded

He wondered what had happened to the curtains. He lay stiffly on the bed, listening, with the old, irritated tightening of the nerves, to the wild and grating hubbub of the Cairo street outside his window, the insane wailing of newsboys, the everlasting iron drip of garry-horses' hooves, the pained yelps of peddlers. The sun, bright and hurtful as hot nickel, cut in through the open windows. On the floor lay the curtains, torn, with bits of cord still running from them to the top of the windows, like a ruptured spider web.

"What happened to the curtains?" he asked. His voice felt dry and sandy in his throat, and the right side of his head began to ache.

Mac was shaving at the washstand. His beard made a crinkly, Spartan sound against the razor. "Last night," Mac said, without turning. "In the excitement."

"What excitement?"

"You pulled the curtains down."

"Why?"

Mac shaved quietly and intently around the short, soldierly mustache. "Don't know," he said. "Either you wanted to throw me out, or throw yourself out, or just tear down the curtains."

"Oh, God!"

Mac scrubbed his face with water. "Pretty drunk, Peter," he said.

"What else did I do?"

"Two lieutenants and a major. In the lounge. Ten minutes of insults."

"A major! Christ!" Peter closed his eyes.

"I think you hit a lieutenant." Mac's voice was muffled in a towel. "Anyway, you hit something. Your hand's all cut up."

Peter opened his eyes and looked at his hand. Across the back of it there was a wide, ugly wound, just beginning to puff up

238

around the edges. As he looked at it, he realized that it was hurting him.

"I poured iodine over it," Mac said. "You won't die."

"Thanks." Peter let his hand drop, licked his dry lips. "What did I say to the major?"

" 'Base wallah.' 'Imperial vulture.' 'Gezira bloodsucker.' 'Headquarters hangman.' "

"That's enough." The right side of Peter's head hurt very strongly for a moment.

"You were a little unfair," Mac said calmly. "He was a nice type. Been in the desert three years. Just come back from Sicily with dysentery. Wounded twice. Been attached to headquarters four days."

"Oh, Christ," Peter said. "Oh, Christ."

The room was silent as Mac put on his shirt and combed his hair.

"Get his name?" Peter asked finally.

"Major Robert Lewis. Might be a good idea to say good morning."

"How about the lieutenants?"

Mac took out his notebook. "MacIntyre and Clark," he read. "They await your pleasure."

Peter sat up and swung his legs over the side of the bed. The room faded and glittered for a moment, and he had to hold on to the bed when he stood up.

"Some day, soon," he said, "I have to stop drinking."

"A little whisky," Mac said kindly, "is good for the soul. Anything I can do for you?"

"No, thanks."

Mac stood at the door.

"Mac . . ."

"Yes, Captain . . . ?" Tiny, astringent, helpful mockery in the title.

"Mac, this is the first time anything like this ever happened to me."

"I know," Mac said softly. He went quietly out of the room.

Peter walked slowly over to the wash basin, looked at himself in the mirror. The familiar long, thin face, the uneven dotted crenelation of his wound across his forehead, the strange dark mark in the eye that had been blind for three weeks, all seeming to tremble slightly now in the bitter sunlight, as it had trembled for two months.

He shaved carefully and went to take a shower. He came back, feeling better, and put on fresh clothes. He switched his tabs with the three pips to his clean shirt, looking absently and automatically to see if there was any lipstick on them. Three and a half years ago, at Arras, there had been lipstick one morning, and he had walked around all day long, ignorant, wondering why smiles hid on sergeants' lips.

Then he went down to apologize to the major.

He sat at his desk, sweating. The heat of Egypt was like the inside of a balloon. The balloon was being constantly filled; the pressure getting greater and greater. Typewriters clicked dryly in the swelling air, and flies, the true owners of Egypt, whirled cleverly and maliciously before his eyes.

Sergeant Brown, his thick glasses clouded with sweat, clumped in and put a stack of papers on his desk, clumped out again. The back of Sergeant Brown's shirt was soaked where he had been pressing against the back of a chair, and sweat ran in trickles down his infantryman legs to the heavy wool socks and gaiters.

Peter stared at the stack of papers. Ruled forms and tiny and intricate notations that had to be gone over slowly, corrected, signed.

Outside, a donkey brayed painfully. It sounded like an immense wooden machine in agony, wood grating against wood, incredibly loud. It made the little, paper-stacked room seem hotter than ever.

Peter reread the letter he had received that morning from Italy. " . . . I am taking the liberty of answering your letter to Col. Sands, who was badly wounded last week. I am afraid there is nothing we can do about requesting your being posted to this regiment, as there is no provision in our establishment for medically graded officers."

The donkey brayed again outside. It sounded like the death of all the animals of Egypt on this hot morning.

Peter stared at the papers on his desk. Three flies danced over them, lighted, swept off. The typewriters rattled flatly in the heat. He took the top paper off the pile, looked at it. The figures leapt and wavered in the heat, and a drop of sweat fell from his forehead and mistily covered a 3, a 7, an 8. His hands glistened in little sick beads, and the paper felt slippery under his fingers. Hobnails sounded on the marble floor in the corridor, ostentatious and over-military among the clerks and filing cabinets. His throat burned dryly with the fifteenth cigarette of the morning.

He stood up jerkily and took his hat and went out. In the corridor he passed Mrs. Burroughs. She was a tall, full-bodied girl who wore flowered prints and always seemed to manage silk stockings. She was going home to England to divorce her husband, who was a lieutenant in India. She was going to marry an American Air-Force major who had been switched to London from Cairo. She was very pretty and she had a soft, hesitant voice, and her bosom was always oppressively soft and noticeable under the flowered prints.

She smiled at him, hesitant, polite, gentle. She had two rosebuds clasped in her dark hair. "Good morning," she said, stopping, her voice cool, shy, inviting in the drab corridor. She always tried to stop him, talk to him.

"Good morning," Peter said stiffly. He never could look squarely at her. He looked down. No silk stockings this morning. The pretty legs bare, the skin firm and creamy. He had a sudden, hateful vision of Mrs. Burroughs landing in London, running to be crushed in the arms of the American major in the press of Waterloo Station, her eyes bright with tears of love and gratitude, her husband, used and forgotten, in India. . . .

"I'm going to Groppi's," he heard himself say, surprisingly. "Tea. Would you like to join me?"

"Sorry," Mrs. Burroughs said, her voice sounding genuinely sorry. "So much work. Some other time. I'd be delighted. . . ."

Peter nodded awkwardly, went out. He hated Mrs. Burroughs.

The street was full of heat, beggars, dirt, children with fly-eaten eyes, roaring army lorries. He put on his hat, feeling his forehead, wet and warm, rebel under the wool. A drunken New Zealander, at eleven o'clock in the morning, wobbled sorrowfully in the full glare of the sun, hatless, senseless, reft of dignity, 7,000 miles from his green and ordered island.

Groppi's was cooler, dark and shaded. The red-fezzed waiters in the long white gaballiehs moved quietly through the pleasant gloom. Two American sergeants with gunners' wings on their shirts solemnly were drinking two ice-cream sodas apiece.

Peter had tea and read the morning paper. The birth rate had gone up in England, and an American magazine had suggested that Princess Elizabeth marry an American. The *Egyptian Mail* reprinted it with approval in a flood of Anglo-American feeling. After six years, somebody said in Parliament, men in the forces were to be sent home. The Russians were pouring across the Dnieper. Peter always saved the Russian news for last. Every step the Russians took was that much nearer home, nearer the rugged and manly weather of Scotland, near Anne. . . .

He tried to think of Anne, what she looked like, what her skin felt like. He looked up at the ceiling and half-closed his eyes to shut out the tea and ice-cream shop, to close out Egypt, summer, war, army, distance, absence, close out everything but his wife. But he couldn't remember what she looked like. He remembered the dress she wore when they were married and the inn they'd stayed at after Dunkirk and what they'd played at the concert the last night in London, and he remembered that he loved her. But her face, the sound of her voice . . . lost. She refused to have photographs taken of her. Some whim or female superstition, far away in England. . . .

He paid and went out and started back to his office. But when he stood in front of the peeling, ornately balconied, sand-bagged building and thought of the small, hot office, the endless papers, the sweat and hobnails, he couldn't go in. He turned and walked slowly down the street. He looked at his watch. Still an hour before the bars opened. He walked on the shady side, erect and soldierly, slowly, like a man with a grave purpose. A horribly dirty woman with a horribly dirty child, as dirty and street-worn as only Egyptians can be, followed him, whining, for half a block. Peter didn't walk any faster, although he felt his nerves jerking at the sound of the woman's voice.

The woman left him finally, and he walked deliberately through the crowded streets stopping from time to time to peer into shop windows. French perfume, women's dresses, mangoes, books, photographs, his mind recorded heavily. He went into the photographer's and had his picture taken, refusing to smile, looking soberly square into the camera, intimidating the photographer. He would send the picture to Anne. Three years. How long could a woman be expected to remember a man? His face would stare solemnly at her morning, noon, and night, crying, "Remember me, remember your husband. . . ."

Out in the street again he resumed his grave pacing down the shady side of the street. Fifteen minutes more and the bars would open. He grinned crookedly to himself as he thought of his pose before the camera, frozen Scotch passion grimly and puritanically peering across three years and two oceans. Anne would probably giggle at the absurdly stern, accusing face.

"Officer, wanna lady, wanna lady?"

Peter looked down. A tiny, filthy ten-year-old boy, barefooted, in a torn, bag-like single garment, was smiling up at him conspiratorially, pulling at his blouse.

"French lady," the boy whispered wickedly. "Fine French lady."

Peter stared at him disbelievingly, then broke into a roar of laughter. The boy, after a moment of doubt, also laughed.

"No, thank you, sir," Peter said.

The boy shrugged, grinned up at him. "Officer," he said, "cigarette?"

Peter gave him a cigarette and lit it for him, and the boy darted off, to try the French lady on a Polish corporal.


The bar had a nice beery smell and was dark and cool and the bartender drew eight glasses at a time, letting the foam settle whitely on the glass rims.

"The two lieutenants," Peter was saying, "were a little stuffy, but the major was fine."

"I knew he would be," Mac said. "I talked to him last night."

"I had breakfast with him"—Peter waved for two more beers—"and he said he guessed he'd be doing the same thing himself if he had to hang around this town five months."

Mac comfortably drained his beer.

"The birth rate in England," Peter said, "has gone up. I read it in the *Mail* this morning. There're three million Englishmen out of the country and the birth rate's rocketing. . . ." He heard his own voice loud and angry and humorless. "How in the name of God do they dare print things like that?" He saw Mac grinning widely, but he couldn't stop. "Who're the fathers? Where're the fathers? Bloody damned newspaper!"

"My," Mac said, "you have it bad today."

Suddenly Peter realized that Mac, placid and tolerant, was bearing a great deal of the burden of Peter's nerves.

"Mac," he said quietly, "forgive me."

"Uh?" Mac looked at him, surprised.

"Wailing Wall Chrome. Agony, Cairo division." Peter shook his head in disgust. "I keep feeding it to you seven days a week."

"Oh, shut up. I've lived with lots worse."

"Any time I get on your nerves, sing out, will you?"

"Sure thing. Drink your beer." Mac was embarrassed.

"I must be going a little crazy." Peter looked at his hands, which had taken to trembling in the last few months. The cigarette jerked minutely between his fingers, in a spasmodic rhythm. "This town. When I was with the regiment . . . Oh, hell . . . ." The truth was that out in the desert, under the guns, on a pint of water a day, and the sudden air often dire with Stukas, he had been much happier. There were no women in the desert, no reminders of a civilized and normal life. There was clean, sterile sand, the noise of armor, thousands of grumbling, good-humored men intimate with an equal death, and above all there was the sense of immense and hardy effort and accomplishment, as first they had held the Afrika Corps and then driven it back. Cairo then had been a beautiful town, two days at a time, a hot bath and unlimited Scotch, and sweet, clean sheets and relief from the guns. But now, under the dry flood of paper, under the stiffness and pettiness of headquarters politics, under the cheap weight of men who had clung to soft jobs for three years, with the streets full of bare-legged girls, with the war on another continent a thousand miles away . . .

Now the regiment, what was left of it, was broken up. Most of them were in graves on the road to Tunis, others were in hospitals, the rest scattered among other units, after the four years that had started in France. Mac, who had been his platoon sergeant at Arras, calmly instructing the untrained men how to load and fire the guns they had never used before, then taking them out into the fresh May fields of France hunting for parachutists. Himself, who had crawled through the German lines to Dunkirk, who had entered Tripoli the first hour, who had blown up in the jeep outside Mareth, with his driver dead in the air beside him . . . Now, both of them clerks in small offices, chained to paper and civil servants.

"Six years," he said, "some bloody MP said we'd be sent home after six years. What do you think a woman thinks when she reads that she'll get her man back in only six years?"

"Always remember," Mac grinned, "what Monty said. 'The war can't last more than seven years. We'll run out of paper.' "

"If only I could get back to England," Peter said, "and sleep with my wife for two nights, everything would be all right. Just two nights."

Mac sighed. He was a quiet, efficient, small, matter-of-fact man, noticeably graying, and sighing was strange and incongruous to him. "Peter," he said, "can I talk plainly?"

Peter nodded.

"Peter, you ought to get yourself a girl."

They sat in silence. Peter played somberly with his beer. In France, even though he had just been married, he had been the gay young officer. Handsome and debonair, he had played joyfully and thoughtlessly with the pretty ladies of the country towns at which he'd been stationed, and in Paris, when he'd had a month there, a charming, beautifully dressed wife of a French captain stationed in Algiers.

But when he'd got back to England with the gray-faced remnants of his regiment, after the hideous, bloody days of the break-through, and had taken his wife silently into his arms, all frivolity, all smallness and lack of faith had seemed wanton and irreligious in the face of so much ruin, such agony. Leaving England for Africa, he had felt that behind him he had to leave the best part of his life orderly and decent.

"Maybe," he said to Mac, "Maybe . . ."

"A man's got to be practical," Mac said. "Three years. Oh, my God!"

Peter had to smile at the drastic expression on the practical man's face.

"You'll just explode," Mac said, "and blow away."

Peter laughed loudly, nervously. "Whisky," he said, "provides certain compensations."

"Whisky," Mac said grimly, "will send you home a doddering wreck. You'll do no one any good that way."

"Maybe. Maybe . . ." Peter shrugged. "Anyway, I hate these women out here. Having the best time of their lives. Ugly, impossible girls no one would ever look at in peacetime, just because there are a hundred men for every woman . . . Snobbish, overconfident . . . Bitches, all of them. A man has to sacrifice all decent, male pride to chase after one of these. . . ." He talked faster and faster, all the bitter observation of the past years flooding to his tongue. "They demand abasement, homage, the ugliest, horrible and meanest of them. Women," he said, "have been among the most horrible of the war's casualties. All humility's gone, all normal value, all friendship. They're man-greedy. They're profiteering on the war, like the worst usurer and manufacturer of machine tools, except that their profits are lieutenants and generals, not cash. After the war," he said, "we should have rehabilitation hospitals for women who have been in troop areas, just like the hospitals for maimed men, to teach them how to live normal lives again. . . ."

Mac was laughing by now, helplessly, into his beer. "Enough," he said. "Enough, John Knox! All I wanted to say is that I have a date tonight, and my girl has a friend who's just come from Jerusalem, and it might do you a world of good just to have dinner with a woman for once. Do you want to go?"

Peter flushed, looked down at the beer-ringed table. "I won't even know how to talk to a woman any more."

"Do you want to go?"

Peter opened his mouth, closed it. "All right," he said, "All right."

"Jerusalem is nice enough . . ." It was on the dance floor at the Auberge des Pyramides, under the stars, with the three great tombs standing huge and a rebuke to time in the darkness just outside the lights and the music. Joyce was talking as they went slowly and painfully around the dance floor. "The city's clean, and the King David's an amusing hotel, but the people're simply dreadful." She had a brittle, drawling voice, pitched just high enough so that everyone nearby could hear clearly what she was saying. "There," she said brightly, as Peter managed a full turn, "we're doing much better, aren't we?"

"Yes," Peter said, sweating in the heavy Nile heat, only slightly tempered by night, as he tried to concentrate on the beat of the music. Joyce's voice distracted him and put him off, and somehow she never seemed to stop talking. She worked in the consular service, and by nine-thirty Peter had a full store of information on the doings of the consulate in Jerusalem for the last year and a half, at which time Joyce had come out from England. He had hardly said a word all night, stammering, half-finishing sentences, suffering, feeling like the clumsiest farmer. Still, she was pretty, most desirable in a full white evening gown ("We always dress in Jerusalem"), with full, sleek shoulders bare and daring under the gay lights.

"That's King Farouk. . . ." For the first time all evening her voice dropped a bit. "Isn't it?"

Peter looked. "Yes," he said.

"Isn't he attractive? What an original beard!"

Peter looked at King Farouk. "He looks like a fat, self-satisfied young man," Peter said, the first full sentence he had got out all evening. "And I understand he grew the beard because he has a terrible case of acne."

"Dance around the edge of the dance floor," Joyce whispered. "I'd like people to see me."

Dutifully and heavily Peter danced around the edge of the floor until the music stopped. He followed Joyce to the table. Joyce smiled vivaciously at seven or eight officers seated at various tables throughout the establishment.

"It's amazing," she said, brightly and loudly, "how many men I know in Cairo." They sat down. There was an awful silence while Peter wondered where in the name of God Mac was, and his girl, and Joyce smiled prettily first at one table, then another.

"Are you married?" Peter heard his voice, crooked and rasping, asking inexplicably. For the first time that evening Joyce gave him her undivided attention.

"Why," she said, looking at him queerly and coldly, "what a strange question!"

"It's just that there's a girl around my office," Peter said, almost dazedly. "Married to a lieutenant in India. Marrying an American major in London . . ." The expression on Joyce's face became more and more strained. "I don't know what made me think of her," Peter said lamely.

"No," Joyce said coldly, "I'm not married."

"I am," Peter said, despairingly.

"Really." Joyce smiled automatically at a colonel four tables away.

"My wife," said Peter, not knowing why he was talking, feeling his tongue too loose from the drinking that had been continuous since six that evening, "my wife is a woman of admirable character, although I can't remember what she looks like. Her name is Anne. She works for the Air Ministry in Manchester. After Dunkirk, I was stationed on the beach at Dover for five months. I used to manage to get away weekends. We'd just stay in one room and just look at each other. After France . . . I felt as though my wife had healed me of a dreadful disease. She healed me of mud and death and friends dying on all sides. She's most beautiful, but I don't remember what she looks like. She's very calm and simple and her voice is low, although I don't remember that, either. I sent her my photograph today. Six years is too long for a man to expect a woman to remember him. Someone ought to tell Parliament that. . . Don't you think?"

Joyce was staring at him, her mouth frozen to one side. "Yes," she said.

"If I could only see her for two nights . . ." Well, finally, the thought crossed his consciousness, the lady from Jerusalem is listening to me. "Right before I came out here, I was moved to another beach. It was raining. Autumn and miserable and barbed wire at the high-tide marks and mines all over the beaches. I called her long-distance and she told me she had a week and asked me if she should come down. I told her no. It was so miserable. Cheap little shacks waiting for the Germans in the rain. I knew we were leaving for Africa and I didn't want our last days together to be dreary, in that abominable place. I told her no, but she said, 'You wait right there. I'm coming down tonight.'" Suddenly, above the dance music in the Valley of the Nile, Peter remembered what his wife's voice had sounded like, merry and sensual and confidently commanding over the faulty wires on that autumn night on a wet beach on the English Channel. "She came down and we had the week together, and the rain and the barbed wire made no difference at all. I've never been so gay, and it was early in the war, and we always had a coal fire and hot rum and lovely heavy breakfasts, with the curtains still drawn. And never a tear when she left. And I started for Africa singing in my heart." He was talking straight ahead to the Pyramids in the ancient desert darkness now, not to the silly, bare-shouldered girl across the table. "I haven't heard from her in two months. Not a letter in two months." He shrugged. "After the war," he said, "I'm going to go in for politics. I'm going to stand for Parliament. There must be somebody in Parliament who knows what a war is like, who knows that one war is enough, six years is too much . . ."

"Why, Joyce, how nice!" It was the colonel, standing gallantly at the table. "Dance?"

Joyce looked doubtfully at Peter. Peter stood up, a little unsteadily. "Delighted," he said ambiguously. Without looking at Peter, Joyce went off with the colonel, smiling impartially at dozens of officers in Sam Browne belts as she danced on the edge of the floor.

Peter hazily watched the flashing plump white dress among the brave khaki and brass pips. He passed his hand over his eyes, thinking, as he remembered his outburst, God, I must be going crazy.

He saw a captain step in and dance with Joyce, then an American major. "The world," he said softly to himself, "is full of American majors." He laughed gently to himself, stood up, walked slowly out of the night club. Outside, with the music thin and distant in his ears, the Pyramids loomed, crumbling in the darkness, in memory of the unremembered dead.

He got into a cab and started for Cairo.

When the cab got to Gezira Island, he tapped the driver on the shoulder. "Sporting Club," he said.

The old, wheezing taxi laboriously turned. "I need a drink," Peter told himself seriously. "I need a drink very badly." He thought of old Mac caught there with two girls and the tremendous bill. He felt bad about it, but he'd pay his share, although it would mean considerably less drinking for the rest of the month. But he couldn't stay with that damned girl. The truth was he couldn't stay with any girl. Anne, unphotographed, in Manchester . . . Still, she should write more often than once every two months. . . .

The bar at Gezira was still open. There were some South Africans and some American fliers lounging against it. One of the American fliers was singing, in a soft Southern voice, "Oh, Susannah, don't you cry for me . . ."

"Scotch," Peter said to the bartender, feeling for the first time that evening a cessation of loneliness, his constant climate.

"Fo' Ah'm gawn't' Alabama, with mah banjo on mah knee . . ." the American pilot sang sweetly and happily.

"Gin and lime," said one of the South Africans, a gigantic captain with huge, bare arms whom the others called Lee. "Gin and lime all around." He turned to Peter. "What're you drinking, Captain?"

"I've ordered, thanks." Peter smiled at him.

"Man says he's ordered," the American pilot sang. "What do you know about that? British captain says he's ordered. Order again and order again, oh, Captain, order again. . . ."

The bartender put two Scotches in front of Peter, grinning. The huge South African captain poured it all into one glass. They lifted their glasses.

"To South Africa," one of the Americans said.

They drank.

"To sergeants." The American who had been singing grinned at a large South African lieutenant with a mustache. The lieutenant looked around him uneasily. "Quiet, please," he said. "I'll be in jail five years."

"This gentleman looks like a gentleman," Lee put his arm around the lieutenant with the mustache. "Doesn't he?"

"Yes," said Peter.

"Jail," said the lieutenant with the mustache.

"He's not a gentleman. He is a sergeant. He is my bloody sergeant from my bloody company."

"Ten years," said the lieutenant with the mustache.

"We're all AWOL, Sergeant Monks, lieutenant for the evening, Lieutenant Fredericks . . ." He waved to a slightly smaller red-headed South African down the bar. "And myself. We're farmers. Independent men. When the bloody O.C. said 'no leaves,' we said farewell. Sixty miles out on the desert for three weeks. Miserable little clerk of an O.C. Sergeant, I said, here's a pip. Take off those bloody stripes. We wish to show you the glories of Shepheard's and Gezira, so that you can come back and dazzle the poor bastards in the other ranks with tales of the high life of Cairo."

"I've been talking to brigadiers all afternoon and evening," Monks complained. "Wearing on the nerves."

"If the O.C. shows up, it's all taped," Lee said. "I grab Monks by one arm, Freddy grabs him by the other. 'We've just arrested the bugger, sir,' we say. 'Impersonating an officer.' ''

"Ten years," Monks said, grinning. "This round is on me."

Peter laughed. He lifted his glass. "To sergeants everywhere." They all drank.

"On my right," said Lee, "is the American Air Force."

The American Air Force raised its glasses at Peter and the pilot who sang started in on "Chattanooga Choo-choo." There were two lieutenants and a twenty-four-year-old major.

"The American Air Force is going home," said Lee. "Their tour is over. Home by way of England. The infantry's tour is never over. Oh, the poor, stinking, bloody infantry, their tour is never over . . ."

"Unskilled labor," one of the pilots said calmly. "We're delicate and highly sensitive mechanisms. We are war-weary. Our Schneiders are low as an Egyptian whore. We've bombed too many places. We've seen too much flak. We are lopsided from wearing ribbons. We are going home now to instruct the young how to shoot."

"I am going home to play with my wife," the twenty-four-year-old major said soberly.

"The infantry is not under the same Awful Strain," said the pilot who had been singing. "All they have to do is walk in and be shot. Their nerves are not stretched to the breaking point like ours. Captain," he said, leaning back and talking to Peter, "you look a little war-weary yourself."

"I'm pretty war-weary," Peter said.

"He looks sensitive," the major said. "He looks fine and sensitive enough to be at least a navigator. He looks like Hamlet on a rough night."

"I was in the tanks," Peter said.

"It's possible," said the major, "to get war-weary in a tank, too, I suppose."

"It's possible," Peter said, grinning.

" . . . breakfast in Carolina . . ." sang the musical pilot.

"When're you leaving for home?" Peter asked.

"6 A.M. tomorrow. 0600 hours, as they say in the army," said the major.

"Five or six glorious days in London among our brave English Allies and cousins," said the other pilot, "and then the Stork Club, the Harvard-Yale football game, all the blonde, full-bosomed, ribbon-conscious, lascivious American girls . . ."

"London," said Peter. "I wish I were going with you."

"Come along," said the major expansively. "We have a nice

250

empty Liberator. Pleased to have you. Closer relations with our British comrades. Merely be at the airport at 0600 hours, as they say in the army.''

"Did you see," asked the singing pilot, "in the *Mail* today? Some idiot wants Princess Elizabeth to marry an American.''

"Excellent idea,'' said the major. "Some upstanding representative citizen of the Republic. Post-war planning on all fronts. My nomination for Prince Escort is Maxie Rosenbloom.''

Everyone considered the suggestion gravely.

"You could do worse,'' the pilot said.

"Infusion of sturdy American stock into an aging dynasty,'' the major said. "The issue would be strongly built, with good left hands. . . .''

"Do you mean it?'' Peter asked. "You really could take me?''

"Delighted,'' the major said.

The singing pilot started in on "All Alone,'' and everyone but Peter joined him. Peter stared unseeingly at the glasses and bottles behind the bar. In three days he could be home. Three days and he could walk into Anne's room, quietly, unannounced, smiling a little tremulously as she looked up unsuspectingly. Maybe it was possible. He had had no leave since he'd come to Africa, except for two weeks' convalescence. He could go immediately to Colonel Foster's apartment, explain to him. Colonel Foster liked him, was very sympathetic. If he gave him a written order, releasing him from duty for twenty-one days, he, Peter, would undertake to get transportation back. Somehow, somehow . . . He would take all the responsibility himself. He was sure that Colonel Foster, who was a good soul, would do it.

Peter stood up straight. He spoke to the American major. "Perhaps I'll see you at six o'clock.''

"Fine,'' the major said heartily. "It's going to be a great trip. We're loaded with Scotch.'' He waved as Peter turned and left the bar.

"All alone, by the telephone . . .'' the wailing, mocking voices quavered in the night. Peter got into a taxicab and gave Colonel Foster's address.

He felt he was trembling. He closed his eyes and leaned back. It was all absolutely possible. England was only three days away. Two weeks there and the desert and the guns and the dying and ruled paper and heat and loneliness and insane expanding tension would disappear. He could face the rest of the war calmly, knowing that he would not explode, would not lose his reason. It was possible. Men were going home to their wives. That American major. All so cheerful and matter-of-fact about it. England in three days, after the three years . . . Colonel Foster would most certainly say yes. Peter was sure of it as the taxi drove up to the dark building where Colonel Foster lived. Peter paid the driver and looked up. The colonel's window was alight, the only one in the entire building. Peter felt his breath coming fast. It was a symbol, an omen. The man was awake. His friend, who could give him England tonight with five strokes of a pen, by luck was wakeful in the quiet night, when all the rest of the city slept around him. It would be irregular, and Colonel Foster would be running some risk, but he had rank enough and was independent enough to take the chance. . . .

Peter rang the night-bell to the side of the locked doors of the apartment building. Far in the depths of the sleeping stone and brick, a forlorn and distant bell sang weirdly.

As he waited for the hall-boy to open the doors, Peter hastily rehearsed his story. No leave in three years. The tension getting worse and worse. Medically graded, no chance of getting to an active unit. Regiment disbanded. Work deteriorating. Given to sudden fits of temper and what could only be described as melancholia, although a doctor wouldn't believe it until it was too late. He knew the British Army couldn't provide transportation, but here were these Americans with an empty Liberator. He'd get back somehow.

As he went over it, in the darkness, with the faraway bell sounding as though it were ringing at the bottom of a troubled sea, Peter was sure the logic was irrefutable; Foster couldn't refuse.

When the hall-boy finally opened the door, Peter sprang past him, raced up the steps, too impatient to take the elevator.

He was panting when he rang Colonel Foster's bell, and the sweat was streaming down the sides of his face. He rang the bell sharply, twice. He heard his breath whistling into his lungs, and he tried to compose himself, so that Colonel Foster would think him absolutely calm, absolutely lucid. . . .

The door opened. The figure at the door was silhouetted against the yellowish light behind it.

"Colonel," Peter said, panting, "I'm so glad you're up. I must talk to you. I hate to disturb you, but . . ."

"Come in." The door was opened wider and Peter strode down the hall, into the living room. He heard the door close and turned around. "I . . . ." he began. He stopped. The man who was standing there was not Colonel Foster. It was a large, red-faced man, bald, in a tattered red bathrobe. He had a mustache and tired eyes and he was holding a book in his hand. Peter looked at the book. *The Poems of Robert Browning*.

The man stood there, waiting, pulling his bathrobe a little tighter, a curious little smile on his weary face.

"I . . . I saw the light, sir," Peter said. "I thought Colonel Foster would be up and I took the liberty of . . . I had some business with . . ."

"Colonel Foster doesn't live here," the man said. His voice was clipped and military, but tired, aging. "He moved out a week ago."

"Oh," Peter said. He suddenly stopped sweating. He swallowed, made a conscious effort to speak quietly. "Do you know where he lives, sir?"

"I'm afraid not. Is there anything I can do, Captain? I'm Colonel Gaines." He smiled, false teeth above the old robe. "That's why when you said Colonel, at the door, I . . . ."

"No, sir," Peter said. "Nothing, sir. I'm dreadfully sorry. This time of night . . . ."

"Oh, that's all right." The man waved a little embarrassedly. "I never go to sleep. I was reading."

"Well . . . Thank you, sir, Good night."

"Uh . . . ." The man looked hesitantly at him, as though he felt that somehow Peter should be helped in some dubious, obscure way. "Uh—perhaps a drink. I have some whisky I was just going to—for myself . . . ."

"No, thank you, sir," Peter said. "I'd better be getting along."

Clumsily, they went down the passage together to the door. The man opened the door. He stood there, red-faced, huge, British, like a living Colonel Blimp, lonely and tired, with Robert Browning in the foreign night.

"Good night, sir."

"Good night. . . ."

The door closed and Peter walked slowly down the dark stairs.

Peter started toward his hotel, but the thought of the disordered room and Mac lying there, steadily asleep, steadily and slightly snoring in the next bed, was impossible.

He walked slowly past the dark policemen standing quietly with their rifles on the street corners. Down the street garry-lights, small and flickering and lonesome, wandered past, and the sound of the horses' hooves was deliberate and weary.

He came to the English Bridge and stood on the banks of the river, looking at the dark water swirling north toward the Mediterranean. Down the river a felucca, its immense sail spread in a soaring triangle, slowly made its way among the shadows from the trees along the shore. Across the river a minaret, poignant with faith, shone sharp and delicate in the moonlight.

Peter felt spent and drained. A nervous and hysteric pulse pulled at his bad eye and a gigantic sob seemed wedged into his throat.

Overhead, far away, there was the sound of a plane. It came nearer, passed across the stars, died away, going somewhere.

The wedge dislodged and the sob broke out like tears and blood.

Peter closed his eyes, and when he opened them again the wild pulse had stopped, his throat was clear. He stared across the river at the minaret, faithful and lovely in the light of the moon, by the side of the old river.

Tomorrow, he thought, tomorrow there may be a letter from home. . . .

# Night in Algiers

It was late at night in Algiers and in the army newspaper office the clatter of typewriters had long since died down. Most of the men had gone to sleep upstairs and the halls were empty. The wisecracks and decisions and sudden laughter were over for the day, and in another building the presses were comfortably turning out the next day's paper.

On the walls, the pictures of all the pretty girls with big bosoms looked a little weary in the dim light. Down on the street outside the Red Cross building, late-traveling soldiers whistled for hitches in the dark and a soldier who had had some wine was singing the "Marseillaise" in English, the brave words and the brave tune floating up a little uncertainly through the darkness until a truck stopped and picked the singer up. In the office the radio was on and Tchaikovsky's piano concerto was coming in, moody and sorrowful, from London.

An assistant editor with sergeant's stripes on his sleeves came in and sat down wearily in front of the radio. He stared at it, remembering many things that had nothing to do with his job, remembering home and what his college campus looked like in June and how it had felt to sail out of New York harbor in the rain.

"Have some wine," said the reporter who was sitting there listening to the music. The reporter had no stripes on his sleeves at all. The assistant editor took the wine and forgot to drink, just sitting there holding the bottle.

"There's a bar in New York," the assistant editor said. "Ralph's. On Forty-fifth Street. Ugly little joint. I like to drink there. Ever been there?"

"Uhuh," the reporter said.

"Scotch whisky," the assistant editor said. "Cold beer."

The concerto ended in wild, mournful thunder and a polite English voice said it had been Toscanini conducting and Horowitz at the piano, the names sounding strange on the night-time African coast. The polite voice said good night and the reporter got Berlin. There were waltzes on from Berlin, very prettily played, lilting through the small, paper-littered room. A polite German voice described the waltzes and once more the violins and trumpets swept out of the radio.

"The Germans," the assistant editor said. "They should be deprived of music for fifty years. Should be part of the peace treaty."

A rewrite man, a corporal, on his way up to bed, stuck his head in. "Anybody want a gumdrop?" He brought out the box. "Just got my rations today."

The assistant editor and the reporter reached out. They chewed consideringly on the gumdrops, listening to the waltz.

"Nice music," the rewrite man said.

"Fifty years," said the assistant editor.

The rewrite man yawned and stretched. "Going to bed," he said, and started out. "Maybe when I wake up tomorrow the war'll be over. Good night." He went out and the assistant editor washed down the rationed gumdrop with a little wine.

"Did you ever eat a gumdrop in civilian life?" he asked.

"No," said the reporter.

"Neither did I." He rolled the wine around reflectively in the bottle. "God, it's dull around here. I wish I could have gone to Italy." The radio turned to Hungarian dances and the assistant editor stared gloomily at it. He drank a little wine. "That's the trouble, though. Now that the invasion has come at last, other guys are covering it. Other guys'll write great stories. I'll be sitting here on my can in Africa. The editor. The assistant editor . . . When I got out of college I wrote better than I do now. Eight years ago." He rubbed his bald spot thoughtfully. "Somehow I got to be an editor. Eight years." He finished the wine. "Maybe I should've got married."

"Probably wouldn't make any difference," said the reporter, who was married.

"Probably not." The assistant editor shrugged. "There was a girl back in college in my sophomore year. She was a year older than me. You had to date her up in October for the spring prom. There was a fellow with a car who used to drive her to breakfast, lunch and dinner and send her flowers every day, but she used to take walks with me and lunch sometimes. She did the most marvelous thing that anyone ever did for me. I was a kid then and maybe it oughtn't to seem like so much to me now, but it still does. She

256

broke a date with this other guy and went to the spring prom with me, I gave her orchids and we went to a couple of speakeasies and it was the best night I ever had in my whole life." He sat back, remembering the orchids and the speakeasies. "I introduced her to a friend of mine that summer. He had a lot of dough and called her long distance three times a week and six months later they got married. You can't blame a girl. Want to see her picture?"

"Yes," the reporter said.

The assistant editor took out the picture, yellowed and raveled at the edges. It was of a pretty, graceful girl, in a white dress, sitting erect, a hint of strength in her face, mixed with ancient coquetry. "I don't know why I keep it," the assistant editor said, looking at the picture. "Maybe for luck." He put it back carefully into his wallet. He leaned back and his thick glasses and square, angular, plain, decent face shone in the dim light, clearly and painfully the face of a man who all his life might expect to find his best friends taking his girl.

"There was another girl. A Danish girl," the assistant editor went on. "I met her at a party in the Village. She'd come down from Boston with a friend, to be an actress. She worked at the Filmarte as an usher. I must have seen the last part of 'Grand Illusion' twelve times."

He smiled.

"I'd go around for the last reel or two of the pictures," he said, "and take her out to Sunnyside. She lived there with her friend. She liked me, but she wouldn't have anything much to do with me, even though I used to sleep out on the living-room couch five times a week. We had a fight and she decided she didn't want to be an actress and she went home to Boston. I guess I would've married her then if I hadn't fought with her so much." He took off his glasses and stared wearily at them. "About six months later she came down to New York on a visit and it was different. She moved right in and we had a wonderful time. We'd go out on weekends in the country. Just drive around in the summertime and stop in for drinks here and there and go swimming and laugh. She met me in Provincetown and we stayed with a Danish family. There was a great party. Provincetown, on Cape Cod. I don't think I've ever had a better time and I keep remembering it. . . . Maybe I should've married her. I don't know."

The assistant editor leaned over and put the bottle down. On the street below, three Frenchmen passed, singing loudly.

"I'm thirty years old and I write worse than I ever did. I don't know what I'll do after the war. Once, when I was in the Engineers,

257

I sent her a letter. She was married, she wrote me, and she was having a kid on May seventeenth. She was going to call it David, after her husband's uncle, she said. She asked me to pray for it. I haven't written back. Well, what's the difference?" He put his glasses on again. "The Filmarte Theatre." He laughed and stood up. "I wish I had two hack writers I could throw stories to and know they'd come out right," he said. "I wouldn't get so tired. Well, it's pretty late. Got to go to bed. Tomorrow's another war."

The radio was sending out American jazz now, the deep familiar horns of America pounding like all the music in all the dance halls and all the night clubs and at all the spring proms any American ever went to, any girl in a white dress ever danced at.

The assistant editor listened, his eyes blinking behind the thick lenses of his glasses. When it was over, he walked into his own room slowly, his shirt dumpy and wrinkled, to take one last look at his desk, and made sure everything was all right before going to bed.

# Gunners' Passage

"In Brazil," Whitejack was saying, "the problem was girls. American girls."

They were lying on the comfortable cots with the mosquito netting looped gracefully over their heads and the barracks quiet and empty except for the two of them and shaded and cool when you remembered that outside the full sun of Africa stared down.

"Three months in the jungle, on rice and monkey meat." Whitejack lit a large, long, nickel cigar and puffed deeply, squinting up at the tin roof. "When we got to Rio, we felt we deserved an American girl. So the Lieutenant and Johnny and myself, we got the telephone directory of the American Embassy, and we went down the list, calling up likely names—secretaries, typists, interpreters, filing clerks . . . ." Whitejack grinned up at the ceiling. He had a large, sunburned, rough face, that was broken into good looks by the white teeth of his smile, and his speech was Southern, but not the kind of Southern that puts a Northerner's teeth on edge.

"It was the Lieutenant's idea, and by the time we got to the Q's he was ready to give up but we hit pay dirt on the S's." Slowly he blew out a long draught of cigar smoke. "Uh-uh," he said, closing his eyes reflectively. "Two months and eleven days of honey and molasses. Three tender and affectionate American girls as loving as the day is long, with their own flat. Beer in the icebox from Sunday to Sunday, steaks big enough to saddle a mule with, and nothing to do, just lie on the beach in the afternoon and go swimmin' when the mood seized yuh. On per diem."

"How were the girls?" Stais asked. "Pretty?"

"Well, Sergeant," Whitejack paused and pursed his lips with thoughtful honesty. "To tell you the truth, Sergeant, the girls the Lieutenant and Johnny Moffat had were as smart and pretty as chipmunks. Mine . . ." Once more he paused. "Ordinarily, my girl would find herself hard put to collect a man in the middle of a full division of infantry soldiers. She was small and runty and

259

she had less curves than a rifle barrel, and she wore glasses. But from the first time she looked at me, I could see she wasn't interested in Johnny or the Lieutenant. She looked at me and behind her glasses her eyes were soft and hopeful and humble and appealing.'' Whitejack flicked the cigar ash off into the little tin can on his bare chest he was using as an ash tray. ''Sometimes,'' he said slowly, ''a man feels mighty small if he just thinks of himself and turns down an appeal like that. Let me tell you something, Sergeant, I was in Rio two months and eleven days and I didn't look at another woman. All those dark-brown women walkin' along the beach three-quarters out of their bathing suits, just wavin' it in front of your face. . . . I didn't look at them. This runty, skinny little thing with glasses was the most lovin' and satisfactory and decent little person a man could possibly conceive of, and a man'd just have to be hog-greedy with sex to have winked an eye at another woman.'' Whitejack doused his cigar, took his ash tray off his chest, rolled over on his belly, adjusted the towel properly over his bare buttocks. ''Now,'' he said, ''I'm going to get myself a little sleep. . . .''

In a moment Whitejack was snoring gently, his tough mountaineer's face tucked childishly into the crook of his arm. Outside the barracks the native boy hummed low and wild to himself as he ironed a pair of suntan trousers on the shady side of the building. From the field, two hundred yards away, again and again came the sliding roar of engines climbing or descending the afternoon sky.

Stais closed his eyes wearily. Ever since he'd got into Accra he had done nothing but sleep and lie on his cot, day-dreaming, listening to Whitejack talk.

''Hi,'' Whitejack had said, as Stais had come slowly into the barracks two days before, ''which way you going?''

''Home,'' Stais had said, smiling wearily as he did every time he said it. ''Going home. Which way you going?''

''Not home.'' Whitejack had grinned a little. ''Not home at all.''

Stais liked to listen to Whitejack. Whitejack talked about America, about the woods of the Blue Ridge Mountains where he had been in the forestry service, about his mother's cooking and how he had owned great dogs which had been extraordinary at finding a trail and holding it, about how they had tried hunting deer in the hills from the medium bomber, no good because of the swirling winds rising from the gorges, about pleasant indiscriminate week-end parties in the woods with his friend Johnny Moffat and the girls from the mill in the next town. . . . Stais had been away from America for nineteen months now and Whitejack's talk made his native country seem present and pleasantly real to him.

"There was a man in my town by the name of Thomas Wolfe," Whitejack had said irrelevantly that morning. "He was a great big feller and he went away to New York to be an author. Maybe you heard of him?"

"Yes," said Stais. "I read two books of his."

"Well, I read that book of his," said Whitejack, "and the people in town were yellin' to lynch him for a while, but I read that book and he got that town down fair and proper, and when they brought him back dead I came down from the hills and I went to his funeral. There were a lot of important people from New York and over to Chapel Hill down for the funeral and it was a hot day, too, and I'd never met the feller, but I felt it was only right to go to his funeral after readin' his book. And the whole town was there, very quiet, although just five years before they were yellin' to lynch him, and it was a sad and impressive sight and I'm glad I went."

And another time, the slow deep voice rolling between sleep and dreams in the shaded heat . . . ."My mother takes a quail and bones it, then she scoops out a great big sweet potato and lays some bacon on it, then she puts the quail in and cooks it slow for three hours, bastin' it with butter all the time . . . . You got to try that some time . . . ."

"Yes," said Stais, "I will."

Stais did not have a high priority number and there seemed to be a flood of colonels surging toward America, taking all the seats on the C-54's setting out westward, so he'd had to wait. It hadn't been bad. Just to lie down, stretched full-out, unbothered, these days, was holiday enough after Greece, and anyway he didn't want to arrive home, in front of his mother, until he'd stopped looking like a tired old man. And the barracks had been empty and quiet and the chow good at the transient mess and you could get Coca-Cola and chocolate milk at the PX. The rest of the enlisted men in Whitejack's crew were young and ambitious and were out swimming all day and going to the movies or playing poker in another barracks all night, and Whitejack's talk was smooth and amusing in the periods between sleep and dreams. Whitejack was an aerial photographer and gunner in a mapping-and-survey squadron and he'd been in Alaska and Brazil and back to the States and now was on his way to India, full of conversation. He was in a Mitchell squadron and the whole squadron was supposed to be on its way together, but two of the Mitchells had crashed and burned on the take-off at Natal, as Whitejack's plane had circled the field, waiting to form up. The rest of the squadron had been held at Natal and Whitejack's plane had been sent on to Accra across the ocean, by itself.

Vaguely and slowly, lying on the warm cot, with the wild song of the Negro boy outside the window, Stais thought of the two Mitchells burning between sea and jungle three thousand miles away, and other planes burning elsewhere, and what it was going to be like sitting down in the armchair in his own house and looking across the room at his mother, and the pretty Viennese girl in Jerusalem, and the DC-3 coming down slowly, like an angel in the dusk to the rough secret pasture in the Peloponnesian hills. . . .

He fell asleep. His bones knit gently into dreams on the soft cot, with the sheets, in the quiet barracks, and he was over Athens again, with the ruins pale and shining on the hills, and the fighters boring in, and Lathrop saying, over the intercom, as they persisted in to a hundred, fifty yards twisting swiftly and shiftily in the bright Greek sky, "They grounded all the students today. They have the instructors up this afternoon. . . ." And, suddenly, and wildly, fifty feet over Ploesti, with Liberators going down into the filth in dozens, flaming. . . . Then swimming off the white beach at Bengasi with the dead boys playing in the mild, tideless swell, then the parachute pulling at every muscle in his body, then the green and forest blue of Minnesota woods and his father, fat and small, sleeping on pine needles on his Sunday off, then Athens again, Athens . . .

"I don't know what's come over the Lieutenant," a new voice was saying as Stais came out of his dream. "He passes us on the field and he just don't seem to see us."

Stais opened his eyes. Novak, a farm boy from Oklahoma, was sitting on the edge of Whitejack's bed, talking. "It has all the guys real worried." He had a high, shy, rather girlish voice. "I used to think they never came better than the Lieutenant . . . Now . . ." Novak shrugged. "If he does see you, he snaps at you like he was General George Patton."

"Maybe," Whitejack said, "maybe seeing Lieutenant Brogan go down in Natal . . . He and Brogan were friends since they were ten years old. Like as if I saw Johnny Moffat go down . . ."

"It's not that." Novak went over to his own cot and got out his writing pad. "It began back in Miami four weeks ago. Didn't you notice it?"

"I noticed it," Whitejack said slowly.

"You ought to ask him about it." Novak started writing a letter.

"You and him are good friends. After all, going into combat now, it's bad, the Lieutenant just lookin' through us when he passes us on the field. You don't think he's drunk all the time, do you?"

"He's not drunk."

"You ought to ask him."

"Maybe I will." Whitejack sat up, tying the towel around his lean middle. "Maybe I will." He looked forlornly down at his stomach. "Since I got into the Army, I've turned pig-fat. On the day I took the oath, I was twenty-eight and one-half inches around the waist. Today I'm thirty-two and three-quarters, if I'm an inch. The Army . . . Maybe I shouldn't've joined. I was in a reserved profession, and I was the sole support of an ailing mother."

"Why did you join?" Stais asked.

"Oh," Whitejack smiled at him, "you're awake. Feeling any better, Sergeant?"

"Feeling fine, thanks. Why did you join?"

"Well . . ." Whitejack rubbed the side of his jaw. "Well . . . I waited and I waited. I sat up in my cabin in the hills and I tried to avoid listenin' to the radio, and I waited and I waited, and finally I went downtown to my mother and I said, 'Ma'am, I just can't wait any longer,' and I joined up."

"When was that?" Stais asked.

"Eight days . . ." Whitejack lay down again, plumping the pillow under his head. "Eight days after Pearl Harbor."

"Sergeant," Novak said, "Sergeant Stais, you don't mind if I tell my girl you're a Greek, do you?"

"No," Stais said gravely. "I don't mind. You know, I was born in Minnesota."

"I know," said Novak, writing industriously. "But your parents came from Greece. My girl'll be very interested, your parents coming from Greece and you bombing Greece and being shot down there."

"What do you mean, your girl?" Whitejack asked. "I thought you said she was going around with a Technical Sergeant in Flushing, Long Island."

"That's true," Novak said apologetically. "But I still like to think of her as my girl."

"It's the ones that stay at home," said Whitejack darkly, "that get all the stripes and all the girls. My motto is: Don't write to a girl once you get out of pillow-case distance from her."

"I like to write to this girl in Flushing, Long Island," Novak said, his voice shy but stubborn. Then to Stais, "How many days were you in the hills before the Greek farmers found you?"

"Fourteen," said Stais.

"And how many of you were wounded?"

"Three. Out of seven. The others were dead."

"Maybe," Whitejack said, "he doesn't like to talk about it, Charley."

"Oh, I'm sorry." Novak looked up, his young, unlined face crossed with concern.

"That's all right," Stais said. "I don't mind."

"Did you tell them you were a Greek, too?" Novak asked.

"When one finally showed up who could speak English."

"That must be funny," Novak said reflectively. "Being a Greek, bombing Greece, not speaking the language . . . Can I tell my girl they had a radio and they radioed to Cairo . . . ?"

"It's the girl of a Technical Sergeant in Flushing, Long Island," Whitejack chanted. "Why don't you look facts in the face?"

"I prefer it this way," Novak said with dignity.

"I guess you can tell about the radio," Stais said. "It was pretty long ago. Three days later, the DC-3 came down through a break in the clouds. It'd been raining all the time and it just stopped for about thirty minutes at dusk and that plane came down throwin' water fifteen feet in the air. . . . We cheered, but we couldn't get up from where we were sitting, any of us, because we were too weak to stand."

"I got to write that to my girl," Novak said. "Too weak to stand."

"Then it started to rain again and the field was hip-deep in mud and when we all got into the DC-3, we couldn't get it started." Stais spoke calmly and thoughtfully, as though he were alone, reciting to himself. "We were just bogged down in that Greek mud. Then the pilot got out—he was a captain—and he looked around, with the rain coming down and all those farmers just standing there, sympathizing with him, and nothing anyone could do and he just cursed for ten minutes. He was from San Francisco and he really knew how to curse. Then everybody started breaking branches off the trees in the woods around that pasture, even two of us who couldn't stand one hour before, and we just covered that big DC-3 complete with branches and waited for the rain to stop. We just sat in the woods and prayed no German patrols would come out in weather like that. In those three days I learned five words of Greek."

"What are they?" Novak asked.

"*Vouno*," Stais said. "That means mountain. *Vrohi:* Rains. *Theos:* God. *Avrion:* Tomorrow. And *yassov:* That means farewell."

"*Yassov*," Novak said. "Farewell."

"Then the sun came out and the field started to steam and nobody said anything. We just sat there, watching the water dry off the grass, then the puddles started to go here and there, then the mud to cake a little. Then we got into the DC-3 and the Greeks pushed and hauled for a while and we broke loose and got out. And those farmers just standing below waving at us, as though they were seeing us off at Grand Central Station. Ten miles farther on we went right over a German camp. They fired at us a couple of times, but they didn't come anywhere close. The best moment of my whole life was getting into that hospital bed in Cairo, Egypt. I just stood there and looked at it for a whole minute, looking at the sheets. Then I got in very slow."

"Did you ever find out what happened to those Greeks?" Novak asked.

"No," said Stais. "I guess they're still there, waiting for us to come back some day."

There was silence, broken only by the slow scratching of Novak's pen, Stais thought of the thin, dark mountain faces of the men he had last seen, fading away, waving, standing in the scrub and short silver grass of the hill pasture near the Aegean Sea. They had been cheerful and anxious to please, and there was a look on the faces that made you feel they expected to die.

"How many missions were you on?" Novak asked.

"Twenty-one and a half," Stais said. He smiled. "I count the last one as half."

"How old are you?" Novak was obviously keeping the Technical Sergeant's girl carefully posted on all points of interest.

"Nineteen."

"You look older," said Whitejack.

"Yes," said Stais.

"A lot older."

"Yes."

"Did you shoot down any planes?" Novak peered at him shyly, his red face uncertain and embarrassed, like a little boy asking a doubtful question about girls. "Personally?"

"Two," Stais said. "Personally."

"What did you feel?"

"Why don't you leave him alone?" Whitejack said. "He's too tired to keep his eyes open, as it is."

"I felt—relieved," Stais said. He tried to think of what he'd really felt when the tracers went in and the Focke-Wolfe started to smoke like a crazy smudge pot and the German pilot fought

265

wildly for half a second with the cowling and then didn't fight wildly any more. There was no way of telling these men, no way of remembering, in words, himself. "You'll find out," he said. "Soon enough. The sky's full of Germans."

"Japs," Whitejack said. "We're going to India."

"The sky's full of Japs."

There was silence once more, with the echo of the word "Japs" rustling thinly in the long, quiet room, over the empty rows of cots. Stais felt the old waving dizziness starting behind his eyes that the doctor in Cairo had said came from shock or starvation or exposure or all of these things, and lay back, still keeping his eyes open, as it became worse and waved more violently when he closed his eyes.

"One more question," Novak said. "Are—are guys afraid?"

"You'll be afraid," Stais said.

"Do you want to send that back to your girl in Flushing?" Whitejack asked sardonically.

"No," said Novak quietly. "I wanted that for myself."

"If you want to sleep," said Whitejack, "I'll shut this farmer up."

"Oh, no," said Stais, "I'm pleased to talk."

"If you're not careful," Whitejack said, "he'll talk about his girl in Flushing."

"I'd be pleased to hear it," said Stais.

"It's only natural I should want to talk about her," Novak said defensively. "She was the best girl I ever knew in my whole life. I'd've married her if I could."

"My motto," said Whitejack, "is never marry a girl who goes to bed with you the first time out. The chances are she isn't pure. The second time—that, of course, is different." He winked at Stais.

"I was in Flushing, Long Island, taking a five-weeks course in aerial cameras," Novak said, "and I was living at the YMCA. . . ."

"This is where I leave." Whitejack got off the bed and put on his pants.

"The YMCA was very nice. There were bathrooms for every two rooms and the food was very good," said Novak, talking earnestly to Stais, "but I must confess, I was lonely in Flushing, Long Island . . . ."

"I will be back," Whitejack was buttoning up his shirt, "for the ninth installment."

"As long as you're going out," Novak said to him, "I wish

266

you'd talk to the Lieutenant. It really makes me feel queer passing him, and him just looking through me like I was a window pane."

"Maybe I'll talk to the Lieutenant. And leave the Sergeant alone. Remember he's a tired man who's been to the war and he needs his rest." Whitejack went out.

Novak stared after him. "There's something wrong with him, too," he said. "Just lying on his back here for ten days, reading and sleeping. He never did that before. He was the liveliest man in the United States Air Force. Seeing those two planes go down . . . It's a funny thing, you fly with fellers all over the world, over America, Brazil, Alaska; you watch them shoot porpoises and sharks in gunnery practice over the Gulf Stream, you get drunk with them, go to their weddings, talk to them over the radio with their planes maybe a hundred feet away, in the air—and after all that flying, in one minute, for no reason, two planes go down. Fourteen fellers you've been livin' with for over a year. . . ." Novak shook his head. "There was a particular friend of Whitejack's in one of those planes. Frank Sloan. Just before we left Miami, they had a big fight. Frank went off and married a girl that Whitejack's been going with off and on for a year, every time we hit Miami. Whitejack told him he was crazy, half the squadron had slept with the lady, and that was true, too, and just to teach him a lesson he'd sleep with her himself after they'd been married. And he did, too. . . ." Novak sighed. "A lot of funny things happen in the Army, when fellers've been together a long time and get to know each other real well. And then, one minute, the Mitchell goes down. I guess Whitejack must've felt sort of queer, watching Frankie burn." Novak had put his writing pad down and now he screwed the top on his fountain pen. "The truth is," he said, "I don't feel so solid myself. That's why I like to talk. Especially to you . . . You've been through it. You're young, but you've been through it. But if it's any bother to you, I'll keep quiet. . . ."

"No," said Stais, still lying back, abstractedly wondering whether the waving would get worse or better, "not at all."

"This girl in Flushing, Long Island," Novak said slowly. "It's easy for Whitejack to make fun of me. The girls fall all over themselves chasing after him; he has no real conception of what it's like to be a man like me. Not very good-looking. Not much money. Not an officer. Not humorous. Shy."

Stais couldn't help grinning. "You're going to have a tough time in India."

"I know," Novak said. "I have resigned myself to not having

a girl until the armistice. How did you do with the girls in the Middle East?" he asked politely.

"There was a nice Viennese girl in Jerusalem," Stais said dreamily. "But otherwise zero. You have to be very good unless you're an officer in the Middle East."

"That's what I heard," Novak said sorrowfully. "Well, it won't be so different to me from Oklahoma. That was the nice thing about this girl in Flushing, Long Island. She saw me come into the jewelry store where she worked and . . . I was in my fatigues and I was with a very smooth feller who made a date with her for that night. But she smiled at me, and I knew if I had the guts I could ask her for a date, too. But of course I didn't. But then later that night I was sitting in my room in the YMCA and my phone rang. It was this girl. The other feller had stood her up, she said, and would I take her out." Novak smiled dimly, thinking of that tremulous moment of glory in the small hotel room far away. "I got my fatigues off in one minute and shaved and showered and I picked her up. We went to Coney Island. It was the first time in my entire life I had ever seen Coney Island. It took three and a half weeks for me to finish my course and I went out with that girl every single night. Nothing like that ever happened to me before in my life—a girl who just wanted to see me every night of the week. Then the night before I was due to leave to join my squadron she told me she had got permission to take the afternoon off and she would like to see me off if I let her. I called at the jewelry shop at noon and her boss shook my hand and she had a package under her arm and we got into the subway and we rode to New York City. Then we went into a cafeteria and had a wonderful lunch and she saw me off and gave me the package. It was Schrafft's candy, and she was crying at the gate there, crying for me, and she said she would like me to write, no matter what . . ." Novak paused and Stais could tell that the scene at the gate, the hurrying crowds, the package of Schrafft's chocolates, the weeping young girl, were as clear as the afternoon sunlight to Novak there on the coast of Africa. "So I keep writing," Novak said. "She's written me she has a Technical Sergeant now, but I keep writing. I haven't seen her in a year and a half and what's a girl to do? Do you blame her?"

"No," said Stais, "I don't blame her."

"I hope I haven't bored you," Novak said.

"Not at all." Stais smiled at him. Suddenly the dizziness had gone and he could close his eyes. As he drifted down into that weird and ever-present pool of sleep in which he half-lived these days, he heard Novak say, "Now I have to write my mother."

Outside, the Negro boy sang and the planes grumbled down from the Atlantic and laboriously set out across the Sahara Desert.

Dreams again. Arabs, bundled in rags, driving camels along the perimeter of the field, outlined against the parked Liberators and waiting bombs, two Mitchells still burning on the shores of Brazil and Frank Sloan burning there and circling above him, Whitejack, who had told him he'd sleep with his wife and had, the hills around Jerusalem, gnarled, rocky, dusty, with the powdered green of olive groves set on slopes here and there, clinging against the desert wind, Mitchells slamming along the gorges of the Blue Ridge Mountains, bucking in the updraughts, their guns going, hunting deer, the Mediterranean, bluer than anything in America, below them on the way home from Italy, coming down below oxygen level, with the boys singing dirty songs over the intercom and leave in Alexandria ahead of them. The girl from Flushing, Long Island, quietly going hand in hand with Novak to Coney Island on a summer's night. . . .

It was Whitejack who awakened him. He woke slowly. It was dark outside and the electric light was shining in his eyes and Whitejack was standing over him, shaking him gently.

"I thought you'd like to know," Whitejack was saying, "your name's on the bulletin board. You're leaving tonight."

"Thanks," Stais said, dimly grateful at being shaken out of the broken and somehow sorrowful dreams.

"I took the liberty of initialing it for you, opposite your name," Whitejack said. "Save you a trip up to the field."

"Thanks," said Stais. "Very kind of you."

"Also," said Whitejack, "there's fried chicken for chow."

Stais pondered over the fried chicken. He was a little hungry, but the effort of getting up and putting on his shoes and walking the hundred yards to the mess hall had to be weighed in the balance. "Thanks. I'll just lie right here," he said. "Any news of your boys?" he asked.

"Yes," said Whitejack. "The squadron came in."

"That's good."

"All except one plane." Whitejack sat down on the end of Stais' cot. His voice was soft and expressionless, under the bright electric light. "Johnny Moffat's plane."

In all the months that Stais had been in the Air Force, on fields to which planes had failed to return, he had learned that there was nothing to say, He was only nineteen years old, but he had learned that. So he lay quiet.

"They got separated in clouds on the way out of Ascension, and they never picked them up again. There's still a chance," Whitejack said, "that they'll drop in any minute." He looked at his watch. "Still a chance for another hour and forty minutes . . ."

There was still nothing to say, so Stais lay silent.

"Johnny Moffat," said Whitejack, "at one time looked as though he was going to marry my sister. In a way, it's a good thing he didn't. It'd be a little hard, being brothers-in-law, on some of the parties the Air Force goes on in one place and another." Whitejack fell silent, looked down at his belly. Deliberately, he let his belt out a notch. He pulled it to, with a severe little click. "That fried chicken was mighty good," he said. "You sure you want to pass it up?"

"I'm saving my appetite," Stais said, "for my mother's cooking."

"My sister," said Whitejack, "was passing fond of Johnny, and I have a feeling when he gets home from the war and settles down, she's going to snag him. She came to me right before I left and she asked me if I would let her have ten acres on the north side of my property and three acres of timber to build their house. I said it was OK with me." He was silent again, thinking of the rolling ten acres of upland meadow in North Carolina and the three tall acres of standing timber, oak and pine, from which it would be possible to build a strong country house. "There's nobody in the whole world I'd rather have living on my property than Johnny Moffat. I've known him for twenty years and I've had six fist fights with him and won them all, and been alone with him in the woods for two months at a time, and I still say that. . . ." He got up and went over to his own cot, then turned and came back. "By the way," he said softly, "this is between you and me, Sergeant."

"Sure," said Stais.

"My sister said she'd murder me for my hide and taller if I ever let Johnny know what was in store for him." He grinned a little. "Women're very confident in certain fields," he said. "And I never did tell Johnny, not even when I was so drunk I was singing 'Casey Jones' naked in the middle of the city of Tampa at three o'clock in the morning." He went over to his musette bag and got out a cigar and thoughtfully lit it. "You'd be surprised," he said, "how fond you become of nickel cigars in the Army."

"I tried smoking," said Stais. "I think I'll wait until I get a little older."

Whitejack sat heavily on his own cot. "Do you think they'll send you out to fight again?" he asked.

Stais stared up at the ceiling. "I wouldn't be surprised," he said. "There's nothing really wrong with me. I'm just tired."

Whitejack nodded, smoking slowly. "By the way," he said, "you heard us talking about the Lieutenant, didn't you?"

"Yes."

"I went out to the field and had a little conversation with him. He's just been sittin' there all day and most of the night since we got here, outside the Operations room, just lookin' and starin' across at the planes comin' in. Him and me, we've been good friends for a long time and I asked him pointblank. I said, 'Freddie,' I said, 'there's a question the boys're askin' themselves these days about you,' And he said, 'What's the matter?' And I said, 'The boys're asking if you've turned bad. You pass 'em and you don't even look at them as though you recognize 'em. What is it, you turn GI after a year?' I said. He looked at me and then he looked at the ground and he didn't say anything for maybe a minute. Then he said, 'I beg your pardon, Arnold. It never occurred to me.' Then he told me what was on his mind." Whitejack looked at his watch, almost automatically, then lifted his head again. "Ever since we got the order to go overseas he's been worrying. About the waist gunner and his navigator."

"What's he worrying about?" For a moment a crazy list of all the thousand things you can worry about in the crew of one airplane flashed through Stais' head.

"They're not fighting men," Whitejack said slowly. "They're both good fellers, you wouldn't want better, but the Lieutenant's been watchin' 'em for a long time on the ground, in the air, at their guns, and he's convinced they won't measure. And he feels he's responsible for taking the Mitchell in and getting it out with as many of us alive as possible and he feels the waist gunner and the navigator're dangerous to have in the plane. And he's makin' up his mind to put in a request for two new men when we get to India, and he can't bear to think of what it'll do to the gunner and the navigator when they find out he's asked to have 'em grounded, and that's why he just sits there outside Operations, not even seein' us when we go by. . . ." Whitejack sighed. "He's twenty-two years old, the Lieutenant. It's a strain, something like that, for a man twenty-two years old. If you see Novak, you won't tell him anything, will you?"

"No," said Stais.

"I suppose things like this come up all the time in any army."

271

"All the time," said Stais.

Whitejack looked at his watch. Outside there was the growing and lapsing roar of engines that had been the constant sound of both their lives for so many months.

"Ah," said Whitejack, "they should've put me in the infantry. I can hit a rabbit at three hundred yards with a rifle; they put me in the Air Force and give me a camera. . . Well, Sergeant, I think it's about time you were movin'."

Slowly, Stais got up. He put on his shoes and put his shaving kit into his musette bag and slung it over his shoulder.

"You ready?" asked Whitejack.

"Yes," said Stais.

"That all the baggage you got—that little musette bag?"

"Yes," said Stais. "I was listed as missing, presumed dead, and they sent all my stuff into the supply room and all my personal belongings home to my mother."

Stais looked around the barracks. It shone in the harsh army light of barracks at night all over the world, by now familiar, homelike, to all the men who passed through them. He had left nothing.

They walked out into the soft, engine-filled night. A beacon flashed nervously across the sky, dimming the enormous pale twinkle of Southern stars for a moment. They walked slowly, stepping cautiously over the ditches dug for the flood rains of the African West Coast.

As they passed the Operations room, Stais saw a young lieutenant slumped down in a wobbly old wicker chair, staring out across the field.

"They come yet?" Whitejack asked.

"No," said the Lieutenant, without looking up.

Stais went into the building and into the room where they had the rubber raft and the patented radio and the cloth painted blue on one side and yellow on the other. A fat middle-aged ATC captain wearily told them about ditching procedure. There were more than thirty people in the room, all passengers on Stais' plane. There were two small, yellow Chinese who were going to be airsick and five bouncing fat Red Cross women, and three sergeants with a lot of Air Force medals, trying not to seem excited about going home, and two colonels in the Engineers, looking too old for this war. Stais only half-listened as the fat captain explained how to inflate the raft, what strings to pull, what levers to move, where to find the waterproofed Bible. . . .

Whitejack was standing outside when Stais started for his plane.

He gave Stais a slip of paper. "It's my home address," he said. "After the war, just come down sometime in October and I'll take you hunting."

"Thank you very much," said Stais gravely. Over Whitejack's shoulder he saw the Lieutenant, still slumped in the wicker chair, still staring fixedly and unrelievedly out across the dark field.

Whitejack walked out to the great plane with Stais, along the oil-spattered concrete of the runway, among the Chinese and loud Red Cross women and the sergeants. They stopped, without a word, at the steps going up to the doorway of the plane and the other passengers filed past them.

They stood there, silently, with the two days of random conversation behind them and Brazil and Athens behind them, and five hundred flights behind them, and Jerusalem and Miami behind them, and the girls from Vienna and the American Embassy and Flushing, Long Island, behind them, and the Greek mountaineers behind them and Thomas Wolfe's funeral, and friends burning like torches, and dogs under treed raccoons in the Blue Ridge Mountains behind them, and a desperate twenty-two-year-old Lieutenant painfully staring across a dusty airfield for ten days behind them, and the Mediterranean and the hospital bed in Cairo and Johnny Moffat wandering that night over the Southern Atlantic, with ten acres of meadow and three acres of timber for his house, and Whitejack's sister waiting for him, all behind them. And, ahead of Stais, home and a mother who had presumed him dead and wept over his personal belongings, and ahead of Whitejack the cold bitter mountains of India and China and the tearing dead sound of the fifties and the sky full of Japs. . . .

"All right, Sergeant," the voice of the Lieutenant checking the passengers. "Get on."

Stais waved, a little broken wave, at Whitejack standing there. "See you," he said, "in North Carolina."

"Some October." Whitejack smiled a little in the light of the floodlamps.

The door closed and Stais sat down in the seat in front of the two Chinese.

"I think these planes are absolutely charming," one of the Red Cross women was saying loudly. "Don't you?"

The engines started and the big plane began to roll. Stais looked out of the window. A plane was landing. It came slowly into the light of the runway lamps and set down heavily, bumping wearily. Stais stared. It was a Mitchell. Stais sighed to himself. As the big C-54 wheeled at the head of the runway, then started clumsily down, Stais put the slip of paper with Arnold Whitejack written on it, and the address, in scrawling, childlike handwriting, into his pocket. And as he saw the Mitchell pull to a stop near the Operations room, he felt for the moment a little less guilty for going home.

# Retreat

The column of trucks wound into the little square beside the Madeleine and stopped there, under the trees. They were furry with dust, the black cross almost indistinguishable even in the bright Paris sunlight under the harsh dry coat they had accumulated in the retreat from Normandy.

The engines stopped and suddenly the square was very quiet, the drivers and the soldiers relaxing on the trucks, the people at the little tables in the cafés staring without expression at the line of vehicles, bullet-scarred and fresh from war against the trees and Greek columns of the Madeleine.

A major at the head of the column slowly raised himself and got out of his car. He stood looking up at the Madeleine, a dusty, middle-aged figure, the uniform no longer smart, the lines of the body sagging and unmilitary. The major turned around and walked slowly toward the Café Bernard across the square, his face grimy and worn and expressionless, with the dust in heavy, theatrical lines in the creases of his face and where his goggles had been. He walked heavily, thoughtfully, past his trucks and his men, who watched him dispassionately and incuriously, as though they had known him for many years and there was nothing more to be learned from him. Some of the men got out of their trucks and lay down in the sunshine on the pavement and went to sleep, like corpses in a town where there has been a little fighting, just enough to produce several dead without doing much damage to the buildings.

The major walked over to the little sidewalk tables of the Café Bernard, looking at the drinkers there with the same long, cold, thoughtful stare with which he had surveyed the Madeleine. The drinkers stared back with the guarded, undramatic faces with which they had looked at the Germans for four years.

The major stopped in front of the table where Segal sat alone, the half-finished glass of beer in his hand. A little twist of a smile pulled momentarily at the German's mouth as he stood there, looking at Segal, small and pinned together with desperate neatness in his five-year-old suit, his shirt stitched and cross-stitched to hold it together, his bald head shining old and clean in the bright sun.

"Do you mind . . . ?" The major indicated the empty chair beside Segal with a slow, heavy movement of his hand.

Segal shrugged. "I don't mind," he said.

The major sat down, spread his legs out deliberately in front of him. "*Garçon*," he said, "two beers."

They sat in silence and the major watched his men sleeping like corpses on the Paris pavement.

"For this drink," the major said, in French, "I wanted to sit with a civilian."

The waiter brought the beers and set them down on the table and put the saucers in the middle, between them. The major absently pulled the saucers in front of him.

"To your health," he said. He raised his glass. Segal lifted his and they drank.

The major drank thirstily, closing his eyes, almost finishing his glass before he put it down. He opened his eyes and licked the tiny scallop of froth from the beer off his upper lip, as he slowly turned his head, regarding the buildings around him. "A pretty city," he said. "A very pretty city. I had to have one last drink."

"You've been at the front?" Segal asked.

"Yes," said the major. "I have been at the front."

"And you are going back?"

"I am going back," the major said, "and the front is going back." He grinned a little, sourly. "It is hard to say which precedes which. . . ." He finished his beer, then turned and stared at Segal. "Soon," he said, "the Americans will be here. How do you feel about that?"

Segal touched his face uncomfortably, "You don't really want a Parisian to answer a question like that," he said, "do you?"

"No." The major smiled. "I suppose not. Though, it's too bad the Americans had to meddle. However, it's too late to worry about that now." Under the warlike dust his face now was tired and quiet and intellectual, not good-looking, but studious and reasonable, the face of a man who read after business hours and occasionally went to concerts without being pushed into it by his wife. He waved to the waiter. "*Garçon*, two more beers." He turned to Segal. "You have no objections to drinking another beer with me?"

Segal looked across at the armored vehicles, the two hundred sprawling men, the heavy machine guns mounted and pointing toward the sky. He shrugged, his meaning cynical and clear.

"No," said the major. "I would not dream of using the German army to force Frenchmen to drink beer with me."

"Since the Germans occupied Paris," Segal said, "I haven't drunk with one or conducted a conversation with one. Four years. As an experience, perhaps, I should not miss it. And now is the time to try it. In a little while it will no longer be possible, will it?"

The major disregarded the jibe. He stared across at his command stretched wearily and incongruously in front of the Greek temple Paris had faithfully erected in her midst. He never seemed to be able to take his eyes off the armor and the men, as though there was a connection there, bitter and unsatisfactory and inescapable, that could never really be broken, even for a moment, in a café, over a glass of beer. "You're a Jew," he said quietly to Segal, "aren't you?"

The waiter came and put the two beers and the saucers on the table.

Segal put his hands into his lap, to hide the trembling and the terror in the joints of the elbows and knees and the despair in all the veins of the body that the word had given rise to in him, each time, every day, since the bright summer days of 1940. He sat in silence, licking his lips, automatically and hopelessly looking for exits and doorways, alleys and subway entrances.

The major lifted his glass. "To your health," he said. "Come on. Drink."

Segal wet his lips with the beer.

"Come on," the major said. "You can tell me the truth. If you don't talk, you know, it would be the easiest thing in the world to call over a sergeant and have him look at your papers. . . ."

"Yes," said Segal. "I'm a Jew."

"I knew it," said the major. "That's why I sat down." He stared at his men with the same look of bondage, devoid of affection, devoid of warmth or loyalty or hope. "There are several questions in my mind you can answer better than anyone."

"What are they?" Segal asked uneasily.

"No rush," said the major. "They'll wait for a minute." He peered curiously at Segal. "You know, it's forbidden for Jews to enter a café in France . . . ?"

"I know," said Segal.

"Also," said the major, "all Jews are instructed to wear the yellow star on their coats. . . ."

277

"Yes."

"You don't wear yours and I find you in a café in broad daylight."

"Yes."

"You're very brave." There was a little note of irony in the major's voice. "Is it worth it for a drink—to risk being deported?"

Segal shrugged. "It isn't for the drink," he said. "Maybe you won't understand, but I was born in Paris, I've lived all my life in the cafés, on the boulevards."

"What is your profession, Mr. . . . ? Mr. . . . ?"

"Segal."

"What do you do for a living?"

"I was a musician."

"Ah," there was an involuntary little tone of respect in the German's voice. "What instrument?"

"The saxophone," said Segal "in a jazz orchestra."

The major grinned. "An amusing profession."

"I haven't played in four years," said Segal. "Anyway, I was getting too old for the saxophone and the Germans permitted me to make a graceful exit. But imagine, for a jazz musician, the cafés are his life, his studio, his club, his places to make love, his library and place of business. If I am not free to sit down on a *terrasse* and have a *vin blanc* in Paris, I might just as well go to a concentration camp. . . ."

"Every man," said the major, "to his own particular patriotism."

"I think," said Segal, starting to rise, "that perhaps I'd better go now. . . ."

"No. Sit down. I have a little time." The German stared once more at his men. "We will arrive in Germany a half hour later, if at all. It doesn't matter. Tell me something. Tell me about the French. We have not behaved badly in France. Yet, I feel they hate us. They hate us, most of them, almost as much as the Russians hate us. . . ."

"Yes," said Segal.

"Fantastic," said the major. "We have been most correct, within the bounds of military necessity."

"You believe that. It's wonderful, but you really believe it." Segal was beginning to forget where he was, whom he was talking to, the argument rising hot within him.

"Of course I believe it."

"And the Frenchmen who have been shot . . . ?"

"The army had nothing to do with it. The SS, the Gestapo . . ."

Segal shook his head. "How many times I have heard that!" he said. "And all the dead Jews, too."

"The army knew nothing about it," the major said stubbornly. "I, myself, have never lifted my hand, or done one bad thing against any Jew in Germany or Poland or here in France. At this point, it is necessary to judge accurately who did what . . . ."

"Why is it necessary?" Segal asked.

"Let us face the facts." The major looked around him suddenly, lowered his voice. "It is very probable now that we are beaten . . . ."

"It is probable," Segal smiled. "It is also probable that the sun will rise sometime about six o'clock tomorrow morning."

"A certain amount of revenge—what you call justice, will be demanded. The army has behaved in a civilized manner and that must not be forgotten."

Segal shrugged. "I do not recall seeing the Gestapo in Paris until after the German army came in. . . . ."

"Ah, well," said the major, "you are not representative. You are a Jew, and naturally a little more bitter, although you seem to have done very well, I must say."

"I've done very well," said Segal. "I am still alive. It is true that my two brothers are no longer alive, and my sister is working in Poland, and my people have been wiped out of Europe, but I have done very well. I have been very clever." He took out his wallet and showed it to the major. The Star of David was tucked in so that it could be snapped out in a moment, and there was a needle already threaded, wound round a piece of yellow cardboard right next to it. "In a tight spot," said Segal, "I could always take out the star and put it on. It took six stitches, exactly." His hand trembled as he closed the wallet and put it away. "Four years, major, imagine four years praying each moment you will have thirty seconds somewhere to sew in six stitches before they ask to look at your papers. I've done very well. I've always found the thirty seconds. And do you know where I slept at night, because I was clever? In the woman's jail. So, when the Gestapo came to my house looking for me, I was comfortably locked in a cell among the whores and shoplifters. I could arrange that because my wife is Catholic and a nurse at the jail. Again, I've done very well. My wife decided finally she had had enough of me. I don't blame her, it's difficult for a woman. It's all right for a year, two years, but then the gesture wears out, you yearn not to have the millstone around your neck. So she decided to divorce me. A very simple procedure for a Christian. You merely go to court and say, 'My husband is a Jew,' and that's the end of it. We have three children, and I have not seen them for a year. Well enough. And the propaganda agencies, who also have no connection to the correct German army, also have done well. The French hate the Germans, but they have been fed the lies for four years and I think maybe they will never quite get over the lies about the Jews. The Germans have various accomplishments to their credit, and this is another one . . .''

"I think perhaps you're being too pessimistic," the major said. "People change. The world goes back to normal, people get tired of hatred and bloodshed.''

"You're getting tired of hatred and bloodshed," said Segal. "I can understand that, after all this time.''

"Myself," said the major, "I never wanted it. Look at me. Fundamentally, I'm not a soldier. Come to Germany after the war and I'll sell you a Citroën. I'm an automobile salesman, with a wife and three children, dressed in uniform.''

"Maybe," said Segal. "Maybe . . . Now we will hear that from many people. Fundamentally, I am not a soldier, I am an automobile salesman, a musician, a pet-fancier, a stamp-collector, a Lutheran preacher, a schoolteacher, anything. . . . But in 1940 we did not hear that as you marched down the boulevards. There were no automobile salesmen then—only captains and sergeants, pilots, artillerists . . . Somehow, the uniform was not such an accident in 1940.''

They sat silent. A passing automobile backfired twice, and one of the sleeping soldiers screamed in his sleep, the noise echoing strangely in the sunny square. One of the other soldiers woke the sleeping man and explained to him what had happened and the sleeper sat up against a truck wheel, wiped his face nervously with his hand, went to sleep again, sitting up.

"Segal," said the major, "after this war is over, it will be necessary to salvage Europe. We will all have to live together on the same continent. At the basis of that, there must be forgiveness. I know it is impossible to forgive everyone, but there are the millions who never did anything. . . .''

"Like you?''

"Like me," said the German. "I was never a member of the Party. I lived a quiet middle-class existence with my wife and three children.''

"I am getting very tired," Segal said, "of your wife and three children.''

The major flushed under the dust. He put his hand heavily on Segal's wrist. "Remember," he said, "the Americans are not yet in Paris.''

"Forgive me," said Segal. "I believed you when you told me I could talk freely.''

The major took his hand off Segal's wrist. "I mean it," he said. "Go ahead. I have been thinking about these things for a long time, I might as well listen to you."

"I'm sorry," said Segal. "I have to go home and it's a long walk, to the other bank."

"If you have no objection," said the major, "I'll drive you there."

"Thank you," said Segal.

The major paid and they walked together across the square, in front of the men, who stared at them both with the same incurious, hostile expressions. They got into the major's car and started off. Segal couldn't help enjoying his first ride in an automobile in four years and smiled a little as they crossed the Seine, with the river blue and pleasant below them.

The major barely looked at where they were going. He sat back wearily, an aging man who had been pushed beyond the limits of his strength, his face worn and gentle now with exhaustion as they passed in front of the great statues that guard the Chambre des Députés. He took off his cap and the fresh wind blew his sparse hair in thin curls.

"I am ready to face the fact," he said, his voice soft and almost pleading, "that there is a price to be paid for what could be called our guilt. We have lost and so we are guilty."

Segal chuckled drily. By this time he was feeling exhilarated by the beer he had drunk, and the ride, and the sense of danger and victory that came with talking to the major in a town full of German troops.

"Perhaps," said the major, "even if we hadn't lost we would be guilty. Honestly, Mr. Segal, for the last two years I have thought that. In the beginning, a man is swept up. You have no idea of the pressure that is applied when a country like Germany goes to war to make a man join in with a whole heart, to try to succeed in the profession of soldiering. But even so, it wasn't the older ones like me . . . It was the young ones, the fanatics, they were like a flood, and the rest of us were carried along. You've seen for yourself . . ."

"I've seen the young ones myself," said Segal. "But also the older ones, sitting at the best restaurants, eating butter and steaks and white bread for four years, filling the theatres, wearing the pretty uniforms, signing orders to kill ten Frenchmen a day, twenty . . ."

"Weakness," said the major. "Self-indulgence. The human

race is not composed of saints. Somewhere, forgiveness has to begin."

Segal leaned over and touched the driver on the shoulder. "Stop here, please," he said in German. "I have to get off."

"Do you live here?" the major asked.

"No. Five streets from here," said Segal. "But with all due respect, major, I prefer not showing a German, any German, where I live."

The major shrugged. "Stop here," he told the driver.

The car pulled over to the curb and stopped. Segal opened the door and got out.

The major held his hand. "Don't you think we've paid?" he asked harshly. "Have you seen Berlin, have you seen Hamburg, were you at Stalingrad, have you any idea what the battlefield looked like at Saint Lô, at Mortain, at Falaise? Have you any notion of what it's like to be on the road with the American air force over you all the time and Germans trying to get away in wagons, on foot, on bicycles, living in holes like animals, like cattle in slaughter pens in an abattoir? Isn't that paying, too?" His face worked convulsively under the dust and it seemed to Segal as though he might break into tears in a moment. "Yes," he said, "yes, we're guilty. Granted, we're guilty. Some of us are more guilty than the rest. What are we to do now? What can I do to wash my hands?"

Segal pulled his arm away. For a moment, helplessly, he felt like comforting this aging, wornout, decent-looking man, this automobile salesman, father of three children, this weary, frightened, retreating soldier, this wavering, hopeless target on the straight, long roads of France. Then he looked at the rigid face of the driver, sitting at attention in the front of the car, with his machine pistol, small, and clever, well-oiled and ready for death in the sling under the windshield.

"What can I do," the major cried again, "to wash my hands?"

Segal sighed wearily, spoke without exultation or joy or bitterness, speaking not for himself, but for the first Jew brained on a Munich street long ago and the last American brought to earth that afternoon by a sniper's bullet outside Chartres, and for all the years and all the dead and all the agony in between. "You can cut your throat," he said, "and see if the blood will take the stain out."

The major sat up stiffly and his eyes were dangerous, cold with anger and defeat, and for a moment Segal felt he had gone too far, that after the four years' successful survival, he was going to die now, a week before the liberation of the city, and for the same moment, looking at the set, angry, beaten face, he did not care. He turned his back and walked deliberately toward his home, the space between his shoulder blades electric and attendant, waiting tightly for the bullet. He had walked ten steps, slowly, when he heard the major say something in German. He walked even more slowly, staring, stiff and dry-eyed, down the broad reaches of the Boulevard Raspail. He heard the motor of the car start up, and the slight wail of the tires as it wheeled around sharply, and he did not look back as the car started back toward the Seine and the Madeleine and the waiting troops sleeping like so many dead by their armored cars before the Madeleine, back along the open, unforgiven road to Germany.

# Act of Faith

"Present it in a pitiful light," Olson was saying, as they picked their way through the mud toward the orderly room tent. "Three combat-scarred veterans, who fought their way from Omaha Beach to—what was the name of the town we fought our way to?"

"Konigstein," Seeger said.

"Konigstein." Olson lifted his right foot heavily out of a puddle and stared admiringly at the three pounds of mud clinging to his overshoe. "The backbone of the army, The noncommissioned officer. We deserve better of our country. Mention our decorations in passing."

"What decorations should I mention?" Seeger asked. "The marksman's medal?"

"Never quite made it," Olson said. "I had a cross-eyed scorer at the butts. Mention the bronze star, the silver star, the Croix de Guerre, with palms, the unit citation, the Congressional Medal of Honor."

"I'll mention them all." Seeger grinned. "You don't think the CO'll notice that we haven't won most of them, do you?"

"Gad, sir," Olson said with dignity, "do you think that one Southern military gentleman will dare doubt the word of another Southern military gentleman in the hour of victory?"

"I come from Ohio," Seeger said.

"Welch comes from Kansas," Olson said, coolly staring down a second lieutenant who was passing. The lieutenant made a nervous little jerk with his hand as though he expected a salute, then kept it rigid, as a slight superior smile of scorn twisted at the corner of Olson's mouth. The lieutenant dropped his eyes and splashed on through the mud. "You've heard of Kansas," Olson said. "Magnolia-scented Kansas."

"Of course," said Seeger. "I'm no fool."

"Do your duty by your men, Sergeant." Olson stopped to wipe the rain off his face and lectured him. "Highest ranking noncom present took the initiative and saved his comrades, at great personal risk, above and beyond tbe call of you-know-what, in the best traditions of the American army.''

"I will throw myself in the breach," Seeger said.

"Welch and I can't ask more," said Olson, approvingly.

They walked heavily through the mud on the streets between the rows of tents. The camp stretched drearily over the Rheims plain, with the rain beating on the sagging tents. The division had been there over three weeks by now, waiting to be shipped home, and all the meager diversions of the neighborhood had been sampled and exhausted, and there was an air of watchful suspicion and impatience with the military life hanging over the camp now, and there was even reputed to be a staff sergeant in C Company who was laying odds they would not get back to America before July Fourth.

"I'm redeployable," Olson sang. "It's so enjoyable . . ." It was a jingle he had composed to no recognizable melody in the early days after the victory in Europe, when he had added up his points and found they only came to 63. "Tokyo, wait for me . . .''

They were going to be discharged as soon as they got back to the States, but Olson persisted in singing the song, occasionally adding a mournful stanza about dengue fever and brown girls with venereal disease. He was a short, round boy who had been flunked out of air cadets' school and transferred to the infantry, but whose spirits had not been damaged in the process. He had a high, childish voice and a pretty baby face. He was very good-natured, and had a girl waiting for him at the University of California, where he intended to finish his course at government expense when he got out of the army, and he was just the type who is killed off early and predictably and sadly in motion pictures about the war, but he had gone through four campaigns and six major battles without a scratch.

Seeger was a large, lanky boy, with a big nose, who had been wounded at Saint Lô, but had come back to his outfit in the Siegfried Line, quite unchanged. He was cheerful and dependable, and he knew his business and had broken in five or six second lieutenants who had been killed or wounded and the CO had tried to get him commissioned in the field, but the war had ended while the paperwork was being fumbled over at headquarters.

"They reached the door of the orderly tent and stopped. "Be brave, Sergeant," Olson said. "Welch and I are depending on you."

"O.K.," Seeger said, and went in.

The tent had the dank, army-canvas smell that had been so much a part of Seeger's life in the past three years. The company clerk was reading a July, 1945, issue of the *Buffalo Courier-Express*, which had just reached him, and Captain Taney, the company CO, was seated at a sawbuck table he used as a desk, writing a letter to his wife, his lips pursed with effort. He was a small, fussy man, with sandy hair that was falling out. While the fighting had been going on, he had been lean and tense and his small voice had been cold and full of authority. But now he had relaxed, and a little pot belly was creeping up under his belt and he kept the top button of his trousers open when he could do it without too public loss of dignity. During the war Seeger had thought of him as a natural soldier, tireless, fanatic about detail, aggressive, severely anxious to kill Germans. But in the past few months Seeger had seen him relapsing gradually and pleasantly into a small-town wholesale hardware merchant, which he had been before the war, sedentary and a little shy, and, as he had once told Seeger, worried, here in the bleak champagne fields of France, about his daughter, who had just turned twelve and had a tendency to go after the boys and had been caught by her mother kissing a fifteen-year-old neighbor in the hammock after school.

"Hello, Seeger," he said, returning the salute in a mild, offhand gesture. "What's on your mind?"

"Am I disturbing you, sir?"

"Oh, no. Just writing a letter to my wife. You married, Seeger?" He peered at the tall boy standing before him.

"No, sir."

"It's very difficult," Taney sighed, pushing dissatisfiedly at the letter before him. "My wife complains I don't tell her I love her often enough. Been married fifteen years. You'd think she'd know by now." He smiled at Seeger. "I thought you were going to Paris," he said. "I signed the passes yesterday."

"That's what I came to see you about, sir."

"I suppose something's wrong with the passes." Taney spoke resignedly, like a man who has never quite got the hang of army regulations and has had requisitions, furloughs, requests for court-martial returned for correction in a baffling flood.

"No, sir," Seeger said. "The passes're fine. They start tomorrow. Well, it's just . . . ." He looked around at the company clerk, who was on the sports page.

"This confidential?" Taney asked.

"If you don't mind, sir."

286

"Johnny," Taney said to the clerk, "go stand in the rain some place."

"Yes, sir," the clerk said, and slowly got up and walked out.

Taney looked shrewdly at Seeger, spoke in a secret whisper. "You pick up anything?" he asked.

Seeger grinned. "No, sir, haven't had my hands on a girl since Strasbourg."

"Ah, that's good." Taney leaned back, relieved, happy he didn't have to cope with the disapproval of the Medical Corps.

"It's—well," said Seeger, embarrassed, "it's hard to say—but it's money."

Taney shook his head sadly. "I know."

"We haven't been paid for three months, sir, and . . ."

"Damn it!" Taney stood up and shouted furiously. "I would like to take every bloody chair-warming old lady in the Finance Department and wring their necks."

The clerk stuck his head into the tent. "Anything wrong? You call for me, sir?"

"No," Taney shouted. "Get out of here."

The clerk ducked out.

Taney sat down again. "I suppose," he said, in a more normal voice, "they have their problems. Outfits being broken up, being moved all over the place. But it is rugged."

"It wouldn't be so bad," Seeger said. "But we're going to Paris tomorrow. Olson, Welch and myself. And you need money in Paris."

"Don't I know it." Taney wagged his head. "Do you know what I paid for a bottle of champagne on the Place Pigalle in September . . . ?" He paused significantly. "I won't tell you. You won't have any respect for me the rest of your life."

Seeger laughed. "Hanging," he said, "is too good for the guy who thought up the rate of exchange."

"I don't care if I never see another franc as long as I live." Taney waved his letter in the air, although it had been dry for a long time.

There was silence in the tent and Seeger swallowed a little embarrassedly, watching the CO wave the flimsy sheet of paper in regular sweeping movements. "Sir," he said, "the truth is, I've come to borrow some money for Welch, Olson and myself. We'll pay it back out of the first pay we get, and that can't be too long from now. If you don't want to give it to us, just tell me and I'll understand and get the hell out of here. We don't like to ask, but you might just as well be dead as be in Paris broke."

Taney stopped waving his letter and put it down thoughtfully. He peered at it, wrinkling his brow, looking like an aged bookkeeper in the single gloomy light that hung in the middle of the tent.

"Just say the word, Captain," Seeger said, "and I'll blow . . ."

"Stay where you are, son," said Taney. He dug in his shirt pocket and took out a worn, sweat-stained wallet. He looked at it for a moment. "Alligator," he said, with automatic, absent pride. "My wife sent it to me when we were in England. Pounds don't fit in it. However . . ." He opened it and took out all the contents. There was a small pile of francs on the table in front of him. He counted them. "Four hundred francs," he said. "Eight bucks."

"Excuse me," Seeger said humbly. "I shouldn't have asked."

"Delighted," Taney said vigorously. "Absolutely delighted." He started dividing the francs into two piles. "Truth is, Seeger, most of my money goes home in allotments. And the truth is, I lost eleven hundred francs in a poker game three nights ago, and I ought to be ashamed of myself. Here . . ." He shoved one pile toward Seeger. "Two hundred francs."

Seeger looked down at the frayed, meretricious paper, which always seemed to him like stage money, anyway. "No, sir," he said, "I can't take it."

"Take it," Taney said. "That's a direct order."

Seeger slowly picked up the money, not looking at Taney. "Some time, sir," he said, "after we get out, you have to come over to my house and you and my father and my brother and I'll go on a real drunk."

"I regard that," Taney said, gravely, "as a solemn commitment."

They smiled at each other and Seeger started out.

"Have a drink for me," said Taney, "at the Café de la Paix. A small drink." He was sitting down to write his wife he loved her when Seeger went out of the tent.

Olson fell into step with Seeger and they walked silently through the mud between the tents.

"Well, *mon vieux?*" Olson said finally.

"Two hundred francs," said Seeger.

Olson groaned. "Two hundred francs! We won't be able to pinch a whore's behind on the Boulevard des Capucines for two hundred francs. That miserable, penny-loving Yankee!"

"He only had four hundred," Seeger said.

"I revise my opinion," said Olson.

They walked disconsolately and heavily back toward their tent.

Olson spoke only once before they got there. "These raincoats," he said, patting his. "Most ingenious invention of the war. Highest saturation point of any modern fabric. Collect more water per square inch, and hold it, than any material known to man. All hail the quartermaster!''

Welch was waiting at the entrance of their tent. He was standing there peering excitedly and short-sightedly out at the rain through his glasses, looking angry and tough, like a big-city hack-driver, individual and incorruptible even in the ten-million colored uniform. Every time Seeger came upon Welch unexpectedly, he couldn't help smiling at the belligerent stance, the harsh stare through the steel-rimmed GI glasses, which had nothing at all to do with the way Welch really was. "It's a family inheritance," Welch had once explained. "My whole family stands as though we were getting ready to rap a drunk with a beer glass. Even my old lady." Welch had six brothers, all devout, according to Welch, and Seeger from time to time idly pictured them standing in a row, on Sunday mornings in church, seemingly on the verge of general violence, amid the hushed Latin and Sabbath millinery.

"How much?" Welch asked loudly.

"Don't make us laugh," Olson said, pushing past him into the tent.

"What do you think I could get from the French for my combat jacket?" Seeger said. He went into the tent and lay down on his cot.

Welch followed them in and stood between the two of them, a superior smile on his face. "Boys," he said, "on a man's errand."

"I can just see us now," Olson murmured, lying on his cot with his hands clasped behind his head, "painting Montmartre red. Please bring on the naked dancing girls. Four bucks worth."

"I am not worried," Welch announced.

"Get out of here." Olson turned over on his stomach.

"I know where we can put our hands on sixty-five bucks." Welch looked triumphantly first at Olson, then at Seeger.

Olson turned over slowly and sat up. "I'll kill you," he said, "if you're kidding."

"While you guys are wasting your time," Welch said, "fooling around with the infantry, I used my head. I went into Reems and used my head."

"Rance," Olson said automatically. He had had two years of French in college and he felt, now that the war was over, that he had to introduce his friends to some of his culture.

"I got to talking to a captain in the air force," Welch said eagerly. "A little fat old paddle-footed captain that never got higher off the ground than the second floor of Com Z headquarters,

289

and he told me that what he would admire to do more than anything else is take home a nice shiny German Luger pistol with him to show to the boys back in Pacific Grove, California.''

Silence fell on the tent and Welch and Olson looked tentatively at Seeger.

"Sixty-five bucks for a Luger, these days," Olson said, "is a very good figure."

"They've been sellin' for as low as thirty-five," said Welch hesitantly. "I'll bet," he said to Seeger, "you could sell yours now and buy another one back when you get some dough, and make a clear twenty-five on the deal."

Seeger didn't say anything. He had killed the owner of the Luger, an enormous SS major, in Coblenz, behind some paper bales in a warehouse, and the major had fired at Seeger three times with it, once knicking his helmet, before Seeger hit him in the face at twenty feet. Seeger had kept the Luger, a long, heavy, well-balanced gun, very carefully since then, lugging it with him, hiding it at the bottom of his bedroll, oiling it three times a week, avoiding all opportunities of selling it, although he had been offered as much as a hundred dollars for it and several times eighty and ninety, while the war was still on, before German weapons became a glut on the market.

"Well," said Welch, "there's no hurry. I told the captain I'd see him tonight around 8 o'clock in front of the Lion D'Or Hotel. You got five hours to make up your mind. Plenty of time."

"Me," said Olson, after a pause. "I won't say anything."

Seeger looked reflectively at his feet and the other two men avoided looking at him. Welch dug in his pocket. "I forgot," he said. "I picked up a letter for you." He handed it to Seeger.

"Thanks," Seeger said. He opened it absently, thinking about the Luger.

"Me," said Olson, "I won't say a bloody word. I'm just going to lie here and think about that nice fat air force captain."

Seeger grinned a little at him and went to the tent opening to read the letter in the light. The letter was from his father, and even from one glance at the handwriting, scrawly and hurried and spotted, so different from his father's usual steady handsome professional script, he knew that something was wrong.

"Dear Norman," it read, "sometime in the future, you must forgive me for writing this letter. But I have been holding this in so long, and there is no one here I can talk to, and because of your brother's condition I must pretend to be cheerful and optimistic all the time at home, both with him and your mother, who has never been the same since Leonard was killed. You're the oldest now, and although I know we've never talked very seriously about anything before, you have been through a great deal by now, and I imagine you must have matured considerably, and you've seen so many different places and people. . . . Norman, I need help. While the war was on and you were fighting, I kept this to myself. It wouldn't have been fair to burden you with this. But now the war is over, and I no longer feel I can stand up under this alone. And you will have to face it some time when you get home, if you haven't faced it already, and perhaps we can help each other by facing it together. . . .''

"I'm redeployable," Olson was singing softly, on his cot. "It's so enjoyable, In the Pelilu mud, With the tropical crud . . ." He fell silent after his burst of song.

Seeger blinked his eyes, at the entrance of the tent, in the wan rainy light, and went on reading his father's letter, on the stiff white stationery with the University letterhead in polite engraving at the top of each page.

"I've been feeling this coming on for a long time," the letter continued, "but it wasn't until last Sunday morning that something happened to make me feel it in its full force. I don't know how much you've guessed about the reason for Jacob's discharge from the army. It's true he was pretty badly wounded in the leg at Metz, but I've asked around, and I know that men with worse wounds were returned to duty after hospitalization. Jacob got a medical discharge, but I don't think it was from the shrapnel wound in his thigh. He is suffering now from what I suppose you call combat fatigue, and he is subject to fits of depression and hallucinations. Your mother and I thought that as time went by and the war and the army receded, he would grow better. Instead, he is growing worse. Last Sunday morning when I came down into the living room from upstairs he was crouched in his old uniform, next to the window, peering out . . ."

"What the hell," Olson was saying, "if we don't get the sixty-five bucks we can always go to the Louvre. I understand the Mona Lisa is back."

"I asked Jacob what he was doing," the letter went on. "He didn't turn around. 'I'm observing,' he said. 'V-1's and V-2's. Buzz-bombs and rockets. They're coming in by the hundreds.' I tried to reason with him and he told me to crouch and save myself from flying glass. To humor him I got down on the floor beside him and tried to tell him the war was over, that we were in Ohio, 4,000 miles away from the nearest spot where bombs had fallen,

291

that America had never been touched. He wouldn't listen. 'These're the new rocket bombs,' he said, 'for the Jews.' ''

"Did you ever hear of the Pantheon?" Olson asked loudly.

"No," said Welch.

"It's free."

"I'll go," said Welch.

Seeger shook his head a little and blinked his eyes before he went back to the letter.

"After that," his father went on, "Jacob seemed to forget about the bombs from time to time, but he kept saying that the mobs were coming up the street armed with bazookas and Browning automatic rifles. He mumbled incoherently a good deal of the time and kept walking back and forth saying, 'What's the situation? Do you know what the situation is?' And he told me he wasn't worried about himself, he was a soldier and he expected to be killed, but he was worried about Mother and myself and Leonard and you. He seemed to forget that Leonard was dead. I tried to calm him and get him back to bed before your mother came down, but he refused and wanted to set out immediately to rejoin his division. It was all terribly disjointed and at one time he took the ribbon he got for winning the Bronze star and threw it in the fireplace, then he got down on his hands and knees and picked it out of the ashes and made me pin it on him again, and he kept repeating, 'This is when they are coming for the Jews.' ''

"The next war I'm in," said Olson, "they don't get me under the rank of colonel."

It had stopped raining by now and Seeger folded the unfinished letter and went outside. He walked slowly down to the end of the company street, and facing out across the empty, soaked French fields, scarred and neglected by various armies, he stopped and opened the letter again.

"I don't know what Jacob went through in the army," his father wrote, "that has done this to him. He never talks to me about the war and he refuses to go to a psychoanalyst, and from time to time he is his own bouncing, cheerful self, playing in tennis tournaments, and going around with a large group of girls. But he has devoured all the concentration camp reports, and I have found him weeping when the newspapers reported that a hundred Jews were killed in Tripoli some time ago.

"The terrible thing is, Norman, that I find myself coming to believe that it is not neurotic for a Jew to behave like this today. Perhaps Jacob is the normal one, and I, going about my business, teaching economics in a quiet classroom, pretending to understand that the world is comprehensible and orderly, am really the mad one. I ask you once more to forgive me for writing you a letter like this, so different from any letter or any conversation I've ever had with you. But it is crowding me, too. I do not see rockets and bombs, but I see other things.

"Wherever you go these days—restaurants, hotels, clubs, trains—you seem to hear talk about the Jews, mean, hateful, murderous talk. Whatever page you turn to in the newspapers you seem to find an article about Jews being killed somewhere on the face of the globe. And there are large, influential newspapers and well-known columnists who each day are growing more and more outspoken and more popular. The day that Roosevelt died I heard a drunken man yelling outside a bar, 'Finally, they got the Jew out of the White House.' And some of the people who heard him merely laughed and nobody stopped him. And on V-E Day, in celebration, hoodlums in Los Angeles savagely beat a Jewish writer. It's difficult to know what to do, whom to fight, where to look for allies.

"Three months ago, for example, I stopped my Thursday night poker game, after playing with the same men for over ten years. John Reilly happened to say that the Jews were getting rich out of this war, and when I demanded an apology, he refused, and when I looked around at the faces of the men who had been my friends for so long, I could see they were not with me. And when I left the house no one said good night to me. I know the poison was spreading from Germany before the war and during it, but I had not realized it had come so close.

"And in my economics class, I find myself idiotically hedging in my lectures. I discover that I am loath to praise any liberal writer or any liberal act and find myself somehow annoyed and frightened to see an article of criticism of existing abuses signed by a Jewish name. And I hate to see Jewish names on important committees, and hate to read of Jews fighting for the poor, the oppressed, the cheated and hungry. Somehow, even in a country where my family has lived a hundred years, the enemy has won this subtle victory over me—he has made me disfranchise myself from honest causes by calling them foreign, Communist, using Jewish names connected with them as ammunition against them.

"And, most hateful of all, I find myself looking for Jewish names in the casualty lists and secretly being glad when I discover them there, to prove that there at least, among the dead and wounded, we belong. Three times, thanks to you and your brothers, I have found our name there, and, may God forgive me, at the expense of your blood and your brother's life, through my tears, I have felt that same twitch of satisfaction. . . .

"When I read the newspapers and see another story that Jews are still being killed in Poland, or Jews are requesting that they be given back their homes in France, or that they be allowed to enter some country where they will not be murdered, I am annoyed with them, I feel they are boring the rest of the world with their problems, they are making demands upon the rest of the world by being killed, they are disturbing everyone by being hungry and asking for the return of their property. If we could all fall through the crust of the earth and vanish in one hour, with our heroes and poets and prophets and martyrs, perhaps we would be doing the memory of the Jewish race a service. . . .

"This is how I feel today, son. I need some help. You've been to the war, you've fought and killed men, you've seen the people of other countries. Maybe you understand things that I don't understand. Maybe you see some hope somewhere. Help me. Your loving father."

Seeger folded the letter slowly, not seeing what he was doing because the tears were burning his eyes. He walked slowly and aimlessly across the dead autumn grass of the empty field, away from the camp.

He tried to wipe away his tears, because with his eyes full and dark, he kept seeing his father and brother crouched in the old-fashioned living room in Ohio and hearing his brother, dressed in the old, discarded uniform, saying, "These're the new rocket bombs. For the Jews."

He sighed, looking out over the bleak, wasted land. Now, he thought, now I have to think about it. He felt a slight, unreasonable twinge of anger at his father for presenting him with the necessity of thinking about it. The army was good about serious problems. While you were fighting, you were too busy and frightened and weary to think about anything, and at other times you were relaxing, putting your brain on a shelf, postponing everything to that impossible time of clarity and beauty after the war. Well, now, here was the impossible, clear, beautiful time, and here was his father, demanding that he think. There are all sorts of Jews, he thought, there are the sort whose every waking moment is ridden by the knowledge of Jewishness, who see signs against the Jew in every smile on a streetcar, every whisper, who see pogroms in every newspaper article, threats in every change of the weather, scorn in every handshake, death behind each closed door. He had not been like that. He was young, he was big and healthy and easy-going and people of all kinds had seemed to like him all his life, in the army and out. In America, especially, what was going on in Europe had seemed remote, unreal, unrelated to him. The chanting, bearded old men burning in the Nazi furnaces, and the dark-eyed women screaming prayers in Polish and Russian and German as they were pushed naked into the gas chambers had seemed as shadowy and almost as unrelated to him as he trotted out onto the Stadium field for a football game, as they must have been to the men named O'Dwyer and Wickersham and Poole who played in the line beside him.

They had seemed more related in Europe. Again and again in the towns that had been taken back from the Germans, gaunt, gray-faced men had stopped him humbly, looking searchingly at him, and had asked, peering at his long, lined, grimy face, under the anonymous helmet, "Are you a Jew?" Sometimes they asked it in English, sometimes French, or Yiddish. He didn't know French or Yiddish, but he learned to recognize the phrase. He had never understood exactly why they had asked the question, since they never demanded anything from him, rarely even could speak to him, until, one day in Strasbourg, a little bent old man and a small, shapeless woman had stopped him, and asked, in English, if he was Jewish.

"Yes," he said, smiling at them.

The two old people had smiled widely, like children. "Look," the old man had said to his wife. "A young American soldier. A Jew. And so large and strong." He had touched Seeger's arm reverently with the tips of his fingers, then had touched the Garand he was carrying. "And such a beautiful rifle . . ."

And there, for a moment, although he was not particularly sensitive, Seeger got an inkling of why he had been stopped and questioned by so many before. Here, to these bent, exhausted old people, ravaged of their families, familiar with flight and death for so many years, was a symbol of continuing life. A large young man in the uniform of the liberator, blood, as they thought, of their blood, but not in hiding, not quivering in fear and helplessness, but striding secure and victorious down the street, armed and capable of inflicting terrible destruction on his enemies.

Seeger had kissed the old lady on the cheek and she had wept and the old man had scolded her for it, while shaking Seeger's hand fervently and thankfully before saying good-bye.

And, thinking back on it, it was silly to pretend that, even before his father's letter, he had been like any other American soldier going through the war. When he had stood over the huge dead SS major with the face blown in by his bullets in the warehouse in Coblenz, and taken the pistol from the dead hand, he had tasted a strange little extra flavor of triumph. How many Jews, he'd thought, has this man killed, how fitting it is that I've killed him. Neither Olson nor Welch, who were like his brothers, would have felt that in picking up the Luger, its barrel still hot from the last shots its owner had fired before dying. And he had resolved that he was going to make sure to take this gun back with him to America, and plug it and keep it on his desk at home, as a kind of vague, half-understood sign to himself that justice had once been done and he had been its instrument.

Maybe, he thought, maybe I'd better take it back with me, but not as a memento. Not plugged, but loaded. America by now was a strange country for him. He had been away a long time and he wasn't sure what was waiting for him when he got home. If the mobs were coming down the street toward his house, he was not going to die singing and praying.

When he was taking basic training he'd heard a scrawny, clerk-like-looking soldier from Boston talking at the other end of the PX bar, over the watered beer. "The boys at the office," the scratchy voice was saying, "gave me a party before I left. And they told me one thing. 'Charlie,' they said, 'hold on to your bayonet. We're going to be able to use it when you get back. On the Yids.' "

He hadn't said anything then, because he'd felt it was neither possible nor desirable to fight against every random overheard voice raised against the Jews from one end of the world to another. But again and again, at odd moments, lying on a barracks cot, or stretched out trying to sleep on the floor of a ruined French farmhouse, he had heard that voice, harsh, satisfied, heavy with hate and ignorance, saying above the beery grumble of apprentice soldiers at the bar, "Hold on to your bayonet. . . ."

And the other stories—Jews collected stories of hatred and injustice and inklings of doom like a special, lunatic kind of miser. The story of the naval officer, commander of a small vessel off the Aleutians, who, in the officers' wardroom, had complained that he hated the Jews because it was the Jews who had demanded that the Germans be beaten first and the forces in the Pacific had been starved in consequence. And when one of his junior officers, who had just come aboard, had objected and told the commander that he was a Jew, the commander had risen from the table and said, "Mister, the Constitution of the United States says I have to serve in the same navy with Jews, but it doesn't say I have to eat at the same table with them." In the fogs and the cold, swelling Arctic seas off the Aleutians, in a small boat, subject to sudden, mortal attack at any moment . . .

And the two young combat engineers in an attached company on D Day, when they were lying off the coast right before climbing down into the landing barges. "There's France," one of them had said.

"What's it like?" the second one had asked, peering out across the miles of water toward the smoking coast.

"Like every place else," the first one had answered. "The Jews've made all the dough during the war."

"Shut up!" Seeger had said, helplessly thinking of the dead, destroyed, wandering, starving Jews of France. The engineers had shut up, and they'd climbed down together into the heaving boat, and gone into the beach together.

And the million other stories. Jews, even the most normal and best adjusted of them, became living treasuries of them, scraps of malice and bloodthirstiness, clever and confusing and cunningly twisted so that every act by every Jew became suspect and blameworthy and hateful. Seeger had heard the stories, and had made an almost conscious effort to forget them. Now, holding his father's letter in his hand, he remembered them all.

He stared unseeingly out in front of him. Maybe, he thought, maybe it would've been better to have been killed in the war, like Leonard. Simpler. Leonard would never have to face a crowd coming for his mother and father. Leonard would not have to listen and collect these hideous, fascinating little stories that made of every Jew a stranger in any town, on any field, on the face of the earth. He had come so close to being killed so many times, it would have been so easy, so neat and final.

Seeger shook his head. It was ridiculous to feel like that, and he was ashamed of himself for the weak moment. At the age of twenty-one, death was not an answer.

"Seeger!" It was Olson's voice. He and Welch had sloshed silently up behind Seeger, standing in the open field. "Seeger, *mon vieux*, what're you doing—grazing?"

Seeger turned slowly to them. "I wanted to read my letter," he said.

Olson looked closely at him. They had been together so long, through so many things, that flickers and hints of expression on each other's faces were recognized and acted upon. "Anything wrong?" Olson asked.

"No," said Seeger. "Nothing much."

"Norman," Welch said, his voice young and solemn. "Norman, we've been talking, Olson and me. We decided—you're pretty attached to that Luger, and maybe—if you—well . . ."

"What he's trying to say," said Olson, "is we withdraw the request. If you want to sell it, O.K. If you don't, don't do it for our sake. Honest."

Seeger looked at them, standing there, disreputable and tough and familiar. "I haven't made up my mind yet," he said.

"Anything you decide," Welch said oratorically, "is perfectly all right with us. Perfectly."

They walked aimlessly and silently across the field, away from camp. As they walked, their shoes making a wet, sliding sound in the damp, dead grass, Seeger thought of the time Olson had covered him in the little town outside Cherbourg, when Seeger had been caught going down the side of a street by four Germans with a machine gun on the second story of a house on the corner and Olson had had to stand out in the middle of the street with no cover at all for more than a minute, firing continuously, so that Seeger could get away alive. And he thought of the time outside Saint Lô when he had been wounded and had lain in a minefield for three hours and Welch and Captain Taney had come looking for him in the darkness and had found him and picked him up and run for it, all of them expecting to get blown up any second.

And he thought of all the drinks they'd had together and the long marches and the cold winter together, and all the girls they'd gone out with together, and he thought of his father and brother crouching behind the window in Ohio waiting for the rockets and the crowds armed with Browning automatic rifles.

"Say," he stopped and stood facing them. "Say, what do you guys think of the Jews?"

Welch and Olson looked at each other, and Olson glanced down at the letter in Seeger's hand.

"Jews?" Olson said finally. "What're they? Welch, you ever hear of the Jews?"

Welch looked thoughtfully at the gray sky. "No," he said. "But remember, I'm an uneducated fellow."

"Sorry, Bud," Olson said, turning to Seeger. "We can't help you. Ask us another question. Maybe we'll do better."

Seeger peered at the faces of his friends. He would have to rely upon them, later on, out of uniform, on their native streets, more than he had ever relied on them on the bullet-swept street and in the dark minefield in France. Welch and Olson stared back at him, troubled, their faces candid and tough and dependable.

"What time," Seeger asked, "did you tell that captain you'd meet him?"

"Eight o'clock," Welch said. "But we don't have to go. If you have any feeling about that gun . . ."

"We'll meet him," Seeger said. "We can use that sixty-five bucks."

"Listen," Olson said, "I know how much you like that gun and I'll feel like a heel if you sell it."

"Forget it," Seeger said, starting to walk again. "What could I use it for in America?"

# The Man with One Arm

I would like complete reports on these three people," Captain Mikhailov was saying. He pushed a slip of paper across the desk to Garbrecht, and Garbrecht glanced at the names. "They are interpreters at the American civil affairs headquarters. The Americans have a charming habit of hiring ex-Nazis almost exclusively for those jobs, and we have found it rewarding to inquire into the pasts of such gentlemen." Mikhailov smiled. He was a short, stocky man with a round, shielded face, and pale, unsmiling eyes, and when he smiled it was like a flower painted unconvincingly on stone.

Garbrecht recognized two of the three names. Mikhailov was right. They were Nazis. It would take some thinking out, later, though, to decide whether to expose them to Mikhailov, or exactly how far to expose them. Garbrecht watched Mikhailov unlock a drawer in his desk and take out some American marks. Methodically, Mikhailov counted the notes out in his square, machine-like hands. He locked the drawer and pushed the money across the desk to Garbrecht.

"There," Mikhailov said, "that will keep you until we see each other next week."

"Yes, Captain," Garbrecht said. He reached out and pulled the money toward him, leaving it on the top of the desk. He took out his wallet, and, slowly, one by one, put the notes into the wallet. He was still slow and clumsy with things like that, because he had not yet learned how to handle things deftly with his left hand, and his right hand and arm were buried behind the field hospital in the brewery fourteen hundred miles away. Mikhailov watched him impassively, without offering aid.

Garbrecht put his wallet away and stood up. His overcoat was thrown over a chair and he picked it up and struggled to get it over his shoulders.

"Till next week," he said.

"Next week," Mikhailov said.

Garbrecht did not salute. He opened the door and went out. At least, he thought, with a nervous sensation of triumph, as he went down the grimy steps past the two plain-clothes men loitering in the dark hall, at least I didn't salute the bastard. That's the third week in a row I didn't salute him.

The plain-clothes men stared at him with a common blank threatening look. By now he knew them too well to be frightened by them. They looked that way at everything. When they looked at a horse or a child or a bunch of flowers, they threatened it. It was merely their comfortable professional adjustment to the world around them, like Mikhailov's smile. The Russians, Garbrecht thought as he went down the street, what a people to have in Berlin!

Garbrecht walked without looking about him. The landscape of the cities of Germany had become monotonous—rubble, broken statues, neatly swept lanes between piled cracked brick, looming blank single walls, shells of buildings, half-demolished houses in which dozens of families somehow lived. He moved briskly and energetically, like everyone else, swinging his one arm a little awkwardly to maintain his balance, but very little of what he saw around him made any impression on him. A solid numbness had taken possession of him when they cut off his arm. It was like the anesthesia which they injected into your spine. You were conscious and you could see and hear and speak and you could understand what was being done to you, but all feeling was absent. Finally, Garbrecht knew, the anesthesia would wear off, but for the present it was a most valuable defense.

"Lieutenant." It was a woman's voice somewhere behind him, and Garbrecht did not look around. "Oh, Lieutenant Garbrecht."

He stopped and turned slowly. Nobody had called him lieutenant for more than a year now. A short, blonde woman in a gray cloth coat was hurrying toward him. He looked at her, puzzled. He had never seen her before, and he wondered if it were she who had called his name.

"Did you call me?" he asked as she stopped in front of him.

"Yes," she said. She was thin, with a pale, rather pretty face. She did not smile. "I followed you from Mikhailov's office."

"I'm sure," Garbrecht said, turning and starting away, "that you have made some mistake."

The woman fell in beside him, walking swiftly. She wore no stockings and her legs showed a little purple from the cold. "Please," she said, "do not behave like an idiot."

Then, in a flat, undemanding voice, she said several things to him that he had thought nobody alive remembered about him, and finally she called him by his correct name, and he knew that there was no escaping it now. He stopped in the middle of the ruined street and sighed, and said, after a long time, "Very well. I will go with you."

There was a smell of cooking in the room. Good cooking, A roast, probably, and a heavy, strong soup. It was the kind of smell that had seemed to vanish from Germany sometime around 1942, and even with all the other things happening to him, Garbrecht could feel the saliva welling helplessly and tantalizingly up from the ducts under his tongue. It was a spacious room with a high ceiling that must have been at one time quite elegant. There was a bricked-up fireplace with a large, broken mirror over it. By some trick of fracture the mirror reflected separate images in each of its broken parts, and it made Garbrecht feel that something shining and abnormal was hidden there.

The girl had ushered him without formality into the room and had told him to sit down and had disappeared. Garbrecht could feel his muscles slowly curling as he sat rigidly in the half-broken wooden chair, staring coldly at the battered desk, the surprising leather chair behind the desk, the strange mirror, the ten-inch high portrait of Lenin which was the only adornment on the wall. Lenin looked down at him from the wall, across the years, through the clumsy heroics of the lithographer, with a remote, ambiguous challenge glaring from the dark, wild eyes.

The door through which he had himself come was opened and a man entered. The man slammed the door behind him and walked swiftly across the room to the desk. Then he wheeled and faced Garbrecht.

"Well, well," the man said, smiling, his voice hearty and welcoming, "here you are. Here you are. Sorry to keep you waiting. Terribly sorry." He beamed across the room, leaning forward hospitably from his position in front of the desk. He was a short, stocky man with a light, pink face, and pale, silky hair that he wore long, possibly in an attempt to hide what might be an increasing tendency to baldness. He looked like an amiable butcher's boy, growing a little old for his job, or the strong man in a tumbling act in a small-time circus, the one on the bottom that the others climbed on. Garbrecht stood up and peered at him, trying to remember if he had ever seen the man before.

"No, no," the man said, waving his pudgy hands, "no, we have never met. Do not trouble your brain. Sit down, sit down.

302

Comfort first. Everything else after.'' He leapt lightly across the room and almost pushed Garbrecht into his chair. "It is a lesson I have learned from our friends, the Americans. How to slouch. Look what they've accomplished merely by spending most of their time on the base of their spines.'' He laughed uproariously, as though the joke were too merry not to be enjoyed, and swept quickly across the room, with his almost leaping, light gait, and hurled himself into the large leather chair behind the desk. He continued beaming at Garbrecht.

"I want to say,'' said Garbrecht, "that I have no notion of why I was asked to come here. I merely came,'' he said carefully, "because the young lady made me curious, and I had an hour to spare, anyway, and . . .''

"Enough, enough.'' The man rocked solidly back and forth in the squeaking chair. "You came. Sufficient. Delighted. Very pleased. Have a cigarette . . .'' With a sudden movement, he thrust out the brass cigarette box that lay on the desk.

"Not at the moment, thank you,'' Garbrecht said, although his throat was quivering for one.

"Ah,'' the fat man said, grinning. "A rarity. Only German known to refuse a cigarette since the surrender. Still, no matter. . . .'' He took a cigarette himself and lighted it deftly. "First, introductions, Lieutenant. My name. Anton Seedorf. Captain, Hermann Goering Division. I keep the title.'' He grinned. "A man saves what he can from a war.''

"I imagine,'' Garbrecht said, "you know my name.''

"Yes.'' Seedorf seemed to bubble with some inward humor. "Oh, yes, I certainly do. Yes, indeed. I've heard a great deal about you. Been most anxious to meet you. The arm,'' he said, with sudden solemnity. "Where was that?''

"Stalingrad.''

"Ah, Stalingrad,'' Seedorf said heartily, as though he were speaking the name of a winter resort at which he had spent a marvelous holiday. "A lot of good souls left there, weren't there, many good souls. A miscalculation. One of many. Vanity. The most terrible thing in the world, the vanity of a victorious army. A most interesting subject for historians—the role of vanity in military disasters. Don't you agree?'' He peered eagerly at Garbrecht.

"Captain,'' Garbrecht said coldly, "I cannot remain here all afternoon.''

"Of course,'' Seedorf said. "Naturally. You're curious about why I invited you here. I understand.'' He pufed swiftly on his cigarette, wreathing his pale head in smoke before the cracked mirror. He jumped up and perched himself on the desk, facing Garbrecht, boyishly. ''Well,'' he said, heartily, ''it is past time for hiding anything. I know you. I know your very good record in the Party . . .''

Garbrecht felt the cold rising in his throat. It's going to be worse, he thought, worse than I expected.

'' . . . promising career in the army until the unfortunate accident at Stalingrad,'' Seedorf was saying brightly, ''loyal, dependable, et cetera; there is really no need to go into it at this moment, is there?''

''No,'' said Garbrecht, ''none at all.'' He stood up. ''If it is all the same to you, I prefer not to be reminded of any of it. That is all past and, I hope, it will soon all be forgotten.''

Seedorf giggled. ''Now, now,'' he said. ''There is no need to be so cautious with me. To a person like you or me,'' he said, with a wide, genial gesture, ''it is never forgotten. To a person who has said the things we have said, who did the things we have done, for so many years, a paid Party official, a good soldier, a good German . . .''

''I am not interested any more,'' Garbrecht said loudly but hopelessly, ''in being what you call a good German.''

''It is not a question,'' Seedorf said, smiling widely and dousing his cigarette, ''of what you are interested in, Lieutenant. I beg your pardon. It is a question of what must be done. Simply that.''

''I am not going to do anything,'' said Garbrecht.

''I beg your pardon once more.'' Seedorf rocked happily back and forth on the edge of the desk. ''There are several little things that you can be very useful doing. I beg your pardon, you will do them. You work for the Russians, collecting information in the American zone. A useful fellow. You also work for the Americans, collecting information in the Russian zone.'' Seedorf beamed at him. ''A prize!''

Garbrecht started to deny it, then shrugged wearily. There might be a way out, but denial certainly was not it.

''We, too, several of us, maybe more than several, could use a little information.'' Seedorf's voice had grown harder, and there was only an echo of jollity left in it, like the sound of laughter dying down a distant alley on a cold night. ''We are not as large an organization at the moment as the Russians; we are not as well equipped for the time being as the Americans . . . but we are even more . . . more . . .'' He chuckled as he thought of the word . . . ''Curious. And more ambitious.''

There was silence in the room. Garbrecht stared heavily at the pale, fat head outlined against the broken mirror with its insane, multiplied reflections. If he were alone, Garbrecht knew he would bend his head and weep, as he did so often, without apparent reason, these days.

"Why don't you stop?" he asked heavily. "What's the sense? How many times do you have to be beaten?"

Seedorf grinned. "One more time, at least," he said. "Is that a good answer?"

"I won't do it," Garbrecht said. "I'll give the whole thing up. I don't want to get involved any more."

"I beg your pardon," said Seedorf happily, "you will give up nothing. It is terrible for me to talk to a man who gave his arm for the Fatherland this way," he said with a kind of glittering facsimile of pity, "but I am afraid the Russians would be told your correct name and Party position from 1934 on, and they would be told of your affiliations with the Americans, and they would be told of your job as adjutant to the commanding officer of Maidanek concentration camp in the winter of 1944, when several thousand people died by orders with your name on them. . . ."

Seedorf drummed his heels softly and cheerfully against the desk. "They have just really begun on their war trials . . . and these new ones will not run ten months, Lieutenant. I beg your pardon for talking this way, and I promise you from now on, we will not mention any of these matters again." He jumped up and came across the room in his swift, round walk. "I know how you feel," he said softly. "Often, I feel the same way. Quit. Quit now, once and for all. But it is not possible to quit. In a little while you will see that and you will be very grateful."

"What is it?" Garbrecht said. "What is it that you want me to do?"

"Just a little thing," Seedorf said. "Nothing at all, really. Merely report here every week and tell me what you have told the Russians and the Americans and what they have told you. Fifteen minutes a week. That's all there is to it."

"Fifteen minutes a week." Garbrecht was surprised that he had actually laughed, "That's all."

"Exactly." Seedorf laughed. "It won't be so bad. There's always a meal to be had here, and cigarettes. It is almost like old times. There!" He stepped back, smiling widely. "I am so happy it is settled." He took Garbrecht's hand and shook it warmly with both his. "Till next week," he said.

Garbrecht looked heavily at him. Then he sighed. "Till next week," he said.

Seedorf held the door open for him when he went out. There was no one else in the corridor and no guards at the door, and he walked slowly down the creaking hall, through the rich smell of cooking, and on into the street and the gathering cold evening air.

He walked blankly through the broken brick wastes toward the American control post, staring straight ahead of him. Next week, he thought, I must ask him what the picture of Lenin is doing on the wall.

The office of Captain Peterson was very different from the bleak room in which Captain Mikhailov conducted his affairs. There was a clerk in the corner and an American flag on the wall, and the busy sound of American typewriters from the next room. There was a water cooler and a warm radiator, and there was a picture of a pretty girl with a small blond child on Peterson's disordered desk. Garbrecht took his coat off and sat down in one of the comfortable looted plush chairs and waited for Peterson. The interviews with Peterson were much less of a strain than the ones with Mikhailov. Peterson was a large young man who spoke good German and, amazingly, fair Russian. He was good-natured and naïve, and Garbrecht was sure he believed Garbrecht's excellently forged papers and innocuous, false record, and Garbrecht's quiet, repeated insistence that he had been anti-Nazi from the beginning. Peterson was an enthusiast. He had been an enthusiast about the war, in which he had performed quite creditably, he was an enthusiast about Germany, its scenery, its art, its future, its people, whom he regarded as the first victims of Hitler. Mikhailov was different. He bleakly made no comment on the official soft tones issuing from Moscow on the subject of the German people, but Garbrecht knew that he regarded the Germans not as the first victims, but as the first accomplices.

Of late, Garbrecht had to admit, Peterson had not seemed quite so enthusiastic. He had seemed rather baffled and sometimes hurt and weary. In the beginning, his naïveté had spread to cover the Russians in a rosy blanket, too. The assignments he gave to Garbrecht to execute in the Russian zone were so routine and so comparatively innocent, that if Garbrecht had had a conscience he would have hesitated at taking payment for their fulfillment.

Peterson was smiling broadly when he came in, looking like a schoolboy who has just been promoted to the first team on a football squad. He was a tall, heavy young man with an excited, swift manner of talking. "Glad to see you, Garbrecht," he said. "I was afraid I was going to miss you. I've been busy as a bartender on Saturday night, hand-carrying orders all over the place, packing, saying good-bye . . ."

"Good-bye?" Garbrecht said, shaken by a small tremor of fear. "Where are you going?"

"Home." Peterson pulled out three drawers from his desk and started emptying them in a swift jumble. "The United States of America."

"But I thought," Garbrecht said, "that you had decided to stay. You said your wife and child were coming over and . . ."

"I know . . ." Peterson threw a whole batch of mimeographed papers lightheartedly into the trash basket. "I changed my mind." He stopped working on the drawers and looked soberly at Garbrecht. "They're not coming here. I decided I didn't want my child to grow up in Europe." He sat down heavily, staring over Garbrecht's head at the molding around the ceiling. "In fact," he said, "I don't think I want to hang around Europe any more myself. In the beginning I thought I could do a lot of good here. Now . . ." He shrugged. "They'd better try someone else. I'd better go back to America and clear my head for a while. It's simpler in a war. You know whom you're fighting and you have a general idea about where he is. Now . . ." Once more the shrug.

"Maybe I'm too stupid for a job like this," he continued. "Or maybe I expected too much. I've been here a year, and everything seems to be getting worse and worse. I feel as though I'm sliding downhill all the time. Slowly, not very perceptibly . . . but downhill. Maybe Germany has always struck everybody the same way. Maybe that's why so many people have always committed suicide here. I'm going to get out of here before I wake up one morning and say to myself, 'By God, they have the right idea.' "

Suddenly he stood up, swinging his big feet in their heavy army shoes down to the floor with a commanding crash. "Come on," he said. "I'll take you in to see Major Dobelmeir. He's going to replace me." Peterson opened the door for Garbrecht, and they went out into the anteroom with the four desks and the girls in uniform typing. Peterson led the way. "I think the United States Army is going to begin to get its money's worth out of you now, Garbrecht," Peterson said, without looking back. "Dobelmeir is quite a different kettle of fish from that nice, simple young Captain Peterson."

Garbrecht stared at the back of Peterson's head. So, he thought coldly, he wasn't so completely fooled by me, after all. Maybe it's good he's going.

But then Peterson opened the door to one of the rooms along the hall and they went in, and Garbrecht took one look at the major's leaf and the heavy, brooding, suspicious face, and he knew that he was wrong; it would have been much better if Peterson had stayed.

Peterson introduced them and the Major said, "Sit down," in flat, heavy-voiced German, and Peterson said, "Good luck, I have to go now," and left. The Major looked down at the papers on his desk and read them stolidly, for what seemed to Garbrecht like a very long time. Garbrecht felt the tension beginning again in his muscles, as it had in Seedorf's room. Everything, he thought, gets worse and worse, more and more complicated.

"Garbrecht," the Major said, without looking up, "I have been reading your reports." He did not say anything else, merely continued to read slowly and effortfully, his eyes covered, his heavy chin creasing in solid fat as he bent his head over the desk.

"Yes?" Garbrecht said finally, because he could no longer stand the silence.

For a moment, Dobelmeir did not answer. Then he said, "They aren't worth ten marks, all of them together, to anybody. The United States Government ought to sue you for obtaining money on false pretenses."

"I am very sorry," Garbrecht said hurriedly, "I thought that that is what was wanted, and I . . ."

"Don't lie." The Major finally lifted his head and stared fishily at him.

"My dear Major . . ."

"Keep quiet," the Major said evenly. "We now institute a new regime. You can do all right if you produce. If you don't, you can go find another job. Now we know where we stand."

"Yes, sir," said Garbrecht.

"I should not have to teach you your business at this late date," the Major said. "There is only one way in which an operation like this can pay for itself; only one rule to follow. All our agents must act as though the nation on which they are spying is an active enemy of the United States, as though the war has, in fact, begun. Otherwise the information you gather has no point, no focus, no measurable value. When you bring me information it must be information of an enemy who is probing our line for weak spots, who is building up various depots of supplies and troops and forces in specific places, who is choosing certain specific fields on which to fight the crucial battles. I am not interested in random, confusing gossip. I am only interested in indications of the disposition of the enemy's strength and indications of his aggressive intentions toward us. Is that clear?''

"Yes, sir," said Garbrecht.

The Major picked up three sheets of clipped-together papers. "This is your last report," he said. He ripped the papers methodically in half and then once more in half and threw them on the floor. "That is what I think of it."

"Yes, sir," said Garbrecht. He knew the sweat was streaming down into his collar and he knew that the Major must have noticed it and was probably sourly amused at it, but there was nothing he could do to stop it.

"This office has sent out its last chambermaid-gossip report," the Major said. "From now on, we will send out only useful military information, or nothing at all. I'm not paying you for the last two weeks' work. You haven't earned it. Get out of here. And don't come back until you have something to tell me."

He bent down once more over the papers on his desk. Garbrecht stood up and slowly went out the door. He knew that the Major did not look up as he closed the door behind him.

Greta wasn't home, and he had to stand outside her door in the cold all evening because the janitress refused to recognize him and let him in. Greta did not get back till after midnight, and then she came up with an American officer in a closed car, and Garbrecht had to hide in the shadows across the street while the American kissed Greta clumsily again and again before going off. Garbrecht hurried across the broken pavement of the street to reach Greta before she retreated into the house.

Greta could speak English and worked for the Americans as a typist and filing clerk, and perhaps something else, not quite so official, in the evenings. Garbrecht did not inquire too closely. Greta was agreeable enough and permitted him to use her room when he was in the American zone, and she always seemed to have a store of canned food in her cupboard, gift of her various uniformed employers, and she was quite generous and warm-hearted about the entire arrangement. Greta had been an energetic patriot before the defeat, and Garbrecht had met her when she visited the hospital where he was lying with his arm freshly severed after the somber journey back from Russia. Whether it was patriotism, pity, or perversity that had moved her, Garbrecht did not know, nor did he inquire too deeply; at any rate, Greta had remained a snug anchorage in the wild years that had passed, and he was fond of her.

"Hello," he said, as he came up behind her. She was struggling with the lock, and turned abruptly, as though frightened.

"Oh," she said. "I didn't think you'd be here tonight."

"I'm sorry," he said. "I couldn't get in touch with you."

She opened the door, and he went in with her. She unlocked the door of her own room, which was on the ground floor, and slammed it irritably behind her. Ah, he thought unhappily, things are bad here, too, tonight.

He sighed. "What is it?" he said.

"Nothing," she said. She started to undress, methodically, and without any of the usual graceful secrecy she ordinarily managed even in the small drab room.

"Can I be of any help?" Garbrecht asked.

Greta stopped pulling off her stockings and looked thoughtfully at Garbrecht. Then she shook her head and yanked at the heel of the right stocking. "You could," she said, contemptuously. "But you won't."

Garbrecht squinted painfully at her. "How do you know?" he asked.

"Because you're all the same," Greta said coldly. "Weak. Quiet. Disgusting."

"What is it?" he asked. "What would you want me to do?" He would have preferred it if Greta had refused to tell him, but he knew he had to ask.

Greta worked methodically on the other stocking. "You ought to get four or five of your friends, the ex-heroes of the German Army," she said disdainfully, "and march over to Freda Raush's house and tear her clothes off her back and shave her head and make her walk down the street that way."

"What?" Garbrecht sat up incredulously. "What are you talking about?"

"You were always yelling about honor," Greta said loudly. "Your honor, the Army's honor, Germany's honor."

"What's that got to do with Freda Raush?"

"Honor is something Germans have only when they're winning, is that it?" Greta pulled her dress savagely over her shoulders. "Disgusting."

Garbrecht shook his head. "I don't know what you're talking about," he said. "I thought Freda was a good friend of yours."

"Even the French," Greta said, disregarding him, "were braver. They shaved their women's heads when they caught them. . . ."

"All right, all right," Garbrecht said wearily. "What did Freda do?"

Greta looked wildly at him, her hair disarranged and tumbled around her full shoulders, her large, rather fat body shivering in cold and anger in her sleazy slip. "Tonight," she said, "she invited the Lieutenant I was with and myself to her house. . . ."

"Yes," said Garbrecht, trying to concentrate very hard.

"She is living with an American captain."

"Yes?" said Garbrecht, doubtfully. Half the girls Greta knew seemed to be living with American captains, and the other half were trying to. That certainly could not have infuriated Greta to this wild point of vengeance.

"Do you know what his name is?" Greta asked rhetorically. "Rosenthal! A Jew. Freda!"

Garbrecht sighed, his breath making a hollow, sorrowful sound in the cold midnight room. He looked up at Greta, who was standing over him, her face set in quivering, tense lines. She was usually such a placid, rather stupid, and easygoing girl that moments like this came as a shocking surprise.

"You will have to find someone else," Garbrecht said wearily, "if you want to have Freda's head shaved. I am not in the running."

"Of course," Greta said icily. "I knew you wouldn't be."

"Frankly," Garbrecht said, trying to be reasonable with her, "I am a little tired of the whole question of the Jews. I think we ought to drop it, once and for all. It was all right for a while, but I think we've probably just about used it all up by now."

"Ah," Greta said, "keep quiet. I should have known better than to expect anything from a cripple."

They both were silent then. Greta continued undressing with contemptuous asexual familiarity, and Garbrecht slowly took his clothes off and got into bed, while Greta, in a black rayon nightgown that her American Lieutenant had got for her, put her hair up in curlers before the small, wavy mirror. Garbrecht looked at her reflection in the mirror and remembered the nervous, multiple reflections in the cracked mirror in Seedorf's office.

He closed his stinging eyes, feeling the lids trembling jumpily. He touched the folded, raw scar on his right shoulder. As long as he lived, he probably would never get over being shocked at the strange, brutal scar on his own body. And he would never get over being shocked when anybody called him a cripple. He would have to be more diplomatic with Greta. She was the only girl he was familiar with, and occasionally there was true warmth and blessed hours of forgetfulness in her bed. It would be ridiculous

311

to lose that over a silly political discussion in which he had no real interest at all. Girls were hard to get these days. During the war it was better. You got a lot of girls out of pity. But pity went out at Rheims. And any German, even a whole, robust one, had a hard time competing with the cigarettes and chocolates and prestige of the victors. And for a man with one arm . . . It had been a miserable day, and this was a fitting, miserable climax to it.

Greta put out the light and got aggressively into bed, without touching him. Tentatively he put his hand out to her. She didn't move. "I'm tired," she said. "I've had a long day. Good night."

In a few moments she was asleep.

Garbrecht lay awake a long time, listening to Greta snore; a wavering, troubling reflection from a street light outside played on his lids from the small mirror across the room.

As he approached the house in which Seedorf kept his head-quarters, Garbrecht realized that he had begun to hurry his pace a little, that he was actually looking forward to the meeting. This was the fourth week that he had reported to the fat ex-Captain, and he smiled a little to himself as he reminded himself of how affectionately he had begun to regard Seedorf. Seedorf had not been at all demanding. He had listened with eager interest to each report of Garbrecht's meetings with Mikhailov and Dobelmeir, had chuckled delightedly here and there, slapped his leg in appreciation of one point or another, and had shrewdly and humorously invented plausible little stories, scraps of humor, to give first to the Russian, then to the American. Seedorf, who had never met either of them, seemed to understand them both far better than Garbrecht did, and Garbrecht had risen steadily in the favor of both Captain Mikhailov and Major Dobelmeir since he had given himself to Seedorf's coaching.

As Garbrecht opened the door of Seedorf's headquarters, he remembered with a little smile the sense of danger and apprehension with which he had first come there.

He did not have to wait long at all. Miss Renner, the blonde who had first talked to him on the street, opened the door to the ex-Captain's room almost immediately.

Seedorf was obviously in high spirits. He was beaming and moving up and down in front of his desk with little, mincing, almost dancing steps. "Hello, hello," he said warmly, as Garbrecht came into the room. "Good of you to come."

Garbrecht never could make out whether this was sly humor on

Seedorf's part, or perfectly automatic good manners, this pretense that Garbrecht had any choice in the matter.

"Wonderful day," Seedorf said. "Absolutely wonderful day. Did you hear the news?"

"What news?" Garbrecht asked cautiously.

"The first bomb!" Seedorf clasped his hands delightedly. "This afternoon at two-thirty the first bomb went off in Germany. Stuttgart! A solemn day. A day of remembrance! After 1918 it took twelve years before the Germans started any real opposition to the Allies. And now . . . less than a year and a half after the surrender . . . the first bomb! Delightful!" He beamed at Garbrecht. "Aren't you pleased?" he asked.

"Very," said Garbrecht diplomatically. He was not fond of bombs. Maybe for a man with two arms, bombs might have an attraction, but for him . . .

"Now we can really go to work." Seedorf hurled himself forcefully into his leather chair behind the desk and stared piercingly out at Garbrecht. "Until now, it hasn't meant very much. Really only developing an organization. Trying out the parts. Seeing who could work and who couldn't. Instituting necessary discipline. Practice, more than anything else. Now the maneuvers are over. Now we move onto the battlefield!"

Professional soldiers, Garbrecht thought bitterly, his new-found peace of mind already shaken, they couldn't get the jargon of their calling out of their thinking. Maneuvers, battlefields . . . The only accomplishment they seemed to be able to recognize was the product of explosion the only political means they really understood and relished, death.

"Lieutenant," Seedorf said, "we have been testing you too. I am glad to say," he said oratorically, "we have decided that you are dependable. Now you really begin your mission. Next Tuesday at noon Miss Renner will meet you. She will take you to the home of a friend of ours. He will give you a package. You will carry it to an address that Miss Renner will give you at the time. I will not hide from you that you will be in a certain danger. The package you will carry will include a timing mechanism that will go into the first bomb to be exploded in the new war against the Allies in Berlin. . . ."

Seedorf seemed to be far away and his voice distant and strange. It had been too good to be true, Garbrecht thought dazedly, the easygoing, undangerous, messenger-boy life that he had thought he was leading. Merely a sly, deadly game that Seedorf had been playing, testing him.

313

"Captain," he whispered, "Captain . . . I can't . . . I can't . . ."

"The beginning," Seedorf said, ecstatically, as though he had not heard Garbrecht's interruption. "Finally, there will be explosions day and night, all over the city, all over the country. . . . The Americans will blame the Russians, the Russians will blame the Americans, they will become more and more frightened, more and more distrustful of each other. They will come to us secretly, bargain with us, bid for us against each other. . . ."

It will never happen, Garbrecht said dazedly to himself, never. It is the same old thing. All during the war they told us that. The Americans would break with the British, the British with the Russians. And here they all were in what was left of Berlin: Cockneys, Tartars from Siberia, Negroes from Mississippi. Men like Seedorf were victims of their own propaganda, men who listened and finally believed their own hopes, their own lies. And, he, Garbrecht, next week, would be walking among the lounging American MP's, with the delicate, deadly machinery ticking under his arm, because of Seedorf's hallucination. Any other nation, Garbrecht thought, would be convinced. They'd look around at the ruin of their cities, at the ever-stretching cemeteries, at the marching enemy troops in the heart of their capital, and they'd say, "No, it did not work." But not the Germans. Goering was just dead in the Nuremberg jail, and here was this fat murderer with the jolly smile who even looked a bit like Goering, rubbing his hands and shouting, "A day of remembrance! The first bomb has exploded!"

Garbrecht felt lost and exhausted and hopeless, sitting in the wooden chair, watching the fat man move nervously and jubilantly behind the desk, hearing the rough, good-natured voice saying, "It took fourteen years last time, it won't take four years this time! Garbrecht, you'll be a full colonel in 1950, one arm and all."

Garbrecht wanted to protest, say something, some word that would stop this careening, jovial, bloodthirsty, deluded lunatic, but he could get no sound out between his lips. Later on, perhaps, when he was alone, he might be able to figure some way out of this whirling trap. Not here, not in this tall, dark room, with the fat, shouting captain, the broken mirror, the somber, incongruous, brooding picture of Lenin, Seedorf's obscure, mocking joke, that hung on the cracked wall.

"In the meantime," Seedorf was saying, "you continue your regular work. By God!" he laughed, "you will be the richest man in Berlin when they all get through paying you!" His voice changed.

It became low and probing. "Do you know two men called Kleiber and Machewski who work out of Mikhailov's office?" He peered shrewdly at Garbrecht.

"No," said Garbrecht after a moment. He knew them. They were both on Mikhailov's payroll and they worked in the American zone, but there was no sense in telling that, yet, to Seedorf.

"No matter," Seedorf laughed, after an almost imperceptible pause. "You will give their names and this address to your American Major." He took a piece of paper out from his pocket and put it down on the desk before him. "You will tell the Major that they are Russian spies and that they can be found at this place." He tapped the paper. "It will be quite a haul for the Major," Seedorf said ironically, "and he will be sure to reward you handsomely. And he will have a very strong tendency after that to trust you with quite important matters."

"Yes," said Garbrecht.

"You're sure," Seedorf said inquiringly, smiling a little at Garbrecht, "you're sure you don't know these men?"

Then Garbrecht knew that Seedorf knew he was lying, but it was too late to do anything about it.

"I don't know them," he said.

"I could have sworn . . ." Seedorf shrugged. "No matter." He got up from the desk, carrying the slip of paper, and came over to the chair where Garbrecht was sitting. "Some day, my friend," he said, putting his hand lightly on Garbrecht's shoulder, "some day you will learn that you will have to trust me, too. As a matter of . . ." He laughed. "A matter of discipline."

He handed Garbrecht the slip of paper and Garbrecht put it in his pocket and stood up. "I trust you, sir," he said flatly. "I have to."

Seedorf laughed uproariously. "I like a good answer," he shouted. "I do like a good answer." He put his arm around Garbrecht in a brotherly hug. "Remember," he said, "my first and only lesson— the one principle in being a hired informer is to tell the man who is paying you exactly what he wishes to hear. Any information must fit into theories which he already holds. Then he will trust you, pay you well, regard you as a more and more valuable employee. However . . ." and he laughed again, "do not try to work this on me. I am different. I don't pay you . . . and therefore, I expect the truth. You will remember that?" He turned Garbrecht around quite roughly and peered into his eyes. He was not smiling now.

"Yes, sir," said Garbrecht. "I will remember it."

"Good." Seedorf pushed him toward the door. "Now go downstairs and talk to Miss Renner. She will make all arrangements."

He pushed Garbrecht gently through the door and closed it sharply behind him. Garbrecht stared at the closed door for a moment, then walked slowly downstairs to Miss Renner.

Later, on the street, on his way to Mikhailov's office, he tried not to think of Seedorf's conversation, or the ingenious, deadly device that even now was waiting for him on the other side of the city.

He felt like stopping and leaning his head against the cold, cracked brick wall of a gutted house he was passing, to weep and weep in the twisting, cutting wind. After so much, after all the fighting, all the death, after the operating room in the brewery at Stalingrad, a man should be entitled to something, some peace, some security. And, instead, this onrushing dilemma, this flirtation with next week's death, this life of being scraped against every rock of the jagged year by every tide that crashed through Germany. Even numbness was no longer possible.

He shuffled on dazedly, not seeing where he was going. He stumbled over a piece of pavement that jutted crazily up from the sidewalk. He put out his hand to try to steady himself, but it was too late, and he fell heavily into the gutter. His head smashed against the concrete, and he felt the hot laceration of broken stone on the palm of his hand.

He sat up and looked at his hand in the dim light. There was blood coming from the dirty, ripped wounds, and his head was pounding. He sat on the curb, his head down, waiting for it to clear before he stood up. No escape, he thought, heavily, there never would be any escape. It was silly to hope for it. He stood up slowly, and continued on his way to Mikhailov's office.

Mikhailov was crouched over his desk, the light of a single lamp making him look froglike and ugly as he sat there, without looking up at Garbrecht. " . . . Tell the man who is paying you exactly what he wishes to hear. . . ." Garbrecht could almost hear Seedorf's mocking, hearty voice. Maybe Seedorf knew what he was talking about. Maybe the Russian was that foolish, maybe the American was that suspicious. . . . Suddenly, Garbrecht knew what he was going to tell Mikhailov.

"Well?" Mikhailov said finally, still peering down at his desk. "Anything important? Have you found out anything about that new man the Americans are using?"

Mikhailov had asked him to find out what he could about Dobelmeir last week, but Garbrecht had silently resolved to keep his mouth shut about the American. If he said too much, if he slipped once, Mikhailov would become suspicious, start prying, set someone on Garbrecht's trail. But now he spoke in a loud, even voice. "Yes," he said. "He is a second generation German-American. He is a lawyer in Milwaukee in civilian life. He was under investigation early in the war because he was said to have contributed to the German-American Bund in 1939 and 1940." Garbrecht saw Mikhailov slowly raise his head and look at him, his eyes beginning to glisten with undisguised interest. It's working, Garbrecht thought, it actually is working. "The case was never pressed," he went on calmly with his invention, "and he was given a direct commission late in the war and sent to Germany on special orders. Several members of his family are still alive in the British zone, Hamburg, and a cousin of his was a U-boat commander in the German Navy and was sunk off the Azores in 1943."

"Of course," said Mikhailov, his voice triumphant and satisfied. "Of course. Typical." He did not say what it was typical of, but he looked at Garbrecht with an expression that almost approached fondness.

"There are two things you might work on for the next few weeks," Mikhailov said. "We've asked everyone working out of this office to pick up what he can on this matter. We are quite sure that the Americans have shipped over a number of atomic bombs to Great Britain. We have reason to believe that they are being stored in Scotland, within easy distance of the airfield at Prestwick. There are flights in from Prestwick every day, and the crews are careless. I would like to find out if there are any preparations, even of the most preliminary kind, for basing a group of B-29's somewhere in that area. Skeleton repair shops, new fuel storage tanks, new radar warning stations, et cetera. Will you see if you can pick up anything?"

"Yes, sir," said Garbrecht, knowing that for Mikhailov's purpose he would make certain to pick up a great deal.

"Very good," said Mikhailov. He unlocked the drawer in his desk and took out the money. "You will find a little bonus here," he said with his mechanical smile.

"Thank you, sir," said Garbrecht, picking up the money.

"Till next week," Mikhailov said.

"Till next week," said Garbrecht. He saluted and Mikhailov returned the salute as Garbrecht went out the door.

Although it was dark and cold outside, and his head was still

317

throbbing from his fall, Garbrecht walked lightly, grinning to himself, as he moved toward the American zone.

He didn't see Dobelmeir till the next morning. "You might be interested in these men," he said, placing before the Major the slip of paper with the names of the men Seedorf had instructed him to denounce. "They are paid agents for the Russians, and the address is written down there, too."

Dobelmeir looked at the names, and a slow, delighted grin broke over his heavy face. "Very, very interesting," he said. "Excellent." His large hand went slowly over the crumpled paper, smoothing it out in a kind of dull caress. "I've had some more inquiries for information about that Professor I asked you to check. Kittlinger. What did you find out?"

Garbrecht had found out, more by accident than anything else, that the Professor, an aging, obscure physics teacher in the Berlin Medical School, had been killed in a concentration camp in 1944, but he was sure that there was no record anywhere of his death. "Professor Kittlinger," Garbrecht said glibly, "was working on nuclear fission from 1934 to the end of the war. Ten days after the Russians entered Berlin, he was arrested and sent to Moscow. No word has been heard since."

"Of course," Dobelmeir said flatly. "Of course."

The atom, Garbrecht thought, with a slight touch of exhilaration, is a marvelous thing. It hands over everything like a magic charm. Mention the atom, and they will solemnly believe any bit of nonsense you feed them. Perhaps, he thought, grinning inwardly, I will become a specialist. Garbrecht, Atomic Secrets Limited. An easy, rich, overflowing, simple field.

Dobelmeir was industriously scratching down the doubtful history of Professor Kittlinger, Atomic Experimenter. For the first time since he had begun working for the Americans, Garbrecht realized that he was actually enjoying himself.

"You might be interested," he said calmly, "in something I picked up last night."

Dobelmeir looked up assiduously from his desk. "Of course," he said gently.

"It probably doesn't amount to anything, just drunken, irresponsible raving . . ."

"What is it?" Dobelmeir leaned forward keenly.

"Three days ago a General Bryansky, who is on the Russian General Staff . . ."

"I know, I know," said Dobelmeir impatiently. "I know who he is. He's been in Berlin for a week now."

"Well," said Garbrecht, deliberately playing with Dobelmeir's impatience, "he made a speech before a small group of officers at the Officers' Club, and later on he got quite drunk, and there are rumors about certain things that he said. . . . I really don't know whether I ought to report anything as vague as this, as I said, just a rumor. . . ."

"Go ahead," Dobelmeir said hungrily. "Let me hear it."

"He is reported to have said that there will be war in sixty days. The atomic bomb is meaningless, he said. The Russian Army can march to the Channel from the Elbe in twenty-five days. Then let the Americans use the atomic bomb on them. They will be in Paris, in Brussels, in Amsterdam, and the Americans won't dare touch them. . . . Of course, I cannot vouch for this, but . . . ."

"Of course he said it," Dobelmeir said. "Or if he didn't, some other of those murderers did." He leaned back wearily. "I'll put it in the report. Maybe it'll make somebody wake up in Washington. And don't worry about reporting rumors. Very often there's more to be learned from a rumor than from the most heavily documented evidence."

"Yes, sir," said Garbrecht.

"I don't know," said Dobelmeir, "whether you heard about the bombing in Stuttgart yesterday."

"Yes, sir. I did."

"I have my own theory about it. There are going to be more, too, take my word for it. I think if you got to the bottom of it, you'd find our friends, the Russians, there. I want you to work on that, see what you can pick up this week. . . ."

"Yes, sir," Garbrecht said. What a wonderful man Seedorf is, Garbrecht thought. How astute, how correct in his intuition. How worthy of faith. He stood up. "Is that all, sir?"

"That's all." Dobelmeir handed him an envelope. "Here's your money. You'll find two weeks' pay I held back in the beginning are added to this week's money."

"Thank you very much, sir," Garbrecht said.

"Don't thank me," said the Major. "You've earned it. See you next week."

"Next week, sir." Garbrecht saluted and went out.

There were two MP's standing at the door, in the clear winter sunshine, their equipment glittering, their faces bored. Garbrecht smiled and nodded at them, amused now, long in advance, as he thought of himself scornfully carrying the delicate parts of the first bomb past them, right under their noses.

He walked briskly down the street, breathing deeply the invigorating air, patting the small bulge under his coat where the money lay. He could feel the numbness that had held him for so long deserting him, but it was not pain that was taking its place, not pain at all.

# The Passion of Lance Corporal Hawkins

Lance Corporal Alfred Hawkins stood on the Haifa dock, his fingers wet on the long nightstick in his hands, the unaccustomed helmet heavy on his head, watching a naval launch slowly bring in the two-masted schooner *Hope*, its decks and tattered rigging swarming with people, who looked like clustered dark bees, so far away, and not like people at all. Please, Lord, Hawkins prayed to himself, standing at ease with his platoon, warm in the yellow Mediterranean sun, please, Lord, keep me from hitting any of them.

"Don't take any nonsense from the buggers," Lieutenant Madox said, standing in front of the platoon. "Whack 'em a couple of times and they'll behave like bloody gentlemen." He turned and peered at the shabby schooner slowly approaching the dock, and Hawkins was sure that the look on the Lieutenant's thick red face was one of pleasurable anticipation. Hawkins looked at the other men of the platoon. Except for Hogan, you couldn't tell anything from their faces. In London once, during the war, Hawkins had overheard an American Air Force major saying, "The British would watch Hitler hanging or their daughters marrying into the Royal Family or their own legs being chopped off at the knee and not change expression by one twitch of the eyebrow. You can't beat an army like that." The American had been drunk, of course, but, looking around him now, and remembering other times, too—like the day outside Caen and the day on the Rhine and the day his company went into the concentration camp at Belsen—Hawkins could understand what the American had been talking about. In ten or fifteen minutes, the men around him might be in the middle of a very mean fight on board the schooner, against clubs and knives, perhaps, and maybe even home-made bombs, and except for Hogan, again, all of them looked as though they were merely lined up for a routine roll call outside their barracks in the morning. And Hogan, of course, was an Irishman, and not the same thing

321

at all. He was a small, thin boy, with a tough, broken-nosed, handsome face, and now he was fidgeting uneasily, his jaw rigid with excitement, pushing his helmet back and forth on his head, shifting his nightstick, breathing loudly enough to be heard over all the small noises of the harbor and the platoon around him.

They were singing now on the schooner. The rising and falling, chanting, foreign melody came thinly and defiantly across the oily green water. Hawkins could understand several words of Hebrew, but he could not make out what the song was about. It sounded wild and somehow menacing, as though it should not be sung in sunshine and in the morning or by women's voices but late at night, in the desert, by lawless and desperate men. Esther had translated two or three Hebrew songs for Hawkins in the last few weeks, and he had noticed that the words "freedom" and "justice" figured in them prominently, but those words did not seem to fit with the flat, dangerous, hoarse music hammering across the harbor from the slowly moving old boat.

Hawkins wished they wouldn't sing. It made it harder if they sang and you knew they were singing about freedom or justice. After all, they were singing to him, and to the other men around him, and what did they expect him to do?

Hawkins closed his eyes, as though by shutting out the sight of the dark-clustered boat inexorably being pushed to the dock, and the clubs, and the transport waiting to take them to the stockade on Cyprus, he could somehow also shut out the sound of the rough, challenging voices of the Jews.

He closed his eyes, his youthful, almost childish face, sweating under the hot helmet, painfully composed, painfully disclosing nothing to the Lieutenant or the men around him or to the eyes of the fugitives he was expected to punish. He closed his eyes. He was uncomfortable in his wool battle dress and the tight canvas belting, and was sorry he was in Palestine, sorry he was in the Army, sorry he was an Englishman, sorry he was alive. This was not what he had expected when he had reënlisted, six months after the war was over. He didn't know exactly what he had expected. He had just known he did not want to live in Southampton, in the foggy weather, among the ruined docks and the torn buildings; in the same house with his father, who had had his arm torn off during a raid in 1941; in the same house with his sister, whose husband had been killed at Bari in 1943; in the same house in which he had lived for such a short while with Nancy, who had later divorced him and married an American sergeant in the port battalion—and that was a soft job for a soldier, wasn't it, during a war. He had just known that after four years in the Army, ever since he was seventeen, he did not want to start looking for a job as a longshoreman on the wrecked wharves, he did not want to stand in a queue collecting the unemployment dole, he did not want the bitter weather of unheated winter England after glimpses of Africa and summer France. And the only thing he had known was soldiering. They had made it a little more attractive—they had raised the pay and promised many rather vague benefits—and, if the truth must be told, the only time anyone had ever really taken care of him was in the Army. It was certain no one was really going to take care of you as a civilian, Socialist government or no Socialist government. Though he had voted for them, of course. He had read all the pamphlets and he knew what he was doing, a common soldier in the Army of the King, the son of a workingman, the grandson of a workingman, the great-grandson of a workingman. That was another thing about the Army. It had given him the chance to read for the first time in his life. Especially the two periods he'd been in the hospital, first with the bullet in his hip and then with the piece of shrapnel he'd picked up twelve days before the end of the war. The hospital library had had a complete set of H. G. Wells, and he had slowly and studiously gone through it all, soberly agreeing with the energetic arguments of the old man. By the time he'd got out of the hospital, he had become a confirmed Socialist, believing that education could change the world, and that violence was a hangover from primitive times, and that year by year the human race was certain to improve. He opened his eyes for a moment and looked at the schooner. It was much closer now, and he could smell it, too. There were perhaps three hundred people jammed onto it, men and women, and they had obviously not had the most complete sanitation facilities. He wished H. G. Wells were on the dock in the uniform of an infantry lance corporal today; it would be interesting to see what he would do.

It had been so much simpler during the war. There were the Germans across the fields, or up on a hill two miles away, and you shot them and they shot you. They had bombed your home and torn the arm off your father's shoulder and killed your brother-in-law, and there were no further decisions to be made about them. And all the men around you felt exactly as you did, no matter who they were. But now . . . There was Lieutenant Madox, who hated all Jews and was delighted with this duty on the dock this morning. Of course, Lieutenant Madox hated everybody, except Englishmen, and if he had been in India or Malaya or France, he would have looked forward to cracking Indian or Malayan or French skulls with equal pleasure. But he happened to be in Palestine, and he happened to be looking forward to hitting Jews. Then there was Private Fleming, a quiet, capable man of thirty-five. Private Fleming was a Communist. Communists, Hawkins knew, did not think much of Zionism, but certainly they didn't believe in braining Jews, and yet there was Private Fleming, an excellent soldier, standing quietly at ease, ready to do his duty, gripping his nightstick like all the others. And there was Hogan, who was one of Hawkins' best friends, with whom he drank beer in Jerusalem and Tel Aviv, and who was a Catholic, like Hawkins, and went to Mass on Sunday morning with him, and whose father had been killed by the British in the trouble in Dublin in 1916. Hogan often went out with him and Esther, too. Esther would bring a friend and they would swim on the beach at Tel Aviv and go to the movies at night when they played musical pictures. Hogan hated the Jews, though, because his second cousin, who was in the Sixth Airborne, had got his foot blown off by a Jewish mine on the Rehovoth Road two months before. What would H. G. Wells have made of the Dublin orphan on the sunny dock this morning, tense with pent-up fury as he glared at the naval launch slowly pushing the tattered, dark, chanting refugees toward him?

And, supposing H. G. Wells had been a Jew, and were standing on the deck of the *Hope* this morning, after the years of murder in Germany, after the displaced persons' camps, after the illegal journey across Europe and the crooked voyage down the Mediterranean, what clever, hopeful statement would he make then, waiting there like an old bull in the knacker's yard, waiting for the clubs and the Cyprian wire?

An Arab laborer walked by, rolling a wheelbarrow. He put the wheelbarrow down in front of the platoon, his long, skinny arms dark mahogany, dangling out of his tattered shirt. He had a little black scraggly beard, and he didn't smell so good, either. He grinned at the soldiers. His teeth were not all there, but when he smiled, he looked childlike and ingratiating, and some of the men smiled back at him. The Arab looked over his shoulder at the approaching boat, grinned more widely, and moved his finger across his Adam's apple in the gesture of throat slitting.

"Get out of here, you filthy old rascal," Lieutenant Madox said, smiling broadly. "Go ahead. Out of the way. We'll have no international incidents on this dock."

The Arab bobbed his head, the grin fixed on his face, and made the throatcutting gesture again, like a child who repeats a trick that he sees has pleased his elders. Then he bent and picked up the handles of the wheelbarrow again and trundled it off, giggling to himself.

Hawkins didn't remember what H. G. Wells had had to say about the Arabs. He was sure there must have been something on the subject, because there was something on every subject in the old man's books, but he couldn't remember. The Arabs, Hawkins had to admit, were much more pleasant to have around than the Jews. For one thing, they did what you told them. For another thing, they weren't likely to get you off in a corner and engage you in a loud political argument. Esther lived in the same house with a family by the name of Freedman, who were German refugees and whose two sons had been in the Jewish Brigade during the war. The two boys lay in wait for Hawkins when he came to call for Esther and battered him with questions like "Why doesn't Britain live up to the Balfour Declaration?" and "Why does Britain allow the Grand Mufti of Jerusalem, who worked with the Nazis during the war, to come back to lead the Arabs from Cairo?" It was very queer, sitting in the small white living room of the apartment house, with your rifle leaning against the wall (from time to time, Division Headquarters ordered that all troops be armed when they left the barracks), drinking tea and eating little sweet cookies that Mrs. Freedman kept pressing on you, debating politely with the two fierce young veterans, who were probably members of the Jewish underground and had probably blown up a sergeant major in the morning.

"It's not fair," he had said to Esther after one such session, when he had finally managed to get her away from the house. "They talk as though I was personally responsible."

Esther had glanced at him obliquely, then looked away. "Maybe," she said softly, "maybe that's what they think about every British soldier."

"Is that what you think?"

Esther had shaken her head and gripped his arm more firmly. "No," she had said gravely, her low, soft voice solemn and warm. "No, I do not think of you as a British soldier." They had been walking along the quiet, white street, in the clear, foreign evening air—his boots making a hob-nailed clatter on the pavement and his rifle sling pulling at his shoulder and the girl beside him in a thin white dress with a blue sweater over it, her hair blowing gently, soft and pale brown, in the stirring wind.

"Listen to them sing," Hogan said, his voice nervous and angry.

"The murderin' heathen! They'll sing a different tune an hour from now, they will!"

Hawkins opened his eyes. The ship was much closer now, and the songs clamored across the water from the packed ship, with the soprano of the women shrill and glittering over the menacing bass of the men's voices. Hogan, Hawkins remembered, also sang songs in another language—in Gaelic—and the words "freedom" and "justice" figured prominently in them, too. They were songs Hogan's grandfather had taught him in memory of his dead father, shot through the throat on a Dublin pavement by men in the same uniform that Hogan was wearing now so far away, seventy-five miles north of Jerusalem.

Hawkins closed his eyes again. It would do no good to watch the boat come nearer, foot by foot. There would be time enough to look, later. He thought of Esther. He had arranged to meet her that night in Tel Aviv and take her to a movie if he got off duty early. He had not known what the duty would be, though, and he doubted if he would tell her later on. Matters were complicated enough with Esther as it was. She looked so cheerful and agreeable, so pretty and young, like the very nicest kind of girl you might meet by a lucky accident at home, but there had been the terrible times when she had suddenly broken down, for no apparent reason, and wept in his arms, wildly and inconsolably, clutching him as though to make certain again and again that he was there and alive. She was a German girl, whose mother and father had been killed in Munich, and whose husband had been caught by the British near Haifa unloading illegal immigrants in 1939. He had been put into a camp, where he had caught typhus and died. The authorities had permitted Esther to visit her husband the day he died, and once Esther had told Hawkins about it, although most of the time they avoided talking about things like that. The husband, who was twenty-four years old and had been a robust, laughing young man (Hawkins had seen his picture), had been wasted by the disease to ninety pounds and was screaming in his delirium when Esther finally saw him. He did not recognize his wife at all when she came into the room, and that, somehow, was Esther's bitterest memory—the screaming, skeleton-like boy turning his head senselessly to the wall in the bare, barred room. Then, after that, all through the war, Esther had been kept under house arrest and had not been permitted to go out into the streets from sunset to dawn. When Hawkins had first known her, she had been quiet, almost fearful, and perhaps it was because she had matched his own shyness and fearfulness so well that he had begun to love her.

For the past several months, whenever Hawkins was waiting somewhere, and closed his eyes, as he was doing now, he had had a recurrent daydream. It was winter in the dream, a cold, windy night, and he and Esther were sitting before a warm fire in their own house. He could never decide whether the house was in England, in a quiet village, or on a farm in Palestine, cupped in the small, old hills, among the orange orchards. They were reading, and occasionally they looked up from their books and smiled at each other, not having to talk, in the firelight. After a time, there was a knock on the door and guests began to come in; not many of them, just good friends. Hogan, with his wild hair plastered down politely. Fleming, with the schoolteacher wife from Leeds he talked about so often. Robinson, who had been in Hawkins' platoon in Africa—it was always hard to remember, especially in a daydream, that Robinson was dead, buried in the small, windy cemetery near Constantine. They talked quietly in the warm room, and Hawkins opened up the tall bottles of heavy beer, and after a while Hogan sang, in his hoarse, accurate boy's voice, the sad, thrilling songs his grandfather had taught him in his father's honor, songs whose words no one understood but whose melodies made you somehow melancholy and proud.

Hawkins blinked and refused himself the pleasure of taking the daydream through to its quiet ending. It was ridiculous to allow himself to moon like that, and it only made it worse when he finally opened his eyes and looked around him. There he was, on the dock, in the hot, bare sun, with the nightstick, waiting for Lieutenant Madox to order him to fight. And in the hills behind him, among the orange groves, people were hiding rifles and knives and machine guns to murder each other in the long winter nights. And in England, from all the letters he got from his family, they were preparing to starve and freeze to celebrate their victory in the war. He was sorry he was not older. Perhaps if he were thirty or forty or fifty, he could understand it better. During the war they had been warm, during the war they had been fed, during the war the Russians had loved them, the Americans had admired them, the French had kissed them when they came into a town; wherever they had gone, they had been heroes and saviors. He remembered the day that the election returns came out. He was still in Germany, in Hamburg, and an American sergeant had come over to him and said, very solemnly, "Soldier, my name is McCarthy. I'm a paid-up C.I.O. member from Indianapolis. I decided I wanted to tell some Englishmen how wonderful I think they are, and you're the first one I've come across since I made the decision. You've

327

shown the whole world how civilized human beings should behave."
The American had been drunk, of course (was it possible that
Americans appreciated other people only when they had ten drinks
under their belts?), but he had shaken Hawkins' hand sternly and
clapped him on the back, and Hawkins had walked away grinning
and feeling proud because he had voted for Attlee and the others
who were going to prove that a country could be run for the benefit
of the workingman without violence or disaster. He was glad the
American wasn't around to see him standing on the dock today
with helmet and nightstick, in this land of widows and orphans,
in this land where there were no whole families, only survivors,
in this land where everyone—every girl on the street, every child
in a schoolroom, every farmer plowing a furrow—had a story like
Esther's, memories like Esther's, nightmares like Esther's, where
the memory of the furnace flickered across every face, the knocking
of the midnight arrest broke into every dream, where agony was
so commonplace that no one even remarked it. What a puzzling,
sad thing it was to be an Englishman today, Hawkins thought,
staring at the boat, which was so close now. If he was in England,
he was caught between cold and hunger, in Palestine between Jew
and Arab, in India between Hindu and Moslem, in the East Indies
between Dutchman and Javanese, and no friends anywhere, no
approval anywhere, just the helmet and the nightstick, the barbed
wire and the Lieutenant, the songs in the strange languages hurled
at your head like hand grenades. You could read all the pamphlets,
vote all the elections, pray all the Sundays, and each day it became
worse, each day made you more of a villain, each day your uniform
was cursed on the streets of more cities, in more languages. He
closed his eyes.

"Hawkins!"

Hawkins jumped and straightened up. Lieutenant Madox was
standing in front of him. "Damn you, Hawkins!" Madox was
saying. "Will you keep your bloody eyes open! Get over here!"

"Yes, sir," said Hawkins. He gripped his club and moved to
where two sailors were swinging a gangplank up to the railing of
the boat. The boat was tied to the dock now, and a terrible stillness
had settled over the people on it.

"Spread out, spread out," Madox was shouting to the platoon.
"Don't let anyone jump onto the dock. Make 'em all come down
the gangplank."

The smell was awful now, and in the silence the Jews stared
down at the Lieutenant and the men of the platoon with cold,
devouring hatred. Over a loudspeaker came a cool, pleasant voice.

328

"Ladies and gentlemen," the voice said, and it sounded like at least a colonel in the Guards, "we wish to do this in as orderly a fashion as possible. You will please come down the gangplank in twos and march to your right and go aboard the vessel moored directly behind your boat. You are going to be transferred to Cyprus, where you will be taken care of in British Army camps. Your sick will be treated and you will be given every consideration possible. Now, if you please, start leaving your vessel."

The voice halted in a mechanical crackle. No one moved.

"All right," Madox said. "Let's get on board."

Slowly and deliberately, the men of the platoon started up the gangplank. Hawkins was right behind the Lieutenant, with Hogan at his side. For a moment, at the top of the gangplank, he stopped. He looked down at the deck of the schooner. There was a blur of eyes, dark, staring, wild; a confusion of gaunt, ravaged faces; a wavering mass of tattered clothing such as might have been recovered from the corpses of a dug-up graveyard. Hawkins tottered momentarily, feeling, dizzily, this has happened to me before, Then he remembered. Belsen, he thought—wherever you turn, it is Belsen. In Belsen, he remembered, there had been the smell, too, and the same eyes, the same clothes, and there had been the old man (although later Hawkins had found out the man was only thirty) who had opened a door of one of the huts and come slowly out, holding his hands in front of him, his hands like claws, his face twisted skull-like and horrible in what Hawkins had later realized the man had meant as a glorious smile of greeting but which at the moment had seemed weird and threatening. Then, just as he had reached Hawkins, he had dropped to the ground, and when Hawkins had bent over him, he had died. But no one here approached Hawkins; there was no expression here that might later be deciphered into a smile. On the other side of the deck, there were the women, and standing, facing the gangplank, were the young men, and then Hawkins knew there was going to be a fight. Crazily, he thought: I'll bet there are some of these people here who will recognize me from Belsen. What will they think of me?

"Come on!" Madox was shouting furiously. "Come on, Hawkins, get in there!"

Slowly, with dreamy obedience, Hawkins moved toward the first line of men. I am not going to hit them, he thought as he walked through the stinking, unreal silence. No matter what, I am not going to hit them. Then he saw Hogan swing and there was the flat, awful noise of the stick hitting a shoulder. Then the screams began, and the shouting, which closed around you in a savage, wild, echoing vault of sound, and the bodies slamming into you, and the spurt of someone's blood, hot and slippery, in your face, and the confused flailing of arms and the black gleam of wood flashing against the yellow sky and a form dropping with a scream out of the rigging. Hawkins tried to keep his arms over his head, so that he wouldn't be pinned in helplessly, but hands grabbed at his club, and stabbed into his face, and he had to move his arms furiously to keep the club from being torn away. Then, suddenly, there was a pair of hands at his throat and he was staring into a dark, grimacing face, the eyes, just six inches from his, pitiless, mad, as the powerful fingers pressed and pressed. Hawkins tried to pull away, but there was no escaping the hands. Oh, God, Hawkins thought, feeling the blood pounding in his head, oh, God, he is going to kill me. No, he wanted to say, you don't understand. I am not doing anything. I was at Belsen. I was one of the people at Belsen. But the hands gripped firmer and firmer, the eyes stared coldly and triumphantly close to his own, as though the man who was choking him were finally taking vengeance for the ghetto in Poland, the death of his children, the locked cars, the whips, the furnaces, the graves of Europe. Hawkins felt his eyes clouding, his throat being torn, his knees slowly crumpling, as he pressed back and back, with the screams and the wet smashing of blows all around him. With his waning strength, he wrenched away. Then he hit the man. The man did not let go. Hawkins hit him again, across the face, and the man's face disappeared in a fuzz of blood, but still the fingers gripped, as strong as ever. Then, again and again, with all the desperate strength in his arms and body, Hawkins lashed out at the man who was trying to strangle him. The man's face seemed to crumble in a red, dissolving tissue, his jaw hanging queer and sidewise in a broken leer, only his eyes, steadfast and full of hatred, still glaring into Hawkins' own. There was a last, convulsive spasm of the fingers at Hawkins' throat; then the man slowly and silently slid down and away. Hawkins stared at him, then fell on top of him, and something crashed across his head, and when he opened his eyes again, he was lying on the dock and everything was very quiet, except for the weeping of women, soft and far away.

Hawkins sat up. The fight was over. Now they were taking the women down the gangplank, and that was where the weeping was coming from—from the raddled bundles of living rags being carried by troopers onto the soil of Palestine and back onto the other ship, thirty-five feet away. Hawkins felt his throat. It was terribly sore, and blood was still oozing from a cut under his ear. He felt sick and lightheaded. He turned his head away from the women. He did not want to look at them. Lying next to him on the dock, very quiet, face downward, was a man. He had on an American Army shirt and a pair of Royal Air Force pants. He was barefooted and his feet were terribly cut and swollen, black with blood. Slowly, Hawkins took the man's shoulder and rolled him over. The eyes were still open. The face was smashed, the jaw leering and dislocated, the teeth broken and red at the roots. But the eyes were open and they were the eyes of the man who had tried to kill Hawkins on board the schooner *Hope*.

Hawkins stood up. It was hard to walk, but he moved slowly over to the gate in the barbed wire at the other end of the dock. Madox was there, sweating but looking pleased.

"Very well done, Hawkins," Madox said. "I watched you. Are you hurt?"

"A little, sir," Hawkins said, surprised at the croaking, strange noise that came from his throat. "Not too bad."

"Good," said Madox. "It's just about finished here. We'll be going back to camp in a minute." He looked solicitously at Hawkins' torn throat. "You're in rather bad shape. You'd better not go with the others in the lorry. I'll take you with me in my jeep."

"Yes, sir," said Hawkins flatly. He walked slowly over to where the jeep was parked and laboriously climbed into the back. He leaned against the canvas. He closed his eyes, thinking of nothing.

Ten minutes later, Madox and his driver got into the jeep, and the jeep rolled slowly through the gate. Hawkins did not look back purposely, but he could not help seeing the dock, the two boats, the old, silent, broken, deserted schooner, and the full transport, beginning to work up steam for the voyage to Cyprus. They were singing again on board the transport, but softer now, and wearily, and Hawkins thought, I must get Esther to translate that song for me. And on the dock, with the Arab laborer, still holding his wheelbarrow, standing curiously over him, lay the dead man, flat and alone. Hawkins closed his eyes as the jeep spurted away from the waterfront.

I wonder, he was thinking, slowly and painfully, because his head did not seem familiar or normal to him any more, I wonder if I can get off tonight to go into Tel Aviv to take Esther to the movies. Then there was the explosion, and even as he felt himself slamming through the air, Hawkins thought, They must have got hold of some Army mines. Then he hit. He moved with crawling,

331

broken slowness, feeling everything slippery and sliding all around him, thinking with dull persistence, I must tell them, they mustn't do this to me, they don't understand, I was at Belsen. Then he lay still.

# The Dry Rock

"We're late," Helen said as the cab stopped at a light. "We're twenty minutes late." She looked at her husband accusingly.

"All right," Fitzsimmons said. "I couldn't help it. The work was on the desk and it had to . . ."

"This is the one dinner party of the year I didn't want to be late for," Helen said. "So naturally . . ."

The cab started and was halfway across the street when the Ford sedan roared into it, twisting, with a crashing and scraping of metal, a high mournful scream of brakes, the tinkling of glass. The cab shook a little, then subsided.

The cabby, a little gray man, turned and looked back, worriedly. "Everybody is all right?" he asked nervously.

"Everybody is fine," Helen said bitterly, pulling at her cape to get it straight again after the jolting.

"No damage done," said Fitzsimmons, smiling reassuringly at the cabby, who looked very frightened.

"I am happy to hear that," the cabby said. He got out of his car and stood looking sadly at his fender, now thoroughly crumpled, and his headlight, now without a lens. The door of the Ford opened and its driver sprang out. He was a large young man with a light gray hat. He glanced hurriedly at the cab.

"Why don't yuh watch where the hell yer goin'?" he asked harshly.

"The light was in my favor," said the cabby. He was a small man of fifty, in a cap and a ragged coat, and he spoke with a heavy accent. "It turned green and I started across. I would like your license, Mister."

"What for?" the man in the gray hat shouted. "Yer load's all right. Get on yer way. No harm done." He started back to his car.

The cabby gently put his hand on the young man's arm. "Excuse

333

me, friend," he said. "It is a five-dollar job, at least. I would like to see your license."

The young man pulled his arm away, glared at the cabby. "Aaah," he said and swung. His fist made a loud, surprising noise against the cabby's nose. The old man sat down slowly on the running board of his cab, holding his head wearily in his hands. The young man in the gray hat stood over him, bent over, fists still clenched. "Didn't I tell yuh no harm was done?" he shouted. "Why didn't yuh lissen t' me? I got a good mind to . . ."

"Now, see here," Fitzsimmons said, opening the rear door and stepping out.

"What d'*you* want?" The young man turned and snarled at Fitzsimmons, his fists held higher. "Who asked for *you?*"

"I saw the whole thing," Fitzsimmons began, "and I don't think you . . ."

"Aaah," snarled the young man. "Dry up."

"Claude," Helen called. "Claude, keep out of this."

"Claude," the young man repeated balefully. "Dry up, Claude."

"Are you all right?" Fitzsimmons asked, bending over the cabby, who still sat reflectively on the running board, his head down, his old and swollen cap hiding his face, blood trickling down his clothes.

"I'm all right," the cabby said wearily. He stood up, looked wonderingly at the young man. "Now, my friend, you force me to make trouble. Police!" he called, loudly. *"Police!"*

"Say, lissen," the man in the gray hat shouted. "What the hell do yuh need to call the cops for? Hey, cut it out!"

*"Police!"* the old cabby shouted calmly, but with fervor deep in his voice. "Police!"

"I ought to give it to yuh good." The young man shook his fist under the cabby's nose. He jumped around nervously. "This is a small matter," he shouted, "nobody needs the cops!"

"Police!" called the cabby.

"Claude." Helen put her head out the window. "Let's get out of here and let the two gentlemen settle this any way they please."

"I apologize!" The young man held the cabby by his lapels with both large hands, shook him, to emphasize his apology. "Excuse me. I'm sorry. Stop yelling police, for God's sake!"

"I'm going to have you locked up," the cabby said. He stood there, slowly drying the blood off his shabby coat with his cap. His hair was gray, but long and full, like a musician's. He had a big head for his little shoulders, and a sad, lined little face and he looked older than fifty, to Fitzsimmons, and very poor, neglected, badly nourished. "You have committed a crime," the cabby said, "and there is a punishment for it."

"Will yuh talk to him?" The young man turned savagely to Fitzsimmons. "Will yuh tell him I'm sorry?"

"It's entirely up to him," Fitzsimmons said.

"We're a half hour late," Helen announced bitterly. "The perfect dinner guests."

"It is not enough to be sorry," said the cab driver. *"Police . . ."*

"Say, listen, Bud," the young man said, his voice quick and confidential, "what's yer name?"

"Leopold Tarloff" the cabby said. "I have been driving a cab on the streets of New York for twenty years, and everybody thinks just because you're a cab driver they can do whatever they want to you."

"Lissen, Leopold," the young man pushed his light gray hat far back on his head. "Let's be sensible. I hit yer cab. All right. I hit you. All right."

"What's all right about it?" Tarloff asked.

"What I mean is, I admit it, I confess I did it, that's what I mean. All right." The young man grabbed Tarloff's short ragged arms as he spoke, intensely. "Why the fuss? It happens every day. Police are unnecessary. I'll tell yuh what I'll do with yuh, Leopold. Five dollars, yuh say, for the fender. All right. And for the bloody nose, another pound. What do yuh say? Everybody is satisfied. Yuh've made yerself a fiver on the transaction; these good people go to their party without no more delay."

Tarloff shook his arms free from the huge hands of the man in the gray hat. He put his head back and ran his fingers through his thick hair and spoke coldly. "I don't want to hear another word. I have never been so insulted in my whole life."

The young man stepped back, his arms wide, palms up wonderingly. "I insult him!" He turned to Fitzsimmons. "Did you hear me insult this party?" he asked.

"Claude!" Helen called. "Are we going to sit here all night?"

"A man steps up and hits me in the nose," Tarloff said. "He thinks he makes everything all right with five dollars. He is mistaken. Not with five hundred dollars."

"How much d'yuh think a clap in the puss is worth?" the young man growled. "Who d'yuh think y'are—Joe Louis?"

"Not ten thousand dollars," Tarloff said, on the surface calm, but quivering underneath. "Not for twenty thousand dollars. My dignity."

"His dignity!" the young man whispered. "For Christ's sake!"

"What do you want to do?" Fitzsimmons asked, conscious of Helen glooming in the rear seat of the cab.

"I would like to take him to the station house and make a complaint," Tarloff said. "You would have to come with me, if you'd be so kind. What is your opinion on the matter?"

"Will yuh tell him the cops are not a necessity!" the young man said hoarsely. "Will yuh tell the bastidd?"

"Claude!" called Helen.

"It's up to you," Fitzsimmons said, looking with what he hoped was an impartial, judicious expression at Tarloff, hoping he wouldn't have to waste any more time. "You do what you think you ought to do."

Tarloff smiled, showing three yellow teeth in the front of his small and childlike mouth, curved and red and surprising in the lined and weatherbeaten old hackie's face. "Thank you very much," he said. "I am glad to see you agree with me."

Fitzsimmons sighed.

"Yer drivin' me crazy!" the young man shouted at Tarloff. "Yer makin' life impossible!"

"To you," Tarloff said with dignity, "I talk from now on only in a court of law. That's my last word."

The young man stood there, breathing heavily, his fists clenching and unclenching, his pale gray hat shining in the light of a street lamp. A policeman turned the corner, walking in a leisurely and abstracted manner, his eyes on the legs of a girl across the street.

Fitzsimmons went over to him. "Officer," he said, "there's a little job for you over here." The policeman regretfully took his eyes off the girl's legs and sighed and walked slowly over to where the two cars were still nestling against each other.

"What are yuh?" the young man was asking Tarloff, when Fitzsimmons came up with the policeman. "Yuh don't act like an American citizen. What are yuh?"

"I'm a Russian," Tarloff said, "But I'm in the country twenty-five years now, I know what the rights of an individual are."

"Yeah," said the young man hopelessly. "Yeah . . . ."

The Fitzsimmonses drove silently to the police station in the cab, with Tarloff driving slowly and carefully, though with hands that shook on the wheel. The policeman drove with the young man in the young man's Ford. Fitzsimmons saw the Ford stop at a cigar store and the young man jump out and go into the store, into a telephone booth.

"For three months," Helen said, as they drove, "I've been trying to get Adele Lowrie to invite us to dinner. Now we've finally managed it. Perhaps we ought to call her and invite the whole party down to night court."

"It isn't night court," Fitzsimmons said patiently. "It's a police station. And I think you might take it a little better. After all, the poor old man has no one else to speak up for him."

"Leopold Tarloff," Helen said. "It sounds impossible. Leopold Tarloff. Leopold Tarloff."

They sat in silence until Tarloff stopped the cab in front of the police station and opened the door for them. The Ford with the policeman and the young man drove up right behind them and they all went in together.

There were some people up in front of the desk lieutenant, a dejected-looking man with long mustaches and a loud, blonde woman who kept saying that the man had threatened her with a baseball bat three times that evening. Two Negroes with bloody bandages around their heads were waiting, too.

"It will take some time," said the policeman. "There are two cases ahead of you. My name is Kraus."

"Oh, my," said Helen.

"You'd better call Adele," Fitzsimmons said. "Tell her not to hold dinner for us."

Helen held her hand out gloomily for nickels.

"I'm sorry," Tarloff said anxiously, "to interrupt your plans for the evening."

"Perfectly all right," Fitzsimmons said, trying to screen his wife's face from Tarloff by bending over to search for the nickels in his pocket.

Helen went off, disdainfully holding her long formal skirt up with her hand, as she walked down the spit- and butt-marked corridor of the police station toward a pay telephone. Fitzsimmons reflectively watched her elegant back retreat down the hallway.

"I am tired," Tarloff said. "I think I will have to sit down, if you will excuse me." He sat on the floor, looking up with a frail, apologetic smile on his red face worn by wind and rain and traffic-policemen. Fitzsimmons suddenly felt like crying, watching the old man sitting there among the spit and cigarette butts, on the floor against the wall, with his cap off and his great bush of musician's gray hair giving the lie to the tired, weathered face below it.

Four men threw open the outside doors and walked into the police station with certainty and authority. They all wore the same light-gray hats with the huge flat brims. The young man who had hit Tarloff greeted them guardedly. "I'm glad you're here, Pidgear," he said to the man who, by some subtle mixture of stance and clothing, of lift of eyebrow and droop of mouth, announced himself as leader.

They talked swiftly and quietly in a corner.

"A Russian!" Pidgear's voice rang out angrily. "There are 10,000 cab drivers in the metropolitan area, you have to pick a Russian to punch in the nose!"

"I'm excitable!" the young man yelled. "Can I help it if I'm excitable? My father was the same way; it's a family characteristic."

"Go tell that to the Russian," Pidgear said. He went over to one of the three men who had come in with him, a large man who needed a shave and whose collar was open at the throat, as though no collar could be bought large enough to go all the way around that neck. The large man nodded, went over to Tarloff, still sitting patiently against the wall.

"You speak Russian?" the man with the open collar said to Tarloff.

"Yes, sir," Tarloff said.

The large man sat down slowly beside him, gripped Tarloff's knee confidentially in his tremendous hairy hand, spoke excitedly, winningly, in Russian.

Pidgear and the young man who had hit Tarloff came over to Fitzsimmons, leaving the other two men in the gray hats, small, dark men with shining eyes, who just stood at the door and looked hotly on.

"My name is Pidgear," the man said to Fitzsimmons, who by now was impressed with the beautiful efficiency of the system that had been put into motion by the young driver of the Ford—an obviously legal mind like Pidgear, a man who spoke Russian, and two intense men with gray hats standing on call just to see justice done, and all collected in the space of fifteen minutes. "Alton Pidgear," the man said, smiling professionally at Fitzsimmons. "I represent Mr. Rusk."

"Yeah," said the young man.

"My name is Fitzsimmons."

"Frankly, Mr. Fitzsimmons," Pidgear said, "I would like to see you get Mr. Tarloff to call this whole thing off. It's an em-

338

barrassing affair for all concerned; nobody stands to gain anything by pressing it."

Helen came back and Fitzsimmons saw by the expression on her face that she wasn't happy. "They're at the soup by now," she said loudly to Fitzsimmons. "Adele said for us to take all the time we want, they're getting along fine."

"Mr. Rusk is willing to make a handsome offer," Pidgear said. "Five dollars for the car, five dollars for the nose . . ."

"Go out to dinner with your husband," Helen muttered, "and you wind up in a telephone booth in a police station. 'Excuse me for being late, darling, but I'm calling from the 8th Precinct, this is our night for street-fighting.' "

"Shhh, Helen, please," Fitzsimmons said. He hadn't eaten since nine that morning and his stomach was growling with hunger.

"It was all a mistake," Pidgear said smoothly. "A natural mistake. Why should the man be stubborn? He is being reimbursed for everything, isn't he? I wish you would talk to him, Mr. Fitzsimmons; we don't want to keep you from your social engagements. Undoubtedly," Pidgear said, eyeing their evening clothes respectfully, "you and the madam were going to an important dinner party. It would be too bad to spoil an important dinner party for a little thing like this. Why, this whole affair is niggling," he said, waving his hand in front of Fitzsimmons' face. "Absolutely niggling."

Fitzsimmons looked over to where Tarloff and the other Russian were sitting on the floor. From Tarloff's face and gestures, even though he was talking in deepest Russian, Fitzsimmons could tell Tarloff was still as firm as ever. Fitzsimmons looked closely at Rusk, who was standing looking at Tarloff through narrow, baleful eyes.

"Why're you so anxious?" Fitzsimmons asked.

Rusk's eyes clouded over and his throat throbbed against his collar with rage. "I don't want to appear in court!" he yelled. "I don't want the whole goddamn business to start all over again, investigation, lawyers, fingerprints . . ."

Pidgear punched him savagely in the ribs, his fist going a short distance, but with great violence.

"Why don't you buy time on the National Broadcasting System?" Pidgear asked. "Make an address, coast to coast!"

Rusk glared murderously for a moment at Pidgear, then leaned over toward Fitzsimmons, pointing a large blunt finger at him.

339

"Do I have to put my finger in your mouth?" he whispered hoarsely.

"What does he mean by that?" Helen asked loudly. "Put his finger in your mouth? Why should he put his finger in your mouth?"

Rusk looked at her with complete hatred, turned, too full for words, and stalked away, with Pidgear after him. The two little men in the gray hats watched the room without moving.

"Claude?" Helen began.

"Obviously," Fitzsimmons said, his voice low, "Mr. Rusk isn't anxious for anyone to look at his fingerprints. He's happier this way."

"You picked a fine night!" Helen shook her head sadly. "Why can't we just pick up and get out of here?"

Rusk, with Pidgear at his side, strode back. He stopped in front of the Fitzsimmonses. "I'm a family man," he said, trying to sound like one. "I ask yuh as a favor. Talk to the Russian."

"I had to go to Bergdorf Goodman," Helen said, too deep in her own troubles to bother with Rusk, "to get a gown to spend the evening in a police station. 'Mrs. Claude Fitzsimmons was lovely last night in blue velvet and silver fox at Officer Kraus's reception at the 8th Precinct. Other guests were the well-known Leopold Tarloff, and the Messrs. Pidgear and Rusk, in gray hats. Other guests included the Russian Ambassador and two leading Italian artillerymen, also in gray hats.' "

Pidgear laughed politely. "Your wife is a very witty woman," he said.

"Yes," said Fitzsimmons, wondering why he'd married her.

"Will yuh for Christ's sake *ask?*" Rusk demanded. "Can it hurt yuh?"

"We're willing to do our part," Pidgear said, "We even brought down a Russian to talk to him and clear up any little points in his own language. No effort is too great."

Fitzsimmons' stomach growled loudly. "Haven't eaten all day," he said, embarrassed.

"That's what happens," Pidgear said. "Naturally."

"Yeah," said Rusk.

"Perhaps I should go out and get you a malted milk," Helen suggested coldly.

Fitzsimmons went over to where Tarloff was sitting with the other Russian. The others followed him.

"Are you sure, Mr. Tarloff," Fitzsimmons said "that you still want to prosecute?"

"Yes," Tarloff said promptly.

340

"Ten dollars," Rusk said. "I offer yuh ten dollars. Can a man do more?"

"Money is not the object." With his cap Tarloff patted his nose, which was still bleeding slowly and had swelled enormously, making Tarloff look lopsided and monstrous.

"What's the object?" Rusk asked.

"The object, Mr. Rusk, is principle."

"You talk to him," Rusk said to Fitzsimmons.

"All right," Officer Kraus said, "you can go up there now."

They all filed in in front of the lieutenant sitting high at his desk.

Tarloff told his story, the accident, the wanton punch in the nose.

"It's true," Pidgear said, "that there was an accident, that there was a slight scuffle after by mistake. But the man isn't hurt. A little swelling in the region of the nose. No more." He pointed dramatically to Tarloff.

"Physically," Tarloff said, clutching his cap, talking with difficulty because his nose was clogged, "physically that's true. I am not badly hurt. But in a mental sense . . ." He shrugged. "I have suffered an injury."

"Mr. Rusk is offering the amount of ten dollars," Pidgear said, "Also, he apologizes; he's sorry."

The lieutenant looked wearily down at Rusk. "Are you sorry?" he asked.

"I'm sorry," said Rusk, raising his right hand. "On the Bible, I swear I'm sorry."

"Mr. Tarloff," the lieutenant said, "if you wish to press charges, there are certain steps you will have to take. A deposition will have to be taken. Have you got witnesses?"

"Here," Tarloff said with a shy smile at the Fitzsimmonses.

"They will have to be present," the lieutenant said sleepily.

"Oh, God," Helen said.

"A warrant will have to be sworn out, there must be a hearing, at which the witnesses must also be present . . ."

"Oh, God," Helen said.

"Then the trial," said the lieutenant.

"Oh, God!" Helen said loudly.

"The question is, Mr. Tarloff," said the lieutenant, yawning, "are you willing to go through all that trouble?"

"The fact is," Tarloff said unhappily, "he hit me in the head without provocation. He is guilty of a crime on my person. He insulted me. He did me an injustice. The law exists for such things.

One individual is not to be hit by another individual in the streets of the city without legal punishment.'' Tarloff was using his hands to try to get everyone, the Fitzsimmonses, the lieutenant, Pidgear, to understand. "There is a principle. The dignity of the human body. Justice. For a bad act a man suffers. It's an important thing . . .''

"I'm excitable," Rusk shouted. "If yuh want, yuh can hit me in the head.''

"That is not the idea," Tarloff said.

"The man is sorry," the lieutenant said, wiping his eyes, "he is offering you the sum of ten dollars; it will be a long, hard job to bring this man to trial; it will cost a lot of the taxpayers' money; you are bothering these good people here who have other things to do. What is the sense in it, Mr. Tarloff?''

Tarloff scraped his feet slowly on the dirty floor, looked sadly, hopefully, at Fitzsimmons. Fitzsimmons looked at his wife, who was glaring at Tarloff, tapping her foot sharply again and again. Fitzsimmons looked back at Tarloff, standing there, before the high desk, small, in his ragged coat and wild gray hair, his little worn face twisted and grotesque with the swollen nose, his eyes lost and appealing. Fitzsimmons shrugged sadly. Tarloff drooped inside his old coat, shook his head wearily, shrugged, deserted once and for all before the lieutenant's desk, on the dry rock of principle.

"O.K.," he said.

"Here," Rusk brought the ten-dollar bill out with magical speed.

Tarloff pushed it away. "Get out of here," he said, without looking up.

No one talked all the way to Adele Lowrie's house. Tarloff opened the door and sat, looking straight ahead, while they got out. Helen went to the door of the house and rang. Silently, Fitzsimmons offered Tarloff the fare. Tarloff shook his head. "You have been very good," he said. "Forget it.''

Fitzsimmons put the money away slowly.

"Claude!" Helen called. "The door's open.''

Fitzsimmons hated his wife, suddenly, without turning to look at her. He put out his hand and Tarloff shook it wearily

"I'm awfully sorry," Fitzsimmons said. "I wish I . . .''

Tarloff shrugged. "That's all right," he said. "I understand." His face, in the shabby light of the cab, worn and old and battered by the streets of the city, was a deep well of sorrow. "There is no time. Principle." He laughed, shrugged. "Today there is no time for anything.''

He shifted gears and the taxi moved slowly off, its motor grinding noisily.

"Claude!" Helen called.

"Oh, shut up!" Fitzsimmons said as he turned and walked into Adele Lowrie's house.

# Noises in the City

Weatherby was surprised to see the lights of the restaurant still lit when he turned off Sixth Avenue and started up the street toward the small apartment house in the middle of the block in which he lived. The restaurant was called the Santa Margharita and was more or less Italian, with French overtones. Its main business was at lunchtime and by ten-thirty at night it was usually closed. It was convenient and on nights when they were lazy or when Weatherby had work to do at home, he and his wife sometimes had dinner there. It wasn't expensive, and Giovanni, the bartender, was a friend, and from time to time Weatherby stopped in for a drink on his way home from the office, because the liquor was good and the atmosphere quiet and there was no television.

He nearly passed it, then stopped and decided he could use a whiskey. His wife had told him she was going to a movie and wouldn't be home before eleven-thirty, and he was tired and didn't relish the thought of going into the empty apartment and drinking by himself.

There was only one customer in the restaurant, sitting at the small bar near the entrance. The waiters had already gone home and Giovanni was changing glasses for the man at the bar and pouring him a bourbon. Weatherby sat at the end of the bar, but there were still only two stools between him and the other customer. Giovanni came over to Weatherby and said, "Good evening, Mr. Weatherby," and put out a glass and poured him a big whiskey, without measuring, and opened a soda bottle and allowed Weatherby to fill the glass himself.

Giovanni was a large, non-Italian-looking man, with an unsmiling, square, severe face and a gray, Prussian-cut head of hair. "How's Mrs. Weatherby tonight?" he asked.

"Fine," Weatherby said. "At least she was fine when I talked to her this afternoon. I've just come from the office."

"You work too hard, Mr. Weatherby," Giovanni said.

344

"That's right." Weatherby took a good long swallow of the whiskey. There is nothing like Scotch, he thought gratefully, and touched the glass with the palm of his hand and rubbed it pleasurably. "You're open late tonight," he said.

"That's all right," Giovanni said. "I'm in no hurry. Drink as much as you want." Although he was talking to Weatherby, Weatherby somehow had the feeling that the words were addressed to the other man at the bar, who was sitting with his elbows on the mahogany, holding his glass in his two hands in front of his face and peering with a small smile into it, like a clairvoyant who sees something undefined and cloudy, but still agreeable, in the crystal ball. The man was slender and graying, with a polite, educated face. His clothes were narrow and modish, in dark gray, and he wore a gay striped bow tie and a button-down oxford white shirt. Weatherby noted a wedding ring on his left hand. He didn't look like the sort of man who sat around alone in bars drinking late at night. The light in the bar was subdued and Weatherby had the impression that in a brighter light he would recognize the man and that he would turn out to be someone he had met briefly once or twice long ago. But New York was like that. After you lived in New York long enough, a great many of the faces seemed tantalizingly familiar to you.

"I suppose," Giovanni said, standing in front of Weatherby, "after it happens, we'll be losing you."

"Oh," Weatherby said, "we'll be dropping in here to eat again and again."

"You know what I mean," Giovanni said. "You plan on moving to the country?"

"Eventually," Weatherby said, "I imagine so. If we find a nice place, not too far out."

"Kids need fresh air," Giovanni said. "It isn't fair to them, growing up in the city."

"No," Weatherby said. Dorothy, his wife, was seven-months pregnant. They had been married five years and this was their first child, and it gave him an absurd primitive pleasure to talk about the country air that his child would breathe as he grew up. "And then, of course, the schools." What joy there was in platitudes about children, once you knew you could have them.

"Mr. Weatherby . . ." It was the other man at the bar. "May I say good evening to you, sir?"

Weatherby turned toward the man, a little reluctantly. He was in no mood for random conversation with strangers. Also, he had

had a fleeting impression that Giovanni regretted the man's advance toward him.

"You don't remember me," the man said, smiling nervously. "I met you eight or ten years ago. In my . . , ah . . . in my shop." He made a slight sibilant sound that might have been the beginning of an embarrassed laugh. "In fact, I think you came there two or three times. . . . There was some question of our perhaps doing some work together, if I remember correctly. Then, when I heard Giovanni call you by name. I couldn't help overhearing. I'm . . . ah . . . Sidney Gosden." He let his voice drop as he spoke his name, as people who are celebrated sometimes do when they don't wish to sound immodest. Weatherby glanced across the bar at Giovanni for help, but Giovanni was polishing a glass with a towel, his eyes lowered, consciously keeping aloof from the conversation.

"Oh . . . uh . . . yes," Weatherby said vaguely.

"I had—have—the shop on Third Avenue," Gosden said. "Antiques, interior decoration." Again the soft, hissing, self-deprecating half-laugh. "It was when I was supposed to do over that row of houses off Beekman Place and you had spoken to a friend of mine . . ."

"Of course," Weatherby said heartily. He still didn't remember the man's name, really, but he remembered the incident. It was when he was just starting in, when he still thought he could make a go of it by himself as an architect, and he had heard that four old buildings on the East Side were going to be thrown together and cut up into small studio apartments. Somebody in one of the big firms, which had turned the job down, had suggested it might be worth looking into and had given him Gosden's name. His memory of his conversation with Gosden was shadowy, fifteen or twenty minutes of rather distracted talk in a dark shop with unlit brass lamps and early-American tables piled one on top of another, a sense of time being wasted, a sense of going up one more dead-end street. "Whatever happened?" he asked.

"Nothing," Gosden said. "You know how those things are. In the end, they merely pulled the whole block down and put up one of those monstrous apartment houses nineteen-stories high. It was too bad. I was terribly impressed with your ideas. I do remember, to this day." He sounded like a woman at a cocktail party, talking swiftly to a man in a corner to hold him there, saying anything that came to mind, to try to keep him from escaping to the bar and leaving her there stranded, with no one to talk to for the rest of the evening, for the rest of her life. "I meant to follow your career," Gosden went on hurriedly. "I was sure you were meant

346

for splendid achievements, but a person is so kept so frantically busy in this city—with nothing important, of course—the best intentions—'' He waved his hand helplessly and let the complicated sentence lapse. "I'm sure I pass buildings you've put up every day, monuments to your talent, without knowing . . ."

"Not really," Weatherby said. "I went in with a big firm." He told the man the name of the firm and Gosden nodded gravely, to show his respect for their works. "I do bits and pieces for them."

"Everything in due time," Gosden said gaily. "So you're one of those young men who are putting us poor New Yorkers into our cold, bright glass cages."

"I'm not so young," Weatherby said, thinking, grimly, *That's* the truth. And, at the most, Gosden could only have been ten years older than he. He drained his drink. Gosden's manner, gushy, importunate, with its hint of effeminacy, made him uncomfortable. "Well," he said, taking out his wallet, "I think I'd better . . ."

"Oh, no, please . . ." Gosden said. There was a surprising note of anguish in his voice. "Giovanni will just lock up the bottles and put me out if you go. Another round, please, Giovanni. Please. And please serve yourself, too. Late at night like this . . ."

"I really must . . ." Weatherby began. Then he saw Giovanni looking at him in a strange, imperative way, as though there were an urgent message he wanted to deliver. Giovanni quickly poured a second Scotch for Weatherby, a bourbon for Gosden and a neat slug of bourbon for himself.

"There," Gosden said, beaming. *"That's* better. And don't think, Mr. Weatherby, that I go around town just offering rounds of drink to *every*body. In fact, I'm parsimonious, unpleasantly parsimonious, my wife used to say, it was the one thing she constantly held against me." He held up his glass ceremoniously. His long narrow hand was shaking minutely, Weatherby noticed, and he wondered if Gosden was a drunkard. "To the cold, beautiful, lonesome glass buildings," Gosden said, "of the city of New York."

They all drank. Giovanni knocked his tot down in one gulp and washed the glass and dried it without changing his expression.

"I do love this place," Gosden said, looking around him fondly at the dim lamps and the gluey paintings of the Ligurian coast that dotted the walls. "It has especial memories for me. I proposed marriage here on a winter night. To my wife," he added hastily, as if afraid that Weatherby would suspect he had proposed marriage to somebody else's wife here. "We never came here often enough

347

after that." He shook his head a little sadly. "I don't know why. Perhaps because we lived on the other side of town." He sipped at his drink and squinted at a painting of sea and mountains at the other end of the bar. "I always intended to take my wife to Nervi. To see the Temple," he said obscurely. "The Golden Bough. As the French would say, Hélas, we did not make the voyage. Foolishly, I thought there would always be time, some other year. And, of course, being parsimonious, the expense always seemed out of proportion . . ." He shrugged and once more took up his clairvoyant position, holding the glass up with his two hands and peering into it. "Tell me, Mr. Weatherby," he said in a flat, ordinary tone of voice, "have you ever killed a man?"

"What?" Weatherby asked, not believing that he had heard correctly.

"Have you ever killed a man?" Gosden for the third time made his little hissing near-laugh. "Actually, it's a question that one might well ask quite frequently, on many different occasions. After all, there must be quite a few people loose in the city who at one time or another have killed a man—policemen on their rounds, rash automobilists, prizefighters, doctors and nurses, with the best will in the world, children with air rifles, bank robbers, thugs, soldiers of the great war . . ."

Weatherby looked doubtfully at Giovanni. Giovanni didn't say anything, but there was something in his face that showed Weatherby the barman wanted him to humor the other man.

"Well," Weatherby said, "I was in the war. . . ."

"In the infantry, with a bayonet, perhaps," Gosden said, in the new, curious, flat, noneffeminate voice.

"I was in the artillery," Weatherby said. "In a battery of 105's. I suppose you could say that . . ."

"A dashing captain," Gosden said, smiling, "peering through binoculars, calling down the fire of the great guns on the enemy headquarters."

"It wasn't exactly like that," Weatherby said. "I was nineteen years old and I was a private and I was one of the loaders. Most of the time I spent digging."

"Still," Gosden persisted, "you could say that you contributed, that by your efforts men had been killed."

"Well," Weatherby said, "we fired off a lot of rounds. Somewhere along the line we probably hit something."

"I used to be a passionate hunter," Gosden said. "When I was a boy. I was brought up in the South. Alabama, to be exact, although I'm proud to say one would never know it from my accent. I once shot a lynx." He sipped thoughtfully at his drink. "It finally became distasteful to me to take the lives of animals. Although I had no feeling about birds. There is something inimical, *prehuman* about birds, don't you think, Mr. Weatherby?"

"I haven't really given it much thought," Weatherby said, sure now the man was drunk and wondering how soon, with decency, he could get out of there and whether he could go without buying Gosden a round.

"There must be a moment of the utmost exaltation when you take a human life," Gosden said, "followed by a wave of the most abject, ineradicable shame. For example, during the war, among your soldier friends, the question must have arisen. . . ."

"I'm afraid," Weatherby said, "that in most cases they didn't feel as much as you would like them to have felt."

"How about you?" Gosden said. "Even in your humble position as loader, as you put it, as a cog in the machinery—how did you feel, how do you feel now?"

Weatherby hesitated, on the verge of being angry with the man. "Now," he said, "I regret it. While it was happening, I merely wanted to survive."

"Have you given any thought to the institution of capital punishment, Mr. Weatherby?" Gosden spoke without looking in Weatherby's direction, but staring at his own dim reflection above the bottles in the mirror above the bar. "Are you pro or con the taking of life by the State? Have you ever made an effort to have it abolished?"

"I signed a petition once, in college, I think."

"When we are young," Gosden said, speaking to his wavery reflection in the mirror, "we are more conscious of the value of life. I, myself, once walked in a procession protesting the hanging of several young colored boys. I was not in the South, then. I had already moved up North. Still, I walked in the procession. In France, under the guillotine, the theory is that death is instantaneous, although an instant is a variable quantity, as it were. And there is some speculation that the severed head as it rolls into the basket is still capable of feeling and thinking some moments after the act is completed."

"Now, Mr. Gosden," Giovanni said soothingly, "I don't think it helps to talk like this, does it, now?"

"I'm sorry, Giovanni," Gosden said, smiling brightly. "I should be ashamed of myself. In a charming bar like this, with a man of sensibility and talent like Mr. Weatherby. Please forgive me. And now, if you'll pardon me, there's a telephone call I have to make."

He got off his stool and walked jauntily, his shoulders thrown back in his narrow dark suit, toward the other end of the deserted restaurant and went through the little door that led to the washrooms and the telephone booth.

"My Lord," Weatherby said. "What's *that* all about?"

"Don't you know who he is?" Giovanni said, in a low voice, keeping his eyes on the rear of the restaurant.

"Only what he just told me," Weatherby said. "Why? Are people supposed to know who he is?"

"His name was in all the papers, two, three years ago," Giovanni said. "His wife was raped and murdered. Somewhere on the East Side. He came home for dinner and found the body."

"Good God," said Weatherby softly, with pity.

"They picked up the guy who did it the next day," Giovanni said. "It was a carpenter or a plumber or something like that. A foreigner from Europe, with a wife and three kids in Queens somewhere. No criminal sheet, no complaints on him previous. He had a job to do in the building and he rang the wrong doorbell and there she was in her bathrobe or something."

"What did they do to him?" Weatherby asked.

"Murder in the first degree," Giovanni said. "They're electrocuting him up the river tonight. That's what *he's* calling about now. To find out if it's over or not. Usually, they do it around eleven, eleven-thirty, I think."

Weatherby looked at his watch. It was nearly eleven-fifteen. "Oh, the poor man," he said. If he had been forced to say whether he meant Gosden or the doomed murderer, it would have been almost impossible for him to give a clear answer. "Gosden, Gosden . . ." he said. "I must have been out of town when it happened."

"It made a big splash," Giovanni said. "For a coupla days."

"Does he come in here and talk like this often?" Weatherby asked.

"This is the first time I heard him say a word about it," Giovanni said. "Usually, he comes in here once, twice a month, has one drink at the bar, polite and quiet, and eats by himself in back, early, reading a book. You'd never think anything ever happened to him. Tonight's special, I guess. He came in around eight o'clock and he didn't eat anything, just sat up there at the bar, drinking slow all night."

"That's why you're still open," Weatherby said.

"That's why I'm still open. You can't turn a man out on a night like this."

"No," Weatherby said. Once more he looked at the door to

the telephone booth. He would have liked to leave. He didn't want to hear what the man would have to say when he came out of the telephone booth. He wanted to leave quickly and be sure to be in his apartment when his wife came home. But he knew he couldn't run out now, no matter how tempting the idea was.

"This is the first time I heard he asked his wife to marry him here," Giovanni said. "I suppose that's why . . ." He left the thought unfinished.

"What was she like?" Weatherby asked. "The wife?"

"A nice, pretty little quiet type of woman," Giovanni said. "You wouldn't notice her much."

The door at the rear of the restaurant opened and Gosden came striding lightly toward the bar. Weatherby watched him, but he didn't see the man look either left or right at any particular table that might have held special memories for him. As he sprang up onto his stool and smiled his quick, apologetic smile, there was no hint on his face of what he had heard over the telephone. "Well," Gosden said briskly, "here we are again."

"Let me offer a round," Weatherby said, raising his finger for Giovanni.

"That is kind, Mr. Weatherby," said Gosden. "Very kind indeed."

They watched Giovanni pour the drinks.

"While I was waiting for the connection," Gosden said, "I remembered an amusing story. About how some people are lucky and some people are unlucky. It's a fishing story. It's quite clean. I never seem to be able to remember risqué stories, no matter how funny they are. I don't know why. My wife used to say that I was a prude and perhaps she was right. I do hope I get the story right. Let me see—" He hesitated and squinted at his reflection in the mirror. "It's about two brothers who decide to go fishing for a week in a lake in the mountains. . . . Perhaps you've heard it, Mr. Weatherby?"

"No," Weatherby said.

"Please don't be polite just for my sake," Gosden said. "I would hate to think that I was boring you."

"No," Weatherby said, "I really haven't heard it."

"It's quite an old story, I'm sure, I must have heard it years ago when I still went to parties and nightclubs and places like that. Well, the two brothers go to the lake and they rent a boat and they go out on the water and no sooner do they put down their lines than one brother has a bite and pulls up the hugest fish. He puts down his line again and once again immediately he pulls up another huge fish. And again and again all day long, And all day long the other brother sits in the boat and never gets the tiniest nibble on his hook. And the next day it is the same. And the day after that, and the day after that. The brother who is catching nothing gets gloomier and gloomier and angrier and angrier with the brother who is catching all the fish. Finally, the brother who is catching all the fish, wanting to keep peace in the family, as it were, tells the other brother that he will stay on shore the next day and let the one who hasn't caught anything have the lake for himself that day. So the next day, bright and early, the unlucky brother goes out by himself with his rod and his line and his most succulent bait and puts his line overboard and waits. For a long time nothing happens. Then there is a splash nearby and a huge fish, the hugest fish of all, jumps out of the water and says, 'Say, Bud, isn't your brother coming out today?' '' Gosden looked anxiously over at Weatherby to see what his reaction was. Weatherby made himself pretend to chuckle.

"I do hope I got it right," Gosden said. "It seems to me to have a somewhat deeper meaning than most such anecdotes. About luck and destiny and things like that, if you know what I mean."

"Yes, it does," Weatherby said.

"People usually prefer off-color stories, I notice," Gosden said, "but as I said, I don't seem to be able to remember them." He drank delicately from his glass. "I suppose Giovanni told you something about me while I was telephoning," he said. Once more his voice had taken on its other tone, flat, almost dead, not effeminate.

Weatherby glanced at Giovanni and Giovanni nodded, almost imperceptibly. "Yes," Weatherby said. "A little."

"My wife was a virgin when I married her," Gosden said. "But we had the most passionate and complete relationship right from the beginning. She was one of those rare women who are made simply for marriage, for wifehood, and nothing else. No one could suspect the glory of her beauty or the depths of her feeling merely from looking at her or talking to her. On the surface, she seemed the shyest and least assertive of women, didn't she, Giovanni?"

"Yes, Mr. Gosden," Giovanni said.

"In all the world there were only two men who could have known. Myself and . . . ." He stopped. His face twitched. "At eleven-o-eight," he said, "they pulled the switch. The man is dead. I was constantly telling her to leave the chain on the door, but she was thoughtless and she trusted all the world. The city is full of wild beasts, it is ridiculous to say that we are civilized. She screamed. Various people in the building heard her scream, but in the city one pays little attention to the noises that emanate from a neighbor's apartment. Later on, a lady downstairs said that she thought perhaps my wife and I were having an argument, although we never fought in all the years we were married, and another neighbor thought it was a program on a television set, and she was thinking of complaining to the management of the building because she had a headache that morning and was trying to sleep.'' Gosden tucked his feet under the barstool rung in an almost girlish position and held his glass up again before his eyes with his two hands. ''It is good of you to listen to me like this, Mr. Weatherby,'' he said. ''People have been avoiding me in the last three years, old customers hurry past my shop without looking in, old friends are out when I call. I depend upon strangers for trade and conversation these days. At Christmas, I sent a hundred-dollar bill anonymously, in a plain envelope, through the mails to the woman in Queens. It was on impulse, I didn't reason it out, the holiday season perhaps. . . . I contemplated asking for an invitation to the . . . the ceremony at Ossining tonight, I thought quite seriously about it, I suppose it could have been arranged. Then, finally, I thought it wouldn't really do any good, would it. And I came here, instead, to drink with Giovanni.'' He smiled across the bar at Giovanni. ''Italians,'' he said, ''are likely to have gentle and understanding souls. And now, I really must go home. I sleep poorly and on principle I'm opposed to drugs.'' He got out his wallet and put down some bills.

''Wait a few minutes,'' Giovanni said, ''until I lock up and I'll walk you home and open your door for you.''

''Ah,'' Gosden said, ''that would be kind of you, Giovanni. It is the most difficult moment. Opening the door. I am terribly alone. After that, I'm sure I'll be absolutely all right.''

Weatherby got off the stool and said to Giovanni, ''Put it on the bill, please.'' He was released now. ''Good night,'' he said to Giovanni. ''Good night, Mr. Gosden.'' He wanted to say more, to proffer some word of consolation or hope, but he knew nothing he could say would be of any help.

''Good night,'' Gosden said, in his bright, breathy voice now. ''It's been a pleasure renewing our acquaintanceship, even so briefly. And please present my respects to your wife.''

Weatherby went out of the door onto the street, leaving Giovanni locking the liquor bottles away and Gosden silently and slowly drinking, perched neat and straight-backed on the barstool.

The street was dark and Weatherby hurried up it toward his doorway, making himself keep from running. He used the stairway,

353

because the elevator was too slow. He opened the metal door of his apartment and saw that there was a light on in the bedroom.

"Is that you, darling?" He heard his wife's drowsy voice from the bedroom.

"I'll be right in," Weatherby said. "I'm locking up." He pushed the extra bolt that most of the time they neglected to use and carefully walked, without haste, as on any night, across the carpet of the darkened living room.

Dorothy was in bed, with the lamp beside her lit and a magazine that she had been reading fallen to the floor beside her. She smiled up at him sleepily. "You have a lazy wife," she said, as he began to undress.

"I thought you were going to the movies," he said.

"I went. But I kept falling asleep," she said. "So I came home."

"Do you want anything? A glass of milk. Some crackers?"

"Sleep," she said. She rolled over on her back, the covers up to her throat, her hair loose on the pillow. He put on his pyjamas, turned off the light, and got into bed beside her and she lifted her head to put it on his shoulder.

"Whiskey," she said drowsily. "Why do people have such a prejudice against it? Smells delicious. Did you work hard, darling?"

"Not too bad," he said, with the freshness of her hair against his face.

"Yum," she said, and went to sleep.

He lay awake for a while, holding her gently, listening to the muffled sounds from the street below. God deliver us from accident, he thought, and make us understand the true nature of the noises arising from the city around us.

# The Indian in Depth of Night

The city lay around Central Park in a deep hush, the four-o'clock-in-the-morning sky mild with stars and a frail, softly rising mist. Now and then a car went secretly by, with a sigh of tires and wind and a sudden small flare of headlights. The birds were still, and the trolley cars and buses; the taxicabs waited silently at scattered corners; the drunks were lying by this time in the doorways; the bums bedded for the night, the lights of the tall choked buildings out, save for a window here and there lit in lust or illness. There was no wind, and the smell of earth, heavy and surprising in the concrete city, rose with the mist.

O'Malley walked slowly from east to west on the rolling footpaths of the park, free now of nurses and children and policemen and scholars and old men retired heartbrokenly from business. The paths were free now of everything but the soft night and the mist and the country smell of spring earth and the endless and complex memory of all the feet that had trod and worn the paths in the green park in the palm of the city's hand.

O'Malley walked slowly, carrying his head with the exaggerated and conscious care of a man who feels he has drunk one whisky past absolute clarity. He breathed deeply of that rare and fragrant early morning air which seemed to O'Malley to have been made especially by God, in assurance of His mercy and benign tolerance, to follow whisky.

O'Malley looked around him at the city slumbering magnificently past the trees of the park and was glad to know his home was there, his work, his future. He walked slowly from east to west, breathing in the quiet air, holding his head carefully, but comfortably.

"Pardon me." A man slipped out in front of him. "Have you got a light?"

O'Malley stopped and struck a match. He held the match to the man's cigarette, noticing the touch of rouge on the cheeks, the long, carefully waved hair, the white trembling hands cupping the match, the slight smear of rouge on the man's lips.

"Thanks." The man lifted his head, looked sidewise, but challengingly, at O'Malley. O'Malley put the matches away and started to move westward, holding his head in gentle balance.

"Lovely night," said the man hurriedly. His voice was shrill and girlish and came from high in his throat, all breath, nervous, almost hysterical. "I adore walking in the park at this time on a night like this. Breathe," he said. "Just breathe the air."

O'Malley breathed the air.

"All alone?" the man asked nervously.

"Uhuh," O'Malley said.

"You're not lonesome?" The man's hands pulled at each other as he talked. "You're not afraid to walk all alone through the park at this hour?"

"No," O'Malley said, ready, with the drinks and the sweetness of the air, and the feeling of living in and, in a way, owning the great city of New York, to pass on a kind word to every living thing. "I never get lonesome and I like to walk through the park when it's empty and dark like this."

The man nodded unhappily. "Are you sure you don't want company?" he asked desperately, looking up at O'Malley with that sidewise and challenging look, like the look of a frightened but determined woman at a man she has decided to catch.

"I'm sure," O'Malley said gently. "I'm sorry." And he left the man with the carefully waved hair standing next to a tree with the little light of the cigarette gleaming in his hand and walked slowly on. He walked on, feeling sorry for the man, feeling good that he had enough of a fund of sympathy and human feeling so that he could sorrow, even slightly, over a man like that, rouged and roaming the park on a sinful and illicit errand, met for sixty seconds in the middle of the night.

"Say, Buddy," another man, small, and even in the darkness, knobby and gnarled, stepped out from behind a tree. "I want a dime."

O'Malley dug dreamily in his pocket. There was nothing there. "I haven't got a dime," he said.

"I want a dime," the man said. O'Malley saw that his face was dark and savage-looking, not a city face, grimy, hard, gleaming in the light of a distant lamppost. The clothes the man wore were too large and improvised and torn, and he continually lifted his arms to slide the sleeves back from his wrist, giving him a supplicant and religious look.

"I told you I haven't got a dime," O'Malley said.

"Gimme a dime!" the little man said loudly. His voice was rough and hoarse, as though he had been shouting in noisy places for years on end.

O'Malley took out his wallet and opened it and showed it to the man. "There's nothing there," he said. "Look."

The man looked. He lifted his arms to free his wrists from his sleeves, looked uneasily over O'Malley's shoulder up at the lamppost. O'Malley put his wallet away.

"Gimme a dollar," the man said.

"I showed you my wallet," O'Malley said. "I haven't got a dollar. I haven't got anything. I'm busted."

The man walked thoughtfully around O'Malley, walking lightly, on his toes, as though he expected to take O'Malley by surprise. "I'll beat you up," he said. "No matter how big you are. I'm a prizefighter. I'm an Indian. I'm a Creek Indian. My name's Billy Elk. Gimme a dime!" He put out his hand as though he was absolutely confident now that he'd convinced O'Malley and the money would be dropped in his hand.

"I'm busted," O'Malley said. "Honest."

Billy Elk circled O'Malley slowly, his large and ragged garments flapping around him. O'Malley stood there, gently willing, in the fragrance and loneliness and peace of the night, to befriend a penniless Creek Indian prizefighter astray far from home in Central Park.

Billy Elk's face creased in thought as he tip-toed around O'Malley. "Give me the wallet," he said suddenly. "I can get a dollar for that."

"It only cost seventy-five cents," O'Malley said.

Billy Elk's face creased in thought again. Only half-consciously now, he walked lightly in a circle around O'Malley, who stood there dreamily, looking up at the towers of the city rearing dark and magnificent against the clear soft sky, with here and there the scattered lights, lust and illness, keeping the city from total sleep in the depths of the night.

Suddenly Billy Elk leaped at him, snatched from his outside breast pocket the fountain pen O'Malley carried there. Billy Elk covered it proudly and lovingly in his gnarled hands, half-bent over it, his dark and savage face lit now by wild satisfaction. "I can get a dollar for this," he said.

"It only cost twenty-five cents," O'Malley said gently. "In the five and ten."

Billy Elk considered the pen in his hands. "All right," he said. "I can get twenty-five."

"Who'll give you twenty-five?" O'Malley asked.

Billy Elk backed up three steps to think about this. He sighed, came up to O'Malley and gave him the pen. O'Malley put the pen in his pocket, smiled in a pleasant, brotherly way at the Indian.

"Give me a dollar!" Billy Elk said harshly.

O'Malley smiled again and patted him on the shoulder. "Good night," he said, and started slowly home.

"If you don't give me the dollar," Billy Elk shouted, keeping pace with him, talking up at him, "I'll report you to the police." O'Malley stopped. "For what?" he asked, smiling dreamily, pleased that the city and the night had produced after the one Scotch too many, this wild and tiny creature.

"For talking to a fairy," Billy Elk shouted. "I saw you!"

"What did you see?" O'Malley asked mildly.

"I saw you with that fairy," Billy Elk said. "I'll take you to a policeman. Don't try to get away. I'm a prizefighter. Keep your hands in your pockets!"

"Take me to a policeman," O'Malley said, feeling somehow that it was his duty, as one of the few citizens of the city awake and moving, to be pleasant, hospitable, at the service of visitors, beggars, lunatics, lost children and young girls fled from home.

They walked out of the park in silence. Billy Elk's face was cast in harsh, savage lines, his eyes glittered, his mouth was set. At a corner on Central Park West, a fat policeman was wearily talking to a cab driver slouched in his seat. All the weight of the night hung over them, the deaths in the hospitals, the pain endured, the crimes committed in the dark hours, the hearts broken and the torture of men betrayed by women while the city slept, distilled and poured down in the bleak lamplight over the officer of the law and the tired man at the wheel of the old cab under the lamppost.

O'Malley stopped ten yards away and Billy Elk strode up to the policeman, who was lamenting the fact that his wife had kidney trouble and that his daughter was free with the boys, although she was only in the third term of high school.

The policeman stopped talking when Billy Elk stopped in front of him, and looked at the Indian slowly, mournfully, expecting only trouble, the night's everlasting gift to him.

"Well?" he asked Billy Elk sadly.

Billy Elk looked fleetingly and wildly over his shoulder at

358

O'Malley, then turned back to the policeman. "Is there an Indian Reservation around here?" he asked loudly.

The policeman, grateful that no murder had turned up, no entry, rape, arson, assault, double-parking committed, thought seriously for a full minute. "No," he said. "I don't know of any Indian Reservation in these parts."

"There's a place called Indian Point," said the cab driver. "It's up the river."

Billy Elk nodded soberly, with ancient dignity, came back to O'Malley and the policeman went on to tell the cab driver that although his daughter was merely sixteen years old she was built in all respects like a full-blooded woman of thirty.

Billy Elk stood in front of O'Malley and smiled, his face suddenly broken by the flash of teeth and gleam of eye into warm childishness. "See," he said. "I'm not such a bad guy."

He waved and departed into the park, slipping silently and expertly among the trees, like Tecumseh's braves and the slippery, valiant red defenders of Kentucky's bloody ground.

O'Malley walked slowly home, breathing deeply the clear morning air, pleased to be in a city in which Indians roamed the streets and went to great lengths to prove their friendliness and goodness of heart.

# Material Witness

Lester Barnum walked down the steps, across the street and around the corner without looking back. He was a small, worn-out, neat, married-looking man, walking slowly, as though he never got enough sleep, his head lowered politely and humbly into his gray overcoat, his gray face pursed vaguely and undramatically over some inner problem.

A year in jail, he thought. He shook his head and turned to look at the huge gray prison that had held him, but he had gone around the corner without realizing it, and the jail and the year were behind him and out of sight. He walked aimlessly on, looking without real interest at the free men about him.

He hadn't liked the men he'd met in prison. In the movies, cellblocks were invariably inhabited by warm, great-hearted, harmless persons, but in the year he had spent behind bars no convicts of that particular type had turned up. There had only been rough, large, desperate men who had put pepper in his coffee, nails in his bed, and occasionally, in moments of extreme emotion, had hit him with mop-handles and slop buckets. And there was always a small, pasty-faced man turning up every month or so, whispering gratingly into his ear in the exercise yard, "Talk an' the next stop is Woodlawn. Fer yer own good . . ."

Everybody took it for granted that he owned some secret, deadly information—the police, the district attorney, the convicts. Barnum sighed as he walked listlessly along the bustling, free streets. He stopped irresolutely at a corner. No direction was more inviting than any other direction, no street offered any final destination. There was no home for him to go to. For the first time in his forty-three years there was no definite, appointed place where his clothes were hanging, his bed ready to be slept in. His wife had gone to St. Louis with an automobile mechanic and had taken his two daughters with her. "I might as well tell you," she'd said flatly in the visiting room at the jail after he'd been there three

360

months. "This has been going on a long time, but now he's going to St. Louis and I guess it's about time you found out." And she'd pulled at one of the curly little hats she was always wearing and adjusted her corset a little angrily as though Barnum had insulted her and she'd started west. And he'd found out that the printing shop he'd worked in for seventeen years had been unionized and his job had been taken over, at a much higher salary, by a Rumanian with a beard.

Barnum whistled bleakly through his teeth, thinking vaguely of the years behind him when he had led an ordinary, simple existence, bringing home the comic papers to his children every evening, dozing after dinner while his wife complained of one thing and another, a plain, unnoticed, uncomplicated life, in which he never talked to such important, improbable persons as district attorneys and Irish detectives, never had pepper put in his coffee by exasperated swindlers and dope-peddlers.

It had all started because he'd turned down Columbus Avenue, instead of Broadway. A year ago he had been walking slowly and quietly home from work, worrying over the fact that the Boss had marched back and forth behind him in the shop all afternoon, muttering, "I can't stand it! There are limits! I can't stand it!" Barnum hadn't known what it was that the Boss couldn't stand, but, vaguely, it had worried him, as there was always the possibility that the thing that the Boss couldn't stand might be Barnum. But he had been walking wearily home, knowing there would be haddock for dinner and that he would have to mind the children that evening because his wife was going to some woman's club where, she said, instruction was to be had in knitting.

Dimly Barnum had felt the evening was not going to be pleasant— dull, aimless, like thousands of other evenings in his life.

Then it had happened. A tall, very dark man had walked swiftly past Barnum, holding his hands in his pockets. Suddenly another man, in a gray hat and topcoat, had leaped out of a doorway and tapped the tall dark man on the shoulder. "Here you are, you son of a bitch," the man in the gray hat had said loudly and the dark man had started to run and the man in the gray hat had pulled a gun from under his armpit and yelled, "Not this time, Spanish!" and shot the dark man four times. The dark man slid quietly to the pavement and the man in the gray coat said, "How do you like that?" and looked once, coldly, at Barnum, who was standing there, with his mouth open. "Aah!" the man in the gray coat said loudly, pulling up one corner of his mouth in a snarl—and then he'd disappeared.

Barnum just stood there looking at the tall dark man who was lying quietly on the sidewalk, looking not so tall now, with the blood coming from him. After a while Barnum closed his mouth. He moved dreamily over to the man lying on the sidewalk. The man's eyes looked up at Barnum, calmly dead.

"Say—say, Mister! What happened?" A man in a butcher's apron was standing next to Barnum, looking down excitedly.

"I saw it," Barnum said slowly. "This fellow walked past me and a man in a gray hat jumped out of a doorway and he said, 'Here you are, you son of a bitch!' and then he said, 'Not this time, Spanish' and he went bang! bang! bang! bang! and he said 'How do you like that?' and he looked at me and he went 'Aaah!' and he disappeared and this gentleman was dead."

"What happened?" A fat lady ran across the street from a millinery shop, shouting as she ran.

"A man's been shot," the butcher said. "He saw it." He pointed at Barnum.

"How did it happen?" the milliner asked, respectfully. Three more men had run up by this time, and four small boys, all looking at the corpse.

"Well," Barnum said, feeling important as the babel of talk died down as he began to speak, "I was walking along and this fellow walked past me and a man in a gray hat jumped out of a doorway and he said, 'Here you are, you son of a bitch!' and this fellow started to run and the man in the gray hat pulled out a gun and he said, 'Not this time, Spanish' and he went bang! bang! bang! bang!" Barnum shouted the bangs and pointed his finger violently at the corpse on the sidewalk. "And he said, 'How do you like that?' and he looked at me and he went 'Aaah!' " Barnum curled his lip into an imitation of the murderer's snarl. "And he disappeared and this gentleman was dead."

By now there were fifty people gathered around Barnum and the corpse. "What happened?" the latest arrival asked.

"I was walking along," Barnum said in a loud voice, conscious of every eye upon him, "and this fellow walked past me. . . ."

"Lissen, Buddy." A small rough-looking man nudged his elbow. "Why don't you go home? You didn't see nuthin'."

"I saw," Barnum said excitedly. "I saw with my own eyes. A man in a gray hat jumped out of a doorway . . ." Barnum leaped to demonstrate, the crowd respectfully falling back to give him room, as Barnum landed catlike, his knees bent but tense. "And he said, 'Here you are, you son of a bitch!' And this fellow"— with a wave for the corpse—"started to run . . ." Barnum took two quick little steps to show how the dead man had started to run " . . . and the man in the gray hat pulled out a gun and said . . ."

"Why don't you go home?" the rough little man said pleadingly. "It's nuthin' to me, but you're only complicating yerself. Why don't you go home?"

Barnum looked at him coldly for a moment.

"Then what happened?" a voice demanded from the crowd.

" 'Not this time, Spanish!' " Barnum cried. "And he went bang! bang! bang! bang!" Barnum moved his hand as though he was firing a heavy gun and fighting the recoil. "And he said, 'How do you like that?' and he looked at me and he went 'Aaah!' " Barnum snarled it out, with every eye upon him, "and he disappeared, and this gentleman was dead."

"As a good friend of yours," the small rough man said earnestly, "I advise you to go home. You didn't see nuthin'. . . ."

"What happened?" A voice shouted across the bobbing heads. By now it seemed to Barnum nearly a thousand people must be congregated around him, all with their eyes fixed eagerly on him, who never, even in his own home, could get three people at one time, even his wife and two children, to listen to him for as long as a minute without interruption.

"I was walking along," Barnum said in a loud, ringing voice, "and this fellow . . ."                                    •

"Mistuh!" The small man shook his head despairingly. "Why're you doing this? What's it goin' to get you? Trouble!"

"This fellow," Barnum went on, disregarding the small, rough man, "walked past me and a man in a gray hat jumped out of a doorway . . ." Once more Barnum demonstrated. " 'There you are, you son of a bitch!' he hollered and this fellow started to run and the man in the gray hat pulled out a gun . . ." Barnum snatched an imaginary pistol from under his armpit, pointed it at the corpse. "And he yelled, 'Not this time, Spanish!' and he went bang! bang! bang! bang! and he said, 'How do you like that?' and he looked at me and he went 'Aaah!' and he disappeared and this gentleman was dead." Barnum was sweating heavily now from his leaps and snarls and the unaccustomed strain of talking so that a thousand people could hear every word, and his eyes were rolling with excitement. "And it was all over," Barnum said dramatically, "and this gentleman was lying there looking up at me before you could blink your eyes."

"Jesus Christ!" one of the four little boys in the inner circle said in deep admiration.

"Whoever you are," the small man said to Barnum, "you're a dope. Remember I told you. Good-bye." And he pushed his way out of the crowd.

A big man with a red face tapped Barnum's arm. He smiled engagingly at Barnum. "Did you really see it?" he asked.

"Did I see it!" Barnum waved his hand. "The bullets went past my head."

"What happened?" the red-faced man asked.

"I was walking along," Barnum began while the red-faced man listened with deep interest. "And this fellow was walking in front of me . . ."

"Louder!" a voice cried deep in the crowd.

"I WAS WALKING ALONG," Barnum shouted, "AND THIS FELLOW WAS WALKING IN FRONT OF ME AND A MAN IN A GRAY HAT . . ." And Barnum went through the story, with gestures, while the red-faced man listened with respect.

"You saw the murderer close up?" the red-faced man inquired.

"Like you." Barnum stuck his face right next to the other man's.

"You'd know his face again if you saw it?"

"Like my wife's . . ."

"Good," said the red-faced man, taking Barnum by the elbow and starting out through the crowd, as the sirens of radio cars howled to a halt at the corner. "You'll come with me to the police station and when we catch the murderer you'll identify him. You're a material witness. I'm glad I found you."

Barnum, a year later, sighed in retrospect. For a whole year the murderer was not caught, and he sat in jail and lost his wife and children and a bearded Rumanian took his job and highwaymen and forgers beat him with mop handles and slop buckets. Every three days he would be taken down to look at some new collection of thugs. Each time he would have to shake his head because the man in the gray hat was not among them and then the young district attorney would say, sneeringly, "You're one hell of a fine material witness, Barnum. Get him the hell out of here!" and the detectives would wearily drag him back to his cell. "We're pertectin' yuh," the detectives would say when Barnum would ask to be freed. "Yuh wanna go out and have 'em blow yer brains out? That was Sammy Spanish that was killed. He's an important figure. You know too much. Take it easy, yuh're getting yer three squares a day, ain't yuh?"

"I don't know anything," Barnum would say wearily, in a low voice, as they locked him into his cell, but they never paid any attention. Luckily, the district attorney got a good job with an insurance company and gave up looking for the murderer of Sammy Spanish, otherwise Barnum was sure he'd have been kept until either he or the district attorney died.

Walking aimlessly down the street, with the year behind him, homeless, wifeless, childless, jobless, Barnum sighed. He stood on a corner, rubbing his chin sadly, trying to decide which way to turn. A car swung around the corner past him, too close to a car parked just below the corner. There was the sound of the grating of fenders and then the forlorn wail of brakes and the crumpling of metal. A man jumped out of the parked car, waving his hands.

"Where the hell do you think you're going?" he cried to the driver of the other car, looking wildly at his mashed fender. "Lemme see your license! Somebody's got to pay for that fender and it ain't going to be me, brother!" While the reckless driver was getting out of his car, the owner of the damaged car turned sadly to Barnum.

"Did you see that?" he asked.

Barnum looked hurriedly at him, at the fender, at the street around him. "Oh, no," he said. "I didn't see anything."

And he turned and walked swiftly back in the direction from which he had come.

# Little Henry Irving

The dice rolled like cavalry across the concrete floor of the academy basement.

"Eight's the point," Eddie said, pulling at the high collar of his cadet's uniform. "Eight, baby, come eight, oh, you eight." He stood up with a grin, dusting the knife-creases at his knees. "Read them," he said.

The Custodian shook his head and sat down backward. "I might just as well lay down and die. On Christmas. How can a man be as unlucky as me on Christmas?"

"Roll for the pot," Eddie offered seductively.

"My better nature says no," the Custodian said.

"Roll you for the pot."

"If I lose I'm cleaned. I won't even be able to buy a pint of beer for my throat on Christmas."

"O.K.," Eddie said offhandedly, starting to rake in the silver, "if you want to quit, losing . . ."

"Roll for the pot," the Custodian said grimly. He put out his last dollar-twenty with the desperate calm of a man signing his will. "Go ahead, Diamond Jim."

Eddie cooed to the dice, held warm and cozy in his hands, and rocked soothingly back and forth on his skinny knees. "The moment has come," he cried softly into his hands. "Little sweethearts . . ."

"Roll!" the Custodian cried irritably. "No poetry!"

"Four and three, five and two, six and one," Eddie coaxed into his hands. "That's all I ask."

"Roll!" the Custodian yelled.

Delicately Eddie spun the dice along the cold hard floor. They stopped like lovers, nestling together against Fate. "Do we read seven?" Eddie asked gently.

"On Christmas!" the Custodian said despairingly.

Eddie carefully counted and sorted his money. "You put up a good fight," he said comfortingly to the Custodian.

"Yeah," the Custodian muttered. "Oh, yeah. A kid like you. Say, how old *are* you, anyway, a million?"

"I am thirteen years old," Eddie said, pocketing the last coins. "But I come from New York."

"You ought to be home with your family. On Christmas. A kid like you. I wish to hell you was home with yer family!"

"In Connecticut," Eddie said, pulling his skimpy uniform jacket down, "nobody knows anything about crap. I'm telling you for your own good."

"You ought to be home with yer family," the Custodian insisted.

A veil of tears came suddenly over Eddie's large dark eyes. "My Pop told me he don't want to see me for a year."

"What'd ye do?" the Custodian asked. "Win his pants from him last Christmas?"

Eddie blew his nose and the tears left his eyes. "I hit my sister with a lamp. A bridge lamp." His mouth tightened in retrospect. "I would do it again. Her name's Diana. She's fifteen years old."

"That's nice," the Custodian said. "You're a fine little boy, all around."

"It took four stitches. She cried for five hours. *Diana!* She said I mighta ruined her beauty."

"Well, it wouldn't do her beauty no good, hitting her with a bridge lamp," the Custodian said reasonably.

"She's going to be an actress. A stage actress."

"That's nice for a girl," the Custodian said.

"Aaah," Eddie snorted. "What's nice about it? She takes lessons from dancing teachers and French teachers and English teachers and horseback teachers and music teachers and Pop is always kissin' her and callin' her his little Bernhardt. She stinks."

"That's no way to talk about yer sister," the Custodian said sternly. "I won't listen to a little boy talkin' like that about his sister."

"Aaah, shut up!" Eddie said bitterly. "Little Bernhardt. Pop's an actor, too. The whole damn family's actors. Except me," he said with somber satisfaction.

"You're a crap player," the Custodian said. "You got nothing to worry about."

"Little Bernhardt. Pop takes her with him all over the country. Detroit, Dallas, St. Louis, Hollywood."

"Hollywood!"

"Me they send to Military Academy."

"Military Academy is good for young minds," the Custodian said loyally.

"Aaah," Eddie said. "Little Bernhardt. I would like to step on her face."

"That's no way to talk."

"She goes in three times a week to see my Pop act. My Pop can act better than anybody since Sir Henry Irving."

"Who says so?" the Custodian wanted to know.

"My Pop," Eddie said "He's a Polack, my Pop. He's got feeling. Real feeling. Everybody says my Pop's got feeling. You oughta see him act."

"I only go to the movies," the Custodian said.

"He's actin' in *The Merchant of Venice*. With a long white beard, you'd never know it was my Pop. When he talks people laugh and cry in the audience. You can hear my Pop's voice for five blocks, I bet."

"That's the kind of actin' I like," the Custodian said.

Eddie threw out his arm in a tragic, pleading gesture. "Hath not a Jew eyes?" he demanded in tones of thunder. "Hath not a Jew hands, organs, dimensions, senses, affections, passions? Like that, that's the way my Pop does it." He sat down slowly on an upturned box. "It's the most beautiful thing in the world, the way my Pop does it," he said softly.

"You shouldn't've hit yer sister with a bridge lamp," the Custodian said morally. "Then you could've been seein' him act tonight."

"He smacked me for fifteen minutes, my Pop. He weighs two hundred and fifteen pounds an' he's built like Lou Gehrig, my Pop, like a truck horse, an' he was swingin' from his heels, but I didn't cry an' I didn't tell him why I hit her with a bridge lamp. I didn't cry one tear. I showed him. His little Bernhardt." Eddie got up with determination. "What the hell, I might just as well spend Christmas in a Military Academy as any place else." He started out into the bleak December afternoon.

"Lissen, Eddie," the Custodian said hurriedly, before Eddie could get through the door, "I wanna ask you a question."

"What?" Eddie asked coldly, sensing what was coming.

"It's Christmas Eve," the Custodian said, preparation in his voice.

"All right," Eddie said, "it's Christmas Eve."

"I'm an old man." The Custodian brushed his white mustache pitifully. "I'm an old man without kith or kin."

"All right," Eddie said.

"Usually on Christmas, Eddie, I buy myself a little pint of something, applejack usually, and I warm my old heart in a corner to forget that I'm deserted by the world. When you get older you'll know what I mean.''

"Yeah," Eddie said.

"This year," the Custodian shifted uneasily, "this year you happen to've won all my money. Now, I was wonderin', if you would . . .''

"No," Eddie said, starting out.

"On Christmas Eve, for an old man, Eddie.''

"You lost," Eddie said without heat. "I won. O.K.''

He left and the Custodian settled down in his carpet-seated rocker next to the furnace. The Custodian rocked mournfully back and forth and shook his head as he watched Eddie go up the cellar steps out into the gray afternoon.

Eddie shambled aimlessly around the winter-bare school grounds. "Military School! Aaah!" he said to himself. He should be home in New York City, blazing with lights, green and red and white lights, filled with people hurrying happily through the streets with packages done up in colored ribbon, and Santa Clauses ringing their little bells on the street corners for the Salvation Army and the thousand movie houses gaping invitingly along the sidewalks. He should go watch Pop act tonight and go to dinner with him afterwards on Second Avenue, and eat duck and potato pancakes and drink spiced wine and go home and listen to Pop sing German songs at the top of his voice, accompanying himself on the piano loudly, until the neighbors complained to the police.

He sighed. Here he was, stuck at a Military Academy in Connecticut, because he was a bad boy. Ever since his sixth birthday he'd been known as a bad boy. He'd had a party on his sixth birthday and he'd had a fine time, with cake, candy, ice cream and bicycles, until his sister Diana had come into the middle of the room and done a scene from *As You Like It* that her English teacher had coached her in. "All the world's a stage," she'd piped in her imitation Boston accent that the English teacher gave her, "and all the men and women in't merely playahs . . .'' At the end of it everybody shouted "Bravo!" and Pop grabbed her and swung her up and cried on her blonde hair and said over and over again, "Little Bernhardt, my little Bernhardt!''

Eddie had thrown a plate of ice cream at her and it had spattered all over Pop and Diana had cried for two hours and he'd been spanked and sent to bed.

"I hate Connecticut," he said to a leafless elm, leaning coldly over the dirty snow on the side of the walk.

Since then he had thrown Diana off a porch, tearing ligaments

369

in her arm; he had run away in a rowboat off the coast of New Jersey and had had to be rescued by the Coast Guard at ten o'clock at night; he had played truant from seven different private and public schools; he had been caught coming out of burlesque houses with older friends; he had disobeyed his father on every possible occasion, and had been beaten three times to the month, standing there proud and stubborn, conscious in those moments at least, as Pop stood over him angry and terrible, that, actor or no actor, he was getting some attention, some evidence of paternal love.

He leaned against a tree and closed his eyes. He was in his Pop's dressing room at the theater and Pop was in his silk bathrobe with pieces of beard stuck here and there over his face and his hair gray with powder. Beautiful women with furs came in, talking and laughing in their womanly musical voices and Pop said, "This is my son, Eddie. He is a little Henry Irving," and the women cried with delight and took him in their arms, among the scented furs and kissed him, their lips cool from the winter outside on his warm red face. And Pop beamed and patted his behind kindly and said, "Eddie, you do not have to go to Military School any longer and you don't have to spend Christmas with your aunt in Duluth, either. You are going to spend Christmas in New York alone with me. Go to the box office and get a ticket for tonight's performance, Row A, center, 'Hath not a Jew eyes? Hath not a Jew hands, organs . . .' Yes, Pop, yes, Pop, yes . . ."

Eddie blinked his eyes and looked around him at the mean wood walls of the Academy. Prison, prison. "I wish you burn," he said with utter hate to the peeling paint and the dead ivy and the ramshackle bell tower. "Burn! *Burn!*"

Abruptly he became quiet. His eyes narrowed and the cast of thought came over his face beneath the stiff short visor of his military cap. He regarded the dreary buildings intently, his lips moving silently over deep, unmentionable thoughts, the expression on his face a hunter's expression, marking down prey for the kill far off in the tangled jungle.

If the school burned down he couldn't sleep in the December woods, could he, they would have to send him home, wouldn't they, and if he was rescued from the burning building Pop would be so grateful that his son was not dead that . . . The school would have to burn down completely and they would never send him back and fire burns from the bottom up and the bottom was the cellar and the only person there was the Custodian, sitting lonely there, longing for his Christmas bottle . . .

With a sharp involuntary sigh, Eddie wheeled swiftly and walked toward the cellar entrance, to seize the moment.

"Lissen," he said to the Custodian, rocking mournfully back and forth next to the furnace. "Lissen, I feel sorry for yuh."

"Yeah," the Custodian said hopelessly. "I can see it."

"I swear. An old man like you. All alone on Christmas Eve. Nothin' to comfort yuh. That's terrible."

"Yeah," the Custodian agreed. "Yeah."

"Not even a single drink to warm yuh up."

"Not a drink. On Christmas!" The Custodian rocked bitterly back and forth. "I might as well lay down and die."

"I got a change of heart," Eddie said deliberately. "How much does a bottle of applejack cost?"

"Well," the Custodian said craftily, "there's applejack and applejack."

"The cheapest applejack," Eddie said sternly. "Who do you think I am?"

"You can get a first-rate bottle of applejack for ninety-five cents, Eddie," the Custodian said in haste. "I would take that kindly. That's a thoughtful deed for an old man in the holiday season."

Eddie slowly assorted ninety-five cents out in his pocket. "Understand," he said, "this ain't a usual thing."

"Of course not, Eddie," the Custodian said quickly. "I wouldn't expect . . ."

"I won it honest," Eddie insisted.

"Sure, Eddie."

"But on Christmas . . ."

"Sure, just on Christmas . . ." The Custodian was on the edge of his rocker now, leaning forward, his mouth open, his tongue licking at the corners of his lips.

Eddie put out his hand with the coins in it. "Ninety-five cents," he said. "Take it or leave it."

The Custodian's hand trembled as he took the money. "You got a good heart, Eddie," he said simply. "You don't look it, but you got a good heart."

"I would go get it for you myself," Eddie said, "only I got to write my father a letter."

"That's all right, Eddie, my boy, perfectly all right. I'll take a little walk into town myself." The Custodian laughed nervously. "The clear air. Pick me up. Thank you, Eddie, you're one of the best."

"Well," Eddie said, starting out. "Merry Christmas."

"Merry Christmas," the Custodian said heartily. "Merry Christmas, my boy, *and* a happy New Year."

And he sang "I saw three ships go sailing by, go sailing by," as Eddie went up the cellar steps.

Five hours later Eddie walked down Forty-fifth Street, in New York City, without an overcoat, shivering in the cold, but happy. He marched across from Grand Central Station through the good-natured holiday crowds, reciting gaily to the lights, the neon signs, the bluecoated policemen, "If you prick us, do we not bleed? if you tickle us, do we not laugh? if you poison us, do we not die?" He crossed Sixth Avenue, turned into the stage-entrance alley of the theater over which the huge sign read in electric bulbs, *The Merchant of Venice* by William Shakespeare. "And if you wrong us, shall we not revenge?" he shouted thickly at the alley walls, as he opened the stage door and ran upstairs to his father's dressing room.

The door was open and his father was sitting at his make-up table, applying grease and false hair carefully, close to the mirror. Eddie sidled in softly.

"Pop," he said, standing at the door. Then again, "Pop."

"Uh." His father touched up an eyebrow with a comb, making it bush out.

"Pop," Eddie said. "It's me."

His father soberly put down the grease-stick, the small comb, the false hair, and turned around.

"Eddie," he said.

"Merry Christmas, Pop," Eddie said, smiling nervously.

"What're you doing here, Eddie?" His father looked him straight and seriously in the eye.

"I'm home, Pop," Eddie said quickly. "I'm home for Christmas."

"I am paying that money-grabbing Military Academy forty-five dollars extra to keep you there and you tell me you are home for Christmas!" The great voice boomed out with the passion and depth that made audiences of fifteen hundred souls shiver in their seats. "A telephone! I want a telephone! Frederick!" he called for his dresser. "Frederick, by God Almighty, a telephone!"

"But, Pop . . ." Eddie said.

"I will talk to those miserable toy soldiers, those uniformed school-ma'ams! Frederick, in the name of God!"

"Pop, Pop," Eddie wailed. "You can't call them."

His father stood up to his six-foot-three magnificence in his red-silk dressing gown and looked down on Eddie, one eyebrow high with mockery on the huge domed forehead. "I can't call them, my son says. Little snot-nose tells me what to do and what not to do."

"You can't call, Pop," Eddie yelled, "because there's nothing to talk to. See?"

"Oh," his father said, with searing irony, "the school has disappeared. Poof! and off it goes. The Arabian Nights. In Connecticut."

"That's why I'm here, Pop," Eddie pleaded rapidly. "There ain't no more school. It burned. It burned right down to the ground. This afternoon. Look, even my overcoat. Look, I don't have an overcoat."

His father stood silent, regarding him soberly through the deepset cold gray eyes under the famous gray brows. One of the famous long thick fingers beat slowly, like the pendulum of doom, on the dressing table, as he listened to his son, standing there, chapped by exposure, in his tight uniform, talking fast, shifting from one foot to another.

"See, Pop, it burned down, I swear to God, you can ask anyone, I was lying in my bed writing a letter and the firemen got me, you can ask them, and there wasn't no place for them to put me and they gave me money for the train and . . . I'll stay here with you, Pop, eh, Pop, for Christmas, what do you say, Pop?" Pleading, pleading . . . His voice broke off under his father's steady, unrelenting stare. He stood silent, pleading with his face, his eyes, the twist of his mouth, with his cold, chapped hands. His father moved majestically over to him, raised his hand, and slapped him across the face.

Eddie stood there, his face quivering, but no tears. "Pop," he said, controlling his voice as best he could. "Pop, what're you hitting me for? It ain't my fault. The school burned down, Pop."

"If the school burned down," his father said in measured tones, "and you were there, it was your fault. Frederick," he said to his dresser, who was standing in the doorway "put Eddie on the next train to his aunt in Duluth." And he turned, immutable as Fate, back to his dressing table and once more carefully started applying false hair to the famous face.

In the train to Duluth an hour later, Eddie sat watching the Hudson River fly past, crying at last.

# The House of Pain

"Tell her Mr. Bloomer wants to see her," Phillip said, holding his hat, standing straight before the elegant, white-handed hotel clerk.

"It's a Mr. Bloomer, Miss Gerry," the hotel clerk said elegantly, looking through Philip's plain, clean face, far across the rich lobby.

Philip heard the famous voice rise and fall in the receiver. "Who the hell is Mr. Bloomer?" the famous, sweet voice said.

Philip moved his shoulders uncomfortably in his overcoat. His country-boy ears, sticking out from his rough hair, reddened.

"I heard that," he said. "Tell her my name is Philip Bloomer and I wrote a play called *The House of Pain.*"

"It's a Mr. Philip Bloomer," the clerk said languidly, "and he says he wrote a play called *A House of Pain.*"

"Did he come all the way up here to tell me that?" the deep rich voice boomed in the receiver. "Tell him that's dandy."

"Let me talk to her, please." Philip grabbed the receiver from the clerk's pale hand. "Hello," he said, his voice shaking in embarrassment. "This is Philip Bloomer."

"How do you do, Mr. Bloomer?" the voice said with charm.

"The thing is, Miss Gerry, this play I wrote," Philip tried to find the subject, the object, the predicate before she hung up, "*The House of Pain.*"

"The clerk said *A House of Pain,* Mr. Bloomer."

"He's wrong," Philip said.

"He's a very stupid man, that clerk," the voice said. "I've told him so many times."

"I went to Mr. Wilkes' office," Philip said desperately, "and they said you still had the script."

"What script?" Miss Gerry asked.

"*The House of Pain,*" Philip cried, sweating. "When I brought it into Mr. Wilkes' office I suggested that you play the leading part and they sent it to you. Now, you see, somebody at the Theatre

374

Guild wants to see the script, and you've had it for two months already, so I thought you mightn't mind letting me have it,''

There was a pause, an intake of breath at the other end of the wire. "Won't you come up, Mr. Bloomer?" Miss Gerry said, her voice chaste but inviting.

"Yes, ma'am," Philip said.

"1205, sir," the clerk said, delicately taking the phone from Philip's hands and placing it softly on its pedestal.

In the elevator Philip looked anxiously at his reflection in the mirror, arranged his tie, tried to smooth down his hair. The truth was he looked like a farm boy, a dairy-hand who had perhaps gone to agricultural school for two years. As far as possible he tried to avoid meeting theater people because he knew nobody would believe that anybody who looked like him could write plays.

He got out of the elevator and went down the softly carpeted hall to 1205. There was a sheet of paper stuck in a clip on the metal door. He braced himself and rang the bell.

Miss Adele Gerry opened the door herself. She stood there, tall, dark-haired, perfumed, womanly, in an afternoon dress that showed a square yard of bosom. Her eyes held the same dark fire that had commanded admiring attention on many stages from Brooks Atkinson, from Mantle, from John Mason Brown. She stood there, her hand lightly on the doorknob, her hair swept up simply, her head a little to one side, looking speculatively at Philip Bloomer in the hallway.

"I'm Mr. Bloomer," Philip said.

"Won't you come in?" Her voice was sweet, simple, direct, fitted exactly to the task of allaying the nervousness of farm boys and dairy-hands.

"There's a note for you on the door," Philip said, glad of one sentence, at least, with which to get inside.

"Oh, thank you," she said, taking it.

"Probably a letter from some secret admirer," Philip said, with a smile, suddenly resolved to be gallant, to fight the farm boy, destroy the dairy-hand.

Miss Gerry took the sheet of paper over to the window, scanned it, her eyes close to it near-sightedly, her whole body beautifully intent on the written word.

"It's a menu," she said, tossing it on a table. "They have lamb stew tonight."

Philip closed his eyes for a moment, hoping that when he opened them, Miss Gerry, the room, the hotel would have disappeared.

"Won't you sit down, Mr. Bloomer?" Miss Gerry said.

He opened his eyes and marched across the room and sat upright on a little gilt chair. Miss Gerry arranged herself beautifully on a sofa, her hand outstretched along the back, the fingers dangling, the legs girlishly tucked in.

"You know, Mr. Bloomer," Miss Gerry said, her voice charmingly playful, "you don't look like a playwright at all."

"I know," Philip said, gloomily.

"You look so healthy." She laughed.

"I know."

"But you *are* a playwright?" She leaned forward intimately, and Philip religiously kept his eyes away from her bosom. This, he suddenly realized, had become the great problem of the interview.

"Oh, yes," he said, looking steadfastly over her shoulder. "Yes, indeed. As I told you over the phone, I came up for my play."

"*The House of Pain.*" She shook her head musingly. "A lovely title. Such a strange title for such a healthy-looking boy."

"Yes, ma'am," Philip said, rigorously holding his head steady, his gaze up.

"It was so good of you to think of me for it," Miss Gerry said, leaning forward even farther, her eyes liquid and grateful enough to project to the third row, balcony. "I've practically been in retirement for three years. I thought nobody even remembered Adele Gerry any more."

"Oh, no," Philip said, gallantly. "I remembered you." He saw that this was bad, but was sure that anything else he might add would be worse.

"The Theatre Guild is going to do your play, Mr. Bloomer?" Miss Gerry asked fondly.

"Oh, no. I didn't say that. I said somebody I knew up there thought it might not be a bad idea to send it around, and since you'd had the play for two months . . ."

Some of the interest fled from Miss Gerry's deep eyes. "I haven't a copy of your play, Mr. Bloomer. My director, Mr. Lawrence Wilkes, has it." She smiled beautifully at him, although the wrinkles showed clearly then. "I was interested in seeing you. I like to keep an eye on the new blood of the theater."

"Thank you," Philip mumbled, feeling somehow exalted. Miss Gerry beamed at him and he felt his eyes, unable to withstand the full glory of her glance, sinking to her bosom. "Mr. Wilkes," he said loudly. "I've seen many of his plays. You were wonderful in his plays. He's a wonderful director."

"He has his points," Miss Gerry said coldly. "But he has limitations. Grave limitations. It is the tragedy of the American theater that there is no man operating in it today who does not suffer from grave limitations.''

"Yes," Philip said.

"Tell me about your play, Mr. Bloomer. Tell me about the part you had in mind for me." She recrossed her legs comfortably, as though preparing for a long session on the sofa.

"Well," Philip said, "it's about a boarding house. A low, dreary, miserable boarding house with bad plumbing and poor devils who can't pay the rent. That sort of thing."

Miss Gerry said nothing.

"The presiding genius of this boarding house," Philip went on, "is a slatternly, tyrannical, scheming, harsh woman. I modeled her on my aunt, who keeps a boarding house."

"How old is she?" Miss Gerry asked, her voice small and flat.

"Who? My aunt?"

"The woman in the play."

"Forty-five." Philip got up and started to stride up and down the room as he talked of his play. "She's continually snooping around, listening at keyholes, piecing together the tragedies of her boarders from overheard snatches, fighting with her family, fighting with . . ." He stopped. "Why, Miss Gerry," he said, "Miss Gerry . . ."

She was bent over on the couch and the tears were dropping slowly and bitterly from her eyes.

"That man," she wept, "that man . . ." She jumped up and swept across to the phone, dialed a number. Unheeded, the tears streamed down through the mascara, eye-shadow, rouge, powder, in dark channels. "That man," she wept, "that man . . ."

Philip backed instinctively against a wall between a table and a chest, his hands spread coldly out behind him. Silently he stood there, like a man awaiting an attack.

"Lawrence!" she cried into the phone. "I'm glad you were home. There's a young man up here and he's offered me a part in his play." The tears coursed bitterly down the dark channels on her cheeks. "Do you know what part it is? I'm going to tell you and then I'm going to throw the young man right the hell out of this hotel!"

Philip cowered against the wall.

"Keep quiet, Lawrence!" Miss Gerry was shouting. "I've listened to your smooth excuses long enough. A woman of forty-five," she wept, her mouth close to the phone, "a bitter, slatternly, ugly, hateful boarding-house keeper who listens at keyholes and fights with her family." Miss Gerry was half bent over in grief now,

377

and she gripped the telephone desperately and clumsily in her two hands. Because her tears were too much for her, she listened and Philip heard a man's voice talking quickly, but soothingly, over the phone.

Finally, disregarding the urgent voice in the receiver, Miss Gerry stood straight. "Mr. Bloomer," she said, her teeth closing savagely over the name, "please tell me why you thought of me for this rich and glamorous role."

Philip braced himself weakly against the wall between the chest and the table. "You see," he said, his voice high and boyish and forlorn, "I saw you in two plays."

"Shut up, for the love of God!" Miss Gerry called into the phone. Then she looked up and with a cold smile, spoke to Philip. "What plays, Mr. Bloomer?"

"*Sun in the East*," Philip croaked, "and *Take the Hindmost*."

A new and deeper flood of tears formed in her dark eyes. "Lawrence," she sobbed into the phone. "Do you know why he's offering me this part? He saw me in two plays. Your two great successes. He saw me playing a hag of sixty in *Sun in the East* and he saw me playing the mother of a goddamned brood of Irish hoodlums in *Take the Hindmost*. You've ruined me, Lawrence, you've ruined me."

Philip slipped out of his niche against the wall and walked quickly over to the window and looked out. Twelve stories, his mind registered automatically.

"*Everybody's* seen me in those parts. Everybody! Now, whenever there's a play with a mother, a crone in it, they say, 'Call up Adele Gerry.' I'm a woman in the full flush of my powers. I should be playing Candida, Hedda, Joan, and I'm everybody's candidate for the hero's old mother! Boarding-house keepers in children's first efforts!"

Philip winced, looking down at Madison Avenue.

"Who did this to me?" Miss Gerry's tones were full, round, tragic. "Who did it? Who cajoled, pleaded, begged, drove me into those two miserable plays? Lawrence Wilkes! Lawrence Wilkes can claim the credit for ruining the magnificent career of a great actress. The famous Lawrence Wilkes, who fooled me into playing a mother at the age of thirty-three!"

Philip hunched his shoulders as the deep, famous voice crowded the room with sound.

"And now you wonder," even at the phone, her wide gesture of shoulder and arm was sharp with irony, "now you wonder why I won't marry you. Send me flowers, send me books, send me tickets to the theater, write me letters telling me you don't care if I go out with other men. From now on I'm going out with the entire garrison of Governor's Island! I'll eat dinner next to you with a different man every night! I hate you, I hate you, Larry, I hate you . . ."

Her sobs finally conquered her. She let the phone drop heedlessly, walked slowly and with pain over to a deep chair and sank into it, damp, bedraggled, undone, like a sorrowing child.

Philip breathed deeply and turned around. "I'm sorry," he said hoarsely.

Miss Gerry waved her hand wearily. "It's not your fault. I've been getting this for three years. You're the agent of events, that's all."

"Thank you," Philip said gratefully.

"A young woman like me," Miss Gerry moaned, looking like a little girl, miserable in the deep chair. "I'll never get a decent part. Never. Never. Mothers! That man has done me in. Don't ever get mixed up with that man. He's an egotistic maniac. He would crucify his grandmother for a second-act curtain." She wiped her eyes in a general smear of cosmetics. "He wants me to marry him." She laughed horribly.

"I'm so sorry," Philip said, feeling finally, because that was all he could say, like a farm boy, a dairy-hand. "I'm so, so sorry."

"He says go up and get your script," Miss Gerry said. "He lives across the street in the Chatham. Just call up from the desk and he'll bring it down."

"Thank you, Miss Gerry," Philip said.

"Come here," she said, the tears departing. He walked slowly over to her and she pulled his head down to her bosom and kissed his forehead and held his ears with her two hands. "You're a nice, clean, stupid boy," she said. "I'm glad to see there's a new crop springing up. Go."

Philip limped to the door, turned there, meaning to say something, saw Adele Gerry sitting in her chair, looking blankly at the floor, with her face a ruin of sorrow and mascara and age. Philip softly opened the door and softly closed it behind him.

He went across to the street, breathing the cold air deeply, and called Lawrence Wilkes on the phone. Philip recognized Wilkes when he got out of the elevator with a copy of *The House of Pain* under his arm. Wilkes was neatly and beautifully dressed and had a hit running and had just been to a barber, but his face was worn and tortured and weary, like the faces of the people in the newsreels who have just escaped an air-raid, but who do not hope to escape the next.

"Mr. Wilkes," Philip said softly.

Wilkes look at Philip and smiled and put his head forgivingly and humorously to one side. "Young man," he said, "in the theater you must learn one thing. Never tell an actress what type of part you think she can play." And he gave Philip *The House of Pain* and turned and went back into the elevator. Philip watched the door close on his well-tailored, tortured back, then sprang out into the street and fled across town to the Theatre Guild.

# A Year to Learn the Language

"*La barbe*," Louise said, "how can you stand the stink?" She was sitting on the floor cross-legged, her bare feet sticking out of her blue jeans, her back against the bookcase. She had on the heavy black tortoise-shell glasses that she used for reading and she was eating miniature éclairs out of a little carton on the floor next to her as she turned the pages of her book. Louise was studying French literature at the Sorbonne for a year, but at the moment was reading *Huckleberry Finn*, in a French translation. French literature was depressing her, she said, and she yearned for a whiff of the Mississippi. She came from St. Louis and at parties she had been heard to say that the Mississippi was the Mother-Water of her life. Roberta wasn't quite sure what this meant, but was secretly impressed by the statement, with its hint of mid-continent mysticism and the liquid boldness of its self-knowledge. Roberta, as far as she knew, had no Mother-Water in her life.

Roberta was at the easel in the middle of the big, dark, cluttered room which she and Louise had shared since they had come to Paris eight months before. Roberta was working on a long thin canvas of Parisian shop windows, trying to overcome the influences of Chagall, Picasso, and Joan Miró, influences that overtook her in disconcerting waves at different periods of the month. She was only nineteen and she worried over her susceptibility to other styles and other people and tried to look at as few paintings as possible.

Louise stood up with a long, swanlike movement, sucking éclair goo off her fingers, shaking her shiny black hair. She went over to the window and threw it open and took several loud, ostentatious breaths of the dank winter afternoon Paris air. "I fear for your health," she said. "I'll bet that if they took a survey, they'd discover that half the painters of history died from silicosis."

"That's a miner's disease," Roberta said, painting placidly. "From the dust. There's no dust in oils."

"I await the result of the survey," Louise said, not giving an inch. She peered out the window down to the street three stories below. "He might even be handsome," she said, "if he ever got a haircut."

"He has beautiful hair," Roberta said, fighting down the almost irresistible impulse to go over to the window and look out. "Anyway, that's the way all the boys wear it these days."

"All the boys," Louise said darkly. She was a year older than Roberta and had already had two affairs, with Frenchmen, that had come out, according to her, disastrously, and she was in an acid and sophisticated period. "Have you got a date with him?" she asked.

"At four o'clock," Roberta said. "He's taking me over to the Right Bank." She poked distractedly at the canvas. The knowledge that Guy was so close made it difficult to concentrate on her work.

Louise looked at her watch. "It's only three-thirty," she said. "What devotion."

Roberta didn't like the ironic tone in Louise's voice but didn't know how to combat it. She wished that Louise would save her sophistication for her own use. Thinking about Guy made Roberta feel trembly and electric and she began to clean her brushes because she couldn't work feeling like that.

"What's he doing?" Roberta asked, trying to sound offhand.

"He's looking yearningly into the window of the butcher shop," Louise said. "They have a specialty today. Rumpsteak. Seven hundred and fifty francs the kilo."

Roberta felt a slight twinge of disappointment. As long as he was there, anyway, it would have been more satisfactory if he had been gazing, yearningly or not, at *her* window. "I think it's perfectly insufferable of Madame Ruffat not to let us have people up here," she said. Madame Ruffat was their landlady. She lived in the same apartment and they shared the kitchen and bathroom with her. She was a little fat woman, stuffed into girdles and grim uplift brassieres, and she had an unpleasant habit of bursting in upon them unannounced and surveying them with a shifty, mistrustful eye, as though she suspected them of being on the verge of despoiling the stained red damask that covered the walls or smuggling in unworthy young men for the night.

"She knows what she's doing," Louise said, still at the window. "Madame Ruffat. She's lived in Paris for fifty years. She understands Frenchmen. You let a Frenchman into your room and you can't get him out until the next war."

"Oh, Louise," Roberta said, "why do you always try to sound so—so disillusioned?"

"Because I *am* disillusioned," Louise said. "And you will be too if you keep going the way you're going."

"I'm not going any way," Roberta said.

"Hah!"

"What does that mean—hah?" Roberta asked.

Louise didn't bother to explain. Instead she peered out the window, with a critical and disapproving expression on her face. "How old does he say he is?" she asked.

"He's twenty-one."

"Has he pounced on you yet?" Louise asked.

"Of course not," Roberta said.

"Then he's not twenty-one." Louise turned away from the window and strode across the room to sink down next to the bookcase again and *Huckleberry Finn* in French and the last éclair.

"Listen, Louise," Roberta said, hoping she was sounding severe and sensible, "I don't interfere with your private life, and I'd appreciate it if you didn't interfere with mine."

"I am merely trying to give you the benefit of my experience," Louise said, her voice a little thick with custard. "My bitter experience. Besides, I promised your mother I'd look after you."

"Forget about my mother, will you? One of the main reasons I came to France was to get away from my mother."

"On your own head," Louise said, turning a page with a little snap. "There's only so much a friend can do."

The rest of the time Roberta was in the room passed in silence. She checked the watercolors in the portfolio she was taking with her and combed her hair and tied a scarf around it and touched her lips with rouge and looked anxiously at herself in the mirror, worrying, as usual, that she looked too young, too blue-eyed, too innocent, too American, too shy, too everlastingly, hopelessly *unready*.

At the door, poised to leave, she said to Louise, who was steadfastly looking down at her book, "I won't be home for dinner."

"One last word," Louise said implacably. "Beware."

Roberta closed the door behind her with a bang and went down the long dark hall, carrying the portfolio. Madame Ruffat was sitting in the salon on a little gilt chair, her back to the window, glaring, above her iron corsets, through the open salon doors into the hallway, playing solitaire and checking on all arrivals and departures. She and Roberta nodded coldly at each other. *Old insufferable witch,* Roberta said under her breath as she manipulated the three locks on the front door with which Madame Ruffat kept the world at bay.

As she descended the dark stairway, with its cavelike odor of underground rivers and cold and forgotten dinners, Roberta felt melancholy and oppressed. When her father, back in Chicago, had told her he'd been able to scrape together enough money for her to paint for twelve months in Paris, saying, "Well, even if nothing else happens, at least you'll have a year to learn the language," Roberta was sure that she was bursting into a new life, a life that would be free, assured, blossoming, open to the fruitful touch of adventure. Instead, what with worrying about everybody's influence on her painting, and the grim surveillance of Madame Ruffat and Louise's constant gloomy warnings, Roberta felt more tied up, uncertain, constrained than ever before.

People had even lied to her about the language. Oh, they had said, in three months, at your age, you'll be speaking like a native. Well, it was eight months, not three, and she had studied the grammar assiduously, and while she could understand most of what was said around her all right, every time she spoke more than five words in French, people replied to her in English. Even Guy, who professed to love her, and whose English sounded like Maurice Chevalier's first movie, insisted upon conducting even the most intimate, the most *French* conversations with her in English.

Sometimes, like this afternoon, she felt as though she would never break the cage of childhood, no matter what she did, that the freedom, the desperate risks and final rewards and punishments of adulthood would forever be beyond her grasp. Stopping for a moment to push the button that buzzed open the door into the street, she had a sickening vision of herself as one of those wispy and virginal old maids, eternally locked in brittle nursery innocence, before whom no one spoke of scandals, death, or passion.

Hugely dissatisfied with herself, she gave a last push to the scarf around her head, hoping for coquetry, and stepped out into the street, where Guy was waiting, in front of the butcher shop, polishing the handlebars of his Vespa. His long, dark, intense Mediterranean face, which Roberta had once, but only once, told Louise looked as though it had been created by Modigliani, broke into a brilliant smile. But this afternoon it didn't have its usual effect on Roberta. "Louise is right," she said cruelly. "You ought to get a haircut."

The smile vanished. In its place appeared a slightly bored, languid, raised-eyebrow expression that at other times had also had a disturbing effect on Roberta, but which did nothing for her, she noted coldly, this afternoon. "Louise," Guy said, wrinkling his nose. "That old bag of tomatoes."

"First of all," Roberta said censoriously, "Louise is my friend and you mustn't talk about my friends like that. Secondly, if you think you're talking American slang, you're way far out. 'Old bag' is possible, if that's what you mean. But nobody's called a girl a 'tomato' in America since before Pearl Harbor. If you must insult my friends, why don't you speak French?"

"*Écoute, mon chou,*" Guy said, in the weary and practically lifeless tone that made him appear so much more grown-up and exciting to Roberta than the breathless and bumbling boys she had known back in Chicago. "I wish to communicate with you and make love to you. Possibly even to marry you. But I do not wish to act as a substitute for the Berlitz School. If you wish to be polite for the rest of the afternoon, you are permitted to climb onto the back seat and I will take you where you wish to go. But if you are going to enervate me you can walk."

This quick and independent harshness, coming from a man who had been waiting patiently for her more than a half-hour in the cold, made Roberta feel deliciously submissive. It gave substance to the statement she had heard (most often from Guy himself), that Frenchmen knew how to treat women and made the boys who had mooned over her on the shores of Lake Michigan seem like debilitated, irresolute children.

"All I said," she said, retreating, "was that maybe you'd look a little better if your hair were shorter."

"Get on," Guy said. He swung onto the saddle of the Vespa and she arranged herself behind him. It was a little awkward, with the huge portfolio which she had to carry under one arm while with the other she gripped Guy around the waist. She wore blue jeans for her expeditions on the machine, because she hadn't liked the swoop of wind under her skirts the one or two times she had worn them, nor the immodest way they sometimes billowed at unexpected moments, which caused pedestrians to look at her with unpleasantly candid appreciation.

She gave Guy the address of the gallery on the Rue Faubourg St. Honoré where she had an appointment with the gallery's director, arranged for by Monsieur Raimond, the painter in whose atelier she studied. "It is a gallery without distinction, Patrini's," M. Raimond had told her, "but the fellow is constantly searching for cheap young people to exploit. And he is amused by Americans. Perhaps, with luck, he will take a watercolor or two and hang them, provisionally, in a back room, for a few days, and see what

385

happens. Just don't sign anything, not anything at all, and no permanent harm can befall you.''

Guy started the Vespa and they dashed off, roaring in and out between cars, buses, bicycles, and pedestrians with doomed looks on their faces. Guy drove at all times with an iron-nerved and debonair disregard of risk. It was an expression of his character, he told Roberta, and a sign of his rebellion against what he called the timid bourgeois love of security of his parents. He lived with his parents because he was still going to school. He was studying to be an engineer and when he was through he was going to build dams in Egypt, railroad bridges in the Andes, roads across India. So he wasn't one of those shaggy and worthless young men who merely hung around St. Germain des Près all day and all night, sponging off foreigners and damning the future, entwined in indiscriminate sex, like the characters in the *nouvelle vague* movies. He believed in love and fidelity and accomplishment, although he was terribly dashing about it all, and far from having pounced on her, as Louise had so uncouthly put it, in the three months Roberta had known him, he hadn't even kissed her once, except on the cheek when they had said good night. "I'm past all that cheap, adolescent promiscuity. When we are ready for each other we will know it,'' he had said loftily; and Roberta had adored him for it, sensing that she was getting the best values of Chicago and Paris in the one package. He had never introduced her to his parents. "They're good, solid citizens *de pauvres mais braves gens,''* he had told Roberta, "but of no interest to anyone but their relatives. One night with them and you'd be bored onto the first boat train back to Le Havre.''

They whistled up the Quai d'Orsay, with the Seine below them, and the Louvre looking like a dream of France across the river, and the wind making Guy's bright scarf and long black hair whip back straight from his head and bringing spots of color to Roberta's cheeks and frozen tears to her eyes. She held onto the waist of Guy's smart sheepskin coat, soaringly content with zigzagging around the city like this through the gray winter afternoon.

Jouncing on the pillion of the noisy little machine, crossing the bridge in front of the Assemblée Nationale, with a portfolio of paintings under her arm and the handsomest boy in Europe speeding her deftly past the obelisk and the stone horses of the Place de la Concorde, on her way to discuss art with a man who had bought and sold twenty thousand pictures in the course of his career, Roberta's doubts left her. She knew that she had been right to leave Chicago, right to come to Paris, right to give her telephone number to Guy three months before when he had asked for it at the party Louise had taken her to at the apartment of her second Frenchman. Omens of happiness and good luck wound around her head like small, almost visible singing birds, and when she dismounted in front of the little gallery on the Rue Faubourg St. Honoré, she faced the unwelcoming door with an athlete's spring and confidence.

"*Écoute, Roberta,*" Guy said, patting her cheek, "*je t'assure que tout va très bien se passer. Pour une femme, tu es un grand peintre, et bientôt tout le monde le saura.*"

She smiled mistily at him, equally grateful for his belief in her and for the delicacy of spirit which had made him declare it in French.

"Now," he said, lapsing into his usual Chevalier English, "I go to do several excruciating errands for Mama. I attend you in a half-hour at Queenie's."

He waved, swung gallantly onto the saddle of the Vespa and, hair and scarf streaming, dodged down the bustling street toward the British embassy. Roberta watched him for a moment, then turned toward the door. In the window of the gallery there was a large painting done in shades of purple that might have represented a washing machine or a nightmare. Roberta scanned it swiftly and thought, It's a cinch I can do better than that, and opened the door and went in.

The gallery was small and plushly carpeted, with many paintings jammed together on the walls, a good many of them by the purple-washing-machine man in the window or his disciples. There was one visitor, a man of about fifty in a coat with a mink collar and a beautiful black Homburg hat. The owner of the gallery, distinguished by a red carnation in his buttonhole and a wary and at the same time predatory expression on a thin, disabused face, stood behind and a little to one side of the man in the fur-trimmed coat. His white hands twitched gently at his sides, as though he were ready instantaneously to produce a blank check or seize the potential client if he showed signs of flight.

Roberta introduced herself to Monsieur Patrini, the owner of the gallery, in her best French, and Patrini said brusquely, in perfect English, "Yes, Raimond says you're not without talent. Here, you can use this easel."

He stood about ten feet away from the easel, frowning slightly, as though he were remembering a dish at lunch that hadn't quite agreed with him, as Roberta took the first watercolor out of her portfolio and placed it on the easel. The sight of the painting did not cause any change in Patrini's expression. He still looked as though he was being mildly haunted by a too-rich sauce or a fish that had been too long in transit from Normandy. He made no comment. Every once in a while his lips twisted minutely, as if in digestive pain, and Roberta took this as a sign of progress and put the next painting on the easel. In the middle of the exhibition, Roberta became conscious that the man in the Homburg hat had given up his examination of the pictures on the walls and was standing off a little to one side, looking at her watercolors as she slid them one by one onto the easel. She was so intent on trying to discover some sign of reaction on Patrini's face that she never even glanced at the man in the Homburg hat throughout the entire performance.

Patrini's lips made a final gaseous twitch.

"There," Roberta said flatly, hating him and resigned to failure, "that's the lot."

"Ummm . . . huh . . . umm," Patrini said. He had a very low bass voice and for a moment Roberta was afraid that he had said something in French and she had been unable to understand it. But then he went on, in English. "There is a certain promise," he said. "Deeply buried."

"Forgive me, *cher ami*," said the man in the Homburg hat. "There is a great deal more than that." His English sounded as if he had lived all his life at Oxford, although he was clearly a Frenchman. "My dear young lady," he went on, taking off his hat and revealing a marvelously barbered head of iron-gray hair, "I wonder if I could bother you further. Would you be good enough to put your paintings all around the gallery so that I might study them and compare them without haste?"

Roberta looked numbly at Patrini. She was sure that she had let her mouth fall open and she shut it with a loud click of teeth. "*Mon cher* Baron," Patrini was saying, his face suddenly transformed by a brilliant, demi-social, demi-commercial smile, "may I present a young American friend of great talent, Miss Roberta James. Miss James, the Baron de Ummhuhzediers."

That was what the name sounded like to Roberta, and she cursed herself again for not having yet gotten the hang of French names, even as she tried to smile graciously at the gray-haired Frenchman. "Of course," she said, her voice an octave too high. "I'd be delighted." She began to grab paintings off the pile on the easel and stand them indiscriminately on the floor against the walls. Patrini, suddenly spry and professional, helped her, and within two minutes, the work of eight months was spread all around the gallery in an impromptu one-woman show.

No word was spoken for a long time. The Baron moved from painting to painting, standing minutes before some of them, passing others quickly, his hands behind his back, a slight, polite smile touching his lips. Occasionally he nodded gently. Roberta stood to one side, anxiously peering at each painting as the Baron approached it, trying to see it anew with those shrewd, experienced eyes. Patrini subtly stood at the window, his back to the room, staring out at the traffic of the busy street outside, the echo of whose passage made a constant *hush-hush* in the carpeted, warm room.

At last the Baron spoke. He was standing in front of a painting Roberta had made at the zoo at Vincennes, of some children in pale blue ski suits looking in at the leopard's cage. "I'm afraid I can't make up my mind," he said, not taking his eyes off the painting. "I can't decide whether I want this one or"—he walked slowly along the wall—"or this one here." He nodded at one of Roberta's latest, one of her shop windows.

"If I may make a suggestion," Patrini said, turning swiftly into the room at the sound of a customer's voice. "Why don't you take them both home for study and make up your mind at your leisure?"

"If the young lady wouldn't mind." The Baron turned deferentially, almost pleadingly, toward Roberta.

"No," Roberta said, struggling to keep from shouting, "I wouldn't mind."

"Excellent," the Baron said crisply, "I'll send my man to pick them up tomorrow morning." He made a little bow, put on his beautiful black hat over his beautiful iron-gray hair and went through the door which Patrini had magically opened for him.

When the Baron had disappeared, Patrini came back briskly into the shop and picked up the two paintings the Baron had chosen. "Excellent," Patrini said. "It confirms an old belief of mine. In certain cases it is advisable for the client to meet the artist at the very beginning." With the two watercolors under his arm, he peered critically at a monochromatic wash of a nude that Roberta had painted at Raimond's studio. "Perhaps I'll keep that one around for a week or two, also," Patrini said. "If I pass the word around that the Baron is interested in your work, it may stir one or two of my other clients in your direction." He picked up the nude, too. "The Baron has a famous collection, as you know, of course."

"Of course," Roberta lied.

"He has several excellent Soutines, quite a few Matisses, and a really first-class Braque. And, of course, like everybody else, several Picassos. When I hear from him, I'll drop you a line." The telephone rang in the little office at the back of the shop and Patrini hurried away to answer it, carrying the three paintings with him. Soon he was involved in an intense, whispered conversation, the tone of which suggested a communication in code between two intelligence agents.

Roberta stood irresolutely for a while in the middle of the shop, then gathered all her paintings and put them back into the portfolio. Patrini was still whispering into the telephone in the office. Roberta went to the door of the office and stood there until he looked up. "*Au revoir, Mademoiselle*," he said, waving a white hand at her gently, and lapsed back into his coded mumble.

Roberta would have preferred more ceremony for the occasion. After all, this was the first time anybody had ever expressed even the vaguest intention of buying a painting of hers. But Patrini gave no indication that he might conclude his conversation before midnight, and he had clearly dismissed her. So she smiled uncertainly at him and left.

Outside, in the cold dusk, she walked lightly and gaily past the glowing, jewel-like windows of the expensive shops, her scarf, her short, dun-colored coat, her blue jeans and flat shoes, and the battered green portfolio under her arm setting her puritanically apart from the furred, perfumed, high-heeled women who constituted the natural fauna of the Rue Faubourg St. Honoré. As she walked among them, museum doors swung open before her in a golden trance and she could almost see huge posters, with her name in severe, long letters—*James*—blossoming on the kiosks and on gallery doors. The invisible birds of joy which had sung around her head earlier in the afternoon now sang more loudly and privately than ever as she approached Queenie's, where Guy was waiting for her.

Superstitiously she decided to tell Guy nothing about what had taken place in the gallery. When it had happened, when the painting (whichever of the two it turned out to be) had been bought and paid for and hung on the Baron's walls, there would be time enough to announce and celebrate. Besides, she didn't want to have to admit to Guy that she hadn't caught the Baron's name and had been too shy and flustered to find it out after he'd gone. She would pass by the gallery in the next day or two and find an opportunity to ask Patrini, casually, to spell it out for her.

Guy was sitting in a corner of the large, crowded café, grumpily looking at his watch, a half-finished glass of pineapple juice on the table in front of him. To Roberta's secret disappointment, he never drank any wine or alcohol. "Alcohol is the curse of France," he said again and again. "Wine has made us a second-rate power." On her own, Roberta hardly ever drank anything at all, but she couldn't help feeling a little cheated at being connected with the one man in France who ordered Coca-Cola or lemonade each time the *sommelier* came up to them in a restaurant and offered the wine card. It was uncomfortably like Chicago.

Guy stood up ungraciously as she approached. "What happens?" he said. "I have been waiting forever. I have drunk three juices of pineapples."

"I'm sorry," Roberta said, setting the portfolio down and slipping into a chair beside Guy's. "The man was busy."

Guy sat down, a little mollified. "How did it pass?"

"Not too badly," Roberta said, fighting the temptation to bubble out the news. "He said he'd be interested in seeing my oils."

"They are all fools," Guy said, pressing her hand. "He will bite his nails when you are famous." He waved to a passing waiter. "*Deux jus d'ananas*," he said. He stared hard at Roberta. "Tell me," he said, "what are your intentions?"

"My intentions?" Roberta said doubtfully. "Do you mean toward you?"

"No." Guy waved rather impatiently. "That will discover itself at the proper time. I mean, in a philosophical sense—your intentions in life."

"Well," Roberta said, speaking hesitantly, because although she had thought about the question for a long time now, she was uncertain about how it would sound put into words. "Well, I want to be a good painter, of course. I want to know exactly what I am doing and why I'm doing it and what I want people to feel when they look at my pictures."

"Good. Very good," Guy said, sounding like an approving teacher to a promising student. "What else?"

"I want my whole life to be like that," Roberta went on. "I don't want to—well—grope. That's what I hate about so many people my age back home—they don't know what they want or how they want to get it, They're—well, they're groping."

Guy looked puzzled. "Grope, groping," he said. "What does that mean?"

"*Tâtonner,*" Roberta said, pleased at this unusual chance to demonstrate her linguistic superiority. "My father is a history student, he specializes in battles, and he's always talking about the fog of war, everybody running around and killing each other and doing the right thing or the wrong thing, winning or losing, without understanding it. . . ."

"Oh, yes," Guy said. "I have heard the phrase."

"My feeling is," Roberta went on, "the fog of war is nothing compared to the fog of youth. The Battle of Gettysburg was crystal clear compared to being nineteen years old. I want to get out of the fog of youth. I want to be *precise*. I don't want anything to be an accident. That's one of the reasons I came to Paris—everybody's always talking about how precise the French are. Maybe I can learn to be like that."

"Do you think I am precise?" Guy asked.

"Enormously. That's one of the things I like best about you."

Guy nodded somberly, agreeing. His eyes, with their heavy fringe of black lashes, glowed darkly. "American," he said, "you are going to be a very superior woman. And you have never been more beautiful." He leaned over and kissed her cheek, still cold from her walk.

"What a lovely afternoon," she said.

They went to see a movie that Guy had heard was very good and after that to a *bistro* on the Left Bank for dinner. Roberta had wanted to go home and leave her portfolio and change her clothes, but Guy had forbidden it. "Tonight," he said mysteriously, "I do not want you to be exposed to the pronouncements of your friend, Louise."

Roberta hadn't paid much attention to the picture. There were big signs plastered all over the outside of the theater saying that it was forbidden for anyone under eighteen years of age and she had been embarrassed by the ironic stare of the man who took the tickets when they went in. She wished she had her passport with her to prove that she was over eighteen. The picture itself was largely incomprehensible to her, as she had difficulty understanding French when it was reproduced mechanically, either in the movies or over public-address systems. In the movie there were the familiar long scenes of young people chatting away in bed together, all needlessly bare and explicit, to Roberta's way of thinking. She half-closed her eyes through much of the showing, recreating, with certain embellishments, the events of the afternoon, and she was hardly conscious of Guy, at her side, who was raising her hand to his lips and kissing her fingertips in an unusual manner throughout the most dramatic moments of the film.

During dinner, he behaved strangely, too. He remained silent for long periods of time, which wasn't like him at all, and stared across the little table at her with a purposeful directness that made Roberta edgy and uneasy. Finally, with the coffee, Guy cleared his throat oratorically, stretched across the table to take both her hands in his and said, "I have decided. The time is ripe. We have reached the inevitable moment."

"What are you talking about?" Roberta asked nervously, conscious of the barman watching them with interest in the empty little restaurant.

"I speak in an adult manner," Guy said. "Tonight we become lovers."

"*Shhhh* . . ." Roberta looked worriedly at the barman and drew her hands away and put them out of reach under the table.

"I cannot live any longer without you," Guy said. "I have borrowed the key to the apartment of a friend of mine. He has gone to visit his family in Tours for the night. It is just around the corner."

Roberta could not pretend to be shocked by Guy's proposal. Like all virgins who come to Paris, she was secretly convinced, or resigned, or delighted, by the idea that she would leave the city in a different condition from that in which she had arrived in it. And at almost any other time in the last three months she probably would have been moved by Guy's declaration and been tempted to accept. Even now, she admired what she considered the sobriety and dignity of the offer. But the same superstitious reserve that had prevented her from telling Guy about her two paintings worked again on her now. When the fate of the paintings was known, she would consider Guy's invitation. Not before. Tonight was out of the question for another reason too. However it was fated finally to happen, of one thing she was sure—she was not going to enter the first love affair of her life in blue jeans.

She shook her head, annoyed with herself because of the flush that warmed her cheeks and neck. She looked down at her plate, because looking across at Guy made her blush more intense. "No, please," she whispered. "Not tonight."

"Why not tonight?" Guy demanded.

"It—it's so abrupt," Roberta said.

"Abrupt!" Guy said loudly. "I have seen you nearly every day for three months now. What are you accustomed to?"

"I'm not accustomed to anything. You know that," she said. "Please, let's not talk about it. Not tonight."

"But I have the apartment for tonight," Guy said. "My friend may not go to Tours for another year." His face was sorrowful and hurt and for the first time since she had known him, Roberta had the feeling that he was in need of comforting. She leaned over and patted his hand sympathetically.

"Don't look like that," she said. "Maybe some other time."

"I warn you," he said with dignity, "the next time it will have to be you who will make the advances."

"I will make the advances," she said, relieved and at the same time obscurely annoyed by his quick surrender. "Now pay the check. I have to get up early tomorrow."

Later on, in her narrow, lumpy bed, under the heavy quilt, she was too excited to sleep. What a day, she thought. I am on the verge of being a painter. I am on the verge of being a woman. Then she giggled softly at the solemnity of the phrase and hugged herself. She was favorably impressed by the quality of her own skin. If Louise had been awake, she would have told her everything. But Louise slept sternly in the bed along the opposite wall, her hair in curlers, her face greased against wrinkles that would not appear for another twenty years. Regretfully Roberta closed her eyes. It was not the sort of day you liked to see end.

Two days later, when she came into the room and turned on the light, she saw a *pneumatique* addressed to her on her bed. It was late in the afternoon and the apartment was cold and empty. Louise was out, and for once Madame Ruffat had not been at her post playing solitaire when Roberta had walked down the hall. Roberta opened the *pneumatique*. "Dear Miss James," it read. "Please get in touch with me immediately. I have some important news for you." It was signed "Patrini."

Roberta looked at her watch. It was five o'clock. Patrini would still be in the gallery. Feeling prickly and lightheaded, she went back along the hall and into the salon, where the telephone was. When Madame Ruffat went out, she locked the dial mechanism with a little padlock, but there was always a chance that for once she had forgotten to do it. But Madame Ruffat had forgotten nothing. The phone was locked. Roberta said, *Insufferable old witch*, three times under her breath, and went into the kitchen to look for the maid. The kitchen was dark and Roberta remembered that it was the maid's day off.

"Oh, damn," Roberta said to herself. "France!" She let herself out of the apartment and hurried down to the café on the corner, where there was a pay telephone. But there was a little damp man with a briefcase in the booth, making notes on a sheet of paper as he talked. From what Roberta could gather over the noise from the bar, the man with the briefcase was involved in a complicated transaction concerning the installation of plumbing fixtures. He gave no sign that he was close to finishing. Paris, Roberta thought unfairly. Everybody's on the phone at all hours of the day and night.

She looked at her watch. It was a quarter past five. Patrini closed the gallery at six. Roberta retreated to the bar and ordered a glass of red wine to soothe her nerves. She would have to chew some gum after to remove the traces of the wine from her breath. She had a date with Guy at seven and it would mean a long lecture if he discovered she'd been drinking. The bar was full of workmen from the quarter, laughing and speaking loudly, obviously not at all concerned with what *their* breaths were going to smell like that evening.

Finally, the plumbing man came out and Roberta leaped into the booth and put in the *jeton*. The line was busy. She remembered the interminable conversation Patrini had engaged in the afternoon she was there and began to get panicky. She tried three times more and each time the line was busy. It was five twenty-five. She rushed out of the booth, paid for her wine and hurried toward the Métro. It was a long trip across the city, but there was nothing else to be done, She couldn't bear the thought of going through the whole night without knowing what Patrini had to say to her.

Even though it was a bitterly cold afternoon, she was perspiring and out of breath from running when she reached the gallery. It was five to six. The lights were still on. The purple man was still represented in the window. Roberta hurled herself through the door. There was nobody in the gallery, but from the office in the back, she heard the secretive whisper of Patrini on the telephone. She had the unreasonable impression that he had been talking like that, in the same position and in the same voice, since the time she had left him two days before. She took a little time to regain her breath, then walked to the rear of the gallery and showed herself at the door to Patrini. He looked up after a while, waved languidly in greeting and continued his conversation. She turned back into the gallery and pretended to be studying a large painting which vaguely reminded her of robins' eggs, magnified thirty times. She was glad for the respite now. It gave her time to compose herself. Patrini, she was sure, was a man who would be adversely affected by signs of excitement or expressions of enthusiasm or gratitude. By the time he came out of the office and approached her, she had frozen her face into lines of mildly amused boredom.

Roberta heard the click of the phone in the office as Patrini hung up. He came up to her like a large soft animal, padding along on the thick carpet. "Good evening, *chère Mademoiselle*," he said. "I called the number you left me this morning, but the lady who answered informed me there was nobody by your name living there."

"That's my landlady," Roberta said. It was an old trick of Madame Ruffat to discourage what she termed the intolerable racket of the telephone bell.

"I wanted to tell you," said Patrini, "that the Baron came by this morning to say that he still couldn't make up his mind which of the two paintings he liked, so he's decided to take them both."

Roberta closed her eyes against the glory of the moment, pretending to be squinting at a painting on the opposite wall. "Really?" she said. "Both of them? He's more intelligent than I thought."

Patrini made a funny sound, as though he were choking, but Roberta forgave him, because at that moment she would have forgiven anybody anything.

"He also asked me to tell you that you're invited to his house for dinner tonight," Patrini went on. "I'm to call his secretary before seven to let him know. *Are* you free for dinner?"

Roberta hesitated. She had the date with Guy at seven and she knew he would appear faithfully at six forty-five and stand waiting on the cold street for her to appear, a gelid victim of Madame Ruffat's detestation of the male sex. For a moment, she hesitated. Then she thought, Artists must be ruthless, or they are not artists. Remember Gauguin. Remember Baudelaire. "Yes," she said offhandedly to Patrini, "I believe I can make it."

"It's number nineteen *bis* Square du Bois de Boulogne," Patrini said. "That's off the Avenue Foch. Eight o'clock. Under no circumstances discuss prices. I will handle that end. Is that understood?"

"I never discuss prices," Roberta said haughtily. She bathed in self-control.

"I will call the Baron's secretary for you," Patrini said. "And tomorrow I will display your nude in the window."

"I may drop by," Roberta said. She knew she had to get out of there fast. She had the feeling that if she had to speak a sentence of more than four words, it would end in a primitive yell of triumph. She started out of the shop. Unexpectedly Patrini held the door open for her. "Young lady," he said, "it's none of my business, but please be careful."

Roberta nodded in an amused manner. She even forgave him that. It was only when she had floated two hundred yards in a westerly direction that she remembered that she still didn't know the Baron's name. It was while she was passing the bayoneted guards of the Palais Matignon that she realized that there were one or two other problems she had to face. She was dressed as she had been dressed all day—for traveling around on foot on the streets of a wet and wintry Paris. She was wearing a raincoat and a scarf and under it a plaid wool skirt and sweater and dark green wool stockings and after-ski boots. It was hardly the costume for a dinner in a mansion off the Avenue Foch. But if she went home to change, Guy would undoubtedly be there, waiting for her, and she didn't have the courage to tell him that she was ditching him this way to dine with a fifty-year-old member of the French nobility. He would be hurt and at the same time cutting and fierce and certainly would make her cry. He made her cry easily when he wanted to. This was one night she couldn't afford to appear red-eyed and damp. No, she decided, the Baron would have to take her in her green stockings. If you wanted to mingle with artists you had to be ready for certain eccentricities.

But she was uneasy about just leaving Guy standing forlornly outside her door on the cold street. He had weak lungs and suffered from severe attacks of bronchitis every winter. She went into a café on the Avenue Matignon and tried to telephone her apartment. But there was no answer. Louise, Roberta thought angrily. Never around the one time you need her. I bet she's starting on her third Frenchman.

Roberta hung up and got back her *jeton*. She stared at the telephone, considering. She could call Guy's apartment of course, and eventually, in the course of the evening, the message might reach him. But the two or three times she had called his home she had gotten his mother, who had a high, irritated voice and who pretended she couldn't understand Roberta's French. Roberta didn't want to expose herself to that sort of treatment tonight. She tossed the *jeton* thoughtfully in the air once or twice and then left the booth. The problem of Guy would have to be put off until tomorrow. Resolutely, as she walked toward the Champs Elysées, in the ugly dark drizzle she put Guy out of her mind. If you were in love, you had to expect to endure a certain amount of pain.

It was a long walk to the Square du Bois de Boulogne and she had difficulty finding it and it was eight-fifteen and she had made a long unnecessary loop in the black rain before she came upon it. Nineteen *bis* was a large forbidding mansion with a Bentley and several smaller cars and two or three chauffeurs parked in front of it. Roberta was surprised to see these signs that there were to be other guests. Somehow, from the tone in which Patrini had said, "Please be careful," she had been sure that it was going to be a cozy little tête-à-tête dinner that the Baron had arranged for himself and his young protégée. In the course of her long walk, Roberta had pondered this and had decided not to be shocked or alarmed at whatever happened, and to behave in a sophisticated and Parisienne manner. Besides, she was sure she could handle any fifty-year-old man, regardless of how many pictures he bought.

She rang the bell, feeling cold and soaked. A butler in white gloves opened the door and stared at her as though he didn't believe the evidence of his eyes. She stepped into the high-ceilinged, mirrored hallway and took off her sopping coat and scarf and handed it to the man. "*Dites au Baron que Mademoiselle James est là, s'il vous plaît,*" she said. But when the man just stood there, gaping at her, holding her coat and scarf at arm's length, she added sharply, *Je suis invitée à diner.*"

"*Oui, Mademoiselle,*" the man said. He hung up her coat on a rack, at a noncontaminating distance from a half-dozen or so mink coats that were ranged there, and disappeared through a door which he carefully closed behind him.

Roberta looked at herself in one of the mirrors in the hallway and quickly attacked the dismal wet tangle of her hair with a comb. She had just succeeded in imposing a rough kind of order on her dank curls when the hallway door opened and the Baron came out. He was dressed in a dinner jacket and he stopped for just the briefest part of a second when he saw her, but then a warm smile broke over his face and he said, "Charming, charming. I'm delighted you could come." He bent over her hand ceremoniously and kissed it, and said, with the quickest edge of a glance at her after-ski boots, "I hope the invitation wasn't at too short notice."

"Well," Roberta said honestly, "I certainly would have changed my shoes if I'd known it was going to be a party."

The Baron laughed as though she had said something immensely witty and squeezed her hand and said, "Nonsense, you're absolutely perfect as you are. Now," he said, taking her arm conspiratorially, "I want to show you something before we join the other guests." He led her down the hall into a sitting room with pink walls, in which a small fire was glowing in the grate. On the wall opposite the fireplace were her two watercolors, handsomely framed, separated by a glorious pencil drawing by Matisse. On another wall there was, indeed, a Soutine.

"How do you like them?" the Baron asked anxiously.

If Roberta had told the Baron how she *really* liked seeing her pictures hanging amid this glorious company, she would have sounded like the last movement of the Ninth Symphony. "OK," she said flatly. "I think they're OK."

The Baron's face was twisted by an almost invisible quick grimace, as though not smiling was causing him considerable pain. He reached into his pocket and took out a check, folded in half, which he pushed into Roberta's hand. "Here," he said. "I hope this strikes you as being enough. I've discussed it with Patrini. Don't worry about his commission. It's all arranged for."

Taking her eyes away from her pictures with difficulty, Roberta unfolded the check and looked at it. The first thing she tried to make out was the Baron's signature, so that she would finally know his name. But the signature was in a wild, spiky French script and there was no deciphering it. Then she looked at the figure. It was for 250 new francs. More than five hundred dollars, her mind registered automatically. Her father sent her one hundred and eighty dollars a month to live on. I will be able to live in France forever, she thought. My God!

She felt herself grow pale and the check shook in her hands. The Baron looked at her, alarmed. "What's the trouble?" he asked. "Isn't it enough?"

"Not at all," Roberta said. "I mean—well, what I mean is, I never dreamed it would be so much. . . ."

The Baron gestured generously. "Buy yourself a new dress," he said. Then, after an involuntary glance at her plaid skirt and old sweater, and obviously fearing that she might feel he was criticizing her taste in clothes, he added, "I mean, do anything you want with it." He took her elbow again. "Now," he said, "I'm afraid we must really join the others. Just remember, whenever you wish to come and look at your work, all you have to do is call me."

He led her gently out of the pink room and across the hall into the salon. It was an enormous room with paintings by Braque and Rouault and Segonzac on the walls and was populated by an orderly mob of Frenchmen in dinner jackets and bare-shouldered and bejeweled Frenchwomen who, moving gracefully between the pieces of gilt and brocade furniture, gave off that high, self-satisfied, musical tone which is educated Parisian conversation at the peak moment of propriety and contentment which that particular society reaches five minutes before dinner is announced.

The Baron introduced her to a great many of the guests, none of whose names Roberta could catch, but who smiled amiably at her or kissed her hand, in the case of the men, as though it were the most natural thing in the world to dine in a house like that with an American girl in green wool stockings and after-ski boots. Two or three of the more elderly gentlemen said complimentary things about her paintings, in English, of course, and one lady said, "It *is* reassuring to see Americans painting like that again," which had an ambiguous note to it, but which Roberta finally decided to consider as praise.

Then, suddenly, she was alone in a corner of the room, with a glass containing an almost colorless liquid in her hand. The Baron had had to go meet some new guests and the last group of people he had introduced her to had melted into other groups in different sections of the room. Roberta kept her eyes rigidly fixed forward, with the idea that if she never looked down once during the evening, she might be able to forget the way she was dressed. Maybe, she thought, if I drink enough, I will finally feel as though I'm wearing something from Dior. She took a sip from her glass. She had never tasted the drink before, but some profound racial knowledge informed her that she had just entered the world of martini drinkers. She didn't like the taste, but she drained the glass. It gave her something to do. A waiter passed with another tray of drinks and she took a second glass and drank it down swiftly and without coughing. The after-ski boots on her feet were rapidly being transformed into shoes by Mancini, and she was sure by now that all the elegant people in the room, although they seemed to have their backs turned to her, were talking about her admiringly.

Before she had time to seek out the waiter and get a third glass, dinner was announced. She made her way among the undulating bare shoulders and the diamond earrings into the dining room. It was lighted by candles and the long table, with its batteries of wineglasses, was covered by an immense pink lace tablecloth. I must write Mother about *this*, Roberta thought, as she looked for her name on its place card. I am in French Society. Like Proust.

She was seated at the very end of the table, next to a bald man, who smiled mechanically at her once, then never looked at her again. Across from her sat another bald man, who was engrossed throughout the dinner by the large blond woman on his left. The Baron was four places down, in the center of the table, as the host, but after one quick friendly glance in her direction, there was no further communication from that quarter. Since the people around her were not speaking to Roberta, they were talking French. They spoke swiftly and elliptically, with their heads turned away from Roberta a good part of the time, and that, combined with the fact that the two martinis had somewhat loosened her control over the language, made the conversation only fitfully comprehensible to her and began to give her a sensation of exile.

She was surprised by the wine waiter, who whispered into her ear as he leaned over and poured her a glass of white wine. She couldn't quite make out what he was saying, but for a moment she thought he was trying to give her his telephone number. "*Comment?*" she said loudly, ready to embarrass him.

"Montrachet, *mil neuf cent cinquante-cinq,*" he whispered again, and she realized that he was merely announcing the wine. It was delicious, besides, and she had two more glasses of it with the cold lobster that was served as the first course. She ate enormously, because she had never tasted food as good, but with a growing sense of hostility toward everybody else at the table, because they paid no more attention to her than if she had been dining alone in the middle of the Bois de Boulogne.

As soup followed lobster, and pheasant followed soup, as Château Lafite 1928 followed Montrachet 1955, Roberta began to look with misty disdain at her fellow guests. First of all, there was nobody at the table, she was sure, under forty. What am I doing in this old people's home? she thought as she took a second helping of pheasant and a large gob of currant jelly. The food only stoked the fires of her anger. These tottering Gallic Babbitts, these stockbrokers and their overdressed, high-pitched women didn't deserve the company of artists if all they did was sit them at the bottom of the table and feed them like charity cases at a soup kitchen and ignore them. Somehow, during the course of the dinner, she had become convinced that all the men present were stockbrokers. She munched on pheasant breast, now bitterly conscious again of her green stockings and tangled hair. She made a forceful attempt to understand what was being said around her and, her linguistic sense sharpened by contempt, she began to get the drift of the several conversations going on within earshot. Somebody said that the rainy summer had been disastrous for the shooting. Somebody said that a strong stand had to be taken in Algeria. Somebody spoke about a play that Roberta hadn't heard of and complained that the second act was outrageous. A lady in a white dress said she had heard from an American friend that President Kennedy had surrounded himself with Communists.

"What nonsense," Roberta said, quite loudly, but nobody even turned his head.

She ate some more pheasant, drank some more wine, and brooded. She began to suffer from a suspicion that she didn't exist. She wondered what she could say to get anyone there to acknowledge the fact that she was alive. It would have to be fairly shocking. She played with various opening statements. "I heard someone mention President Kennedy. I happen to be very close to the family. I wonder if it would interest anyone here to know that the President plans to remove all American troops from France by August." *That*'d make them look up from their plates for a few seconds, she thought grimly.

Or perhaps a more personal attack would serve better. Something like, "I must apologize for having been late this evening, but I was speaking over the cable to the Museum of Modern Art in New York. They want to buy four of my oils, but my agent wants me to wait until my one-man show this autumn."

Snobs, she thought, looking around her fiercely, I'll bet that'd swing the conversation around a bit.

But she sat dumbly, knowing she would never say anything, ignominiously trapped in her youth, her outlandish clothes, her ignorance, her infuriating shyness. Proust, she thought with huge self-scorn. French society!

Belligerence stirred within her. As she glared around her, over the crystal lip of her glass, the other people there seemed frivolous and false, with their talk of a bad season for pheasants, and their outrageous second acts, and their Communists surrounding the President. She glared at the Baron, so vainly barbered and foppishly perfect, and began to hate him most of all. I know what *he's* after, she muttered to herself, into the wineglass, and he's not going to get it.

She ate some more, heartily.

Her hatred for the Baron grew tropically. He'd invited her as a freak, to amuse his friends, she decided, and he'd hung her paintings in the same room with the Matisse and the Soutine as a joke, because he knew as well as she did that they didn't belong there. The minute she left, after he'd made his pass and failed, he'd have one of the butlers in white gloves take the paintings down and put them in the basement or the attic or the cook's bathroom, where they belonged.

Suddenly the vision of Guy, standing, faithful and frozen, outside her window in the winter night, swam before her. Tears welled in her eyes at the thought of how heartless she'd been to him and how much better he was than all these chattering gluttons at the table. She remembered how much he loved her and how he respected her and how pure he was and how happy she could make him just by lifting her little finger, so to speak. Sitting there with her plate heaped with breast of pheasant and purée of marrons, and her glass filled once more with a 1928 Bordeaux, she felt that it was intolerable that she wasn't with Guy at that moment and she could feel her immortal soul being corrupted second by second within her.

Abruptly, she stood up. Her chair would have fallen if one of the men in white gloves hadn't leaped and caught it. She stood very straight, wondering if she was as pale as she felt. All conversation ceased and every eye was turned upon her.

"I'm terribly sorry," she said, addressing the Baron. "I have a very important telephone call to make."

"Of course, my dear," the Baron said. He stood, but with a sharp little gesture kept the other men seated. "Henri will show you where the telephone is."

A waiter stepped forward, wooden-faced, from his station against the wall. Walking erectly, keeping her head high, her after-ski boots making a curious but not unmusical noise on the polished floor, she followed the waiter out of the silent room. The door closed behind her. I will never enter that room again, she thought. I will never see any of those people again. I have made my choice. My eternal choice.

Her knees felt cloudy and she was not conscious of the effort of walking as she followed Henri across the hall and into the pink salon.

"Voilà, Mademoiselle," Henri said, pointing to a phone on an inlaid table. "Désirez-vous que je compose le numéro pour vous?" "Non," she said coldly. "Je le composerai moi-même, merci." She waited until he had left the room, then sat down on the couch next to the phone. She dialed the number of Guy's home. While she listened to the buzzing in her ear, she stared at her paintings on the opposite wall. They looked pallid and ordinary and influenced by everybody. She remembered how exalted she had been when the Baron had led her into the room to show her the pictures so short a time ago. I am a pendulum, she thought, I am a classic manic-depressive. If I came from a rich family they would send me to a psychiatrist. I am not a painter. I must give up wearing blue jeans. I must devote myself to being a good woman and making a man happy. I must never drink again.

403

"*Allô! Allô!*" a woman's irritated voice said over the phone. It was Guy's mother.

Speaking as clearly as possible, Roberta asked if Guy was home. Guy's mother pretended not to understand Roberta at first and made her repeat the question twice. Then, sounding enraged, Guy's mother said yes, her son was home, but was sick in bed with a fever, and could talk to no one. Guy's mother seemed dangerously ready to hang up at any moment, and Roberta spoke urgently, in an attempt to get a message through before the phone went dead.

Guy's mother kept saying, "*Comment? Comment? Qu'est-ce que vous avez dit?*" in a shrill crescendo of annoyance.

Roberta was trying to say that she would be home in an hour, and that, if Guy felt well enough to get out of bed, she would like him to call her, when there was the sound of male shouts over the phone, and then thumping noises, as though there was a struggle going on for the instrument. Then she heard Guy's voice, panting. "Roberta? Where are you? Are you all right? What happened?"

"I'm a bitch," Roberta whispered. "Forgive me."

"Never mind that," Guy said. "Where are you?"

"I'm surrounded by the most terrible people," Roberta said. "It serves me right. I behaved like an idiot. . . ."

"Where are you?" Guy shouted. "What's the address?"

"Nineteen *bis* Square du Bois de Boulogne," Roberta said. "I'm awfully sorry you're sick. I wanted to see you and tell you—"

"Don't move," Guy said. "I'll be there in ten minutes."

There was an off-instrument cascade of French from Guy's mother, and then the click as Guy hung up. Roberta sat there a moment, the pain of her wounds beginning to vanish, soothed by the swift, dependable voice of love on the telephone. I must deserve him, she thought religiously. I must deserve him.

She stood up and went over and stared at her paintings. She would have liked to be able to scratch out her signature, but the paintings were covered with glass, and it wasn't possible.

She went out into the hall and put on her coat and tied her scarf around her head. The house seemed silent and empty. None of the men in white gloves were to be seen and whatever the guests were saying about her in the dining room was mercifully muffled by distance and a series of closed doors. She took a last look around, at the mirrors, the marble, the mink. This is not for me, she thought without regret. Tomorrow she would find out the Baron's name from Patrini and send him a dozen roses with a note of apology for her bad manners. Otherwise, she would never be able to face her mother again. She wondered if her mother had ever gone through a night like this when she was nineteen.

She opened the door softly and slipped out. The Bentley and the other cars were still there, and the chauffeurs standing in the cold, sad attendance of the rich, were grouped in the mist under a lamppost. Roberta leaned against the iron fence of the Baron's house, feeling her head clearing in the cold night air. Soon she was chilled to the bone, but doing penance for the hours Guy had spent outside her window, she didn't move or try to keep warm.

Sooner than she had dared to hope she heard the roar of the Vespa and saw the familiar figure of Guy, dangerously angled, as he sped through the narrow passage into the square. She went out under the lamppost so he could see her and when he skidded to a halt in front of her, she threw her arms around him, not caring that the chauffeurs were all watching. "Thank you, thank you," she whispered. "Now take me away from here. Quick!"

Guy kissed her cheek briefly, and squeezed her. She got on the pillion behind him and held him tight as he started the Vespa. They surged out between the dark buildings and into the Avenue Foch. For a moment, that was enough—the speed, the fresh cold wind, the crisp feel of his coat between her arms, the sense of escape, as they crossed the Avenue Foch and headed down the empty boulevard toward the Arc, shimmering insubstantially under its floodlights in the thin mist.

She held Guy closely, whispering into the fleece collar of his coat, too low for him to hear, "I love you, I love you." She felt holy and clean, as though she had been delivered from the danger of mortal sin.

As they approached the Etoile, Guy slowed down and turned his head. His face looked drawn and tense. "Where to?" he said.

She hesitated. Then she said, "Do you still have the key to your friend's apartment? The one who went to Tours?"

Guy started violently and the Vespa skidded and they only recovered their balance at the very last moment.

He pulled the Vespa over to the curb and stopped. He twisted around to face her. For a fleeting instant she had the feeling that he looked frightened. "Are you drunk?" he asked.

"Not any more. *Do* you have the key?"

"No," Guy said. He shook his head in despair. "He came back from Tours two days ago. What are we going to do?"

"We can go to a hotel," Roberta said. She was surprised to hear the words come out of her mouth. "Can't we?"

"What hotel?"

"Any hotel that will let us in," Roberta said.

Guy gripped her arm above the elbow, hard. "Are you sure you know what you are doing?"

"Of course." She smiled at him. She was enjoying doing this wicked planning for them. Somehow, it helped wipe out the memory of all the gaucheries she had committed that night. "Didn't I tell you I would make all the advances? I'm now making the advances."

Guy's lips trembled. "American," he said, "you are magnificent." Roberta thought he was going to kiss her, but he didn't seem to trust himself to go that far yet. He turned again on the saddle and started the Vespa. Now he drove with the care of a man transporting a load of precious porcelain on a rough mountain road.

They wound through the eighth arrondissement, passing hotel after hotel, but none of them seemed to attract Guy. He would hesitate as he saw one ahead of him, then shake his head and mumble something to himself and keep the Vespa at cruising speed. Roberta had never realized there were so many hotels in Paris. She was beginning to feel terribly cold, but she said nothing. This was Guy's town and she had had no experience in these matters. If he had some perfect image of a hotel for this occasion and would be satisfied with nothing less, she would ride half across the city behind him without complaint.

They crossed the Pont Alexandre III and swept up and around the Invalides into the Faubourg St. Germain, through dark, discreet streets, where huge mansions reared behind high walls. Even here, there were a surprising number of hotels, large ones, small ones, luxurious ones, modest ones, hotels brightly lit and hotels that seemed to be dozing in low lamplight. Still, Guy kept on.

Finally, in a section of the city that Roberta had never visited before, near the Avenue des Gobelins, on a street that seemed on the verge of becoming a slum, Guy came to a halt. A dim light illuminated a sign that read Hôtel du Cardinal, Tout Confort. There was no indication which Cardinal was being commemorated here and the paint was chipped and flaky on the lettering of Tout Confort.

"I have found it," Guy said. "I have heard about this place from a friend. It is very welcoming, he said."

Roberta dismounted stiffly. "It looks very nice," she said hypocritically.

"If you will stay here and guard the machine," Guy said, "I

will go in and make the arrangements." He seemed distracted and avoided looking Roberta in the eye. He was feeling for his wallet as he went into the hotel, like a man in a crowd at a sporting event who is worried about pickpockets.

Roberta stood with her hand possessively on the saddle of the Vespa, trying to put herself into the proper frame of mind for what lay ahead of her. She wished she had had a third martini. She wondered if there were going to be mirrors on the ceiling, and Watteau-like paintings of nymphs. She hadn't heard about much in Paris, but she had heard about *that*.

I must behave with grace, gaiety and beauty, she thought. This must be a lyrical experience.

She wished Guy would come out. Standing out there alone in the dark protecting the Vespa made her nervous. It wasn't the *idea* of making love that bothered her, she told herself, it was the practical details, like what expression to put on her face when she passed the clerk in the lobby. In the movies that Guy took her to see, the girls, even though they were only seventeen or eighteen years old, never seemed to be bothered by these problems. They were graceful as panthers, sensual as Cleopatra, and they slipped into bed as naturally as eating lunch. Of course, they were French, and that helped. Well, Guy was French. She was comforted by this thought. Still, for the first time in some months, she wished Louise were at her side for a moment or two, and she regretted the questions she hadn't asked on those nights when Louise had come home late and eager to talk.

Guy came out of the hotel. "It's all right," he said. "The man is permitting me to station the Vespa in the lobby." Guy took the Vespa by the handle bars and trundled it up the steps and through the door into the lobby of the hotel. Roberta followed him, wondering if she ought to help him with the machine, because he seemed to be panting with the effort of getting it up the steps.

The lobby was narrow and dark, with only one light over the clerk at the desk. The clerk was an old man with thin gray hair, He looked at her with a dead, all-knowing eye. "*Soixante-deux,*" he said. He gave Guy the key and went back to reading a newspaper that he had spread out on his desk.

There was no elevator and Roberta followed Guy up three flights of a narrow staircase. The carpet on the staircase was scuffed and smelled dusty. Guy had some trouble getting the key into the lock of the door of Number 62, and muttered under his breath as he struggled with it. Then the lock gave way and Guy opened the

407

door and turned on the light. He squeezed Roberta's arm as she went past him into the room.

There were no mirrors on the ceiling and no nymphs on the walls. It was a small, plain room with a narrow brass bed, a yellow wooden armchair, a table with a scruffy piece of blotting paper on it, and a tattered screen in one corner concealing a bidet, all under the blue glare of the single bare bulb hanging on a braided wire from the ceiling. And it was bitterly cold, with the cold of many unforgiving winters concentrated between the stained walls.

"Oh," Roberta said in a small, desolate whisper.

Guy put his arms around her from behind. "Forgive me," he said, "I forgot to take any money with me, and all I had in my pocket was seven hundred francs. Ancient francs."

"That's all right," Roberta said. She turned and tried to smile at him. "I don't mind."

Guy took off his coat and threw it over the chair. "After all," he said, "it is only a *place*. There is no sense in being sentimental about *places*, is there?" He avoided looking at her and kept blowing on his knuckles, which were red with cold. "Well," he said, "I suppose you ought to undress."

"You first," Roberta said, almost automatically.

"My dear Roberta," Guy said, blowing assiduously on his knuckles, "everybody knows that in a situation like this, the girl always undresses first."

"Not this girl," Roberta said. She sat down in the armchair, crushing Guy's coat. It was going to be difficult, she realized, to behave with grace and gaiety.

Guy stood over her, breathing hard, His lips were blue with cold. "Very well," he said, "I will give in to you. This once. But you must promise not to look."

"I have no desire to look," Roberta said with dignity.

"Go to the window and keep your back turned," Guy said.

Roberta stood up and went to the window. The curtains were threadbare and smelled like the carpet on the staircase. Behind her, she heard the sounds of Guy's undressing. Oh, God, she thought, I never imagined it was going to be like this. Twenty seconds later, she heard the creak of the bed. "All right," he said, "you can look now."

He was under the covers, his face dark and gaunt on the grayish pillow. "Now you," he said.

"Turn your head to the wall," Roberta said. She waited until Guy turned his head to the wall. Then she undressed swiftly, laying her clothes neatly over the disorderly pile Guy had left on the chair. Icy, she hurried under the covers. Guy was clamped along the wall on the other side of the bed and she didn't touch him. He was trembling, making the bedclothes quiver.

With a violent movement he turned toward her. He still didn't touch her, "*Zut*," he said, "the light is still on."

They both looked up at the light. The bulb stared down at them, like the night clerk's eye.

"You forgot to turn it off," Guy said accusingly.

"I know," she said. "Well, turn it off. I'm not budging from this bed."

"You were the last one up," Guy said plaintively.

"I don't care," she said.

"That is absolutely unfair," said Guy.

"Unfair or not," Roberta said, "I'm staying right here." Even as she spoke, she had the impression that she had had a conversation very much like this somewhere before in her life. Then she remembered. It had been with her brother, who was two years younger than she, and it had been in a cottage in a summer resort, when she was six years old. The echo disturbed her.

"But you're on the outside," Guy said. "I'll have to climb over you."

Roberta thought this over for a moment. She knew she couldn't bear the thought of his touching her, even accidentally, with the light still on. "Stay where you are," she said. With a convulsive movement she threw back the covers, leaped out of bed and fled across the room. She switched off the light and hurled herself back into bed, pulling the covers up around her neck.

Guy was trembling more than ever. "You are *exquise*," he said. "I cannot bear it." This time he hadn't turned his face away. He reached out his hand and touched her. Involuntarily, she gasped and gave a little jump. His hand was like a fistful of ice. Disastrously, he began to weep. Roberta lay rigid and alarmed on her side of the bed, as Guy sobbed heartbrokenly.

"It is awful," he said, between sobs. "I do not blame you for pulling away. It is not the way it should be at all. I am too clumsy, too stupid. I do not know anything. It serves me right. I have been lying to you for three months. . . . ."

"Lying?" Roberta asked, remaining absolutely still. "What do you mean?"

"I have been playing a role," Guy said brokenly. "I have no experience. I am not studying to be an engineer. I am still in the *lycée*. I am not twenty-one years old. I am only sixteen."

"Oh." Roberta closed her eyes slowly, blotting out the night. "Why did you do that?"

"Because you would not have looked at me otherwise," he said. "Is that not true?"

"Yes," Roberta said, "it is true." She opened her eyes, because you couldn't keep your eyes closed forever.

"If only it had not been so cold," Guy wept, "if only I had more than seven hundred francs, you would never have known."

"Well, I know now," Roberta said. No wonder he only drank pineapple juice, she thought. How can I be so inaccurate? Will I ever change?

Guy sat up. "I suppose I ought to take you home," he said. His voice was broken, dead, devoid of hope.

She wanted to go home. She thought of her single bed with longing. She wanted to retreat and stay hidden and start everything, her whole life, all over again. But there was no starting all over again with the echo of that forlorn, childish voice to haunt her. She put out her hand and touched his shoulder. "Lie down," she said gently.

After a moment, Guy slid down and lay motionless, away from her, on his side of the bed. She moved toward him and took him in her arms. He put his head high on her shoulder, his lips touching her throat. He sobbed once. She held him and after a while they were both warm under the covers. He sighed and fell asleep.

She dozed fitfully during the night and woke each time to feel the warm, slender, adolescent body curled trustingly against her. She kissed the top of Guy's head with modesty and pity and affection.

In the morning, she got out of bed without waking him and dressed quickly. She drew back the curtains. It was a sunny day. Guy was sleeping, flat on his back, under the covers, his face defenseless and happy. She went over to him and touched his forehead with her fingertips. He woke and stared up at her.

"It's morning," she whispered. "You'd better get up. It's time for you to go to school." She smiled at him and after a while he smiled gravely up at her. He sprang out of bed and began to get dressed. She watched him candidly.

They went down to the lobby. The night clerk was still on duty. He regarded them dully, thinking a night clerk's thoughts. Roberta nodded to him without shame or embarrassment, and helped Guy trundle the Vespa out of the lobby and down the steps to the street. They mounted the Vespa and sped through the morning traffic, and in ten minutes were at the entrance to the building in which Roberta lived. Guy stopped the Vespa and they both got off. Guy seemed to have trouble speaking. He started several sentences with, "Well, I . . ." and, "Someday I suppose I should . . ." In the morning light his face looked very very young. Finally, playing nervously with the brake handle, his eyes downcast, he said, "Do you hate me?"

"Of course not," Roberta said. "It was the most wonderful night of my life." At last, she thought exultantly, I'm learning to be accurate.

Guy looked up uncertainly, searching her face for signs of mockery. "Will I ever see you again?" he asked.

"Of course," she said lightly. "Tonight. As usual."

"Oh, God," he said. "If I do not get out of here I am going to cry again."

Roberta leaned over and kissed his cheek. He swung back onto the saddle of the Vespa and spurted down the street, swift and showy and careless of danger.

She watched him disappear, then entered the building, moving serenely, womanly, amused, innocent, pleased with herself. She climbed the dark stairway and put her keys into the locks of Madame Ruffat's door. But she hesitated a moment before turning the last key. She made a firm resolve. Never, NEVER would she tell Louise that Guy was only sixteen years old.

She chuckled, turned the key and went in.

# The Greek General

"I did it," Alex kept saying. "I swear I did it."

"Tell me more stories," Flanagan said, standing right over him, "I love to hear stories."

"I swear to God," Alex said, beginning to feel scared.

"Come on!" Flanagan jerked Alex to his feet. "We are going to visit New Jersey. We are going to revisit the scene of the crime, except there was no crime."

"I don't understand," Alex said hurriedly, putting on his coat and going down the stairs between Flanagan and Sam, leaving his door unlocked. "I don't understand at all."

Sam drove the car through the empty night streets, and Alex and Flanagan sat in the back seat.

"I did everything very careful," Alex said in a troubled voice. "I soaked the whole goddamn house with naphtha. I didn't forget a single thing. You know me, Flanagan, I know how to do a job . . ."

"Yeah," Flanagan said, "The efficiency expert. Alexander. The Greek general. Only the house didn't burn. That's all."

"I honestly don't understand it." Alex shook his head in puzzlement. "I put a fuse into a pile of rags that had enough naphtha on it to wash a elephant. I swear to God."

"Only the house didn't burn," Flanagan said stubbornly. "Everything was dandy, only the house didn't burn. I would like to kick you in the belly."

"Now, lissen, Flanagan," Alex protested, "what would you want to do that for? Lissen, I meant well. Sam," he appealed to the driver, "you know me, ain't I got a reputation . . .?"

"Yeah," Sam said, flatly, not taking his eyes off the traffic ahead of him.

"Jesus, Flanagan, why would I want to run out? Answer me that, what's there in it for me if I run out? I ask you that simple question."

412

"You give me a pain in the belly," Flanagan said. "A terrible pain, Alexander." He took out a cigarette and lit it, without offering one to Alex, and looked moodily out at the policeman who was taking their toll money at the Holland Tunnel entrance.

They rode in silence through the tunnel until Sam said, "This is some tunnel. It's an achievement of engineering. Look, they got a cop every hundred yards."

"You give me a pain in the belly, too," Flanagan said to Sam. So they rode in silence until they came to the skyway. The open starlit sky seemed to loosen Flanagan up a little. He took off his derby and ran his fingers through his sandy hair with a nervous unhappy motion.

"I had to get mixed up with you," he said to Alex. "A simple little thing like burning down a house and you gum it up like flypaper. Twenty-five thousand dollars hanging by a thread. Christ!" he said bitterly. "Maybe I ought to shoot you."

"I don't understand it," Alex said miserably. "That fuse shoulda reached the naphtha in two hours. It shoulda burned like a gas stove."

"You Greek general."

"Lissen, Flanagan," Alex said, tough and businesslike. "I don't like the way you talk. You talk like I threw the job away on purpose. Lissen, do you think I'd throw five thousand bucks out the window like that?"

"I don't know what you'd do," Flanagan said, lighting another cigarette. "I don't think you got enough brains to come in outa the rain. That's my honest opinion."

"Five thousand bucks is five thousand bucks," Alex insisted. "With money like that I could open a poolroom and be a gentleman for the rest of my life." He looked up at the ceiling of the car and spoke softly. "I always wanted to operate a poolroom." Then, harshly, to Flanagan, "You think I'd give up a chance like that? What do you think—I'm crazy?"

"I don't think nothing," Flanagan said stubbornly. "All I know is the house didn't burn. That's all I know."

He looked stonily out his window and there was quiet in the car as it raced across the Jersey meadows through the stockyard, fertilizer, glue-factory smells, and turned off on the fork to Orangeburg. Two miles out of the town they stopped at an intersection and McCracken came out from behind a tree and got into the car. Sam started the car again even before McCracken was seated. McCracken was not in uniform and there was a harried frown on his face. "This is the nuts," McCracken said even before he got

413

the car door closed. "This is wonderful. This is a beautiful kettle of fish."

"If you just come to cry," Flanagan said bluntly, "you can get right out now."

"I have been sitting around in the police station," McCracken wailed, "and I have been going crazy,"

"All right. All right!" Flanagan said.

"Everything worked just like we planned," McCracken went right on, pounding his hand on his knee. "Ten minutes before eleven o'clock an alarm was turned in from the other end of town and the whole damned fire department went charging out to put out a brush fire in a vacant lot. I waited and waited and for two hours there was no sign of a fire from the Littleworth house. Twenty-five thousand bucks!" He rocked back and forth in misery. "Then I called you. What're you doing, playing a game?"

Flanagan gestured toward Alex with his thumb. "Look at him. There's the boy. Our efficiency expert. I would like to kick him in the belly."

"Lissen," Alex said coolly and reasonably. "Something went wrong. A mistake. All right."

"What's all right about it?" McCracken shouted. "You tell me! Lissen, Alex, I get four thousand bucks a year for bein' Chief of Police of this town, I can't afford to get mixed up in mistakes."

"I will do the job over," Alex said soothingly. "I will do it good this time."

"You better," Flanagan said grimly. "You'll be served up as pie if you make another mistake."

"That's no way to talk," Alex said, hurt.

"That's the way I talk," Flanagan said. "Sam, go to the Littleworth house."

The car barely stopped for Alex to jump out in front of the Littleworth house. "We'll be back in ten minutes," Flanagan said as he closed the door. "Find out what went wrong. *Alex!*" he said with loathing.

Alex shrugged and looked up at the huge pile of the Littleworth house, black against the sky. By all rights it should've been just a heap of ashes by now with insurance experts probing in the remains to estimate how much damage was done. Why couldn't it've burned? Alex wept inwardly, why couldn't it? Five thousand dollars, he thought as he went swiftly and quietly across the dark lawn. A nice comfortable poolroom, with the balls clicking like music and the boys buying Coca-Cola at ten cents a bottle between shots and the cash register ringing again and again. A gentleman's life. No wondering every time you saw a cop was he looking for you. Why couldn't it've burned?

He slipped silently through the window that he had left open and padded along the thick carpet to the library, his flashlight winking on and off cautiously in the dark hall. He went directly to the pile of rags in the corner, over which still hung the faint odor of naphtha. He played the flashlight on the fuse that he had carefully lighted before slipping out the window. Only ashes remained. The fuse had burned all right. Uncertainly he touched the rags. They were dry as sand. "Nuts," he said softly in the silent library. "Nuts. Smart guy!" He hit his head with both his hands in irritation. "What a smart guy!" He kicked the pile of rags bitterly and went back along the hall and jumped out the window and walked out across the lawn and waited for Flanagan and Sam behind a tree, smoking a cigarette.

Alex breathed deeply, looking around him. This was the way to live, he thought, peering at the big houses set behind trees and lawns off in the darkness, fresh air and birds and quiet, going off to Palm Beach when you wanted your house burned down and you didn't want to know anything about it. He sighed, blotting out his cigarette against the tree. A well-run poolroom ought to be good for six, seven thousand dollars a year. You could live very respectable in Flatbush on six, seven thousand dollars a year, there were trees there, all over the place, and squirrels, live squirrels, in the gardens. Like a park, like a real park, that's how people ought to live . . .

The car drew up to him and Flanagan opened the door and leaned out.

"Well, general?" Flanagan asked without humor.

"Look, Flanagan," Alex said seriously, talking in whispers, "something went wrong."

"No!" Flanagan said with bitter irony. "No! Don't tell me!"

"Do you want to make jokes?" Alex asked. "Or do you want to hear what happened?"

"For God's sake," McCracken whispered, his voice tense and high, "don't be a comedian, Flanagan. Say what you got to say and let's get outa here!" He looked anxiously up and down the street. "For all I know a cop's liable to come walkin' up this street any minute!"

"Our Chief of Police. Old Iron Nerves," Flanagan said.

"I'm sorry I ever got into this," McCracken said hoarsely, "Well, Alex, what the hell happened?"

"It's very simple," Alex said, "I set a two-hour fuse and the naphtha evaporated."

"Evaporated?" Sam said slowly. "What's that, evaporated?"

"He's a student, our boy, Alex," Flanagan said. "He knows big words. Evaporated. You dumb Greek! You efficiency expert! You stupid sonofabitch! Trust you to burn down a house! Evaporated! You ought to be washing dishes! *Alexander!*" Deliberately Flanagan spit at Alex.

"You oughtn't to say that," Alex said, wiping his face. "I did my best."

"What're we going to do now?" McCracken wailed. "Somebody tell me what we're going to do now."

Flanagan leaned way over and grabbed Alex fiercely by the collar. "Lissen, Alexander," he said right into Alex's face, "you're goin' back in that house and you're settin' fire to that house, and you're settin' fire to it good! Hear me?"

"Yeah," Alex said, his voice trembling. "Sure I hear you, Flanagan. You don't have to tear my collar off. Say, lissen, Flanagan, this shirt cost me eight bucks . . ."

"You are setting fire to this house personally now," Flanagan's grip tightened on the collar. "You are giving this fire the benefit of your personal attention, see? No fuse, no evaporated, nothing, understand?"

"Yeah," Alex said. "Sure, Flannagan."

"You will be served up as pie, anything goes wrong," Flanagan said slowly, his pale mean eyes glaring straight into Alex's.

"Why don't you leave go my collar?" Alex said, choking a little. "Lissen, Flanagan, this shirt cost me . . ."

Flanagan spat into his face again. "I would like to kick you in the belly," he said. He let go Alex's collar and pushed Alex's face with the heel of his hand.

"Say, Flanagan . . ." Alex protested as he stumbled back.

The car door slammed. "Move, Sam," Flanagan said, sitting back.

The car spurted down the street. Alex wiped his face with a shaking hand. "Oh, Jesus," he said to himself as he walked back across the completely dark lawn to the house. He heard a sparrow cheep in the three o'clock morning hush and he nearly cried under the peaceful trees.

Once in the house, though, he became very businesslike. He went upstairs to where he had set out buckets of naphtha and brought them down in pairs. He tore down all the drapes from the ground-floor windows and piled them at the farther end of the long hall that ran along one side of the house. Then he took all the linen covers off the furniture and piled them on top of the drapes. He went down to the cellar and brought up three egg boxes full of excelsior and put the excelsior on top of the piled cloth. It made a heap about seven feet high at the end of the hall. He worked grimly, swiftly, ripping cloth when it wouldn't give way easily, running up and down steps, sweating in his overcoat, feeling the sweat roll down his neck onto his tight collar. He soaked every piece of furniture with naphtha, then came out and poured ten gallons of naphtha over the pile at the end of the hall. He stepped back, the acrid smell sharp in his nostrils, and surveyed his work with satisfaction. If that didn't work you couldn't burn this house down in a blast-oven. When he got through with it, the home of the Littleworths would be hot. No mistake this time. He got a broom and broke off the handle and wrapped it heavily with rags. He soaked the rags with naphtha until the liquid ran out of the saturated cloth to the floor. He whistled comfortably under his breath "There'll be a hot time in the old town tonight" as he opened the window wide behind him at the end of the hall that was opposite the huge pile of cloth and excelsior. It was a narrow hall, but long. A distance of thirty-five feet separated him from the pyre at the other end.

"There'll be a hot time in the old town tonight," he sang under his breath as he took out a match from the dozen he had lying loose in his pocket. He stood next to the open window, prepared to jump swiftly out as he struck the match, put it to his heavy torch. The torch flared up wildly in his hand and he hurled it with all his strength straight down the hall to the pile of naphtha-soaked cloth and excelsior at the other end. It landed squarely on the pile. For a moment nothing happened. Alex stood, ready at the window, his eyes shining in the fierce light of the flaring torch. Alex smiled and kissed his fingers at the other end of the hall.

Then the whole hall exploded. The pile of cloth became a single huge ball of flame and hurtled down the hall like a flaming shell to the open window behind Alex. With a scream sick in his throat, lost in the immense roar of the exploding house, Alex dove to the floor just as the ball of flame shot over him and through the window to the pull of the open air beyond, carrying his hat and his hair, like smoke going up a chimney to the pull of the sky.

When he came to there was a dusty burned smell in his nostrils. Without surprise he saw that the carpet under his face was quietly afire, burning gently, like coal in a grate. He hit the side of his head three times to put out the fire in what remained of his hair, and sat up dully. Coughing and crying, he dove down to the floor again, escaping the smoke. He crawled along the burning carpet foot by foot, his hands getting black and crisp under him as he slowly made his way to the nearest door. He opened the door and crawled out onto a side porch. Just behind him the hall beams collapsed and a column of flame shot up through the roof, as solid as cement. He sighed and crawled to the edge of the porch and fell off five feet to the loam of a flower bed. The loam was hot and smelled from manure, but he lay there gratefully for a moment, until he realized that something was wrong with his hip. Stiffly he sat up and looked at his hip. Flames were coming out through his overcoat from inside and he could smell his skin broiling. Neatly he unbuttoned his coat and hit at the flames, curling up from the pocket where he had the dozen matches. When he put out the fire on his hip he crawled out to the lawn, shaking his head again and again to clear it, and sat behind a tree. He slid over and went out again, his head on a root.

Far off, far off a bell clanged again and again. Alex opened his eyes, singed of their lashes, and listened. He heard the fire trucks turn into the street. He sighed again and crawled, clinging to the cold ground, around the back of the house and through a bare hedge that cut his swelling hands, and away from the house. He stood up and walked off behind a high hedge just as the first fireman came running down toward the back of the house.

Directly, but slowly, like a man walking in a dream, he went to McCracken's house. It took forty minutes to walk there, walking deliberately down alleys and back streets in the dark, feeling the burned skin crack on his knees with every step.

He rang the bell and waited. The door opened slowly and McCracken cautiously put his face out.

"My God!" McCracken said and started to slam the door, but Alex had his foot in the way.

"Lemme in," Alex said in a hoarse broken voice.

"You're burned," McCracken said, trying to kick Alex's foot out of the doorway. "I can't have nothing to do with you. Get outa here."

Alex took out his gun and shoved it into McCracken's ribs. "Lemme in," he said.

McCracken slowly opened the door. Alex could feel his ribs shaking against the muzzle of the gun. "Take it easy," McCracken said, his voice high and girlish with fright. "Lissen, Alex, take it easy."

They stepped inside the hall and McCracken closed the door.

McCracken kept holding on to the doorknob to keep from sliding to the floor from terror, "What do you want from me, Alex?" His necktie jumped up and down with the strain of talking. "What can I do for you?"

"I want a hat," Alex said, "and I want a coat."

"Sure, sure, Alex. Anything I can do to help . . ."

"Also I want for you to drive me to New York."

McCracken swallowed hard. "Now, look, Alex," he wiped his mouth with the back of his hand to dry the lips, "let's be reasonable. It's impossible for me to drive you to New York. I got a four-thousand-dollar job. I'm Chief of Police. I can't take chances like . . ."

Alex started to cry. "I'll give it to you right in the guts. So help me."

"All right, Alex, all right," McCracken said hurriedly. "What're you crying about?"

"It hurts. I can't stand it, it hurts so much." Alex weaved back and forth in the hallway in pain. "I got to get to a doctor before I croak. Come on, you bastard," he wept, "drive me to the city!"

All the way to Jersey City Alex cried as he sat there, jolting in the front seat, wrapped in a big coat of McCracken's, an old hat slipping back and forth on his burnt head as the car sped east into the dawn. McCracken gripped the wheel with tight, sweating hands, his face drawn and pale. From time to time he glanced sidewise fearfully at Alex.

"Yeah," Alex said once when he caught McCracken looking at him. "I'm still here. I ain't dead yet. Watch where you're goin', Chief of Police."

A block from the Jersey entrance of the Holland Tunnel, McCracken stopped the car.

"Please, Alex," he pleaded, "don't make me take you across to New York. I can't take the chance."

"I gotta get to a doctor," Alex said, licking his cracked lips. "I gotta get to a doctor. Nobody's gonna stop me from getting to a doctor. You're goin' to take me through the tunnel and then I'm goin' to let you have it because you're a bastard. You're an Irish bastard. Start this car." He rocked back and forth in the front seat to help him with the pain. "Start this car!" he shouted.

Shaking so that it was hard for him to control the car, McCracken drove Alex all the way to the St. George Hotel in Brooklyn where Flanagan lived. He stopped the car and sat still, slumped exhausted over the wheel.

"O.K., Alex," he said. "Here we are. You're gonna be a good

guy, aren't you, Alex, you're not goin' to do anythin' you're goin' to be sorry for, are you? Remember, Alex, I'm a family man, I'm a man with three children. Come on, Alex, why don't you talk? Why would you want to hurt me?''

"Because you're a bastard," Alex said painfully because his jaws were stiffening. "I got a good mind to. You didn't want to help me. I had to make you help me."

"I got a kid aged two years old," McCracken cried. "Do you want to make a orphan of a two-year-old kid? Please, Alex. I'll do anything you say."

Alex sighed. "Go get Flanagan."

McCracken jumped out quickly and came right back with Flanagan and Sam. Alex smiled stiffly when Flanagan opened the door of the car and saw Alex and whistled. "Nice," Flanagan said. "Very nice."

"Look at him," Sam said, shaking his head. "He looks like he been in a war."

"You ought to a' seen what I done to the house," Alex said. "A first-class job."

"Are you goin' to pass out, Alex?" Sam asked anxiously.

Alex waved his gun pointlessly two or three times and then pitched forward, his head hitting the dashboard with a smart crack, like the sound of a baseball bat on a thrown ball.

When he opened his eyes he was in a dark, meagerly furnished room and Flanagan's voice was saying, "Lissen, Doc, this man can't die. He's gotta come through, understand? It is too hard to explain away a dead body. It can't be done. I don't care if he loses both legs and both arms and if it takes five years, but he's got to pull through."

"I should never've gotten mixed up in this," McCracken's voice wailed. "I was a damn fool. Risking a four-thousand-dollar-a-year job. I ought to have my head examined."

"Maybe he will and maybe he won't," a strange professional voice said. "That is a well-done young man."

"It looks to me," Sam's voice said, "as if he's marked special delivery to Calvary Cemetery."

"Shut up!" Flanagan said. "And from now on nobody says a word. This is a private case. Alexander. The lousy Greek.''

Alex heard them all go out before he dropped off again.

For the next five days, the doctor kept him full of dope, and Flanagan kept Sam at his bedside with a towel for a gag, to keep him quiet when the pain became too much to bear. He would start to yell and Sam would shove the towel into his mouth and say soothingly, "This is a respectable boarding house, Alex. They don't like noise." And he could scream all he wanted to into the towel and bother no one.

Ten days later the doctor told Flanagan, "All right. He'll live."

Flanagan sighed. "The dumb Greek," he said, patting Alex on his bandaged head. "I would like to kick him in the belly. I am going out to get drunk." And he put on his derby hat, square on his head, and went out.

Alex lay in one position for three months in the furnished room. Sam played nursemaid, feeding him, playing rummy with him, reading the sporting news to him.

At times when Sam wasn't there Alex lay straight on his bed, his eyes half-closed, thinking of his poolroom. He would have a neon sign, "Alex's Billiard Parlor" going on and off and new tables and leather chairs just like a club. Ladies could play in "Alex's Billiard Parlor" it would be so refined. He would cater to the better element. Maybe even a refined free lunch, cold meats and Swiss cheese. For the rest of his life he would be a gentleman, sitting behind a cash register with his jacket on. He smiled to himself. When Flanagan gave him his money he would go straight to the pool parlor on Clinton Street and throw his money down on the counter. Cold cash. This was hard-earned money, he nearly died and there were days he'd wished he could die, and his hair was going to grow in patches, like scrub grass on a highway, for the rest of his life, but what the hell. You didn't get nothing for nothing. Five thousand dollars, five thousand dollars, five thousand dollars . . .

On June first he put on his clothes for the first time in three months and twelve days. He had to sit down after he pulled his pants on because the strain hit him at the knees. He got completely dressed, dressing very slowly, and being very careful with his necktie, and then sat down to wait for Flanagan and Sam. He was going to walk out of that lousy little room with five thousand dollars flat in his wallet. Well, he thought, I earned it, I certainly did earn it.

Flanagan and Sam came in without knocking.

"We're in a hurry," Flanagan said. "We're going to the Adirondacks. The Adirondacks in June are supposed to be something. We came to settle up."

"That's right," Alex said. He couldn't help but smile, thinking about the money. "Five thousand dollars. Baby!"

"I think you are making a mistake," Flanagan said slowly.

"Did you say five thousand dollars?" Sam asked politely.

"Yeah," Alex said. "Yeah. Five thousand bucks, that's what we agreed, isn't it?"

"That was in February, Alex," Flanagan explained calmly. "A lot of things've happened since February."

"Great changes have taken place," Sam said. "Read the papers."

"Stop the kiddin'," Alex said, weeping inside his chest. "Come on, stop the bull."

"It is true, general," Flanagan said, looking disinterestedly out the window, "that you was supposed to get five thousand dollars. But doctor bills ate it all up. Ain't it too bad? It's terrible, how expensive doctors are, these days."

"We got a specialist for you, Alex," Sam said. "Nothing but the best. He's very good on gunwounds too. But it costs."

"You lousy Flanagan," Alex shouted. "I'll get you. Don't think I won't get you!"

"You shouldn't yell in your condition," Flanagan said smoothly.

"Yeah," Sam said. "The specialist says you should relax."

"Get out of here," Alex said through tears. "Get the hell out of here."

Flanagan went over to the dresser drawer and took out Alex's gun. Expertly, he broke it and took out the shells and slipped them into his pocket. "This is just in case your hot Greek blood gets the better of you for a minute, Alex," he said. "That would be too bad."

"Lissen, Flanagan," Alex cried, "ain't I going to get anything? Not anything?"

Flanagan looked at Sam, then took out his wallet, threw a fifty-dollar bill at Alex. "Outa my own pocket," he said. "My Irish generosity."

"Some day," Alex said, "I'm going to give it to you. Wait and see. Remember."

Flanagan laughed. "The efficiency expert. Look, Alexander, you ought to get out of this business. Take the advice of an older man. You ain't got the temperament for it."

"I'm going to give it to you," Alex said stubbornly. "Remember what I said."

"The general," Flanagan laughed. "The terrible Greek." He came over and hit Alex's head back with the heel of his hand. "So long, Alexander."

He left the room.

Sam came over and put his hand on Alex's shoulder. "Take care of yourself, Alex," he said. "You've been under a big strain." And he followed Flanagan.

Alex sat for ten minutes, dry-eyed, in his chair. His nose was bleeding a little from Flanagan's push. He sighed and got up and put his coat on. He bent and picked up the fifty-dollar bill and put it in his wallet. He slipped the empty pistol into his topcoat pocket and went out slowly into the warm June sunshine. He walked slowly the two blocks to Fort Greene Park and sat down panting on the first bench. He sat there reflectively for a few minutes, shaking his head sadly from time to time. Finally he took the gun out of his pocket, looked secretly around him, and dropped it into the waste can next to the bench. It fell with a soft dry plop on the papers in the can. He reached into the can and got out a discarded newspaper and turned to the Help Wanted section. He blinked his eyes in the glare of the sun off the newsprint and traced down the page with his finger to "Help Wanted, Boys." He sat there in the warm June sunshine, with his topcoat on, making neat little checks with a pencil on the margin of the page.

# The Green Nude

As a young man, Sergei Baranov, although he preferred painting large still lifes of red apples, green pears, and very orange oranges, joined the Red Army and did a mild amount of damage in several engagements against the Whites around Kiev. He was a sturdy, good-humored, dreamy youth who did not like to refuse anyone anything, and since all his friends were joining the Revolution he went along and served faithfully and cheerfully, eating the soldier's black bread, sleeping on the soldier's straw, pulling the trigger of his ancient rifle when the people around him ordered him to do so, advancing bravely when everyone else was advancing, and running in fear of his life when that seemed like the necessary thing to do. When the Revolution was over, he retired from the military, equipped with a modest decoration for an action at which he was not present, and took up quarters in Moscow and began once more to paint red apples, green pears, and very orange oranges. All his friends were enthusiastically convinced that the Revolution was an excellent thing, and Sergei, never one to strike out on his own, amiably and decorously concurred. The truth was that he was only really interested in his highly colored fruits and vegetables and when, in his studio or in the café which he frequented, discussions would start about Lenin and Trotsky or the new economic program, he would laugh his hearty and agreeable laugh and say, bashfully, "Eh, who knows? It is for the philosophers." Besides, being a decorated hero of the Revolution and an artist to boot, he was treated well, and was assigned an excellent studio with a skylight and permitted heavy laborer's rations. His paintings, too, were warmly approved by everyone, since he had the trick of making all his garden products seem marvelously edible. They sold without delay and his work was to be seen in the homes and offices of many quite-important officials of the new regime, warm and appetizing globs of color on the otherwise bleak and functional walls.

When, in 1923, he met and conquered an ample and beautiful

young lady from Soviet Armenia, his painting took a new turn. He began to paint nudes. Since his technique remained the same, despite the change in subject matter, his success increased in leaps and bounds. As edible as ever, his paintings now combined the most satisfactory features of the orchard and the harem, and examples of his work, rosy, healthy, and very round, were much sought after by even more important officials of the regime.

He undoubtedly would have continued thus to this day, happily producing a succession of canvases of hearty, lightly clad, appetizing girls, alternating with piled heaps of oversized purple grapes and bananas, going from success to success, honor to honor, if he had not met, at a literary party, the woman who was finally to become his wife.

Anna Kronsky was one of those sharp-featured and overpoweringly energetic women that the liberation of women from the nursery and kitchen has turned loose on the male world. Angular, voracious, and clever, with a tongue like an iron clapper in a new bell, racked by indigestion and a deep contempt for the male sex, she was the sort of woman who in this country would run a store or report wars for the Luce publications. As one of her friends said of her, in attempting to put his finger on the exact difference between Anna and her more gentle contemporaries, "Anna does not make up her face when she goes out in the morning—she hones it."

In Moscow, at the time Sergei met her, she had gravitated inexorably into the education system. With twenty-three day nurseries for the children of working parents under her supervision, and a staff of over five hundred cowed men and women, she had already made her mark on the new population of the growing state. The children under her care were known as the cleanest and most precocious in the Soviet Union, and it was not until 1938 that a routine survey of neurotic diseases disclosed the fact that the graduates of Anna Kronsky's immaculate creches led all other population groups of the nation by three to one in absolute nervous breakdowns.

In a necessarily incomplete study, prepared by a thoughtful Artillery Colonel during a slow month on the Southern front in 1944, the estimate was made that the ministrations of Anna Kronsky to the rising generation had cost the Red Army more manpower than a full armored brigade of the Nazi 9th Army. However, the study was accepted with a grain of salt by the Colonel's superiors, since his OGPU dossier revealed that he had been the lover of Miss Kronsky between the dates of August third and August seventh, 1922, and had sent into headquarters a fervent request for transfer to Archangel on August eighth of the same year.

It was this lady, who, flanked by a heroic poet and an aging test-pilot, set her eyes on the sturdy Baranov as he came through the door, and, in one moment of iron speculation, made the decision that was to transform the painter's life, Her carborundum eyes glittering, she crossed the room, introduced herself to her prey, ignored the beautiful girl from Soviet Armenia who had come with Baranov, and started the necessary process which resulted three months later in marriage. Just what it was that made Baranov so immediately attractive to her, none of her friends could decide. Perhaps she saw, in the painter's simple docility and good-humored health, evidence of a fine digestion and an uncomplicated nervous system, excellent attributes for the husband of a busy lady executive who came home each night jangled and worried with the day's thousand cares, Whatever the reasons, Anna left no escape possible for Sergei. He had a tearful scene with his beloved Soviet Armenian, painted one last, pink, fruity nude, and helped carry the poor girl's meager belongings to the new room Anna had managed to find for her in a slum section three-quarters of an hour away from the center of town. Then Anna moved in, bringing with her a new bedspread, three packing cases of pamphlets and reports, and a large goose-neck lamp.

The marriage seemed from the beginning to be a thoroughly happy one, and there was only one noticeable change in Baranov, outside of a subtle, but growing tendency toward silence in company. He no longer painted nudes. Not one painting, not one sketch, not even a wash from the waist up, of the ripe, unclad female form, came from his studio. Confined once more entirely to the vegetable world, he seemed to have mastered a new understanding of the problems of the apple, the orange, and the pear. As edible as ever, a new dust seemed to be powdered over his work, a haunting and melancholy fragrance, as though the fruit he chose to paint came now from autumnal boughs, the last sweet bounty of the closing year, the final, nostalgic yield of trees and vines through whose dying leaves and frozen branches the cruel winds of winter were already moaning.

This new development in Baranov's work was greeted with respectful praise by critics and public alike and examples of the new phase were hung in many museums and public places. Success did not change him, however. More silent than ever, he painted steadily, experimenting with beets and pumpkins in ever darker reds and yellows, going everywhere with his sallow and brilliant wife, listening with model attention night after night as she monopolized conversations in literary, artistic, political, educational, and industrial circles. Once, it is true, at the request of his wife, he went to one of her nurseries and started a painting of a group of children he saw there. He painted for about an hour, then put his brush down, tore the canvas in half and had it burned in the stove, and went into the men's room, where he was reported sobbing uncontrollably. This story was not believed by anyone, as it was retailed by a young teacher who had crossed swords with Anna Kronsky and who was removed later at her instigation as unreliable. Whatever the truth of the matter was, Baranov returned to his studio and went back to his beets and pumpkins.

It was about this time that he took to painting at night, using the goose-neck lamp that Anna had brought with her as part of her dowry. They had their own apartment by now, as a result of their double importance, more than a mile away from the studio, and the sturdy though now slightly bent figure of the painter, trudging through the snow late at night, was a common sight on the almost deserted streets between his home and his studio. He became very secretive, locking his door at all times, and when friends asked him about his current work, he would merely smile vaguely and politely and change the subject. Anna, of course, never asked him about his work, as she was a very busy woman, and it was not until the opening of his one-man show, an affair attended by many of the intellectual élite of the government and the arts, that she saw for the first time the painting that had engaged her husband for the past many months.

It was a nude. But it was like no nude that Baranov had painted before. There was no touch of pink anywhere on the enormous and frightening canvas. The prevailing color was green, that green that lurks in the sky before cyclones and hurricanes, sallow, lurid, oppressive to the eye. The figure itself, of a slack-breasted and lank-haired woman with a wrinkled abdomen and stringy but somehow violent loins, was also done in mottled green, and the staring and demonic eyes under the dry brow were another shade of the dominant hue. The mouth, the most fearful feature of the work, was done in dead black and somehow gave the startling impression of howling speech, as though the painter had caught his model in a full flood of maniac oratory. The mouth seemed to fill the canvas, indeed the entire room, with a tumbling, morbid, glittering torrent of horrid rhetoric, and it was to be noticed that the viewers attempted, uneasily, to avoid, as much as possible, looking at that particular section of the work. The background, so different from Baranov's usual arrangement of carefully painted, richly figured materials, was spume and wreckage, jagged stony ruins of temples and tenements against a green and charcoal sky. The only recognizable link with Baranov's past work was a cherry tree in the right foreground. But the tree was stunted and uprooted; a green fungus ate at the branches; a thick and snakelike vine wound murderously around the suffering trunk, and minutely painted green worms munched among the unripe fruit. The entire effect was of madness, genius, energy, disaster, sorrow, and despair.

When Anna Kronsky Baranov entered the room, people were standing in muted groups, staring with horrid fascination at the new painting. "Great," she heard Suvarnin, the critic for *The Sickle*, mutter. And, "Incredible," whispered Levinoff, the painter, as she passed him.

Baranov himself was standing in a corner, shyly and excitedly accepting the awed congratulations of friends. Anna stared incredulously at the painting, then again at her husband, who, with his rosy complexion and pleasantly smiling, obedient face, looked not one whit different from the man she had known all these years. She started to go over to congratulate him, although the painting seemed very unlifelike to her, but she was intercepted by two men who ran a tractor factory in Rostov, and she became so interested in lecturing to them about tractor manufacture that she forgot to mention anything about the painting to Baranov until much later in the evening.

From time to time, various of the guests stole sidelong and speculative glances at Anna, especially when she happened to be standing in front of her husband's masterpiece. Although Anna was conscious of their regard and also conscious of something vaguely disturbing in their eyes, she dismissed the feeling, since she was well-used by now to glances of varying intensity from her subordinates in the halls and offices of the nurseries under her command. The real reason for the hurried, measuring appraisals of the people in the gallery she never discovered and no one in the Soviet Union had the courage to apprise her of it. The wild and nightmare face that topped the terrible body of the green nude bore a family resemblance to Anna Kronsky that no amount of stylization on the part of the artist could erase. Sisters, twin souls, the painted and the living woman existed in a hideous relationship that escaped the notice of none. The only other person in Moscow who did not know that the artist had painted his wife's portrait was the man who went home obediently each night with her. Ignorant and happy in his new glory, Sergei Baranov took his wife to the ballet that night to celebrate and later ordered three bottles of champagne at a café, most of which was drunk by the two tractor men from Rostov.

The week following the opening of the show marked the highpoint of Sergei Baranov's early life. Feted, pointed out wherever he went, especially when accompanied by his wife, saluted in the press, urged to create murals to cover acres of walls, he swam in a bright stream of praise. The critic Suvarnin, who had barely acknowledged his greeting before this, even deigned to come to Baranov's studio to interview him, and, breaking all precedent, appeared sober.

"Tell me," said Suvarnin, squinting at Baranov through his pale, cold eyes, those eyes which had riddled holes in so many canvases before this, "tell me how a man who has only painted fruit before this comes to do such a painting."

"Well," said Baranov, who had recaptured some of his early loquacity and expansiveness in the past week, "well, it happened something like this. As you know, if you have seen any of my painting recently, my work has become more and more melancholy."

Suvarnin nodded thoughtfully, agreeing.

"The palette became more and more subdued. Brown, dark brown, entered increasingly into the canvases. The fruit . . . well, the truth is, the fruit began to be withered, frostbitten, sad, I would come here to my studio and I would sit down and cry. For an hour. Two hours at a time. All by myself. I began to dream every night. Dreams of death, dreams of trains going out of stations, dreams of boats leaving me on the dock, in the rain, dreams of being buried alive and being sniffed at by dark brown foxes and other small animals . . ." Baranov spoke with lively animation, as a perfectly healthy man might describe symptoms of a dreadful disease which he has suffered and proudly conquered. "The worst dream, and one that I had over and over again, was that I was in a small room and it was crowded with women, only women. All the women could talk, but I couldn't. I tried. I moved my lips. My tongue quivered between my teeth. The conversation around me filled the air deafeningly like locomotive whistles and French horns. And I could not make a sound. You have no idea how terrible this simple thing can be. It was like being committed each night to a new kind of awful prison. I began to fear going to bed. I would come and stare at the blank canvas on my easel, at the arrangement of potatoes and eggplants on which I intended to work, and I could not move my fingers to the brushes. An artist, as you know, must create out of his emotions. How could I transfer how I felt into the image of an eggplant, into potatoes? I felt I was lost. I felt I would never be able to paint again. I contemplated suicide."

Suvarnin nodded. He even thought of making notes, something he hadn't done for twenty years, since he was of the firm opinion that accuracy in reporting was the foe of creative criticism. He put his hand into his pocket for a pencil, but discovered he had neglected to bring one along with him. He took his hand out of his pocket and gave up the thought of taking notes.

"Suicide," Baranov repeated, flushed with joy at having the redoubtable Suvarnin pay such close attention to his confession. "I moaned. I shrieked." Baranov knew that he had done no such thing, and had, in fact, merely gloomed silently in front of the easel, but he felt that these active expressions of passion would sit well with the critic, as indeed they did, "I cried out. I despaired." Suvarnin moved restively, glancing instinctively at the vodka bottle on the table, and licking the corner of his mouth, and Baranov hurried on, feeling anxiously that he had perhaps gone a little far with his synonyms. "I slashed out blindly at the canvas. I did not guide my hand. I did not search for colors. I did not look at the potatoes or the eggplant. My terrors painted through me. I was the instrument of my dreams. I hardly looked to see what I was doing. I painted all night long, one night after another. I did not know what I was doing . . ." By now Baranov had forgotten that he was trying to make an impression. By now he was letting the simple truth pour out. "All I knew was, that as the painting grew, a great weight was being lifted from me. My subconscious was being delivered from its prison. When I slept, I no longer dreamed of being struck dumb or being nosed by dark brown foxes. Now my dreams were of vineyards in the springtime and large-breasted young women I wished to approach on the streets. Finally, when I was finished, and I sat back and looked at the green nude and the ruins, I was as surprised by what I had done as if I had come into my studio and found that another man, a complete stranger, had used my easel while I was away on holiday. And I was grateful to him, whoever he was. And I was grateful to the green lady on the canvas. Between them," Baranov said simply, "they had delivered me from Hell."

Suvarnin stood up and silently shook the painter's hand. "Out of anguish," he said finally, "comes the great art. Out of the depths of despair only can we reach to the skies. Look at Dostoyevsky."

Baranov nodded, although a little uneasily, as he had tried to read *The Brothers Karamazov* three times and had never got past page 165. But Suvarnin did not press the point. "Read my article on Saturday," he said modestly. "I think you will be pleased."

"Thank you," Baranov said humbly, resolving to call Anna immediately Suvarnin left to impart to her the heady news. "I am in your debt."

"Nonsense," said Suvarnin, with the concision and gift for a phrase that had made his reputation secure in a dozen cities. "Art is in your debt. And now," he asked, "what is the next painting going to be?"

Baranov smiled happily. "Cherries," he said. "Six kilos of red cherries in a wicker basket. They are being delivered here at two o'clock from the market."

"Good," said Suvarnin. They shook hands once more and the critic departed, with only one tentative glance at the vodka bottle.

Baranov sat down, waiting dreamily for the arrival of the cherries, thinking, as he sat there, Perhaps it is time that I started a scrapbook for my reviews.

On Saturday, Baranov opened the magazine with trembling fingers. There, on the page with Suvarnin's photograph, was a streaming black title, "FILTH IN THE GALLERIES." Baranov blinked. Then he began to read. "Last week," Suvarnin had written, "the Counter-Revolution struck one of its most audacious blows at Russian Art. From the bestial brushes of one, Sergei Baranov, who has until now concealed his heretical infamies under bushels of rotten fruit, and who now feels that he can come out boldly and shamelessly in his true colors, we have received a nauseating sample of decadent, bourgeois 'art.' "

Baranov sat down, trying to get air into his aching lungs. Then he forced himself to read on. "In this gangrenous excrescence," Suvarnin continued, using what Baranov, even in his extremity, recognized as a pet phrase, "the dying world of Capitalism, allied with the Trotskyst bandits, has served notice on the Soviet Union that its minions and agents have wormed their way into the heart of the fatherland's cultural life. By what treachery and corruption the notorious Baranov managed to get his monstrosity hung on a gallery wall, we shall leave to the public prosecutor to discover. But while waiting for the reports on the investigation that will surely take place, we of the art world must join ranks to defend ourselves. We must not permit the insidious Baranov and others of his ilk, slavishly devoted to the fads and aberrations of their plutocratic masters, to desecrate our walls with these samples of dada-istic despair, reactionary cubism, retrogressive abstractionism,

431

surrealistic archaism, aristocratic individualism, religiostic mysticism, materialistic Fordism."

Baranov put the magazine down carefully. He did not have to read further. He had read it often enough before so that he could have recited the rest of the piece without glancing once more at the page. He sat on his stool, his world in ruins, staring unhappily at the six kilos of bright red cherries, arranged prettily in their wicker basket.

There was a knock on the door. Before he could say, "Come in," the door opened and Suvarnin came in. The critic went directly to the table and poured himself five fingers of vodka and drained it. Then he turned to Baranov, "I see," he said, gesturing toward the still-open magazine, "that you've read the piece."

"Yes," said Baranov hoarsely.

"Here," said Suvarnin, taking some manuscript pages out of his pocket. "You might be interested in reading what I wrote originally."

Baranov numbly took the sheets and stared at them. Suvarnin poured himself another drink while Baranov read through swimming eyes, " . . . a great new unfolding of talent . . . a courageous grappling with the problems of doubt and disillusionment which are the beginning of understanding . . . a blazing display of technical ability . . . a pioneering plunge into the depths of the modern psyche in paint . . ."

Baranov pushed the pages aside. "What . . . what happened?" he asked dimly.

"The Committee," Suvarnin said. "They saw your painting. Then they saw my review. They asked me to make certain changes," he said delicately. "That Klopoyev, the president of the committee, the one who has made eighty-four portrait heads of Stalin, he was especially anxious."

"What's going to happen to me now?"

Suvarnin shrugged. "Nothing good," he said. "As a friend, I advise you . . . leave the country." He went over and picked up the manuscript sheets of his first review. He tore them into small pieces, made a little pile of them on the floor and put a match to them. He watched until the flame had burnt itself out, then carefully scattered the ashes with his foot. He finished the vodka, drinking this time directly from the bottle, and went out.

Baranov did not dream that night. He was up all night listening to his wife.

She spoke vigorously from eight in the evening until eight the next morning, a full-length address in which every relevant topic was stated and developed with a balance and fullness which Edmund Burke, in another country and a more leisurely century, would have wholeheartedly admired. She had been notified that afternoon that their apartment was being taken over by a cellist with a cousin on the Central Committee and she had been removed from her position as head of the nursery system at five P.M. and relegated to the post of assistant dietician at a ward for backward and criminally inclined children in a penal camp some thirty kilometers outside Moscow. With these facts as a springboard and with her audience of one wanly rooted against the bedpillows, she ran through her eloquent twelve hours of recrimination without noticeably pausing for breath and without repeating herself.

"Ruined," she said clearly, with no sign of hoarseness, as the eight o'clock factory whistles sounded outside, "we are completely ruined. And for what? For an idiotic, senseless daub that no one can make head or tail of! A man wants to be a painter. All right! It is childish—but all right, I do not complain. A man wants to paint apples. Silly? All right. But apples can be understood. Apples do not have political implications. Apples do not turn into bombshells. But this . . . this naked witch . . . Why? Why have you done this to me? Why?"

Dumbly, Baranov leaned against the pillows, staring at his wife.

"Come," Anna called. "Come, you must have something to say. You can't sit without speaking forever. Say something. Say one word."

"Anna," Baranov said brokenly, "Anna . . . please . . . ." He hesitated. He wanted to say, "Anna, I love you," but he thought better of it.

"Well," Anna demanded. "Well?"

"Anna," Baranov said, "let us have hope. Maybe it will all blow over."

Anna glared at him coldly. "Nothing," she said, "nothing blows over in Moscow."

Then she got dressed and went out to the penal camp to report to her new job in the kitchen there.

Anna's prediction proved only too well founded. Attacks which made Suvarnin's article seem like an unrestrained paean of praise by comparison were loosed on him in newspapers and magazines all over the Soviet Union. *The New Masses*, in New York City, which had never before mentioned his name, printed, opposite a full page pen and ink drawing of Stalin by Klopoyev, a heated diatribe which called him, among other things, a "traitor to the working class of the world, a lecher after Western fleshpots, a Park Avenue sensationalist, a man who would be at home drawing cartoons for *The New Yorker*." In a follow-up article, a writer who later joined the Catholic Church and went to work for Metro-Goldwyn-Mayer preparing scenarios for a dog star used the Baranov case to point out that Michelangelo had been the first proponent of Socialist-realism. In Moscow, a painters' congress, led by the fiery Klopoyev, dropped Baranov from the Painters' Union by the customary vote of 578 to nothing. On one morning, between the hours of ten and twelve, every painting of Baranov's disappeared from every wall in Russia on which they had been hanging. Baranov's studio, which he had held for ten years, was taken from him and given to a man who drew signs for the Moscow subway. Two large plainclothesmen appeared and followed Baranov day and night for three months. His mail was always late and always opened. Anna Kronsky discovered a dictaphone under the sink in the kitchen in which she now worked. Old friends crossed over to the other side of the street when they spotted Baranov in the distance and he no longer found it possible to get tickets for the ballet or the theater. A woman he had never seen before claimed that he was the father of her illegitimate child and when the case came to trial he lost and was ordered to pay 90 rubles a week for her support and only barely avoided being sent to a work-camp.

Sensing which way the wind was blowing, Baranov put an old camel's hair brush and the goose-neck lamp into a bag, and haggard and thin, with Anna at his side, fled the country.

Six months later, in the summer of 1929, Baranov and Anna were established in Berlin. The climate of the German capital at that time was most propitious for artists, and Baranov, who had set to work industriously painting oranges, lemons, and apples, in his early edible style, enjoyed an immediate success. "We will be very happy here," Anna prophesied, correctly. "You will paint only fruits and vegetables. You will use dark colors very sparingly. You will avoid nudes and political implications. You will keep your mouth shut and permit me to do all the talking."

Baranov was only too happy to obey these simple and salutary injunctions. Aside from a certain vagueness of outline, a kind of subtle mist, which seemed to arise from the artist's subconscious hesitancy to come out too definitely on any subject, even the exact location of a lemon on a tablecloth, his work compared very favorably with the first canvases he had done when he returned from the Revolution. He prospered. His cheeks filled out and grew rosy again and he developed a little paunch. He took a small chalet for the summer in Bavaria and rented a superb studio near the Tiergarten. He learned to sit in rathskellers and drink Munich beer and say, with a hearty laugh, when politics was discussed, as it often was in those days, "Eh, who knows? That is for the philosophers."

When Suvarnin, who had slid from official suspicion to official ostracism in Moscow, as a result of his first, unpublished tribute to Baranov, appeared in Berlin, looking somewhat the worse for wear, Baranov generously took him in and let the critic live in the spare room under the studio, even managing a warm, reminiscent chuckle when Suvarnin told him that the green nude had the most conspicuous place in a new museum for decadent art in Leningrad.

Anna found herself a position as a physical-training instructress in one of the new organizations for young women that were springing up at the time and soon became noted for the vigor of her programs. She turned out battalions of iron-thewed females with enormous hips who could march eighteen hours a day through plowed country and who could, bare-handed, disarm strong men equipped with rifles and bayonets. When Hitler came to power, she was called into the government and given command of the entire women's training program for Prussia and Saxony. Much later, the Bureau of Statistics for the Women's Motherhood-and-National-Honor-Front put out a report disclosing that the graduates of Anna's classes led all other Germans in incidence of miscarriage and death in childbirth seven to one, but by that time, of course, the Baranovs had left the country.

Between 1933 and 1937, the life the Baranovs led was very much as it had been in the good days in Moscow. Baranov painted steadily, and his ripe fruit was hung on many famous walls, including, it was said, the Fuehrer's private gas-proof bomb shelter under the Chancellery, where it considerably brightened the otherwise rather austere atmosphere. Much in demand socially because of Anna's prominence and Baranov's good humor, the couple attended a constant round of parties, at which Anna, as usual, monopolized the conversation, holding forth at great length and with her famous clarity and sharpness on such matters as military tactics, steel production, diplomacy, and the upbringing of children.

It was during this period, friends later recalled, that Baranov seemed to grow more and more silent. At parties, he would stand near Anna, listening attentively, munching on grapes and almonds, answering questions with absent-minded monosyllables. He began to fall off in weight, too, and his eyes had the look about them of a man who slept poorly and had bad dreams. He began to paint at night, locking his door, pulling down the blinds, his studio lit by the functional glare of the goose-neck lamp.

It came as a complete surprise, both to Anna and the Baranovs' friends, when the green nude was discovered. Suvarnin, who had seen both the original and the Berlin canvas, has said that, if possible, the second was even better than the first, although the main figure was, in conception at least, almost identical in the two paintings. "The anguish," said Suvarnin, who at that time was employed by the government as a roving critic of official architecture, a post, he sensibly figured, in which errors of judgment could not be as spectacular and dangerous as those that might be made in the field of easel painting, "the anguish by now in the painting seemed intolerable. It was heroic, gigantic, god-size. Baranov had plunged to the sub-cellars of despair. [Perhaps it was because I knew of Baranov's nightmares, particularly the one in which he could not say a word in a roomful of conversing women, that I got so strong an impression that this was all humanity, locked in dumbness, protesting, wordlessly and hopelessly, against the tragic predicament of life.] I liked especially the nice new touch of the dwarf hermaphrodite nude, done in pink, being nosed in the left foreground by a brace of small dark brown animals."

It is doubtful that Baranov was rash enough to contemplate showing the painting publicly. (Whatever necessity drove him to re-creating his masterpiece was adequately served by its completion and his memories of the damage he had suffered in Moscow must have been too fresh to allow him to court disaster in Berlin by unveiling his work.) But the matter was taken out of his hands, by the Gestapo, who, in their routine weekly search of the homes and offices of all people who read foreign newspapers (a habit to which Baranov was foolishly addicted) came upon the green nude on the very day Baranov had finished it. The two detectives were simple fellows, but they were well-enough imbued with National Socialist culture to sense defection and heresy here. Arranging for reinforcements and throwing a cordon around the building, they called the chief of the bureau which dealt in these matters. One hour later, Baranov was under arrest and Anna had been removed from her post and sent to work as an assistant dietician in a home for unwed mothers near the Polish border. As was the case in Moscow, no one, not even a fire-eating Colonel in an SS Armored division with whom Anna had quite an intimate relationship, ever dared point out to Anna that her husband had not gone out of his home for his model.

Baranov was questioned by the Gestapo for one month. The questioning, more or less routine, during the course of which Baranov lost three teeth and was twice condemned to death, was aimed largely at getting Baranov to deliver over his lists of accomplices and fellow-conspirators and to confess to certain acts of sabotage in nearby airplane factories which had been committed in the past several months. While he was in the hands of the Gestapo, Baranov's painting was put on public view in a large exhibition arranged by the Propaganda Ministry to acquaint the population with the newest trends in decadent and un-German art. The exhibition was enormously successful and was attended by a hundred thousand more people than had ever witnessed a showing of paintings in Berlin until that time.

On the day that Baranov was released from jail, considerably stooped and doomed to eat soft foods for some months to come, the leading critic of the Berlin *Tageblatt* came out with the official judgment on the painting. Baranov bought a paper and read, "This is Judaeo-Anarchism at its most insolent peak. Egged on by Rome (there was a new addition in the background of the ruins of a village church), with the connivance of Wall Street and Hollywood, under orders from Moscow, this barbaric worm of a Baranov, né Goldfarb, has insinuated himself into the heartland of German culture in an attempt to bring discredit on our German health and our German institutions of justice. It is a pacifistic attack on our Army, Navy and Air Force, a vile Oriental slander of our glorious German women, a celebration of the lecherous so-called psychology of the Viennese ghetto, a noxious fume from the Paris sewers of the French degenerates, a sly argument from the British Foreign office for their bloodthirsty Imperialism. With our usual reticent dignity, we Germans of the German art world, we monitors of the proud and holy German soul, must band together and demand, in respectful, firm, reserved tones, that this gangrenous excrescence on our national life be expunged. Heil Hitler!"

That night, in bed with Anna, who had luckily managed to get a three-day leave to welcome her husband home, listening to what was now a standard twelve-hour lecture on his wife's part, Baranov looked back with something like fondness on the comparatively delicate phrasing of the *Tageblatt* critic.

The next morning he saw Suvarnin. Suvarnin noted that despite the physical ravages of the past month, his friend seemed to have regained some secure inner peace, some great lessening of the weight of an impalpable but soul-destroying burden. Also, despite the night of oratory he had just passed through and the thirty days of police handling, he seemed rested, as if he had been sleeping well recently.

"You shouldn't have done it," Suvarnin said with mild reproach.

"I know," said Baranov. "But I couldn't help it. It just came out."

"Do you want some advice?"

"Yes."

"Leave the country," Suvarnin said. "Fast."

But Anna, who liked Germany and was convinced that she could win her way up the ladder once more, refused. And it was inconceivable to Baranov that he go without her. But in the next three months, he was twice beaten up severely on the street by SA gangs and a man who lived three blocks away who resembled him slightly was kicked to death by five young men by mistake; all his paintings were collected and officially burned; he was accused by his janitor of homosexuality and was given a suspended sentence after a trial of four days; he was arrested and questioned for twenty-four hours when he was caught carrying a camera past the Chancellery on the way to a pawnshop and the camera was confiscated. All this would not have shaken Anna in her determination to remain in Germany, but when proceedings were put under way to have Baranov sterilized as a threat to the German bloodstream, she crossed the border with him into Switzerland in the middle of a snowstorm.

It took the Baranovs more than a year to get to America, but as Sergei walked down 57th Street in New York City, staring at the windows of the art galleries, in which the most extreme styles of painting, from lurid surrealism to sugary naturalism were peacefully on display, he felt that all his trials and troubles had been worthwhile because they had eventually brought him to this harbor. Gratefully and emotionally he made application within the first week for citizenship for Anna and himself. As further demonstration of his new-born allegiance he even took to watching the Giants play at the Polo Grounds, although it never became quite clear to him what, exactly, the players were doing around second base, and he patriotically developed a taste for Manhattan cocktails, which he rightly assumed to be the native drink.

The next few years were the happiest of the Baranovs' lives. Critics and patrons alike found that the soft-voiced Russian brought a mysterious European flavor, melancholy and classic, to homely American tomatoes and cucumbers, and his shows almost invariably sold out at good prices. A large wine company used Baranov grapes on all their labels and advertising and a large Baranov still life of a basket of oranges was bought by a California packing company and blown up into twenty-four sheets and plastered on billboards from one end of the country to the other. Baranov bought a small house in Jersey, not far from New York, and when Suvarnin turned up, having left Germany with a price on his head because he had been overheard, in his cups, saying that the German Army could not reach Moscow in three weeks, Baranov gladly invited the critic to live with them.

Heady with his new sense of freedom, Baranov even went so far as to paint a nude, very pink and firm-fleshed, from memory. But Anna, who by this time was attached to a nationally circulated news magazine as an authority on Communism and Fascism, was very firm in her handling of the situation. She ripped the painting to shreds with a breadknife and dismissed the robust, apple-cheeked Czech girl who did their cooking, although the girl went to the rather extreme length of having a reputable physician testify to her virginity in an attempt to retain her position.

Anna's success in America, where men have long been conditioned to listen to women, and where her particular brand of crisp, loquacious efficiency was regarded with stunned fascination by her male colleagues, was even more dazzling than any she had enjoyed in Europe. By the end of the war the magazine for which she worked had put her in charge of the departments of Political Interpretation, Medicine for Women, Fashion, Books, and, of course, Child Care. She even got a job for Suvarnin on the magazine, reviewing motion-pictures, a job he held until the autumn of '47, when he lost his eyesight.

Anna became a well-known figure in Washington, testifying at great length as a friendly witness before several important committees, discoursing on such varied subjects as the sending of subversive literature through the mails and the effect of sex education in the public school systems of several Northern states. She even had the exhilarating experience of having her girdle pinched in an elevator by a senior Senator from the West. As was inevitable, she was invited to countless dinners, receptions, congresses, and parties, and to all of them Baranov faithfully escorted her. In the beginning, living in the free atmosphere of literary and artistic America, Baranov had seemed to shed the taciturnity that had set in during the last part of his years in Moscow. He laughed frequently, he sang old Red Army songs without much urging, he insisted on mixing Manhattans at the homes of his friends, he spoke up on all subjects with disarming and agreeable gusto. But after a while he began to sink back into his old silences. Munching peanuts, occasionally muttering a monosyllable he would stand by Anna's side at parties, watching her closely, listening with strange concentration as she spoke out, clearly and fully, on the destiny of the Republican Party, trends in the theater, and the intricacies of the American Constitution. It was at this time, too, that Baranov began to have trouble sleeping. His weight fell off and he began to work at night.

Half-blind as he was, Suvarnin saw what was happening. Excitedly, he waited for the great day. In advance, he composed once more the stirring tribute to his friend's genius that he had first written so long ago in Moscow. Suvarnin was one of those writers who hates to see any word of his go unpublished and the fact that nearly twenty years had passed since he had been forced to jettison his appreciation only made him more eager to get it finally into print. Also, it was a great relief to write about painting again, after the long months of Betty Grable and Van Johnson.

On the morning that, Anna being in the city and the house quiet, Baranov came to him and said, "I would like you to come into my studio," Suvarnin found himself trembling. Stumbling a little, he hurried out of the house and followed Baranov across the driveway to the barn which had been converted into a studio. He peered through his darkening eyes for a long time at the enormous canvas. "This," he said humbly, "this is the great one. Here," he took out some manuscript papers from his pocket, "here, read what I have to say about it."

When he had finished reading his friend's eulogy, Baranov wiped a tear from his eye. Then he went over to Suvarnin and kissed him. There was no question this time about hiding the masterpiece. Baranov rolled it up carefully, put it in a case, and with Suvarnin at his side, drove in with it to his dealer. However, by silent agreement, he and Suvarnin tactfully refrained from telling Anna anything about the matter.

Two months later Sergei Baranov was the new hero of the world of art. His dealer had to put up velvet ropes to contain the crowds who came to see the green nude. Suvarnin's tribute now seemed pale and insubstantial in the torrent of adjectives poured out by the other critics. Picasso was mentioned in the same sentence as Baranov countless times and several writers brought up the name of El Greco. Bonwit Teller had six green nudes in their windows, wearing lizard shoes and draped with mink. A Baranov Grapes and Local Cheese, which the painter had sold in 1940 for two hundred dollars, brought fifty-six hundred dollars at an auction.

The Museum of Modern Art sent a man around to arrange about a retrospective show. The World Good Will Association, whose letterhead boasted the names of many dozen legislators and leaders of industry, requested it as the leading item in a show of American art which they proposed to send, at government expense, to fourteen European countries. Even Anna, to whom, as usual, no one dared mention the interesting resemblance of painter's wife and painter's model, seemed pleased, and for a whole evening allowed Baranov to speak without interrupting once.

At the opening of the show of American art, which was being revealed in New York preliminary to its trip overseas, Baranov was the center of attention. Photographers took his picture in all poses, toying with a Manhattan, munching on a smoked salmon canapé, talking to the wife of an Ambassador, looking up gravely at his masterpiece, surrounded by admirers. It was the crowning moment of his life and if he had been struck dead that midnight he would have expired happily. In fact, later on, looking back at that evening, from the vantage point of the events that followed, Baranov often bitterly wished that he *had* died that night.

For, one week later, on the floor of Congress, an economy-minded representative, enraged at what he called the irresponsible money-squandering proclivities of the Administration, which had put up good American dollars to send this sinister travesty on America to our late allies, demanded a thorough investigation of the entire enterprise. The lawmaker went on to describe the main exhibit, a green nude by a Russian foreigner, as sickening twaddle, Communist-inspired, an insult to American womanhood, a blow to White Supremacy, atheistic, psychological, un-American, sub-versive, Red-Fascistic, not the sort of thing he would like his fourteen-year-old daughter to see either alone or accompanied by her mother, decadent, likely to inspire scorn for the Republic of the United States in foreign breasts, calculated aid to Stalin in the cold war between America and the Soviet Union, a slap in the face to the heroes of the Berlin air lift, injurious to trade, an offense to our neighbors to the South, artistic gangsterism, a natural result of our letting down our immigration barriers, proof of the necessity of Federal censorship of the press, the radio, and the movies, and a calamitous consequence of the Wagner Labor Relations Act.

Other developments followed quickly. A conservative, mellow-voiced radio commentator, broadcasting from Washington, announced that he had warned the country over and over again that New Deal paternalism would finally spawn just such monstrosities and hinted darkly that the man responsible for the painting had entered the United States illegally, being put ashore from a submarine by night with a woman he alleged to be his wife.

Several newspaper chains took up the matter in both their editorial and news columns, sending their least civil employees down to the Baranov farm to question the culprit and reporting that a samovar stood in a place of honor in the Baranov living room and that the outside of the studio was painted red. One editor demanded to know why no cover from the *Saturday Evening Post* was included in the collection of paintings. Leaders of the American Legion filed a formal protest against sending the paintings in question over to the lands where our boys had fought so bravely so shortly before and pointing out that Baranov was not a veteran.

The House Committee on Un-American Activities served a subpoena on both Baranovs and put a tap on their telephone wires, hiring a man who knew Russian to monitor it. At the hearing, it was brought out that Baranov in 1917, 1918, and 1919 had served in the Red Army, and the Bureau of Immigration was publicly denounced for allowing such doubtful human material into the country. Ministers of all three religions circulated a petition calling upon the government to halt the shipment of the paintings to Europe, a place which all knew was badly shaken in the department of religious faith as it was. A well-known jurist was quoted as saying he was tired of modern art experts and that he could paint a better picture than the green nude with a bucket of barn paint and a paperhanger's brush. A psychiatrist, quoted in a national magazine, said that the painting in question had obviously been done by a man who felt rejected by his mother and who had unstable and violent tendencies which were bound to grow worse with the years. The FBI threw in a squad of investigators who conducted interviews with seventy-five friends of the Baranovs and discovered that the couple had subscriptions to the Book-of-the-Month Club, *House and Garden*, and the *Daily News*, and that they often spoke Russian in front of their servants.

A cross was burned on the Baranov lawn on a rainy evening, but even so, wind-blown sparks ignited a privy on a neighbor's property and reduced it to the ground. Irate, the neighbor fired a shotgun at the Baranovs' Siamese cat, nicking it twice in the rear.

The local Chamber of Commerce petitioned the Baranovs to move away, as they were giving the town a bad name, just at a time when they were trying to attract a plumbing factory to set up business there.

A Communist civil-liberties group held a mass meeting to raise funds for Baranov, who denounced them. They, in turn, denounced the Baranovs and demanded that they be deported to Russia.

The Treasury Department, attracted by the commotion, went over Baranov's last five income-tax returns and disallowed several items and sent in a bill for an additional eight hundred and twenty dollars. The Baranovs' citizenship papers were carefully scanned and it was revealed that Mrs. Baranov had lied about her age.

At a radio forum on the subject "What Should We Do with the Green Nude?" Baranov's name was hissed by the audience every time it was mentioned and the next day the postmaster in a small Massachusetts town announced that a mural of cranberry pickers and fishermen that Baranov had painted for the post-office in the days of the WPA would be torn down.

Anna Baranov, due to the unwelcome publicity given her, was deprived by her editor first of the Department of Political Interpretation, then of Medicine for Women, then of Books and Fashion, and finally, of Child Care, after which she was allowed to resign.

Baranov moved through all this in a dull haze, dreading more than anything else the long hours of mounting rhetoric which were loosed on him by his wife between midnight and eight each morning. Occasionally, huddled for disguise into the turned-up collar of his overcoat, he would go to the gallery where the disputed painting still hung, and would stare mournfully and puzzledly at it. When, one day, the director of the gallery took him aside, and told him, not unkindly, that in response to certain pressures, the authorities had decided to disband the show and not send it to Europe after all, he wept.

That night, he was sitting alone, slumped in a wooden chair in the middle of his cold studio. The blinds were drawn because of the habit the small boys of the neighborhood had developed of hurling rocks through the windows at any moving shadows they saw within. In Baranov's hand he held a small world atlas, opened to a map of the Caribbean and Central America, but he did not look at it.

The door opened and Suvarnin came in. He sat down without a word.

Finally, Baranov spoke, without looking at his friend. "I was at the gallery today," he said, his voice low and troubled. "I looked at the painting for a long time. Maybe it's my imagination," he said, "but I thought I noticed something."

"Yes?"

"Suddenly," Baranov said, "the painting reminded me of someone. I thought and thought who it could be. Just now I remembered. Suvarnin," he twisted anxiously in his chair to face the critic, "Suvarnin, have you ever noticed that there was any resemblance there to my wife, Anna?"

Suvarnin said nothing for a while. He closed his movie-destroyed eyes thoughtfully and rubbed his nose. "No," he said, finally. "Not the slightest."

Baranov smiled wanly. "Oh, what a relief," he said. "It would be a terrible shock to her." He spread the book on his knees and stared down at the small red and blue countries of the warm middle Atlantic. "Suvarnin," he said, "have you ever been to the Caribbean?"

"No," said Suvarnin.

"What sort of fruit," Baranov asked, peering at the map, "do you think a man could find to paint in Costa Rica?"

Suvarnin sighed and stood up. "I will go pack my things," he said heavily, and went out, leaving Baranov alone in the cold studio, staring at his brightly colored, repetitious map.

# The Climate of Insomnia

Cahill let himself into the silent house, softly closing the door behind him. He hung up his hat and coat, noticing the pleasant, frail smell of damp and night that came up from the cloth. Then he saw the note on the telephone table. It was scrawled in the maid's grave, childish handwriting, which always amused him a little when he saw it. "Mr. Reeves called," the message read. "He must talk to you. Very important, he says."

Cahill started to take up the phone under the mirror. Then he glanced at his watch. It was past one. Too late, he decided; it will have to wait till morning. He looked at himself in the dim glass, noting with satisfaction that his face was still thin and rather young-looking and that his eyes, despite the three drinks after the meeting that night, were not bloodshot. With dissatisfaction, he noted also that the gray was gaining over the black at his temples and that the lines under his eyes were now permanent. He sighed with agreeable melancholy, thinking gently: Older, older . . .

He put out the light and started upstairs. He was a large, bulky man, but he moved gracefully up the carpeted steps of his home. He touched the smooth wood of the banister, smelling the mixed but orderly aromas of living that the house breathed into the still darkness—the lemony fragrance of furniture polish, the autumnal dust of chrysanthemums from the living room, the hint of his wife's perfume, lingering here after the day's comings and goings.

He walked past the adjoining doors behind which slept his son and his daughter. He thought of the dark-haired, seventeen-year-old girl lying neatly in the quilted bed, the almost womanly mouth relaxed back into childishness by sleep. He brushed the door with his fingertips sentimentally. As he passed his son's door, he could hear a low, dreamy mumble, then, more clearly, Charlie's voice calling, "Intercept! Intercept!" Then the voice stopped. Cahill grinned, reflecting on what vigorous, simple dreams of green fields and sunny afternoons visited the sleep of his fifteen-year-old son.

445

Cahill, the miser, he thought, quietly going past the closed doors, counting his treasures at midnight.

He went into the bathroom and undressed there, so as not to wake his wife. After he had put on his pajamas and slippers, he stood for a moment in front of the medicine chest, debating whether or not to take the sedative for his stomach that Dr. Manners had prescribed for him on Tuesday. He patted his stomach thoughtfully. It bulged a little, as it had been doing for seven or eight years now, but it felt relaxed and healthy. The hell with it, he thought. I am going to break the Tyranny of the Pill.

Unmedicined, he put out the bathroom light and padded into the bedroom. He sat carefully on the edge of his bed and silently took off his slippers, moving with domestic caution, watching his wife, in the next bed. She did not stir. A little moonlight filtered in through the curtained windows and softly outlined the head against the pillows. She slept steadily, not moving even when Cahill inadvertently knocked against the base of the lamp on the bed table, making a resonant metallic noise. She looked young, pretty, defenseless in the obscure light, although Cahill noticed, with a grimace, that she had her hair up in curlers, leaving only a small bang loose in front as a sop to marital attractions. A woman must be awfully certain of her husband, he thought, to appear in bed night after night in those grim ringlets. He grinned to himself as he got under the covers, amused at his strong feelings on the subject.

As the warmth of the blankets slowly filled in around him, he stretched, enjoying the softness of the bed, his muscles luxuriously delivering him over to the long weariness of the day. The curtains, folded in moonlight, rustled gently at the windows. A fragile, tenuous sense of peace settled drowsily upon him. His son and his daughter slept youthfully and securely beyond the bedroom wall. His first class the next morning was not until ten o'clock. His wife confidently clamped her hair in ludicrous curls, knowing nothing could disturb her marriage. At the meeting, he had spoken quite well, and Professor Edwards, who was the head of the department, had come over afterward and approved of it. In the next morning's second class, Philosophy 12, there were three of the brightest young people in the college—two boys and a girl, and the girl was rather pretty, too—and they had all made it plain that they admired him enormously, and were constantly quoting him in the classes of other instructors. Cahill moved softly under the covers as the pleasant, half-formed images of contentment drifted

446

across his brain. Tomorrow, he thought, will be clear and warmer—that's what the paper says. I'll wear my new brown tweed suit.

Just before he dozed off, he thought of the message from Joe Reeves. Important, he thought a little irritably, important—now, what could that be? He twitched a little, uneasily, nearly coming back to wakefulness. Then, with the steady breathing of his wife sounding from the next bed, he dropped off to sleep.

The siren must have been wailing for some time before Cahill woke, because it entered harshly into his dream, and somehow he was back in London, in the cold billet, and the planes were overhead and the guns were going off, and he had the old feeling that neighbors were dying by chance in burning buildings on the street outside his window. He could feel himself moaning softly and shivering under the blankets and hoping he would be alive in the morning, and then he awoke.

He gazed blindly at the dark ceiling, feeling the cold, unreasonable sweat come out on his body. What is it? he thought. What is it? Then he realized that he was at home, in his own bed, and that the war was over. The noise of the siren howled down the quiet street outside—a police car going to investigate a burglary or pick up a drunk—echoing among the untouched homes, behind their undamaged lawns. He shook his head, irritated with himself for his nervousness. He looked across at his wife. She slept, unperturbed, her breath coming evenly, her arms primly down at her sides, her captured hair untossed on the pillow, happily beyond the reach of sirens and the memory of sirens.

He felt tremblingly awake. Every sound now reached him clearly and with individual significance: the wind troubling the curtains in a starched rhythm; the insubstantial creak of the stairs reacting to the obscure strain that years put upon old houses; the distant crashing of a truck's gears past a faraway street corner, attacking all insomniacs within a radius of a mile; the even intake and exhalation of his wife's breath, too mild to be called a snore but now as annoying as a suddenly loud clock, holding the hours of the night too strictly to account, reminding the would-be sleeper that every moment of wakefulness now would be answered by weariness tomorrow.

Cahill looked at the low radium gleam of the clock on the bed table. Four-thirty. He fell back onto his pillow heavily. Too late to take a sleeping pill. If he took a pill now, he'd be doped all day; he wouldn't have time to sleep it off. The ubiquitous problem of modern civilization, he thought: Is it too late for a pill? Too early? Which way will it be worse tomorrow? All over the country, sleepy, nervous hands reaching out for the clock, troubled heads calculating, It will wear off in six hours, but I have to get up in four. Sleep, he thought, the first great natural resource to be exhausted by modern man. The erosion of the nerves, not to be halted by any reclamation project, private or public.

He lay rigid in his bed, conscious now of various dull, unpleasant sensations in his body. His eyelids felt harsh and granular and seemed to scrape his eyeballs when he blinked. He was too warm, but a damp breeze from the window felt cold and uncomfortable on his forehead. The muscles of his right leg felt cramped, and he had a curious sensation that the tendon running up from his ankle had grown too short during the night. His stomach, just under the diaphragm, was moving in little spasms. He put his hand on the spot and felt the sick, erratic fluttering. He could taste the whiskey he had drunk, high and sour in his throat. That damned siren, he thought. I was feeling so well . . .

Then Cahill remembered the message. It must be something really pressing, he thought, for Joe Reeves to call like that. Cahill couldn't recall another occasion, in all the time he'd known Joe, when Joe had left that sort of a message for him. Early in his college career, Joe had decided to be urbane, debonair, off-hand, and his manner of treating all matters light-handedly and without urgency had become, if anything, more pronounced with the years. And there was nothing off-handed about leaving a disturbing note like that waiting for a man to pick up at one o'clock in the morning. After all, he saw Joe almost every day, at lunch. You'd think a man could wait until noon the next day. Unless it was a matter of the most drastic importance . . .

Cahill twisted restlessly in his bed, trying to keep his eyes closed, sullenly inviting sleep. I will think about this tomorrow, he thought. I will think about this tomorrow. But the restful emptiness of mind he sought evaded him. Unpleasantly, he remembered that Joe had good reason to call him. Subconsciously, he realized, he had been waiting for just such a message, and dreading it. For the twentieth time, he wondered if Joe had heard what he, Cahill, had said about him at the Faculty Club two weeks before. He had felt guilty about it ever since, and ashamed of himself. Even giving himself the excuse that he had drunk a little too much had not helped. In a discussion about teaching techniques, the subject of Joe's popularity with his classes had come up, and Cahill had said cruelly, ''Joe Reeves charms his classes into believing they're learning a great deal about economics when what they're really learning is how charming Joe Reeves can be.'' It was a stupid thing to say, even though it was partly true, and Lloyd and Evarts, who had been listening to him, had chuckled maliciously. Reeves had seemed rather cool for the last two weeks, and Cahill was almost certain that the remark had got back to him, as was almost inevitable in the narrow companionship of a college town. It was too bad. He and Joe Reeves had been close friends for over twenty years, and even though the relationship by now had more the form than the substance of the earlier friendship (how really remain friendly with any man after you are married?), it was silly to risk it for a light and mischievous judgment over a glass of whiskey. And it didn't even represent what Cahill really felt about Reeves. True, there was a superficiality about Reeves, especially in recent years, that came with his easy success with everyone—university presidents, faculty wives, students—but buried beneath that were the shrewdness, the good sense, the honorable instincts that had attracted Cahill to him in the first place. Jealousy, Cahill thought, ashamed of himself. How can a grown man give himself to it so easily? Probably, Cahill thought, Reeves had heard about the remark the very next morning and had mulled it over for the last two weeks, growing angrier and angrier, until this evening, when he had decided to have a showdown with Cahill about it. And Cahill couldn't deny having said it, or disguise in any way the envy and criticism that had called it forth, and that would be the end of the friendship. Joe, for all his easy assurance, was terribly touchy, vain, unforgiving. Cahill pondered on what it would be like not to be friendly with Joe. They had gone through college together, travelled through Europe together, lent each other money, books, opinions, neckties, celebrated together, mourned, exulted together. Even now, they and their wives had dinner together once or twice a week and made free of each other's homes in a carefully preserved informality that was pleasant, if not quite honest, and that kept alive for them a kind of gentle memory of their exciting younger days. And now, for a phrase, for a drop of wanton acid, to lose it all.

Cahill stared bitterly at the ceiling. The tongue, he thought, grows looser and more destructive with the years. Give a talkative man enough listeners and he will bring down stone with his indiscretions.

The curtains scraped in their humble starch at the windows, rasping across his consciousness. Of course, Cahill thought, it is possible that Joe did not hear what I said about him. The message could be about a dozen other things. What things? Joe was so intimately connected with his life, with the people and events of his past, with the problems and promises of the present, that the message might be concerned with his wife, his children, his job, his health, his finances, anything.

Edith moved a little in the next bed, sighing—a forlorn, sleep-bound, homeless, unremembered intake of breath—then settled back into that steady almost snore. Cahill looked over at her shadowed face. She slept, resting, secure, masked, giving no information, volunteering no help. Suddenly, he disliked and mistrusted her. Just to be so calmly and happily unconscious at a moment like this, when her husband lay awake, remorseful and torn by doubt, was a kind of willful absence, a tacit infidelity, a form of uncaring callousness.

Cahill considered his wife coldly. Her face looked surprisingly young. Twenty-eight, you might say—thirty. Frivolity, he thought, has preserved her youth. Age needed some assistance from thought and feeling to carve lines into a face, and in Edith's case age had had to work unaided. Still, she looked pretty, attractive, despite the net and curlers. Why was she so finickingly careful about the way she looked? Not for his sake, that was sure. Another man? How could anyone ever possibly know? Lectures in other towns took him away from home quite often. And then there were the whole long days that were hers to spend unquestioned. Maybe Joe had something to say on this subject—something that couldn't wait.

Unwillingly, Cahill remembered the evening, the week before, at the Crowells', when he'd gone out onto the darkened porch and come upon Joe and Edith sitting close to each other, both of them speaking in low, urgent whispers. They'd seemed embarrassed when they saw Cahill, and Edith had looked startled. And Joe's rather heavy standard joke about being caught in the act had not served to clear the air. Cahill had been troubled for a moment; then he had dismissed it from his mind. There could be a hundred reasons, all innocent, for Joe and Edith to be talking secretly together. They'd always been friendly, right from the beginning. They kissed each time they met, Cahill suddenly recalled. Why was that? He, Cahill, never kissed Joe's wife, except ceremonially, on New Year's Eve and birthdays. The whole modern world, Cahill thought with distaste, kisses too damned much. Sly, without innocence, full of subtle invitation and hidden implication, these public embraces of the married. And, considered coldly, Joe was ripe for experiment. He and his wife didn't get along at all well. She bored Joe; that was plain enough. He was impatient with her in discussions, and she often gave the impression that she had been crying before guests arrived. And she was one of those women who are always going off on long visits to their families, in the Midwest. No woman who had a happy married life remained that attached to her mother and father. And in those bachelorlike periods God knew what Joe did with himself. Also, Cahill remembered, Joe had not been spectacularly celibate in his youth, and in his speech, at least, gave no indication that he had reformed. Another thing: Edith, Cahill remembered, always laughed at Joe's jokes. Damaging, Cahill thought, very damaging. She laughed markedly seldom at his. Well, the truth was he wasn't terribly witty, and a woman might be expected to catch on in eighteen years of marriage. He mourned briefly over the fact that he was not witty, and mourned even more bitterly because now, at the age of forty, he realized it. When he was younger, he had had a higher opinion of himself. Edith had laughed at his jokes then, and so had other people, but now he knew that it was not wit so much as the good humor and vitality of youth that had created an air of cheerfulness about him. That was gone, there was no doubt about that, and it would be unseemly and embarrassing to pretend it wasn't. I must turn, as gracefully as possible, he thought, into a grave old man. Let people like Joe Reeves, who had the talent, say the bright things. He thought of Reeves, with his arched, actor's eyebrows and his dry, knowing delivery, at the center of things at parties, surrounded by eagerly listening, easily laughing people. Of course, Cahill thought bleakly, that's bound to be attractive to women. Also, Reeves wasn't fat. He had never exercised in all his life, but he was still as thin and straight and young-looking as ever. God has a vicious habit, Cahill thought, of putting all the gifts in one basket. Weighing the matter objectively, a woman would have to be crazy to prefer Cahill to Joe Reeves. Cahill thought of all the stories he'd heard, through the years, of good friends who had switched wives. And of the man he had met during the war who had arrived back from Europe to find his brother and his wife waiting for him on the dock with the brave, honorable, up-to-date news that they were in love with each other and wanted to marry, but not without his permission. What permission would he be able to give Joe Reeves and his sleeping wife, and what permission had they already given themselves?

Hating Edith, Cahill twitched under the rumpled covers and groaned softly. I should have taken the pill when I woke up, regardless of the time, he thought.

It might not be Edith, Cahill thought, violently keeping his eyes shut; it might be about the Mitchell girl. There was no doubt about it, he'd been a fool about that, and trouble waited there inevitably. Dora Mitchell had been in one of his classes the year before and had decided that she was in love with him. She was nineteen years old, with a dark, unstable look to her and a kind of solemn, uncertain beauty that Cahill thought most attractive. They had met several times out of class, by accident. (At least, Cahill had thought it was by accident until Dora had told him that she waited for him outside his classroom and on the steps of the library building.) And then, more times than he wished to remember, Cahill had met her in quiet bars and had taken her on drives to the country and to a small inn for tea, fifteen miles out of town. He had been flattered by her devotion, and some obscure, middle-aged hunger in him had fed on her youth and her ingenuous high estimate of him. He had known enough, of course, never to touch her. In fact, he had never even kissed her. But who, seeing them together in a clandestine corner of the Red Wheel Inn—the animated, unaccustomedly high-spirited man and the tall, adoring girl—would ever believe that? And he knew they'd been observed several times. And, besides that, Dora had once or twice wept and rather hysterically declared she could not go on this way and had even suggested, with the melodrama born of a hundred movies full of Other Women, that she have a heart-to-heart talk with Edith.

Cahill shuddered in his bed. It was all too possible that Dora had gone to Reeves, whom she knew, and unburdened herself to him, sobbing and overflowing with grandiose, youthful passion. Perhaps she had been to see Reeves that very night, and that's why Reeves had been so anxious to have Cahill call him. Tenderness, Cahill thought, the blind, many-edged weapon for the cutting down of fools. Bitterly, he made himself imagine what it would be like the day his own daughter, Elizabeth, herself only two years younger than Dora, found out (from a malicious sorority sister, a newspaper report, from a process server for divorce proceedings, from Dora herself over ice-cream sodas after a basketball game). Grotesque, he thought, for a few hours of gentle conversation, for an illusory, ephemeral buttressing of the vanity, for the titillating suggestion of sin without the sin itself, to risk so much! Maybe, he thought despairingly, I should go to a psychoanalyst; the urge for self-destruction has overcome me.

That, of course, was out of the question. He couldn't afford it. He could be as mad as Peter the Great, or as any lunatic screaming in a padded cell, and he couldn't pay the first bill of the rawest young practitioner, just past his initial reading of Freud and Jung.

452

Absolutely sane or raving like an ape in a tree, he would still have to conduct classes in Philosophy 22, Philosophy 12, Philosophy 53A, for Students in Pre-Educational Courses. Money. He thought about money and groaned again. Still three payments on the car. Elizabeth's tuition, due in two weeks. Butter, how many cents a pound? Roast beef once a week, eighty cents a pound, and Charles, his son, and Margaret, the maid, between them devoured four whole ribs each time. Insurance, he calculated in the darkness, in a well-remembered, dreadful nighttime litany, taxes, clothes, dentist, doctor, gifts to his wife's large family, amusement. Perhaps, he thought, Reeves had called him to tell him about promotion. God knew he was up for it, and Old Man Edwards was almost due to retire, and that would leave some room near the top. Reeves was very friendly with the president. Dinner there once a month. First names and private confidences. Reeves had been in to see the president that afternoon. Cahill knew because Lloyd, in his own department, who had all the gossip of the university at his fingertips, had told him so. Perhaps Reeves had been given the good word and wanted to pass it on. Cahill played luxuriously with the idea of promotion. Twelve, fifteen hundred more a year. No more Philosophy 53A, the dullest course in the curriculum. No eight-o'clock classes. Then the glow passed. Probably, he thought, it's the other way around. The president had never been any more than polite to him, and it was to be remembered that he had been passed over twice on the promotion lists, for Kennedy and O'Rourke, younger men than he. It wouldn't be too surprising, all things considered, if they had decided to get rid of him. He was far from being the most popular instructor on the campus. To be absolutely honest, he wouldn't blame them for firing him. Ever since he'd come back from the war, the job had bored him. Not that there was anything else that he particularly wanted to do. Just sit, perhaps, and stare into an open fire. Drink more whiskey than was good for him. Not pretend to anyone that he knew anything much, or not pretend he thought it was valuable that anyone learn anything much. Dangerous doctrine for professors, assistant professors, instructors, tutors. Probably others had caught on. Come to think of it, the last time he had seen the president at a faculty meeting, the president had been . . . frosty. That was the word—frosty. Purge by frost. Execution, university style. The polite death among the library shelves. He could almost hear Joe Reeves' troubled voice on the phone, warning him, trying to break it to him gently, trying to cheer him up with lies about other jobs, in other colleges.

Cahill lay in bed thinking about what it would be like not to have a job. Rent, taxes, roast beef, tuition, clothes. The advantage of marrying a rich wife. Nothing, finally, was crucial. There was always the net of fat relatives to fall back on, like a high-wire artist who slipped in the circus. Edith's father had worked for the Pennsylvania Railroad and had retired on a pension of a hundred and thirty-five dollars a month. Not much of a net there. Cahill thought of the rich wives he might have married. Rowena . . . Rowena what? Twenty years ago, in Chicago. Shipping. Father in Lake steamers. How could a man be expected to marry a girl named Rowena? Also, she had weighed a hundred and seventy pounds. No exaggeration. Maybe a hundred and eighty. Amorous as the gilded fly, too. Who wanted a wife like that, Lake steamers or no Lake steamers, especially at that weight? Anyway, that had been his one chance of marrying into wealth. Some people were lucky, of course. They met pretty girls, very nice, whose fathers controlled the Chase National Bank or owned mining empires in Central America. Still, if he had married Rowena—Rowena Grumman, that was it; good God, what a name—he wouldn't be trembling like this tonight. Seven hundred dollars in the bank, debts three fifty-five, and that was that. One month and then relief. For this relief, very little thanks. He supposed that nine-tenths of the people in the country walked, as he did, on this thin edge of disaster all their lives, smiling, dissembling, not sleeping some nights, hoping their nerve would hold out as they saw the edge crumbling, crumbling. And then the people in China, scouring sidewalks for lost grains of rice, running before the armies with two pans and a blanket on their backs, dying politely, with Oriental good manners, of starvation. Maybe Reeves ought to call them up, too. Perhaps he had an important message for the Chinese as well. Still, all the philosophical identification in the world would not help if the frost set in. Somehow, he thought regretfully, I should have arranged things better. Somewhere, I missed a chance, was too lazy, too stupid, too complacent.

Of course, Reeves might be calling him about something entirely different. Maybe Elizabeth. Reeves had a nephew, name of Richard, and he and Elizabeth had been seeing a good deal of each other recently. Fact was, last Saturday night Cahill had surprised them kissing at the door. Quite a shock. Item: What do you do when you see your seventeen-year-old daughter kissing the nephew of your best friend? Bringing up a daughter was a little like sitting over one of those dud bombs that had been dropped into cellars during the war. A year might go by, two years. Nothing might happen. Or, the world was full of women who had gone bad, and at one time they had all been seventeen and some father's dewy darling. Ministers' daughters, admirals' daughters, daughters of the leaders of society. How could any father know what obscure, shameful invitations of the flesh his daughter was accepting and succumbing to among the college pennants and dimity and framed photographs in the next room? And Elizabeth was no help. She had always been a secretive, self-willed child, going her own way, disdainful of help or advice, not lying, exactly, but never telling any more of the truth than she was forced to. He tried to think of her as someone else's daughter, in order to get an objective impression of her. Handsomely developed, prematurely womanly, he would have to say, with a promising, challenging look in her eye, a hidden, guarded sensuality, very much like her mother's. Oh, God, he thought torturedly, I hope the message isn't about her!

Or Reeves might want to talk to him about Charlie. Cahill considered the question of Charlie. In addition to eating an enormous amount of expensive roast beef when he got the chance, Charlie did very badly in his studies (was it possible that he was fundamentally stupid?) and got into trouble regularly with all authorities. A smooth-tongued truant, a brawler in schoolyards, a mischievous vandal in locker rooms, Charlie had been the occasion, again and again, for long visits of apology on the part of Cahill to parents of broken-nosed children, angry and insulted teachers, even, once, to the police station, when Charlie had broken into the country-club tennis shop and stolen a dozen cans of balls and two lengths of chrome twist. At what moment did the high-spirited schoolboy turn into the juvenile delinquent? Cahill thought of Charlie's sly, blond, unruly face. Consider your son objectively. What did you see? The insolence of the radio-and-comic-book age. The violence and irresponsibility of the double- and triple-featured generation of movie gangsters and movie sensualists. The restless superficiality of the book haters, who slid into whiskey, divorce courts, bankruptcy, worse, as the years wore on. Cahill had a vision of himself at the age of seventy, supporting his son, paying various blonde women alimony for him, bailing him out of magistrates' courts, and trying to hush up charges of drunken driving and cop-fighting. Tomorrow, he thought gloomily, I am going to have a serious talk with that young man. Though who knew what good it might do? John Dillinger's father probably had several talks with his son on the farm back in Indiana, and old Mr. Capone no doubt had the parish priest in to talk sternly to his dark-eyed boy in the crowded home in Brooklyn.

Cahill hoped that Reeves was not going to talk to him about Charlie when they finally met the next day.

The bed now seemed intolerably warm, and Cahill could feel the sweat collecting in the crease of his chest. He threw back the covers. They made a loud, electric crackle and static electricity from the friction jumped in strange blue flashes around him. Edith stirred a little at the noise but did not wake. Cahill glared gloomily at her, listening to her breathe. If she had been home, as she had said she was going to be, that evening, it would have been she who had talked to Reeves. He'd have given her some inkling of what it was he wanted to talk to Cahill about and he'd have been spared this agonizing night of conjecture. Tomorrow, Cahill thought, I'm going to damn well ask her a question or two, too. No, he thought, I'll be sly. If I seem to be quizzing her, she'll get suspicious or angry and sulk for days, and there'll be hell to pay around the house, and I'll have to give in to her on everything from now to Easter Sunday. I'll be nonchalant, elaborately offhand—pretend to be reading the paper, mix it up with questions about the kids, surprise her into revelations, if there are any. Then he was ashamed of himself for plotting this way against his wife, sleeping so trustfully and innocently in the next bed. He had an impulse to go over to her and hold her in his arms. He even sat up, tentatively. Then he thought better of it. Edith was terribly grouchy when he woke her in the middle of the night, and could be depended on to make him suffer for it the next day. He stared at her, resenting her. The business of the two beds, now. Until the war, they'd slept in one big old bed, as married people should. You felt really married, two people defending themselves as a unit against the world, if each night you retired into the warm fortress of the marital bed. Two beds brought with them the inevitable warning of division, oneness, loneliness, rejection. And when he'd come back from the war, Edith had said she couldn't sleep that way any more, she'd got too used to sleeping alone. And, like a fool, he'd consented. The two beds, with the extra mattresses and blankets, had cost nearly three hundred dollars, too. All his terminal-leave pay. Your bonus for fighting the war was that your wife made you sleep alone. Beds fit for heroes to sleep in—singularly.

It was silly to worry about that any more. It was a battle he'd lost, definitely, a long time ago. Each night to its own insomnia. Tonight, he thought—by now a little light-headed and oratorical,

456

even in his thoughts—we take up the problem of the message of Joseph Reeves.

The thing was to systematize it, attack the problem scientifically. Like *Time* magazine: Business, Politics, National Affairs, Science, Religion, Sex. Everything in its neat, crisp department. Two minutes with each one and you're ready with enough facts and opinions to carry you until the next publication date.

National Affairs. In the twentieth century, Reeves had said at lunch three days before, National Affairs had become a euphemism for butchery. Butchery accomplished, butchery in progress, butchery contemplated. Slaughter in three tenses, with a corresponding rise in the budget. In the last few months, Reeves had become more and more obsessed with the idea of war. At the same lunch, they'd had a gloomy conversation about the possibility that it would break out soon. Reeves, so optimistic about other things, sombrely dug around in newspapers and magazines to find new and disturbing items about the imminence of conflict and the dreadful new tools that might be employed. Cahill had even tried to avoid Reeves recently, because it was a subject he preferred not to reflect on. And his friend's dark flood of statistics about the range of atomic missiles and the mortal potential of biologic agents was not calculated to improve the delicate lunchtime appetite. Also, Reeves had made an unpleasant survey of the various and all too frequent occasions in history on which whole nations and, in fact, whole civilizations had committed suicide, deducing from that that it was entirely possible, and, indeed, probable, that in the next few years just such a widespread immolation would take place. To preserve his sanity, Cahill thought, resentfully trying to crowd Reeves' apocalyptic arguments out of his mind, a man must keep himself from speculating on these matters. Impotent and haunted, frozen in the slow, massive tide of events beyond his control, the night waker could only hope to ignore the question, or at least think about it in daylight, when the nerves were steadier. War, he thought angrily and helplessly, war. He remembered the cemeteries of Normandy and the sound shells made going over his head. At this moment, in a dozen places on the crust of the earth, machine guns were flicking and men were joyfully and devotedly putting other men to death and inviting the Americans, the Russians, the Berbers, the Malayans, the Yugoslavs, the Finns, and the Bulgars to join them.

Read a newspaper, listen to a news broadcast, wake for a quarter hour in your own bed some time before dawn, and death came familiarly to hand. When he'd come home in 1945, he'd thought all that was behind him. My limit, he always said—not seriously,

457

but meaning it, too—is one war. But other people, of more influence, seemed to have other limits. It was one thing, at the age of thirty-three, bravely to don the uniform and sail off to a relatively old-fashioned war, in which comprehensible weapons like machine guns and bombs were being used. It was quite another, seven years later, a sedentary forty, to contemplate exposing yourself to the atom and the microbe, feeling, too, all the while, that your well-run home, enclosing your wife and children, might at any moment dissolve in radioactive dust or become the harbor for the germs of plague. He looked over at his wife, comfortably at rest. How, he wondered, does anyone sleep this year?

The dim light of dawn was washing through the curtains now. God, Cahill thought, his hot eyes resentfully taking it in, I am going to be a wreck today. Masochistically, he continued with his list. Politics. There we have a subject, he reflected, to keep a man's eyes open a night or two. According to Lloyd again, after Reeves had visited the president's office that afternoon, he had been called into a secret session of the committee of state senators who were down from the capital investigating Communist influence on the campus. Lloyd, who had been active in several questionable organizations for years, and who didn't trust Reeves, had been none too happy about that. "A company man," Lloyd had said resentfully, in Cahill's presence. "He'd sell his best friend for a smile from the stockholders." Lloyd had peered meaningfully at Cahill when he said it, too, and Cahill was sure that the phrase "his best friend" had not been a random choice of words. Cahill thought of various things that Reeves might have told the committee and twitched uneasily. Back in the years before the war, when Communism was an almost respectable doctrine, Cahill had been on various committees with people he was sure belonged to the Party, and had let his name be used again and again on a flood of well-meaning petitions and statements that, if not promulgated by the Communists, certainly had their endorsement. Once, he and Reeves had even gone to a kind of polite, open Party meeting, at which several people he knew had made amorphous speeches about Communism's being twentieth-century Americanism, and stuff like that. He had even been invited to join, he remembered, although he couldn't remember who had actually come up to him and spoken the fateful words. He hadn't joined, and he'd never gone to another meeting, but what if the committee, armed with informers' information, demanded of him whether he had ever attended a meeting and if he had ever been asked to join. What would he do? Perjure himself, and say he had never gone, or tell the truth and leave himself open to the next question. Was Professor Kane there? Did Mr. Ryan, instructor in chemistry, make a speech about the working of the Communist Party? Will you kindly look over this list of names and check off the ones you can swear were present? What do you do in a situation like that? Professor Kane had been there and had made a speech, but Cahill knew that he had quietly resigned from the Party at the time of the Pact and had had no more to do with it. Still, who knew what Kane had told the committee? Kane was a friend of his, and needed the job. And if Cahill told the truth, Kane would be out of his job, disgraced, in a month. And poor Ryan. He'd been suspended on suspicion already, and his wife was sick, and he'd had to pay a lawyer to defend him. And, Communist or no, he'd always seemed to Cahill to be a very decent, shy, undangerous man. Cahill had given Ryan fifty dollars toward his defense, secretly, in cash. It was hard to understand just why. He was opposed to Ryan's politics, but he liked Ryan and felt sorry for him, and fifty dollars was not much, one way or another. Cahill had told Reeves about the fifty dollars and had even asked Reeves to help, too. Reeves, coldly, saying Ryan had it coming to him, had refused. What if Reeves had been trapped into saying something about the fifty dollars to the committee? What could Cahill tell them when he was questioned? How would he act? Would he be brave, considered, honorable? Just what was honorable in a situation like this? Was there honor in perjury? Or did honor lie in destroying your friends? Or destroying yourself? Did he actually believe that Ryan, for example, was an innocent, idealistic fellow, or did he believe that Ryan, the soft-voiced, scholarly, shyly smiling family man Ryan, was a potential traitor, a patient murderer, a dangerous conspirator against all the values that he, Cahill, held dear? I am too weary, Cahill thought pettishly, to decide this this morning. What if they asked about the meeting? What day was it? What year? Who invited you? The mists of memory shifted thickly around the fact. Whatever you answered was bound to be wrong. And if you said honestly, "I don't remember," how would that look on the record and in the newspapers? Like evasion, guilt, worthy only of disbelief and disdain.

So much for the crisp, neat two minutes of Politics. It was simpler in a magazine, where another issue was coming out in seven days, with another capsule of highly polished, anonymous, streamlined facts. A new man, Cahill thought, should be published every week, under a different title, anonymously. Each issue built around a different fact. The honorable man. The perjured man. The sensual man. The devout man. The economic man. Fifty-two times a year, something new and interesting in each copy. No irreconcilable facts to be found in any single volume. For Christmas, we plan to give you the friendly man, to be followed shortly by the betraying man, all in fine, unlimited editions. And, as a dividend to our subscribers, bound in blood, stitched with nerve ends, and illustrated by the leading artists of the age, with copious notes, the doubtful man, on which our editors have been working continuously for three hundred years at great personal expense.

There was a soft, sighing sound at the window, and Cahill saw that the wind had grown stronger and that it had begun to snow. A thin shower of snow sifted in through the open window, making a pale pattern on the floor. Fair and warmer, Cahill thought angrily, that's what the forecasters said. The liars of science, portentously surrounded by inaccurate instruments, confidently deluding you with false visions of the future. Like Dr. Manners, armed with stethoscope and X-ray, patting him heartily on the back last Tuesday, telling him of course he occasionally must expect to feel a twinge here, a pain there; he was not as young as he used to be. How many men died on Sunday who had been told during the week by their doctors that they were not as young as they used to be? The breezy assumption on the part of the medical profession that agony was the ordinary condition of life. Manners, he thought resentfully, would be considerably less breezy with himself if it were his chest that trembled to the tone of pain, secret and until now distant, but there, warning, definite. Experimentally, Cahill lifted his left arm and stretched it. Again, as always in the last few months, there was the small answering pressure, dull, lurking, cross his chest, across his heart. "A slight irregularity," Manners had said. "Just nerves. Nothing to worry about." Nothing for Manners to worry about, perhaps. And the constriction across the stomach; that, too, according to Manners, was nerves. Nerves, the modern equivalent for Fate, the substitute for the medieval Devil, which attacked mankind in the form of obscure, and often mortal, ills. Nerves, the perfect formula for the lazy diagnostician. Or—and Cahill could feel his breath catching in his throat at the thought—perhaps Manners, out of kindness, was hiding the true information from him. A hearty clap on the back, an innocuous prescription for sugar water and belladonna, and, after the door had closed, a thoughtful, sorrowful shrug, and the fateful entry in the case history of Philip Cahill "Prognosis negative."

Cahill put the palm of his hand under his pajama jacket, on the warm skin of his abdomen, as though by the touch of flesh on flesh he might discover the dreadful secret that lay there. Within him, under his hand, he could feel a faint, erratic quivering. Not good, he thought, not good at all. His mind touched regretfully on the edge of the word he was afraid to say. The papers were so damned full of it, the posters on the buses, even the radio. And if it occurred in the stomach, it was fatal at least eighty per cent of the time, and you almost never found out about it before it was too late. Maybe that was what Reeves had called about. Maybe Manners had gone to Reeves and explained to him and asked what Reeves thought should be done. The services that friends had to do for each other. You start out as gay children, playing tennis with each other, racing each other across the lakes of summer, roaring jubilantly together on your first drunks, and twenty years later, all that far in the past, you have to go in and announce to your friend that his death is at hand.

Ridiculous, Cahill thought. I'm not going to lie here any longer. He got out of bed and stood up. His legs felt weary and uncertain, and there was the tense, stretched sensation in his stomach as he put on his robe and slippers. He looked over at Edith. She still slept, the rhythm of her breathing unchanged. Walking slowly, his slippers shuffling across the rug, he went silently out of the bedroom. He descended the stairs, holding the banister, shivering a little in the night-frozen house. In the hall below, he went over to the telephone, on the table under the mirror. He hesitated, staring at the phone. The clock in the living room said ten minutes to seven. He picked up the phone and dialed Joe Reeves' number. While he listened to the long succession of buzzes in the receiver, he stared at himself in the mirror. His face was haggard, his eyes thick and glazed and encircled completely by muddy blue shadows. His rumpled hair looked slack and lustreless, his face exhausted and—hunted. He looked for a moment, then turned his back on the mirror.

Finally, there was the sound of someone picking up the receiver at the other end. Whoever it was fumbled a long time with the instrument, and Cahill said impatiently, "Hello! Hello!" Then he heard a sleepy, dark voice mumbling irritatedly, "Mr. Reeves' residence. Who that calling?"

"Hello," Cahill said eagerly. "Violet?"

"Yes. This Violet. Who calling?"

"Violet," Cahill said, making his voice even and clear, because he remembered with what suspicion Violet regarded the telephone, "this is Mr. Cahill."

"Who?"

"Cahill. Mr. Cahill."

"It's an awful early hour of the mawnin', Mr. Cahill," Violet said aggrievedly.

"I know," Cahill said, "but Mr. Reeves has a message for me. He especially asked me to call him as soon as I could. Is he up yet?"

"I dunno, Mr. Cahill," said Violet. He could hear her yawn enormously at the other end of the wire. "He's not here."

"What's that?"

"He's gone. Went last night. He and Mis' Reeves. They gone for the weekend. I'm the only livin' soul in the house. And"— her voice took on a tone of impatient complaint—"I'm freezin' here in my night shirt in this drafty old hall."

Cahill could sense that Violet was on the verge of hurling the receiver down on the hook—an amusing trick of hers, with which she concluded telephone conversations in mid-message. It was not amusing now. "Violet," he said urgently, "don't hang up. Where did they go?"

"Don't ask me," Violet said. "They didn't tell me. You know Mr. Reeves. He was sittin' around the house last night, real restless, like he is, and all of a sudden he jumped up and said to Mis' Reeves, 'Let's get into the car and get away from here for a couple of days.' They just packed one little bag. Mis' Reeves was wearing slacks and she didn't even bother to change 'em, They just gone for a ride, I guess. They'll be back by Monday, never you worry."

Slowly, Cahill put the receiver down. He looked up and saw that Elizabeth was standing at the foot of the stairs, in an almost transparent nightgown, her bathrobe carelessly open and hanging loose from her shoulders. Her dark hair was down, flowing thickly around her throat. Her face was creamy with sleep and her eyes were half closed in an amused, almost condescending smile. "Daddy," she said, "who on earth are you calling at this fantastic hour? One of your other girls?"

Cahill stared dully at her. Through the frail rayon of her nightdress, he could see, very plainly, the swell of her breasts, rising generously from the exposed, rich skin of her bare bosom. "None of your business," he said harshly. "Now go upstairs. And when you come down again, make sure you're decently covered! This is your home. It is not a burlesque house! Is that clear?"

He could see the incredulous, hurt grimace gripping her features, and then the blush, rising from her bosom, flaming on her cheeks. "Yes," she said faintly. "Yes, Daddy." She turned, hugging her robe around her ashamedly. Cahill watched her walk slowly and painfully up the stairs. He wanted to say something, call her back, but by now he knew there was nothing to say and that the child would not come back.

He went into the living room and sank into a chair, feeling cold. Wildly, he contemplated the thought of living until Monday.

# Goldilocks at Graveside

She was surprised to see him in the church. She hadn't known he was in Los Angeles. And there had only been the one notice in the one newspaper—"Ex-State Dept. Officer Dies. William MacPherson Bryant died last night at the Santa Monica Hospital, after a long illness. Entering the foreign service in 1935, he held posts in Washington, Geneva, Italy, Brazil and Spain, before resigning for reasons of health in 1952. The couple were childless and he is survived only by his widow, who, under her maiden name, Victoria Simmons, is the editress of the Women's Page of this newspaper."

The church was almost empty, as Bryant had made no friends since they moved West, and there was just a scattering of people from the paper, who came as a matter of courtesy to the widow, so Victoria saw Borden almost immediately. It was a dark, rainy day, and he was sitting alone, in the rear of the church, near the door, but his blond head was unmistakable. Irrelevantly, while paying only half-attention to what the minister was saying, Victoria remembered the secret nickname by which, among the three of them, Borden had been called—Goldilocks.

There were only two cars in the cortege to the cemetery, but Borden found room in the second car and stood bareheaded in the rain during the ceremony at the grave. Victoria observed that he was now dyeing his hair and that, although at a distance there was still an appearance of boyish good looks about him, up close his face was lined by fine wrinkles and seemed dusted over by uncertainty and fatigue.

As she walked away from the grave, an erect, veiled, middle-aged, slender woman, tearless behind the black cloth, Borden asked her if he could drive back with her. Since she had come out to the cemetery with only the minister and there was plenty of room, she said yes. Borden's voice had changed, too. Like his

464

dyed hair, it pretended to a youthfulness and energy that she remembered and that was no longer there.

The minister was silent most of the way back to town. Victoria had only met him for the first time the day before, when she was making the arrangements for the funeral. Neither she nor her husband had been members of the congregation and the minister had that slightly aggrieved expression that one remarks on the faces of the representatives of religion when they know they are only being used out of necessity and not out of faith.

Among the three of them they spoke no more than thirty words on the way back into town. The minister got off at the church and after his embarrassed little handshake, Borden asked Victoria if he could accompany her home. She was in perfect control of herself—all her tears had been shed years before—and she told him she didn't need any help. In fact, she had planned to sit down directly at her desk when she got home and start working on the full page for the Sunday issue, both because it needed doing and as a remedy against melancholy. But Borden persisted, with the same light good manners and concern for the welfare of others that had made him so popular in the years of their friendship.

With the minister gone, Victoria asked for a cigarette. She threw back her veil as Borden offered her a cigarette from a flat gold case and lighted both hers and his own with a flat gold lighter. There was something a little displeasing to Victoria in the action of his hands. She would have been hard put to explain why. They seemed, for lack of a better word, *exaggerated*.

They drove in silence for a minute or two. "Was he happy," Borden asked, "those last few years?"

"No," she said.

"What a waste," Borden sighed. The sigh, she was sure, was not only for her husband. "He was an able man, an able man." The tone was pompous. For that moment he might have been a politician making a speech at the dedication of a statue, much delayed, to the dead of a half-forgotten war.

"What did he do after he retired?" Borden asked.

"He read," she said.

"Read?" Borden sounded puzzled. "Is that all?"

"Yes. My job on the paper supported us well enough."

"I didn't know you were any kind of writer," Borden said.

"Necessity," she said. "I used to get A's in English courses in college." They both smiled.

"Is Clare here with you?" Victoria asked.

465

Borden looked at Victoria strangely, as though he suspected her of sarcasm. "Didn't you hear?"

"Hear what?"

"We were divorced six years ago. She married an Italian. He owns race horses. She won't come to America."

"I'm sorry," she said.

He shrugged. "It wasn't much of a marriage." His voice was flat and careless. "We put on a good show for a few years, while it still did any good. After that—*Adieu, Chérie.* . . ."

"What are you doing out here?" Victoria asked.

"Well," he said, "after the debacle, Clare and I wandered around Europe for a while, but it never was the same. The jobs I might have had I didn't want and we had enough money so that I didn't *have* to work—and there was always that little whispering when we came into a room. Maybe we only imagined it, but . . ."

"You didn't imagine it," Victoria said.

They drove in silence for a while. Then he asked her for her telephone number and wrote it down, with exaggeratedly neat little strokes of a small gold pencil in a handsome leather notebook.

"When you feel like," he said, "please call me and we can have dinner." He gave her his card. "Borden Staines," it read. "Bottega del Mezzogiorno—Styles for Men."

"I'm there every day," he said, "after eleven o'clock."

She had passed the shop many times. The name on the window had always struck her as pretentious and foolish. After all, in English, it only meant "The South Shop." The place was elegant, expensive, and displayed gaudy shirts and ties and Italian sweaters and things like that, all a little too showy for her taste. She had never gone in.

"I bought it five years ago," Borden said. "I decided I had to do *something*." He smiled a little apologetically. "It's amazing how well it's done. I must say it never occurred to me that I would wind up as a Beverly Hills haberdasher. Anyway, it keeps me busy."

The car stopped in front of the apartment house in which Victoria lived. It was still raining, but Borden hurried out to open the door for her and sent the driver on his way, saying that he preferred to walk a bit. "You're sure you don't mind being alone?" he said. "You know, I'd be delighted to come up and . . ."

"Thank you, no," she said.

"Well . . ." he said, uncertainly, "I felt I just had to come. After all, we had so many good times together, all of us . . ." His voice trailed off.

"It was very good of you to come, Borden," she said.

"I have a confession to make," Borden said. He looked uneasily around him, as though fearful of being overheard. "I did see you that afternoon, Vicky. When you smiled and I turned away. I've always felt foolish about it and guilty and I . . ."

"What afternoon?" Victoria said. She turned and opened the lobby door.

"You don't remember. . . ?" He stared at her, his eyes suspicious and searching.

"What afternoon, Borden?" she repeated, standing with her hand on the doorknob.

"I guess I was mistaken," he said. "It isn't important." He smiled at her, with his almost-perfect imitation of boyishness, and kissed her lightly on the cheek, good-bye now, probably good-bye forever, and walked off, very trim and young-looking in his smart raincoat, with his blond hair glistening with rain.

She went upstairs and unlocked the door. She threw off her hat and veil and walked aimlessly around the empty apartment. The apartment was nondescript. Nobody ever comes here, the apartment said, this is merely a place where two people once took shelter. Temporarily. Reduced now. To one.

Without emotion, Victoria looked at a photograph of her husband in a silver frame. It had been taken more than ten years ago. It was a sober portrait, posed carefully in a studio, and her husband looked serious and responsible, the sort of man who gets elected, young, to the board of trustees of the university from which he was graduated. You could not imagine his ever wearing any of the clothes displayed in the window of a California shop called "Bottega del Mezzogiorno."

There was work laid out all over the desk, but she couldn't get herself to sit down and finish it. The meeting with Borden had started too many memories. It was so unexpected that it had unsettled her in a way that her husband's death, long awaited, had not.

She went to the closet where she kept her files and pulled down a carton. The carton had "1953" written in large numerals on its label. She leafed through the pages until she came upon what she was looking for. It was a folder, neatly held together by clasps, with about twenty-five typewritten pages in it.

She sat down in a chair near the window, which was still streaming with rain, and put on her glasses and started to read. It was the first time in at least ten years that she had even glanced at the folder.

"From the Desert," she read. "A short story by V. Simmons."

467

She made a little grimace and reached over and picked up a pencil and blacked out the V. Simmons. Then she settled back and started to read.

Naturally, *she read*, I am not going to sign my real name to this. If the reader persists to the end, the reason will be plain to him.

If I am ever successful in the attempt to become a writer, it will be quite easy for me to keep my identity hidden. I have never written anything before and in all the years since I have been married, I have put down in answer to all questionnaires and official requests, *Occupation: Housewife*. I am still making beds and cooking three meals a day and going into town twice a week to do the shopping and we have no neighbors and we have made no friends who might see the typewriter on my desk or the ream of cheap paper which I was sensible enough to buy in C—, the large city which is fifty miles away from where we live. I have taken the precaution, also, of renting a postal box in the same city under the pseudonym which I intend to use and all communications from publishers and editors will be delivered to me there. When I have to send any of the things I plan to write through the mails, I shall make the trip to the city and mail the manuscripts in an ordinary envelope at a time when the traffic in the post office is at its peak and a rather plain, modestly dressed, middle-aged woman standing momentarily before the outgoing slot in the wall can most probably pass unnoticed.

All these measures must seem rather excessive to the reader, but until recently my husband and I have been leading our lives in an atmosphere of surveillance, of rumors of hidden microphones, intercepted mail and confidential reports of private conversations with friends. While I am sure the rumors were more lurid than the facts, there was never any means of discovering just how lurid they were and I have become accustomed to a permanent quiver of uneasiness. Even living as we do now, on the bare face of the desert, with no servants and not another house in sight, and no telephone for the curious, the malicious, or the inquiring to listen in on, I cannot rid myself of the posture of suspicion.

Our habit of isolation has been accepted on strange terms in the town in which I do our shopping. My husband never goes into town and the people of the town know, of course, that we receive no visitors. Somehow, the shopkeepers, and the postmistress, who are my only points of contact with the town, have decided that my husband is suffering from consumption and has come here to take advantage of the dryness of the climate and the tranquillity of the desert. Naturally, we have said nothing to disabuse them. John, my husband (that is not his real name, of course), was never well known enough to have his name in the newspapers, and the events leading to his retirement were handled, largely by luck, with circumspection.

My decision to try to write came slowly and from a variety of reasons. I found myself with a great deal of time on my hands, as the work of the house, which is a small and simple one, can be done in three or four hours a day. Since his arrival here, my husband has become less and less communicative and spends the greater part of his time reading in a corner of the patio, protected by the wall from the wind, or staring, for hours on end, at the mountains which rim our desert to the north and east. The question of money will begin to be of importance within the next year and I have reached the conclusion that my husband, at the age of forty-five, will never work again.

When we first came here, I supposed that our retreat was only to be temporary, while my husband came to terms with his defeat and gathered his forces for an effort in a new direction. In the beginning he sent out several letters a week to old friends and acquaintances with the suggestion that, after a prolonged vacation of perhaps six months, he would be ready to work again. He understood that in the field of public service his usefulness was probably at an end, at least in the foreseeable future, but he felt that a man of his education and experience, especially abroad, could be of considerable value in a variety of private enterprises. The tone and quality of the responses to his letters, especially from men who had been his friends since his college days, proved disillusioning, although in this instance, as always, he showed nothing, on the surface, of his disappointment. For three months now he has not written a letter to anyone.

My husband has never told me that he has given up hope but I know him too well to require direct statements from him. I spy on him. I read his letters. I covertly watch his expression every moment I am with him. When we eat a new dish I scan his face minutely for signs of approval. When we still had friends I could tell, almost to the second, when a friendship was beginning to bore him, and I would take steps immediately to bring the relationship painlessly to an end. In matters that are secret between a man and wife and which, as a writer, despite the present style, I do not intend to discuss, I have made myself a connoisseur of his pleasure. When he reads a book, I read it immediately after. I am a dossier of his likes and dislikes, his moods, his satisfactions. I do not do all this out of jealousy or a sick, female love of possession, I do it so that at all times I can amuse and interest him and I do it for him and not for myself and I do it out of gratitude.

My husband is an extraordinary man, with an appearance that is studiedly ordinary. He wears the correct, unobtrusive clothes of his caste and he has his hair cut short and brushed straight back, although he has a long, bony face and a bold nose and the shortness of hair above it makes the proportions somehow unpleasing. Once, when he and I spent a vacation alone on an island in the Caribbean, he permitted his hair to grow and he developed a full, thick black moustache. Suddenly, his face assumed its proper proportions and character. With the deep tan that he acquired on the beach and on a small sailing vessel that we rented, he looked like the photographs of the young men, dedicated and spirited, who go on expeditions to climb the Himalayas. But when the time came to return to his post, he shaved the moustache and clipped his hair, so that his face assumed once more the unremarkable expression and not quite harmonious proportions behind which he protects himself.

His manner, like his appearance, is designed, too, for disguise rather than display. He is a snob who is unfailingly polite to his inferiors and carefully disinterested in the presence of people whom he admires. He is subject to fierce and sudden tempers which he controls, with an exhausting expense of will, by forcing himself, at the moment when he is under the greatest stress, to speak slightly more slowly and with a hesitant and lowered voice. He is perfectly confident of his intelligence and has a deep contempt for the powers of most of the men with whom he has had to work, but he has spent endless hours listening to their ramblings and pretending to take their proposals into consideration. He is a man tortured by ambition without limit and he has unfailingly refrained from using all the hundred expedients by which his less gifted colleagues have won advancement. Racked, as I know, by passion, he has hardly even reached for my hand in public or allowed himself even the most casual expression of interest in the presence of the beautiful women who frequented the society in which we moved for so long a time. Avid for the touch of destiny, he has not moved a step in its direction.

This is the man who sits now day after day, reading in the silent desert sunlight, wearing, even here, the neat collar and tie and gray jacket of his working days, protected by the patio wall from the constant wind.

If he wishes to remain here, alone with me, for the rest of his life, I am content. Since, situated as we are, there is no other way to earn money, and both our families having long since succumbed into the economic morass so that there is no help to be hoped for from them, I have taken to the typewriter. We do not need much to keep us going in this remote place and while I have had no experience in the field of letters I am encouraged by the dismal quality of the writing which is published daily in this country. Certainly, a person of education, and one who has been close to the center of important affairs, as I have for nearly twenty years, should, with such pitiful standards to meet, be able to sustain a modest existence on almost the barest level of literacy.

I admit that I look forward to the experience with pleasure. I am a plain and vindictive woman who has had to remain silent in the company of fools and self-seekers for a long time and in the process of paying them off, I feel there should be profit both for me and whatever readers I may attract who have not been irremediably numbed by the floods of sentimentality, violence and hypocrisy which pour forth from our presses.

Writers of the first class, I have read somewhere, are invariably men or women with an obsession. While I do not deceive myself about my merits or the grandeur of the heights I might ultimately reach, I share that one thing with them. I have an obsession. That obsession is my husband and it is of him that I shall write.

My husband came of a family that, in another country or other times, might fairly be called aristocratic. The family fortune held out long enough so that he went to the proper schools and was graduated from the proper college, in the same class with a surprising number of men who have since done extremely well in business and in the government. Unsympathetic to commerce and springing from a family which has a long tradition of public office, my husband applied for the Foreign Service. This was at a time when the other departments of the government were being thrown open to hordes of noisy and unpleasant careerists, of doubtful origin, painful manners, and the most imperfect education. The Service, because of its rigid system of selection and its frank prejudice in favor of intellectual and conservative young men of good family, was the one enclave in a welter of shallow egalitarianism in which a gentleman might serve his country without compromise.

My husband, who never spared himself when there was a question of work, was given one good post after another. He was never popular, but he was always respected and at the time he married me, four years after his first appointment, we both could reasonably suppose that in time he would rise to the most important positions in the Service. During the war he was given a mission of the utmost danger and delicacy, and performed it so well that he was told, personally, by the Secretary, that he was responsible for saving the lives of a considerable number of Americans.

Just after the war, he was appointed to the Embassy at X—. (Forgive me for these old-fashioned symbols. At this moment in our country's history candor is foolhardy, reprisals devastating.) I did not accompany my husband to X—. It was at that time that I found it necessary to undergo an operation which turned out to be not so simple as my doctor had hoped. A second operation was considered advisable, complications developed, and it was six months before I could join my husband. In those six months of living alone in a turbulent city, my husband became involved with the two people who, it turned out, were to destroy him. The first was Munder (the name, like all others I shall use, is an invention, of course), who at that time was making a brilliant record for himself as first secretary of the embassy. John and he had been friendly at college and the friendship was renewed and strengthened in the embassy, helped in great part by their recognition in each other of similar ambitions, equal devotion to their jobs, and complementary temperaments. The ambassador at that time was an amiable and lazy man who was pleased to turn over the real work of the embassy to his subordinates, and between them, Munder and my husband were, in an appreciable degree, responsible for the carrying-out of directives from Washington and the formulation of local policy. It was at that period that the Communists were profiting most, throughout Europe, from the post-armistice confusions, and the success of the Embassy at X—in tactfully shoring up a government favorable to the interests of the United States was in no small measure due to the efforts of Munder and my husband. In fact, it was because of this that some time later Munder was recalled to Washington, where he played, for several years, a leading part in the formulation of policy. His prominence, as it so often does, finally resulted in his downfall. When the time came to offer up a sacrifice to the exasperation and disappointments of the electorate, Munder, because of his earlier distinction, was treated in such a manner that he decided to resign. While they did not understand it at the time, his friends and aides in the Service were also marked for eventual degradation, or, what is almost as bad, stagnation in humiliatingly unimportant posts.

The other person my husband became involved with was a woman. She was the wife of a diplomat from another country, a distinguished idiot who foolishly permitted himself to be sent off on distant missions for months at a time. She was that most dangerous of combinations—beautiful, talkative, and sentimental; and it was only a question of time before she blundered into a scandal. It was my husband's misfortune that her luck ran out during his tenure as her lover. As it later turned out, it might just as well have been any one of three or four other gentlemen, all within the diplomatic community, which the lady favored exclusively for her activities.

I knew, of course, almost from the beginning, although I was four thousand miles away, of what was going on. Friends, as they always do, saw to that. I will not pretend that I was either happy with the news or surprised by it. In marriages like mine, in which the partners are separated for months on end and the woman is, like me, rather drab and no longer young, it would take a fool to expect perfect fidelity from a passionate and attractive man. I do not know of a single marriage within the circle of my friends and acquaintants which has not required, at one point or another, a painful act of forgiveness on the part of one or both of the partners, to ensure the survival of the marriage. I had no intention of allowing the central foundations of my life to be laid in ruins for the fleeting pleasure of recrimination or to satisfy the busy hypocrisy of my friends. I did not hurry my convalescence, confident that when I appeared on the scene a workable *modus vivendi* would gradually be achieved.

Unhappily, when my husband told the lady of my impending arrival and announced to her that that would mean the end of their relationship, she made one of those half-hearted attempts at suicide with which silly and frivolous women try to prove to themselves and their lovers that they are not silly and frivolous. The lady telephoned my husband just after she took the pills, and was unconscious, in negligee, in her apartment, when he arrived. He did what was necessary and stayed with her at the hospital until he was assured by the doctors that she was out of danger. Luckily, the people at the hospital were civilized and sympathetic, and my husband managed, with a minimum of bribery, to keep the entire matter out of the newspapers. There was a wave of rumor, of course, in certain circles of the city, and there was no doubt a quite accurate estimate of the situation current for a week or two; but in Europe present scandal blends easily into centuries of anecdote, and when the lady appeared two weeks later, looking as pretty as ever, on her husband's arm at a diplomatic reception, the event seemed safely in the past.

My husband recounted the entire story to me on the first afternoon after my arrival. I listened and told him I would say no more about

473

it and we have not mentioned the matter again to this day. I think I can honestly say that I have not permitted the incident to change, in the smallest particular, our relations with each other.

It is at this point in my story that I begin to perceive some of the problems that a writer faces. To make understandable what has happened it has been necessary to explain, as fully as I have, the background and personality of my husband, the kind of marriage we enjoy, and the stages and accidents of his career. But none of these things has its proper meaning unless it is viewed in relationship to the climate in which he worked and in which we lived and the pressures to which he was subjected. A more skillful writer would no doubt manage to include as much information of this nature as was necessary in a well-contrived series of dramatic scenes, so that the reader, while being held in suspense and amused by the brisk conflict of personalities, would be brought, almost without his realizing it, adequately prepared, to the climax of the story. There are two reasons why I have not attempted to do this. In the first place, I find it beyond my still undeveloped powers. And secondly, in my reading, I have found, for my own tastes, that the writers who did this particular thing most deftly were the ones I finally could not stomach.


There are crucial days in the lives of men and women, as in the lives of governments and armies; days which may begin like all other days, ordinary and routine, with no warning of the crises ahead and which end with cabinets fallen, battles lost, careers brought to a sudden and catastrophic halt.

The crucial day for my husband was clear and warm, in late spring, when the waters of the harbor of the port in which he was serving as vice-consul were blue and calm. At breakfast we decided the season was well enough advanced so that we could dine thereafter on the terrace of our apartment and I told my husband that I would search in the shops that day for a pair of hurricane lamps to shield the candles on our table in the evening. Two friends were coming in after dinner for bridge, and I asked my husband to bring home with him a bottle of whiskey. He left the apartment, as usual, neat, brushed, deliberate, unmistakably American, despite his many years abroad, among the lively pedestrian traffic of our quarter.

My husband is a methodical man, with a trained memory, and when I asked him, later on, for my own purposes, exactly what took place that morning he was able to tell me, almost word for word. The consul had gone north for several days and my husband was serving temporarily as chief of the office. When he reached the office he read the mail and despatches, none of which was of immediate importance.

Just as he had finished reading, Michael Laborde came into the office. (Remember, please, that all names used here are fictitious.) Michael had the office next to my husband's and he wandered in and out through a connecting door, almost at will. He was no more than thirty years old and held a junior post in the commercial side of the consulate. He was personable, though weak, and my husband considered him intelligent. He was lonely in the city and we had him to dinner at least once a week. He had a quick, jumpy mind and he was always full of gossip and my husband has confessed that he enjoyed the five-minute breaks in the day's routine which Laborde's visits afforded. This morning, Michael came into the office, smoking a cigarette, looking disturbed.

"Holy God," he said, "that Washington."

"What is it now?" my husband asked.

"I got a letter last night," Michael said. "Friend of mine works in the Latin-American section. They're howling in anguish. People're getting dumped by the dozen, every day."

"A certain amount of deadwood . . . ." my husband began. He is always very correct in questions like this, even with good friends.

"Deadwood, hell!" Michael said. "They're cutting the living flesh. And they're going crazy on the pansy hunt. My friend says he heard they have microphones in half the hotels and bars in Washington and they've caught twenty of them already, right out of their own mouths. And no nonsense about it. No looking at the record for commendations, no fooling around about length of service or anything. A five-minute interview and then out—as of close of business that day."

"Well," my husband said, smiling, "I don't imagine you have to worry about that too much." Michael had something of a reputation locally as a ladies' man, being a bachelor, and, as I have said, quite personable.

"I'm not worried about myself—not about that, anyway," Michael said. "But I'm not so sure about the principle. Official purity. Once people declare for purity they're not satisfied until they nail you to the wood. And my friend wrote me to be careful what I say in my letters. My last letter had scotch tape on it. And I never use scotch tape."

"Your friend is too nervous," my husband said.

"He says Il Blanko has ninety paid spies in Europe," said Michael. Il Blanko was Michael's epithet for the senator who was freezing the Foreign Service into a permanent attitude of terror.

"My friend says the damndest people are reporting back all the time. He says they sit next to you in restaurants and write down the jokes when you're not looking."

"Eat at home," my husband said. "Like me."

"And he says he's heard of a new wrinkle," Michael went on. "Some crank you never heard of decides he doesn't like you and he sends an anonymous letter to the FBI saying he saw you flying the flag upside down on the Fourth of July or that you're living with two eleven-year-old Arab boys and then he sends a copy to some hot-eyed congressman and a couple of days later the congressman gets up waving the letter and saying, 'I have here a copy of information that is at this moment resting in the files of the FBI,' and the next thing you know you're in the soup."

"Do you believe that?" my husband asked.

"How the hell do I know what to believe? I'm waiting for the rumor that they've discovered a sane man on F Street," Michael said. "Then I'm going to apply for home leave to see for myself." He doused his cigarette and went back into his own office.

My husband sat at his desk, feeling, as he told me later, annoyed with Michael for having brought up matters which, to tell the truth, had been lying close to the surface of John's consciousness for some time. John had been passed over for promotion twice and his present appointment, even when the most optimistic face had been put upon it, could only be regarded as a sign that, at the very least, he was out of favor in certain influential quarters in the Service. For more than a year he had had moments of uneasiness about his own mail and had, without specifically admitting it to himself, taken to keeping the tone and contents of his letters, even to intimate friends, mildly noncommittal. As he sat there, he remembered, disquietingly, that several personal letters among those he had received in the last few months had had scotch tape on the flaps of the envelopes. And in the course of his duties in the visa and passport sections he had received information through intelligence channels on various applicants, of a surprisingly intimate nature, information which must have been gathered, he realized, in the most unorthodox manner. And in recent months he had been visited, with annoying frequency, by investigators, persistent and humorless young men, who had questioned him closely for derogatory information about colleagues of his, going back in time as far as 1933. Since all this, as the investigators always pointed out, was merely routine, my husband was conscious of the fact that the very same young men must certainly be making the same inquiries about himself.

476

My husband is a realist and was not one of those who considered these activities merely wanton persecution of the department. An actor in it himself, he realized better than most the obscure and fearful nature of the struggle which was taking place in the world and the necessity for measures of defense; treachery existed, and he regarded as ingenuous those of his friends and acquaintances who pretended it did not. It was only in the current vagueness of definition and limits of the term that he was uneasy. Trained to assess guilt and innocence by definite standards, and, as a result of his extended service in Europe, having grown into a habit of tolerance of political diversity, he could not help but feel that perhaps he would be considered old-fashioned and not sufficiently severe by his superiors. The custom he had fallen into of discussing with me all invitations, with a view to avoiding being associated, even in the most casual way, with anyone who might conceivably discredit him, was, while necessary, increasingly irksome. The pleasure of society, to be truly enjoyed, must have a certain automatic and spontaneous quality, and in the last year or so all that had vanished. To judge, professionally, the virtue of colleagues and applicants, is one thing—it is quite another to be forced, on the most innocent occasions, to speculate on the politics, the discretion, the potential future disgrace, of dinner companions and tourists to whom one is introduced, by chance, in a bar.

John's speculation was interrupted by the arrival of Trent. Trent was an executive of an American oil company which had an office in the city. He was a large, soft-spoken man, from Illinois, a little older than my husband. John occasionally played golf with him and considered him a friend. My husband rose and shook Trent's hand and offered him a chair. They talked for several moments about inconsequential matters before Trent settled down to the business that had brought him to the consulate.

"There's something I want your advice about," Trent said. He looked uncomfortable and uncharacteristically ill-at-ease. "You're mixed up in this particular line and you know what's going on better than I do. I've been over here a long time. I read the magazines from home every week, but it's hard to tell from them just how serious something like this would be. I have a problem, John."

"What is it?" my husband asked.

Trent hesitated, and took out a cigar and bit the end off without lighting it. "Well," he said, finally, laughing sheepishly, "I was once asked to join the Communist Party."

"What?" my husband asked, surprised. Trent is a large, expensively dressed man with carefully brushed gray hair and he looks the perfect image of what, in fact, he is—an ambitious, successful business executive. "What did you say?"

"I said I was asked to join the Communist Party," Trent repeated.

"When?" my husband asked.

"In 1932," Trent said. "When I was in college. The University of Chicago."

"Yes?" my husband said, puzzled, not understanding what Trent wanted from him.

"What am I supposed to do about it?" Trent asked.

"*Did* you join?" my husband asked.

"No." Trent said. "Though I'll admit to you that I thought about it for a long time."

"Then I don't quite see what the problem is," my husband said.

"The man who asked me to join," Trent said, "was an instructor. In the Economics Department. He was one of those young ones, in tweed jackets, who'd been to Russia. He'd have the bright boys up to his apartment for beer and a bull session once a week and we'd talk about sex and God and politics and feel pretty damned intelligent about everything. In those days he seemed like one hell of a guy. . . ."

"Yes?" My husband was still puzzled.

"Well," Trent said, "I see they're going after the colleges now, the committees, I mean, and I wonder if I oughtn't to send in his name."

At that moment, my husband decided to be careful. He realized then that he didn't know Trent very well, despite the afternoons on the golf course. He picked up a pencil and pulled a pad over toward him. "What's the man's name?" he asked.

"No," Trent said, "I don't want to get you mixed up in it. And I'm not sure yet that I want to get mixed up in it myself."

"Where's the man now?" my husband asked.

"I don't know," said Trent. "He's not at Chicago any more. I used to correspond with him for a few years and then it petered out. For all I know he's dead now or he's taken up yoga."

"What, exactly," my husband asked, a little sharply, "is it that you want from me?"

"I just wanted your opinion," said Trent. "To sort of help me make up my mind."

"Send in his name."

"Well . . ." Trent said uncertainly. "I'll see. We used to be pretty good friends and I thought a lot of him and something like this could do a man a lot of harm and it's more than twenty years ago. . . ."

"You asked me for advice," my husband said. "My advice is send in his name."

At this moment, the door opened and the consul came in, without knocking. He hadn't been expected back for two days and my husband was surprised to see him.

"Oh, I didn't realize you had someone with you," the consul said. "As soon as you're through, I'd like to see you in my office, please."

"I'm just going," Trent said, standing up. "Thanks. Thanks for everything." He shook hands and went out.

The consul closed the door carefully behind him and turned toward my husband. "Sit down, John," he said. "I have some very grave news for you."

The consul was a young man, not much older than Michael. He was one of those fortunate young men who appear to swim upward, in any organization, without any apparent effort on their own part. He had clever, slender good looks and he always seemed to manage to be evenly and healthily tanned. He had been married, within the last year, to a very pretty girl, the only daughter of a wealthy family, and the two of them together had the valuable reputation of being an amusing couple, and were much in demand for parties and long weekends at famous houses. He was a young man whose career his elders delighted to advance and he had been clearly singled out almost from the very beginning of his service, for high position. My husband, from whom he differed in luck and temperament so markedly, shared the common attitude toward him, and willingly and almost with pleasure took on the extra duties that the consul's full social schedule prevented the consul from fulfilling. That is not to say that my husband was not deeply envious of him. My husband was too conscious of his own worth and his solid achievements in the service not to feel a sense of injustice when he contemplated their comparative positions and their probable futures. And besides, while they were both attached to the embassy at X—, my husband had occupied a position of considerably greater importance and no man takes easily to seeing a younger man moved over his head into authority. But an attitude of envy, affection, and devotion, all mingled together, is less rare in a hierarchy than is generally thought possible.

Alone among his fellow workers, Michael Laborde did not think much of the consul, and called him slightingly, because of his light blond hair and his unfailing luck, Goldilocks. I must admit

479

that I, too, was not so completely charmed by the consul as my husband. There was something that I found vaguely unpleasant and false about him, although I was careful not to give any intimation of this to my husband. I also kept to myself a curious little incident in which the consul and I were the only participants. I was out shopping one afternoon by myself and had stopped in front of a window for a moment, when I looked up to see the consul coming out of a doorway just a few feet away. He looked, as always, neat and beautifully dressed. He was not wearing a hat and his hair was wet and newly brushed, as though he had just taken a shower. He took a step in my direction and I began to smile in greeting, when he suddenly turned, without giving any sign of recognition, and walked swiftly away. I was certain he had seen me and there was in his whole performance a sense of embarrassment which was unusual for him. I watched him turn the corner and started on my own way, puzzled. Then, out of curiosity, I stopped and retraced my steps and went to the doorway from which the consul had emerged. The names of the six occupants of the building were on the side of the door and I recognized only one. It was the name of a young American, who was reputed to have a large independent income and who had settled, in the last three months, in our city. I had met him once or twice at parties, and even if his reputation had not preceded him, I would have been able, from his manner of walking and talking, to judge him immediately for what he was. Of course, if the consul had merely nodded to me and said Hello in the normal manner it would never have occurred to me to look at the names on the doorplates.

"I came down from the embassy earlier than I expected," the consul said, when my husband had seated himself, "because I had to tell you this myself. You're suspended, John, as of close of business this day."

My husband has told me, speaking of that moment, that he experienced a curious sense of relief. Subconsciously and without apparent reason, for almost two years, he had been living in expectation of hearing just those words. Now that they had been finally said, it was almost as though a burden had been lifted from his shoulders. Certainty, even of so disastrous a nature, was, for a flicker in time, more comfortable to bear than continuing doubt.

"Repeat that, please," my husband said.

"You're suspended," the consul said, "and I advise you to resign immediately."

"I'm permitted to resign?" my husband asked.

480

"Yes," said the consul. "Friends of yours have been working for you behind the scenes and they've managed that."

"What's the complaint against me?" my husband asked. Curiously enough, despite his premonitions of the last two years, he had, up until that moment, no inkling of what the complaint would be.

"It's a morals charge, John," the consul said. "And if you fight it, that much is bound to get out and you know what people will think."

"They'll think that I've been kicked out for homosexuality," my husband said.

"Well, not the people who really know you," said the consul. "But everyone else . . ."

"And if I fight it and win?"

"That's not possible, John," the consul said. "They've had people after you and they know all about the lady who tried to commit suicide. They have statements from the doctor, from the porter at the lady's apartment, from somebody at the embassy who went out and did some detective work on his own and then tipped them off."

"Who was that?" my husband asked.

"I can't say," the consul said, "and you'll never find out."

"But it happened more than five years ago," my husband said.

"That makes no difference," said the consul. "It happened."

"If I resign suddenly, like this," my husband said, "the people who don't think it's because of homosexuality will think it's because I'm a security risk—or disloyal."

"I told you," the consul said, "that everybody concerned has agreed to keep it as quiet as possible."

"Still," my husband said, "these things always leak a little."

"A little," the consul admitted. "Perhaps the best thing would be for you to leave as quietly as possible and go to some place where you're not known for a year or so and let it blow over."

"What if I were to go to all the people I've worked for in the Service," my husband said, "and got statements from them about the value of my work for those periods while I was with them— that is, a defense of my record to balance against this one extra-curricular offense—"

"There are no extracurricular offenses any more," the consul said.

"Still," my husband persisted. "What if I got the statements— some of them from people very high in the government by now—"

"It wouldn't do any good," the consul said.

481

"Even so," my husband said, "perhaps I'd like to try. Would you make such a statement for me?"

The consul hesitated for a moment. "No," he said.

"Why not?" my husband asked.

"For several reasons," the consul said. "Remember, you're being treated leniently. You're being permitted to resign and people have agreed to do their best to keep it quiet. If you oppose them, you're bound to anger someone who'll talk and you'll find yourself all over the newspapers and dismissed summarily, to boot. Secondly, if I give you a statement, no matter how closely I keep it to a professional evaluation of your work in this consulate, I'll seem to be encouraging you in your opposition and lining myself up on your side. Believe me, John," the consul said, and according to my husband, he sounded sincere, "if I thought it would help you, I'd do it, But knowing that it would *hurt* you, it's out of the question."

My husband nodded, collected his things, and walked out of his office for the last time. He came home and told me what had happened. We cancelled the bridge party I had intended to give and discussed the matter the better part of the night. A good deal of the time we spent speculating on the identity of the person at the embassy who had taken it on himself to track down John's story. We could fix on no one and to this day we have no hint as to who it might possibly have been.

In the morning John sent in his resignation and two weeks later we flew to America. We bought a car and set out West, looking for a small, quiet place, in which we could live cheaply and without neighbors. We had a lovely trip and we enjoyed the richness of the scenery and talking once more to Americans, after being so long abroad.

We found our little house, by luck. After five minutes of inspecting it and surveying the empty desert lying on all sides of it, we made our minds up and have not regretted the decision for a moment. I have rearranged the furniture to suit our tastes and had two large bookcases built for John's books. The hurricane lamps I bought the day John worked for the last time serve us wonderfully for our dinners in the patio under the starry desert sky.

There was only one incident in all the time that made me feel that perhaps our plan for ourselves was not going to work out, and it was entirely due to my thoughtlessness that it happened at all. Several months ago, on one of my trips to town, I bought a fashion magazine which had in it an article, illustrated by photographs, entitled, with typical vulgarity, "Fashionable Americans

Abroad." There, pictured on a snowy terrace at St. Moritz was the consul and his wife. They were both deeply tanned and smiling widely. They looked, I must confess, very handsome and young and lucky in their skiing clothes. Thinking, foolishly, that it would amuse my husband, I passed him the magazine, saying, "He still manages to get around, doesn't he?"

My husband looked for a long time at the photograph and gave it back to me, finally, without a word. That night, he went for a long walk across the desert and did not come back until just before dawn, and when I saw him the next morning, his face looked old and ravaged, as though he had spent the night in bitter struggle. The peace and forgetfulness that I had thought we were achieving were all vanished from his face and for once, in my presence, his defenses were gone and all the violence of his pride, his endless ambition, his baffled jealousy, were plainly evident, all focussed and brought to an unbearably painful point in the smiling image of the man he had once admired and served so faithfully.

"Never do anything like that to me again," he said, in the morning, and although we had not spoken a word to each other for nearly twelve hours, I knew what he meant.

But it is all over now, although it took the better part of three months, and during that time my husband said hardly a word to me, hardly even read—but spent the days staring across the desert and the nights staring into the fire, like a bankrupt going over his accounts again and again, running the losses through his head, in helpless, silent hysteria. But this morning I came in from town with a letter from Michael, who, alone among our old friends, continued to correspond with us. It was a short letter and my husband read it quickly, standing up, and without changing his expression. When he had finished he handed the letter to me.

"Read this," he said.

"Dear Children," the letter began, in Laborde's hasty scrawl. "Just a note to keep you *au courant*. The weather's beastly, the natives sullen, and the consulate is rocking. Goldilocks is out. Resigned suddenly, as of two days ago, with no explanation. Except that at every cocktail party and every bar where English is spoken, the guess is Kinsey. The first bit of poison leaked three days ago in a column in Washington. Goldilocks and bride, tearstained, departed yesterday for an Alp, to ponder the irony of destiny. Burn this letter and keep a bed warm for me in the desert. Love . . ."

I folded the letter and gave it back to my husband. He put it thoughtfully into his pocket. "Now," he said, "what do you think of that?"

He did not expect an answer and I said nothing. He took a turn around the small patio, touching the sun-warmed adobe wall, and stopped in front of me once more. "Poor man," he said, and the pity was real and revivifying. "He was doing so well."

He took another turn around the patio and said, "What do you think happened?"

"I don't know," I said. "I suppose somebody sent a letter to somebody."

"Somebody sent a letter to somebody," he repeated, nodding gently. He looked at me for what seemed like a long time, searchingly. Then he touched my hand and smiled in a very strange manner.

"Do you know what I've been thinking?" he said. "I've been thinking it might be a nice idea if we both got into the car and drove into C— and bought a good bottle of wine for dinner."

"Yes," I said, "that would be a very nice idea."

I went in and changed and then we drove down the long, straight fifty miles to C—. We bought a bottle of Bordeaux that my husband said was of a quality he hadn't expected to find so deep in the heart of America. He seemed delighted with the crowds on the streets and the things in the windows and insisted upon buying me a very pretty little cotton dress, in a green plaid design, that he saw in a shop.

We drove home and I prepared the dinner and we sat out under the stars and ate it slowly. The Bordeaux, my husband said, was exceptionally good, and we became quite tipsy over the unaccustomed wine, and we laughed unreasonably as we sat across from each other at the table and if there had been anybody there to see us, he would have thought that we were very happy indeed, that night.

Victoria put the folder down.

The story had never been printed. There had been three rejection slips and she had given up. The editors during that period were cowardly, she told herself. She had started four or five more stories and never finished them. Wishing does not make a writer, nor education, nor injustice, nor suffering. The house was sold, at a profit, and they moved to Los Angeles.

She looked at the photograph of her husband, grave, soberly lighted, falsely calm, falsely honorable. She was not sorry he was dead.

She looked out the window. It was still raining. The rain on the window drowned the drowning world outside. It had turned out to be a good day for funerals. A good day for questions, too. Victoria. Victory. Victory over what?

What sort of love could it have been that demanded that price for its survival? In a time of sharks, must all be sharks? Who was the monster who had sat, in the pretty new dress—proud, wily, subservient, dining under the desert stars, and had smiled in pleasure and complicity at the man across the table, enjoying the wine?

*The blond hair had been wet that day, too, although Borden was young then and had not yet begun to use dye.*

# Mixed Doubles

As Jane Collins walked out onto the court behind her husband, she felt once more the private, strong thrill of pride that had moved her again and again in the time she had known him. Jane and Stewart had been married six years, but even so, as she watched him stride before her in that curious upright, individual, half-proud, half-comic walk, like a Prussian drill sergeant on his Sunday off, Jane felt the same mixture of amusement and delight in him that had touched her so strongly when they first met. Stewart was tall and broad and his face was moody and good-humored and original, and Jane felt that even at a distance of five hundred yards and surrounded by a crowd of people, she could pick him out unerringly. Now, in well-cut white trousers and a long-sleeved Oxford shirt, he seemed elegant and a little old-fashioned among the other players, and he looked graceful and debonair as he hit the first few shots in the preliminary rallying.

Jane was sensibly dressed, in shorts and tennis shirt, and her hair was imprisoned in a bandanna, so that it wouldn't get into her eyes. She knew that the shorts made her look a little dumpy and that the handkerchief around her head gave her a rather skinned and severe appearance, and she had a slight twinge of female regret when she looked across the net and saw Eleanor Burns soft and attractive in a prettily cut tennis dress and with a red ribbon in her hair, but she fought it down and concentrated on keeping her eye on the ball as Mr. Croker, Eleanor's partner, sliced it back methodically at her.

Mr. Croker, a vague, round, serious little man, was a neighbor of the Collinses' hosts. His shorts were too tight for him, and Jane knew, from having watched him on previous occasions, that his face would get more serious and more purple as the afternoon wore on, but he played a steady, dependable game and he was useful when other guests were too lazy or had drunk too much at lunch to play in the afternoon.

Two large oak trees shaded part of the court, and the balls flashed back and forth, in light and shadow, making guitarlike chords as they hit the rackets, and on the small terrace above the court, where the other guests were lounging, there was the watery music of ice in glasses and the bright flash of summer colors as people moved about.

How pleasant this was, Jane thought—to get away from the city on a weekend, to this cool, tree-shaded spot, to slip all the stiff bonds of business and city living and run swiftly on the springy surface of the court, feeling the country wind against her bare skin, feeling youth in her legs, feeling, for this short Sunday hour at least, free of desks and doors and weekday concrete.

Stewart hit a tremendous overhead smash, whipping all the strength of his long body into it, and the ball struck the ground at Eleanor's feet and slammed high in the air. He grinned. "I'm ready," he said.

"You're not going to do that to me in the game, are you?" Eleanor asked.

"I certainly am," Stewart said. "No mercy for women. The ancient motto of the Collins family."

They tossed for service, and Stewart won. He served and aced Eleanor with a twisting, ferocious shot that spun off at a sharp angle.

"Jane, darling," he said, grinning, as he walked to the other side, "we're going to be sensational today."

They won the first set with no trouble. Stewart played very well. He moved around the court swiftly and easily, hitting the ball hard in loose, well-coached strokes, with an almost exaggerated grace. Again and again, the people watching applauded or called out after one of his shots, and he waved his racket, smiling at them, and said, "Oh, we're murderous today." He kept humming between shots—a tuneless, happy composition of his own—like a little boy who is completely satisfied with himself, and Jane couldn't help smiling and adoring him as he light-heartedly dominated the game and the spectators and the afternoon, brown and dashing and handsome in his white clothes, with the sun flooding around him like a spotlight on an actor in the middle of the stage.

Occasionally, when Stewart missed a shot, he would stand, betrayed and tragic, and stare up at the sky and ask with mock despair, "Collins, why don't you just go home?" And then he would turn to Jane and say, "Janie, darling, forgive me. Your husband's just no good."

And even as she smiled at him and said, "You're so right,"

she could sense the other women, up on the terrace, looking down at him, their eyes speculative and veiled and lit with invitation as they watched.

Jane played her usual game, steady, unheroic, getting almost everything back quite sharply, keeping the ball in play until Stewart could get his racket on it and kill it. They were a good team. Jane let Stewart poach on her territory for spectacular kills, and twice Stewart patted her approvingly on the behind after she had made difficult saves, and there were appreciative chuckles from the spectators at the small domestic vulgarity.

Stewart made the last point of the set on a slamming deep backhand that passed Eleanor at the net. Eleanor shook her head and said, "Collins, you're an impossible man," and Croker said stolidly, "Splendid. Splendid," and Stewart said, grinning, "Something I've been saving for this point, old man."

They walked off and sat down on a bench in the shade between sets, and Croker and Jane had to wipe their faces with towels and Croker's alarming purple died a little from his cheeks.

"That overhead!" Eleanor said to Stewart. "It's absolutely frightening. When I see you winding up, I'm just tempted to throw away my poor little racket and run for my life."

Jane lifted her head and glanced swiftly at Stewart to see how he was taking it. He was taking it badly, smiling a little too widely at Eleanor, being boyish and charming. "It's nothing," he said. "Something I picked up on Omaha Beach."

That, too, Jane thought bitterly. Foxhole time, too. She ducked her head into her towel to keep from saying something wifely. This is the last time, she thought, feeling the towel sticky against her sweaty forehead, the last time I am coming to any of these weekend things, always loaded with unattached or semi-attached, man-hungry, half-naked, honey-mouthed girls. She composed her face, so that when she looked up from the towel she would look like a nice, serene woman who merely was interested in the next set of tennis.

Eleanor, who had wide green eyes, was staring soberly and unambiguously over the head of her racket at Stewart, and Stewart, fascinated, as always, and a little embarrassed, was staring back. Oh, God, Jane thought, the long stare, too.

"Well," she said briskly, "I'm ready for one more set."

"What do you say," Stewart asked, "we divide up differently this time? Might make it more even. Croker and you, Jane, and the young lady and me."

"Oh," said Eleanor, "I'd be a terrible drag to you, Stewart. And besides, I'm sure your wife loves playing on your side."

"Not at all," Jane said stiffly. The young lady! How obvious could a man be?

"No," said Croker surprisingly. "Let's stay the way we are." Jane wanted to kiss the round purple face, a bleak, thankful kiss. "I think we'll do better this time. I've been sort of figuring out what to do with you, Collins."

Stewart looked at him briefly and unpleasantly, then smiled charmingly. "Anything you say, old man. I just thought . . ."

"I'm sure we'll do better," Croker said firmly. He stood up. "Come on, Eleanor."

Eleanor stood up, lithe and graceful in her short dress, which whipped around her brown legs in the summer wind. Never again, Jane thought, will I wear shorts. Dresses like that, even if they cost fifty dollars apiece, and soft false bosoms to put in them, too, and no bandanna, even if I'm blinded on each shot.

Stewart watched Eleanor follow Croker onto the court, and Jane could have brained him for the buried, measuring glint in his eye.

"Let's go," Stewart said and under his breath, as they walked to their positions on the base line. He added, "Let's really show the old idiot this time, Jane."

"Yes, dear," Jane said, and pulled her bandanna straight and tight around her hair.

The first three games were ludicrously one-sided. Stewart stormed the net, made sizzling, malicious shots to Croker's feet, and purposely made him run, so that he panted pitifully and grew more purple than ever, and from time to time muttered to Jane, "Ridiculous old windbag," and "I thought he had me figured out," and "Don't let up, Janie, don't let up."

Jane played as usual, steady, undeviating, as predictably and sensibly as she always played. She was serving in the fourth game and was at 40–15 when Stewart dropped a shot just over the net, grinning as Croker galloped heavily in and barely got his racket on it. Croker's return wobbled over Stewart's head and landed three inches beyond the base line.

"Nice shot," she heard Stewart say. "Just in."

She looked at him in surprise. He was nodding his head emphatically at Croker.

Eleanor was at the net on the other side, looking at Stewart. "It looked out to me," she said.

"Not at all," Stewart said. "Beautiful shot. Serve them up, Janie."

Oh, Lord, Jane thought, now he's being sporting.

Jane made an error on the next point and Croker made a placement for advantage and Stewart hit into the net for the last point, and it was Croker's and Eleanor's game. Stewart came back to receive the service, not humming any more, his face irritable and dark.

Croker suddenly began to play very well, making sharp, sliding, slicing shots that again and again forced Stewart and Jane into errors. As they played, even as she swung at the ball, Jane kept remembering the shot that Stewart had called in, that had become the turning point of the set. He had not been able to resist the gallant gesture, especially when Eleanor had been standing so close, watching it all. It was just like Stewart. Jane shook her head determinedly, trying to concentrate on the game. This was no time to start dissecting her husband. They had had a lovely weekend till now and Stewart had been wonderful, gay and funny and loving, and criticism could at least be reserved for weekdays, when everything else was dreary, too. But it *was* just like Stewart. It was awful how everything he did was all of a piece. His whole life was crowded with gestures. Hitting his boss that time in the boss's own office with three secretaries watching, because the boss had bawled him out. Giving up his R.O.T.C. commission and going into the Army as a private, in 1942. Giving five thousand dollars, just about the last of their savings, to Harry Mather, for Mather's business, just because they had gone to school together, when everyone knew Mather had become a hopeless drunk and none of his other friends would chip in. To an outsider, all these might seem the acts of a generous and rather noble character but to a wife caught in the consequences . . .

"Damn these pants," Stewart was muttering after hitting a ball into the net. "I keep tripping over them all the time."

"You ought to wear shorts, like everyone else," Jane said.

"I will. Buy me some this week," Stewart said, taking time out and rolling his cuffs up slowly and obviously. Jane had bought him three pairs of shorts a month before, but he always pretended he couldn't find them, and wore the long trousers. His legs are surprisingly skinny, Jane thought, hating herself for thinking it, and they're hairy, and his vanity won't let him. . . . She started to go for a ball, then stopped when she saw Stewart going for it.

He hit it out to the backstop. "Janie, darling," he said, "at least stay out of my way."

"Sorry," she said. Stewie, darling, she thought, Stewie, be careful. Don't lay it on. You're not really like this. I know you're not. Even for a moment, don't make it look as though you are.

Stewart ended the next rally by hitting the ball into the net. He stared unhappily at the ground. "The least they might do," he said in a low voice to Jane, "is roll the court if they invite people to play on it."

Please, Stewie, Jane begged within herself, don't do it. The alibis. The time he forgot to sign the lease for the apartment and they were put out and he blamed it on the lawyer, and the time he lost the job in Chicago and it was because he had gone to the wrong college, and the time . . . By a rigorous act of will, Jane froze her eyes on the ball, kept her mind blank as she hit it back methodically again and again.

Eleanor and Croker kept winning points. Croker had begun to chop every ball, spinning soft, deceptive shots that landed in midcourt and hardly bounced before they fell a second time. The only way that Jane could return them was to hit them carefully, softly, just getting them back. But Stewart kept going in on them furiously, taking his full, beautiful swing, sending the ball whistling into the net or over the court into the backstop. He looked as pretty and expert as ever as he played, but he lost point after point.

"What a way to play tennis," he grumbled, with his back to his opponents. "Why doesn't he play ping-pong or jacks?"

"You can't slam those dinky little shots like that," Janie said. "You have to get them back soft."

"You play your game," Stewart said, "and I'll play mine."

"Sorry," Jane said. Oh, Stewart, she mourned within her.

Stewart went after two more of Croker's soft chops, each time whipping his backhand around in his usual, slightly exaggerated, beautiful stroke, and each time knocking the ball into the net.

I can't help it, Jane thought. That *is* the way he is. Form above everything. If he were hanging over a cliff, he'd let himself fall to the rocks below rather than risk being ungraceful climbing to safety to save his life. He always has to pick up the check in bars and restaurants, no matter whom he is with or how many guests there are at the table, always with the same lordly, laughing, slightly derisive manner, even if we are down to our last fifty dollars. And when they had people in to dinner, there had to be two maids to wait on table, and French wines, and there always had to be those special bottles of brandy that cost as much as a vacation in the country. And he became so cold and remote when Jane argued with him about it, reminding him they were not rich and there was no sense in pretending they were. And his shoes. She blinked her eyes painfully, getting a sudden vision, there in the sun and shadow, of the long row of exquisite shoes, at seventy dollars a pair, that he insisted upon having made to his order. How ridiculous, she thought, to allow yourself to be unnerved at your husband's taste in shoes, and she loyally reminded herself how much a part of his attraction it had been in the beginning that he was always so beautifully dressed and so easy and graceful and careless of money.

The score was 4–3 in favor of Eleanor and Croker. Stewart's shots suddenly began to work again, and he and Jane took the next game with ease. Stewart's grin came back then, and he cheerfully reassured Jane, "Now we're going to take them." But after winning the first two points of the next game he had a wild streak and missed the base line by a few inches three times in a row, and they eventually lost the game.

I will make no deductions from this, Jane told herself stonily as she went up to the net for Stewart's serve. Anybody is liable to miss a few shots like that—anybody. And yet, how like Stewart! Just when it was most important to be steady and dependable. . . . The time she'd been so sick and the maid had quit, and Jane lay, broken and miserable, in bed for three weeks, with no one to take care of her except Stewart . . . He had been charming and thoughtful for the first week, fixing her meals, reading to her, sitting at her side for hours on end, cheerful and obliging, making her illness gently tolerable. And then he had suddenly grown nervous and abrupt, made vague excuses to leave her alone, and vanished for hours at a time, only to come back and hastily attend her for a few moments and vanish again, leaving her there in the rumpled bed, staring, lonely and shaken, at the ceiling as dusk faded into night and night into morning. She had been sure there was another girl then and she had resolved that when she was well and able to move around again, she would come to some decision with him, but as unpredictably as his absences had begun, they stopped. Once more he was tender and helpful, once more he sat at her side and nursed her and cheered her, and out of gratitude and love she had remained quiet and pushed her doubts deep to the back of her mind. And here they were again, in the middle of a holiday afternoon, foolishly, in this most unlikely place, during this mild, pointless game, with half a dozen people lazily watching, laughing and friendly, over their drinks.

She looked at him a few moments later, handsome and dear and familiar at her side, and he grinned back at her, and she was ashamed of herself for the thoughts that had been flooding through her brain. It was that silly girl on the other side of the net who had started it all, she thought. That practiced, obvious, almost automatic technique of flattering the male sex. That meaningless, rather pitiful flirtatiousness. It was foolish to allow it to throw her into the bitter waters of reflection. Marriage, after all, was an up-and-down affair and in many ways a fragile and devious thing, and was not to be examined too closely. Marriage was not a bank statement or a foreign policy or an X-ray photograph in a doctor's hand. You took it and lived through it, and maybe, a long time later—perhaps the day before you died—you totalled up the accounts, if you were of that turn of mind, but not before. And if you were a reasonable, sensible, mature woman, you certainly didn't do your additions and subtractions on a tennis court every time your husband hit a ball into the net. Jane smiled at herself and shook her head.

"Nice shot," she said warmly to Stewart as he swept a forehand across court, past Croker, for a point.

But it was still set point. Croker placed himself to receive Stewart's service, tense and determined and a little funny-looking, with his purple face and his serious round body a little too tight under his clothes. The spectators had fallen silent, and the wind had died, and there was a sense of stillness and expectancy as Stewart reared up and served.

Jane was at the net and she heard the sharp twang of Stewart's racket hitting the ball behind her and the riflelike report as it hit the tape and fell away. He had just missed his first service.

Jane didn't dare look around. She could feel Stewart walking into place, in that stiff-backed, pleasant way of his, and feel him shuffling around nervously, and she couldn't look back. Please, she thought, please get this one in. Helplessly, she thought of all the times when, just at the crucial moment, he had failed. Oh, God, this is silly, she thought. I mustn't do this. The time he had old man Sawyer's account practically in his hands and he got drunk. On the sporting pages, they called it coming through in the clutch. There were some players who did and some players who didn't, and after a while you got to know which was which. If you looked at it coldly, you had to admit that until now Stewart had been one of those who didn't. The time her father died, just after her sister had run off with the vocalist in that band, and if there had been a man around, taking hold of things, her father's partner wouldn't't've been able to get away with most of the estate the way he did, and the vocalist could have been frightened off. One day's strength and determination, one day of making the right move at the right time . . . But after the funeral, Stewart had pulled out and gone to Seattle on what he had said was absolutely imperative business, but that had never amounted to anything anyway, and Jane's mother and sister, and Jane, too, were still paying for that day of failure.

She could sense Stewart winding up for his service behind her back. Somewhere in her spine she felt a sense of disaster. It was going to be a double fault. She knew it. No, she thought, I mustn't. He isn't really like that. He's so intelligent and talented and good, he can go so far. She must not make this terrible judgment on her husband just because of the way he played tennis. And yet, his tennis was so much like his life. Gifted, graceful, powerful, showy, flawed, erratic . . .

Please, she thought, make this one good. Childishly, she felt, If this one is good it will be a turning point, a symbol, his whole life will be different. She hated herself for her thoughts and stared blankly at Eleanor, self-consciously alert and desirable in her pretty dress.

Why the hell did she have to come here this Sunday? Jane thought despairingly.

She heard the crack of the racket behind her. The ball whistled past her, hit the tape, rolled undecidedly on top of the net for a moment, then fell back at her feet for a double fault and the set.

"Too bad." She turned and smiled at Stewart, helplessly feeling herself beginning to wonder how she would manage to find the six weeks it would take in Reno. She shook her head, knowing that she wasn't going to Reno, but knowing, too, that the word would pass through her thoughts again and again, more and more frequently, with growing insistence, as the days went by.

She walked off the court with Stewart, holding his hand.

"The shadows," Stewart was saying. "Late in the afternoon, like this. It's impossible to see the service line."

"Yes, dear," Jane said.

# A Wicked Story

The curtain came down and the applause began. The theatre was warm now, after the three long acts, and Robert Harvey applauded lightly, only from the wrists, because he didn't want to sweat. He was a big, heavy man, and he had found that when he permitted himself enthusiasm in the overheated midtown auditoriums, he came away soaking wet. He had once caught a bad cold that way, going out into a rainstorm after *A Streetcar Named Desire*, and he had learned to temper his gratitude, moving his hands politely but making very little noise. The curtain went up again and the cast took their bows, smiling widely because the play had been running three months and was going to run at least a year and they were all eating. Robert regarded them coolly, thinking, Well, they certainly aren't worth four-eighty a seat. What has happened, he thought, to the plays I used to see when I was a younger man?

Virginia, in the next seat, was applauding briskly. Her eyes were shining, as they did when she was enjoying herself. Robert decided not to say anything about the four-eighty a seat when he talked to her later about the play. The actors were taking individual curtain calls now, and when the girl who played the cynical friend of the heroine came on, Robert clapped his hands quite powerfully, risking perspiration, because he had met her once at a party. Besides, she was not a bad-looking girl, with longish black hair, cut in an unusual way, and large blue eyes. She was a bit too big and eventually she was going to be fat and you had the feeling she never was going to get very far as an actress, but none of these things would be crucial for several more years. Robert felt the beads of perspiration coming out on his forehead, and he was glad when the girl, after a bosomy curtsy, went off into the wings.

The lights came on and the Harveys moved slowly up the aisle in the newly disturbed waves of perfume and fur. Virginia said, "That was a very nice little play, wasn't it?" and Robert nodded, hoping that there were no relatives of the playwright within earshot.

495

In the lobby, as he put on his coat, he saw a young man with a yellow muffler who was leaning against the box-office window staring at Virginia. In a more realistic society, he thought, taking Virginia's arm and moving her toward the street, you would be permitted to walk over and punch the nose of any man who looked at your wife that way.

They spurted across the street among the taxis, Virginia fleet on her high heels, and went through the alley, between the stage doors and the gay posters for musical comedies. There were three hits playing on the next street, and the people flowing from the theatres sounded good-natured and jubilant, and you knew that they would remain that way for at least another half hour, and it was pleasant to be among them in the windless, cold night air. The lights of the restaurant across the street were warm among the dark buildings, and the doorman, while not effusive, was agreeably polite as he swung the door open for them. The headwaiter was a little chillier than the doorman and seated them at the rear of the restaurant, although there were several empty tables closer to the entrance. Robert humbly accepted the table, thinking philosophically, Well, this is a theatrical restaurant; there are dozens of places where they'd put me near the front of the room and actors'd be lucky to get through the door.

Virginia settled herself on the banquette with a hundred small subsiding movements, then took out her glasses and carefully surveyed the room. After a minute, she put the glasses down on the table and turned toward Robert. "What're you smiling at?" she asked.

"Because you're so pleased," said Robert.

"Who says I'm pleased?"

"You examined the terrain and you said to yourself, 'Isn't this nice? I'm prettier than any of them,' and now you can enjoy your supper."

"Oh, you're so sharp," Virginia said. She smiled. "You're such a sharp man."

The waiter came, and they ordered spaghetti and half a bottle of Chianti, and watched the restaurant fill up with people who had been to the theatre and actors who still had traces of greasepaint around their collars and tall, astonishing-looking girls in mink coats from the musicals across the street. Robert ate hungrily and drank his wine slowly, nursing it.

"That play tonight," Virginia was saying, delicately winding spaghetti on her fork against a spoon, "was all right and I enjoyed it while I was there, but I'm getting tired of how awful all the female characters are in plays these days. All the women always are drunks or nymphomaniacs or they drive their sons crazy or they ruin the lives of two or three people an act. If I were a playwright, I'd write a nice, old-fashioned play in which the heroine is pure and beautiful and makes a man out of her husband, even though he's weak and drinks too much and occasionally robs his boss to bet on the horses."

"If you were a playwright, you'd be in Hollywood," Robert said.

"Anyway, I bet it'd be a big success," Virginia insisted. "I bet people are just dying to go to see a play that they can come out of and say, 'Yes, that's just how Mother was the time Dad had his trouble down at the bank and those two men in plainclothes came to see him from New York.' "

"If anything like that comes up," Robert said comfortably, "you go to see it some matinée. By yourself."

"And all the actresses these days. They try to act so ordinary. Just like anybody you'd meet in the street. Sometimes you wonder how they dare charge you admission to watch them. When I was a little girl, actresses used to be so affected you'd *know* you had to pay to see them, because you'd never meet anybody like that in real life in a million years."

"How did you like Duse?" Robert asked. "What did you think of Bernhardt when you were ten?"

"Don't be so witty. You know what I mean. That girl you liked so much tonight, for example . . ."

"Which girl I liked so much?" Robert asked, puzzled.

"The big one. The one that played the friend."

"Oh, that one," Robert said. "I didn't like her so much."

"You certainly sounded as though you did. I thought your hands'd be a bloody pulp by the time she got off the stage."

"I was just being neighborly," Robert said. "I met her once at a party."

"Whose party?" Virginia stopped eating.

"The Lawtons'. She went to school with Anne Lawton," Robert said. "Didn't you meet her?"

"I didn't go to that party. I had the flu that week." Virginia sipped her wine. "What's her name?"

"Carol Something. Look at the program."

"I left the program in the theatre. Was she nice?"

Robert shrugged. "I only talked to her for five minutes. She told me she came from California and she hates working for television and she was divorced last year but they're still good friends. The usual kind of talk you get at the Lawtons'."

"She looks as though she came from California," Virginia said, making it sound like a criticism.

"Oakland," Robert said. "It's not exactly the same thing."

"There she is now," said Virginia. "Near the door."

Robert looked up. The girl was alone and was making her way down the center of the room. She wasn't wearing a hat, and her hair looked careless, and she had on a shapeless polo coat and flat shoes, and Robert decided, looking at her, that actresses were getting plainer every year. She stopped briefly once or twice to greet friends at other tables, then headed for a table in the corner, where a group of three men and two women were waiting for her. Robert realized that she was going to pass their table, and wondered if he ought to greet her. The party at which they'd met had been almost two months before, and he had a modest theory that people like actresses and book publishers and movie directors never remembered anyone they met who wasn't in a related profession. He doubted whether the girl would recognize him, but he arranged a slight, impersonal smile on his face, so that if she did happen to remember, he would seem to be saluting her. If she just passed by, Robert hoped that it would merely look as though he were responding with polite amusement to one of Virginia's remarks.

But the girl stopped in front of the table, smiling widely. She put out her hand and said, "Why, Mr. Harvey, isn't it nice seeing you again!"

She wasn't any prettier close up, Robert decided, but when she smiled, she seemed friendly and simple, and her voice sounded as though she really was glad to see him again after the five minutes in the noisy corner at the Lawtons' two months ago. Robert stood up and took her hand. "Hello," he said. "May I present my wife. Miss Byrne."

"How do you do, Miss Byrne," Virginia said. "We were just talking about you."

"We saw your show tonight," Robert said. "We thought you were very good indeed."

"Aren't you dear to say that," the girl said. "I love to hear it, even if you don't mean it at all."

"What about the man who wrote the play?" Virginia asked. "He must be rather strange."

"Mother trouble." Miss Byrne glanced significantly up at the ceiling. "All the young writers coming into the theatre these days seem to have the same thing. You'd think it'd be the war that would be haunting them, but it isn't at all. It's only Mama.''

Virginia smiled. ''Not only young writers,'' she said. ''Is this your first play, Miss Byrne?''

''Heavens, no,'' the girl said. ''I've been in three others. *Regret, The Six-Week Vacation.* . . . I don't even remember the name of the third one. Turkeys. Here today and closed by Saturday.''

Virginia turned to Robert. ''Did you happen to see any of them, dear?'' she asked.

''No,'' Robert said, surprised. He never went to the theatre without Virginia.

''Three other plays,'' Virginia went on pleasantly, sounding genuinely interested. ''You must have been in New York quite a long time.''

''Two years,'' Miss Byrne said. ''A single blink of the eye of a drama critic.''

''Two years,'' Virginia said, politely. She turned to Robert again. ''Where did you say Miss Byrne came from? Hollywood?''

''Oakland,'' Robert said.

''New York must be quite exciting,'' Virginia said. ''After Oakland.''

''I love it,'' Miss Byrne said, sounding young and enthusiastic. ''Even with the flops.''

''I'm so sorry,'' Virginia said. ''Keeping you standing there like that, talking on and on about the theatre. Wouldn't you like to sit down and join us for a drink?''

''Thanks,'' the girl said, ''I really can't. They're waiting for me over in the corner.''

''Some other time, perhaps,'' Virginia said.

''I'd love it,'' said Miss Byrne. ''It's been fun meeting you, Mrs. Harvey. Mr. Harvey told me about you. I do hope we see each other again. Good night.'' She waved and smiled widely again and strode over toward her waiting friends.

Robert sat down slowly. There was silence at the table for a moment.

''It's a hard life,'' Virginia said after a while, ''for actresses, isn't it?''

''Yes.''

''*The Six-Week Vacation,*'' Virginia said. ''No wonder it failed, with a title like that. Did she play the lead in it, that girl?''

''I don't know,'' Robert said, waiting. ''I told you I didn't see it.''

"That's right," Virginia said. "You told me."

They were silent again. Virginia began to twist the stem of her wineglass with little, jerky movements. "You told me," she repeated. "It's too bad she couldn't have a drink with us. We might have learned a great deal about the theatre tonight. I find people in the theatre so fascinating. Don't you?"

"What's the matter with you?" Robert asked.

"Nothing," Virginia said flatly. "There's nothing the matter with me at all. Are you finished with your food?"

"Yes."

"Let's pay the check and get out of here."

"Virginia . . ." Robert said, drawling the name out complainingly.

"Rah-ahbert . . ." Virginia said, mimicking him.

"All right," said Robert. "What is it?"

"I said nothing."

"I know what you said. What is it?"

Virginia lifted her eyes and looked at him closely. "Miss Byrne," she said. "I thought you didn't know her name."

"Oh," Robert said. "Now it's turning into one of those evenings."

"It's not turning into any kind of evening. Get the check," Virginia said. "I want to go home."

"Waiter!" Robert called. "The check, please." He stared at Virginia. She was beginning to look martyred. "Listen," Robert said. "I didn't know her name."

"Carol Something," said Virginia.

"It came to me just as she got to the table. While I was standing up. Hasn't that ever happened to you?"

"No," said Virginia.

"Well, it's a common phenomenon."

Virginia nodded. "Very common," she said, "I'm sure."

"Don't you believe me?"

"You haven't forgotten a girl's name since you were six years old," Virginia said. "You remember the name of the girl you danced with once the night of the Yale game in 1935."

"Gladys," Robert said. "Gladys McCreary. She played field hockey for Bryn Mawr."

"No wonder you were so eager to get to the Lawtons' that night."

"I wasn't eager to get to the Lawtons' that night," Robert said, his voice beginning to rise. "And anyway I didn't even know she existed. At least be logical."

"I had a hundred and three fever," Virginia said, pitying herself

500

all over again for the damp eyes, the hot forehead, the painful cough of two months earlier. "I was just lying there all alone, day after day . . ."

"Don't make it sound as though you were on the point of death for the whole winter," Robert said loudly. "You were in bed three days, and on Saturday you went to lunch in a snowstorm."

"Oh," Virginia said, "you can remember that it snowed one Saturday two months ago, but you can't remember the name of a girl you talked to for hours at a party, that you exchanged the most intimate confidences with."

"Virginia," Robert said, "I'm going to get up on this seat and scream at the top of my voice."

"Divorced, she said, but they're still good friends. I'll bet they are. I'll bet that girl is good friends with a lot of people. How about you and *your* ex-wife?" Virginia demanded. "Are you good friends with her, too?"

"You know as well as I do," Robert said, "that the only time I see my ex-wife is when she wants the alimony adjusted."

"If you keep talking in that tone of voice, they'll never let you in this restaurant again," Virginia whispered.

"Let's get out of here," Robert said blindly. "Waiter, where's that check?"

"She's thick." Virginia stared at Miss Byrne, who was sitting with her back to them twenty feet away, talking brightly and waving a cigarette. "Through the middle. Grotesquely thick."

"Grotesquely," Robert agreed.

"You don't fool me," Virginia said, "I know your tastes."

"Oh, God," Robert murmured.

"Always pretending to be such a connoisseur of beautiful women," Virginia said, "and secretly what you really like are old-fashioned, disgusting brood mares."

"Oh, God," Robert said again.

"Like that Elise Cross," Virginia rolled on, "two summers ago on the Cape. She always looked as though she had to be packed into her girdle under pressure. And whenever I looked around for you at a party, you both were gone, out on the dunes."

"I thought we had agreed never to discuss that subject again," Robert said with dignity.

"What subject am I permitted to discuss?" Virginia demanded. "The United Nations?"

"There never was anything between me and Elise Cross. Not anything. And you know it," Robert said firmly and convincingly. It was true that there had been something, but that had been two years ago, and he hadn't seen Elise Cross since then, or anyone else, for that matter. And anyway it had been summertime then, and he had been drunk a good deal of the time for a reason he could no longer recall, and the people around them had been of that peculiar, handsome, neurotic, wife-changing type that appears at places like that in August and infects the atmosphere. He had been ashamed of himself by Labor Day and had resolved to change his ways once and for all. Now he felt blameless and aggrieved at being called upon to defend himself after all that abstinence.

"You spent more time on the beach than the Coast Guard," Virginia said.

"If the waiter doesn't come with the check," Robert said, "I'm going to walk out of here and they can follow me in a taxi if they want their money."

"I should have known," Virginia said, and there was a remote throb in her voice. "People told me about you before we were married. I knew your reputation."

"Look, that was more than five years ago," Robert said doggedly. "I was younger then and more energetic and I was married to a woman I didn't like and who didn't like me. I was unhappy and lonely and restless—"

"And now?"

"And now," Robert said, thinking how wonderful it would be to get up and walk away from his wife for six or seven months, "and now I am married to a woman I love and I am settled and profoundly happy. I haven't had lunch or a drink with anyone for years. I barely tip my hat to women I know when I pass them in the street."

"And what about that fat actress over there?"

"Look," Robert said, feeling hoarse, as though he had been shouting into the wind for hours. "Let's get it straight. I met her at a party. I spoke to her for five minutes. I don't think she's very pretty. I don't think she's much as an actress. I was surprised when she recognized me. I forgot her name. Then I remembered her name when she came to the table."

"I suppose you expect me to believe that." Virginia smiled coldly.

"I certainly do. Because it's an exact statement of fact."

"I saw that smile," Virginia said. "Don't think I didn't."

"What smile?" Robert asked, honestly puzzled.

"Why, Mr. Harvey," Virginia said, cooing, "isn't it nice seeing you again? And then the teeth and the girlish crinkling of the nose and the long, direct stare . . ."

"Finally," Robert said to the waiter, who was leaning over the table, putting the check down. "Don't go away." Robert counted out some bills, feeling his hands shaking minutely with rage. He watched the waiter going toward the cashier's desk, near the kitchen, for change. Then he spoke, trying to keep his voice under control. "Now," he said, turning back to Virginia, "what, exactly, did you mean by that?"

"I may not be very smart," Virginia said, "but if there's one thing I have, it's intuition. Especially where you're concerned. And anyway that smile was unmistakable."

"Now, wait a minute." Robert felt his fists opening and closing spasmodically. "It's charming of you to think, even after being married to me for five years, that women just drop at my feet after speaking to me for five minutes, but I have to disillusion you. It has never happened to me. Never," he said slowly and distinctly and with some disappointment.

"If there's one thing I can't stand, it's fake modesty," Virginia said. "I've seen you looking at yourself in the mirror, approving of yourself by the hour, pretending you were shaving or looking for gray hairs. And," she added bitterly, "I've talked to your mother. I know how she brought you up. Drilling it into your head that the whole panting female sex was after you because you were a Harvey and you were so dazzling—"

"Good God," Robert said. "Now we have my mother, too."

"She has a lot to answer for," Virginia said, "your mother. Don't think she hasn't."

"All right," Robert said. "My mother is a low, terrible woman and everybody agrees on that. But what has that got to do with the fact that a woman I met at a party happened to smile at me?"

"Happened," Virginia said.

"I still don't see how it could be my fault," Robert said, trying to sound patient. "I can't control the way people smile in restaurants."

"It's always your fault," Virginia said. "Even if you don't say a word. It's just the way you come into the room and stand there and decide to look . . . male."

Robert jumped up, pushing the table back. "I can't stand it," he said. "I can't stand it any more. The hell with the change."

Virginia stood up, too, her face rigid. "I have an idea," Robert said as he helped her on with her coat. "Let's you and I not talk to each other for a week."

"Fine," said Virginia crazily. "That's perfectly fine with me."

503

She walked swiftly toward the door, through the middle of the restaurant, without looking back.

Robert watched her striding down the narrow aisle between the tables, her black coat floating behind her. He wished that he had a worse temper. He wished that he had a temper so bad that he could stay out all night and get drunk.

The waiter came with the change, and Robert fumbled with the tip. Over the waiter's shoulder he saw Miss Byrne swing her head slowly toward him. Everybody else at her table was talking animatedly. For the first time, Robert looked at her carefully. It *is* true, he thought numbly. Most women these days *are* too damn thin.

Then Miss Byrne smiled at him. Her nose crinkled and her teeth showed and she seemed to be looking at him for a long time. He felt flattered and considerably younger and very curious. And as he dropped his eyes and left a large tip for the waiter, he knew, helplessly, that he was going to call her next day and he knew what her voice was going to sound like on the telephone.

Then he got his coat and hurried out of the restaurant after his wife.

# Age of Reason

He had the dream only once—in December. He thought about it for a few moments the next morning, and forgot about it until one evening in April, ten minutes before his plane was scheduled to take off. Then, suddenly, it returned to him. Always, when he was about to board a plane, there was a slight tremor; an awareness of risk, however small and controlled; a slight, subconscious realization that each flight might end with death; a hidden knowledge that there was a small, lurking fatality in winds and cloud and valves and wings, and that no amount of airline skill and care and advertising could ever absolutely dispel it. It was that usual minute, buried twinge of disaster that made him remember the dream as he stood at the gate with his wife and sister, looking out at the dark field and the huge, substantial plane and the flickering lights that marked the runways.

The dream had been a simple one. In it, somehow, his sister Elizabeth had died, and he had, in a resigned and hopeless way, followed the coffin to the cemetery and watched with dry eyes as it was lowered into the ground, and then he had returned home. And somehow, in the dream, it had all happened on May 14th. The date had been absolutely clear and definite and had given the dream a real, tragic sense that it might not otherwise have had. When he woke, he tried to figure out why May 14th, an obscure day five months in the future, had been chosen so relentlessly and specifically by his dreaming mind, but it was no use. There were no birthdays in his family in May, no anniversaries, and nothing in particular had ever happened to him or anyone he knew on that day. He had laughed a little, sleepily, to himself, gently touched Alice's bare shoulder in the bed beside him, and had risen and gone to work, in the sensible, everyday atmosphere of drafting boards and blueprints, without saying a word then or later to her or anyone else about the dream.

And then—laughing at the way his five-year-old daughter had

sleepily and carelessly said good-bye when he had left the apartment, standing there with the noise of engines filling the fresh April evening air, kissing his sister Elizabeth good-bye—the dream came back. Elizabeth was as rosy and sturdy as ever, a cheerful, pretty girl who looked as though she had just come triumphantly off a tennis court or from a swimming meet, and if there was any touch of doom hanging over her, it was very well hidden.

"Bring me back Cary Grant," Elizabeth said as she brushed his cheek.

"Of course," Roy said.

"I now leave you two to say a fond farewell," Elizabeth said. "Alice, give him his last-minute instructions. Tell him to behave himself."

"I've already briefed him for this mission," Alice said. "No girls. No more than three Martinis before dinner. Telephone me and report twice weekly. Get on the plane and get home the minute the job is done."

"Two weeks," Roy said. "I swear I'll be back in two weeks."

"Don't have too good a time." Alice was smiling but on the verge of tears, as she always was every time he went anyplace without her, even overnight to Washington.

"I won't," Roy said. "I promise to be miserable."

"Good enough." Alice laughed.

"No old telephone numbers secreted on your person?" Elizabeth asked.

"No." There had been a period in Roy's life, just before he married Alice, when he had been quite lively, and during the war some of his friends had come back from Europe with lurid and highly fictionized tales of wild times in Paris and London, and to the women of his family he seemed more dashing and unstable than was the fact.

"God," he said, "it'll be a relief getting away from this female board of directors for a few days."

He and Alice went up to the gate.

"Take care of yourself, darling," Alice said softly.

"Don't worry." He kissed her.

"I hate this," Alice said, holding on to him. "We're always saying good-bye. This is the last time. From now on, no matter where you go, I'm going with you."

"All right." Roy smiled down at her.

"Even if you only go to Yankee Stadium."

"Couldn't be more pleased." He held her tightly for a moment, dear and familiar and forlorn, left behind this way. Then he walked out to the plane. He turned as he started to climb into it, and waved. Alice and Elizabeth waved back, and he noticed again how much alike they looked, standing together, like two sisters in a pretty family, both of them blond and fair, trim, with little tricks of movement and holding themselves that were almost identical.

He turned and went into the plane, and a moment later the door was shut behind him and the plane started rolling toward the end of the runway.

Ten days later, over the phone between Los Angeles and New York, Roy told Alice she would have to come West. "Munson says it's going to take six months," Roy said, "and he's promised me a place to live, and you are hereby invited."

"Thanks," Alice said. "Tell Munson I would like to kick him in the teeth."

"Can't be helped, baby," Roy said. "Commerce above all. You know."

"Why couldn't he have told you before you went out? Then you could've helped me close up the apartment and we could've gone out together."

"He didn't know before I came out," Roy said patiently. "The world is very confused these days."

"I would like to kick him in the teeth."

"O.K." Roy grinned. "You come out and tell him yourself. When do you arrive? Tomorrow?"

"There's one thing you've got to learn, Roy," Alice said. "I am not a troop movement. You can't say, 'Civilian Alice Gaynor will report three thousand miles from here at 4 P.M. tomorrow,' and expect it to happen."

"O.K., you're not a troop movement. When?"

Alice chuckled. "You sound nice and anxious."

"I *am* nice and anxious."

"That's good."

"When?"

"Well"—Alice hesitated thoughtfully—"I have to get Sally out of school, I have to send some things to storage, I have to rent the apartment, I have to get plane reservations—"

"When?"

"Two weeks," Alice said, "if I can get the reservations all right. Can you wait?"

"No," Roy said.

"Neither can I." They both laughed. "Have you been very gay out there?"

Roy recognized the tentative, inquiring tone and sighed to himself.

"Dull as mud," he said. "I stay in in the evenings and read. I've read six books and I'm halfway through General Marshall's report on the conduct of the war."

"There was one evening you didn't read." Alice's voice was careful and purposely light.

"All right," Roy said flatly. "Let's hear it."

"Monica came in from the Coast Tuesday and she called me. She said she saw you with a beautiful girl at a fancy restaurant."

"If there was any justice," Roy said, "they would drop Monica on Bikini Atoll."

"She had long black hair, Monica said."

"She was absolutely right," Roy said. "The girl had long black hair."

"Don't shout. I can hear perfectly well."

"What Monica neglected to say was that it was Charlie Lewis's wife—"

"She said you were alone."

"—and Charlie Lewis was twenty feet away, in the men's room."

"Are you sure?"

"No. Maybe he was in the ladies' room."

"It may be funny to you, but with your history—"

"I will match my history with any husband's," Roy said.

"I hate your sense of humor on this subject." Alice's voice began to tremble a little, and Roy relented.

"Listen, baby," he said softly. "Get out here quick. Quick as you can. Then we can stop this nonsense."

"I'm sorry." Alice's voice was soft and repentant. "It's just that we've been away from each other for so long in these last few years. I'm foolish and jittery. Who's paying for this call?"

"The company."

"That's good." Alice chuckled. "I'd hate to fight on our own money. Do you love me?"

"Get out here quick."

"Do you consider that an answer to my question?"

"Yes."

"O.K.," Alice said. "So do I. Good-bye, darling. See you soon."

"Kiss Sally for me," said Roy.

"I will. Good-bye."

Roy hung up. First he shook his head a little wearily, remembering the argument; then he smiled, remembering the end of the conversation. He got up from his chair and went over to the calendar on the desk, to try to figure what day he could expect his wife and child.

The telegram came three days later: "RESERVATIONS ON 2 O'CLOCK FLIGHT MAY 14. WILL ARRIVE BURBANK AT 10 P.M. YOUR TIME. PLEASE SHAVE. LOVE, ALICE."

Roy grinned as he reread the telegram, then became conscious of a sensation of uneasiness that refused to be crystallized or pinned down. He walked around all that day with that undefined sense of trouble, and it wasn't until he was dozing off to sleep that night that it suddenly became clear to him. He woke and got out of bed and read the telegram again. May 14th. He képt the lamp on and lit a cigarette and sat up in the narrow bed in the impersonal hotel room and slowly allowed the thing to take control.

He had never been a superstitious man, or even a religious man, and he had always laughed at his mother, who had a fund of dreams and predictions and omens of good and evil at her command. Alice had one or two superstitious habits—like not talking about anything that she wanted to have happen, because she was sure it wouldn't happen if it were mentioned or hoped for too much— but he had always scorned them, too. During the war, when every magazine assured the world that there were no atheists in foxholes, he had never prayed, even in the most gloomy and dangerous times. He had never, in all his adult life, done anything as a result of superstition or premonition. He looked around him at his efficiently furnished, bright, twentieth-century room and felt foolish to be awake now in the heel of the night, chasing phantoms and echoing warnings and scraps of old dreams through the sensible channels of his engineer's mind.

The dream, of course, had been explicit. His sister was to die on May 14th. But dreams never were what they seemed to be, and Elizabeth and Alice looked so much alike, and they were always together and such good friends. . . . He knew enough about dreams to understand that it would be a simple transference in that shadowy, whimsical world—a wife for a sister, a sister for a wife. And now, of all the days in the year, his wife and child had picked May 14th to fly the three thousand miles over the rivers and mountains of the continent from New York to California.

He put out the light much later, with nothing decided, and tried to sleep. He stared up at the dark ceiling, listening to the occasional swift swoosh of a car on the street outside, hurrying home through the waning night. For a man who didn't believe in Fate, he thought, who saw the world in terms of simple cause and effect; who felt that no act was inevitable, that what was going to happen tomorrow or the next second was in no place determined and was everlastingly variable; who felt that no man's death or burial place was fixed, that no event was recorded in any future book, that the human race got hints or warnings from no supernatural source—this was a ludicrous and profitless way to spend a night. For a man who walked under ladders, cheerfully broke mirrors, never had his palm read or his fortune told from cards, he felt that he was behaving idiotically, and yet he couldn't sleep.

In the morning he called New York.

"Alice," he said, "I want you to come by train."

"What's the matter?" she said.

"I'm afraid of the plane." He heard her laugh incredulously over the phone. "I'm afraid of the plane," he repeated stubbornly.

"Don't be silly," Alice said. "They haven't had an accident with that plane yet, and they won't start now."

"Even so—"

"And I'm not going to try to keep Sally amused for three days in a roomette," Alice said. "It would take me the whole summer to recover."

"Please," Roy said.

"And I couldn't get train reservations for weeks," Alice said, "and the apartment's rented and everything. What's come over you?" Her voice sounded suspicious and wary.

"Nothing," Roy said. "It's just that I'm worried about flying."

"Good God!" Alice said. "You've flown two hundred thousand miles in all sorts of contraptions."

"I know," Roy said. "That's why I'm worried."

"Are you drunk?" Alice asked.

"Alice, darling," Roy sighed. "It's eight o'clock in the morning out here."

"Well, you sound queer."

"I've been up all night, worrying."

"Well, stop worrying. I'll see you on the fourteenth. Are you sure you're all right?"

"Yes."

"This is a very strange telephone call, I must say."

"I'm sorry."

They talked for a moment more, but quite coldly, and Roy hung up feeling dissatisfied and defeated.

He called again two days later and tried once more.

"Don't ask any questions," he said. "Just do this for me, and I'll explain when you get out here. If you want to come on the plane, that's all right, but don't come on the fourteenth. Come on the fifteenth or sixteenth or seventeenth. Any other day. But not on the fourteenth.''

"Roy,'' Alice said, "you've got me terribly worried. What's come over you? I've asked Elizabeth and she says that this doesn't sound like you at all.''

"How is she?'' Roy asked.

"Elizabeth is fine. She tells me to ignore you and come out as scheduled.''

"Tell her to mind her own damned business.'' Roy had been working hard and sleeping badly and his voice was raw and nervous, and Alice reacted to it.

"I think I know what's going on,'' she said coldly. "Monica told me there's a big party at the Condons' on the fourteenth, and you've probably promised to take someone else, and a wife would be a big handicap—''

"Oh, God, will you stop that!'' Roy shouted into the phone.

"I haven't been married to you for seven years for nothing,'' Alice said. "I'm not blind.''

"Come out today!'' Roy shouted. "Come out tomorrow! Come out the thirteenth! Only not the fourteenth!''

"You know as well as I do that if I give up my reservations, I won't get another until June. If you don't want to see me any more, tell me. You don't have to go through all this rigmarole.''

"Alice, darling,'' Roy pleaded, "I assure you I want to see you.''

"Well, then, stop this nonsense or tell me what it's all about.''

"Alice, it's this way,'' he began, resolved to tell her, no matter how much of an idiot it made him feel, but there was a click on the wire and then three thousand miles of whispering silence. By the time he got Alice back on the phone, ten minutes later, he felt too ridiculous, felt that he could not live with himself or his wife if he at this late date exposed himself as a silly, undependable man with a brain gone soft and nervous and irresponsible after all the sane, dependable years.

"I haven't anything else to say,'' he told Alice when the operator finally made the connection, "except that I love you very much and I couldn't bear it if anything ever happened to you.''

He heard Alice crying softly at the other end of the wire. "We have to be together soon,'' she said. "This is awful. And please don't call me any more, Roy, darling. You're acting so strangely, and after I talk to you, the most miserable ideas grab hold of me. Will it be all right when I get out there?''

"It'll be wonderful, darling,'' Roy said.

"And you'll never go away without me again? Never?"

"Never." He could close his eyes and see her crouched like a little girl over the phone in the bedroom of their quiet, pleasant home, both her hands on the instrument, her pretty, clever face screwed up with grief and longing, and it was hard to say anything more. "Good night," he said. "Be careful."

He hung up and stared wildly at the blank wall on the other side of the room, knowing he wouldn't sleep again that night.

There was an early fog on the morning of May 14th, and Roy stared at it, hot-eyed and lightheaded from lack of sleep, and went out and walked along the quiet, gray streets, with only police cars and milk-delivery carts disturbing the soft, thick dawn.

California, he thought; it's always foggy in the morning, fog is general in California before eight, and it's a different time and a different weather on the coast of the Atlantic, and her plane isn't due to leave for hours yet.

It must be the war, he thought. This would never have happened to me before the war. I thought I came out all right, but maybe I was overconfident. All the cemeteries, with the young men tucked away in the sand and spring grass, and the old ladies in black lace dresses dying on the next street in London in the air raids. A man's imagination was bound to take a morbid turn, finally. I must take hold of myself, he told himself reasonably. I'm the man who always felt sane, balanced, healthy in all situations, who always scorned mediums and table tappers, priests and psychoanalysts.

The fog was beginning to lift, and he stopped to stare at the distant smudge of mountains that stood guard over the eastern approaches of the city. Planes had to come in steeply over them and circle the city and land from the westward side. A strip of blue appeared above the mountains and widened and widened, and the fog melted away in wisps among the ugly, fat palm trees that lined the street, and soon the sun was shining on the dewy lawns, and the sky looked clear and blue from Beverly Hills to Scotland.

He went back to his hotel and lay down without even taking his shoes off. Some time later he woke up. Vaguely, in the moment before waking, there was a confusion of planes going down in puffs of smoke, like the newsreel of an air battle, and Sally's voice over it, regretfully saying, as she always did at bedtime, "Do I *really* have to go to sleep now? I'm terribly wide-awake."

He looked at the clock. It was one-forty in New York. They were at the airport now, and the big plane was waiting on the field, with the mechanics fiddling on it and the men checking the gas tanks. The hell with it, he thought. I don't care how foolish I seem.

He picked up the phone. "La Guardia Field, New York," he said.

"There will be a slight delay," the operator sang. "I will call you."

"This is very important," Roy said. "Urgent."

"There will be a slight delay," the operator said in exactly the same tones. "I will call you."

He hung up and went to the window and stared out. The sky stretched, radiant and clear, over the hills toward New York. I'll tell her the whole thing, he thought, idiotic or not. Forbid her to get on the plane. We can laugh about it later. I'll take the first plane back myself and fly back with them. That'll prove to her it has nothing to do with anything here.

He went and got out his valise and put three shirts in it, then picked up the phone again. Five minutes later he got the airport, but it took another five minutes to get through to the station manager for the airline.

"My name is Gaynor"—Roy's voice was high and hurried— "and this is a very unusual request, so please listen carefully."

"What was that name, sir?"

"Gaynor. G-a-y-n-o-r."

"Oh, yes, Gaynor. Like the dive." The distant voice laughed politely at its own joke. "What can I do for you, sir?"

"My wife and child—"

"You will have to speak louder, please."

"My wife and child!" Roy shouted. "Mrs. Alice Gaynor, on the two-o'clock flight to Los Angeles. I want you to stop them—"

"What did you say?"

"I said I wanted you to stop them. They are not to take the plane. My wife and child. Mrs. Alice Gaynor. The two-o'clock flight to Los Angeles—"

"I'm afraid that's impossible, Mr. Gaynor." The voice was puzzled but polite.

"It can't be impossible. All you have to do is announce it over the public-address system and—"

"Impossible, sir. The two-o'clock flight is just taking off at this moment. I'm terribly sorry. Is there anything else I can do for you?"

513

"No," Roy said flatly, and put the phone down. He sat on the edge of his bed for a moment, then got up and went to the window. He looked out at the bright sky and the green-and-yellow mountains. He remained standing there, staring at the mountains, waiting for the call from the airline.

# Peter Two

It was Saturday night and people were killing each other by the hour on the small screen. Policemen were shot in the line of duty, gangsters were thrown off roofs, and an elderly lady was slowly poisoned for her pearls, and her murderer brought to justice by a cigarette company after a long series of discussions in the office of a private detective. Brave, unarmed actors leaped at villains holding forty-fives, and ingénues were saved from death by the knife by the quick thinking of various handsome and intrepid young men.

Peter sat in the big chair in front of the screen, his feet up over the arm, eating grapes. His mother wasn't home, so he ate the seeds and all as he stared critically at the violence before him. When his mother was around, the fear of appendicitis hung in the air and she watched carefully to see that each seed was neatly extracted and placed in an ashtray. Too, if she were home, there would be irritated little lectures on the quality of television entertainment for the young, and quick-tempered fiddling with the dials to find something that was vaguely defined as educational. Alone, daringly awake at eleven o'clock, Peter ground the seeds between his teeth, enjoying the impolite noise and the solitude and freedom of the empty house. During the television commercials Peter closed his eyes and imagined himself hurling bottles at large unshaven men with pistols and walking slowly up dark stairways toward the door behind which everyone knew the Boss was waiting, the bulge of his shoulder holster unmistakable under the cloth of his pencil-striped flannel jacket.

Peter was thirteen years old. In his class there were three other boys with the same given name, and the history teacher, who thought he was a funny man, called them Peter One, Peter Two (now eating grapes, seeds and all), Peter Three, and Peter the Great. Peter the Great was, of course, the smallest boy in the class. He weighed only sixty-two pounds, and he wore glasses, and in games he was always the last one to be chosen. The class always laughed when the history teacher called out "Peter the Great," and Peter Two laughed with them, but he didn't think it was so awfully funny.

He had done something pretty good for Peter the Great two weeks ago, and now they were what you might call friends. All the Peters were what you might call friends on account of that comedian of a history teacher. They weren't *real* friends, but they had something together, something the other boys didn't have. They didn't like it, but they had it, and it made them responsible for each other. So two weeks ago, when Charley Blaisdell, who weighed a hundred and twenty, took Peter the Great's cap at recess and started horsing around with it, and Peter the Great looked as if he was going to cry, he, Peter Two, grabbed the cap and gave it back and faced Blaisdell. Of course, there was a fight, and Peter thought it was going to be his third defeat of the term, but a wonderful thing happened. In the middle of the fight, just when Peter was hoping one of the teachers would show up (they sure showed up plenty of times when you didn't need them), Blaisdell let a hard one go. Peter ducked and Blaisdell hit him on the top of the head and broke his arm. You could tell right off he broke his arm, because he fell to the ground yelling, and his arm just hung like a piece of string. Walters, the gym teacher, finally showed up and carried Blaisdell off, yelling all the time, and Peter the Great came up and said admiringly, "Boy, one thing you have to admit, you sure have a hard head."

Blaisdell was out of class two days, and he still had his arm in the sling, and every time he was excused from writing on the blackboard because he had a broken arm, Peter got a nice warm feeling all over. Peter the Great hung around him all the time, doing things for him and buying him sodas, because Peter the Great's parents were divorced and gave him all the money he wanted, to make up to him. And that was O.K.

But the best thing was the feeling he'd had since the fight. It was like what the people on the television must feel after they'd gone into a room full of enemies and come out with the girl or with the papers or with the suspect, leaving corpses and desolation behind them. Blaisdell weighed a hundred and twenty pounds but that hadn't stopped Peter any more than the fact that the spies all had two guns apiece ever stopped the F.B.I. men on the screen. They saw what they had to do and they went in and did it, that was all. Peter couldn't phrase it for himself, but for the first time

516

in his life he had a conscious feeling of confidence and pride in himself.

"Let them come," he muttered obscurely, munching grape seeds and watching the television set through narrowed eyes, "just let them come."

He was going to be a dangerous man, he felt, when he grew up, but one to whom the weak and the unjustly hunted could safely turn. He was sure he was going to be six feet tall, because his father was six feet tall, and all his uncles, and that would help. But he would have to develop his arms. They were just too thin. After all, you couldn't depend on people breaking their bones on your head every time. He had been doing pushups each morning and night for the past month. He could only do five and a half at a time so far, but he was going to keep at it until he had arms like steel bars. Arms like that really could mean the difference between life and death later on, when you had to dive under the gun and disarm somebody. You had to have quick reflexes, too, of course, and be able to feint to one side with your eyes before the crucial moment. And, most important of all, no matter what the odds, you had to be fearless. One moment of hesitation and it was a case for the morgue. But now, after the battle of Peter the Great's cap, he didn't worry about that part of it, the fearless part. From now on, it would just be a question of technique.

Comedians began to appear all over the dial, laughing with a lot of teeth, and Peter went into the kitchen and got another bunch of grapes and two tangerines from the refrigerator. He didn't put on the light in the kitchen and it was funny how mysterious a kitchen could be near midnight when nobody else was home, and there was only the beam of the light from the open refrigerator, casting shadows from the milk bottles onto the linoleum. Until recently he hadn't liked the dark too much and he always turned on lights wherever he went, but you had to practice being fearless, just like anything else.

He ate the two tangerines standing in the dark in the kitchen, just for practice. He ate the seeds, too, to show his mother. Then he went back into the living room, carrying the grapes.

The comedians were still on and still laughing. He fiddled with the dial, but they were wearing funny hats and laughing and telling jokes about the income tax on all the channels. If his mother hadn't made him promise to go to sleep by ten o'clock, he'd have turned off the set and gone to bed. He decided not to waste his time and got down on the floor and began to do pushups, trying to be sure to keep his knees straight. He was up to four and slowing down when he heard the scream. He stopped in the middle of a pushup and waited, just to make sure. The scream came again. It was a woman and it was real loud. He looked up at the television set. There was a man there talking about floor wax, a man with a mustache and a lot of teeth, and it was a cinch *he* wasn't doing any screaming.

The next time the scream came there was moaning and talking at the end of it, and the sound of fists beating on the front door. Peter got up and turned off the television, just to be sure the sounds he was hearing weren't somehow being broadcast.

The beating on the door began again and a woman's voice cried "Please, please, *please* . . ." and there was no doubt about it any more.

Peter looked around him at the empty room. Three lamps were lit and the room was nice and bright and the light was reflected off the grapes and off the glass of the picture of the boats on Cape Cod that his Aunt Martha painted the year she was up there. The television set stood in the corner, like a big blind eye now that the light was out. The cushions of the soft chair he had been sitting in to watch the programs were pushed in and he knew his mother would come and plump them out before she went to sleep, and the whole room looked like a place in which it was impossible to hear a woman screaming at midnight and beating on the door with her fists and yelling, "Please, please, *please* . . ."

The woman at the door yelled "Murder, murder, he's killing me!" and for the first time Peter was sorry his parents had gone out that night.

"Open the door!" the woman yelled. "Please, *please* open the door!" You could tell she wasn't saying please just to be polite by now.

Peter looked nervously around him. The room, with all its lights, seemed strange, and there were shadows behind everything. Then the woman yelled again, just noise this time. Either a person is fearless, Peter thought coldly, or he isn't fearless. He started walking slowly toward the front door. There was a long mirror in the foyer and he got a good look at himself. His arms looked very thin.

The woman began hammering once more on the front door and Peter looked at it closely. It was a big steel door, but it was shaking minutely, as though somebody with a machine was working on it. For the first time he heard another voice. It was a man's voice, only it didn't sound quite like a man's voice. It sounded like an animal in a cave, growling and deciding to do something unreasonable. In all the scenes of threat and violence on the television set, Peter had never heard anything at all like it. He moved slowly toward the door, feeling the way he had felt when he had the flu, remembering how thin his arms looked in the mirror, regretting that he had decided to be fearless.

"Oh, God!" the woman yelled. "Oh, God, don't do it!"

Then there was some more hammering and the low, animal sound of the beast in the cave that you never heard over the air, and he threw the door open.

Mrs. Chalmers was there in the vestibule, on her knees, facing him, and behind her Mr. Chalmers was standing, leaning against the wall, with the door to his own apartment open behind him. Mr. Chalmers was making that funny sound and he had a gun in his hand and he was pointing it at Mrs. Chalmers.

The vestibule was small and it had what Peter's mother called Early American wallpaper and a brass light fixture. There were only the two doors opening on the vestibule, and the Chalmerses had a mat in front of theirs with "Welcome" written on it. The Chalmerses were in their mid-thirties, and Peter's mother always said about them, "One thing about our neighbors, they *are* quiet." She also said that Mrs. Chalmers put a lot of money on her back.

Mrs. Chalmers was kind of fat and her hair was pretty blond and her complexion was soft and pink and she always looked as though she had been in the beauty parlor all afternoon. She always said "My, you're getting to be a big boy" to Peter when she met him in the elevator, in a soft voice, as though she was just about to laugh. She must have said that fifty times by now. She had a good, strong smell of perfume on her all the time, too.

Mr. Chalmers wore pince-nez glasses most of the time and he was getting bald and he worked late at his office a good many evenings of the week. When he met Peter in the elevator he would say, "It's getting colder," or "It's getting warmer," and that was all, so Peter had no opinion about him, except that he looked like the principal of a school.

But now Mrs. Chalmers was on her knees in the vestibule and her dress was torn and she was crying and there were black streaks on her cheeks and she didn't look as though she'd just come from the beauty parlor. And Mr. Chalmers wasn't wearing a jacket and he didn't have his glasses on and what hair he had was mussed all over his head and he was leaning against the Early American wallpaper making this animal noise, and he had a big, heavy pistol in his hand and he was pointing it right at Mrs. Chalmers.

"Let me in!" Mrs. Chalmers yelled, still on her knees. "You've got to let me in. He's going to kill me. *Please!*"

"Mrs. Chalmers . . ." Peter began. His voice sounded as though he were trying to talk under water, and it was very hard to say the "s" at the end of her name. He put out his hands uncertainly in front of him, as though he expected somebody to throw him something.

"Get inside, you," Mr. Chalmers said.

Peter looked at Mr. Chalmers. He was only five feet away and without his glasses he was squinting. Peter feinted with his eyes, or at least later in his life he thought he had feinted with his eyes. Mr. Chalmers didn't do anything. He just stood there, with the pistol pointed, somehow, it seemed to Peter, at both Mrs. Chalmers and himself at the same time. Five feet was a long distance, a long, long distance.

"Good night," Peter said, and he closed the door.

There was a single sob on the other side of the door and that was all.

Peter went in and put the uneaten grapes back in the refrigerator, flicking on the light as he went into the kitchen and leaving it on when he went out. Then he went back to the living room and got the stems from the first bunch of grapes and threw them into the fireplace, because otherwise his mother would notice and look for the seeds and not see them and give him four tablespoons of milk of magnesia the next day.

Then, leaving the lights on in the living room, although he knew what his mother would say about that when she got home, he went into his room and quickly got into bed. He waited for the sound of shots. There were two or three noises that might have been shots, but in the city it was hard to tell.

He was still awake when his parents came home. He heard his mother's voice, and he knew from the sound she was complaining about the lights in the living room and kitchen, but he pretended to be sleeping when she came into his room to look at him. He didn't want to start in with his mother about the Chalmerses, because then she'd ask when it had happened and she'd want to know what he was doing up at twelve o'clock.

He kept listening for shots for a long time, and he got hot and damp under the covers and then freezing cold. He heard several sharp, ambiguous noises in the quiet night, but nothing that you could be sure about, and after a while he fell asleep.

In the morning, Peter got out of bed early, dressed quickly, and went silently out of the apartment without waking his parents. The vestibule looked just the way it always did, with the brass lamp and the flowered wallpaper and the Chalmerses' doormat with "Welcome" on it. There were no bodies and no blood. Sometimes when Mrs. Chalmers had been standing there waiting for the elevator, you could smell her perfume for a long time after. But now there was no smell of perfume, just the dusty, apartment-house usual smell. Peter stared at the Chalmerses' door nervously while waiting for the elevator to come up, but it didn't open and no sound came from within.

Sam, the man who ran the elevator and who didn't like him, anyway, only grunted when Peter got into the elevator, and Peter decided not to ask him any questions. He went out into the chilly, bright Sunday-morning street, half expecting to see the morgue wagon in front of the door, or at least two or three prowl cars. But there was only a sleepy woman in slacks airing a boxer and a man with his collar turned up hurrying up from the corner with the newspapers under his arm.

Peter went across the street and looked up to the sixth floor, at the windows of the Chalmerses' apartment. The Venetian blinds were pulled shut in every room and all the windows were closed.

A policeman walked down the other side of the street, heavy, blue and purposeful, and for a moment Peter felt close to arrest. But the policeman continued on toward the avenue and turned the corner and disappeared and Peter said to himself, They never know anything.

He walked up and down the street, first on one side, then on the other, waiting, although it was hard to know what he was waiting for. He saw a hand come out through the blinds in his parents' room and slam the window shut, and he knew he ought to get upstairs quickly with a good excuse for being out, but he couldn't face them this morning, and he would invent an excuse later. Maybe he would even say he had gone to the museum, although he doubted that his mother would swallow that. Some excuse. Later.

Then, after he had been patrolling the street for almost two hours, and just as he was coming up to the entrance of his building, the door opened and Mr. and Mrs. Chalmers came out. He had on his pince-nez and a dark-gray hat, and Mrs. Chalmers had on her fur coat and a red hat with feathers on it. Mr. Chalmers was holding the door open politely for his wife, and she looked, as

521

she came out the door, as though she had just come from the beauty parlor.

It was too late to turn back or avoid them, and Peter just stood still, five feet from the entrance.

"Good morning," Mr. Chalmers said as he took his wife's arm and they started walking past Peter.

"Good morning, Peter," said Mrs. Chalmers in her soft voice, smiling at him. "Isn't it a nice day today?"

"Good morning," Peter said, and he was surprised that it came out and sounded like good morning.

The Chalmerses walked down the street toward Madison Avenue, two married people, arm in arm, going to church or to a big hotel for Sunday breakfast. Peter watched them, ashamed. He was ashamed of Mrs. Chalmers for looking the way she did the night before, down on her knees, and yelling like that and being so afraid. He was ashamed of Mr. Chalmers for making the noise that was not like the noise of a human being, and for threatening to shoot Mrs. Chalmers and not doing it. And he was ashamed of himself because he had been fearless when he opened the door, but had not been fearless ten seconds later, with Mr. Chalmers five feet away with the gun. He was ashamed of himself for not taking Mrs. Chalmers into the apartment, ashamed because he was not lying now with a bullet in his heart. But most of all he was ashamed because they had all said good morning to each other and the Chalmerses were walking quietly together, arm in arm, in the windy sunlight, toward Madison Avenue.

It was nearly eleven o'clock when Peter got back to the apartment, but his parents had gone back to sleep. There was a pretty good program on at eleven, about counterspies in Asia, and he turned it on automatically, while eating an orange. It was pretty exciting, but then there was a part in which an Oriental held a ticking bomb in his hand in a roomful of Americans, and Peter could tell what was coming. The hero, who was fearless and who came from California, was beginning to feint with his eyes, and Peter reached over and turned the set off. It closed down with a shivering, collapsing pattern. Blinking a little, Peter watched the blind screen for a moment.

Ah, he thought in sudden, permanent disbelief, after the night in which he had faced the incomprehensible, shameless, weaponed grownup world and had failed to disarm it, ah, they can have that, that's for kids.

# The Sunny Banks of the River Lethe

Hugh Forester always remembered everything. He remembered the dates of the Battle of New Cold Harbor (May 31–June 12, 1864); he remembered the name of his teacher in the first grade (Webel; red-haired; weight, one-forty-five; no eyelashes); he remembered the record number of strikeouts in one game in the National League (Dizzy Dean, St. Louis Cards, July 30, 1933, seventeen men, against the Cubs); he remembered the fifth line of "To a Skylark" (Shelley: "In profuse strains of unpremeditated art"); he remembered the address of the first girl he ever kissed (Prudence Collingwood, 248 East South Temple Street, Salt Lake City, Utah; March 14, 1918); he remembered the dates of the three partitions of Poland and the destruction of the Temple (1772, 1793, 1795, and 70 A.D.); he remembered the number of ships taken by Nelson at the Battle of Trafalgar (twenty), and the profession of the hero of Frank Norris's novel *McTeague* (dentist); he remembered the name of the man who won the Pulitzer Prize for history in 1925 (Frederic L. Paxson), the name of the Derby winner at Epsom in 1923 (Papyrus), and the number he drew in the draft in 1940 (4726); he remembered the figures for his blood pressure (a hundred and sixty-five over ninety; too high), his blood type (0), and his vision (forty over twenty for the right eye and thirty over twenty for the left); he remembered what his boss told him when he was fired from his first job ("I'm getting a machine to do the job"), and what his wife said when he proposed to her ("I want to live in New York"); he remembered the correct name of Lenin (Vladimir Ilyich Ulyanov), and what caused the death of Louis XIV (gangrene of the leg). He also remembered the species of birds, the mean depths of the navigable rivers of America; the names, given and assumed, of all the Popes, including the ones at Avignon; the batting averages of Harry Heilmann and Heinie Groh; the dates of the total eclipses of the sun since the reign of Charlemagne; the speed of sound; the location of the tomb of D. H. Lawrence; all of the *Rubáiyát* of Omar Khayyám; the population of the lost settlement of Roanoke; the rate of fire of the Browning automatic rifle; the campaigns of Caesar in Gaul and Britain; the name of the shepherdess in *As You Like It* and the amount of money he had in the Chemical Bank & Trust on the morning of December 7, 1941 ($2,367.58).

Then he forgot his twenty-fourth wedding anniversary (January 25th). His wife, Narcisse, looked at him strangely over breakfast that morning, but he was reading the previous night's newspaper and thinking, They will never get it straight in Washington, and he didn't pay much attention. There was a letter from their son, who was at the University of Alabama, but he put it in his pocket without opening it. It was addressed only to him, so he knew it was a request for money. When Morton wrote his dutiful, familial notes they were addressed to both his parents. Morton was at Alabama because his marks had not been high enough to get him into Yale, Dartmouth, Williams, Antioch, the College of the City of New York, or the University of Colorado.

Narcisse asked if Hugh wanted fish for dinner and he said yes, and Narcisse said that fish was criminally expensive, too, and he said yes, and she asked if anything was the matter and he said no and kissed her and walked out of the apartment to the 242nd Street subway station and stood all the way down to the office, reading the morning newspaper. Narcisse's parents had lived in France for some time and that was where the name came from; by now he was used to it. As he read his newspaper in the crowded car he wished, mildly, that most of the people whom people wrote about in the newspapers would vanish.

Hugh was the first one in the office, and he went to his cubbyhole and sat at his desk, leaving the door open, enjoying the empty desks and the sound of silence. He remembered that Narcisse's nose had twitched at the breakfast table and that she had seemed about to cry. He wondered briefly why, but knew that he would be told in good time, and dismissed it. Narcisse cried between five and eight times a month.

The company for which he worked was putting out a one-volume encyclopedia, absolutely complete, on Indian paper, with seven hundred and fifty illustrations. There was some talk of its being called the Giant Pocket Encyclopedia, but no final decision had as yet been reached. Hugh was working on the "S"s. Today he had Soap, Sodium, Sophocles, and Sorrento before him. He remembered that Maxim Gorki had lived in Sorrento, and that of the hundred and twenty-three plays that Sophocles wrote, only seven had been discovered. Hugh was not actually unhappy at his work except when Mr. Gorsline appeared. Mr. Gorsline was the owner and editor-in-chief of the house, and believed in standing behind the backs of his employees, silently watching them at their labors. Whenever Mr. Gorsline came into the room, Hugh had the curious feeling that blood was running slowly over his groin.

Mr. Gorsline was gray-haired, wore tweed suits, had the face and figure of a picador, and had started with calendars. The house still put out a great variety of calendars—pornographic, religious and occasional. Hugh was very useful on calendars because he remembered things like the death of Oliver Cromwell (September 3, 1658) and the date on which Marconi sent the first wireless message across the Atlantic (December 12, 1901) and the date of the first steamboat run from New York to Albany (August 17, 1807).

Mr. Gorsline appreciated Hugh's peculiar talents and was relentlessly paternal about his welfare. Mr. Gorsline was a believer in homeopathic medicines and the health-giving properties of raw vegetables, particularly eggplant. He was also opposed to glasses, having thrown his away in 1944 after reading a book about a series of exercises for the muscles of the eyes. He had persuaded Hugh to discard his glasses for a period of seven months in 1948, during which time Hugh had suffered from continual headaches, for which Mr. Gorsline had prescribed minute doses of a medicine from a homeopathic pharmacy which made Hugh feel as though he had been hit in the skull with bird shot. Now whenever Mr. Gorsline stood behind Hugh, he stared at Hugh's glasses with the stubborn, Irredentist expression of an Italian general surveying Trieste. Hugh's health, while not actively bad, was shabby. He had frequent, moist colds, and his eyes had a tendency to become bloodshot after lunch. There was no hiding these lapses or the fact that in cold weather he had to make several trips an hour to the men's room. At such times, Mr. Gorsline would break his customary silence to outline diets designed to improve the tone of the nasal passages, the eyes and the kidneys.

During the morning, Mr. Gorsline came into Hugh's room twice. The first time, he stood behind Hugh's chair without saying a word for five minutes, then said, "Still on Sodium?" and left. The next time, he stood silently for eight minutes, then said, "Forester, you're putting on weight. White bread," and left. Each time, Hugh had the familiar feeling in the groin.

Just before lunch, Hugh's daughter came into his office. She kissed him and said, "Many happy returns of the day, Daddy," and gave him a small oblong package with a bow of colored ribbon on top of it. Clare was twenty-two and had been married four years but she refused to stop saying "Daddy." Hugh opened the package, feeling confused. There was a gold-topped fountain pen in it. It was the fourth fountain pen Clare had given him in the last six years, two on birthdays and the third on Christmas. She had not inherited her father's memory.

"What's this for?" Hugh asked.

"Daddy!" Clare said. "You're kidding."

Hugh stared at the pen. He knew it wasn't his birthday (June 12th). And it certainly wasn't Christmas (December 25th).

"It can't be," Clare said incredulously. "You didn't *forget!*"

Hugh remembered Narcisse's face at breakfast, and the twitching of her nose. "Oh, my," he said.

"You better load yourself with flowers before you set foot in the house tonight," Clare said. She peered anxiously at her father. "Daddy, are you all right?" she asked.

"Of course I'm all right," Hugh said, annoyed. "Everybody forgets an anniversary once in a while."

"Not you, Daddy."

"Me, too. I'm human, too," he said, but he felt shaken. He unscrewed the top of the pen and wrote TWENTY-FOUR YEARS, in capitals, on a pad, keeping his head down. He now owned eight fountain pens. "It's just what I needed, Clare," he said, and put it in his pocket. "Thank you very much."

"You haven't forgotten that you promised to take me to lunch, have you?" Clare had phoned the day before to make the appointment for lunch, because, she told Hugh, she had some serious problems to discuss.

"Of course not," Hugh said briskly. He put on his overcoat, and they went out together. Hugh ordered sole, then changed to a lamb chop, because he remembered that Narcisse had said at breakfast they were to have fish for dinner. Clare ordered roast chicken and Waldorf salad, and a bottle of wine, because, she said, the afternoons became less sad after a bottle of wine. Hugh didn't understand why a pretty twenty-two-year-old girl needed wine to keep her from being sad in the afternoons, but he didn't interfere.

While Clare was going over the wine card, Hugh took Morton's letter out of his pocket and read it. Morton was asking for two hundred and fifty dollars. It seemed that he had borrowed a fraternity brother's Plymouth and gone into a ditch with it after a dance and the repairs had come to a hundred and twenty-five dollars. There had been a girl with him, too, and her nose had been broken and the doctor had charged a hundred dollars for the nose and Morton had promised to pay. Then, there was ten dollars for two books in a course on ethics and fifteen dollars just, as Morton phrased it, to make it a round number. Hugh put the letter back in his pocket without saying anything about it to Clare. At least, Hugh thought, it wasn't as bad as last year, when it looked as though Morton was going to be kicked out of school for cheating on a calculus examination.

As Clare ate her chicken and drank her wine, she told her father what was troubling her. Mostly, it was Freddie, her husband. She was undecided, she said as she ate away steadily at her chicken, whether to leave him or have a baby. She was sure Freddie was seeing another woman, on East Seventy-eighth Street, in the afternoons, and before she took a step in either direction she wanted Hugh to confront Freddie man to man and get a statement of intentions from him. Freddie wouldn't talk to her. Whenever she brought the subject up, he left the house and went to a hotel for the night. If it was to be a divorce, she would need at least a thousand dollars from Hugh for the six weeks in Reno, because Freddie had already told her he wouldn't advance a cent for any damn thing like that. Besides, Freddie was having a little financial trouble at the moment. He had overdrawn against his account at the automobile agency for which he worked, and they had clamped down on him two weeks ago. If they had the baby, the doctor Clare wanted would cost eight hundred dollars, and there would be at least another five hundred for the hospital and nurses, and she knew she could depend on Daddy for that.

She drank her wine and talked on as Hugh ate silently. Freddie, she said, was also five months behind in his dues and greens fees at the golf club, and they were going to post his name if he didn't pay by Sunday, and that was *really* urgent, because of the disgrace, and Freddie had behaved like an absolute savage around the house ever since he received the letter from the club secretary.

"I told him," Clare said, with tears in her eyes and eating steadily, "I told him I would gladly go out and work, but he said he'd be damned if he'd let people say he couldn't support his own wife, and, of course, you have to respect a feeling like that. And he told me he wouldn't come to you for another cent, either, and you can't help admiring him for that, can you?"

"No," Hugh said, remembering that his son-in-law had borrowed

527

from him, over a period of four years, three thousand eight hundred and fifty dollars and had not paid back a cent. "No, you can't. Did he know you were going to come and talk to me today?"

"Vaguely," Clare said, and poured herself another glass of wine. As she carefully harvested the last bits of apple and walnut from her salad, Clare said she didn't really like to burden him with her problems but he was the only one in the whole world whose judgment she really trusted. He was so solid and sensible and smart, she said, and she didn't know any more whether she really loved Freddie or not and she was so confused and she hated to see Freddie so unhappy all the time about money and she wanted to know whether Hugh honestly felt she was ready for motherhood at the age of twenty-two. By the time they finished their coffee, Hugh had promised to talk to Freddie very soon about the woman on Seventy-eighth Street and to underwrite either the trip to Reno or the obstetrician, as the case might be, and he had made a half promise about the back dues and the greens fees.

On the way to the office, Hugh bought an alligator handbag for Narcisse for sixty dollars and worried sharply, for a moment, about inflation as he wrote out the check and handed it to the salesgirl.

It was a little difficult to work after lunch, because he kept thinking about Clare and what she had been like as a little girl (measles at four, mumps the year after, braces from eleven to fifteen, acne between fourteen and seventeen). He worked very slowly on Sorrento. Mr. Gorsline came in twice during the afternoon. The first time he said, "Still on Sorrento?" and the second time he said, "Who the hell cares if that Communist Russian wrote a book there?"

In addition to the usual sensation in the groin, Hugh noticed a quickening of his breath, which was almost a gasp, when Mr. Gorsline stood behind him during the afternoon.

After work, he went into the little bar on Lexington Avenue where he met Jean three times a week. She was sitting there, finishing her first whisky, and he sat down beside her and squeezed her hand in greeting. They had been in love for eleven years now, but he had kissed her only once (V-E Day), because she had been a classmate of Narcisse's at Bryn Mawr and they had decided early in the game to be honorable. She was a tall, majestic woman who, because she had led a troubled life, still looked comparatively young. They sat sadly and secretly in sad little bars late in the afternoon and talked in low, nostalgic tones about how different everything could have been. In the beginning, their conversation had been more animated, and for a half hour at a time Hugh had recovered some of the optimism and confidence that he had had as a young man who had taken all the honors at college, before it had become apparent that a retentive memory and talent and intelligence and luck were not all the same thing.

"I think, very soon," Jean said while he was sipping his drink, "we'll have to give this up. It isn't going anywhere, really, is it, and I just don't feel right about it. I feel guilty. Don't you?"

Until then, it hadn't occurred to Hugh that he had done anything to feel guilty about, with the possible exception of the kiss on V-E Day. But now that Jean had said it, he realized that he probably would feel guilty from now on, every time he entered the bar and saw her sitting there.

"Yes," he said sadly. "I suppose you're right."

"I'm going away for the summer," Jean said. "In June. When I come back I'm not going to see you any more."

Hugh nodded miserably. The summer was still five months away, but behind him he had a sense of something slipping, with a rustling noise, like a curtain coming down.

He had to stand in the subway all the way home, and the car was so crowded that he couldn't turn the pages of his newspaper. He read and reread the front page, thinking, I certainly am glad I wasn't elected President.

It was hot in the train, and he felt fat and uncomfortable jammed among the travellers, and he had a new, uneasy feeling that his flesh was overburdening him. Then, just before he came to Two hundred and forty-second Street, he realized that he had left the alligator bag on his desk in the office. He felt a little tickle of terror in his throat and knees. It was not so much that, empty-handed, he faced an evening of domestic sighs, half-spoken reproaches, and almost certain tears. It was not even so much the fact that he mistrusted the cleaning woman who did his office every night and who had once (November 3, 1950), he was sure, taken a dollar and thirty cents' worth of airmail stamps from the upper right-hand drawer. But, standing there in the now uncrowded car, he had to face the fact that twice in one day he had forgotten something. He couldn't remember when anything like that had ever happened to him before. He touched his head with his fingertips, as though there might be some obscure explanation to be found that way. He decided to give up drinking. He drank only five or six whiskies a week, but the induction of partial amnesia by alcohol was a well-established medical principle, and perhaps his level of tolerance was abnormally low.

The evening passed as he had expected. He bought some roses at the station for Narcisse, but he couldn't tell her about the alligator bag left on his desk, because he figured, correctly, that that would only compound the morning's offense. He even suggested that they return to the city for an anniversary dinner, but Narcisse had had the whole day alone to augment her self-pity and brood upon her martyrdom, and she insisted on eating the fish, which had cost ninety-three cents a pound. By ten-thirty she was crying.

Hugh slept badly and got to the office early the next morning, but even the sight of the alligator bag, left squarely in the middle of the desk by the cleaning woman, did not raise his spirits. During the day he forgot the names of three of Sophocles' plays *(Oedipus at Colonus, Trachiniae,* and *Philoctetes)* and the telephone number of his dentist.

It started that way. Hugh began to make more and more frequent trips to the reference library on the thirteenth floor, dreading the trip through the office, because of the way his fellow-workers commenced to look at him, curious and puzzled, as he traversed the room again and again in the course of an hour. One day he forgot the titles of the works of Sardou, the area of Santo Domingo, the symptoms of silicosis, the definition of syndrome, and the occasion of the mortification of Saint Simeon Stylites.

Hoping it would pass, he said nothing about it to anyone—not even to Jean, in the little bar on Lexington Avenue.

Mr. Gorsline took to standing for longer and longer periods behind Hugh's desk, and Hugh sat there, pretending to be working, pretending he didn't look haggard, his jowls hanging from his cheekbones like gallows ropes, his brain feeling like a piece of frozen meat that was being nibbled by a wolf. Once, Mr. Gorsline muttered something about hormones, and once, at four-thirty, he told Hugh to take the afternoon off. Hugh had worked for Mr. Gorsline for eighteen years and this was the first time Mr. Gorsline had told him to take an afternoon off. When Mr. Gorsline left his office, Hugh sat at his desk, staring blindly into terrifying depths.

One morning, some days after the anniversary, Hugh forgot the name of his morning newspaper. He stood in front of the news dealer, staring down at the ranked *Times* and *Tribunes* and *News* and *Mirrors,* and they all looked the same to him. He knew that for the past twenty-five years he had been buying the same paper each morning, but now there was no clue for him in their makeup or in their headlines as to which one it was. He bent down and peered more closely at the papers. The President, a headline announced, was to speak that night. As Hugh straightened up, he realized he no longer remembered the President's name or whether he was a Republican or a Democrat. For a moment, he experienced what could be described only as an exquisite pang of pleasure. But he knew it was deceptive, like the ecstasy described by T. E. Lawrence on the occasion when he was nearly beaten to death by the Turks.

He bought a copy of *Holiday*, and stared numbly at the colored photographs of distant cities all the way down to the office. That morning, he forgot the date on which John L. Sullivan won the heavyweight championship of the world, and the name of the inventor of the submarine. He also had to go to the reference library because he wasn't sure whether Santander was in Chile or Spain.

He was sitting at his desk that afternoon, staring at his hands, because for an hour he had had the feeling that mice were running between his fingers, when his son-in-law came into the office.

"Hi, Hughie, old boy," his son-in-law said. From the very first night his son-in-law had appeared at the house, he had been unfalteringly breezy with Hugh.

Hugh stood up and said "Hello—" and stopped. He stared at his son-in-law. He knew it was his son-in-law. He knew it was Clare's husband. But he couldn't remember the man's name. For the second time that day he experienced the trilling wave of pleasure that he had felt at the newsstand when he realized he had forgotten the name and political affiliations of the President of the United States. Only this time it seemed to last. It lasted while he shook hands with his son-in-law and all during the trip down in the elevator with him, and it lasted in the bar next door while he bought his son-in-law three Martinis.

"Hughie, old boy," his son-in-law said during the third Martini, "let's get down to cases. Clare said you had a problem you wanted to talk to me about. Spit it out, old boy, and let's get it over with. What have you got on your mind?"

Hugh looked hard at the man across the table. He searched his brain conscientiously, but he couldn't think of a single problem that might possibly involve them. "No," Hugh said slowly. "I have nothing in particular on my mind."

His son-in-law kept looking at Hugh belligerently while Hugh was paying for the drinks, but Hugh merely hummed under his breath, smiling slightly at the waitress. Outside, where they stood for a moment, his son-in-law cleared his throat once and said,

"Now, look here, old boy, if it's about—" but Hugh shook his hand warmly and walked briskly away, feeling deft and limber.

But back in his office, looking down at his cluttered desk, his sense of well-being left him. He had moved on to the "T"'s by now, and as he looked at the scraps of paper and the jumble of books on his desk, he realized that he had forgotten a considerable number of facts about Tacitus and was completely lost on the subject of Taine. There was a sheet of notepaper on his desk with the date and the beginning of a salutation: "Dear . . ."

He stared at the paper and tried to remember who it was he had been writing to. It was five minutes before it came to him; the letter was to have been to his son, and he had meant, finally, to enclose the check for the two hundred and fifty dollars, as requested. He felt in his inside pocket for his checkbook. It wasn't there. He looked carefully through all the drawers of his desk, but the checkbook wasn't there, either. Shaking a little, because this was the first time in his life that he had misplaced a checkbook, he decided to call up his bank and ask them to mail him a new book. He picked up the phone. Then he stared at it blankly. He had forgotten the telephone number of the bank. He put the phone down and opened the classified telephone directory to "B." Then he stopped. He swallowed dryly. He had forgotten the name of his bank. He looked at the page of banks. All the names seemed vaguely familiar to him, but no one name seemed to have any special meaning for him. He closed the book and stood up and went over to the window. He looked out. There were two pigeons sitting on the sill, looking cold, and across the street a bald man was standing at a window in the building opposite, smoking a cigarette and staring down as though he were contemplating suicide.

Hugh went back to his desk and sat down. Perhaps it was an omen, he thought, the thing about the checkbook. Perhaps it was a sign that he ought to take a sterner line with his son. Let him pay for his own mistakes for once. He picked up his pen, resolved to write this to Alabama. "Dear . . ." he read. He looked for a long time at the word. Then he carefully closed his pen and put it back in his pocket. He no longer remembered his son's name.

He put on his coat and went out, although it was only three-twenty-five. He walked all the way up to the Museum, striding lightly, feeling better and better with each block. By the time he reached the Museum, he felt like a man who has just been told that he has won a hundred-dollar bet on a fourteen-to-one shot. In the Museum, he went and looked at the Egyptians. He had

532

meant to look at the Egyptians for years, but he had always been too busy.

When he got through with the Egyptians, he felt wonderful. He continued feeling wonderful all the way home in the subway. He no longer made any attempt to buy the newspapers. They didn't make any sense to him. He didn't recognize any of the people whose names appeared in the columns. It was like reading the Karachi *Sind Observer* or the Sonora *El Mundo*. Not having a paper in his hands made the long ride much more agreeable. He spent his time in the subway looking at the people around him. The people in the subway seemed much more interesting, much more pleasant, now that he no longer read in the newspapers what they were doing to each other.

Of course, once he opened his front door, his euphoria left him. Narcisse had taken to looking at him very closely in the evenings, and he had to be very careful with his conversation. He didn't want Narcisse to discover what was happening to him. He didn't want her to worry, or try to cure him. He sat all evening listening to the phonograph, but he forgot to change the record. It was an automatic machine and it played the last record of the second Saint-Saëns piano concerto seven times before Narcisse came in from the kitchen and said, "I'm going out of my mind," and turned it off.

He went to bed early. He heard Narcisse crying in the next bed. It was the third time that month. There were between two and five more times to go. He remembered that.

The next afternoon, he was working on Talleyrand. He was bent over his desk, working slowly but not too badly, when he became conscious that there was someone standing behind him. He swung in his chair. A gray-haired man in a tweed suit was standing there, staring down at him.

"Yes?" Hugh said curtly. "Are you looking for someone?"

The man, surprisingly, turned red, then went out of the room, slamming the door behind him. Hugh shrugged incuriously and turned back to Talleyrand.

The elevator was crowded when he left for the day, and the hall downstairs was thronged with clerks and secretaries hurrying out of the building. Near the entrance, a very pretty girl was standing, and she smiled and waved at Hugh over the heads of the homeward-bound office workers. Hugh stopped for an instant, flattered, and was tempted to smile back. But he had a date with Jean, and anyway he was too old for anything like that. He set his face and hurried out in the stream of people. He thought he heard a kind of wail, which sounded curiously like "Daddy," but he knew that was impossible, and didn't turn around.

He went to Lexington Avenue, enjoying the shining winter evening, and started north. He passed two bars and was approaching a third when he slowed down. He retraced his steps, peering at the bar fronts. They all had chromium on them, and neon lights, and they all looked the same. There was another bar across the street. He went and looked at the bar across the street, but it was just like the others. He went into it, anyway, but Jean wasn't there. He ordered a whisky, standing at the bar, and asked the bartender, "Have you seen a lady alone in here in the last half hour?"

The bartender looked up at the ceiling, thinking. "What's she look like?" he asked.

"She—" Hugh stopped. He sipped his drink. "Never mind," he said to the bartender. He laid a dollar bill on the counter and went out.

Walking over to the subway station he felt better than he had felt since he won the hundred-yard dash at the age of eleven at the annual field day of the Brigham Young Public School in Salt Lake City on June 9, 1915.

The feeling lasted, of course, only until Narcisse put the soup on the table. Her eyes were puffed, and she had obviously been crying that afternoon, which was curious, because Narcisse never cried when she was alone. Eating his dinner, conscious of Narcisse watching him closely across the table, Hugh began to feel the mice between his fingers again. After dinner, Narcisse said, "You can't fool me. There's another woman." She also said, "I never thought this would happen to me."

By the time Hugh went to bed, he felt like a passenger on a badly loaded freighter in a winter storm off Cape Hatteras.

He awoke early, conscious that it was a sunny day outside. He lay in bed, feeling warm and healthy. There was a noise from the next bed, and he looked across the little space. There was a woman in the next bed. She was middle-aged and was wearing curlers and she was snoring and Hugh was certain he had never seen her before in his life. He got out of bed silently, dressed quickly, and went out into the sunny day.

Without thinking about it, he walked to the subway station. He watched the people hurrying toward the trains and he knew that he probably should join them. He had the feeling that somewhere in the city to the south, in some tall building on a narrow street, his arrival was expected. But he knew that no matter how hard he tried he would never be able to find the building. Buildings these days, it occurred to him suddenly, were too much like other buildings.

He walked briskly away from the subway station in the direction of the river. The river was shining in the sun and there was ice along the banks. A boy of about twelve, in a plaid mackinaw and a wool hat, was sitting on a bench and regarding the river. There were some schoolbooks, tied with a leather strap, on the frozen ground at his feet.

Hugh sat down next to the boy. "Good morning," he said pleasantly.

"Good morning," said the boy.

"What're you doing?" Hugh asked.

"I'm counting the boats," the boy said. "Yesterday I counted thirty-two boats. Not counting ferries. I don't count ferries."

Hugh nodded. He put his hands in his pockets and looked down over the river. By five o'clock that afternoon he and the boy had counted forty-three boats, not including ferries. He couldn't remember having had a nicer day.

# The Man Who Married a French Wife

*The habit had grown on him. Now it had assumed the shape of a nightly ritual. When he sat down in the commuters' train at Grand Central, he opened the French newspaper first. He read with difficulty, because he had only begun to teach himself the language after he had come back from Europe, and that was more than a year ago. Finally, he read almost the entire paper, the list of accidents and crimes on the second page, the political section, the theatrical section, even the sports page. But what he turned to first, always, was the account of the* attentats, *and* plastiquages, *the assassinations and bombings and massacres that were being perpetrated in Algeria and throughout France by the Secret Army, in rebellion against the government of General de Gaulle.*

*He was looking for a name. For more than a year he hadn't found it. Then, on a rainy spring evening, as the crowded train, full of suburbia's prisoners, pulled out of the station, he saw it. There had been eleven bombings in Paris the night before, the paper reported. A bookshop had been blown up, a pharmacy, the apartments of two officials, the home of a newspaperman. The newspaperman had been cut around the head, but his days, as the phrase went in French, were not in danger.*

*Beauchurch put the paper under the seat. This was one newspaper he wasn't going to take home with him.*

*He sat staring out the window, now sluiced with rain, as the train came up from the tunnel and raced along Park Avenue. Matters hadn't worked out exactly as predicted, but close enough, close enough. He stared out through the window and the year vanished and the tenements and rainy roofs of New York were replaced by the afternoon streets of Paris. . . .*

Beauchurch went into a *tabac* and by means of pantomime and pointing got the cigar he wanted. It was the second cigar of the afternoon. At home he never smoked a cigar until after dinner, but he was on holiday, and he had had a fine lunch with two old friends, and Paris was brisk and strange and amusing around him, and the second cigar gave him an added feeling of luxury and well-being. He lit the cigar carefully and strolled along the rich street, admiring the shop windows and the way the women looked and the last light of the autumn sun on Napoleon atop his high green pillar. He looked into a famous jeweler's shop and half-decided to be terribly extravagant and buy a clip for his wife. He went in and priced the clip and came out shaking his head. A little farther on he stopped at a bookshop and bought her a large, beautifully printed volume containing colored prints of the École de Paris. The book was expensive, but it felt like a bargain after the clip.

Ginette wasn't crazy about jewelry, anyway. Luckily. Because until the last year or so, when Beauchurch had been taken in as a partner in the law firm for which he had worked ever since he'd gotten his degree, he and Ginette had had to be very canny about money. What with the children and taxes and building the house near Stamford, there was very little left over for things like diamond clips. Besides, Beauchurch thought, she's so beautiful and smart she doesn't need diamonds. He smiled to himself at this clever and flattering rationalization.

Then, a half-block from the hotel, he saw her. She was about twenty yards ahead of him and there were quite a few people between them, but there was no mistaking that bright, neat head and the straight, disciplined way she held herself as she walked. But she wasn't alone. She was with a man in a raincoat and a soft green Tyrolian kind of hat, and she was holding his arm as they walked slowly toward the hotel on the corner of the Rue de Rivoli. They were talking earnestly, Ginette's face turned to the man, as he guided her among the pedestrians, and from time to time they stopped, as though the gravity of their conversation had halted them.

As he watched them, Beauchurch felt his sense of well-being, of luxury, of pleasure at being in this city for the first time in his life, suddenly sliding away from him. She was so obviously involved with the man in the raincoat, so fixed, concerned, intimate, so patently oblivious of everything else around her, that she gave Beauchurch the feeling that if he went up to her and stood in front of her it would be some time before she would recognize him or acknowledge him as her husband. After nearly thirteen years of marriage, the intensity of his wife's connection with a stranger on a foreign street made Beauchurch feel lost, disavowed, and for one moment he faced the realization that it was possible that one day she would leave him.

He made himself stop and look in a window, to free himself from the coupled image. His reflection in the window was solid, reasonable, reassuring, that of a man in his middle thirties, not bad-looking, in abounding health, with a twist of humor about the mouth. It was the reflection of a man who was plainly not capricious or given to neurotic fantasies, the reflection of a man who could be depended upon in crises to act with intelligence and decision, a man who would not be hurried into hasty judgments or shaken by baseless fears.

Staring into the window, he made himself examine the possible meanings of what he had seen. His wife had said she was having lunch with her mother. Since Beauchurch had already had several dinners with the old lady and since she couldn't speak English and he couldn't speak French, he had felt that his duty as visiting son-in-law had been fairly discharged by now and he had begged off, to lunch with other friends. But it was past four o'clock by now. Lunch was a long time over, even in Paris. Even if she had seen her mother, Ginette would have had plenty of time for other rendezvous between then and now. Ginette had grown up in Paris and had visited France alone twice since their marriage, and the man in the raincoat could have been any one of a hundred old friends or acquaintances met by accident on the street. But the memory of what Ginette and the man in the raincoat had looked like together twenty paces in front of him canceled out the notion of accident and made the words "friend" or "acquaintance" seem inadequate and false.

On the other hand, in thirteen years of marriage, Ginette had never even for a moment given the slightest indication that she had ever been interested in any other man, and the last time she had been in Paris to see her mother, she had cut her stay short by two weeks because, she said, she hadn't been able to bear to be separated any longer from Beauchurch and the children. And on this visit, which by now had lasted nearly three weeks, they had been together almost every moment of every day, except for those evasive hours when women disappear into hairdressers' salons and the fitting rooms of couturiers.

Another thing to be considered—if she had anything to hide what would she be doing a few doors from the hotel, where she might expect to see her husband at any moment? Unless she didn't want to hide it, whatever it might be, unless she deliberately wanted to provoke . . . Provoke what?

*Provoke what?*

He made himself remain absolutely still in front of the window, not shifting his weight by so much as an ounce, not moving a finger. He had taught himself this little trick of immobility a long time ago, for the times when he was tempted to lash out, to act rashly, to give way to anger or impatience. As a young man he had been violent and passionate. He had been thrown out of two preparatory schools and one college. He had avoided court-martial in the Army only through the unexpected benevolence of a Major he had grossly insulted. He had been a nervy, blind fighter, a quick maker of enemies, intolerant, sometimes brutal with men and women both. He had made himself over, slowly and with pain, because he had been intelligent enough to realize that he was skirting destruction. Or, rather, he had made over his surface, his behavior. He had known what he wanted to be like, what he had to be like to reach the goals he had set for himself. He was clear, at an early age, what those goals were. They included financial security, a reputation for probity and hard work, a loving, honorable marriage and decent children, and, later on, political power and a high federal judgeship. All these things, he knew, would elude him if he did not keep himself sternly in hand at all times. He had forced himself to act slowly, to swallow fury, to present to the world the image of a calm, balanced, judicious man. Even with Ginette he had managed, almost completely, to preserve that image. The cost was high, but until now it had been worth it. At his core, he still knew himself to be violent, sudden, ready for explosion, fatally ready to destroy himself for the satisfaction of a moment's anger, a moment's desire. The deliberateness of his movements, the softness of his speech, the formal air of privacy with which he surrounded himself were the calculated means by which he preserved himself. Looking like the safest of men, he felt himself continually in danger. Seemingly even-tempered and rational, he fought a daily battle within himself against rage and irrationality, and lived in dread of the day when the useful, admirable, sham character with which he masked his inner turbulence would crack and vanish.

*Provoke, provoke . . .*

Beauchurch shrugged. He took one last look at the tall, sensible, well-dressed reflection of himself in the window and turned toward the hotel. By now Ginette and the man had disappeared. Beauchurch covered the few yards to the hotel entrance rapidly, threw away his cigar, and went in.

Ginette and the man were standing at the concierge's desk in the lobby. The man had taken his hat off and was turning it slowly in his hands. As Beauchurch came up to them, he heard Ginette saying to the concierge, "Est-ce que Monsieur Beauchurch est rentré?" which was one of the few sentences he could understand in the French language.

"Bonjour, Madame," Beauchurch said, smiling, and carefully keeping his face normal. "Can I help you?"

Ginette turned. "Tom," she said, "I was hoping you were back." She kissed his cheek. To Beauchurch she seemed strained and ill-at-ease. "I want you to meet a friend of mine. Claude Mestre. My husband."

Beauchurch shook the man's hand. The fleeting contact gave him an impression of dryness and nerves. Mestre was tall and thin, with a high, domed brow and smooth chestnut hair. He had deep-set, worried, gray eyes and a long straight nose. He was a good-looking man, but his face was pale and seemed tired, as though he were overworked. He smiled politely as he greeted Beauchurch, but there was an obscure appeal buried in the smile.

"You don't have to go out again, do you, Tom?" Ginette asked. "We can sit down somewhere and have a drink, can't we?"

"Of course," Beauchurch said.

"I do not wish to spoil your afternoon," Mestre said. His accent was strong, but he spoke slowly and clearly, pronouncing every syllable loyally. "You have so little time in Paris."

"We have nothing to do until dinner," Beauchurch said. "I'd love a drink."

They went toward the bar, past a long alley where old ladies were taking tea. The bar was a huge hall, dark, almost deserted, with the tarnished gold-leaf and mahogany elegance of a nineteenth-century palace. Ginette squeezed Beauchurch's arm as they went through the door, which Mestre held open for them. Close to her, Beauchurch was conscious of the strong, pleasing scent of Ginette's perfume.

"How was your mother?" Beauchurch asked, as they traversed the room, toward the high windows which looked out on the Tuileries.

"Fine," Ginette said. "She was disappointed you couldn't come to lunch."

"Tell her, next time," Beauchurch said. They gave their coats to the waiter and sat down. Beauchurch handed the package containing the book of prints to the waiter, too, without telling Ginette what was in it.

"This is rather sinister, this bar, isn't it?" Mestre said, looking around him. "It is rather like a place for ghosts to come and drink."

"I imagine it was pretty gay here," Beauchurch said, "in 1897."

The waiter came and they all ordered whiskey and Beauchurch was conscious again of Ginette's perfume when she leaned toward him slightly to allow him to light a cigarette for her. He saw, or imagined he saw, a cool, speculative expression on Mestre's face, as though the Frenchman was trying to judge the nature of the relations between the husband and wife across the table from him, in the moment in which they briefly approached each other over the flare of the lighter.

There were two large Americans at the bar, their voices making a bass background rumble of sound in the room, with an occasional phrase here and there suddenly intelligible across the bare tables. " . . . The problem," one of the men was saying, "is with the Belgian delegation. They're sullen and suspicious. I understand perfectly why, but . . ." Then the voice sank back into a rumble again.

"Claude is a journalist," Ginette said, in her hostessy, introducing-the-guests-at-a-party voice. "He's one of the leading journalists in France. That's how I found him. I saw his name in the paper."

"I congratulate you," Beauchurch said. "On being a journalist, I mean. Like everybody else in America, when I was young, I wanted to be a newspaperman. But nobody would give me a job." Saw his name in a newspaper, he thought. I was right. She called him. It wasn't any accidental meeting on the street.

Mestre shrugged. "Perhaps I should be the one to congratulate you," he said. "For not getting the job. There are moments when I consider the man who gave me my first job on a newspaper as a deadly enemy." He sounded weary and disabused. "For example—I could never hope to dress my wife in the charming manner in which Ginette is dressed or afford a six-week tour of Europe in the middle of the Autumn like you."

That's a damned envious, unpleasant thing for a man to say, Beauchurch thought. "Oh," he said. "You're married."

"Forever," Mestre said.

"He has four children," Ginette said. A trifle too quickly, Beauchurch thought.

"I am personally attempting to redress the demographic imbalance that Napoleon left as his heritage to France." Mestre smiled ironically as he said it.

"Have you seen his children?" Beauchurch asked Ginette.

"No," she said. She volunteered no further information.

541

The waiter came and served their drinks. Mestre lifted his glass. "To a happy stay in this happy country," he said, his voice still carrying the edge of irony. "And a quick return."

They drank. There was an uncomfortable silence.

"What's your specialty?" Beauchurch asked, to bridge the silence. "I mean, is there any particular field that you write about?"

"War and politics," Mestre said. "The prize assignments."

"That's enough to keep you busy, I imagine," Beauchurch said.

"Yes. There are always enough fools and brutes to keep a man busy," Mestre said.

"What do you think is going to happen here, in France?" Beauchurch said, resolved to be polite and keep the conversation going until he could find some inkling of why Ginette had wanted him to meet this man.

"What do you think is going to happen here?" Mestre repeated. "It is becoming the new form of greeting in France. It has practically replaced *Bonjour* and *Comment ça va.*" He shrugged. "We are going to have trouble."

"Everybody is going to have trouble," Beauchurch said. "In America, too."

"Do you think," Mestre fixed him with his cold, ironic glance, "that in America you will have violence and political murder and civil war?"

"No," Beauchurch said. "Is that what you think is going to happen here?"

"To a certain extent," Mestre said, "it has already happened."

"And you think it will happen again?" Beauchurch asked.

"Probably," said Mestre. "But in a more aggravated form."

"Soon?"

"Sooner or later," Mestre said.

"That's very pessimistic," Beauchurch said.

"France is composed exclusively of pessimists," said Mestre. "If you stay here long enough, you will discover that."

"If it does come, who do you think will win?" Beauchurch asked.

"The worst elements," said Mestre. "Not permanently, perhaps. But for a period. Unfortunately, the period will have to be lived through. It will not be pleasant."

"Tom," Ginette said, "I think maybe I'd better explain about Claude." She had been listening intently to Mestre, watching his face anxiously as he spoke. "Claude works for a liberal newspaper here and it's already been confiscated several times by the Government because of articles he wrote about Algeria."

"It is getting so that when an article by me appears and the journal is not confiscated," Mestre said, "that I examine myself for signs of cowardice."

Self-pity, Beauchurch thought, combined with deep self-satisfaction. He liked the man less and less, the more he talked.

"There's something else, Tom," Ginette said. She turned to Mestre. "You don't mind if I tell him, do you, Claude?"

"If you think it will interest him . . ." Claude shrugged. "Americans are not liable to take things like that very seriously."

"I'm a very serious American," Beauchurch said, letting his annoyance show for the first time. "I read *Time* magazine almost every week."

"Now you are making fun of me," Mestre said. "I do not blame you. It is my fault." He looked around him vaguely. "Is it possible to have another drink?"

Beauchurch signaled the waiter and made a circular motion with his hand, indicating another round for everyone. "What's the something else, Ginette?" he asked, trying to keep the irritation from his voice.

"The letters and the telephone calls," Ginette said.

"What letters and telephone calls?"

"Threatening to kill me," Mestre said lightly. "The letters are usually addressed to me. The telephone calls to my wife. Naturally, being a woman, she gets rather upset. Especially since there are periods during which she receives five or six a day."

"Who writes them?" Beauchurch asked. He wished he could disbelieve the man, but there was something about the way he was talking now that put the seal of truth upon what he said. "Who makes the calls?"

Mestre shrugged. "Who knows? Cranks, elderly widows, practical jokers, retired army officers, assassins. . . . They never sign their names, of course. It is not terribly new. The anonymous letter has always played an honorable role in French literature."

"Do you think they mean it?" Beauchurch asked.

"Sometimes." Mestre looked up as the waiter came over with the drinks and didn't speak again until the man had gone off once more. "When I am tired or depressed or it's raining, I think they mean it. At any rate, *some* of them undoubtedly mean it."

"What do you do about it?"

"Nothing," Mestre said, sounding surprised. "What is there to do?"

"You could go to the police, for one thing," Beauchurch said.

"In America one would undoubtedly go to the police," Mestre

said. "Here . . ." He made a grimace and took a long sip of his drink. "I am not on particularly good terms with the police at the moment. In fact, I am of the opinion that my mail is often opened and from time to time I am followed and my phone is tapped."

"That's disgraceful," Beauchurch said.

"I like your husband," Mestre said lightly, almost playfully, to Ginette. "He finds things like this disgraceful. It is very American."

"We've had times like that in America, too," Beauchurch said, defending the level of venality of his native land. "And not so long ago, either."

"I know, I know," Mestre said. "I do not mean to imply that I believe that America is a fairyland which is completely untouched by the special diseases of our age. Still, as I say, in America, one would go to the police. . . ."

"Do you *really* think that somebody may try to kill you?" Beauchurch asked. Irrelevantly, he thought, This is a hell of a way to be spending a holiday, talking about things like this.

"Not just now perhaps," Mestre said calmly, as though he were surveying, with judicial impartiality, an abstract problem that had no personal relation to him. "But once the trouble starts, almost certainly."

"Just how do you think the trouble will start?" Somehow, after the weeks of enjoying the peaceful glittering city, with its overflowing shops, its air of bustling activity, its range of pleasures, it was impossible to believe that it would soon be given over to violence and bloodshed.

"How will it start?" Mestre repeated. He squinted thoughtfully over Beauchurch's shoulder into the mahogany depths of the bar, as though trying to formulate there some picture of the future that lay in wait for the city. "I am not in on the councils of the heroes, you understand," he smiled slightly, "so I can only speculate. It depends upon the General, of course. On the state of his health— physical and political. On his powers of survival. At the moment, we are in a period of *détente*. The plotters are waiting. The murderers remain more or less under cover. But if the General is brought down—by failure, by overconfidence, by old age, by anything— then we can expect certain events to follow."

"What?" Beauchurch asked.

"Perhaps an uprising of the troops in Algiers," Mestre said, "a landing on the aerodromes, a movement among the police, the emergence of secretly armed and trained bodies of commandoes in various parts of the country, to take over the seats of government and the radio and television stations, the capture or assassination of certain leading political figures. The usual. There is no mystery any more about these things. Only the timing is problematical.''

Beauchurch turned to his wife. "Do you believe all this?"

"Yes," she said.

"Do any of your other friends talk like this?"

"Almost all of them," she said.

"And you"—Beauchurch turned back, almost accusingly to Mestre—"what do you intend to do if it happens?"

"I shall offer my services to the government," Mestre said. "That is, if I can find the government, and if it has not already locked me up somewhere by then."

"Christ," Beauchurch said, "what a thing it is to be a Frenchman."

"It has its compensations," Mestre said. "Some of the time."

"All right," Beauchurch said to Ginette, "I'm briefed. Only I don't know what for. Why did you want me to hear all this?"

There was an exchange of glances between Mestre and Ginette, and once more Beauchurch had the fleeting sensation of being an outsider, conspired against.

Mestre leaned over and touched Ginette's hand lightly. "Permit me to explain, my dear," he said. He lifted his glass and drank, like an orator playing for time. "Mr. Beauchurch," he began formally, "your wife has been good enough to suggest that perhaps you would be willing to help me. . . ." He waited for Beauchurch to say something, but Beauchurch remained unhelpfully silent.

"It is, unhappily, a question of money," Mestre said.

Good God, Beauchurch thought, all this lead-up to ask for a loan! He was annoyed with Ginette for having gone along with this elaborate manipulation. He could feel his face settling into refusing lines as he waited for Mestre to continue.

"If anything happens," Mestre went on, looking uncomfortable, "as I believe it will, I may have to try to escape from France. Or at least, my wife and my children would be better off out of the country. In any event, I would feel considerably relieved if I had some money safely in another country, to tide me over at least some part of the period of exile that I foresee as a possibility for myself and my family. A numbered account in Switzerland, for example, that either my wife or myself could draw on without formalities. . . ."

"I told Claude we were going to Geneva on Thursday," Ginette said. There was a tone of defiance in her voice, Beauchurch thought, as she said this. "It would be the simplest thing in the world for us to do."

"Now let me get this straight," Beauchurch said to Ginette. "Have you promised your friend that we would lend him a certain amount of money for—" Mestre looked stupefied as he listened, and Beauchurch stopped in mid-sentence. "Have I misunderstood something?" he asked.

"I'm afraid you have," Mestre said. He seemed embarrassed and angry. "There was never any question of a loan. What right would I have to ask a man I had never seen in my life to lend me even a hundred francs?"

"Ginette," Beauchurch said, "I think you'd better explain."

"A French citizen has no right to take money out of France," Ginette said. "Or, anyway, very little. And since we're going to Switzerland, I thought we could do it for Claude."

"As I understand it," Beauchurch said, "nobody has a right to take much money out of France, not even Americans."

"Two hundred and fifty new francs," Mestre said.

"But the customs people never bother Americans," Ginette said. "They never even open your bags. And if they do happen to ask you how many francs you have on you, you say a hundred or so, and that's the end of it."

"Still," Beauchurch persisted, "technically we'd be breaking the law."

"Technically," Ginette said impatiently. "What difference would it make?"

"My dear friends," Mestre said, "please . . ." He spread his hands above the table pacifically. "I beg you not to argue on my account. If you have the slightest hesitation, I understand perfectly. . . ."

"Let me ask you a question, Mr. Mestre," Beauchurch said. "Supposing we hadn't happened to come to France at this time, Ginette and I, and supposing she hadn't called you up—what would you have done?"

Mestre sucked in his cheeks thoughtfully. When he spoke, he spoke slowly and carefully. "I suppose I would have tried to get someone else to do it for me. But I would be very—very—" He searched for the word. "Very uneasy. As I told you, I am sure that from time to time I am under surveillance. I could only entrust something like this to a very close friend—whose relationship with me would be likely to compromise him. With bad luck, the friend might fall under suspicion, especially if he crossed the frontier to another country. Any Frenchman is likely to be searched upon trying to leave the country. He is likely to be questioned. In the times that I see ahead of us, the questioning that will be taking place here in France is liable to be most strict." He smiled wanly at his understatement. "I would not like to have to depend upon the endurance or the good will or the discretion of any of my friends at that time for my safety. Still, that is no reason for you to concern yourself with me. A man who is in danger and demands help is always such a bore. One has only to remember how annoyed everybody was with the refugees during the war." He looked around for the waiter and signaled him to come over. "I would be most pleased," Mestre said, "if you would permit me to pay for the drinks."

"Wait a minute," Beauchurch said. "How much would you want me to take to Switzerland for you?"

"Four million francs," Mestre said. "Old francs, that is."

"That's only about eight thousand dollars, Tom," Ginette said.

"I know," Beauchurch said. He took the check from the waiter's hand, over Mestre's protest. He paid the waiter and stood up. "Let me think about this and talk it over with Ginette. She has your number. We'll call you tomorrow."

Mestre stood up too. "If you don't mind," he said, "I would prefer to call you. The fewer calls I get, the better. . . ."

" . . . In Africa, for example," one of the Americans at the bar was saying, "the old system of competitive bribery is breaking down. But nobody's found anything better. . . ."

Beauchurch followed Mestre and Ginette out of the room, down the alley of old ladies still taking their tea, solidly anchored among their fur coats, their poodles, their pastries, oblivious to all plots, troop movements, fighting in the streets. A dark phalanx of widows, bedecked with the jeweled trophies of their victories, they remained firm and reassuring against all the assaults of change. In that corridor of elaborately coifed, silvery heads, Mestre's fearful words of prophecy seemed like the insubstantial report of a child's dream.

In the lobby, Mestre kissed Ginette's hand, made a formal little bow to Beauchurch and went off. He was bent over surprisingly, Beauchurch noticed, for a man so young, and his walk was heavy and without resilience. When he put on his soft green hat, he did it carelessly, with no attempt at dash. Whatever he was, Beauchurch decided, he was no professional lady-killer. But when Beauchurch turned toward Ginette, he thought he detected a certain emotion in her eyes, only partially concealed. But whether it was desire or pity, it was impossible to tell.

They went up to their room in silence. The sense of holiday

they had shared since their arrival in Paris had entirely gone, and the high-ceilinged old room looked chilly and clumsily furnished in the light of the inadequate lamps. Ginette hung up her coat and pushed listlessly at her hair before the mirror. Beauchurch put the package with the book in it on a table and looked out the window at the gardens of the Tuileries across the traffic-jammed street below him. All the trees were bare and the people hurrying past the newly lit lampposts looked harassed and cold.

Beauchurch heard the bed creak as Ginette sat down on it. "That four million francs," she said. "That's his life savings. That's all he has in the world."

Beauchurch said nothing. He continued to stare out the window at the dark gardens.

"If you won't take it through for him," Ginette said, "I will."

Beauchurch took a deep breath. He turned deliberately away from the windows. "That was a stupid thing to say," he said.

Ginette looked at him coldly, with hostility. "Was it?" she said. "I suppose so." She swung her legs up on the bed and lay back, staring at the ceiling. "Still, I mean it."

"It would make an interesting headline," Beauchurch said. "Wife of New York Lawyer Held in Paris for Smuggling Banknotes. Husband Claims Ignorance of Wife's Activities."

"Does that mean you're not going to help Claude?" Ginette's voice was flat and she kept squinting up at the ceiling.

"It means that in general I am a law-abiding citizen," Beauchurch said. "It means that when I am a guest in a country I prefer not to cheat my hosts."

"Oh," Ginette said. "What a lucky thing it is to be an American. And a Puritan. How convenient it can be."

"It also means that I am balancing the risks against the advantages," said Beauchurch.

"There are no advantages," Ginette said. "There's nothing to balance. A man's in trouble, and we can help him. That's all."

"A lot of men are in trouble," Beauchurch said. "The question is, why do we pick out this particular one to help."

"You didn't like him, did you?"

"Not much," Beauchurch said. "He's self-important and impressed with his own intelligence, and he has a condescending attitude toward Americans."

Unexpectedly, Ginette laughed.

"What are you laughing about?" Beauchurch demanded.

"Because you're so accurate," Ginette said. "That's exactly what he's like. He's the perfect model of the French intellectual."

548

She laughed again. "I must tell him that you ticked him off exactly. He'll be furious."

Beauchurch regarded his wife puzzledly. Her laughter was real, and what she had just said was certainly not the sort of thing a woman would say about a man who attracted her. But against this, there was the enduring vision of the two of them so deeply engrossed in each other on the street in front of the hotel, and Ginette's persistence in pushing Beauchurch to Mestre's rescue.

Beauchurch sat down on the edge of the bed. "The question is," he repeated, "why do we pick out this particular one to help."

Ginette lay quiet for a moment, her arms along her sides, her hands flat on the brocaded bed cover. "Because he's a friend," she said. She waited. Then she said, "That's not quite enough, is it?"

"Not quite," said Beauchurch.

"Because he's French and I was born in Paris," Ginette said. "Because he's talented, because I agree with his politics, because the people who want to kill him are vile. . . ." She stopped and waited again. Beauchurch still said nothing. "That's not quite enough, either, is it?" Ginette said, staring at the ceiling.

"Not quite," said Beauchurch.

"Because he was my lover," Ginette said, without emphasis, looking up at the ceiling. "Did you expect that?"

"I suppose so," Beauchurch said.

"A long time ago," Ginette said. "During the war. He was the first one."

"How many times have you seen him since we've been married?" Beauchurch said. He didn't look at his wife, but he listened intently for a tone of falsehood in her voice. Ginette was not a liar, but a question like this had never come up between them before, and Beauchurch believed that on this subject almost all women, and all men, too, for that matter, lied almost all the time.

"I've seen him twice since 1946," Ginette said. "Yesterday and today."

"Why did you decide, after all these years, to see him yesterday?"

Ginette reached over to the bedtable and took a cigarette out of a pack that was lying there. Automatically, Beauchurch lit it for her. She lay back, her head on the bolster, blowing the smoke straight up. "I don't know why," she said. "Curiosity, nostalgia, guilt—the feeling that middle age was rushing up on me and I wanted to be reminded of a time when I was young—a feeling that maybe I wouldn't see Paris again for a long time and I wanted

549

to straighten out certain memories. . . . I don't know, Don't you ever want to see your first girl again?''

"No," Beauchurch said.

"Well, maybe women're different. Or Frenchwomen. Or me." She squinted at the ceiling through the cigarette smoke. "You're not worried about what went on, are you?"

"No," Beauchurch said. He didn't say anything about the realization he had had on the street that it was possible for her one day to leave him.

"We had two beers at the Dome, because he once took me there on my birthday," Ginette said. "And after the first ten minutes it was all politics and his problem and the thing about Switzerland. Which I brought up, by the way, in case you're thinking of blaming him."

"I'm not blaming him for anything," Beauchurch said. "Still— why didn't you tell me about him yesterday?"

"I was playing with the idea of just taking the money in myself and not worrying you about it at all. Then I decided, today, that that wouldn't be fair to you, and that you had to talk to Claude yourself. I was right about that, wasn't I?" She lifted her head inquisitively.

"Yes," he said.

"I didn't realize that you'd turn so severe," Ginette said. "You didn't behave like your usual self with him at all. You're usually so pleasant with new people. And you were against him from the beginning."

"That's true," Beauchurch said. He offered no explanations. "Look," he said, "you don't have to tell me any of this if you don't want to."

"I do want to," Ginette said. "So you'll understand why I think I have to help him if I can. So you'll understand him better. So you'll understand *me* better."

"Don't you think I understand you?" Beauchurch asked, surprised.

"Not well enough," Ginette said. "We're so reticent with each other, so polite, so careful never to say anything to each other that might disturb or hurt. . . ."

"Is that wrong?" Beauchurch said. "I've always thought that was one of the reasons our marriage has been so solid."

"Solid," Ginette said vaguely. "What marriage is solid?"

"What the hell are you driving at?" Beauchurch asked.

"I don't know," Ginette said listlessly. "Nothing. Maybe I'm homesick, only I'm not sure where my home is. Maybe we shouldn't have come to Paris. Maybe because I was a silly young girl when I was in Paris, I must behave like a silly young girl here, even now when I'm a sober American matron. I *do* look like a sober American matron, don't I, Tom?''

"No," he said.

"I walk along the street and I forget who I am, I forget how old I am, I forget my American passport," she said, speaking softly. "I'm eighteen years old again, there are gray uniforms all over the streets, I'm trying to decide whether I'm in love or not, I change my mind at every corner, I'm wildly happy. Don't be shocked. I wasn't happy because there was a war and the Germans were here, I was happy because I was eighteen years old. A war isn't all one color, even in an occupied country. Hold my hand, please." She put her hand out toward him on the bed cover and he covered it with his, clasping the long, cool fingers, the soft palm, feeling the thin metal of the wedding ring. "We've never confessed enough, you and I," she said. "A marriage needs a certain amount of confession and we've skimped each other." She pressed his fingers. "Don't worry. There won't be any flood. There's no scandalous list. Claude was the only one until I married you. I'm hardly the popular American idea of a Frenchwoman at all. Are you surprised by any of this?"

"No," Beauchurch said. When he had met Ginette, when she had first come over to America on a scholarship, just after the war, she had still been a rather gawky girl, intent on her studies, slender and lovely, but not coquettish or sensual. When they had married she had been unpracticed, reserved, and the sensuality had come later, after months of marriage.

"He wanted to marry me," she went on. "Claude. I was at the Sorbonne. Immersed in Medieval History. It was one of the few safe subjects while the Germans were here. They didn't care much what people said about Charlemagne or St. Louis or the cathedral at Rouen. He was three or four years older than I. Very handsome and fierce-looking. It's not there now, is it?"

"No," Beauchurch said. "Not really."

"How quickly it goes." She shook her head, as though to stop herself from continuing this line of thought. "He wrote plays. He didn't show them to anyone because he didn't want to have any plays put on in Paris while the Germans were still here. Then, after the war, nobody put them on, anyway. I suppose he really wasn't much of a playwright. After the Liberation of Paris, it turned out he hadn't only been writing plays during the Occupation. He'd been in the Resistance and he was put into the Army and that winter he was badly wounded outside Belfort. He was in the hospital nearly two years. They changed him, those years. He became bitter, he hated what was happening to France, to the whole world. He had no hope for anything except . . . well, except for us, him and me. Whatever hope he had in the world he bound up in me. I promised to marry him when he got out, but then the scholarship came along, the chance to go to America . . . . He pleaded with me not to go, or to marry him before I went. He kept saying I'd find someone else in America, that I'd forget him, forget France. He made me swear that no matter what happened I'd come back and see him before I married anyone else. I swore I'd do it. It wasn't hard to do—I loved him—I was sure there'd never be anybody else. Anyway, he was still in the hospital—he had to recover first, establish himself at something, we didn't have a penny between us. Then I met you. I tried. I held back as much as I could. Didn't I?" Her voice was harsh, demanding; before the image of her lover lying broken in his hospital bed so many years ago she was justifying the actions of the girl breaking out of adolescence, newly emerged from the privations and fears of war. "I did everything I could, didn't I?"

"Yes," Beauchurch said, remembering the times he'd been ready to give her up, furious at her hesitations, her incomprehensible fluctuations. Now, after the long marriage, the children, the closely linked lives, they were comprehensible. He wondered if he would have been happier if he'd known, if the marriage would have been better or worse, if he would have behaved differently, loved her more or less. "Why didn't you tell me then?" he asked.

"It was my problem," she said. "It was between him and me. Anyway, I didn't go back. I didn't tell him anything until the day of the wedding. I sent him a cable. I asked him not to write me. I asked him to forgive me."

The days of weddings, Beauchurch thought. The brides at telegraph offices. *Forgive me.* Four thousand miles away. *It is over, it is too late. . . . You were in the hospital too long. Love.* "Well," he said, being cruel to her and to himself, "do you regret it now?" He remembered the phrase Mestre had used. "You could have spent your time redressing the demographic imbalance of France, as the man said."

"It's not too late," she said flatly. "Even now." She was angry and she was reacting to the jibe. "If you must know, he still wants to marry me."

"As of when?"

"As of this afternoon," she said.

"Four children and all?" Beauchurch said. "To say nothing of his wife and your husband and *your* children."

"I told him it was absurd," Ginette said. "We had it all out three years ago."

"Three years ago?" Beauchurch said. "I thought you said you'd only seen him twice since 1946—yesterday and today."

"I was lying," Ginette said, evenly. "Of course I saw him when I was here before, I would have had to be a monster not to see him. I saw him every day."

"I'm not going to ask you what happened," Beauchurch said. He stood up. He felt shaken, confused. The light through the ornate lampshades was dusty and melancholy, and his wife's face, turned away now, was in evening shadow, hidden, unfamiliar. Her voice was cold and distant and devoid of affection. Whatever happened to the holiday? he thought. He went over and poured himself a drink from the bottle on the table near the window. He didn't ask Ginette if she wanted one. The whiskey bit at his throat.

"Nothing happened," Ginette said. "I think I would have had an affair with him, if he had asked me. . . ."

"Why?" Beauchurch asked. "Do you still love him?"

"No," she said. "I don't know why. Atonement, restitution. . . . Anyway, he didn't ask me., It was marriage or nothing, he said. He couldn't bear losing me again, he said."

Beauchurch's hands trembled as he brought the glass to his lips again. A wave of anger toward the man engulfed him, at the arrogance, the egotism, of that permanent, despairing, broken, unwavering love. He put the glass down slowly to keep from throwing it against the wall. He stood immobile, closing his eyes. If he made the slightest movement, he was afraid of what it would lead to. The thought of Mestre and Ginette sitting at café tables during a distant Parisian summer, conferring, cold-bloodedly offering and refusing terms for the looting of his life, was infinitely harder to bear than the thought of their two bodies clasped in bed together. It was less innocent; it lacked the grace and normality of the pardonable weaknesses of the flesh; it ignored, as though they had never existed, the fair claims Beauchurch had established in the years of marriage; it was a conspiracy against him by enemies who were the more hateful because they had never made themselves known to him. If Mestre had been in the room that moment Beauchurch would have gladly killed him. "God damn him," Beauchurch said. He was surprised at how routine, how calm, his voice sounded. He opened his eyes, looked down at Ginette. If she said the wrong thing now, he felt that he would strike her and leave the room, the country, leave everything, once and for all.

"That's why I came home two weeks earlier the last time I was here," Ginette said. "I couldn't stand it any more. I was afraid I'd give in. I ran away."

"I'd prefer it," Beauchurch said, "if you said you ran back."

Ginette turned her head and stared steadily out of the shadows at him. "Yes," she said, "that's better. That's what I mean. I ran back."

She said the right thing, Beauchurch thought. It took a little coaching, but finally it was the right thing. "And in the future," he said, "when you come to France, to Paris, are you going to see him again?"

"Yes," she said. "I suppose so. How can we escape each other?" She lay in silence for a moment. "Well, there it is," she said. "The whole story. I should have told you long ago. Now—are you going to help him?"

Beauchurch looked down at her lying on the bed, the bright hair, the small delightful head, the womanly face with the hesitant touches of girlhood still faintly evident there, the slender, warm, well-known, deeply loved body, the long competent hands lying flat on the bedspread, and he knew there would be no violence, no flight that evening. He knew, too, that he was more than ever inextricably entwined with her, with her memories, her wounds, betrayals, her other country, with her foreign dangers, her decisions, agonies, responsibilities, her lies, her commitments to renounced loves. He sat down beside her and leaned over and kissed her forehead gently. "Of course," he said. "Of course I'll help the bastard."

She laughed a little, softly, and brought up her hand and touched his cheek. "We won't come to Paris again for a long time," she said.

"I don't want to talk to him, though," Beauchurch said, holding her hand against his cheek. "You make all the arrangements."

"Tomorrow morning," she said. She sat up. "I sincerely hope that package is for me," she said.

"It is," he said. "It is that very thing."

She swung lightly out of bed and crossed the room, her stockinged feet making no noise on the faded old carpet. She unwrapped the package neatly, folding the paper carefully and making a little skein of the string. "It is just what I wanted," she said, as she picked up the book and ran her hand over the cover.

"I was going to buy you a diamond," Beauchurch said. "But I thought it would be crass."

"What a narrow escape," she said. She smiled at him. "Now," she said, "come in and talk to me and give me a drink while I take my bath. Then we'll go out and have a sinful, expensive dinner. Just you and me."

Carrying the book, she went into the bathroom. Beauchurch sat on the bed, squinting at the yellowish patterns of the old paint on the opposite wall, measuring his pain and his happiness. After a while he stood up and poured two good drinks and carried the glasses into the bathroom. Ginette was lying deep in the huge old tub, holding the book out of the water, gravely turning the pages. Beauchurch set her glass down on the rim of the tub and sat down on a chair facing her, next to a large, full-length mirror, whose surface, beaded with steam, mistily reflected the marble, the brass, the shining tiles of the warm, out-sized room, shaped for a more spacious age. He sipped at his drink and looked soberly at his wife, stretched out in the shimmering, fragrant water, and knew that the holiday was repaired. More than the holiday. And more than repaired.

# Voyage Out, Voyage Home

Constance sat impatiently in the little chair in the first-class cabin, taking occasional sips of the champagne that Mark had sent. Mark had been called out of town and hadn't been able to come, but he'd sent champagne. She didn't like champagne, but she didn't know what else to do with it, so she drank it. Her father stood in front of the porthole, drinking, too. From his expression, Constance could guess that he didn't like champagne either. Or perhaps he didn't like this particular vintage. Or he didn't like it because Mark had sent it. Or maybe it wasn't the champagne at all but just that he was embarrassed.

Constance knew that she was looking sullen, and she tried to change the set of her face, because she also knew that she looked younger, childish, sixteen, seventeen, when she was sullen. She was sure that everything she did with her face at that moment made her look more sullen than ever, and she wished the horn would blow and her father would get off the ship.

"You'll probably drink a lot of this," her father said. "In France."

"I don't expect to stay in France long," she said. "I'm going to look for someplace quiet." Her voice sounded to her as though it were coming out of the nursery, wailing and spiteful and spoiled. She tried to smile at her father. The last few weeks in the apartment, while the argument had been going on and the hostility had been so close to the surface, had been painful to her, and now, in the last ten minutes before the ship pulled away, she wanted to recapture an earlier, easier relationship as far as she could. So she smiled, but she had the impression that the smile was crafty and cold and coquettish. Her father turned around and looked vaguely out the porthole at the covered wharf. It was rainy and there was a cold wind blowing and the men on the dock waiting to throw off the lines looked miserable.

"It's going to be a choppy night," her father said. "Have you got the Dramamine?"

The hostility returned, because he asked about the Dramamine. At a moment like that. "I won't need Dramamine," Constance said shortly. She took a long drink of the champagne. The label on the bottle was impeccable, like all Mark's gifts, but the wine was sourish and acidy.

Her father turned back toward her. He smiled at her, and she thought, bitterly, This is the last time he's going to get away with patronizing me. He stood there, a robust, confident, healthy, youngish-seeming man, looking privately amused, and Constance thought, How would you like it if I just got out of here and walked off this precious boat—how would you ever like it?

"I envy you," her father said. "If someone had only sent me to Europe when I was twenty . . ."

Twenty, twenty, Constance thought. He's always harping on twenty. "Please, Father, let's cut that out," she said. "I'm here and I'm going and it's all settled, but let's spare ourselves the envy."

"Every time I happen to remind you that you're twenty," her father said mildly, "you react as though I'd insulted you."

He smiled, pleased with himself that he was so damned perceptive, that he understood her so well, that he was not one of those fathers whose children slide irrevocably away from them into mysterious, modern depths.

"Let's not discuss it," Constance said, pitching her voice low. When she remembered, she always made a point of pitching her voice low. It sometimes made her sound forty years old on the telephone, or like a man.

"Have a great time," her father said. "Go to all the bright places. And if you decide you want to stay on, just let me know. Maybe I'll be able to come over and join you for a few weeks—"

"Three months from now," Constance said crisply, "to this day, I'll be coming up the harbor."

"Whatever you say, my dear."

When he said "my dear," Constance knew he was humoring her. She couldn't bear being humored there in the ugly little cabin, with the weather bad outside, and the ship ready to leave, and the sounds of people saying goodbye, laughing loudly, in the next room. If she had been on better terms with her father, she would have cried.

557

The horn blew for visitors to go ashore, and her father came and kissed her, holding her for an extra second, and she tried to be polite. But when he said, very seriously, "You'll see—three months from now you'll thank me for this," she pushed him back, furious with him for his obnoxious assurance, and mournful at the same time that they, who had been so close to each other, were no longer friends.

"Goodbye," she said, her voice choked and not pitched low. "The whistle's blowing. Goodbye."

He picked up his hat, patted her shoulder, hesitated a moment at the door, looking thoughtful but not disturbed, and went out into the corridor and disappeared among the other visitors who were streaming up toward the gangplank and the shore.

When she was sure her father was off, Constance went up to the boat deck and stood there, alone in the sharp, blowy rain, watching the tugs pull the ship into the stream. As the ship went slowly downriver into the harbor and then headed into open water, she shivered in the wintry air, and, approving of herself a little for the grandeur of the sentiment, thought, I am approaching a continent to which I have no connection.

Constance braced herself against the crossbar of the lift as she approached the mid-point of the hill. She made sure that her skis were firmly in the ruts as she came up onto the flat section of packed snow where there was a short line of skiers who had come down only halfway and were waiting to pick up empty hooks and go back to the top. She always felt a little uncertain here, because if you were alone on one side of the T bar, the first person in the line would swing into place alongside you and there would be an extra, sudden pull as the new weight caught that could throw you off balance. She saw that there was a man waiting for the place next to her, and she concentrated on keeping erect gracefully as he settled into place beside her. He did it smoothly, and they skidded easily past the waiting line. She was conscious that he was looking across at her, but she was too occupied for the moment with the terrain in front of her to turn her head.

"Oh, I know you," the man said as they started safely up the hill again, leaning against the pull of the bar, their skis bumping a little in the ruts. "You're the grave young American."

Constance looked at him for the first time. "And you," she said, because everybody talked to everybody else on the hills, "you're the gay young Englishman."

"Half right," he said. He smiled. His face was a skier's brown, with an almost girlish flush of blood along the cheekbones. "At least, one-third right." She knew his name was Pritchard, because she had heard people talking to him in the hotel. She remembered hearing one of the ski teachers say about him, "He is too reckless. He thinks he is better than he actually is. He does not have the technique for so much speed." She glanced across at him and decided he *did* look reckless. He had a long nose—the kind that doesn't photograph well but that looks all right just the same, especially in a long, thin face. Twenty-five, Constance thought, twenty-six. No more. He was leaning easily against the bar, not holding on with his hands. He took off his gloves and fished a package of cigarettes out of his pockets and offered them to Constance. "Players," he said. "I hope you won't hate me."

"No, thank you," Constance said. She was sure that if she tried to light a cigarette she would fall off the lift.

He lit his cigarette, bending over a little and squinting over his cupped hands as the smoke twisted up past his eyes. He had long, thin hands, and ordinarily you had the feeling that people with hands like that were nervous and easily upset. He was tall and slender, and his ski pants were very downhill, Constance noted, and he wore a red sweater and a checked scarf. He had the air of a dandy, but a dandy who was amused at himself. He moved easily on his skis, and you could tell he was one of the people who weren't afraid of falling.

"I never see you in the bar," he said, tossing the match into the snow and putting on his gloves.

"I don't drink," she said, not quite telling the truth.

"They have Coca-Cola," he said. "Switzerland, the forty-ninth state."

"I don't like Coca-Cola."

"Used to be one of the leading British colonies," he said, grinning. "Switzerland. But we lost it, along with India. Before the war, in this town, the English covered the hills like the edelweiss. If you wanted to find a Swiss between January 1st and March 13th, you had to hunt with dogs."

"Were you here before the war?" Constance asked, surprised.

"With my mother. She broke a leg a year."

"Is she here now?"

"No," he said. "She's dead."

I must be careful, Constance thought, avoiding looking at the man beside her, not to ask people in Europe about their relatives. So many of them turn out to be dead.

"It used to be very gay," he said, "the hotels swarming, and dances every night, and everybody dressing for dinner, and singing 'God Save the King' on New Year's. Did you know it was going to be this quiet?"

"Yes," Constance said. "I asked the man at the travel bureau in Paris."

"Oh. What did he say?"

"He said everybody was a serious skier here and went to bed by ten o'clock."

The Englishman glanced at her momentarily. "You're not a serious skier, are you?"

"No. I've only been two or three times before."

"You're not one of the delicate ones, are you?"

"Delicate?" Constance looked at him, puzzled. "What do you mean?"

"You know," he said, "the advertisements. Schools for delicate children. Swiss for t.b."

Constance laughed. "Do I look as though I have t.b.?"

He regarded her gravely, and she felt plump and unaustere and a little too bosomy in her tight clothes. "No," he said. "But you never can tell. Did you ever read *The Magic Mountain*?"

"Yes," she said, feeling proud that she could show she was not completely uncultured, although American and very young, and remembering that she had skipped the philosophic discussions and cried over the death of the cousin. "I read it. Why?"

"The sanitarium it was written about isn't far from here," Pritchard said. "I'll show it to you someday when the snow's bad. Do you think this place is sad?"

"No," she said, surprised. "Why?"

"Some people do. The mixture. The pretty mountains and the healthy types walloping down the hills, risking their necks and feeling marvellous, and the people with the bad lungs hanging on, watching them and wondering if they're ever going to leave here alive."

"I guess I didn't think about it," Constance admitted honestly.

"It was worse right after the war," he said. "There was a boom here right after the war. All the people who hadn't eaten enough or had been living underground or in prison and who had been frightened so long—"

"Where're they now?"

Pritchard shrugged. "Dead, discharged, or destitute," he said. "Is it true that people refuse to die in America?"

"Yes," she said. "It would be an admission of failure."

He smiled and patted her gloved hand, which was clutching

tightly onto the middle bar. "You mustn't be angry that we're jealous," he said. "It's the only way we can show our gratitude." Gently, he loosened her fingers from the wood. "And you mustn't be so tight when you ski. Not even with your fingers. You mustn't even frown until you go in for tea. The drill is—loose, desperate, and supremely confident."

"Is that how you are?"

"Mostly desperate," he said.

"What are you doing on this little beginners' slope, then?" Constance asked. "Why didn't you take the *téléphérique* up to the top?"

"I twisted my ankle yesterday," Pritchard said. "Overrated myself. The February disease. Out of control and into a gully, with a great deal of style. So today I can only do slow, majestic turns. But tomorrow we attack that one once more—" He gestured up toward the peak, half closed in by fog, with the sun a wet, pale ball above it, making it look forbidding and dangerous. "Come along?" He looked at her inquiringly.

"I haven't been up there yet," Constance said, regarding the mountain respectfully. "I'm afraid it's a little too much for me so far."

"You must always do things that are a little too much for you," he said. "On skis. Otherwise, where's the fun?"

They were silent for several moments, moving slowly up the hill, feeling the wind cut across their faces, noticing the quiet and the queer, fogged mountain light. Twenty yards ahead of them, on the preceding bar, a girl in a yellow parka moved evenly upward like a bright, patient doll.

"Paris?" Pritchard said.

"What's that?" He jumps around entirely too much, Constance thought, feeling heavy.

"You said you came from Paris. Are you one of those nice people who come here to give us your government's money?"

"No," said Constance. "I just came over on a—well, on a vacation. I live in New York, really. And French food makes me break out."

He looked at her critically. "You look completely unbroken out now," he said. "You look like the girls who advertise soap and beer in American magazines." Then he added hastily. "If that's considered insulting in your country, I take it back."

"And the men in Paris," she said.

"Oh. Are there men in Paris?"

"Even in the museums. They follow you. With homburg hats.

561

Looking at you as though they're weighing you by the pound. In front of religious pictures and everything.''

"Girl I knew, English girl," Pritchard said, "was followed from Prestwick, Scotland, to the tip of Cornwall by an American gunner in 1944. Three months. No religious pictures, though, as far as I know."

"You know what I mean. It's an impolite atmosphere," she said primly, knowing he was making fun of her in that straight-faced English way but not knowing whether to be offended or not.

"Were you brought up in a convent?"

"No."

"It's amazing how many American girls sound as though they were brought up in a convent. Then it turns out they drink gin and roar in bars. What do you do at night?"

"Where? At home?"

"No. I know what people do at night in America. They look at television," he said. "I mean here."

"I—I wash my hair," she said defensively, feeling foolish. "And I write letters."

"How long are you staying up here?"

"Six weeks."

"Six weeks." He nodded, and swung his poles to his outside hand, because they were nearing the top. "Six weeks of shining hair and correspondence."

"I made a promise," she said, thinking, I might as well let him know now, just in case he's getting any ideas. "I promised someone I'd write him a letter a day while I was gone."

Pritchard nodded soberly, as though sympathizing with her. "Americans," he said as they came to the top and slid out from the T bar onto the flat place. "Americans baffle me."

Then he waved his poles at her and went straight down the hill, his red sweater a swift, diminishing gay speck against the blue-shadowed snow.

The sun slipped between the peaks, like a gold coin in a gigantic slot, and the light got flat and dangerous, making it almost impossible to see the bumps. Constance made her last descent, falling twice and feeling superstitious, because it was always when you said, "Well, this is the last one," that you got hurt.

Running out and coming to a stop on the packed snow between two farmhouses at the outskirts of the town, she kicked off her skis with a sense of accomplishment and relief. Her toes and fingers were frozen, but she was warm everywhere else and her cheeks were bright red and she breathed the thin, cold air with a mountain sense of tasting something delicious. She felt vigorous and friendly, and smiled at the other skiers clattering to a stop around her. She was brushing the snow of the last two falls off her clothes, so that she would look like a good skier as she walked through the town, when Pritchard came down over the last ridge and flicked to a stop beside her.

"I see you," he said, bending to unlock his bindings, "but I won't tell a soul."

Constance gave a final, self-conscious pat to the icy crystals on her parka. "I only fell four times all afternoon," she said.

"Up there, tomorrow"—he made a gesture of his head toward the mountain—"you'll crash all day."

"I didn't say I was going up there." Constance buckled her skis together and started to swing them up to her shoulder. Pritchard reached over and took them from her. "I can carry my own skis," she said.

"Don't be sturdy. American girls are always being sturdy about inessential points." He made a big V out of the two pairs of skis on his shoulders, and they started walking, their boots crunching on the stained, hard snow of the road. The lights came on in the town, pale in the fading light. The postman passed them, pulling his sled with his big dog yoked beside him. Six children in snowsuits on a linked whip of sleds came sliding down out of a steep side street and overturned in front of them in a fountain of laughter. A big brown horse with his belly clipped to keep the ice from forming there slowly pulled three huge logs toward the station. Old men in pale-blue parkas passed them and said *"Grüezi,"* and a maid from one of the houses up the hill shot out on a little sled, holding a milk can between her knees as she rocketed around the turns. They were playing a French waltz over at the skating rink, and the music mingled with the laughter of the children and the bells on the horse's bridle and the distant, old-fashioned clanging of the gong at the railroad station, announcing a train's departure.

"Departure," the station bell said, insistent among the other sounds.

There was a booming noise far off in the hills, and Constance looked up, puzzled. "What's that?" she asked.

"Mortars," said Pritchard. "It snowed last night, and the patrols have been out all day firing at the overhangs. For the avalanches."

There was another shot, low and echoing, and they stopped and listened. "Like old times," Pritchard said as they started walking again. "Like the good old war."

563

"Oh," said Constance, feeling delicate, because she had never heard guns before. "The war. Were you in it?"

"A little." He grinned. "I had a little war."

"Doing what?"

"Night fighter," he said, shifting the yoke of skis a little on his shoulders. "I flew an ugly black plane across an ugly black sky. That's the wonderful thing about the Swiss—the only thing they shoot is snow."

"Night fighter," Constance said vaguely. She had been only twelve years old when the war ended, and it was all jumbled and remote in her memory. It was like hearing about the graduating class two generations before you in school. People were always referring to names and dates and events that they expected you to recognize, but which you could never quite get straight. "Night fighter. What was that?"

"We flew interceptor missions over France," Pritchard said. "We'd fly on the deck to avoid the radar and flak, and hang around airfields making the Hun miserable, waiting for planes to come in slow, with their wheels down."

"Oh, I remember now," Constance said firmly. "You're the ones who ate carrots. For night vision."

Pritchard laughed. "For publication we ate carrots," he said. "Actually, we used radar. We'd locate them on the screen and fire when we saw the exhaust flares. Give me a radar screen over a carrot any day."

"Did you shoot down many planes?" Constance asked, wondering if she sounded morbid.

*"Grüezi,"* Pritchard said to the owner of a *pension* who was standing in front of his door looking up at the sky to see if it was going to snow that night. "Twenty centimetres by morning. Powder."

"You think?" the man said, looking doubtfully at the evening sky.

"I guarantee," Pritchard said.

"You're very polite," the man said, smiling. "You must come to Switzerland more often." He went into his *pension,* closing the door behind him.

"A couple," Pritchard said carelessly. "We shot down a couple. Should I tell you how brave I was?"

"You look so young," Constance said.

"I'm thirty," said Pritchard. "How old do you have to be to shoot down a plane? Especially poor, lumbering transports, running

564

out of gas, full of clerks and rear-echelon types, wiping their glasses and being sorry the airplane was ever invented.''

In the hills, there was the flat sound of the mortars again. Constance wished they'd stop. ''You don't look thirty,'' she said to Pritchard.

''I've led a simple and salutary life. Here,'' he said. They were in front of one of the smaller hotels, and he put the skis in the rack and jammed the poles into the snow beside them. ''Let's go in here and get a simple and salutary cup of tea.''

''Well,'' said Constance, ''I really—''

''Make the letter two pages shorter tonight, and more intense.'' He took her elbow gently, barely touching it, as he guided her toward the door. ''And polish your hair some other night.''

They went into the bar and sat down at a heavy, carefully carved wood table. There were no other skiers in the bar—just some village men sitting under the chamois antlers on the wall, quietly playing cards on felt cloths and drinking coffee out of small, stemmed glasses.

''I told you,'' Pritchard said, taking off his scarf. ''This country is being overrun by the Swiss.''

The waitress came over, and Pritchard ordered, in German.

''What did you ask for?'' Constance asked, because she could tell it wasn't only tea.

''Tea and lemon and black rum,'' said Pritchard.

''Do you think I ought to have rum?'' she asked doubtfully.

''Everybody in the whole world should have rum,'' he said. ''It will keep you from committing suicide in the twilight.''

''You speak German, don't you?''

''I speak all the dead languages of Europe,'' he said. ''German, French, Italian, and English. I was carefully educated for a world of interchangeable currency.'' He sat back, rubbing the knuckles of one hand against the palm of the other, to warm them. His head was leaning against the wood-panelled wall and he was smiling at her and she couldn't tell whether she was uncomfortable or not. ''Let me hear you say 'Hi-ho, Silver.' ''

''What?'' she asked, puzzled.

''Isn't that what people say in America? I want to perfect my accent for the next invasion,'' he said.

''They stopped that,'' she said, thinking, My, he's a jumpy boy, I wonder what happened to him to make him that way. ''They don't say it any more. It's out of date.''

''All the best things go out of date so quickly in your country,'' he said regretfully. ''Observe the Swiss.'' He gestured with his head toward where the men were playing. "That game has been going on since 1910," he said. "Living among the Swiss is so placid. It's like living alongside a lake. Many people can't stand it, of course. You remember that joke about the Swiss in that film about Vienna?"

"No," Constance said. "What film?" This is the first time, she thought, I've ever called a movie a film. I must be careful.

"One of the characters says, 'The Swiss haven't had a war in a hundred and fifty years and what have they produced? The cuckoo clock.' I don't know." Pritchard shrugged. "Maybe it's better to live in a country that invents the cuckoo clock than one that invents radar. Time is nothing serious to a cuckoo clock. A little toy that makes a silly, artificial sound every half hour. For people who invent radar, time is ominous, because it's the difference between the altitude of a plane and the location of the battery that's going to bring it down. It's an invention for people who are suspicious and are thinking of ambush. Here's your tea. As you see, I'm making a serious effort to amuse you, because I've been watching you for five days and you give the impression of a girl who cries herself to sleep several times a week."

"How much of this stuff do I put in?" Constance asked, confused by the flood of talk, holding the glass of rum, and carefully making sure not to look at Pritchard.

"Half," he said. "You have to have something in reserve for the second cup."

"It smells good," Constance said, sniffing the fragrance that rose from the cup after she had measured out half the glass of rum and squeezed the lemon into it.

"Perhaps"—Pritchard prepared his own cup—"perhaps I'd better talk only on impersonal subjects."

"Perhaps that would be better," Constance said.

"The chap who receives all those letters," Pritchard said. "Why isn't he here?"

Constance hesitated for a moment. "He works," she said.

"Oh. That vice." He sipped his tea, then put down his cup and rubbed his nose with his handkerchief. "Hot tea does that to you, too?"

"Yes."

"Are you going to marry him?"

"You said impersonal."

"So. The marriage is arranged."

"I didn't say that."

"No. But you would have said no if it wasn't."

Constance chuckled. "All right," she said. "Arranged. Anyway, approximately arranged."

"When?"

"When the three months're up," she said, without thinking.

"Is that a law in New York?" Pritchard asked. "That you have to wait three months? Or is it a private family taboo?"

Constance hesitated. Suddenly, she felt that she hadn't really talked to anyone in a long time. She had ordered meals and asked directions in railroad stations and said good morning to the people in shops, but everything else had been loneliness and silence, no less painful because she had imposed it on herself, Why not, she thought, selfishly and gratefully. Why not talk about it, for once?

"It's my father," she said, twisting her cup. "It's his idea. He's against it. He said wait three months and see. He thinks I'll forget Mark in three months in Europe."

"America," Pritchard said. "The only place left where people can afford to act in an old-fashioned manner. What's the matter with Mark? Is he a fright?"

"He's beautiful," Constance said. "Melancholy and beautiful."

Pritchard nodded, as though noting all this down. "No money, though," he said.

"Enough," said Constance. "At least, he has a good job."

"What's the matter with him, then?"

"My father thinks he's too old for me," Constance said. "He's forty."

"A grave complaint," Pritchard said. "Is that why he's melancholy?"

Constance smiled. "No. He was born that way. He's a thoughtful man."

"Do you only like forty-year-old men?" Pritchard asked.

"I only like Mark," said Constance. "Although it's true I never got along with the young men I knew. They—they're cruel. They make me feel shy—and angry with myself. When I go out with one of them, I come home feeling crooked."

"Crooked?" Pritchard looked puzzled.

"Yes. I feel I haven't behaved like me. I've behaved the way I think the other girls they've gone out with have behaved. Coquettish, cynical, amorous. Is this too complicated?"

"No."

"I hate the opinions other people have of me," Constance said, almost forgetting the young man at the table with her, and talking bitterly, and for herself. "I hate being used just for celebrations, when people come into town from college or from the Army.

Somebody for parties, somebody to maul on the way home in the taxi. And my father's opinion of me.'' She was getting it out for the first time. ''I used to think we were good friends, that he thought I was a responsible, grown-up human being. Then when I told him I wanted to marry Mark, I found out it was all a fraud. What he really thinks of me is that I'm a child. And a child is a form of idiot. My mother left him when I was ten and we've been very close since then, but we weren't as close as I thought we were. He was just playing a game with me. Flattering me. When the first real issue came up, the whole thing collapsed. He wouldn't let me have my own opinion of me at all. That's why I finally said all right to the three months. To prove it to him once and for all.'' She looked suddenly, distrustfully, at Pritchard to see whether he was smiling. ''Are you being amused at me?''

''Of course not,'' he said. ''I'm thinking of all the people I've known who've had different opinions of me than I've had of myself. What a frightening idea.'' He looked at her speculatively, but it was hard for her to tell how serious he was. ''And what's your opinion of yourself?''

''It's not completely formed yet,'' she said slowly. ''I know what I want it to be. I want to be responsible and I don't want to be a child and I don't want to be cruel—and I want to move in a good direction.'' She shrugged, embarrassed now. ''That's pretty lame, isn't it?''

''Lame,'' Pritchard said, ''but admirable.''

''Oh, I'm not admirable yet,'' she said. ''Maybe in ten years. I haven't sorted myself out completely yet.'' She laughed nervously. ''Isn't it nice,'' she said, ''you're going away in a few days and I'll never see you again, so I can talk like this to you.''

''Yes,'' he said. ''Very nice.''

''I haven't talked to anyone for so long. Maybe it's the rum.'' Pritchard smiled. ''Ready for your second cup?''

''Yes, thank you.'' She watched him pour the tea and was surprised to notice that his hand shook. Perhaps, she thought, he's one of those young men who came out of the war drinking a bottle of whisky a day.

''So,'' he said. ''Tomorrow we go up to the top of the mountain.''

She was grateful to him for realizing that she didn't want to talk about herself any more and switching the conversation without saying anything about it.

''How will you do it—with your ankle?'' she asked.

''I'll get the doctor to put a shot of Novocain in it,'' he said. ''And for a few hours my ankle will feel immortal.''

"All right," she said, watching him pour his own tea, watching his hand shake. "In the morning?"

"I don't ski in the morning," he said. He added the rum to his tea and sniffed it appreciatively.

"What do you do in the morning?"

"I recover, and write poetry."

"Oh." She looked at him doubtfully. "Should I know your name?"

"No," he said. "I always tear it up the next morning."

She laughed, a little uncertainly, because the only other people she had ever known who wrote poetry had been fifteen-year-old boys in prep school. "My," she said, "you're a queer man."

"Queer?" He raised his eyebrows. "Doesn't that mean something a little obscene in America? Boys with boys, I mean."

"Only sometimes," Constance said, embarrassed. "Not now. What sort of poetry do you write?"

"Lyric, elegiac, and athletic," he said. "In praise of youth, death, and anarchy. Very good for tearing. Shall we have dinner together tonight?"

"Why?" she asked, unsettled by the way he jumped from one subject to another.

"That's a question that no European woman would ever ask," he said.

"I told the hotel that I was going to have dinner up in my room."

"I have great influence at the hotel," he said. "I think I may be able to prevent them from taking the tray up."

"Besides," Constance said, "what about the lady you've been having dinner with all week—the French lady?"

"Good." He smiled. "You've been watching me, too."

"There're only fifteen tables in the whole dining room," Constance said uncomfortably. "You can't help . . ." The French lady was at least thirty, with a short, fluffed haircut and a senselessly narrow waist. She wore black slacks and sweaters and very tight, shiny belts, and she and Pritchard always seemed to be laughing a great deal together over private jokes in the corner in which they sat every night. Whenever Constance was in the room with the French lady, she felt young and clumsy.

"The French lady is a good friend," Pritchard said, "but Anglo-Saxons are not *nuancé* enough for her, she says. The French are patriots down to the last bedsheet. Besides, her husband is arriving tomorrow."

"I think I'd really rather stick to my plan," Constance said formally. She stood up. "Are we ready to go?"

He looked at her quietly for a moment. "You're beautiful," he said. "Sometimes it's impossible to keep from saying that."

"Please," she said. "Please, I do have to go now."

"Of course," he said. He stood up and left some money on the table. "Whatever you say."

They walked the hundred yards to their hotel in silence. It was completely dark now, and very cold, and their breath crystallized in little clouds before their mouths as they walked.

"I'll put your skis away," he said, at the door of the hotel.

"Thank you," she said in a low voice.

"Good night. And write a nice letter," he said.

"I'll try," she said. She turned and went into the hotel.

In her room, she took off her boots but didn't bother changing her clothes. She lay down on her bed, without putting on the lights, and stared at the dark ceiling, thinking, Nobody ever told me the English were like that.

"Dearest," she wrote. "Forgive me for not writing, but the weather has been glorious and for a little while I've just devoted myself to making turns and handling deep snow. . . . There's a young man here, an Englishman," she wrote conscientiously, "who's been very nice, who has been good enough to act as an instructor, and even if I say it myself, I'm really getting pretty good. He was in the R.A.F. and his father went down with the Hood and his mother was killed in a bombing—"

She stopped. No, she thought, it sounds tricky. As though I'm hiding something, and putting in the poor, dead, patriotic family as artful window dressing. She crumpled the letter and threw it in the wastebasket. She took out another sheet of paper. "Dearest," she wrote.

There was a knock on the door, and she called "*Ja,*"

The door opened and Pritchard came in. She looked up in surprise. In all the three weeks, he'd never come to her room. She stood up, embarrassed. She was in her stocking feet, and the room was littered with the debris of the afternoon's skiing—boots standing near the window, sweaters thrown over a chair, gloves drying on the radiator, and her parka hanging near the bathroom door, with a little trickle of melting snow running down from the collar. The radio was on, and an American band was playing "Bali Ha'i" from an Armed Forces station in Germany.

Pritchard, standing in front of the open door, smiled at her.

"Ah," he said, "some corner of a foreign room that is forever Vassar."

Constance turned the radio off. "I'm sorry," she said, waving vaguely and conscious that her hair was not combed. "Everything's such a mess."

Pritchard went over to the bureau and peered at Mark's picture, which was standing there in a leather frame. "The receiver of letters?" he asked.

"The receiver of letters." There was an open box of Kleenex on the bureau, and an eyelash curler, and a half-eaten bar of chocolate, and Constance felt guilty to be presenting Mark so frivolously.

"He's very handsome." Pritchard squinted at the photograph.

"Yes," Constance said. She found her moccasins and put them on, and felt a little less embarrassed.

"He looks serious." Pritchard moved the Kleenex to get a better view.

"He *is* serious," said Constance. In all the three weeks that she had been skiing with Pritchard, she had said hardly anything about Mark. They had talked about almost everything else, but somehow, by a tacit agreement, they had avoided Mark. They had skied together every afternoon and had talked a great deal about the necessity of leaning forward at all times, and about falling relaxed, and about Pritchard's time in public school in England, and about his father, and about the London theatre and American novelists, and they had talked gravely about what it was like to be twenty and what it was like to be thirty, and they had talked about Christmastime in New York and what football weekends were like at Princeton, and they had even had a rather sharp discussion on the nature of courage when Constance lost her nerve in the middle of a steep trail late one afternoon, with the sun going down and the mountain deserted. But they had never talked about Mark.

Pritchard turned away from the picture. "You didn't have to shoe yourself for me," he said, indicating her moccasins. "One of the nicest things about skiing is taking those damned heavy boots off and walking around on a warm floor in wool socks."

"I'm engaged in a constant struggle not to be sloppy," Constance said.

They stood there, facing each other in silence for a moment. "Oh," Constance said. "Sit down."

"Thank you," Pritchard said formally. He seated himself in the one easy chair. "I just came by for a minute. To say goodbye."

"Goodbye," Constance repeated stupidly. "Where're you going?"

"Home. Or at least to England. I thought I'd like to leave you my address," Pritchard said.

"Of course."

He reached over and picked up a piece of paper and her pen and wrote for a moment. "It's just a hotel," he said. "Until I find a place of my own." He put the paper down on the desk but kept the pen in his hand, playing with it. "Give you somebody else to write to," he said. "The English receiver of letters."

"Yes," she said.

"You can tell me what the snow's like," he said, "and how many times you came down the mountain in one day and who got drunk at the bar the night before."

"Isn't this sudden?" Constance asked. Somehow, after the first few days, it had never occurred to her that Pritchard might leave. He had been there when she arrived and he seemed to belong there so thoroughly, to be so much a part of the furniture of the place, that it was hard to conceive of being there without him.

"Not so sudden," Pritchard said. He stood up. "I wanted to say goodbye in private," he said. She wondered if he was going to kiss her. In all the three weeks, he hadn't as much as held her hand, and the only times he had touched her had been when he was helping her up after a particularly bad fall. But he made no move. He stood there, smiling curiously, playing with the pen, unusually untalkative, as though waiting for her to say something. "Well," he said, "will I see you later?"

"Yes," she said.

"We'll have a farewell dinner. They have veal on the menu, but I'll see if we can't get something better, in honor of the occasion." He put the pen down carefully on the desk. "Until later," he said, and went out, closing the door behind him.

Constance stared at the closed door. Everybody goes away, she thought. Unreasonably, she felt angry. She knew it was foolish, like a child protesting the end of a birthday party, but she couldn't help feeling that way. She looked around the room. It seemed cluttered and untidy to her, like the room of a silly and careless schoolgirl. She shook her head impatiently and began to put things in place. She put the boots out in the hall and hung the parka in the closet and carried the box of Kleenex into the bathroom and gave the half bar of chocolate to the chambermaid. She straightened the coverlet of the bed and cleaned the ashtray and, on a sudden impulse, dropped the eyelash curler into the wastebasket. It's too piddling, she thought, to worry about curling your eyelashes.

Pritchard ordered a bottle of Burgundy with dinner, because Swiss wine, he said, was too thin to say farewell on. They didn't talk much during dinner. It was as though he had already departed a little. Once or twice, Constance almost started to tell him how grateful she was for his patience with her on the hills, but somehow it never came out, and the dinner became more and more uncomfortable for both of them. Pritchard ordered brandy with the coffee, and she drank it, although it gave her heartburn. The three-piece band began to play for the evening's dancing while they were drinking their brandy, and then it was too noisy to talk.

"Do you want to dance?" he asked.

"No," she said.

"Good," he said. "I despise dancing."

"Let's get out of here," Constance said. "Let's take a walk."

They went to their rooms to get some warm clothes, and Pritchard was waiting for her outside the hotel door when she came down in her snow boots and the beaver coat her father had given her the year before. Pritchard was leaning against a pillar on the front porch and she stared at him for a moment before he turned around, and she was surprised to see how tired and suddenly old he seemed when he was unaware that he was being watched.

They walked down the main street, with the sounds of the band diminishing behind them. It was a clear night, and the stars shone above the mountains, electrically blue. At the top of the highest hill, at the end of the *téléphérique*, a single light glittered from the hut there, where you could warm yourself before the descent, and buy spiced hot wine and biscuits.

They walked down to the bottom of the street and crossed over onto the path alongside the dark skating rink. The ice reflected the stars dimly and there was the noise of water from the brook that ran along one side of the rink and scarcely ever froze.

They stopped at a small, snow-covered bridge, and Pritchard lit a cigarette. The lights of the town were distant now and the trees stood around them in black silence. Pritchard put his head back, with the smoke escaping slowly from between his lips, and gestured up toward the light on top of the mountain.

"What a life," he said. "Those two people up there. Night after winter night alone on top of the hills, waiting for the world to arrive each morning." He took another puff of the cigarette. "They're not married, you know," he said. "Only the Swiss

573

would think of putting two people who weren't married on top of a hill like that. He's an old man and she's a religious fanatic and they hate each other, but neither of them will give the other the satisfaction of taking another job.'' He chuckled as they both looked at the bright pinpoint above them. ''Last year there was a blizzard and the *téléphérique* didn't run for a week and the power lines were down and they had to stay up there for six days and nights, breaking up chairs for firewood, living off chocolate and tins of soup, and not talking to each other.'' He stared reflectively at the faraway high light. ''It will do as a symbol this year for this pretty continent,'' he said softly.

Suddenly Constance knew what she had to say, ''Alan''—she moved squarely in front of him—''I don't want you to go.''

Pritchard flicked at his cigarette. ''Six days and six nights,'' he said. ''For their hardness of heart.''

''I don't want you to go.''

''I've been here for a long time,'' he said. ''I've had the best of the snow.''

''I want you to marry me,'' Constance said.

Pritchard looked at her. She could see he was trying to smile. ''That's the wonderful thing about being twenty years old,'' he said. ''You can say things like that.''

''I said I want you to marry me.''

He tossed away his cigarette. It glowed on the snow. He took a step toward her and kissed her. She could taste the fumed grape of the brandy faint on his lips. He held her for a moment, then stepped back and buttoned her coat, like a nurse being careful with a little girl. ''The things that can happen to a man,'' he said. He shook his head slowly.

''Alan,'' Constance said.

''I take it all back,'' Pritchard said. ''You're not at all like the girls who advertise soap and beer.''

''Please,'' she said. ''Don't make it hard.''

''What do you know about me?'' He knocked the snow off the bridge railing and leaned against it, brushing the snow off his hands with a dry sound. ''Haven't you ever been warned about the young men you're liable to meet in Europe?''

''Don't confuse me,'' she said. ''Please.''

''What about the chap in the leather frame?''

Constance took a deep breath. She could feel the cold tingling in her lungs. ''I don't know,'' she said. ''He's not here.''

Pritchard chuckled, but it sounded sad. ''Lost,'' he said. ''Lost by an ocean.''

"It's not only the ocean," she said.

They walked in silence again, listening to the sound of their boots on the frozen path. The moon was coming up between the peaks and reflecting milkily off the snow.

"You ought to know one bit of information," Pritchard said in a low voice, looking down at the long shadow the moon cast on the path ahead of him. "I've been married."

"Oh," Constance said. She was very careful to walk in the footprints of the others who had tamped the path down before her.

"Not gravely married," Pritchard said, looking up. "We were divorced two years ago. Does that make a difference to you?"

"Your business," Constance said.

"I must visit America someday," Pritchard said, chuckling. "They are breeding a new type."

"What else?" Constance asked.

"The next thing is unattractive," Pritchard said. "I don't have a pound. I haven't worked since the war. I've been living off what was left of my mother's jewelry. There wasn't much and I sold the last brooch in Zurich last week. That's why I have to go back, even if there were no other reasons. You can see," he said, grinning painfully, "you've picked the prize of the litter."

"What else?" Constance asked.

"Do you still want to hear more?"

"Yes."

"I would never live in America," Pritchard said. "I'm a weary, poverty-stricken, grounded old R.A.F. type, and I'm committed to another place. Come on." He took her elbow brusquely, as though he didn't want to talk any more. "It's late. We'd better get to the hotel."

Constance hung back. "You're not telling me everything," she said.

"Isn't that enough?"

"No."

"All right," he said. "I couldn't go with you to America if I wanted to."

"Why not?"

"Because they wouldn't let me in."

"Why not?" Constance asked, puzzled.

"Because I am host to the worm," Pritchard said.

"What're you talking about?"

"Swiss for delicate," he said harshly. "They kicked D. H. Lawrence out of New Mexico and made him die along the Riviera

575

for it. You can't blame them. They have enough diseases of their own. Now let's go back to the hotel."

"But you seem so healthy. You ski—"

"Everybody dies here in the best of health," Pritchard said. "It goes up and down with me. I almost get cured, then the next year"—he shrugged and chuckled soundlessly—"the next year I get almost uncured. The doctors hold their heads when they see me going up in the lift. Go home," he said. "I'm not for you. I'm oppressed. And you're not oppressed. It is the final miscegenation. Now shall we go back to the hotel?"

Constance nodded. They walked slowly. The town on the hill ahead of them was almost completely dark now, but they could hear the music of the dance band, thin and distant in the clear night air.

"I don't care," Constance said as they came to the first buildings. "I don't care about anything."

"When I was twenty—" Pritchard said. "When I was twenty I once said the same thing."

"First, we'll be practical," Constance said. "You'll need money to stay here. I'll give it to you tomorrow."

"I can't take your money."

"It's not mine," Constance said. "It's my father's."

"England is forever in your debt," Pritchard said. He was trying to smile. "Be careful of me."

"What do you mean?"

"I am beginning to feel as though I can be consoled."

"What's wrong with that?"

"It can prove to be mortal," Pritchard whispered, taking her clumsily and bulkily in his arms, "for those of us who are inconsolable."

When they woke in the morning, they were solemn at first, and disconnectedly discussed the weather, which was revealed through the not quite closed curtains to be gray and uncertain. But then Pritchard asked, "How do you feel?" and Constance, taking her time and wrinkling her eyebrows in a deep attempt to be accurate, said, "I feel *enormously* grown up." Pritchard couldn't help roaring with laughter, and all solemnity was gone. They lay there comfortably discussing themselves, going over their future like misers, and Constance was worried, although not too seriously, about scandalizing the hotel people, and Pritchard said that there was nothing to worry about—nothing that foreigners could do could scandalize the Swiss—and Constance felt more comfortable than ever at being in such a civilized country.

They made plans about the wedding, and Pritchard said they'd go to the French part of Switzerland to get married, because he didn't want to get married in German, and Constance said she was sorry she hadn't thought of it herself.

Then they decided to get dressed, because you could not spend the rest of your life in bed, and Constance had a sorrowful, stinging moment when she saw how thin he was, and thought, conspiratorially, Eggs, milk, butter, rest. They went out of the room together, bravely determined to brazen it out, but there was no one in the corridor or on the stairway to see them, so they had the double pleasure of being candid and being unobserved at the same time, which Constance regarded as an omen of good luck. They discovered that it was almost time for lunch, so they had some kirsch first, and then orange juice and bacon and eggs and wonderful, dark coffee in the scrubbed, wood-panelled dining room, and in the middle of it tears came into Constance's eyes and Pritchard asked why she was crying and she said, "I'm thinking of all the breakfasts we're going to eat together." Pritchard's eyes got a little wet then, too, as he stared across the table at her, and she said, "You must cry often, please."

"Why?" he asked.

"Because it's so un-English," she said, and they both laughed.

After breakfast, Pritchard said he was going up the hill to make a few runs and asked if she wanted to go with him, but she said she felt too melodious that day to ski, and he grinned at the "melodious."

She said she was going to write some letters, and he grew thoughtful. "If I were a gentleman, I'd write your father immediately and explain everything," he said.

"Don't you dare," she said, meaning it, because she knew her father would be over on the next plane if he got a letter like that.

"Don't worry," he said. "I'm not that much of a gentleman."

She watched him stride off between the snowbanks with his red sweater and his skis, looking boyish and jaunty, and then went to her room and wrote a letter to Mark, saying that she had thought it over and that she was sorry but she had decided it was a mistake. She wrote the letter calmly, without feeling anything, cozy in her warm room. She didn't mention Pritchard, because that was none of Mark's business.

Then she wrote a letter to her father and told him that she had broken off with Mark. She didn't mention Pritchard in the letter to her father, either, because she didn't want him over on the next plane, and she didn't say anything about coming home. All that could wait.

She sealed the letters, then lay down dreamily to nap, and slept without dreaming for more than an hour. She dressed for the snow and went to the post office to mail the letters and walked down to the skating rink to watch the children on the ice, and on her way back to the hotel she stopped at the ski shop and bought Pritchard a lightweight yellow sweater, because soon the sun would be very hot all day and the clothes of winter would all be too warm.

She was in the bar, waiting unhurriedly for Pritchard, when she heard that he was dead.

Nobody had come to tell her, because there was no particular reason for anybody to come to tell her.

There was an instructor with whom Pritchard had sometimes skied talking in the bar to some Americans, and he was saying, "He was out of control and he miscalculated and he went into a tree and he was dead in five minutes. He was a jolly fine fellow"— the ski teacher had learned his English from his British pupils before the war—"but he went too fast. He did not have the technique to handle the speed."

The ski teacher did not sound as though it were routine to die on skis, but he did not sound surprised. He himself had had many of his bones broken, as had all his friends, crashing into trees and stone walls and from falls in the summertime, when he was a guide for climbers, and he sounded as though it were inevitable, and even just, that from time to time people paid up to the mountain for faults of technique.

Constance stayed for the funeral, walking behind the black-draped sled to the churchyard and the hole in the snow and the unexpected dark color of the earth after the complete white of the winter. No one came from England, because there was no one to come, although the ex-wife telegraphed flowers. A good many of the villagers came, but merely as friends, and some of the other skiers, who had known Pritchard casually, and as far as anyone could tell, Constance was just one of them.

At the grave, the ski teacher, with the professional habit of repetition common to teachers, said, "He did not have the technique for that much speed."

Constance didn't know what to do with the yellow sweater, and she finally gave it to the chambermaid for her husband.

Eight days later, Constance was in New York. Her father was waiting for her on the pier and she waved to him and he waved back, and she could tell, even at that distance, how glad he was to see her again. They kissed when she walked off the gangplank, and he hugged her, very hard, then held her off at arm's length and stared at her delightedly, and said, "God, you look absolutely wonderful! See," he said, and she wished he hadn't said it, but she realized he couldn't help himself. "See—wasn't I right? Didn't I know what I was talking about?"

"Yes, Father," she said, thinking, How could I ever have been angry with him? He's not stupid or mean or selfish or uncomprehending—he is merely alone.

Holding her hand the way he used to do while they took walks together when she was a little girl, he led her into the customs shed, to wait for her trunk to come off the ship.

# Tip on a Dead Jockey

Lloyd Barber was lying on his bed reading *France-Soir* when the phone rang. It was only two o'clock in the afternoon, but it was raining for the fifth consecutive day and he had no place to go anyway. He was reading about the relative standing of the teams in the Rugby leagues. He never went to Rugby games and he had no interest in the relative standings of Lille and Pau and Bordeaux, but he had finished everything else in the paper. It was cold in the small, dark room, because there was no heat provided between ten in the morning and six in the evening, and he lay on the lumpy double bed, his shoes off, covered with his overcoat.

He picked up the phone, and the man at the desk downstairs said, "There is a lady waiting for you here, M. Barber."

Barber squinted at himself in the mirror above the bureau across from the bed. He wished he was better-looking. "Did she give her name?" he asked.

"No, Monsieur. Should I demand it?"

"Never mind," Barber said. "I'll be right down."

He hung up the phone and put on his shoes. He always put the left one on first, for luck. He buttoned his collar and pulled his tie into place, noticing that it was frayed at the knot. He got into his jacket and patted his pockets to see if he had cigarettes. He had no cigarettes. He shrugged, and left the light on vindictively, because the manager was being unpleasant about the bill, and went downstairs.

Maureen Richardson was sitting in the little room off the lobby, in one of those age-colored plush chairs that fourth-rate Parisian hotels furnish their clientele to discourage excessive conviviality on the ground floor. None of the lamps was lit, and a dark, dead, greenish light filtered in through the dusty curtains from the rainy street outside. Maureen had been a young, pretty girl with bright, credulous blue eyes when Barber first met her, during the war, just before she married Jimmy Richardson. But she had had two children since then and Richardson hadn't done so well, and now she was wearing a worn cloth coat that was soaked, and her complexion had gone, and in the greenish lobby light she seemed bone-colored and her eyes were pale.

"Hello, Beauty," Barber said. Richardson always called her that, and while it had amused his friends in the squadron, he had loyally stuck to it, and finally everyone had picked it up.

Maureen turned around quickly, almost as though he had frightened her. "Lloyd," she said. "I'm so glad I found you in."

They shook hands, and Barber asked if she wanted to go someplace for a coffee.

"I'd rather not," Maureen said. "I left the kids with a friend for lunch and I promised I'd collect them at two-thirty and I don't have much time."

"Sure," Barber said. "How's Jimmy?"

"Oh, Lloyd . . ." Maureen pulled at her fingers, and Barber noticed that they were reddened and the nails were uneven. "Have you seen him?"

"What?" Barber peered through the gloom at her, puzzled. "What do you mean?"

"Have you seen him?" Maureen persisted. Her voice was thin and frightened.

"Not for a month or so," Barber said. "Why?" He asked it, but he almost knew why.

"He's gone, Lloyd," Maureen said. "He's been gone thirty-two days. I don't know what I'm going to do."

"Where did he go?" Barber asked.

"I don't know." Maureen took out a pack of cigarettes and lit one. She was too distracted to offer the pack to Barber. "He didn't tell me." She smoked the cigarette avidly but absently. "I'm so worried, I thought maybe he'd said something to you—or that you'd bumped into him."

"No," Barber said carefully. "He didn't say anything."

"It's the queerest thing. We've been married over ten years and he never did anything like this before," Maureen said, trying to control her voice. "He just came to me one night and he said he'd got leave of absence from his job for a month and that he'd be back inside of thirty days and he'd tell me all about it when he got back, and he begged me not to ask any questions."

"And you didn't ask any questions?"

"He was acting so strangely," Maureen said. "I'd never seen him like that before. All hopped up. Excited. You might even say happy, except that he kept going in all night to look at the kids.

581

And he's never given me anything to worry about in the—the girl department," Maureen said primly. "Not like some of the other boys we know. And if there was one thing about Jimmy, it was that you could trust him. So I helped him pack."

"What did he take?"

"Just one Valpak," Maureen said. "With light clothes. As though he was going off on a summer vacation. He even took a tennis racket."

"A tennis racket," Barber nodded, as though it were the most natural thing in the world for husbands to take tennis rackets along when disappearing. "Did you hear from him at all?"

"No," Maureen said. "He told me he wouldn't write. Did you ever hear of anything like that?" Even in her anguish, she permitted herself a tone of wifely grievance. "I knew we shouldn't have come to Europe. It's different for you. You're not married and you were always kind of wild anyway, not like Jimmy—"

"Did you call his office?" Barber asked, interrupting. He didn't want to hear how wild people thought he was, or how unmarried.

"I had a friend call," Maureen said. "It would look too fishy—his wife calling to ask where he was."

"What did they say?"

"They said that they had expected him two days ago but he hadn't come in yet."

Barber took one of Maureen's cigarettes and lit it. It was the first one in four hours and it tasted wonderful. He had a little selfish twinge of gratitude that Maureen had come to his hotel.

"Lloyd, do you know anything?" Maureen asked, worn and shabby in her damp, thin coat in the foggy green light.

Barber hesitated. "No," he said. "But I'll put in a couple of calls and I'll telephone you tomorrow."

They both stood up. Maureen pulled on gloves over her reddened hands. The gloves were worn and greenish black. Looking at them, Barber suddenly remembered how neat and shining Maureen had been when they first met, in Louisiana, so many years before, and how healthy and well-dressed he and Jimmy and the others had been in their lieutenants' uniforms with the new wings on their breasts.

"Listen, Beauty," Barber said. "How are you fixed for dough?"

"I didn't come over for that," Maureen said firmly.

Barber took out his wallet and peered judiciously into it. It wasn't necessary. He knew exactly what was there. He took out a five-thousand-franc note. "Here," he said, handing it to her. "Try this on for size."

582

Maureen made a motion as though to give it back to him. "I really don't think I should . . ." she began.

"Sh-h-h, Beauty," Barber said. "There isn't an American girl in Paris who couldn't use five *mille* on a day like this."

Maureen sighed and put the bill in her pocketbook. "I feel terrible about taking your money, Lloyd."

Barber kissed her forehead. "In memory of the wild blue yonder," he said, pocketing the wallet, with its remaining fifteen thousand francs, which, as far as he knew, would have to last him for the rest of his life. "Jimmy'll give it back to me."

"Do you think he's all right?" Maureen asked, standing close to him.

"Of course," Lloyd said lightly and falsely. "There's nothing to worry about. I'll call you tomorrow. He'll probably be there, answering the phone, getting sore at me for sucking around his wife when he's out of town."

"I bet." Maureen smiled miserably. She went through the cavelike murk of the lobby, out into the rainy street, on her way to pick up the two children, who had been sent out to lunch at the home of a friend.

Barber went to his room and picked up the phone and waited for the old man downstairs to plug in. There were two suitcases standing open on the floor, with shirts piled in them, because there wasn't enough drawer space in the tiny bureau supplied by the hotel. On top of the bureau there were: a bill, marked overdue, from a tailor; a letter from his ex-wife, in New York, saying she had found an Army pistol of his in the bottom of a trunk and asking him what he wanted her to do with it, because she was afraid of the Sullivan Law; a letter from his mother, telling him to stop being a damn fool and come home and get a regular job; a letter from a woman in whom he was not interested, inviting him to come and stay with her in her villa near Eze, where it was beautiful and warm, she said, and where she needed a man around the house; a letter from a boy who had flown as his waist-gunner during the war and who insisted that Barber had saved his life when he was hit in the stomach over Palermo, and who, surprisingly, had written a book since then. Now he sent long, rather literary letters at least once a month to Barber. He was an odd, intense boy, who had been an excitable gunner, and he was constantly examining himself to find out whether he and the people he loved, among whom he rather embarrassingly included Barber, mostly because of the eight minutes over Palermo, were living up to their

583

promise. "Our generation is in danger," the boy had typed in the letter on the bureau, "the danger of diminution. We have had our adventures too early. Our love has turned to affection, our hate to distaste, our despair to melancholy, our passion to preference. We have settled for the life of obedient dwarfs in a small but fatal sideshow."

The letter had depressed Barber and he hadn't answered it. You got enough of that sort of thing from the French. He wished the ex-waist-gunner would stop writing him, or at least write on different subjects. Barber hadn't answered his ex-wife, either, because he had come to Europe to try to forget her. He hadn't answered his mother, because he was afraid she was right. And he hadn't gone down to Eze, because no matter how broke he was, he wasn't selling that particular commodity yet.

Stuck into the mirror above the bureau was a photograph of himself and Jimmy Richardson, taken on the beach at Deauville the summer before. The Richardsons had taken a cottage there, and Barber had spent a couple of weekends with them. Jimmy Richardson was another one who had attached himself to Barber during the war. Somehow, Barber was always being presented with the devotion of people whose devotion he didn't want. "People hang on to you," a girl who was angry at him once told him, "because you're an automatic hypocrite. As soon as somebody comes into the room, you become gay and confident."

Jimmy and he had been in bathing trunks when the picture was snapped, and Barber was tall and blessed with a blond, California kind of good looks next to Jimmy, who seemed like a fat, incompetent infant, standing there with the sunny sea behind him.

Barber peered at the photograph. Jimmy didn't look like the sort of man who would ever be missing from anywhere for thirty-two days. As for himself, Barber thought wryly, he looked automatically gay and confident.

He leaned over and took the picture down and threw it into a drawer. Then, holding the phone loosely, he stared around him with distaste. In the glare of the unshaded lamp, the dark woodwork looked gloomy and termite-ridden, and the bed, with its mottled velours spread, the color of spoiled pears, looked as though it had been wallowed on by countless hundreds of obscenely shaped men and women who had rented the room for an hour at a time. For a second, he was piercingly homesick for all the rooms of all the Hotel Statlers he had slept in and all the roomettes on trains between New York and Chicago, and St. Louis and Los Angeles.

There was a whistling, staticlike sound in the phone, and he shook himself and gave the number of the George V. When he got the George V, he asked for M. Smith, Mr. Bert Smith. After a while, the girl said M. Smith was no longer at the hotel. Barber asked hurriedly, before the girl could cut him off, whether M. Smith was expected to return shortly or if he had left a forwarding address. No, the girl said after a long wait, he was not expected to return and there was no forwarding address.

Barber hung up. He was not surprised about Bert Smith. He was a man who wandered mysteriously from hotel to hotel, and he might have used a half-dozen names besides Smith since Barber had spoken to him last.

With a conscious effort, Barber tried not to think about Jimmy Richardson or his wife, who was called, as a friendly squadron joke, Beauty, or about Jimmy Richardson's two small sons.

Scowling, Barber went over to the window. The winter rain of Paris was seeping down into the narrow street, blurring it with the unproductive malice of city rain, chipping colorlessly at the buildings opposite, making it impossible to imagine what they had looked like when they were new. A workman was unloading cases of wine from a truck, looking persecuted by the weather, the Paris sound of clinking bottles muted and made hollow and mournful by the flow of gray water from the skies and from window ledges and signs and rolled awnings. It was not a day for a husband to be missing, for a friend to be missing. It was not a day to be alone or to have only fifteen thousand francs in your pocket or to be in a narrow hotel room where the heat was off from ten in the morning till six at night. It was not a day to be without a job or cigarettes or lunch. It was not a day on which to examine yourself and realize that no matter how many excuses you gave yourself, you were going to wind up knowing that, finally, you were responsible.

Barber shook himself again. There was no sense in just staying in the room all day. If he was going to do any good, he would have to find Bert Smith. He looked at his watch. It was nearly two-thirty. He tried to remember all the places he had ever seen Bert Smith at two-thirty in the afternoon. The fancy restaurant near the Rond-Point, where the movie people and the French newspaper owners and the rich tourists ate; the bistro on the Boulevard Latour-Maubourg, on the Left Bank; the restaurants at Auteuil and Longchamp and St. Cloud. Barber looked at the newspaper. They were running at Auteuil today.

If he was not at the races and if he was still in Paris, Bert Smith was likely to be in one art gallery or another in the middle of the afternoon. Bert Smith was an art lover, or at least he bought pictures, shrewdly and knowingly. Since Smith lived in hotel rooms, which were unlikely places for a collection, it was probable that he bought paintings on speculation or as an agent or, when they were important ones that the government did not wish to have leave the country, to be smuggled out of France.

Barber had also seen Smith late in the afternoons in the steam room at Claridge's, a small, round man with surprisingly well-shaped legs, sitting in the vapor, wrapped in a sheet, growing pinker and pinker, smiling luxuriously in the steam, sweating off the fat that he had accumulated in many years of eating in the best restaurants in Europe.

He had also seen Smith several times around six o'clock in the evening in the barbershop at the George V getting shaved, and after that in the bar upstairs, and in the bar at the Relais Plaza and the English bar downstairs at the Plaza-Athénée. And late at night he had seen him at various night clubs—L'Eléphant Blanc, Carroll's, La Rose Rouge . . .

Barber thought unhappily of the last fifteen thousand francs in his wallet. It was going to be a long, wet, hard, expensive day. He put on his hat and coat and went out. It was still raining, and he hailed a taxi and gave the driver the address of the restaurant near the Rond-Point.

It had started about two months before, in the stand at Auteuil just before the sixth race. The day was misty and there weren't many spectators, and Barber had not been doing very well, but he had got a tip on the sixth race, on an eight-to-one shot. He put five thousand down on the nose and climbed high up in the stand to get a good view of the race.

There was only one other spectator near him in the stand, a small, round man wearing an expensive-looking velours hat, and carrying a pair of binoculars and a rolled umbrella, like an Englishman. He smiled at Barber and nodded. As Barber smiled back politely, he realized that he had seen the man many times before, or his brother, or a half-dozen other men who looked like him, in restaurants and in bars and on the street, usually with tall girls who might have been lower-class mannequins or upper-class tarts.

The man with the umbrella moved over to him along the damp concrete row of seats. He had little, dapper feet and a bright necktie, and he had a well-cared-for, international kind of face, with large, pretty dark eyes, fringed by thick black lashes. He had what Barber had come to call an import-export face. It was a face that was at the same time bland, cynical, self-assured, sensual, hopeless, and daring, and its owner might be Turkish or Hungarian or Greek or he might have been born in Basra. It was a face you might see in Paris or Rome or Brussels or Tangier, always in the best places, always doing business. It was a face, you felt somehow, that was occasionally of interest to the police.

"Good afternoon," the man said, in English, tipping his hat. "Are you having a lucky day?" He had an accent, but it was difficult to place it. It was as though as a child he had gone to school everywhere and had had ten nurses of ten different nationalities.

"Not bad," Barber said carefully.

"Which do you like in this one?" The man pointed with his umbrella at the track, where the horses were gingerly going up to the distant starting line on the muddied grass.

"Number Three," Barber said.

"Number Three." The man shrugged, as though he pitied Barber but was restrained by his good breeding from saying so. "How is the movie business these days?" the man asked.

"The movie business went home a month ago," Barber said, slightly surprised that the man knew anything about it. An American company had been making a picture about the war, and Barber had had four lucky, well-paid months as a technical expert, buckling leading men into parachutes and explaining the difference between a P-47 and a B-25 to the director.

"And the blond star?" the man asked, taking his glasses away from his eyes. "With the exquisite behind?"

"Also home."

The man moved his eyebrows and shook his head gently, indicating his regret that his new acquaintance and the city of Paris were now deprived of the exquisite behind. "Well," he said, "at least it leaves you free in the afternoon to come to the races." He peered out across the track through the glasses. "There they go."

No. 3 led all the way until the stretch. In the stretch, he was passed rapidly by four other horses.

"Every race in this country," Barber said as the horses crossed the finish line, "is a hundred metres too long." He took out his tickets and tore them once and dropped them on the wet concrete.

He watched with surprise as the man with the umbrella took out some tickets and tore them up, too. They were on No. 3, and Barber could see that they were big ones. The man with the umbrella dropped the tickets with a resigned, half-amused expression on his face, as though all his life he had been used to tearing up things that had suddenly become of no value.

"Are you staying for the last race?" the man with the umbrella asked as they started to descend through the empty stands.

"I don't think so," Barber said. "This day has been glorious enough already."

"Why don't you stay?" the man said. "I may have something."

Barber thought for a moment, listening to their footsteps on the concrete.

"I have a car," the man said. "I could give you a lift into town, Mr. Barber."

"Oh," Barber said, surprised, "you know my name."

"Of course," the man said, smiling. "Why don't you wait for me at the bar? I have to go and cash some tickets."

"I thought you lost," Barber said suspiciously.

"On Number Three," the man said. From another pocket he took out some more tickets and waved them gently. "But there is always the insurance. One must always think of the insurance," he said. "Will I see you at the bar?"

"O.K.," Barber said, not because he hoped for anything in the way of information on the next race from the man with the umbrella but because of the ride home. "I'll be there. Oh—by the way, what's your name?"

"Smith," the man said. "Bert Smith."

Barber went to the bar and ordered a coffee, then changed it to a brandy, because coffee wasn't enough after a race like that. He stood there, hunched over the bar, reflecting sourly that he was one of the category of people who never think of the insurance. Smith, he thought, Bert Smith. More insurance. On how many other names, Barber wondered, had the man lost before he picked that one?

Smith came to the bar softly, on his dapper feet, smiling, and laid a hand lightly on Barber's arm. "Mr. Barber," he said, "there is a rumor for the seventh race. Number Six."

"I never win on Number Six," Barber said.

"It is a lovely little rumor," Smith said. "At present, a twenty-two-to-one rumor."

Barber looked at the man doubtfully. He wondered briefly what there was in it for Smith. "What the hell," he said, moving toward the seller's window. "What have I got to lose?"

He put five thousand francs on No. 6 and superstitiously remained at the bar during the race, drinking brandy. No. 6 won, all out, by half a length, and, although the odds had dropped somewhat, paid eighteen to one.

Barber walked through the damp twilight, across the discarded newspapers and the scarred grass, with its farmlike smell, patting his inside pocket with the ninety thousand francs in a comforting bulge there, pleased with the little man trotting beside him.

Bert Smith had a Citroën, and he drove swiftly and well and objectionably, cutting in on other cars and swinging wide into the outside lane to gain advantage at lights.

"Do you bet often on the races, Mr. Barber?" he was saying as they passed a traffic policeman, forlorn in his white cape on the gleaming street.

"Too often," Barber said, enjoying the warmth of the car and the effects of the last brandy and the bulge in his pocket.

"You like to gamble?"

"Who doesn't?"

"There are many who do not like to gamble," Smith said, nearly scraping a truck. "I pity them."

"Pity them?" Barber looked over at Smith, a little surprised at the word. "Why?"

"Because," Smith said softly, smiling, "in this age there comes a time when everyone finds that he is forced to gamble—and not only for money, and not only at the seller's window. And when that time comes, and you are not in the habit, and it does not amuse you, you are most likely to lose."

They rode in silence for a while. From time to time, Barber peered across at the soft, self-assured face above the wheel, lit by the dashboard glow. I would like to get a look at his passport, Barber thought—at all the passports he's carried for the last twenty years.

"For example," Smith said, "during the war . . ."

"Yes?"

"When you were in your plane," Smith said, "on a mission. Weren't there times when you had to decide suddenly to try something, to depend on your luck for one split second, and if you hesitated, if you balked at the act of gambling—sssszt!" Smith took one hand from the wheel and made a gliding, falling motion, with his thumb down. He smiled across at Barber. "I suppose you are one of the young men who were nearly killed a dozen times," he said.

"I suppose so," Barber said.

"I prefer that in Americans," Smith said. "It makes them more like Europeans."

"How did you know I was in the war?" Barber said. For the first time, he began to wonder if it was only a coincidence that Smith had been near him in the stand before the sixth race.

Smith chuckled. "You have been in Paris how long?" he said. "A year and a half?"

"Sixteen months," Barber said, wondering how the man knew *that*.

"Nothing very mysterious about it," Smith said. "People talk at bars, at dinner parties. One girl tells another girl. Paris is a small city. Where shall I drop you?"

Barber looked out the window to see where they were. "Not far from here," he said. "My hotel is just off the Avenue Victor Hugo. You can't get in there with a car."

"Oh, yes," Smith said, as though he knew about all hotels. "If it doesn't seem too inquisitive," he said, "do you intend to stay long in Europe?"

"It depends."

"On what?"

"On luck." Barber grinned.

"Did you have a good job in America?" Smith asked, keeping his eyes on the traffic ahead of him.

"In thirty years, working ten hours a day, I would have been the third biggest man in the company," Barber said.

Smith smiled. "Calamitous," he said. "Have you found more interesting things to do here?"

"Occasionally," Barber said, beginning to be conscious that he was being quizzed.

"After a war it is difficult to remain interested," Smith said. "While it is on, a war is absolutely boring. But then when it is over, you discover peace is even more boring. It is the worst result of wars. Do you still fly?"

"Once in a while."

Smith nodded. "Do you maintain your license?"

"Yes."

"Yes, that's wise," Smith said.

He pulled the car sharply in to the curb and stopped, and Barber got out.

"Here you are," Smith said. He put out his hand, smiling, and Barber shook it. Smith's hand was softly fleshed, but there was a feeling of stone beneath it.

"Thanks for everything," Barber said.

"Thank you, Mr, Barber, for your company," Smith said. He held Barber's hand for a moment, looking across the seat at him. "This has been very pleasant," he said. "I hope we can see each other again soon. Maybe we are lucky for each other."

"Sure," Barber said, grinning. "I'm always at home to people who can pick eighteen-to-one shots."

Smith smiled, relinquishing Barber's hand. "Maybe one of these days we'll have something even better than an eighteen-to-one shot," he said.

He waved a little and Barber closed the car door. Smith spurted out into the traffic, nearly causing two *quatre chevaux* to pile up behind him.

It had taken two weeks for Smith to declare himself. From the beginning, Barber had known that something was coming, but he had waited patiently, curious and amused, lunching with Smith in the fine restaurants Smith patronized, going to galleries with him and listening to Smith on the subject of the Impressionists, going out to the race tracks with him and winning more often than not on the information Smith picked up from tight-lipped men around the paddocks. Barber pretended to enjoy the little, clever man more than he actually did, and Smith, on his part, Barber knew, was pretending to like *him* more than he actually did. It was a kind of veiled and cynical wooing, in which neither party had yet committed himself. Only, unlike more ordinary wooings, Barber for the first two weeks was not sure in just which direction his desirability, as far as Smith was concerned, might lie.

Then, late one night, after a large dinner and a desultory tour of the night clubs, during which Smith had seemed unusually silent and abstracted, they were standing in front of Smith's hotel and he made his move. It was a cold night, and the street was deserted except for a prostitute with a dog, who looked at them without hope as she passed them on the way to the Champs-Elysées.

"Are you going to be in your hotel tomorrow morning, Lloyd?" Smith asked.

"Yes," Barber said. "Why?"

"Why?" Smith repeated absently, staring after the chilled-looking girl and her poodle walking despairingly down the empty, dark street. "Why?" He chuckled irrelevantly. "I have something I would like to show you," he said.

"I'll be in all morning," Barber said.

"Tell me, my friend," Smith said, touching Barber's sleeve lightly with his gloved hand. "Do you have any idea why I have been calling you so often for the last two weeks, and buying you so many good meals and so much good whiskey?"

"Because I am charming and interesting and full of fun," Barber said, grinning. "And because you want something from me."

Smith chuckled, louder this time, and caressed Barber's sleeve. "You are not absolutely stupid, my friend, are you?"

"Not absolutely," said Barber.

"Tell me, my friend," Smith said, almost in a whisper. "How would you like to make twenty-five thousand dollars?"

"What?" Barber asked, certain that he had not heard correctly.

"Sh-h-h," Smith said. He smiled, suddenly gay. "Think about it. I'll see you in the morning. Thank you for walking me home." He dropped Barber's arm and started into the hotel.

"Smith!" Barber called.

"Sh-h-h." Smith put his finger playfully to his mouth. "Sleep well. See you in the morning."

Barber watched him go through the glass revolving doors into the huge, brightly lit, empty lobby of the hotel. Barber took a step toward the doors to follow him in, then stopped and shrugged and put his collar up, and walked slowly in the direction of his own hotel. I've waited this long, he thought, I can wait till morning.

Barber was still in bed the next morning when the door opened and Smith came in. The room was dark, with the curtains drawn, and Barber was lying there, half asleep, thinking drowsily, Twenty-five thousand, twenty-five thousand. He opened his eyes when he heard the door open. There was a short, bulky silhouette framed in the doorway against the pallid light of the corridor.

"Who's that?" Barber asked, without sitting up.

"Lloyd. I'm sorry," Smith said. "Go back to sleep. I'll see you later."

Barber sat up abruptly, "Smith," he said. "Come in."

"I don't want to disturb—"

"Come in, come in." Barber got out of bed and, barefooted, went over to the window and threw back the curtains. He looked out at the street. "By God, what do you know?" he said, shivering and closing the window. "The sun is shining. Shut the door."

Smith closed the door. He was wearing a loose gray tweed overcoat, very British, and a soft Italian felt hat, and he was carrying a large manila envelope. He looked newly bathed and shaved, and wide awake.

Barber, blinking in the sudden sunshine, put on a robe and a pair of moccasins and lit a cigarette. "Excuse me," he said. "I want to wash." He went behind the screen that separated the washbasin and the *bidet* from the rest of the room. As he washed, scrubbing his face and soaking his hair with cold water, he heard Smith go over to the window. Smith was humming, in a soft, true, melodious tenor voice, a passage from an opera that Barber knew he had heard but could not remember. Aside from everything else, Barber thought, combing his hair roughly, I bet the bastard knows fifty operas.

Feeling fresher and less at a disadvantage with his teeth washed and his hair combed, Barber stepped out from behind the screen.

"Paris," Smith said, at the window, looking out. "What a satisfactory city. What a farce." He turned around, smiling. "Ah," he said, "how lucky you are. You can afford to put water on your head." He touched his thin, well-brushed hair sadly. "Every time I wash my hair, it falls like the leaves. How old did you say you are?"

"Thirty," Barber said, knowing that Smith remembered it.

"What an age." Smith sighed. "The wonderful moment of balance. Old enough to know what you want, still young enough to be ready for anything." He came back and sat down and propped the manila envelope on the floor next to the chair. "Anything." He looked up at Barber, almost coquettishly. "You recall our conversation, I trust," he said.

"I recall a man said something about twenty-five thousand dollars," Barber said.

"Ah—you do remember," Smith said gaily. "Well?"

"Well what?"

"Well, do you want to make it?"

"I'm listening," Barber said.

Smith rubbed his soft hands together gently in front of his face, his fingers rigid, making a slight, dry, sliding sound. "A little proposition has come up," he said. "An interesting little proposition."

"What do I have to do for my twenty-five thousand dollars?" Barber asked.

"What do you have to do for your twenty-five thousand dollars?" Smith repeated softly. "You have to do a little flying. You have flown for considerably less, from time to time, haven't you?" He chuckled.

"I sure have," Barber said. "What else do I have to do?"

"Nothing else," Smith said, sounding surprised. "Just fly. Are you still interested?"

"Go on," said Barber.

"A friend of mine has just bought a brand-new single-engine plane. A Beechcraft, single engine. A perfect, pleasant, comfortable, one-hundred-per-cent dependable aircraft," Smith said, describing the perfect little plane with pleasure in its newness and its dependability. "He himself does not fly, of course. He needs a private pilot, who will be on tap at all times."

"For how long?" Barber asked, watching Smith closely.

"For thirty days. Not more." Smith smiled up at him. "The pay is not bad, is it?"

"I can't tell yet," Barber said. "Go on. Where does he want to fly to?"

"He happens to be an Egyptian," Smith said, a little deprecatingly, as though being an Egyptian were a slight private misfortune, which one did not mention except among friends, and then in lowered tones. "He is a wealthy Egyptian who likes to travel. Especially back and forth to France. To the South of France. He is in love with the South of France. He goes there at every opportunity."

"Yes?"

"He would like to make two round trips from Egypt to the vicinity of Cannes within the next month," Smith said, peering steadily at Barber, "in his private new plane. Then on the third trip he will find that he is in a hurry and he will take the commercial plane and his pilot will follow two days later, alone."

"Alone?" Barber asked, trying to keep all the facts straight.

"Alone, that is," Smith said, "except for a small box."

"Ah," Barber said, grinning. "Finally the small box."

"Finally." Smith smiled up at him delightedly. "It has already been calculated. The small box will weigh two hundred and fifty pounds. A comfortable margin of safety for this particular aircraft for each leg of the journey."

"And what will there be in the small two-hundred-and-fifty-pound box?" Barber asked, cool and relieved now that he saw what was being offered to him.

"Is it absolutely necessary to know?"

"What do I tell the customs people when they ask me what's in the box?" Barber said. " 'Go ask Bert Smith'?"

"You have nothing to do with customs people," Smith said. "I assure you. When you take off from the airport in Cairo, the box is not on board. And when you land at the airport at Cannes, the box is not on board. Isn't that enough?"

Barber took a last pull at his cigarette and doused it. He peered thoughtfully at Smith, sitting easily on the straight-backed chair in the rumpled room, looking too neat and too well dressed for such a place at such an hour. Drugs, Barber thought, and he can stuff them . . .

"No, Bertie boy," Barber said roughly. "It is not enough. Come on. Tell."

Smith sighed. "Are you interested up to now?"

"I am interested up to now," Barber said.

"All right," Smith said regretfully. "This is how it will be done. You will have established a pattern. You will have been in and out of the Cairo airport several times. Your papers always impeccable. They will know you. You will have become a part of the legitimate routine of the field. Then, on the trip when you will be taking off alone, everything will be perfectly legitimate. You will have only a small bag with you of your personal effects. Your flight plan will show that your destination is Cannes and that you will come down at Malta and Rome for refuelling only. You will take off from Cairo. You will go off course by only a few miles. Some distance from the coast, you will be over the desert. You will come down on an old R.A.F. landing strip that hasn't been used since 1943. There will be several men there. . . . Are you listening?"

"I'm listening." Barber had walked to the window and was standing there, looking out at the sunny street below, his back to Smith.

"They will put the box on board. The whole thing will not take more than ten minutes," Smith said. "At Malta, nobody will ask you anything, because you will be in transit and you will not leave the plane and you will stay only long enough to refuel. The same thing at Rome. You will arrive over the south coast of France in the evening, before the moon is up. Once more," Smith said, speaking as though he was savoring his words, "you will be just a little off course. You will fly low over the hills between Cannes and Grasse. At a certain point, you will see an arrangement of lights. You will throttle down, open the door, and push the box out, from a height of a hundred feet. Then you will close the door and turn toward the sea and land at the Cannes airport. Your papers will be perfectly in order. There will have been no deviations from your flight plan. You will have nothing to declare. You will walk away from the airplane once and for all, and we will pay you the twenty-five thousand dollars I have spoken of. Isn't it lovely?"

"Lovely," Barber said. "It's just a delicious little old plan, Bertie boy." He turned away from the window. "Now tell me what will be in the box."

Smith chuckled delightedly, as though what he was going to say was too funny to keep to himself. "Money," he said. "Just money."

"How much money?"

"Two hundred and fifty pounds of money," Smith said, his eyes crinkled with amusement. "Two hundred and fifty pounds of tightly packed English notes in a nice, strong, lightweight metal box. Five-pound notes."

At that moment, it occurred to Barber that he was speaking to a lunatic. But Smith was sitting there, matter-of-fact and healthy, obviously a man who had never for a minute in all his life had a single doubt about his sanity.

"When would I get paid?" Barber asked.

"When the box was delivered," Smith said.

"Bertie boy . . ." Barber shook his head reprovingly.

Smith chuckled. "I have warned myself that you were not stupid," he said. "All right. We will deposit twelve thousand five hundred dollars in your name in a Swiss bank before you start for the first time to Egypt."

"You trust me for that?"

Fleetingly the smile left Smith's face. "We'll trust you for that," he said. Then the smile reappeared. "And immediately after the delivery is made, we will deposit the rest. A lovely deal. Hard currency. No income tax. You will be a rich man. Semi-rich." He chuckled at his joke. "Just for a little plane ride. Just to help an Egyptian who is fond of the South of France and who is naturally a little disturbed by the insecurity of his own country."

"When will I meet this Egyptian?" Barber asked.

"When you go to the airfield to take off for your first flight," Smith said. "He'll be there. Don't you worry. He'll be there. Do you hesitate?" he asked anxiously.

"I'm thinking," Barber said.

"It's not as though you were involved in your own country," Smith said piously. "I wouldn't ask a man to do that, a man who had fought for his country in the war. It isn't even as though it had anything to do with the English, for whom it is possible you have a certain affection. But the Egyptians . . ." He shrugged and bent over and picked up the manila envelope and opened it. "I have all the maps here," he said, "if you would like to study them. The route is all marked out, but, of course, it would be finally in your hands, since it would be you who was doing the flying."

Barber took the thick packet of maps. He opened one at random. All it showed was the sea approaches to Malta and the location of the landing strips there. Barber thought of twenty-five thousand dollars and the map shook a little in his hands.

"It is ridiculously easy," Smith said, watching Barber intently. "Foolproof."

Barber put the map down. "If it's so easy, what are you paying twenty-five thousand bucks for?" he said.

Smith laughed. "I admit," he said, "there may be certain little risks. It is improbable, but one never knows. We pay you for the improbability, if you want to put it that way." He shrugged. "After all, after a whole war you must be somewhat hardened to risks."

"When do you have to know?" Barber asked.

"Tonight," Smith said. "If you say no, naturally we have to make other plans. And my Egyptian friend is impatient."

"Who is we?" Barber asked.

"Naturally," Smith said, "I have certain colleagues."

"Who are they?"

Smith made a small regretful gesture. "I am terribly sorry," he said, "but I cannot tell you."

"I'll call you tonight," said Barber.

"Good." Smith stood up and buttoned his coat and carefully put the soft Italian felt hat on his head, at a conservative angle. He played gently and appreciatively with the brim. "This afternoon, I will be at the track. Maybe you would like to join me there."

"Where're they running today?"

"Auteuil," Smith said. "Jumping today."

"Have you heard anything?"

"Perhaps," Smith said. "There is a mare who is doing the jumps for the first time. I have spoken to the jockey and I have been told the mare has responded in training, but I'll hear more at three o'clock."

"I'll be there."

"Good," Smith said enthusiastically. "Although it is against my interests, of course, to make you too rich in advance." He chuckled. "However, for the sake of friendship . . . Should I leave the maps?"

"Yes," said Barber.

"Until three o'clock," Smith said as Barber opened the door. They shook hands, and Smith went out into the corridor, a rich, tweedy, perfumed figure in the impoverished light of the pallid hotel lamps.

Barber locked the door behind him and picked up the packet of maps and spread them on the bed, over the rumpled sheets and blankets. He hadn't looked at aerial maps for a long time. Northern Egypt. The Mediterranean. The island of Malta. Sicily and the Italian coast. The Gulf of Genoa. The Alpes-Maritimes. He stared

597

at the maps. The Mediterranean looked very wide. He didn't like to fly over open water in a single-engined plane. In fact, he didn't like to fly. Since the war, he had flown as little as possible. He hadn't made any explanations to himself, but when he had had to travel, he had gone by car or train or boat whenever he could.

Twenty-five thousand dollars, he thought.

He folded the maps neatly and put them back into the envelope. At this point, the maps weren't going to help.

He lay down on the bed again, propped against the pillows, with his hands clasped behind his head. Open water, he thought. Five times. Even that wouldn't be too bad. But what about the Egyptians? He had been in Cairo briefly during the war. He remembered that at night the policemen walked in pairs, carrying carbines. He didn't like places where the policemen carried carbines. And Egyptian prisons . . .

He moved uneasily on the bed.

Who knew how many people were in on a scheme like this? And it would only take one to cook you. One dissatisfied servant or accomplice, one greedy or timid partner . . . He closed his eyes and almost saw the fat, dark uniformed men with their carbines walking up to the shiny, new little plane.

Or suppose you blew a tire or crumpled a wheel on the landing strip? Who knew what the strip was like, abandoned in the desert since 1943?

Twenty-five thousand dollars.

Or you would think you were making it. The box would be on the seat beside you and the coast of Egypt would be falling off behind you and the sea stretching blue below and ahead and the engine running like a watch—and then the first sign of the patrol. The shimmering dot growing into . . . What did the Egyptian Air Force fly? Spitfires, left over from the war, he supposed. Coming up swiftly, going twice as fast as you, signalling you to turn around . . . He lit a cigarette. Two hundred and fifty pounds. Say the box alone—it would have to be really solid—weighed a hundred and fifty pounds. How much did a five-pound note weigh? Would there be a thousand to a pound? Five thousand multiplied by a hundred, with the pound at two-eighty. Close to a million and a half dollars.

His mouth felt dry, and he got up and drank two glasses of water. Then he made himself sit down on the chair, keeping his hands still. If there was an accident, if for any reason you failed to come through with it . . . If the money was lost, but you were saved. Smith didn't look like a murderer, although who knew what murderers looked like these days? And who knew what other people he was involved with? My colleagues, as Smith called them, who would then be your colleagues. The wealthy Egyptian, the several men at the old R.A.F. landing strip in the desert, the people who were to set out the lights in the certain arrangement in the hills behind Cannes—How many others, sliding across frontiers, going secretly and illegally from one country to another with guns and gold in their suitcases, the survivors of war, prison, denunciation—How many others whom you didn't know, whom you would see briefly in the glare of the African sun, as a running figure on a dark French hillside, whom you couldn't judge or assess and on whom your life depended, who were risking prison, deportation, police bullets for their share of a box full of money . . .

He jumped up and put on his clothes and went out, locking the door. He didn't want to sit in the cold, disordered room, staring at the maps.

He walked around the city aimlessly for the rest of the morning, looking blindly into shopwindows and thinking of the things he would buy if he had money. Turning away from a window, he saw a policeman watching him incuriously. Barber looked speculatively at the policeman, who was small, with a mean face and a thin mustache. Looking at the policeman, Barber remembered some of the stories about what they did to suspects when they questioned them in the back rooms of the local prefectures. An American passport wouldn't do much good if they picked you up with five hundred thousand English pounds under your arm.

This is the first time in my life, Barber thought curiously, walking slowly on the crowded street, that I have contemplated moving over to the other side of the law. He was surprised that he was considering it so calmly. He wondered why that was. Perhaps the movies and the newspapers, he thought. You get so familiar with crime it becomes humanized and accessible. You don't think about it, but then, suddenly, when it enters your life, you realize that subconsciously you have been accepting the idea of crime as an almost normal accompaniment of everyday life. Policemen must know that, he thought, all at once seeing things from the other side. They must look at all the shut, ordinary faces going past them and they must know how close to theft, murder, and defaulting everyone is, and it must drive them crazy. They must want to arrest everybody.

While Barber was watching the horses move in their stiff-legged, trembling walk around the paddock before the sixth race, he felt a light tap on his shoulder.

"Bertie boy," he said, without turning around.

"I'm sorry I'm late," Smith said, coming up to the paddock rail beside Barber. "Were you afraid I wouldn't come?"

"What's the word from the jock?" Barber asked.

Smith looked around him suspiciously. Then he smiled. "The jockey is confident," Smith said. "He is betting himself."

"Which one is it?"

"Number Five."

Barber looked at No. 5. It was a light-boned chestnut mare with a delicate, gentle head. Her tail and mane were braided, and she walked alertly but not too nervously, well-mannered and with a glistening coat. Her jockey was a man of about forty, with a long, scooped French nose. He was an ugly man, and when he opened his mouth, you saw that most of his front teeth were missing. He wore a maroon cap, with his ears tucked in, and a white silk shirt dotted with maroon stars.

Barber, looking at him, thought, It's too bad such ugly men get to ride such beautiful animals.

"O.K., Bertie boy," he said. "Lead me to the window."

Barber bet ten thousand francs on the nose. The odds were a comfortable seven to one. Smith bet twenty-five thousand francs. They walked side by side to the stands and climbed up together as the horses came out on the track. The crowd was small and there were only a few other spectators that high up.

"Well, Lloyd?" Smith said. "Did you look at the maps?"

"I looked at the maps," Barber said.

"What did you think?"

"They're very nice maps."

Smith looked at him sharply. Then he decided to chuckle. "You want to make me fish, eh?" he said. "You know what I mean. Did you decide?"

"I . . ." Barber began, staring down at the cantering horses. He took a deep breath. "I'll tell you after the race," he said.

"Lloyd!" The voice came from below, to the right, and Barber turned in that direction. Toiling up the steps was Jimmy Richardson. He had always been rather round and baby-plump, and Parisian food had done nothing to slim him down, and he was panting, his coat flapping open, disclosing a checkered vest, as he hurried toward Barber.

"How are you?" he said breathlessly as he reached their level.

He clapped Barber on the back. "I saw you up here and I thought maybe you had something for this race. I can't figure this one and they've been murdering me all day. I'm lousy on the jumps."

"Hello, Jimmy," Barber said. "Mr. Richardson. Mr. Smith."

"Pleased to meet you," Richardson said. "How do you spell it?" He laughed loudly at his joke. "Say, really, Lloyd, do you know anything? Maureen'll murder me if I go home and tell her I went into the hole for the afternoon."

Barber looked across at Smith, who was watching Richardson benignly. "Well," he said, "Bertie boy, here, thinks he heard something."

"Bertie boy," Richardson said, "please . . ."

Smith smiled thinly. "Number Five looks very good," he said. "But you'd better hurry. They're going to start in a minute."

"Number Five," Richardson said. "Roger. I'll be right back." He went galloping down the steps, his coat flying behind him.

"He's a trusting soul, isn't he?" Smith said.

"He was an only child," Barber said, "and he never got over it."

Smith smiled politely. "Where do you know him from?"

"He was in my squadron."

"In your squadron." Smith nodded, looking after Richardson's hurrying, diminishing figure on the way to the seller's window. "Pilot?"

"Uh-huh."

"Good?"

Barber shrugged. "Better ones got killed and worse ones won every medal in the collection."

"What is he doing in Paris?"

"He works for a drug company," Barber said.

The bell rang and the horses raced toward the first jump.

"Your friend was too late, I'm afraid," Smith said, putting his binoculars to his eyes.

"Yep," Barber said, watching the bunched horses.

No. 5 fell on the fourth jump. She went over with two other horses, and suddenly she was down and rolling. The pack passed around her. The fourth jump was far off down the track, and it was hard to see what, exactly, was happening until, a moment later, the mare struggled to her feet and cantered after the pack, her reins broken and trailing. Then Barber saw that the jockey was lying there motionless, crumpled up clumsily on his face, with his head turned in under his shoulder.

"We've lost our money," Smith said calmly. He took his binoculars from his eyes and pulled out his tickets and tore them and dropped them.

"May I have those, please?" Barber reached over for the binoculars. Smith lifted the strap over his head, and Barber trained the glasses on the distant jump where the jockey was lying. Two men were running out to him and turning him over.

Barber adjusted the binoculars, and the figures of the two men working on the motionless figure in the maroon-starred shirt came out of the blur into focus. Even in the glasses, there was something terribly urgent and despairing in the movements of the distant men. They picked the jockey up between them and started running clumsily off with him.

"Damn it!" It was Richardson, who had climbed up beside them again. "The window closed just as I—"

"Do not complain, Mr. Richardson," Smith said. "We fell at the fourth jump."

Richardson grinned. "That's the first bit of luck I had all day."

Down below, in front of the stands, the riderless mare was swerving and trotting off down the track to avoid a groom who was trying to grab the torn reins.

Barber kept the glasses on the two men who were carrying the jockey. Suddenly, they put him down on the grass, and one of the men bent down and put his ear against the white silk racing shirt. After a while, he stood up. Then the two men started to carry the jockey again, only now they walked slowly, as though there was no sense in hurrying.

Barber gave the glasses back to Smith. "I'm going home," he said. "I've had enough of the sport for one day."

Smith glanced at him sharply. He put the glasses to his eyes and stared at the men carrying the jockey. Then he put the glasses into their case and hung the case by its strap over his shoulder. "They kill at least one a year," he said in a low voice. "It is to be expected in a sport like this. I'll take you home."

"Say," Richardson said. "Is that fellow dead?"

"He was getting too old," Smith said. "He kept at it too long."

"Holy man!" Richardson said, staring down the track. "And I was sore because I came too late to bet on him. That was some tip." He made a babyish grimace. "A tip on a dead jock."

Barber started down toward the exit.

"I'll come with you," Richardson said. "This isn't my lucky day."

The three men went down under the stands without speaking. People were standing in little groups, and there was a queer rising, hissing sound of whispering all over the place, now that the news was spreading.

When they reached the car, Barber got into the back, allowing Richardson to sit next to Smith, on the front seat. He wanted to be at least that much alone for the time being.

Smith drove slowly and in silence. Even Richardson spoke only once. "What a way to get it," he said as they drove between the bare, high trees. "In a lousy, three-hundred-thousand-franc claiming race."

Barber sat in the corner, his eyes half closed, not looking out. He kept remembering the second time the two men had picked up the jockey. Smith's selection for the afternoon, Barber thought. He closed his eyes altogether and saw the maps spread out on the bed in his room. The Mediterranean, the wide reaches of open water. He remembered the smell of burning. The worst smell. The smell of your dreams during the war. The smell of hot metal, smoldering rubber, Smith's tip.

"Here we are," Smith was saying.

Barber opened his eyes. They were stopped at the corner of the dead-end street down which was the entrance to his hotel. He got out.

"Wait a minute, Bertie boy," Barber said. "I have something I want to give you."

Smith looked at him inquiringly. "Can't it wait, Lloyd?" he asked.

"No. I'll just be a minute." Barber went into his hotel and up to his room. The maps were folded in a pile on the bureau, except for one, which was lying open beside the others. The approaches to Malta. He folded it quickly and put all the maps into the manila envelope and went back to the car. Smith was standing beside the car, smoking, nervously holding on to his hat, because a wind had come up and dead leaves were skittering along the pavement.

"Here you are, Bertie boy," Barber said, holding out the envelope.

Smith didn't take it. "You're sure you know what you're doing?" he said.

"I'm sure."

Smith still didn't take the maps. "I'm in no hurry," he said softly. "Why don't you hold on to them another day?"

"Thanks, no."

Smith looked at him silently for a moment. The fluorescent street lamps had just gone on, hard white-blue light, and Smith's smooth face looked powdery in the shadows under his expensive hat, and his pretty eyes were dark and flat under the curled lashes.

"Just because a jockey falls at a jump—" Smith began.

"Take them," Barber said, "or I'll throw them in the gutter."

Smith shrugged. He put out his hand and took the envelope. "You'll never have a chance like this again," he said, running his finger caressingly over the envelope edge.

"Good night, Jimmy." Barber leaned over the car and spoke to Richardson, who was sitting there watching them, puzzled. "Give my love to Maureen."

"Say, Lloyd," Richardson said, starting to get out. "I thought maybe we could have a couple of drinks. Maureen doesn't expect me home for another hour yet and I thought maybe we could cut up some old touches and—"

"Sorry," Barber said, because he wanted, more than anything else, to be alone. "I have a date. Some other time."

Smith turned and looked thoughtfully at Richardson. "He always has a date, your friend," Smith said. "He's a very popular boy. I feel like a drink myself, Mr. Richardson. I would be honored if you'd join me."

"Well," Richardson said uncertainly, "I live way down near the Hôtel de Ville and—"

"It's on my way," Smith said, smiling warmly.

Richardson settled back in his seat, and Smith started to get into the car. He stopped and looked up at Barber. "I made a mistake about you, didn't I, Lloyd?" he said contemptuously.

"Yes," Barber said. "I'm getting too old. I don't want to keep at it too long."

Smith chuckled and got into the car. They didn't shake hands. He slammed the door, and Barber watched him pull sharply away from the curb, making a taxi-driver behind him jam on his brakes to avoid hitting him.

Barber watched the big black car weave swiftly down the street, under the hard white-blue lights. Then he went back to the hotel and up to his room and lay down, because an afternoon at the races always exhausted him.

An hour later, he got up. He splashed cold water on his face to wake himself, but even so he felt listless and empty. He wasn't hungry and he wasn't thirsty and he kept thinking about the dead jockey in his soiled silks. There was no one he wanted to see. He put on his coat and went out, hating the room as he closed the door behind him.

He walked slowly toward the Étoile. It was a raw night and a fog was moving in from the river, and the streets were almost empty, because everybody was inside eating dinner. He didn't

604

look at any of the lighted windows, because he wasn't going to buy anything for a long time. He passed several movie houses, neon in the drifting fog. In the movies, he thought, the hero would have been on his way to Africa by now. He would nearly be caught several times in Egypt, and he would fight his way out of a trap on the desert, killing several dark men just in time on the airstrip. And he would develop engine trouble over the Mediterranean and just pull out, with the water lapping at the wing tips, and he would undoubtedly crash, without doing too much damage to himself, probably just a photogenic cut on the forehead, and would drag the box out just in time. And he would turn out to be a Treasury agent or a member of British Intelligence and he would never doubt his luck and his nerve would never fail him and he would not end the picture with only a few thousand francs in his pocket. Or, if it was an artistic picture, there would be a heavy ground mist over the hills and the plane would drone on and on, desperate and lost, and then, finally, with the fuel tanks empty, the hero would crash in flames. Battered and staggering as he was, he would try to get the box out, but he wouldn't be able to move it, and finally the flames would drive him back and he would stand against a tree, laughing crazily, his face blackened with smoke, watching the plane and the money burn, to show the vanity of human aspiration and greed.

Barber grinned bleakly, rehearsing the scenarios in front of the giant posters outside the theatres. The movies do it better, he thought. They have their adventures happen to adventurers. He turned off the Champs-Elysées, walking slowly and aimlessly, trying to decide whether to eat now or have a drink first. Almost automatically, he walked toward the Plaza-Athénée. In the two weeks that he had been wooed by Smith, they had met in the English bar of the Plaza-Athénée almost every evening.

He went into the hotel and downstairs to the English bar. As he came into the room, he saw, in the corner, Smith and Jimmy Richardson.

Barber smiled. Bertie boy, he thought, are you ever wasting your time. He stood at the bar and ordered a whiskey.

" . . . fifty missions," he heard Richardson say. Richardson had a loud, empty voice that carried anywhere. "Africa, Sicily, Italy, Yugo—"

Then Smith saw him. He nodded coolly, with no hint of invitation. Richardson swivelled in his chair then, too. He smiled uncomfortably at Barber, getting red in the face, like a man who has been caught by a friend with his friend's girl.

Barber waved to them. For a moment, he wondered if he ought to go over and sit down and try to get Richardson out of there. He watched the two men, trying to figure out what they thought of each other. Or, more accurately, what Smith thought of Richardson. You didn't have to speculate about Jimmy. If you bought Jimmy a drink, he was your friend for life. For all that he had been through—war and marriage and being a father and living in a foreign country—it had still never occurred to Jimmy that people might not like him or might try to do him harm. When you were enjoying Jimmy, you called it trustfulness. When he was boring you, you called it stupidity.

Barber watched Smith's face carefully. By now, he knew Smith well enough to be able to tell a great deal of what was going on behind the pretty eyes and the pale, powdered face. Right now, Barber could tell that Smith was bored and that he wanted to get away from Jimmy Richardson.

Barber turned back to his drink, smiling to himself. It took Bertie boy just about an hour, he thought, an hour of looking at that good-natured empty face, an hour of listening to that booming, vacant voice, to decide that this was no man to fly a small box of five-pound notes from Cairo to Cannes.

Barber finished his drink quickly and went out of the bar before Smith and Richardson got up from the table. He had nothing to do for the evening, but he didn't want to get stuck with Jimmy and Maureen Richardson for dinner.

And now it was almost two months later and nobody had heard from Jimmy Richardson for thirty-two days.

In the whole afternoon of searching, Barber had not come upon any trace of Bert Smith. He had not been at the restaurants or the track or the art galleries, the barbershop, the steam bath, the bars. And no one had seen him for weeks.

It was nearly eight o'clock when Barber arrived at the English bar of the Plaza-Athénée. He was wet from walking in the day's rain, and tired, and his shoes were soggy and he felt a cold coming on. He looked around the room, but it was almost empty. Indulging himself, thinking unhappily of all the taxi fares he had paid that day, he ordered a whiskey.

Barber sipped his whiskey in the quiet room, thinking circularly, I should have said something. But what could I have said? And Jimmy wouldn't have listened. But I should have said something. *The omens are bad, Jimmy, go on home. . . . I saw a plane crashing at the fourth jump, I saw a corpse being carried across dead grass by Egyptians, Jimmy, I saw silks and maps stained by blood.*

I had to be so damned superior, Barber thought bitterly. I had to be so damned sure that Jimmy Richardson was too stupid to be offered that much money. I had to be so damned sure that Bert Smith was too clever to hire him.

He hadn't said any of the things he should have said, and it had all wound up with a frantic, husbandless, penniless girl pleading for help that could only be too late now. Penniless. Jimmy Richardson had been too stupid even to get any of the money in advance.

He remembered what Jimmy and Maureen had looked like, smiling and embarrassed and youthfully important, standing next to Colonel Sumners, the Group Commander, at their wedding in Shreveport. He remembered Jimmy's plane just off his wing over Sicily; he remembered Jimmy's face when he landed at Foggia with an engine on fire; he remembered Jimmy's voice singing drunkenly in a bar in Naples; he remembered Jimmy the day after he arrived in Paris, saying, "Kid, this is the town for me, I got Europe in my blood."

He finished his drink and paid and went upstairs slowly. He went into a phone booth and called his hotel to see if there were any messages for him.

"Mme. Richardson has been calling you all day," the old man at the switchboard said. "Ever since four o'clock. She wanted you to call her back."

"All right," Barber said. "Thank you." He started to hang up.

"Wait a minute, wait a minute," the old man said irritably. "She called an hour ago to say she was going out. She said that if you came in before nine o'clock, she would like you to join her at the bar of the Hotel Bellman."

"Thanks, Henri," Barber said. "If she happens to call again, tell her I'm on my way." He went out of the hotel. The Bellman was nearby, and he walked toward it slowly, even though it was still raining. He was in no hurry to see Maureen Richardson.

When he reached the Bellman, he hesitated before going in, feeling too tired for this, wishing Maureen could be put off at least until the next day. He sighed, and pushed the door open.

The bar was a small one, but it was crowded with large, well-dressed men who were taking their time over drinks before going out to dinner. Then he saw Maureen. She was sitting in a corner, half turned away from the room, her shabby, thin coat thrown back over her chair. She was sitting alone and there was a bottle of champagne in a bucket in a stand beside her.

Barber went over to her, irritated by the sight of the champagne. Is that what she's doing with my five thousand francs, he thought, annoyed. Women are going crazy, too, these days.

He leaned over and kissed the top of her head. She jumped nervously, then smiled when she saw who it was. "Oh, Lloyd," she said, in a funny kind of whisper. She jumped up and kissed him, holding him hard against her. There was a big smell of champagne on her breath and he wondered if she was drunk. "Lloyd, Lloyd . . ." she said. She pushed him away a little, holding on to both his hands. Her eyes were smeary with tears and her mouth kept trembling.

"I came as soon as I got your message," Lloyd said, trying to sound practical, afraid Maureen was going to break down in front of all the people in the bar. She kept standing there, her mouth working, her hands gripping his avidly. He looked down, embarrassed, at her hands. They were still reddened and the nails were still uneven, but there was an enormous ring glittering, white and blue, on her finger. It hadn't been there when she came to his hotel, and he knew he had never seen her with a ring like that before. He looked up, almost frightened, thinking, What the hell has she started? What has she got herself into?

Then he saw Jimmy. Jimmy was making his way among the tables toward him. He was smiling broadly and he had lost some weight and he was dark brown and he looked as though he had just come from a month's vacation on a southern beach.

"Hi, kid," Jimmy said, his voice booming across the tables, across the barroom murmur of conversation. "I was just calling you again."

"He came home," Maureen said. "He came home at four o'clock this afternoon, Lloyd." She sank suddenly into her chair. Whatever else had happened that afternoon, it was plain that she had had access to a bottle. She sat in her chair, still holding on to one of Barber's hands, looking up, with a shimmering, half-dazed expression on her face, at her husband.

Jimmy clapped Barber on the back and shook hands fiercely. "Lloyd," he said. "Good old Lloyd. *Garçon!*" he shouted, his voice reverberating through the whole room. "Another glass. Take your coat off. Sit down. Sit down."

Lloyd took his coat off and sat down slowly.

"Welcome home," he said quietly. He blew his nose. The cold had arrived.

"First," Jimmy said, "I have something for you." Ceremoniously he dug his hand into his pocket and brought out a roll of ten-thousand-franc notes. The roll was three inches thick. He took off one of the notes. "Maureen told me," he said seriously. "You were a damn good friend, Lloyd. Have you got change of ten?"

"I don't think so," Barber said. "No."

*"Garçon,"* Jimmy said to the waiter, who was putting down a third glass, "get me two fives for this, please." When he spoke French, Jimmy had an accent that made even Americans wince.

Jimmy filled the three glasses carefully. He lifted his glass and clinked it first against Barber's and then against Maureen's. Maureen kept looking at him as though she had just seen him for the first time and never hoped to see anything as wonderful again in her whole life.

"To crime," Jimmy said. He winked. He made a complicated face when he winked, like a baby who has trouble with a movement of such subtlety and has to use the whole side of its face and its forehead to effect it.

Maureen giggled.

They drank. It was very good champagne.

"You're having dinner with us," Jimmy said. "Just the three of us. The victory dinner. Just Beauty and me and you, because if it hadn't been for you . . ." Suddenly solemn, he put his hand on Barber's shoulder.

"Yes," said Barber. His feet were icy and his trousers hung soddenly around his wet socks and he had to blow his nose again.

"Did Beauty show you her ring?" Jimmy asked.

"Yes," Barber said.

"She's only had it since six o'clock," Jimmy said.

Maureen held her hand up and stared at her ring. She giggled again.

"I know a place," Jimmy said, "where you can get pheasant and the best bottle of wine in Paris and . . ."

The waiter came back and gave Jimmy the two five-thousand-franc notes. Dimly, Barber wondered how much they weighed.

"If ever you're in a hole," Jimmy said, giving him one of the notes, "you know where to come, don't you?"

"Yes," Barber said. He put the note in his pocket.

He started to sneeze then, and ten minutes later he said he was sorry but he didn't think he could last the evening with a cold like that. Both Jimmy and Maureen tried to get him to stay, but he could tell that they were going to be happier without him.

He finished a second glass of champagne, and said he'd keep in touch, and went out of the bar, feeling his toes squish in his wet shoes. He was hungry and he was very fond of pheasant and actually the cold wasn't so bad, even if his nose kept running all the time. But he knew he couldn't bear to sit between Maureen and Jimmy Richardson all night and watch the way they kept looking at each other.

He walked back to his hotel, because he was through with taxis, and went up and sat on the edge of his bed in his room, in the dark, without taking his coat off. I better get out of here, he thought, rubbing the wet off the end of his nose with the back of his hand. This continent is not for me.

# The Inhabitants of Venus

He had been skiing since early morning, and he was ready to stop and have lunch in the village, but Mac said, "Let's do one more before eating," and since it was Mac's last day, Robert agreed to go up again. The weather was spotty, but there were occasional clear patches of sky, and the visibility had been good enough to make for decent skiing for most of the morning. The teleferique was crowded and they had to push their way in among the bright sweaters and anaracs and the bulky packs of the people who were carrying picnic lunches and extra clothing and skins for climbing. The doors were closed and the cabin swung out of the station, over the belt of pine trees at the base of the mountain.

The passengers were packed in so tightly that it was hard to reach for a handkerchief or light a cigarette. Robert was pressed, not unpleasurably, against a handsome young Italian woman with a dissatisfied face, who was explaining to someone over Robert's shoulder why Milan was such a miserable city to live in in the wintertime. "Milano si trova in un bacino deprimente," the woman said, "bagnato dalla pioggia durante tre mesi all'anno. E, nonostante il loro gusto per l'opera, i Milanesi non sono altro volgari materialisti che solo il denaro interessa," and Robert knew enough Italian to understand that the girl was saying that Milan was in a dismal basin which was swamped by rain for three months a year and that the Milanese, despite their taste for opera, were crass and materialistic and interested only in money.

Robert smiled. Although he had not been born in the United States, he had been a citizen since 1944, and it was pleasant to hear, in the heart of Europe, somebody else besides Americans being accused of materialism and a singular interest in money.

"What's the Contessa saying?" Mac whispered, across the curly red hair of a small Swiss woman who was standing between Robert and Mac. Mac was a lieutenant on leave from his outfit in Germany. He had been in Europe nearly three years and to show that he was

611

not just an ordinary tourist, called all pretty Italian girls Contessa. Robert had met him a week before, in the bar of the hotel they were both staying at. They were the same kind of skiers, adventurous and looking for difficulties, and they had skied together every day, and they were already planning to come back at the same time for the next winter's holiday, if Robert could get over again from America.

"The Contessa is saying that in Milan all they're interested in is money," Robert said, keeping his voice low, although in the babble of conversation in the cabin there was little likelihood of being overheard.

"If I was in Milan," Mac said, "and she was in Milan, I'd be interested in something else besides money." He looked with open admiration at the Italian girl. "Can you find out what run she's going to do?"

"What for?" Robert asked.

"Because that's the run I'm going to do," Mac said, grinning. "I plan to follow her like her shadow."

"Mac," Robert said, "don't waste your time. It's your last day."

"That's when the best things always happen," Mac said. "The last day." He beamed, huge, overt, uncomplicated, at the Italian girl. She took no notice of him. She was busy now complaining to her friend about the natives of Sicily.

The sun came out for a few minutes and it grew hot in the cabin, with some forty people jammed, in heavy clothing, in such a small space, and Robert half-dozed, not bothering to listen any more to the voices speaking in French, Italian, English, Schweizerdeutsch, German, on all sides of him. Robert liked being in the middle of this informal congress of tongues. It was one of the reasons that he came to Switzerland to ski, whenever he could take the time off from his job. In the angry days through which the world was passing, there was a ray of hope in this good-natured polyglot chorus of people who were not threatening each other, who smiled at strangers, who had collected in these shining white hills merely to enjoy the innocent pleasures of sun and snow.

The feeling of generalized cordiality that Robert experienced on these trips was intensified by the fact that most of the people on the lifts and on the runs seemed more or less familiar to him. Skiers formed a kind of loose international club and the same faces kept turning up year after year in Mégève, Davos, St. Anton, Val d'Isère, so that after a while you had the impression you knew almost everybody on the mountain. There were four or five Americans whom Robert was sure he had seen at Stowe at Christmas and who had come over in one of the chartered ski-club planes that Swissair ran every winter on a cut-rate basis. The Americans were young and enthusiastic and none of them had ever been in Europe before and they were rather noisily appreciative of everything—the Alps, the food, the snow, the weather, the appearance of the peasants in their blue smocks, the chic of some of the lady skiers and the skill and good looks of the instructors. They were popular with the villagers because they were so obviously enjoying themselves. Besides, they tipped generously, in the American style, with what was, to Swiss eyes, an endearing disregard of the fact that a service charge of fifteen percent was added automatically to every bill that was presented to them. Two of the girls were very attractive, in a youthful, prettiest-girl-at-the-prom way, and one of the young men, a lanky boy from Philadelphia, the informal leader of the group, was a beautiful skier, who guided the others down the runs and helped the dubs when they ran into difficulties.

The Philadelphian, who was standing near Robert, spoke to him as the cabin swung high over a steep snowy face of the mountain. "You've skied here before, haven't you?" he said.

"Yes," said Robert, "a few times."

"What's the best run down this time of day?" the Philadelphian asked. He had the drawling, flat tone of the good New England schools that Europeans use in their imitations of upper-class Americans when they wish to make fun of them.

"They're all okay today," Robert said.

"What's this run everybody says is so good?" the boy asked. "The . . . the Kaiser something or other?"

"The Kaisergarten," Robert said. "It's the first gully to the right after you get out of the station on top."

"Is it tough?" the boy asked.

"It's not for beginners," Robert said.

"You've seen this bunch ski, haven't you?" The boy waved vaguely to indicate his friends. "Do you think they can make it?"

"Well," Robert said doubtfully, "there's a narrow steep ravine full of bumps halfway down, and there're one or two places where it's advisable not to fall, because you're liable to keep on sliding all the way, if you do. . . ."

"Aah, we'll take a chance," the Philadelphian said. "It'll be good for their characters. Boys and girls," he said, raising his voice, "the cowards will stay on top and have lunch. The heroes will come with me. We're going to the Kaisergarten. . . ."

"Francis," one of the pretty girls said. "I do believe it is your sworn intention to kill me on this trip."

"It's not as bad as all that," Robert said, smiling at the girl, to reassure her.

"Say," the girl said, looking interestedly at Robert, "haven't I seen you someplace before?"

"On this lift, yesterday," Robert said.

"No." The girl shook her head. She had on a black, fuzzy, lambskin hat, and she looked like a high-school drum majorette pretending to be Anna Karenina. "Before yesterday. Someplace."

"I saw you at Stowe," Robert confessed. "At Christmas."

"Oh, that's where," she said. "I saw you ski. Oh, my, you're *silky.*"

Mac broke into a loud laugh at this description of Robert's skiing style.

"Don't mind my friend," Robert said, enjoying the girl's admiration. "He's a coarse soldier who is trying to beat the mountain to its knees by brute strength."

"Say," the girl said, looking a little puzzled. "You have a funny little way of talking. Are you American?"

"Well, yes," Robert said. "I am now. I was born in France."

"Oh, that explains it," the girl said. "You were born among the crags."

"I was born in Paris," Robert said.

"Do you live there now?"

"I live in New York," Robert said.

"Are you married?" The girl asked anxiously.

"Barbara," the Philadelphian protested, "behave yourself."

"I just asked the man a simple, friendly question," the girl protested. "Do you mind, monsieur?"

"Not at all."

*"Are* you married?"

"Yes," Robert said.

"He has three children," Mac added helpfully. "The oldest one is going to run for president at the next election."

"Oh, isn't that too bad," the girl said. "I set myself a goal on this trip. I was going to meet one unmarried Frenchman."

"I'm sure you'll manage it," Robert said.

"Where is your wife? Now?" the girl said.

"In New York."

"Pregnant," Mac said, more helpful than ever.

"And she lets you run off and ski all alone like this?" the girl asked incredulously.

614

"Yes," Robert said. "Actually, I'm in Europe on business, and I sneaked off ten days."

"What business?" the girl asked.

"I'm a diamond merchant," Robert said. "I buy and sell diamonds."

"That's the sort of man I'd like to meet," the girl said. "Somebody awash with diamonds. But unmarried."

"Barbara!" the Philadelphian said.

"I deal mostly in industrial diamonds," Robert said. "It's not exactly the same thing."

"Even so," the girl said.

"Barbara," the Philadelphian said, "pretend you're a lady."

"If you can't speak candidly to a fellow American," the girl said, "who can you speak candidly to?" She looked out the Plexiglas window of the cabin. "Oh, dear," she said, "it's a perfect monster of a mountain, isn't it? I'm in a *fever* of terror." She turned and regarded Robert carefully. "You *do* look like a Frenchman," she said. "Terribly polished. You're definitely *sure* you're married?"

"Barbara," the Philadelphian said forlornly.

Robert laughed and Mac and the other Americans laughed and the girl smiled under her fuzzy hat, amused at her own clowning and pleased at the reaction she was getting. The other people in the car, who could not understand English, smiled good-naturedly at the laughter, happy, even though they were not in on the joke, to be the witnesses of this youthful gaiety.

Then, through the laughter, Robert heard a man's voice nearby, saying, in quiet tones of cold distaste, "Schaut euch diese dummen amerikanischen Gesichter an! Und diese Leute bilden sich ein, sie wären berufen, die Welt zu regieren."

Robert had learned German as a child, from his Alsatian grandparents, and he understood what he had just heard, but he forced himself not to turn around to see who had said it. His years of temper, he liked to believe, were behind him, and if nobody else in the cabin had overheard the voice or understood the words that had been spoken, he was not going to be the one to force the issue. He was here to enjoy himself and he didn't feel like getting into a fight or dragging Mac and the other youngsters into one. Long ago, he had learned the wisdom of playing deaf when he heard things like that, or worse. If some bastard of a German wanted to say, "Look at those stupid American faces. And these are the people who think they have been chosen to rule the world," it made very little real difference to anybody, and a grown-up man ignored it if he could. So he didn't look to see who had said it, because he knew that if he picked out the man, he wouldn't be able to let it go. This way, as an anonymous, though hateful voice, he could let it slide, along with many of the other things that Germans had said during his lifetime.

The effort of not looking was difficult, though, and he closed his eyes, angry with himself for being so disturbed by a scrap of overheard malice like this. It had been a perfect holiday up to now and it would be foolish to let it be shadowed, even briefly, by a random voice in a crowd. If you came to Switzerland to ski, Robert told himself, you had to expect to find some Germans. Though each year now there were more and more of them, massive, prosperous-looking men and sulky-looking women with the suspicious eyes of people who believe they are in danger of being cheated. Men and women both pushed more than was necessary in the lift lines, with a kind of impersonal egotism, a racial, unquestioning assumption of precedence. When they skied, they did it grimly, in large groups, as if under military orders. At night, when they relaxed in the bars and *stublis*, their merriment was more difficult to tolerate than their dedicated daytime gloom and Junker arrogance. They sat in red-faced platoons, drinking gallons of beer, volleying out great bursts of heavy laughter and roaring glee-club arrangements of students' drinking songs. Robert had not yet heard them sing the Horst Wessel song, but he noticed that they had long ago stopped pretending that they were Swiss or Austrian or that they had been born in the Alsace. Somehow, to the sport of skiing, which is, above all, individual and light and an exercise in grace, the Germans seemed to bring the notion of the herd. Once or twice, when he had been trampled in the teleferique station, he had shown some of his distaste to Mac, but Mac, who was far from being a fool under his puppy-fullback exterior, had said, "The trick is to isolate them, lad. It's only when they're in groups that they get on your nerves. I've been in Germany for three years and I've met a lot of good fellows and some *smashing* girls."

Robert had agreed that Mac was probably right. Deep in his heart, he wanted to believe that Mac was right. Before and during the war the problem of the Germans had occupied so much of his waking life, that V-E Day had seemed to him a personal liberation from them, a kind of graduation ceremony from a school in which he had been forced to spend long years, trying to solve a single, boring, painful problem. He had reasoned himself into believing that their defeat had returned the Germans to rationality. So, along with the relief he felt because he no longer ran the risk of being killed by them, there was the almost as intense relief that he no longer had especially to *think* about them.

Once the war was over, he had advocated reestablishing normal relations with the Germans as quickly as possible, both as good politics and simple humanity. He drank German beer and even bought a Volkswagen, although if it were up to him, given the taste for catastrophe that was latent in the German soul, he would not equip the German Army with the hydrogen bomb. In the course of his business he had very few dealings with Germans and it was only here, in this village in the Graubunden, where their presence was becoming so much more visible each year, that the *idea* of Germans disturbed him any more. But he loved the village and the thought of abandoning his yearly vacation there because of the prevalence of license plates from Munich and Dusseldorf was repugnant to him. Maybe, he thought, from now on he would come at a different time, in January, instead of late in February. Late February and early March was the German season, when the sun was warmer and shone until six o'clock in the evening. The Germans were sun gluttons and could be seen all over the hills, stripped to the waist, sitting on rocks, eating their picnic lunches, greedily absorbing each precious ray of sunlight. It was as though they came from a country perpetually covered in mist, like the planet Venus, and had to soak up as much brightness and life as possible in the short periods of their holidays to be able to endure the harshness and gloom of their homeland and the conduct of the other inhabitants of Venus for the rest of the year.

Robert smiled to himself at this tolerant concept and felt better-disposed toward everyone around him. Maybe, he thought, if I were a single man, I'd find a Bavarian girl and fall in love with her and finish the whole thing off then and there.

"I warn you, Francis," the girl in the lambskin hat was saying, "if you do me to death on this mountain, there are three Juniors at Yale who will track you down to the ends of the earth."

Then he heard the German voice again. "Warum haben die Amerikaner nicht genügend Verstand," the voice said, low but distinctly, near him, the accent clearly Hochdeutsch and not Zurichois or any of the other variations of Schweizerdeutsch, "ihre dummen kleinen Nutten zu Hause zu lassen, wo sie hingehören?"

Now, he knew there was no avoiding looking and there was no avoiding doing something about it. He glanced at Mac first, to see if Mac, who understood a little German, had heard. Mac was huge and could be dangerous, and for all his easy good nature, if he had heard the man say, "Why don't the Americans have the

617

sense to leave their silly little whores at home where they belong?" the man was in for a beating. But Mac was still beaming placidly at the Contessa. That was all to the good, Robert thought, relieved. The Swiss police took a dim view of fighting, no matter what the provocation, and Mac, enraged, was likely to wreak terrible damage in a fight, and would more than likely wind up in jail. For an American career soldier on duty in Frankfurt, a brawl like that could have serious consequences. The worst that can happen to me, Robert thought, as he turned to find the man who had spoken, is a few hours in the pokey and a lecture from the magistrate about abusing Swiss hospitality.

Almost automatically, Robert decided that when they got to the top, he would follow the man who had spoken out of the car, tell him quietly, that he, Robert, had understood what had been said about Americans in the car, and swing immediately. I just hope, Robert thought, that whoever it is isn't too damned large.

For a moment, Robert couldn't pick out his opponent-to-be. There was a tall man with his back to Robert, on the other side of the Italian woman, and the voice had come from that direction. Because of the crowd, Robert could only see his head and shoulders, which were bulky and powerful under a black parka. The man had on a white cap of the kind that had been worn by the Afrika Corps during the war. The man was with a plump, hard-faced woman who was whispering earnestly to him, but not loudly enough for Robert to be able to hear what she was saying. Then the man said, crisply, in German, replying to the woman, "I don't care how many of them understand the language. Let them understand," and Robert knew that he had found his man.

An exhilarated tingle of anticipation ran through Robert, making his hands and arms feel tense and jumpy. He regretted that the cabin wouldn't arrive at the top for another five minutes. Now that he had decided the fight was inevitable, he could hardly bear waiting. He stared fixedly at the man's broad, black-nylon back, wishing the fellow would turn around so that he could see his face. He wondered if the man would go down with the first blow, if he would apologize, if he would try to use his ski poles. Robert decided to keep his own poles handy, just in case, although Mac could be depended upon to police matters thoroughly if he saw weapons being used. Deliberately Robert took off his heavy leather mittens and stuck them in his belt. The correction would be more effective with bare knuckles. He wondered, fleetingly, if the man was wearing a ring. He kept his eyes fixed on the back of the man's neck, willing him to turn around. Then the plump woman noticed his stare. She dropped her eyes and whispered something to the man in the black parka and after several seconds, he finally turned around, pretending that it was a casual, unmotivated movement. The man looked squarely at Robert and Robert thought, If you ski long enough you meet every other skier you've ever known. At the same moment, he knew that it wasn't going to be a nice simple little fist fight on the top of the mountain. He knew that somehow he was going to have to kill the man whose icy blue eyes, fringed with pale blond lashes, were staring challengingly at him from under the white peak of the Afrika Corps cap.

It was a long time ago, the winter of 1938, in the French part of Switzerland, and he was fourteen years old and the sun was setting behind another mountain and it was ten below zero and he was lying in the snow, with his foot turned in that funny, unnatural way, although the pain hadn't really begun yet, and the eyes were looking down at him. . . .

He had done something foolish, and at the moment he was more worried about what his parents would say when they found out than about the broken leg. He had gone up, alone, late in the afternoon, when almost everybody else was off the mountain, and even so he hadn't stayed on the normal *piste*, but had started bushwacking through the forest, searching for powder snow that hadn't been tracked by other skiers. One ski had caught on a hidden root and he had fallen forward, hearing the sickening dry cracking sound from his right leg, even as he pitched into the snow.

Trying not to panic, he had sat up, facing in the direction of the *piste*, whose markers he could see some hundred meters away, through the pine forest. If any skiers happened to come by, they might just, with luck, be able to hear him if he shouted. For the moment, he did not try to crawl toward the line of poles, because when he moved a very queer feeling flickered from his ankle up his leg to the pit of his stomach, making him want to throw up.

The shadows were very long now in the forest, and only the highest peaks were rose-colored against a frozen green sky. He was beginning to feel the cold and from time to time he was shaken by acute spasms of shivering.

I'm going to die here, he thought, I'm going to die here tonight. He thought of his parents and his sister probably having tea, comfortably seated this moment in the warm dining room of the chalet two miles down the mountain, and he bit his lips to keep back the tears. They wouldn't start to worry about him for another hour or two yet, and then when they did, and started to do something about finding him, they wouldn't know where to begin. He had known none of the seven or eight people who had been on the lift with him on his last ride up and he hadn't told anybody what run he was going to take. There were three different mountains, with their separate lifts, and their numberless variations of runs, that he might have taken, and finding him in the dark would be an almost hopeless task. He looked up at the sky. There were clouds moving in from the east, slowly, a black high wall, covering the already darkened sky. If it snowed that night, there was a good chance they wouldn't even find his body before spring. He had promised his mother that no matter what happened, he would never ski alone, and he had broken the promise and this was his punishment.

Then he heard the sound of skis, coming fast, making a harsh, metallic noise on the iced snow of the *piste*. Before he could see the skier, he began to shout, with all the strength of his lungs, frantically, *"Au secours! Au secours!"*

A dark shape, going very fast, appeared high up for a second, disappeared behind a clump of trees, then shot into view much lower down, almost on a level with the place where Robert was sitting. Robert shouted wildly, hysterically, not uttering words any more, just a senseless, passionate, throat-bursting claim on the attention of the human race, represented, for this one instant at sunset on this cold mountain, by the dark, expert figure plunging swiftly, with a harsh scraping of steel edges and a *whoosh* of wind, toward the village below.

Then, miraculously, the figure stopped, in a swirl of snow. Robert shouted wordlessly, the sound of his voice echoing hysterically in the forest. For a moment the skier didn't move and Robert shook with the fear that it was all a hallucination, a mirage of sight and sound, that there was no one there on the beaten snow at the edge of the forest, that he was only imagining that he was shouting, that with all the fierce effort of his throat and lungs, he was mute, unheard.

Suddenly, he couldn't see anything any more. He had the sensation of a curtain sinking somewhere within him, of a wall of warm liquid inundating the ducts and canals of his body. He waved his hands weakly and toppled slowly over in a faint.

When he came to, a man was kneeling over him, rubbing his cheeks with snow. "You heard me," Robert said in French to the man. "I was afraid you wouldn't hear me."

"Ich verstehe nicht," the man said. "Nicht parler Französisch."

"I was afraid you wouldn't hear me," Robert repeated, in German.

"You are a stupid little boy," the man said severely, in clipped, educated German. "And very lucky. I am the last man on the mountain." He felt Robert's ankle, his hands hard but deft. "Nice," he said ironically, "very nice. You're going to be in plaster for at least three months. Here—lie still. I am going to take your skis off. You will be more comfortable." He undid the long leather thongs, working swiftly, and stood the skis up in the snow. Then he swept the snow off a stump a few yards away and got around behind Robert and put his hands under Robert's armpits. "Relax," he said. "Do not try to help me." He picked Robert up.

"Luckily," he said, "you weigh nothing. How old are you?— eleven?"

"Fourteen," Robert said.

"What's the matter?" the man said, laughing. "Don't they feed you in Switzerland?"

"I'm French," Robert said.

"Oh," the man's voice went flat. "French." He half-carried, half-dragged Robert over to the stump and sat him down gently on it. "There," he said, "at least you're out of the snow. You won't freeze—for the time being. Now, listen carefully. I will take your skis down with me to the ski school and I will tell them where you are and tell them to send a sled for you. They should get to you in less than an hour. Now, whom are you staying with in town?"

"My mother and father. At the Chalet Montana."

"Good." The man nodded. "The Chalet Montana. Do they speak German, too?"

"Yes."

"Excellent," the man said. "I will telephone them and tell them their foolish son has broken his leg and that the patrol is taking him to the hospital. What is your name?"

"Robert."

"Robert what?"

"Robert Rosenthal," Robert said. "Please don't say I'm hurt too badly. They'll be worried enough as it is."

The man didn't answer immediately. He busied himself tying Robert's skis together and slung them over his shoulder. "Do not worry, Robert Rosenthal," he said, "I will not worry them more than is necessary." Abruptly, he started off, sweeping easily through the trees, his poles held in one hand, Robert's skis balanced across his shoulders with his other hand.

His sudden departure took Robert by surprise and it was only when the man was a considerable distance away, already almost

621

lost among the trees, that Robert realized he hadn't thanked the man for saving his life. "Thank you," he shouted into the growing darkness. "Thank you very much."

The man didn't stop and Robert never knew whether he had heard his cry of thanks or not. Because after an hour, when it was completely dark, with the stars covered by the cloud that had been moving in at sunset from the east, the patrol had not yet appeared. Robert had a watch with a radium dial. Timing himself by it, he waited exactly one hour and a half, until ten minutes past seven, and then decided that nobody was coming for him and that if he hoped to live through the night he would somehow have to crawl out of the forest and make his way down to the town by himself.

He was rigid with cold by now, and suffering from shock. His teeth were chattering in a frightening way, as though his jaws were part of an insane machine over which he had no control. There was no feeling in his fingers any more and the pain in his leg came in ever-enlarging waves of metallic throbbing. He had put up the hood of his parka and sunk his head as low down on his chest as he could, and the cloth of the parka was stiff with his frosted breath. He heard a whimpering sound somewhere around him and it was only after what seemed to him several minutes that he realized the whimpering sound was coming from him and that there was nothing he could do to stop it.

Stiffly, with exaggerated care, he tried to lift himself off the tree stump and down into the snow without putting any weight on his injured leg, but at the last moment he slipped and twisted the leg as he went down. He screamed twice and lay with his face in the snow and thought of just staying that way and forgetting the whole thing, the whole intolerable effort of remaining alive. Later on, when he was much older, he came to the conclusion that the one thing that made him keep moving was the thought of his mother and father waiting for him, with anxiety that would soon grow into terror, in the town below him.

He pulled himself along on his belly, digging at the snow in front of his face with his hands, using rocks, low-hanging branches, snow-covered roots, to help him, meter by meter, out of the forest. His watch was torn off somewhere along the way and when he finally reached the line of poles that marked the packed snow and ice of the *piste* he had no notion of whether it had taken him five minutes or five hours to cover the hundred meters from the place he had fallen. He lay, panting, sobbing, staring at the lights of the town far below him, knowing that he could never reach them, knowing that he had to reach them. The effort of crawling through the deep snow had warmed him again and his face was streaming with sweat, and the blood coming back into his numbed hands and feet jabbed him with a thousand needles of pain.

The lights of the town guided him now, and here and there he could see the marker poles outlined against their small, cosy Christmasy glow. It was easier going, too, on the packed snow of the *piste* and from time to time he managed to slide ten or fifteen meters without stopping, tobogganing on his stomach, screaming occasionally when the foot of his broken leg banged loosely against an icy bump or twisted as he went over a steep embankment to crash against a level spot below. Once he couldn't stop himself and he fell into a swiftly rushing small stream and pulled himself out of it five minutes later with his gloves and stomach and knees soaked with icy water. And still the lights of the town seemed as far away as ever.

Finally, he felt he couldn't move any more. He was exhausted and he had had to stop twice to vomit and the vomit had been a gush of blood. He tried to sit up, so that if the snow came that night, there would be a chance that somebody would see the top of his head sticking out of the new cover in the morning. As he was struggling to push himself erect, a shadow passed between him and the lights of the town. The shadow was very close and with his last breath he called out. Later on, the peasant who rescued him said that what he called out was "Excuse me."

The peasant was moving hay on a big sled from one of the hill barns down to the valley, and he rolled the hay off and put Robert on instead. Then, carefully braking and taking the sled on a path that cut back and forth across the *piste*, he brought Robert down to the valley and the hospital.

By the time his mother and father had been notified and had reached the hospital, the doctor had given him a shot of morphine and was in the middle of setting the leg. So it wasn't until the next morning, as he lay in the gray hospital room, sweating with pain, with his leg in traction, that he could get out any kind of coherent story and tell his parents what had happened.

"Then I saw this man skiing very fast, all alone," Robert said, trying to speak normally, without showing how much the effort was costing him, trying to take the look of shock and agony from his parents' set faces by pretending that his leg hardly hurt him at all, and that the whole incident was of small importance. "He heard me and came over and took off my skis and made me comfortable on a tree stump and he asked me what my name was and where my parents were staying and he said he'd go to the ski school and tell them where I was and to send a sled for me and then he'd call you at the Chalet and tell you they were bringing me down to the hospital. Then, after more than an hour, it was pitch dark already, nobody came and I decided I'd better not wait any more and I started down and I was lucky and I saw this farmer with a sled and . . ."

"You were very lucky," Robert's mother said flatly. She was a small, neat, plump woman, with bad nerves, who was only at home in cities. She detested the cold, detested the mountains, detested the idea of her loved ones running what seemed to her the senseless risk of injury that skiing involved, and only came on these holidays because Robert and his father and sister were so passionate about the sport. Now she was white with fatigue and worry, and if Robert had not been immobilized in traction she would have had him out of the accursed mountains that morning on the train to Paris.

"Now, Robert," his father said, "is it possible that when you hurt yourself, the pain did things to you, and that you just *imagined* you saw a man, and just imagined he told you he was going to call us and get you a sled from the ski school?"

"I didn't imagine it, Papa," Robert said. The morphine had made him feel hazy and heavy-brained and he was puzzled that his father was talking to him that way. "Why do you think I might have imagined it?"

"Because," said his father, "nobody called us last night until ten o'clock, when the doctor telephoned from the hospital. And nobody called the ski school, either."

"I didn't imagine him," Robert repeated. He was hurt that his father perhaps thought he was lying. "If he came into this room I'd know him right off. He was wearing a white cap, he was a big man with a black anarac, and he had blue eyes, they looked a little funny, because his eyelashes were almost white and from a little way off it looked as though he didn't have any eyelashes at all. . . ."

"How old was he, do you think?" Robert's father asked. "As old as I am?" Robert's father was nearly fifty.

"No," Robert said. "I don't think so."

"Was he as old as your uncle Jules?" Robert's father asked.

"Yes," Robert said. "Just about." He wished his father and mother would leave him alone. He was all right now. His leg was in plaster and he wasn't dead and in three months, the doctor said, he'd be walking again, and he wanted to forget everything that had happened last night in the forest.

"So," Robert's mother said, "he was a man of about twenty-five, with a white cap and blue eyes." She picked up the phone and asked for the ski school.

Robert's father lit a cigarette and went over to the window and looked out. It was snowing. It had been snowing since midnight, heavily, and the lifts weren't running today because a driving wind had sprung up with the snow and there was danger of avalanches up on top.

"Did you talk to the farmer who picked me up?" Robert asked.

"Yes," said his father. "He said you were a very brave little boy. He also said that if he hadn't found you, you couldn't have gone on more than another fifty meters. I gave him two hundred francs. Swiss."

"Shhh," Robert's mother said. She had the connection with the ski school now. "This is Mrs. Rosenthal again. Yes, thank you, he's doing as well as can be expected," she said, in her precise, melodious French. "We've been talking to him and there's one aspect of his story that's a little strange. He says a man stopped and helped him take off his skis last night after he'd broken his leg, and promised to go to the ski school and leave the skis there and ask for a sled to be sent to bring him down. We'd like to know if, in fact, the man did come into the office and report the accident. It would have been somewhere around six o'clock." She listened for a moment, her face tense. "I see," she said. She listened again. "No," she said, "we don't know his name. My son says he was about twenty-five years old, with blue eyes and a white cap. Wait a minute. I'll ask." She turned to Robert. "Robert," she said, "what kind of skis did you have? They're going to look and see if they're out front in the rack."

"Attenhoffer's," Robert said. "One meter seventy. And they have my initials in red up on the tips."

"Attenhoffer's," his mother repeated over the phone. "And they have his initials on them. R.R., in red. Thank you. I'll wait."

Robert's father came back from the window, dousing his cigarette in an ashtray. Underneath the holiday tan of his skin, his face looked weary and sick. "Robert," he said, with a rueful smile, "you must learn to be a little more careful. You are my only male heir and there is very little chance that I shall produce another."

"Yes, Papa," Robert said. "I'll be careful."

His mother waved impatiently at them to be quiet and listened again at the telephone. "Thank you," she said. "Please call me if you hear anything." She hung up. "No," she said to Robert's father, "the skis aren't there."

"It can't be possible," Robert's father said, "that a man would leave a little boy to freeze to death just to steal a pair of skis."

"I'd like to get my hands on him," Robert's mother said. "Just for ten minutes. Robert, darling, think hard. Did he seem . . . well . . . did he seem *normal?*"

"He seemed all right," Robert said. "I suppose."

"Was there any other thing about him that you noticed? Think hard. Anything that would help us find him. It's not only for us, Robert. If there's a man in this town who would do something like that to you, it's important that people know about him, before he does something even worse to other boys . . ."

"Mama," Robert said, feeling close to tears under the insistence of his mother's questioning, "I told you just the way it was. Everything. I'm not lying, Mama."

"What did he *sound* like, Robert?" his mother said. "Did he have a low voice, a high voice, did he sound like us, as though he lived in Paris, did he sound like any of your teachers, did he sound like the other people from around here, did he. . . ?"

"Oh . . ." Robert said, remembering.

"What is it? What do you want to say?" his mother said sharply.

"I had to speak German to him," Robert said. Until now, with the pain and the morphine, it hadn't occurred to him to mention that.

"What do you mean you had to speak German to him?"

"I started to speak to him in French and he didn't understand. We spoke in German."

His father and mother exchanged glances. Then his mother said, gently, "Was it real German? Or was it Swiss-German? You know the difference, don't you?"

"Of course," Robert said. One of his father's parlor tricks was giving imitations of Swiss friends in Paris speaking in French and then in Swiss-German. Robert had a good ear for languages, and aside from having heard his Alsatian grandparents speaking German since he was an infant, he was studying German literature in school and knew long passages of Goethe and Schiller and Heine by heart. "It was German, all right," he said.

There was silence in the room. His father went over to the window again and looked out at the snow falling in a soft blurred curtain outside. "I knew," his father said quietly, "that it couldn't just have been for the skis."

In the end, his father won out. His mother wanted to go to the police and get them to try to find the man, even though his father pointed out that there were perhaps ten thousand skiers in the town for the holidays, a good percentage of them German-speaking and blue-eyed, and trainloads arriving and departing five times a day. Robert's father was sure that the man had left the very night Robert had broken his leg, although all during the rest of his stay in the town, Mr. Rosenthal prowled along the snowy streets and in and out of bars searching among the faces for one that answered Robert's description of the man on the mountain. But he said it would do no good to go to the police and might do harm, because once the story got out there would be plenty of people to complain that this was just another hysterical Jewish fantasy of invented injury. "There're plenty of Nazis in Switzerland, of all nationalities," Robert's father told his mother, in the course of an argument that lasted weeks, "and this will just give them more ammunition, they'll be able to say, 'See, wherever the Jews go they start trouble.'"

Robert's mother, who was made of sterner stuff than her husband, and who had relatives in Germany who smuggled out disturbing letters to her, wanted justice at any cost, but after a while even she saw the hopelessness of pushing the matter any further. Four weeks after the accident, when Robert could finally be moved, as she sat beside her son in the ambulance that was to take them both to Geneva and then on to Paris, she said, in a dead voice, holding Robert's hand, "Soon, we must leave Europe. I cannot stand to live any more on a continent where things like this are permitted to happen."

Much later, during the war, after Mr. Rosenthal had died in Occupied France and Robert and his mother and sister were in America, a friend of Robert's, who had also done a lot of skiing in Europe, heard the story of the man in the white cap, and told Robert he was almost sure he recognized the man from the description Robert gave of him. It was a ski instructor from Garmisch, or maybe from Obersdorf or Freudenstadt, who had a couple of rich Austrian clients with whom he toured each winter from one ski station to another. The friend didn't know the man's name, and the one time Robert had been in Garmisch, it had been with French troops in the closing days of the war, and of course nobody was skiing then.

Now the man was standing just three feet from him, his face, on the other side of the pretty Italian woman, framed by straight black lines of skis, his eyes looking coolly, with insolent amusement, but without recognition, at Robert, from under the almost albino eyelashes. He was approaching fifty now and his face was fleshy but hard and healthy, with a thin, set mouth that gave a sense of control and self-discipline to his expression.

Robert hated him. He hated him for the attempted murder of a fourteen-year-old boy in 1938; he hated him for the acts that he must have condoned or collaborated in during the war; he hated him for his father's disappearance and his mother's exile; he hated him for what he had said about the pretty little American girl in the lambskin hat; he hated him for the confident impudence of his glance and the healthy, untouched robustness of his face and neck; he hated him because he could look directly into the eyes of a man he had tried to kill and not recognize him; he hated him because he was here, bringing the idea of death and shamefully unconsummated vengeance into this silvery holiday bubble climbing the placid air of a kindly, welcoming country.

And most of all he hated the man in the white cap because the man betrayed and made a sour joke of the precariously achieved peace that Robert had built for himself, with his wife, his children, his job, his comfortable, easygoing, generously forgetful Americanism, since the war.

The German deprived him of his sense of normalcy. Living with a wife and three children in a clean, cheerful house was not normal; having your name in the telephone directory was not normal; lifting your hat to your neighbor and paying your bills was not normal; obeying the law and depending upon the protection of the police was not normal. The German sent him back through the years to an older and truer normality—murder, blood, flight, conspiracy, pillage, and ruins. For a while Robert had deceived himself into believing that the nature of everyday could change. The German in the crowded cabin had now put him to rights. Meeting the German had been an accident, but the accident had revealed what was permanent and nonaccidental in his life and the life of the people around him.

Mac was saying something to him, and the girl in the lambskin hat was singing an American song in a soft, small voice, but he didn't hear what Mac was saying and the words of the song made no sense to him. He had turned away from looking at the German and was looking at the steep stone face of the mountain, now almost obscured by a swirling cloud, and he was trying to figure out how he could get rid of Mac, escape the young Americans, follow the German, get him alone, and kill him.

He had no intention of making it a duel. He did not intend to give the man a chance to fight for his life. It was punishment he was after, not a symbol of honor. He remembered other stories of men who had been in concentration camps during the war who had suddenly confronted their torturers later on and had turned them in to the authorities and had the satisfaction of witnessing their execution. But whom could he turn the German over to—the Swiss police? For what crime that would fit into what criminal code?

Or he could do what an ex-prisoner had done in Budapest three or four years after the war, when he had met one of his jailers on a bridge over the Danube and had simply picked the man up and thrown him into the water and watched him drown. The ex-prisoner had explained who he was and who the drowned man was and had been let off and had been treated as a hero. But Switzerland was not Hungary, the Danube was far away, the war had finished a long time ago.

No, what he had to do was follow the man, stay with him, surprise him alone somewhere on the slopes, contrive a murder that would look like an accident, be out of the country before anyone asked any questions, divulge nothing to anyone, leave the body, if possible, in an isolated place where the snow would cover it and where it would not be found till the farmers drove their herds high up into the mountains for the summer pasturage. And he had to do it swiftly, before the man realized that he was the object of any special attention on Robert's part, before he started to wonder about the American on his tracks, before the process of memory began its work and the face of the skinny fourteen-year-old boy on the dark mountain in 1938 began to emerge from the avenging face of the grown man.

Robert had never killed a man. During the war, he had been assigned by the American Army as part of a liaison team to a French division, and while he had been shot at often enough, he had never fired a gun after arriving in Europe. When the war was over, he had been secretly thankful that he had been spared the necessity of killing. Now he understood—he was not to be spared; his war was not over.

"Say, Robert . . ." It was Mac's voice finally breaking through into his consciousness. "What's the matter? I've been talking to you for thirty seconds and you haven't heard a word I said. Are you sick? You look awfully queer, lad."

"I'm all right," Robert said. "I have a little headache. That's all. Maybe I'd better eat something, get something warm to drink. You go ahead down by yourself."

"Of course not," Mac said. "I'll wait for you."

"Don't be silly," Robert said, trying to keep his tone natural and friendly. "You'll lose the Contessa. Actually, I don't feel much like skiing any more today. The weather's turned lousy." He gestured at the cloud that was enveloping them. "You can't see a thing. I'll probably take the lift back down. . . ."

"Hey, you're beginning to worry me," Mac said anxiously. "I'll stick with you. You want me to take you to a doctor?"

"Leave me alone, please, Mac," Robert said. He had to get rid of Mac and if it meant hurting his feelings now, he'd make it up to him some way, but later. "When I get one of these headaches I prefer being alone."

"You're sure now?" Mac asked.

"I'm sure."

"Okay. See you at the hotel for tea?"

"Yes," Robert said. After murder, Robert thought, I always have a good tea. He prayed that the Italian girl would put her skis on immediately and move off quickly once they got to the top, so that Mac would be gone before Robert had to start off after the man in the white cap.

The cabin was swinging over the last pylon now and slowing down to come into the station. The passengers were stirring a bit, arranging clothes, testing bindings, in preparation for the descent. Robert stole a quick glance at the German. The woman with him was knotting a silk scarf around his throat, with little wifely gestures. She had the face of a cook. Neither she nor the man looked in Robert's direction. I will face the problem of the woman when I come to it, Robert thought.

The cabin came to a stop and the skiers began to disembark. Robert was close to the door and was one of the first people out. Without looking back, he walked swiftly out of the station and into the shifting grayness of the mountaintop. One side of the mountain dropped off in a sheer, rocky face next to the station and Robert went over and stood on the edge, looking out. If the German, for any reason, happened to come over near him to admire the view or to judge the condition of the *piste* of the Kaisergarten, which had to be entered some distance farther on, but which cut back under the cliff much lower down, where the slope became more gradual, there was a possibility that one quick move on Robert's part would send the man crashing down to the rocks some hundred meters below, and the whole thing would be over. Robert turned and faced the exit of the station, searching in the crowd of brightly dressed skiers for the white cap.

He saw Mac come out with the Italian girl. He was talking to her and carrying her skis and the girl was smiling warmly. Mac waved at Robert and then knelt to help the girl put on her skis. Robert took a deep breath. Mac, at least, was out of the way. And the American group had decided to have lunch on top and had gone into the restaurant near the station.

The white cap was not to be seen. The German and the woman had not yet come out. There was nothing unusual about that. People often waxed their skis in the station, where it was warm, or took time to go to the toilets downstairs before setting out on their runs. It was all to the good. The longer the German took, the fewer people there would be hanging around to notice Robert when he set out after him.

Robert waited on the cliff's edge. In the swirling, cold cloud, he felt warm, capable, powerful, curiously light-headed. For the first time in his life he understood the profound, sensual pleasure of destruction. He waved gaily at Mac and the Italian girl as they moved off together on the traverse to one of the easier runs on the other side of the mountain.

Then the door to the station opened again and the woman who was with the German came out. She had her skis on and Robert realized that they had been so long inside because they had put their skis on in the waiting room. In bad weather people often did that, so that they wouldn't freeze their hands on the icy metal of the bindings in the biting wind outdoors. The woman held the door open and Robert saw the man in the white cap coming through the opening. But he wasn't coming out like everybody else. He was hopping, with great agility, on one leg. The other leg was cut off in mid-thigh and to keep his balance the German had miniature skis fixed on the end of his poles, instead of the usual thonged baskets.

Through the years, Robert had seen other one-legged skiers, veterans of Hitler's armies, who had refused to allow their mutilation to keep them off the mountains they loved, and he had admired their fortitude and skill. But he felt no admiration for the man in the white cap. All he felt was a bitter sense of loss, of having been deprived, at the last moment, of something that had been promised to him and that he had wanted and desperately needed. Because he knew he was not strong enough to murder a cripple, to punish the already punished, and he despised himself for his weakness.

He watched as the man made his way across the snow with crablike cunning, hunched over his poles with their infants' skis on the ends. Two or three times, when the man and the woman came to a rise, the woman got silently behind the man and pushed him up the slope until he could move under his own power again.

The cloud had been swept away and there was a momentary burst of sunlight and in it, Robert could see the man and the woman traverse to the entrance to the run, which was the steepest one on the mountain. Without hesitation, the man plunged into it, skiing skillfully, courageously, overtaking more timid or weaker skiers who were picking their way cautiously down the slope.

Watching the couple, who soon became tiny figures on the white expanse below him, Robert knew there was nothing more to be done, nothing more to wait for, except a cold, hopeless, everlasting forgiveness.

The two figures disappeared out of the sunlight into the solid bank of cloud that cut across the lower part of the mountain. Then Robert went over to where he had left his skis and put them on. He did it clumsily. His hands were cold because he had taken off his mittens in the teleferique cabin, in that hopeful and innocent past, ten minutes ago, when he had thought the German insult could be paid for with a few blows of the bare fist.

He went off, fast, on the run that Mac had taken with the Italian girl, and he caught up with them before they were halfway down. It began to snow when they reached the village and they went into the hotel and had a hilarious lunch with a lot of wine and the girl gave Mac her address and said he should be sure to look her up the next time he came to Rome.

# In the French Style

Beddoes got in from Egypt in the middle of the morning. He went to his hotel and shook hands with the concierge and told him that the trip had been fine but that Egyptians were impossible. From the concierge he found out that the city was crowded, as usual, and that the price of the room had gone up once more, as usual.

"The tourist season now lasts twelve months a year," the concierge said, giving Beddoes his key. "Nobody stays home any more. It is exhausting."

Beddoes went upstairs and told the porter to put his typewriter in the closet, because he didn't want to see it for a while. He opened the window and looked out with pleasure at the Seine flowing past. Then he took a bath and put on fresh clothes and gave Christina's number over the telephone to the woman at the switchboard. The woman at the switchboard had an insulting habit of repeating numbers in English, and Beddoes noticed, with a smile, that that had not changed. There was the familiar hysteria on the wires as the woman on the switchboard got Christina's number. The telephone in Christina's hotel was down the hall from her room, and Beddoes had to spell the name slowly—Mlle. "T" for Théodore, "A" for André, "T" for Théodore, "E" for Edouard—before the man on the other end understood and went away to tell Christina an American gentleman demanded her on the telephone.

Beddoes heard Christina's footsteps coming down the hall toward the telephone and he thought he could tell from the sound that she was wearing high heels.

"Hello," Christina said. There was a sudden crackle on the wire as Christina spoke, but even so Beddoes could recognize the breathless, excited tone of her voice. Christina answered the phone as though she expected each call to be an invitation to a party.

"Hi, Chris," Beddoes said.

"Who's this?"

"The voice of Egypt," said Beddoes.

"Walter!" Christina said happily. "When did you get in?"

"This minute," Beddoes said, lying by an hour to please her. "Are you wearing high heels?"

"What?"

"You're wearing high heels, aren't you?"

"Wait a minute while I look," Christina said. Then, after a pause, "Did you turn psychic in Cairo?"

Beddoes chuckled. "Semi-Oriental fakery," he said. "I brought back a supply. Where're we going for lunch?"

"Walter!" Christina said. "I'm in despair."

"You have a date."

"Yes. When are you going to learn to cable?"

"That's O.K.," Beddoes said carelessly. He made a point of never sounding disappointed. He had a feeling that if he asked Christina to break the date she would, but he also made a point of never pleading for anything. "We'll make it later."

"How about a drink this afternoon?"

"We can start with that," Beddoes said. "Five?"

"Make it five-thirty," Christina said.

"Where're you going to be?" Beddoes asked, minutely annoyed at the postponement.

"Near the Étoile" Christina said.

"Alexandre's?"

"Fine," Christina said. "Will you be on time for once?"

"Be more polite," Beddoes said, "the first day the man comes to town."

"*A tout à l'heure,*" Christina said.

"What did you say, Ma'am?"

"All the kids are speaking French this year." Christina laughed. "Isn't it nice to have you back in town."

There was a click as she hung up. Beddoes put the phone down slowly and went over to the window. He stared at the river, thinking that this was the first time in a long while that Christina hadn't come over immediately when he arrived in Paris. The river appeared cold and the trees were bare and the sky looked as though it had been gray for months. But with all that, the city looked promising. Even the sunless, snowless winter weather couldn't prevent Paris from looking promising.

He had lunch with a man from the A.P. who had just come back from America. The man from the A.P. said that things were in unholy shape in America and that even if you ate in drugstores it cost at least a dollar and a half for lunch and Beddoes ought to be damned glad he wasn't there.

Beddoes got to the café a little late, but Christina hadn't arrived. He sat on the glass-enclosed terrace, next to the huge window, feeling it cold from the winter afternoon against his sleeve. The terrace was crowded with women drinking tea and men reading the evening newspapers. Outside, under the trees, a little parade was forming, the veterans of some World War I unit, huddling, middle-aged, and chilled in their overcoats, with their flags and decorations, preparing to walk behind an Army band up to the Arch and put a wreath on the tomb in memory of comrades who had fallen in battles that no one any longer remembered. The French, Beddoes thought sourly, because Christina was late and the afternoon had failed its promise, are always finding occasions to block traffic. They have an endless supply of dead to celebrate.

He ordered a beer, because he had drunk too much at lunch. He had also eaten too much, in the first wave of gluttony after Egyptian food. His stomach felt uncomfortable, and he was suddenly very tired from all the miles he had traveled in the past twenty-four hours. After the age of thirty-five, he thought, in evening melancholy, no matter how swift the plane, how calm the air, how soft the cushion, the bones record the miles inexorably. He had turned thirty-five three months before and he had begun to reflect uneasily upon age. He stared at his face in mirrors, noticing wrinkles under his eyes and gray in his beard when he shaved. He remembered hearing that aging ballplayers shaved two and three times a day to keep managers and sportswriters from seeing the telltale flecks in beard stubble. Maybe, he thought, career men in the foreign service ought to do the same thing. Seventy minus thirty-five leaves thirty-five, he thought. It was an equation that came ominously to mind, especially late in the afternoon, more and more often after the midway anniversary. He stared out through the cold glass at the shuffling veterans, ranked shabbily behind their flags, their breath, mingled with cigarette smoke, rising in little clouds above their heads. He wished they'd start marching and get away from there. "Veteran" was a word that suddenly fell on his ear with an unpleasant sound.

He also wished that Christina would arrive. It wasn't like her to be late. She was one of those rare girls who always got to places exactly on the appointed hour. Irrelevantly, he remembered that she also dressed with great speed and took only a minute or two to comb her hair. She had blond hair, cut in the short Parisian manner, which left the back of her neck bare. Beddoes thought about the back of Christina's neck and felt better.

They would give themselves a gay evening, he thought. One should not permit himself to feel tired or old in Paris. If the feeling ever gets chronic, he told himself, I'll move away for good.

He thought about the evening ahead of him. They'd wander around to a couple of bars, avoiding their friends and not drinking too much, and go to a *bistro* in the markets where there were thick steaks and a heavy red wine, and after that maybe they'd go to the night club where there was a queer, original puppet show and three young men who sang funny songs that, unlike so many night-club songs, really did turn out to be funny. When you came out into the street after their act you were charmed and amused and you had the sense that this was the way a man should feel in Paris at two o'clock in the morning.

The night before he left for Cairo, he had taken Christina there. The prospect of going back on this first night home gave him an unexplained but pleasant feeling of satisfactory design. Christina had looked very pretty, the prettiest girl in the room full of handsome women, he'd thought, and he had even danced, for the first time in months. The music was supplied by a pianist and a man who got quivering, rich sounds from an electric guitar, and they played those popular French songs that always made you feel how sweet was love in the city, how full of sorrow and tempered regret.

The music had made Christina a little moony, he remembered, which was strange for her, and she had held his hand during the show, and kissed him when the lights went out between numbers. Her eyes had filled with tears for a moment and she had said, "What am I going to do without you for two months?" when he spoke of his departure the next morning. He had felt, a little warily, because he was affected, too, that it was lucky he was leaving, if she was moving into that phase. That was the pre-yearning-for-marriage phase, and you had to be on guard against it, especially late at night, in Paris, in darkened rooms where pianists and electric guitars played songs about dead leaves and dead loves and lovers who were separated by wars.

Beddoes had been married once, and he felt, for the time being, that that was enough. Wives had a tendency to produce children, and sulk and take to drink or other men when their husbands were called away to the other side of the earth for three or four months at a time on jobs.

He had been a little surprised at Christina. Yearning was not in her line. He had known her, although until recently not very well, almost from the time she arrived from the States four years before. She did some modeling for photographers and was pretty enough to have done very well at it, except that, as she said, she felt too silly making the fashionable languorous, sexy grimaces that were demanded of her. She knew how to type and take dictation and she found odd jobs with American businessmen who had work for a month or two at a time in Paris. She had picked up French immediately, and drove a car, and from time to time she got curious little jobs as a companion for old American ladies who wanted to tour through the château country or into Switzerland. She never seemed to need any sleep (even now she was only about twenty-six) and she would stay up all night with anybody and she went to all the parties and had had, to Beddoes' knowledge, affairs with two friends of his—a free-lance photographer and an Air Transport Command pilot who had been killed in a crash outside Frankfurt. You could telephone her at any hour of the day or night without making her angry and you could introduce her into any group and be pleased with the way she behaved. She always knew which *bistro* was having a rage at the moment and who was singing at which night club and which new painter was worth seeing and who was in town and who was going to arrive next week and which little hotels outside Paris were pleasant for lunch or a weekend. She obviously didn't have much money, but she dressed charmingly, French enough to amuse her French friends and not so French that she made Americans feel she was trying to pretend she was European. All in all, while she was not a girl of whom your grandmother was likely to approve, she was, as Beddoes had once told her, an ornament to the wandering and troubled years of the second half of the twentieth century.

The veterans started to move off, the banners flapping a little in the dusk as the small parade turned past the TWA office and up the Champs-Elysées. Beddoes watched them, thinking vaguely of other parades, other banners. Then he saw Christina striding diagonally across the street, swift and sure of herself in the traffic. She could live in Europe the rest of her life, Beddoes thought, smiling as he watched her, and all she'd have to do would be to walk ten steps and everybody would know she had been born on the other side of the ocean.

He stood when she opened the door into the terrace. She was hatless, and Beddoes noticed that her hair was much darker than he remembered and she was wearing it longer. He kissed her on both cheeks as she came up to the table. "Welcome," he said. "In the French style."

She hugged him momentarily. "Well, now," she said, "here's the man again."

She sat down, opening her coat, and smiled across the table at him. Her cheeks were flushed from the cold and her eyes were shining and she looked glitteringly young.

"The spirit of Paris," Beddoes said, touching her hand on the table. "American division. What'll it be to drink?"

"Tea, please. I'm so glad to see you."

"Tea?" Beddoes made a face. "Anything wrong?"

"No," Christina shook her head. "I just want tea."

"That's a hell of a drink to welcome a traveler home on," Beddoes said.

"With lemon, please," Christina said.

Beddoes shrugged, and ordered one tea from the waiter.

"How was Egypt?" Christina asked.

"Was I in Egypt?" Beddoes stared at Christina, enjoying her face.

"That's what it said in the papers."

"Oh, yes," Beddoes said. "A new world struggling to be born," he said, his voice deep and expert. "Too late for feudalism, too early for democracy . . ."

Christina made a face. "Lovely phrases for the State Department archives," she said. "I mean over a drink how is Egypt."

"Sunny and sad," Beddoes said. "After two weeks in Cairo you feel sorry for everybody. How is Paris?"

"Too late for democracy," Christina said, "too early for feudalism."

Beddoes grinned and leaned across the little table and kissed her gently. "I mean over a kiss," he said, "how is Paris?"

"The same," Christina said. She hesitated. "Almost the same."

"Who's around?"

"The group," Christina said carelessly. "The usual happy exiles. Charles, Boris, Anne, Teddy . . ."

Teddy was the free-lance photographer. "You see much of him?" Beddoes asked, very lightly.

"Uh?" Christina smiled, just a little, at him.

"Merely checking." Beddoes grinned.

"No, I haven't," Christina said. "His Greek's in town."

"Still the Greek?"

"Still the Greek," Christina said.

The waiter came and placed the tea in front of her. She poured it into the cup and squeezed the lemon. She had long, competent fingers, and Beddoes noticed that she no longer used bright nail polish.

"Your hair," he said. "What happened?"

Christina touched her hair absently. "Oh," she said. "You noticed?"

"Where're the blondes of yesteryear?"

"I decided to go natural." Christina stirred her tea. "See what that was like for a change. Like it?"

"I haven't decided yet. It's longer, too."

"Uh-huh. For the winter. The back of my neck was cold. People say it makes me look younger."

"They're absolutely right," Beddoes said. "You now look exactly eleven."

Christina smiled and lifted her cup to him. "To those who return," she said.

"I don't accept toasts in tea," Beddoes said.

"You're a finicky, liquor-loving man," Christina said, and placidly sipped at her tea.

"Now," Beddoes said, "the evening. I thought we might skip our dear friends and go to that place in the markets for dinner, because I'm dying for a steak, and after that—" He stopped. "What's the matter? Can't we have dinner together?"

"It's not that, exactly." Christina kept her head down and stirred her tea slowly. "I have a date—"

"Cancel him," Beddoes said promptly. "Cancel the swine."

"I can't really." Christina looked soberly up at him. "He's coming to meet me here any minute now."

"Oh," Beddoes nodded. "That makes it different, doesn't it?"

"Yes."

"Can't we shake him?"

"No," Christina said. "We can't shake him."

"The man doesn't live who can't be shaken," said Beddoes. "Old friend, you say, who just arrived from the horrors of the desert, just escaped dysentery and religious wars by the skin of his teeth, needs soothing, you say, and tender attention for his shattered nerves, et cetera."

Christina was smiling, but shaking her head. "Sorry," she said. "It can't be done."

"Want me to do it?" Beddoes said. "Man to man. See here, old fellow, we're all grown-up, civilized human beings—That sort of thing?"

"No," Christina said.

"Why not?" Beddoes asked, conscious that he was breaking a

639

long-standing and until now jealously adhered-to rule about not pleading for anything. "Why can't we?"

"Because I don't want to," Christina said.

"Oh," said Beddoes. "The wind is in that direction."

"Variably," Christina said softly, "in that direction. We could all have dinner together. The three of us. He's a very nice man. You'd like him."

"I never like any man the first night I'm in Paris," Beddoes said.

They sat in silence for a moment while Beddoes remembered all the times that Christina had said over the phone, "O.K., it's sinful, but I'll brush him. Meet you at eight." It was hard to believe, sitting across from her, noticing that there was no obvious change in the way she looked at him, in the way she touched his hand, that she wouldn't say it in the next minute or so.

"Two months is a long time, isn't it?" Beddoes said. "In Paris?"

"No," Christina said. "It's not a long time. In Paris or anywhere else."

"Hello, Christina." It was a tall, rather heavy-set young man, smiling and blond, who was standing, holding a hat, next to the table. "I found the place all right." He leaned over and kissed her forehead.

Beddoes stood up.

"Jack," Christina said, "this is Walter Beddoes. John Haislip. Dr. Haislip."

The two men shook hands.

"He's a surgeon," Christina said as Haislip gave his hat and coat to the attendant and sat down beside her. "He nearly had his picture in *Life* last year for something he did with kidneys. In thirty years he's going to be enormously famous."

Haislip chuckled. He was a big, placid, self-confident-looking man, with the air of an athlete, who was probably older than he looked. And just with one glance Beddoes could tell how the man felt about Christina. Haislip wasn't hiding anything in that department.

"What'll you drink, Doctor?" Beddoes asked.

"Lemonade, please."

"*Un citron pressé*," Beddoes said to the waiter. He peered curiously at Christina, but she was keeping her face straight.

"Jack doesn't drink," Christina said. "He says it isn't fair for people who make a living out of cutting other people up."

"When I retire," Haislip said cheerfully, "I'm going to soak it up and let my hands shake like leaves in the wind." He turned to Beddoes. You could tell that it took a conscious wrench for him to stop looking at Christina. "Did you have a good time in Egypt?" he asked.

"Oh," Beddoes said, surprised. "You know about my being in Egypt?"

"Christina's told me all about you," Haislip said.

"I swore a solemn oath that I was going to forget Egypt for a month once I got here," Beddoes said.

Haislip chuckled. He had a low, unforced laugh and his face was friendly and unself-conscious. "I know how you feel," he said. "The same way I feel about the hospital sometimes."

"Where is the hospital?" Beddoes asked.

"Seattle," Christina said quickly.

"How long have you been here?" Beddoes saw Christina glance at him obliquely as he spoke.

"Three weeks," said Haislip. He turned back toward Christina, as though he could find comfort in no other position. "The changes that can take place in three weeks. My Lord!" He patted Christina's arm and chuckled again. "One more week and back to the hospital."

"You here for fun or for business?" Beddoes asked, falling helplessly into the pattern of conversation of all Americans who meet each other abroad for the first time.

"A little of both," Haislip said. "There was a conference of surgeons I was asked to attend, and I moseyed around a few hospitals on the side."

"What do you think of French medicine now you've had a chance to see some of it?" Beddoes asked, the investigator within operating automatically.

"Well"—Haislip managed to look away from Christina for a moment—"they function differently from us over here. Intuitively. They don't have the equipment we have, or the money for research, and they have to make up for it with insight and intuition." He grinned. "If you're feeling poorly, Mr. Beddoes," he said, "don't hesitate to put yourself in their hands. You'll do just about as well here as anyplace else."

"I feel all right," Beddoes said, then felt that it had been an idiotic thing to say. The conversation was beginning to make him uncomfortable, not because of anything that had been said but because of the way the man kept looking, so openly and confessingly and completely, at Christina. There was a little pause and Beddoes had the feeling that unless he jumped in, they would sit in silence forever. "Do any sightseeing?" he asked lamely.

"Not as much as I'd like," Haislip said. "Just around Paris. I'd've loved to go down south this time of the year. That place Christina keeps talking about. St. Paul de Vence. I guess that's about as different from Seattle as a man could wish for and still get running water and Christian nourishment. You've been there, haven't you, Mr. Beddoes?"

"Yes," Beddoes said.

"Christina told me," said Haislip. "Oh, thank you," he said to the waiter who put the lemonade down in front of him.

Beddoes stared at Christina. They had spent a week together there early in the autumn. He wondered what, exactly, she had told the Doctor.

"We'll make it the next trip," Haislip said.

"Oh," said Beddoes, noting the "we" and wondering whom it included. "You planning to come over again soon?"

"In three years," Haislip carefully extracted the ice from his lemonade and put it on the saucer. "I figure I can get away for six weeks in the summer every three years. People don't get so sick in the summertime." He stood up. "Pardon me," he said, "but I have to make a couple of telephone calls."

"Downstairs and to the right," Christina said. "The woman'll put the calls through for you. She speaks English."

Haislip laughed. "Christina doesn't trust my French," he said. "She says it's the only recognizable Puget Sound accent that has ever been imposed upon the language." He started away from the table, then stopped. "I sincerely hope you'll be able to join us for dinner, Mr. Beddoes."

"Well," Beddoes said, "I made a tentative promise I'd meet some people. But I'll see what I can do."

."Good." Haislip touched Christina's shoulder lightly, as though for some obscure reassurance, and walked away between the tables.

Beddoes watched him, thinking unpleasantly, Well, one thing, I'm better-looking, anyway. Then he turned to Christina. She was stirring the tea leaves at the bottom of her cup absently with her spoon. "That's why the hair is long and natural," Beddoes said. "Isn't it?"

"That's why." Christina kept stirring the tea leaves.

"And the nail polish."

"And the nail polish."

"And the tea."

"And the tea."

"What did you tell him about St. Paul de Vence?"

"Everything."

"Look up from that damned cup."

Slowly Christina put down the spoon and raised her head. Her eyes were glistening, but not enough to make anything of it, and her mouth was set, as with an effort.

"What do you mean by everything?" Beddoes demanded,

"Everything."

"Why?"

"Because I don't have to hide anything from him."

"How long have you known him?"

"You heard," Christina said. "Three weeks. A friend of mine in New York asked him to look me up."

"What are you going to do with him?"

Christina looked directly into his eyes. "I'm going to marry him next week and I'm going back to Seattle with him."

"And you'll come back here three years from now for six weeks in the summertime, because people don't get so sick in the summertime," Beddoes said.

"Exactly."

"And that's O.K.?"

"Yes."

"You said that too defiantly," Beddoes said.

"Don't be clever with me," Christina said harshly. "I'm through with all that."

"Waiter!" Beddoes called. "Bring me a whiskey, please." He said it in English, because for the moment he had forgotten where he was, "And you," he said to Christina. "For the love of God, have a drink."

"Another tea," Christina said.

"Yes, Madame," said the waiter, and went off.

"Will you answer some questions?" Beddoes asked.

"Yes."

"Do I rate straight answers?"

"Yes."

Beddoes took a deep breath and looked through the window. A man in a raincoat was walking past, reading a newspaper and shaking his head.

"All right," Beddoes said. "What's so great about him?"

"What can I be expected to say to that?" Christina asked. "He's a gentle, good, useful man. And now what do you know?"

"What else?"

"And he loves me." She said it in a low voice. In all the time they'd been together, Beddoes hadn't heard her use the word before. "He loves me," Christina repeated flatly.

"I saw," said Beddoes. "Immoderately."

"Immoderately," Christina said.

"Now let me ask another question," Beddoes said. "Would you like to get up from this table and go off with me tonight?"

Christina pushed her cup away, turning it thoughtfully. "Yes," she said.

"But you won't," said Beddoes.

"No."

"Why not?"

"Let's talk about something else," said Christina. "Where're you going on your next trip? Kenya? Bonn? Tokyo?"

"Why not?"

"Because I'm tired of people like you," Christina said clearly. "I'm tired of correspondents and pilots and promising junior states-men. I'm tired of all the brilliant young men who are constantly going someplace to report a revolution or negotiate a treaty or die in a war. I'm tired of airports and I'm tired of seeing people off. I'm tired of not being allowed to cry until the plane gets off the ground. I'm tired of being so damned prompt. I'm tired of answering the telephone. I'm tired of all the spoiled, hung-over international darlings. I'm tired of sitting down to dinner with people I used to love and being polite to their Greeks. I'm tired of being handed around the group. I'm tired of being more in love with people than they are with me. That answer your question?"

"More or less," Beddoes said. He was surprised that no one at any of the other tables seemed to be paying any special attention to them.

"When you left for Egypt," Christina went on, her voice level, "I decided. I leaned against that wire fence watching them refueling all those monstrous planes, with the lights on, and I dried the tears and I decided. The next time, it was going to be someone who would be shattered when I took off."

"And you found him."

"I found him," Christina said flatly. "And I'm not going to shatter him."

Beddoes put out his hands and took hers. They lay limp in his grasp. "Chris . . ." he said. She was looking out the window. She sat there, outlined against the shining dusk beyond the plate glass, scrubbed and youthful and implacable, making him remember, confusedly, the first time he had met her, and all the best girls he had ever known, and what she had looked like next to him in the early-morning autumnal sunlight that streamed, only three months before, into the hotel room in the south, which overlooked the brown minor Alps and the distant sea. Holding her hands, with the familiar touch of the girlish fingers against his, he felt that if he could get her to turn her head everything would be different.

"Chris . . ." he whispered.

But she didn't turn her head. "Write me in Seattle," she said, staring out the window, which was streaked with moisture and in which the lights from within the café and the lights from the restaurant across the street were reflected and magnified and distorted.

Beddoes let her hands go. She didn't bother to move them. They lay before her, with their pale nail polish glistening dully, on the stained wood table. Beddoes stood up. "I'd better go." It was difficult to talk, and his voice sounded strange to him inside his head, and he thought, God, I'm getting senile, I'm tempted to cry in restaurants. "I don't want to wait for the check," he said. "Tell your friend I'm sorry I couldn't join you for dinner and that I apologize for leaving him with the check."

"That's all right," Christina said evenly. "He'll be happy to pay."

Beddoes leaned over and kissed her, first on one cheek, then on the other. "Good-bye," he said, thinking he was smiling. "In the French style."

He got his coat quickly and went out. He went past the TWA office to the great boulevard and turned the corner, where the veterans had marched a half hour before. He walked blindly toward the Arch, where the laurel leaves of the wreath were already glistening in the evening mist before the tomb and the flame.

He knew that it was a bad night to be alone and that he ought to go in somewhere and telephone and ask someone to have dinner with him. He passed two or three places with telephones, and although he hesitated before each one, he didn't go in. Because there was no one in the whole city he wanted to see that night.

# Then We Were Three

Munnie Brooks was awakened by the sound of two shots outside the window. He opened his eyes and looked at the ceiling. By the quality of the light, even through the drawn curtains, he could tell that it was sunny outside. He turned his head. In the other bed Bert was still asleep. He slept quietly, the blankets neat, in control of his dreams. Munnie got out of his bed and, barefooted, in his pajamas, went over to the window and parted the curtains.

The last mists of morning were curling up from the fields, and far off and below, the sea was smooth in the October sunlight. In the distance, along the curve of the coast, the Pyrenees banked back in green ridges toward a soft sky. From behind a haystack more than a hundred yards away, beyond the edge of the hotel terrace, a hunter and his dog appeared, walking slowly, the hunter reloading. Watching him, Munnie remembered, with mild, gluttonous pleasure, that he had had partridge, newly killed and plump with the summer's feeding, for dinner the night before.

The hunter was an old man, dressed in fisherman's blue and wearing fisherman's rubber boots. He moved solidly and carefully behind his dog, through the cut stubble. When I am an old man, thought Munnie, who was twenty-two, I hope I look and feel like that on an October morning.

He opened the curtains wider and looked at his watch. It was after ten o'clock. They had been up late the night before, all three of them, at the casino in Biarritz. Earlier in the summer, when they had been on the Côte d'Azur, a paratroop lieutenant on leave had showed them a foolproof system for beating the roulette table, and whenever they could, they frequented casinos. The system took a lot of capital and they had never made more than 8000 francs in one night among them on it, and sometimes it meant sitting up till three o'clock in the morning following the wheel, but they hadn't lost yet, either, since they met the lieutenant. It had made their trip unexpectedly luxurious, especially when they got to places where there was a casino. The system ignored the numbers and concentrated on the red and the black and involved a rather complicated rhythm of doubling. The night before they had won only 4500 francs and it had taken them until two o'clock, but still, waking late, with the weather clear and an old man hunting birds outside your window, the thousand-franc notes on the dresser added a fillip of luck and complacency to the morning.

Standing there, feeling the sun warm on his bare feet and smelling the salt and hearing the distant calm mutter of the surf, remembering the partridge and the gambling and everything else about the summer that had just passed, Munnie knew he didn't want to start home that morning as they had planned. Staring down at the hunter following his dog slowly across the brown field on the edge of the sea, Munnie knew that when he was older he would look back upon the summer and think, Ah, it was wonderful when I was young. This double ability to enjoy a moment with the immediacy of youth and the reflective melancholy of age had made Bert say to him, half seriously, half as a joke, "I envy you, Munnie. You have a rare gift—the gift of instantaneous nostalgia. You get twice your investment out of everything."

The gift had its drawbacks. It made moving away from places he liked difficult for Munnie and packed all endings and farewells with emotion, because the old man who traveled within him was always saying, in his autumnal whisper, it will never be like that again.

But putting an end to this long summer, which had stretched into October, was going to be more painful than any other finish or departure that Munnie had known. These were the last days of the last real holiday of his life, Munnie felt. The trip to Europe had been a gift from his parents upon his graduation from college and now when he went back, there they would all be on the dock, the kind, welcoming, demanding faces, expecting him to get to work, asking him what he intended to do, offering him jobs and advice, settling him lovingly and implacably into the rut of being a grownup and responsible and tethered adult. From now on all holidays would be provisional, hurried interludes of gulped summertime between work and work. The last days of your youth, said the old man within. The boat docks in seven days.

Munnie turned and looked at his sleeping friend. Bert slept tranquilly, extended and composed under his blankets, his sunburned long thin nose geometrically straight in the air. This would change, too, Munnie thought. After the boat docked they would never be as close again. Never as close as on the rocks over the sea in Sicily or climbing through the sunny ruins at Paestum or chasing the two English girls through the Roman nightclubs. Never as close as the rainy afternoon in Florence when they talked, together, for the first time, to Martha. Never as close as on the long, winding journey, the three of them packed into the small open car, up the Ligurian coast toward the border, stopping whenever they felt like it for white wine or a swim at the little beach pavilions with all the small, brightly colored pennants whipping out in the hot Mediterranean afternoon. Never as close as the conspiratorial moment over the beers with the paratrooper in the bar of the casino at Juan-les-Pins, learning about the unbeatable system. Never as close as in the lavender, hilarious dawns, driving back to their hotel gloating over their winnings, with Martha dozing between them. Never as close as on the blazing afternoon at Barcelona, sitting high up on the sunny side, sweating and cheering and shading their eyes as the matador walked around the ring holding up the two bull's ears, with the flowers and the wineskins sailing down around him. Never as close at Salamanca and Madrid and on the road through the straw-colored, hot, bare country up to France, drinking sweet, raw Spanish brandy and trying to remember how the music went that the gypsies danced to in the caves. Never so close, again, finally, as here in this small whitewashed Basque hotel room, with Bert still asleep, and Munnie standing at the window watching the old man disappear with his dog and his shotgun, and upstairs in the room above them, Martha, sleeping, as she always did, curled like a child, until they came in, as they always did, together, as though they didn't trust themselves or each other to do it alone, to wake her and tell her what they planned to do for the day.

Munnie threw the curtains wide open and let the sun stream in. If there's one boat that I have a right to miss in my life, he thought, it's the one that's sailing from Le Havre the day after tomorrow.

Munnie went over to Bert's bed, stepping carefully over the clothes that were crumpled on the floor. He poked Bert's bare shoulder with his finger. "Master," he said, "rise and shine." The rule was that whoever lost in tennis between them had to call the other Master for twenty-four hours. Bert had won the day before 6–3, 2–6, 7–5.

"It's after ten." Munnie poked him again.

Bert opened both eyes and stared coldly at the ceiling. "Do I have a hangover?" he asked.

"We only had one bottle of wine amongst us for dinner," said Munnie, "and two beers after."

"I do not have a hangover," Bert said, as if the news depressed him. "But it's raining outside."

"It's a bright, hot sunny morning," Munnie said.

"Everybody always told me it rained all the time on the Basque coast," said Bert, lying still, complaining.

"Everybody is a liar," Munnie said. "Get the hell out of bed."

Bert swung his legs slowly over the side of the bed and sat there, thin, bony and bare from the waist up, in his pajama pants that were too short for him and from which his big feet dangled loosely. "Do you know why American women live longer than American men, Fat Man?" he asked, squinting at Munnie in the sunlight.

"No."

"Because they sleep in the morning. My ambition," Bert said, lying back on the bed again but with his legs still over the side, "is to live as long as the American Woman."

Munnie lit a cigarette and tossed one to Bert, who managed to light it without lifting his head from the blanket. "I had an idea," Munnie said, "while you were wasting the precious hours of your childhood sleeping."

"Put it in the suggestion box." Bert yawned and closed his eyes. "The management will give a buffalo hide saddle to every employee who presents us with an idea that is put into practice by the . . ."

"Listen," Munnie said eagerly. "I think we ought to miss that damned boat."

Bert smoked in silence for a moment, narrowing his eyes and pointing his nose at the ceiling. "Some people," he said, "are born boat-missers and train-missers and plane-missers. My mother, for example. She once saved herself from getting killed by ordering a second dessert at lunch. The plane left just as she got to the field and came down in flames thirty-five minutes later. Not a single survivor. It was ice cream, with crushed fresh strawberries . . ."

"Come on, Bert." Sometimes Munnie got very impatient with Bert's habit of going off on tangents while he was making up his mind. "I know all about your mother."

"In the springtime," Bert said, "she goes mad for strawberries. Tell me, Munnie, have you ever missed anything in your life?"

"No," Munnie said.

"Do you think it's wise," Bert asked, "at this late stage, to fiddle with the patterns of a lifetime?"

Munnie went into the bathroom and filled a glass with water. When he came back into the bedroom, Bert was still lying on the bed, his legs dangling over the side, smoking. Munnie stood over him, then slowly tipped the glass over Bert's bare brown chest. The water splashed a little and ran in thin trickles over Bert's ribs onto the sheets.

"Ah," Bert said, still smoking. "Refreshing."

They both laughed and Bert sat up.

"All right, Fat Man," Bert said. "I didn't know you were serious."

"My idea," said Munnie, "is to stay here until the weather changes. It's too sunny to go home."

"What'll we do about the tickets?"

"We'll send a telegram to the boat people and tell them we'll take passage later. They've got a waiting list a mile long. They'll be delighted."

Bert nodded judiciously. "What about Martha?" he asked. "Maybe she has to get to Paris today."

"Martha doesn't have to go anyplace. Anytime," Munnie said. "You know that."

Bert nodded again. "The luckiest girl in the world," he said.

Outside the window there was the sound of the shotgun again. Bert turned his head, listening. There was a second report. "My," Bert said, running his tongue over his teeth, "that was wonderful partridge last night." He stood up, looking, in his flapping pajama pants, like a boy who would be a good prospect for the college crew if he could be induced to eat heavily for a year. He had been chubby until he went into the Army, but by the time he got out in May, he was long and stringy and his ribs showed. When she wanted to make fun of him, Martha told him he looked like an English poet in his bathing trunks. He went to the window and Munnie crossed over and stood beside him, looking out over the mountains and the sea and the sunlight.

"You're right," Bert said. "Only an idiot would dream of starting home on a day like this. Let's go tell Martha the party's still on."

They dressed quickly, in espadrilles and cotton trousers and tennis shirts and went upstairs together and into Martha's room, without knocking. The wind was making one of the shutters rap against the window, but Martha was still asleep, curled around herself, only the top of her head showing above the blanket, the hair dark and tangled and short. The pillow was on the floor.

Munnie and Bert stood in silence for a moment, looking down at the curled, blanketed figure and the dark head, each of them convinced that the other did not know what he was thinking.

650

"Awake," Bert said softly. "Awake to glory." He went over to the bed and touched the top of Martha's head. Watching him, Munnie could feel the tips of his own fingers twitching electrically.

"Please," Martha said, her eyes still closed. "It's the middle of the night."

"It's nearly noon," Munnie said, lying by nearly two hours, "and we have to tell you something."

"Tell it to me," said Martha, "and get out of here."

"The Fat Man here," said Bert, standing at her head, "has come up with an idea. He wants us to stay here until it begins to rain. How do you feel about it?"

"Of course," Martha said.

Bert and Munnie smiled at each other, because they felt they understood her so well. "Martha," said Bert, "you're the only perfect girl alive."

Then they went out of the room to give her a chance to get dressed.

They had met Martha Holm in Florence. They seemed to have the same ideas about which museums and which churches to go to and they kept bumping into her and she was alone and obviously American and as Bert said, they didn't come prettier, and finally they started talking to each other. Maybe it was because they had first seen her in the Uffizi Gallery among the Botticellis that gave Munnie the idea but he thought privately, that, aside from the fact that her hair was short and dark and irregularly cut, she looked like the Primavera, tall, slender, and girlish, with a long narrow nose and deep, brooding, dangerous eyes. He felt extravagant and embarrassed to be thinking things like this about a twenty-one-year-old American girl who wore slacks and had gone for a year to Smith, but he couldn't help himself. He never told Martha about it and, of course, he never said a word on the subject to Bert.

Martha knew a lot of people in and around Florence (later on, it turned out that she knew a lot of people in and around everyplace) and she got them invited to a tea in Fiesole at a villa where there was a swimming pool and to a party at which Munnie found himself dancing with a Contessa. Martha had been in Europe for nearly two years and she was wonderful at telling you what places to go to and what places were traps, and she spoke Italian and French, and she was ready when you told her to be ready, and she didn't scream for pity when she had to walk a few blocks on her own two feet, and she laughed at Bert's and Munnie's jokes and made some of her own, and she didn't giggle, weep or sulk, which put her several notches above every other girl Munnie had ever known.

After they had been together for three days in Florence and were due to start for Portofino and France, it seemed unbearable just to leave her behind. As far as Munnie and Bert could tell, she had no plans of her own. "I tell my mother," Martha explained, "that I'm taking courses at the Sorbonne, and it's almost true, at least in the wintertime."

Martha's mother lived in Philadelphia, after three divorces, and every once in a while, Martha said, she sent back a photograph, so that when she finally did arrive back home, there wouldn't be an embarrassing moment on the dock when her mother wouldn't recognize her.

So Munnie and Bert talked it over very seriously and sat at a café table with Martha in the Piazza del Signoria and ordered coffee and put it up to her.

"What we've decided," Bert said, with Munnie sitting beside him, silently agreeing, "is that the Brooks-Carboy unguided tour of Europe could use you, as interpreter, hotel-finder, and chief taster of foreign foods. Aside from supplying a welcome feminine touch. Are you interested?"

"Yes," Martha said.

"We'd like to know if we could mesh schedules, more or less," Munnie said.

Martha smiled. "I'm on a schedule of drift," she said. "Didn't you know?"

"Does that mean," Munnie asked, because he liked to have everything absolutely clear, "that you want to come along?"

"It means that I want to come along very much," said Martha, "and I was hoping you'd ask me." She looked at each of them for exactly the same number of seconds, cheerful, grateful, ready for anything.

"Now," said Bert, "Munnie and I have talked it over and we're going to lay it on the line. Something like this has to be planned out in advance or there comes a dark and hideous night of disaster. We've thought up a good, workable set of rules and if you agree, off we go tomorrow. If not—no harm done—and we hope you spend a pleasant summer."

"Get to it, Bert," Munnie said, impatiently. "Don't recite the preamble to the Constitution."

"Rule Number One," Bert said, with Martha sitting still, nodding, gravely listening, "rule number one is basic. No entanglements. Munnie and I're old friends and we've planned this summer for years and we've been having a wonderful time and we don't want to wind up fighting duels with each other or anything like that.

652

Now, I know women . . ." He paused, daring either of them to smile. They didn't smile.

"He wouldn't have said that," Munnie explained, "before the Army."

"What do you know about women?" Martha asked, being serious.

"What I know is that women're always busy choosing," Bert went on. "They come into a room and if there're five men present, their minds get to work like a business machine, punching holes. First Choice, Second Choice, Acceptable, Perhaps, Impossible."

"Oh, my." Martha began to laugh. She covered her mouth with her hand apologetically and tried to straighten her face. "Forgive me. Munnie . . . do you believe this?"

"I don't know," he said embarrassedly, "I haven't had Bert's advantages. I wasn't in the Army."

"I'll even tell you how you'd choose," Bert said, "between Munnie and me, so you won't have to wonder or waste your time."

"Tell me," Martha said. "Do tell me."

"In the beginning," said Bert, "the tendency is to choose me. I'll go into the reasons some other time. Then, after a while, the switch sets in, and Munnie gets the final decision."

"Poor Bert," Martha said, chuckling. "How awful for you! Only winning the opening game of the season all the time. Why are you telling me all this?"

"Because you've got to promise not to choose anybody," Bert said. "And if you *do* choose, you have to go to the grave with your secret."

"To the grave," Martha repeated, trying to be solemn.

"Until the boat sails," Bert said, "we treat each other like brothers and sister, and that's all. *D'accord?*"

"*D'accord,*" Martha said.

"Good." Bert and Munnie nodded at each other, pleased with how reasonable everybody was.

"Rule Number Two," Bert said, "if after a while we get to feel you're a nuisance—we say farewell and you leave. No tears. No recriminations. No scenes. Just a friendly shake of the hand and off to the nearest railroad station. *D'accord?*"

"*D'accord* two times," Martha said.

"Rule Number Three—everybody pays exactly one-third of the expenses."

"Of course," said Martha.

"Rule Number Four," Bert went on, like the director of a company explaining a plan of operations to his board, "everybody is free to go wherever he or she wants to, and with anyone else

653

whoever, and no questions asked. We are not an inseparable unit, because inseparable units are boring. O.K.?''

''A free, loose confederation of sovereign states,'' Martha said. ''I got it. Whomever.''

They all shook hands on it, surrounded by the looming oversized statues, and started out together early the next morning, after figuring out a way to squeeze Martha into the car and strap her baggage onto the back, and it all couldn't have worked out better. There hadn't been a single argument all summer, although they had discussed, among other things, sex, religion, politics, marriage, the choice of careers, the position of women in modern society, the theatre in New York and Paris, and the proper size of bathing costumes for young girls on the beaches of Italy, France and Spain. And when Bert had taken up with a plump little blonde American girl in St. Tropez for a week or so, it hadn't seemed to disturb Martha for a minute, even when the girl moved into the hotel they were staying at and frankly installed herself in the room next to Munnie's and Bert's.

The truth was, nothing seemed to disturb Martha very much. She greeted the events of each day with a strange and almost dreamlike placidity. She seemed to make no decisions herself and whatever decisions the others made, regardless of how they turned out, she accepted with exactly the same good-natured, smiling, rather vague approval. Linked in Munnie's mind with this pleasant will-lessness was Martha's extraordinary talent for sleeping. If nobody went in to awaken her in the morning, she would sleep on till noon, till two o'clock in the afternoon, even if she had gone to bed early the evening before. It wasn't anything physical, either, because she didn't need the sleep and never suggested, herself, that it was time to go to bed, no matter how late they stayed up at night or at what hour she had arisen in the morning. She never wrote any letters and rarely received any, since she hardly ever remembered to leave a forwarding address when they moved. When she needed money she would wire the bank in Paris that handled her allowance, and when it came she spent it carelessly. She took almost no interest in clothes and the reason she cut her hair short the way she did, she told Bert and Munnie, was that she didn't want to be bothered having to comb it all the time.

When the three of them talked about what they would like to do with their lives, she was vaguer than ever. ''I don't know,'' she said, shrugging, smiling, seeming to be mildly and indulgently puzzled about herself. ''I suppose I'll just hang around. Wait and see. For the moment I'm on a policy of float. I don't see anybody else our age doing anything so damned attractive. I'm waiting for a revelation to send me in a permanent direction. I'm in no hurry to commit myself, no hurry at all . . ."

In a curious way, Martha's lack of direction made her much more interesting to Munnie than all the other girls he had ever known, the positive but limited girls who knew they wanted to be married and have babies and join a country club, the girls who wanted to go on the stage and be famous, the girls who wanted to become editors or deans of women's colleges. Martha hadn't settled for anything yet, Munnie felt, because nothing good enough had come up. And there was always the chance, he believed, that when she finally did commit herself it would be for something huge, original and glorious.

The only way that the plans hadn't worked out as outlined in Florence had been that, except for the week of the plump blonde in St. Tropez, they had been an inseparable unit, but that was only because all three of them enjoyed being with one another better than being with anyone else. It wouldn't have worked if Martha had been a different kind of girl, if she had been a coquette or greedy or foolish, and it wouldn't have worked if Munnie and Bert hadn't been such good friends and hadn't trusted each other so completely, and finally, it wouldn't have worked if they had all been a little older. But it *had* worked, at least up until the first week of October, and with luck, it would continue to work, until they kissed Martha good-bye and got on the boat train, and started for home.

They lay on the deserted beach until nearly two o'clock and then took a swim. They had a race, because the water was cold, and it was the best way to keep warm. The race was a short one, only about fifty yards, and Munnie was completely out of breath by the time he finished, trying to keep up with Martha. Martha won easily and was floating serenely on her back when Munnie came up to her, blowing heavily and fighting to get air in his lungs.

"It would be a different story," Munnie said, grinning, but a little ashamed, "if I didn't have asthma."

"Don't be gloomy about it," Martha said, kicking her legs gently. "Women're more naturally buoyant."

They both stood up and watched Bert plowing doggedly up toward them.

"Bert," Martha said, as he reached them and stopped, "you're the only man I know who looks like an old lady driving an electric automobile when he swims.''

"My talents," said Bert, with dignity, "run in another direction."

They went in then, shouting and pink from the cold water and waving their arms. They dressed on the beach, under the big towel, one after another, for modesty's sake. Martha wore slacks that came down only to the middle of her calf and a fisherman's jersey, striped blue and white. Watching her arrange her clothes with light careless movements, Munnie felt that never in his life would he see again anything so gay and obscurely touching as Martha Holm, dressed in a sailor's striped shirt, on a sunny beach, shaking the sea water out of her short, dark hair.

They decided to have a picnic rather than to go to a restaurant for lunch and they got into the little two-seater MG that Munnie's brother had left for him, when he had had his summer in Europe the year before. With Martha sitting on the cushioned brake in the middle they went into town and bought a cold chicken and a long loaf of bread and a piece of Gruyère cheese. They borrowed a basket from the fruit dealer from whom they bought a huge bunch of blue grapes and picked up two bottles of pink wine and got back into the car and drove all around the harbor to the old fort, which had been besieged and which had fallen at other times but which was used now in the summertime as a school to teach young people how to sail. They parked the car and walked out along the broad, bleached top of the sea wall, carrying the basket and the wine and the big, slightly damp towel, to serve as a tablecloth.

From the wall they could see the wide stretch of the oval harbor, empty now except for a dory with a homemade sail heading toward the point of Sainte Barbe, and the deserted beach and the white and red buildings of Saint Jean de Luz. The boatyard near the fort was crammed with small blue Snipe-class boats, lashed down and on blocks for the winter, and from somewhere in the distance came the faint sound of hammering, lonely and out-of-season, where a single workman was putting new planks into the bow of a small fishing vessel. Out at sea, almost lost against the gray-blue wash of the horizon, the boats of the tuna fleet bobbed in the swell. The tide was out and the waves rolled in, white and spumy, but not ominous, over the slanting uncovered rocks on which the sea wall was built. Close to the wall, on the bay side, the ruined, circular bastions of the old wall, which the sea had broken in another century, loomed out of the quiet water, irregular, crumbling, useless, looking somehow Roman and reminding Munnie of aqueducts that had brought mountain water to cities that had long since vanished and dungeons in which the last prisoners had died five hundred years before.

They didn't go all the way out to the end of the wall, which was separated from the middle section of the breakwater by a wide channel through which the shipping entered and left the harbor. Even on the calmest day, Munnie felt something wild and dangerous out there on the flat point of stone, where the full force of the unbroken ocean probed, however quietly, at the guarded waters of the bay and the land beyond. Munnie suffered a little from vertigo and when he looked down the sheer sides of the wall into the shifting green depths and the fringe of foam he had a helpless picture of himself caught there below, or plunging down to fight against the tides and the rocks and the waves coming and going and crossing each other with upcurling tips of spray. He didn't say anything about it, of course, but he was grateful when Martha said, "This is good enough," before they had gone very far, and he carefully helped weight the towel down as a tablecloth squarely in the middle of the wall.

There was a little wind, capricious and sporadically chilly, but Bert took off his shirt, to maintain his tan. Munnie, who had a soft, rather full growth of fuzzy reddish hair on his chest, and who was embarrassed by it, said that the wind was too cold for undressing. Bert glanced at him ironically, because he knew how Munnie felt about his chest, but he didn't say anything.

As Martha cut up the chicken and arranged the cheese and bread and grapes on pieces of paper in the center of the towel, where they could all get at them neatly, Bert cocked his head, listening to the distant, slow, rhythmic hammering from the boatyard. "Whenever I hear that noise in a place like this," he said, "it reminds me of the end of *The Cherry Orchard*. Everything melancholy and closed up and ready to die and the autumn setting in . . ."

"Whenever I hear it," Martha said, arranging the grapes, "I think, 'Divorce, divorce.' "

"That's the difference," said Bert, "between Russia and America." He walked over to the edge of the wall and stood there, his toes dangerously over the brink, staring out at the horizon, a tall, spare, loose-limbed figure, reciting, his arms ritually upraised, "Break, break, break, On thy cold gray stones, O, sea, And I would that my heart could utter, The thoughts that arise in me . . ."

"Lunch is on," Martha said, sitting cross-legged and pushing her sleeves above the elbows, her bare arms, under the bunched jersey, brown and surprisingly full and solid for such a slender girl. She took a piece of chicken and bit into it and said, "It's the only kind of picnic that makes picnics worthwhile. And no ants."

Munnie drank some of the wine from the bottle, because they had neglected to bring glasses, and broke a piece of bread off the long loaf and took some of the dark meat. Bert sat on the other side of Martha, folding his long legs down in slow motion. He reached for a piece of chicken, and said, as he munched at it, "Do you think a bright, sober young American would make a fortune setting up a factory in France to manufacture paper plates and paper cups?"

"It would spoil all the ineffable medieval charm," Martha said.

"Oh, that old, lowdown, ineffable, medieval, greasy-paper charm," Bert said. "Trust a woman to notice things like that, eh, Munnie?" He lifted his eyebrow in an exaggerated, theatrical leer. "God, isn't it lucky we walked into that gallery in Florence and found Martha? Otherwise, you know what our summer would've been like? We'd have been delivered over to all the female riffraff of Europe—all those Italian movie starlets, bursting out of their shirtwaists, all those skinny French models, all those hungry-eyed, golden-brown American divorcees, smelling from Arpège. God, Munnie, doesn't it make you feel as though Something was watching over you that day in the museum? Tell me the truth, Fat Man, doesn't it make you feel supernaturally serene?"

"Where did you ever learn to talk like that?" Martha asked, sitting cross-legged, placidly lifting the wine bottle to her lips.

"My grandfather was a Baptist preacher in Memphis, Tennessee," Bert said, "and he taught me to fear the Lord, read the Bible, relish corn, and speak in balanced sentences." He stood up and waved the drumstick of the chicken at the Atlantic Ocean. "Repent, ye sinners, because ye have swum in the warm waters, and ogled the virgins . . ." He made a bow in Martha's direction. "And ye have played at the tables and ye have neglected to send postcards home. Repent, because ye have found pleasure and ye have missed the boat."

"Do you want some cheese?" Martha asked.

"With mustard." Bert sat down again. He peered thoughtfully at Munnie. "What do you think, Munnie?" he asked. "Are we really as happy as we feel or do we only *think* we're this happy? The philosopher's everlasting cud—illusion or reality. Is this wall stone?" he demanded oratorically. "Is this ocean blue, this water wet? Is this girl beautiful? Is this money we have in our pockets or is it really coupons for prizes that were given away in Duluth in 1922 by a tobacco company that went bankrupt the first Thursday after the crash? Is this the good wine of France we're drinking or is it vinegar spiked with blood and seawater? Rosé de Béarn," he said, reading the label on the bottle. "It seems real, doesn't it, but *is* it? Are we three over-privileged, white-toothed, splendid young American princes, visiting our greatest colony, or are we, without knowing it, pitiful refugees, in flight, with our backs to the sea? . . . Have you read a newspaper this morning, do you know the answer? Are we friends and brothers, or will we betray each other by sunset? Search the lady for daggers."

"Holy man," Martha said, "the self-starter got loose."

Munnie smiled dreamily, in appreciation of Bert's performance. He himself was literal and direct and always said exactly what he meant and no more. But he was entertained by Bert's flights of rhetoric and appreciated Bert much the way a man with no talent, but a love for music, appreciates a friend who is a skillful pianist and who generously performs at just the right moments, without being asked. It went all the way back to the time when they were both sixteen and in school together and Bert used to make scandalous improvisations in blank verse about the assumed sexual habits of the middle-aged and slightly bald lady who taught them chemistry. It got Bert into trouble from time to time because he was recklessly brave and once he started he let himself be carried away and say outrageous things, no matter who was listening. Just this summer, they had had to fight four young Germans in a *brasserie* in Nice and run from the police because of one of his performances. Bert had struck up a conversation with the young men and asked them where they came from and they had said, after a little hesitation, that they were Swiss. "What part of Switzerland?" Bert had asked blandly. "Düsseldorf? Hamburg?"

The Germans, who were large, solid men, had looked uncomfortable and turned away from him toward the beers that were standing on the bar in front of them, but Bert wouldn't leave it alone. "The part of Switzerland I find most charming," Bert said loudly, "is Belsen. So rural, so cosy, so full of memories. What I always have said is that Switzerland would have won the war if it hadn't been stabbed in the back by the watchmakers. And a good thing, too."

"Cut it out," Munnie had whispered, and Martha had shaken her head warningly too, and pulled at Bert's arm. "There're four of them. They'll murder us."

But Bert had gone right on. "I'm proud to tell you gentlemen," he had said, smiling broadly, "that I have always been a believer in a Greater Switzerland and there are plenty of good, red-blooded

Americans who go right along with me." The Germans were muttering among themselves by now and Munnie took off his watch and slipped it into his pocket because he didn't want it broken when the fight began.

"Shut up, Bert," Martha said. "They're going to hit you with a beermug."

"Now, boys," Bert went on, lifting his glass, "I'd like you to join me in a toast to the greatest little old Swiss of them all, that kindly, sweet old lovable fellow, Adolf Hitler, and after that we'll all join in singing Switzerland Über Alles. I'm sure you know the words . . ."

Munnie had edged around by now and when the first German swung, he grabbed the man's arm and clubbed him twice with his right hand. The Germans were slow, but strong, and very angry, and by the time Munnie dragged Bert to the door, he had a bloody nose and Bert's coat collar was half torn off and all the waiters were screaming for the police.

The three of them ran through the back streets of Nice, hearing confused shouting dying down behind them. Bert was chuckling as he ran, and shaking his right hand, which was numb from a German skull, and he kept saying to Munnie, "What part of Switzerland you from, Bud? Leipzig? Nuremberg?"

A half hour later, when they were sitting safely in a bar along the Promenade des Anglais, it had begun to seem funny to Martha and Munnie, too, and for the rest of the summer, whenever any one of them did something that seemed objectionable or foolish, the others would ask, incredulously, "What part of Switzerland are *you* from?"

Now Bert was sitting, waving the wine bottle gently, beaming out at the bay. "I think I am going to start a new kind of travel service. Out-of-season tours to slightly rundown resorts. I'll write a brochure, entitled 'Know Bliss! Be Unfashionable! Get Away from Your Fellow Man on Your Next Vacation!' Do you think your father would be inclined to put up the dough to get us started, Munnie?"

Bert had an unshakable belief that Munnie's father was enormously wealthy and avid for unusual business opportunities, which Bert was happy to find for him. The opportunities had included the planting of an avocado grove near Grasse, and the building of a 4000-foot *téléphérique* for skiing in a village of twenty-two houses in the Spanish Pyrenees. All of Bert's projects, aside from involving great outlays of capital on the part of Munnie's father, also included the necessity of Bert's remaining permanently in Europe as manager.

"Munnie," Bert said, "don't you think we ought to send your father a cable?"

"No," said Munnie.

"The chance of a lifetime," Bert said. "What does he want to hold on to all that money for? The inheritance people'll just take it from him in the hideous end. Well, I'll find something. That's not the only way to turn a dollar." He peered speculatively at Martha, who was eating the grapes by now. "Martha," he said, "do you know that you represent a source of vast potential income?"

"I'm going to donate my body to science," Martha said, "at the age of eighty-five."

"The essential thing," said Bert, "is not to marry an American."

"Report that man to a committee," Martha said.

"America is not the place for a pretty woman," Bert went on. "The houses're getting too small, the help too expensive, a beauty suddenly finds herself in a cosy little nest in Scarsdale surrounded by television sets and labor-saving devices and invitations to join the Parent-Teachers Association. A beautiful woman does better in a country which is decaying a little, and rather uneconomically run—like France. You could marry a nice forty-five-year-old man with a clean mustache and large, rolling feudal estates on the banks of the Loire. Wonderful shooting in the autumn and good, light wines grown on the property and dozens of servants taking off their caps and bowing when the station wagon went by. Your husband would adore you and invite all your friends down to keep you happy and he'd leave you alone a good deal of the time when he went up to Paris to attend to his affairs and have his doctor probe his liver."

"Where do you fit into this picture?" Martha asked.

"He'd be one of the friends invited to keep you happy," Munnie said. He wasn't enjoying the conversation. Even though Bert was joking, Munnie knew that actually Bert would approve if Martha *did* go out and marry an old man with a lot of money. Just the other day, when they had been talking about the careers that might lie ahead of them, Bert had said, "The important thing is to recognize your gift and then use it. And the best way to use it is to keep you from the insufferable boredom of work. Now your gift—" he had grinned at Martha "—your gift is beauty. That's easy. You use it on a man and the sky's the limit. My gift is a double one, but in the long run less hopeful. I have charm . . ." He grinned more widely, making fun of himself. "And I don't give a damn. Still, if I'm clever enough and don't rise to the wrong bait, I may go a long way on it. As for Munnie . . ." He shook his head doubtfully. "His gift is virtue. Poor sod. What can he do with that?"

Now, sitting on the corner of the towel, picking the grapes appreciatively off their stems, one by one, Bert was shaking his head. "No," he said, "I won't be one of the invited friends. I'm a permanent fixture. I'm the overseer of the estates, the curious American with no ambition who likes to live in France on the banks of the pretty river. I walk around in an old tweed jacket smelling a little from horses and new wine barrels, loved by one and all, making wry comments on the state of the world, playing backgammon in front of the fire with the mistress of the house when her husband is away, and going up the stairs later, with the last glass of Armagnac in my hand, to entertain her in my wry, American way in the ancestral bed . . ."

"Ah," Martha said, "how idyllic!"

"Every age," Bert said gravely, "to its own particular idyll. This is this year, among the wars."

Munnie felt very uncomfortable and when he looked over at Martha he felt even more uncomfortable, because she was laughing. They had laughed together at a lot of things since Florence, and they had covered all the subjects, but Munnie didn't want to hear Martha laughing now at this.

He stood up. "I think I'm going down the wall a way," he said, "and take a siesta. Wake me when you want to go."

He walked about thirty yards, carrying a sweater to use as a pillow, and as he stretched out on the smooth sun-warmed stone, he heard Martha and Bert laughing together, the laughter private and small in the wide, bright emptiness.

Closing his eyes against the glare of the sun, listening to the distant laughter, Munnie realized that he was in pain. The pain was not localized and it had a curious, evasive quality. Just when Munnie felt, *There, I've got it, it's in my throat,* it slipped away, not to disappear, but to put vague, sharp, almost detectable fingers somewhere else. Then, lying there, with the curtain of heat on his eyelids, Munnie understood that what he was feeling was not pain, but sorrow.

The sorrow was deep and complex, and was composed of many elements—a sense of deprivation, a shadow of impending departure, a nostalgia for memories that were moving irrevocably away from innocence, a confusion of emotion more profound than anything he had ever experienced before in his life. Engulfed and shaken as he was, Munnie also knew that if, telepathically affected, Martha would stop laughing with Bert and get up and walk the thirty yards along the wall to where he lay, and if she were to sit down beside him and touch his hand, all would instantaneously be well.

But she didn't move, and he heard her laugh more loudly at something that Bert had said and which Munnie couldn't hear.

Suddenly, Munnie knew what he was going to do. As soon as he was on the boat, and all bargains were over, all rules no longer in effect, he was going to write Martha and ask her to marry him. Clumsily, he began to compose the letter in his mind, *This will come as a surprise to you, I suppose, because all summer long I never said a word, but I didn't realize for a long time what had been happening to me, and besides there was the arrangement you and Bert and I made in Florence to keep everything on a purely friendly basis, which I am happy we did. But now I'm on the boat and I feel free to tell you how I feel about you. I love you and I want to marry you. I don't know how you feel about me, but maybe the arrangement kept you from saying anything, just the way it did me. Anyway, I hope so. I am going to get a job and get settled just as soon as I get home, and then you could come back and meet my family and all that . . .*

The letter stopped writing itself inside his head. He thought of his mother sitting down having tea with Martha, saying, "You say your mother lives in Philadelphia? And your father . . . oh . . . Do try one of these cakes. And you say you met Munnie in Florence and then just you and he and Bert went all around Europe for the rest of the summer all together . . . Lemon, cream?"

Munnie shook his head. He'd handle his mother when the time came. He went back to writing the imaginary letter.

*You said once that you didn't know what you wanted to do with yourself, that you were waiting for some kind of revelation to send you in a permanent direction. Maybe you'll laugh at me for offering myself as a revelation, but maybe you'll feel that marrying me will . . .*

Munnie shook his head disgustedly. God, even if she was crazy in love with him, he thought, a sentence like that would queer it forever.

*I don't know about you and other men,* he went on jumpily in his head. *You never seemed interested in anybody else while you were with us and you never mentioned anybody else in any particular way and as far as I could tell you never showed any preference between Bert and me . . .*

Munnie opened his eyes and turned his head to look at Bert and Martha. They were sitting close together, almost head to head, facing each other, talking in low, serious voices.

He remembered Bert's description of what he called his gift. I have charm and I don't give a damn. Well, Munnie thought, with satisfaction, even if she overlooked the egotism, that can't have attracted her so much. And besides, there was that open and avowed blonde in St. Tropez. If Bert had planned to do anything with Martha, or if Martha, as Bert had predicted, was interested in making a choice, that certainly would have put an end to it, wouldn't it? Bert, Munnie decided, could be the amusing, bachelor friend of the family. The best kind.

Munnie dozed a little, a succession of warm and delicious images pouring through his mind. Martha coming off the airplane at Idlewild, because after getting his letter the boat was too slow, and walking away from the runway into his arms. Martha and he waking late on a Sunday morning in their own apartment and deciding to doze for another hour and then go out to breakfast. Martha coming into a party on his arm and a slight, approving, envious, subtle hush sweeping the room for a moment, because she was so beautiful. Martha . . .

Someone was shouting. Far off, someone was shouting.

Munnie opened his eyes and blinked, thinking, puzzled. Now, why did anyone shout in my dream?

The cry came again and Munnie stood up and looked out at the bay. In the water, at least three hundred yards away, was a small boat. It was the dory they had seen before. It had capsized and it was low in the water and there were two figures clinging to it. As he watched, he heard the cry again, wordless, desperate. A hand and arm flashed in the sunlight, waving.

Munnie turned and looked over at Bert and Martha, They were stretched out, their heads together on the towel, their bodies making a wide V, sleeping.

"Bert!" Munnie called. "Martha! Get up!"

Bert stirred, then sat up, rubbing his eyes. The shout came again, wailing, from the bay.

"Out there," Munnie said, pointing. Bert swung around, still sitting, and looked at the capsized boat and the two almost-submerged figures clinging to it, a man and a woman. "Good God," Bert said. "What do they think they're doing there?" He nudged Martha. "Wake up," he said, "and watch the shipwreck."

The boat lay almost motionless in the water, only shifting a little as the two figures moved, changing their positions. As Munnie watched, he saw the man push off from the boat and start to swim toward the beach. The man swam slowly and every thirty seconds he stopped and shouted and waved. After each stop he slid under, then reappeared, splashing and frantic.

"Oh, my," Bert said. "He's leaving her out there!"

Bert was standing by now, with Martha at his side, peering across the bay. The man had a good three hundred yards to go before he could touch down on the beach and with his screaming and waving and going under twice a minute, it didn't look as though he was going to make it. The woman who had been left hanging on to the boat shouted from time to time, too, and her voice sounded shrill and angry as it floated across the glittering quiet water.

Finally, Munnie could make out what the swimmer was shouting. *"Au secours! Je noye, je noye!"* Munnie felt a little flicker of annoyance with him. It seemed melodramatic and overdone to be shouting "I'm drowning," especially in such a powerful voice, on a peaceful afternoon in the calm, sunny bay. He went over to the edge of the wall, joining Bert and Martha.

"He seems to be doing all right," Bert said. "He's got a nice, strong stroke there."

"He's going to have to do a little explaining later," Martha said "leaving his girl friend out there like that."

As they watched, the man went under again. He seemed to stay under a long time and Munnie began to feel his mouth get very dry, watching the spot where the man had disappeared. Then the man surfaced again, this time with his shoulders and arms bare, white and glistening against the deep blue water. He had taken off his shirt underwater and a moment later the shirt came up and floated away, billowing soddenly. The man shouted again. By now it was plain that he was calling directly to the three of them, standing on the wall. The man started swimming again, thrashing heavily.

Munnie scanned the beach and the wharf on which the Snipes were put up on blocks for the winter. There wasn't a boat of any kind he could use, or even a length of rope. He listened for the sound of the hammer they had heard when they had first come onto the wall. Then he realized it had stopped a long time ago, while they were still eating. Far across, on the other side of the bay, there was no movement in front of the houses that faced the water and there were no swimmers or fishermen or children playing anywhere in sight. The entire world of stone, sand and sea that afternoon seemed to be given over to the three of them standing on the wall, and the woman clinging to the bottom of the capsized boat calling shrilly and angrily to the half-naked man struggling in the water and moving slowly and painfully away from her.

Why couldn't this have happened in August? Munnie thought irritably. He looked down at the water rippling in gentle regular swells against the base of the wall. It wasn't very deep now, with the tide out, four or five feet at the most, and huge chunks of rock and concrete broke the surface irregularly. If you jumped it was a drop of at least fifteen feet and there would be no avoiding the rocks.

Munnie looked, almost embarrassedly, across at Martha and Bert. Martha was squinting and there were lines on her forehead. She was biting her thumbnail absently like a little girl puzzling over a problem in school. Bert seemed critical and mildly interested, as though he were watching the performance of an acrobat in a third-rate circus.

"The damn fool," Bert said mildly. "If he couldn't handle a boat any better than that you'd think he'd have had the sense to stick close to the shore."

"Frenchmen," Martha said. "They think they can do anything." She went back to chewing on her nail.

The man called again, aiming it at them.

"What're we going to do?" Munnie asked.

"Bawl the stupid bastard out," Bert said, "when he comes ashore, for being such a lousy sailor."

Munnie peered at the swimmer. He was going more slowly now and he seemed to be settling deeper in the water after each stroke. "I don't think he's going to make it," Munnie said.

"Well," said Bert, "that'll be too bad."

Martha said nothing.

Munnie swallowed dryly. Later on, he thought, I won't be able to bear remembering today, standing here, watching a man drown.

Then another picture flicked before his eyes. It was sharp and clear and there was nothing missing. It was of Bert and Martha and himself standing in front of a French policeman, seated at a desk, with his cap on, scratching away with a leaking fountain pen in a little black book.

"So," the policeman was saying, "you wish to report a drowning?"

"Yes."

"So—you saw this gentleman, some distance from the shore, waving at you, and then he disappeared?"

"Yes."

"And the lady?"

"The last we saw of her she was still holding on to the boat, floating out to sea."

"Ah. And—uh—what steps did you take, personally?"

"We . . . we came here and reported it."

"Oh, yes. Of course." More scratching in the book. A hand reaching out. "Your passports, please." A quick riffling through the pages and one short, coldly smiling glance as the policeman tossed them on the desk. "Ah, Americans, all of you . . ."

The man out in the water went under again for a second.

Munnie tried to swallow again. This time he couldn't manage it.

"I'm going to go get him," he said. But for a moment he didn't move, as though, somehow, just saying it would fix everything, put the man on dry land, right the boat, stop the screams.

"It's two hundred and fifty yards at least from the beach," Bert said, very calmly. "And then two hundred and fifty yards back, or a little less, with a crazy Frenchman holding on to your neck."

Munnie listened gratefully. "Yes," he said. "At least."

"You never swam five hundred yards in your life," Bert said, sounding friendly and reasonable.

The man screamed again and now his voice was hoarse and terrified.

Munnie started walking swiftly along the wall, back to where there was a narrow flight of steps leading down to the little beach in front of the fort. He didn't run because he didn't want to be out of breath when he went into the water.

"Munnie!" he heard Bert call behind him. "Don't be a damn fool!"

Even as he started down the steep flight of steps, slippery with moss, Munnie noticed that Martha hadn't said anything. When he got down to the beach he trotted across it, at the water line, to get to the point nearest the man. He stopped, breathing heavily, and waved at the swimmer, encouraging him. Now, down at water level, it looked a good deal more than two hundred and fifty yards. He kicked off his shoes and tore off his shirt. The wind felt cold on his skin. He took off his pants, tossing them to one side on the sand, and stood there in his shorts. He hesitated. They were old shorts and they had torn at the crotch and he had mended them, clumsily, himself. He had a sudden picture of his body washed ashore and people noticing the shabby mending job and smiling a little. He unbuttoned the shorts, his fingers fumbling thickly at the buttons and let the shorts drop to the sand. As he walked deliberately into the water, he thought, She's never seen me naked, I wonder what she thinks.

He scraped his toes on a rock and the pain made the tears come into his eyes. He kept walking until the water was up to his chest, then pushed off and began to swim. The water was cold and his skin felt tight and frozen almost at once. He tried not to swim too fast, so that he would have some strength left when he reached the drowning man. Whenever he looked up to see how far he'd gone it seemed to him that he had hardly moved at all, and it was hard to keep going in a straight line. Somehow he always seemed to be veering to his left, in the direction of the wall, and he had to keep correcting himself all the time. Once, he looked up at the wall, searching for Bert and Martha. He couldn't see them and he had a moment of panic. What the hell have they done? he thought. They've left. He turned over on his back, losing precious seconds, and saw them on the beach, standing at the water's edge, watching him. Of course, he thought.

He turned over and kept on swimming methodically toward the Frenchman. Whenever he picked his head out of the water, the Frenchman seemed to be screaming, and just as far away as ever. He decided not to look again for a while. It was too discouraging.

Then his arms began to feel tired. It can't be, he thought. I haven't even gone fifty yards yet. Still, the muscles between his shoulders and his elbows seemed to be contracted, twisting his bones, and there was a deep ache of weariness in the back of his arms. His right hand began to cramp a little, too, and he let it flutter loosely through the water, which slowed him down, but he didn't know what else to do about it. The cramp reminded him that he had eaten not very long before and had a lot of wine and grapes and cheese. As he swam, with the water a green blur in his eyes and the slow, steady push of it going past his ears, he remembered his mother, in all the summers of his boyhood, on the shores of the lake in New Hampshire, saying, "No swimming for at least two hours after meals." Sitting on a little wooden chair, under a striped umbrella, watching the children play on the narrow, pebbly beach.

The back of his neck and the base of his skull started to ache now, and his thoughts wavered across his consciousness, disconnected and slippery. He had never liked swimming much, he remembered. He just went in to cool off and play around. Swimming had always seemed like a boring sport. The same old thing, over and over again, lift one arm, lift the other arm, kick, lift one arm, lift the other arm, kick, never really get anyplace. And he had never learned to keep the water out of his ears and sometimes he'd feel deaf for hours and the water wouldn't come out until he'd gone to bed and slept on one side for a long time.

His arms began to feel numb and he rolled more and more, in an effort to get his shoulders into the job, and he seemed to be swimming lower in the water than he ever had before. There's no sense in wasting time, he thought, making himself worry about something else besides his arms, I might as well figure out what to do once I get there. Laboriously, he tried to phrase what he would say to the man in French when he approached him. *Monsieur, J'y suis. Doucement. Doucement.* He would stay off from the man and try to calm him down before grabbing him. Dimly, he remembered having seen a demonstration of life-saving at a pool when he was fourteen years old. He hadn't paid much attention, because the boy behind him had surreptitiously kept flicking at him with a wet towel. But there was something about letting yourself sink if the drowning man put his arms around your neck, then twisting and putting your hand under his chin and pushing back. He hadn't believed it when he was fourteen years old and he didn't believe it now. It was one of those things that looked good in practice, on dry land. Then there were all the stories about hitting people on the chin and knocking them out. More dry land. He had never knocked anybody out in his whole life. His mother hated fighting. *Monsieur, soyez tranquille. Roulez sur votre dos, s'il vous plaît.* Then he'd go in and grab him by the hair and start towing him, sidestroke. If the man understood him. He had an awful lot of trouble getting Frenchmen to understand his accent, especially here in the Basque country. Martha had no trouble at all. They all said what a charming accent she had. Well, why not, after all that time at the Sorbonne? She should have come with him as an interpreter, if for nothing else. *Tournez sur votre dos.* That was better.

He swam heavily and slowly, his eyes beginning to smart from the salt water. When he lifted his head there were white and silver spots before his eyes and everything seemed to be blurred and he couldn't really see anything much. He kept on swimming. After fifty strokes he decided he'd stop and tread water and look around. The idea of treading water now seemed like the greatest pleasure ever vouchsafed the human race.

He started to count the strokes. Fourteen, fifteen, sixteen . . . Lord, he thought, what if he's bald? He tried to remember what the man's head had looked like, far out, splashing away from the overturned boat. There had been a funny pale gleam. Bald, Munnie decided desperately. Nothing is going to go right.

He started counting strokes all over again. By the time he got to thirty-five he knew he would have to stop for a while. He made himself do five more, then stopped and rolled over on his back, gasping and blowing water and looking up at the sky. He got his breath back and turned again and trod water, searching for the Frenchman.

He blinked his eyes and rubbed them with the back of his hand, sinking up to his mouth as he did so. The Frenchman wasn't there. Oh, God, he thought, he went down.

Then he heard the chugging and twisted in the water. A fishing boat was bearing away from the spot where Munnie had last seen the Frenchman, and was going toward the overturned dory. Munnie trod water, watching while the tuna boat stopped, and two fishermen reached down and pulled the woman on board. The tuna boat, Munnie realized, must have been coming up from the south, concealed by the little headland on which the fort was built, and must have coasted along the seaward side of the wall and entered the channel while he was swimming blindly out from the beach.

The men on the tuna boat threw a line onto the dory, then swung around and headed for Munnie. He waited for it, fighting his lungs. The tuna boat, painted blue, and slow and old, approached him, looking big and safe as it drew nearer. Munnie saw grinning, tanned wide faces, capped by blue berets in the bow, and he waved, with great effort, as the tuna boat slowed down and came to a stop next to him.

"Ça va?" a fisherman shouted, grinning down at him. A cigarette, burned almost to the end, hung plastered to his lips.

Munnie managed to smile. "Ça va bien," he called. "Très bien."

The man who had been rescued came to the rail, still naked to the waist, and peered curiously down at Munnie. Munnie saw that he had plenty of hair. The Frenchman didn't say anything. He was a fat young man with a hurt and dignified expression on his face. At his side appeared a woman. She had been heavily made up and the seawater had done a great deal of damage to the rouge and mascara. She stared furiously down at Munnie, then turned to the Frenchman. She grabbed him by both ears and shook him. "Crapaud!" she said loudly. "Espèce de cochon."

The Frenchman closed his eyes and allowed his head to be shaken, keeping his face sad and dignified. The fisherman grinned more broadly.

"*Alors*," one of the fishermen said, throwing a line out toward Munnie, "*allons*-y."

Munnie looked longingly at the line. Then he remembered that he was naked. He shook his head. One thing that was not going to happen to him that afternoon was to be fished out of the sea naked in front of that woman pulling her friend's ears and calling him a pig and a toad. "I'm O.K.," Munnie said, up to the brown, tough amused faces, used to all sorts of comical, salty accidents and escapes. "*Je suis O.K.* I want to swim. I mean—*Je voudrais bien nager*."

"O.K., O.K." the fishermen said laughing, as though what he had said was enormously witty. They pulled in the line and waved and the tuna boat swung around and started in toward the harbor, towing the dory. As it went, over the sound of the engine, Munnie could still hear the sound of the woman screaming.

Well, Munnie thought, watching the boat sail off, at least they understood me.

Then he turned and looked at the beach. It looked miles away and Munnie was surprised that he had swum that far. He had never swum that far before in his life. On the beach, at the water line, with the tower of the fort behind them, Bert and Martha were standing, small, sharp figures, throwing long shadows now in the declining sun.

Taking a deep breath, Munnie started to swim in.

He had to turn over and float every ten yards or so and for a while it seemed to him that he wasn't moving at all, only going through the motions of swimming, but finally, putting his feet down, he touched bottom. It was still fairly deep, up to his chin, and he pulled his feet up and stubbornly kept on swimming. And as a gesture, which he didn't try to understand, even as he did it, he swam all the way in, making himself spurt and do a proper crawl, until the water was so shallow that his fingertips scraped the sand.

Then he stood up. He wavered a little, but he stood up and, making himself smile, walked slowly, naked, with the water streaming off him, toward where Bert and Martha stood next to the little pile of his clothes on the beach.

"Well," Bert said as Munnie came up to them, "what part of Switzerland are *you* from, Bud?"

As he bent over and picked up the towel and began to dry himself, shivering under the rough cloth, Munnie heard Martha laugh.

He rubbed himself dry. He took a long time, shivering badly, too weary and not interested enough to try to cover his nakedness. They drove back to the hotel in silence and when Munnie said that he thought he'd lie down and try to rest for a while, they both agreed that it was probably the best thing to do.

He slept uneasily, his ears half deaf and stopped with water and the blood pounding in them like a distant, fitful sea. When Bert came in and said it was time for dinner, Munnie told him he wasn't hungry and that he wanted to rest. "We're going to the Casino after dinner," Bert said. "Should we stop by and pick you up?"

"No," Munnie said. "I don't feel lucky tonight."

There was a little silence in the darkened room. Then Bert said, "Good night. Sleep well, Fat Man," and went out.

Alone, Munnie lay staring at the shadowed ceiling, thinking. *I'm not fat. Why does he call me that? He only started it in the middle of the summer.* Then he slept again and only awakened when he heard the car drive up outside the hotel and the steps going softly up the stairs, past his door, to the floor above. He heard a door open and close gently upstairs and he made himself shut his eyes and try to sleep.

When he awoke the pillow was wet, where the water had run out of his ears, and he felt better. When he sat up the blood stopped pounding inside his head, too. He turned on the lamp and looked at Bert's bed. It was empty. He looked at his watch. It was four-thirty.

He got out of bed and lit a cigarette and went to the window and opened it. The moon was just going down and the sea was milky and was making an even, grumbling sound, like an old man complaining about the life that lay behind him.

For a moment, he wondered where he would have been at this hour if the tuna boat hadn't come in around the breakwater. Then he doused his cigarette and began to pack. It didn't take long, because they had been traveling light all summer.

When he finished he made sure that the extra key for the car was on his ring. Then he wrote a short note for Bert, telling him that he'd decided to take off for Paris. He hoped to get to Paris in time to catch the boat. He hoped this wouldn't inconvenience Bert too much and he knew that Bert would understand. He didn't mention Martha.

He carried his bag out to the car through the dark hotel and threw the bag into the empty space next to the driver's seat. He put on a raincoat and a pair of gloves and started the car and drove carefully out the driveway, without looking back to see whether the sound of the engine had awakened anyone or whether anyone had come to a window to watch him leave.

There was mist in the low places on the road, and he drove slowly, feeling it wet against his face. With the sighing regular noise of the windshield wipers and the steady, damp light of the headlights on the road ahead of him almost hypnotizing him, he drove mechanically, not thinking of anything at all.

It was only far past Bayonne, when the dawn had broken and he had cut off the lights and the road stretched gray and glistening through the dark pine aisles of Les Landes, that he allowed himself to remember the day and night that had just passed. And then all he could think was, It's my fault. I let the summer go on one day too long.

# God Was Here But He Left Early

"Be lugubrious, Love," she remembered, as she ran the bell. Bert
had said that on the phone when he had called her back from
London. "They dote on sorrow. Suggest suicide. Just the merest
hint, Love. Name me if you want. Everybody knows how weird
I am, even in Geneva, and they'll sympathize. I'm sure it'll be
all right. Three of my friends have been and have lived happily
ever after."

Bert's vocabulary was airy but he was familiar with trouble in
fifteen countries; he was a friend of outlaws; the police in several
cities had taken an interest in him, he knew everybody's name
and address and what they could be used for. Thinking about Bert,
his pleasure in complication, she smiled in the dark corridor before
the closed door. She heard steps. The door opened. She went in.

"You are how old, Mrs. Maclain?"

"Thirty-six," Rosemary said.

"You are American, of course."

"Yes."

"Your home?"

"New York." She had decided not to let him know she spoke
French. It would make her seem more helpless. Adrift, non-com-
municating in foreign lands.

"You are married?"

"Divorced, five years ago."

"Children?"

"A daughter. Eleven years old."

"Your . . . uh . . . condition dates back how far?"

"Six weeks."

"You're sure?" He spoke English precisely. He had studied in
Pennsylvania. He was a small, youngish, precise man with neatly
brushed brown hair in a neat brown office. There was a pale
ceramic blankness about his face, like a modestly designed dinner
plate. He was alone. He had opened the door for her himself.

Diplomas and degrees in several languages hung on the brownish, neutral walls. There was no noise from the street. It was a sunny day. She didn't feel lugubrious.

"Perfectly," she said.

"Your health?"

"Physically . . ." She hesitated. There was no sense in lying. "Physically—I suppose I'd say normal."

"The man?"

"I'd prefer not to talk about it."

"I'm afraid I must insist."

Inventions. *We were to be married but he was killed in a car crash. In an avalanche. I discovered in time that there was a strong streak of insanity in his family. He's a Catholic and Italian and married and as you know there's no divorce in Italy and besides, I have to live in New York. He was a Hindu. He promised to marry me and disappeared. It was a sixteen-year-old boy in a wagon-lit and he had to go back to school.* Absurd. All absurd.

The psychiatrist sat there in his brown office, patient, in ambush, prepared for lies.

"He's married." The truth. "Happily married." Perhaps more or less the truth. "He has two small children. He's much younger than I." Demonstrably true.

"Does he know?"

"No." Absurdity, too, has its limits. A senseless weekend in the mountains with a man you never had met before in your life and finally didn't much like and whom you never really wanted to see again. She had always been a fastidious woman and had never before done anything like that and certainly would never do it again. But you couldn't go surging in on a man ten years younger than you, bear down on him in the bosom of his 16th Arrondissement family, and whine away like a schoolgirl about being seduced because of two meaningless nights during a snowstorm. Caught. She frowned as she thought of the word. The vulgarity was inescapable. She wasn't even sure she had his address. He had written it down the last morning, she remembered, and said that if she ever came to Paris . . . But she had been sleepy and glad to get him out of the room and she wasn't sure whether she had put the slip of paper in her bag. His business address, he had said. The sanctity of the *foyer*. Frenchmen.

"No, he doesn't know," she said.

"Don't you think you ought to tell him?"

"What good would it do? Two people worrying instead of one." Although she couldn't see him worrying. Shrug. American woman coming to Europe not even knowing how to. . . . "You see," she said, "it was terribly casual. In a ski resort. You know how ski resorts are . . ."

"I do not ski." He said it proudly. He was a serious practitioner. He did not devote his time to frivolity. He did not pay good money to break his legs. She began to dislike him in waves. The brown suit was hideous.

"I was drunk." Not true. "He helped me to my room." Not true. "I didn't know it was happening, really." The brown suit twitched. "He behaved in a very ungentlemanly fashion. . . ." Was it really her own voice? "If I *did* tell him, he would only laugh. He's a Frenchman." Perhaps she had something there. The mutual loathing of the Swiss and French. Calvin versus Madame de Pompadour. Geneva humiliated by Napoleon's troops. One Frenchman less in the world. Or demi-Frenchman. "By his attitude, I could tell he would have no sense of responsibility." Now she sounded as though she were translating from a policeman's testimony. She hoped the brown suit didn't notice. It was important to seem spontaneous, too distraught to be artful. Besides, what she had said was probably accurate. Jean-Jacques would have no reason to feel responsible. As far as he knew she might well go to bed with three different men a week. She had taken him to her room after knowing him only twenty-four hours. *Pourquoi moi, Madame? Pourquoi pas quelqu'un d'autre?* She could imagine the polite, disinterested tone, the closed-down, non-giving thin expression on the thin, handsome lady-killer face, still tan with the mountain sun. Jean-Jacques! If an American woman had to take a French lover, the name didn't have to be *that* French. The hyphen. It was so banal. She cringed now, thinking of the weekend. And her own name. Rosemary. People called Rosemary do not have abortions. They get married in white veils and take advice from their mothers-in-law and wait in station wagons in the evenings in green suburbs for commuting husbands.

"What are your means of support, Madame?" the psychiatrist asked. He sat extraordinarily still, his hands ceramically pale on the green of the desk blotter before him. When she first had come into his office she had been aware that he had swiftly made a judgment on the way she was dressed. She had dressed too well for pity. Geneva was an elegant city. Suits from Dior, Balenciaga, Chanel, glittering in front of the banks and advertisements for chronometers. "Does your ex-husband pay you alimony?"

"He pays for our daughter. I support myself."

"Ah. You are a working woman." If his voice were ever allowed to express anything, he would have expressed surprise.

"Yes."

"What is the nature of your work?"

"I am a buyer."

"Yes?" Of course she was a buyer. Everybody bought things. She knew she had to explain. "I buy things for a department store. Foreign things. Italian silks, French antiques, old glass, English silver."

"I see. You travel extensively." Another mark against her. If you traveled extensively, you should not be made pregnant while skiing. There was something that didn't hang together in the story. The pale hands, without moving, indicated distrust.

"I am in Europe three or four months a year."

"*Donc, Madame,*" he said, "*vous parlez français.*"

"*Mal,*" she said. "*Très mal.*" She made the *très* sound as comically American as she could.

"You are quite free?" He was attacking her, she felt.

"More or less." Too free. If she hadn't been so free, she wouldn't be here now. She had broken off a three-year affair, just before she had come to Europe. In fact, that was why she had stayed in Europe so long, had asked for her holiday in winter rather than in August, to let it all settle down. When the man had said he could get his divorce now and they could marry, she had realized he bored her. Rosemary was certainly the wrong name for her. Her parents should have known.

"What I mean is the milieu in which you live is a liberal one," said the doctor, "the atmosphere is tolerant."

"In certain respects," she said, retreating. She wanted to get up and run out of the room. "Do you mind if I smoke?"

"Forgive me for not offering you a cigarette sooner. I myself do not smoke, so I sometimes forget." He didn't ski and he didn't smoke. There were probably many other things he didn't do. He leaned over and took the lighter from her hands, steadily held the flame to her cigarette. Her hands were shaking. Authentically.

There was a little flare of the psychiatrist's nostril, disapproving of the smoke in his office. "When you travel, Madame, who occupies himself with your daughter? Your ex-husband?"

"A maid. I have full custody." Americanism. Probably stir up some subconscious European aversion. "He lives in Denver. I try to make my trips as short as possible."

"A maid," the man said. "Financially, you could bear the expense of another child."

677

She began to feel panic, small electric twinges behind her knees, a tide in her stomach. The man was her enemy. She shouldn't have depended upon Bert. What did Bert really know about these things? "I'm afraid if it was discovered that I was to have a child I would lose my job. At my age. Ridicule is as dangerous as. . . ." She couldn't think of a forceful comparison. "Anyway, America isn't as free as all that, Doctor. And my husband would sue for custody of my daughter and would most probably win it. I would be considered an unfit mother. My husband is very bitter toward me. We do not speak. We. . . ." She stopped. The man was looking down at his immobile hands. She had a vision of herself explaining it all to her daughter. *Frances, darling, tomorrow the stork is going to bring you a present* . . . "I can't bear the thought," she said. "It would ruin my life." Oh God. She had never thought she would ever bring out a sentence like that. *He isn't going to do it, he isn't going to sign the paper, he isn't.* "As it is, even now, I have days of deep depression, I have unreasonable fears that people come into my room when I sleep, I lock the doors and windows, I hesitate to cross streets, I find myself weeping in public places, I . . ." Be lugubrious, Bert had said. It wasn't difficult, it turned out. "I don't know what I would do, I really don't know, it's so ludicrous. . . ." She wanted to cry, but not in front of that glazed face.

"I suggest these are phases, Madame. Temporary phases. It is my feeling that you will recover from them. It is also my feeling that neither your life nor your mental health will be put into serious danger by having this child. And as you no doubt are aware, I am only permitted, by Swiss law, to advise interruption of pregnancy when . . ."

She stood up, stubbing out the cigarette in the ashtray. "Thank you," she said. "You have my address. You know where to send the bill."

He stood up and escorted her to the door and opened it for her. *"Adieu, Madame."* He bowed slightly.

Outside, she walked quickly down the steep cobbles, toward the lake. There were many antique shops on the narrow street, clean, quaintly timbered, eighteenth century. Too picturesque by half for a day like this. She stopped in front of a shop and admired a leather-topped desk, a fine mahogany sideboard. Swiss law. But it had *happened* in Switzerland. They had no right to, it wasn't *just*. When she thought this, even the way she was feeling, she

678

had to laugh. A customer coming out of the shop glanced at her curiously.

She went down to the lake and looked at the fountain frothing in its snowy column, a flag for swans, high out of the water, and the excursion boats moving sedately like 1900, out toward Ouchy, Vevey, Montreux, in the sunshine.

She felt hungry. Her appetite these days was excellent. She looked at her watch. It was time for lunch. She went to the best restaurant she knew in the town and ordered *truite au bleu*. If you're in a country try the specialties of the country. She had a bottle of white wine that was grown farther down the lake.

Travel in Europe, the advertisements in the magazines announced. Relax in Switzerland.

The afternoon loomed before her, endless.

She could get on one of the steamers and throw herself overboard, in her smart suit, into the blue, polluted lake. Then, when they fished her out, she could go, still dripping, to the man in the brown room and confer once more with him on the subject of her mental health.


"Barbaric," Jean-Jacques was saying. "It is a barbaric country. In France, of course, we are even more barbaric." They were sitting at a table on the *terrasse* of the Pavillon Royal in the Bois de Boulogne, overlooking the lake. The trees were mint-green, the sun surprisingly hot, there were tulips, the first oarsmen of the season were gliding out on the brown water in the rented boats, a young American was taking a photograph of his girl to prove when he got home that he had been in the Bois de Boulogne. The girl was dressed in bright orange, one of this season's three colors, and was laughing, showing American teeth.

Rosemary had been in Paris three days before she had called Jean-Jacques. She had found the scribbled piece of paper in her valise. Business address. Legible foreign handwriting. *Très bien* in *orthographe* in the Ecole Communale. The good little clever boy at the small desk. Finding the folded scrap of paper had brought back the smell of the tidy, scrollwork hotel room on the mountain. Old wood, the odor of pine through the open window, the peppery tang of sex between the sheets. She had nearly thrown the address away again. Now she was glad she hadn't. Jean-Jacques was being human. Not French. He had sounded cautious but pleased on the phone, had offered lunch. In Paris his name hadn't seemed too— too, well, foreordained. In Paris the hyphen was not objectionable.

She had spent the three days without speaking to anyone she

knew in Paris. She had used the telephone once, to call Bert, in London. He had been sympathetic, but useless. He was on his way to Athens. Athens was swinging these days. If any ideas occurred to him among the Greeks, he would cable. Never fear, Love, something will turn up. Enjoy Paris, Love.

She was in a hotel on the Left Bank, not her usual hotel on the Rue Mont Tabor where she was known. She didn't want to see anybody she knew. She was going to think everything out sensibly, by herself. Step one, step two, step three, step one, step two, step. . . . Then she had the sensation that her brain was turning around on itself, inverting, like an Op Art painting. Whorls and squares, making illusory patterns that started and ended at the same point. Then suddenly she had to talk to someone. About anything. She hadn't really meant to tell JeanJacques. What was the use? But then, in the restaurant near her hotel (*sole bonne femme*, a bottle of Pouilly Fumé), he had been so solicitous, he had guessed so quickly that something was wrong, he was so good-looking in his dark suit and narrow tie, so *civilized*, it had all come out. She had laughed quite a lot as she told the story, she had made a humorous character out of the man in the brown suit, she had been brave and worldly and flippant and Jean-Jacques hadn't asked *Pourquoi moi?*, but had said "This must be discussed seriously," and had driven her out to the Bois in his lady-killing British racing green sports car for brandy and coffee in the sunshine. (They must have a four-hour lunch period in his office, she thought.) Sitting there, watching the young men row past the tulips, she didn't regret the snowy weekend quite so much. Maybe not at all. It had amused her, she remembered, to take him away from the tight-flanked young beauties who were lying in wait for him. She remembered the ignoble sense of triumph with which she had managed it, older than all the rest, a hesitant novice skier approaching middle age, not swooping down the slopes like those delicious, devouring children. Jean-Jacques held her hand lovingly on the iron table in the sunshine and she felt wickedly pleased all over again. Not pleased enough to go to bed with him again, she had made that clear. He had accepted that graciously. Frenchmen were much maligned, she thought.

When he had taken out his wallet to pay the bill in the restaurant she had gotten a glimpse of a photograph of a young woman behind a celluloid shield. She had insisted upon his showing it to her. It was his wife, a smiling, serene, lovely girl, with wide-spaced grey eyes. She didn't like the mountains, she hated skiing, he said. He went on weekends alone. Their own business. Each marriage to its own rules. She, Rosemary, would not intrude, could not intrude. Jean-Jacques was sitting there, holding her hand not as a lover, but as a friend whom she needed, who had committed himself, unselfishly, to help her.

"Of course," Jean-Jacques was saying, "whatever it costs, I will . . ."

"I don't need *that* sort of help," she said quickly.

"How much time do you have?" he asked. "I mean, when do you have to be back home?"

"I should be there now."

"And America?"

She took her hand out of his. She remembered some of the stories friends of hers had told her. The darkened rooms in doubtful neighborhoods, the money paid in cash in advance, the sleazy nurses, the criminal doctors, the staggering home two hours later, hurried out of doors which bore no nameplates. "Anything better than my sweet native land," she said.

"I've heard," Jean-Jacques said. "A little." He shook his head. "What countries we inhabit." He scowled, looking across the blare of tulips at the idiocy of nations.

Her mind began to feel like Op Art again.

"I am to go to Switzerland for the weekend. Spring skiing." He gave an apologetic little shrug. "It has been arranged weeks ago. I will stop in Zurich. I have friends there. I will try to find a more sympathetic doctor."

"Psychiatrist."

"Of course. I will be back on Tuesday. Can you wait?"

More Op Art. "Yes." Another week.

"Unfortunately, I must go to Strasbourg tomorrow," he said. "On business. I am to go on to Switzerland directly from there. I will not be able to entertain you in Paris."

"That's all right. I'll entertain myself." Entertain, there's a word. "It's very good of you." Inane, but she wanted to make up in some way for earlier, unspoken judgments on him.

He looked at his watch.

There is always the moment, she thought, when a man, the best of men, looks at his watch.

The phone was ringing in her room when she opened the door. "Eldred Harrison here," a soft British voice said in the receiver. "I'm a friend of Bert's. Like everybody else." A little laugh. "He said you were alone in Paris and I must take care of you. Are you free for dinner?"

"Well. . . ." She prepared her refusal.

"I'm dining with some friends. A small party. We could come by your hotel and pick you up."

She looked around her hotel room. Stained, Wateauesque wallpaper, bulbs too dim to read by. The room joined her brain in Op Art patterns. A week to wait. She couldn't just sit in the room and wait seven days.

"That's very good of you, Mr. Harrison."

"I look forward to it." He didn't say it heartily, but softly and tentatively. "Shall we say eight?"

"I'll be ready," she said.

"At five minutes to eight she was sitting in the hotel lobby. Her hair was pulled back severely and she had put on her most shapeless dress. She didn't want to attract anybody this week, not even an Englishman.

Exactly at eight, a couple came into the lobby. The girl was young, with pale hair and Slavic bones. She was pretty, a little chubby, like a child, and seemed anxious to smile. She obviously didn't have much money to spend on her clothes. Jean-Jacques would have liked her, but he would take her to out-of-the-way restaurants. The man was tall, with greying, well-brushed hair and his hint of a self-deprecating stoop, the discreet cut of his patterned grey suit, went with the voice on the telephone. After the first glance, Rosemary sat there, her ankles crossed primly, waiting. The man spoke to the concierge in French and the concierge indicated Rosemary, sitting near the window. The couple came over. They both smiled.

"I hope we haven't kept you waiting, Mrs. Maclain," Harrison said.

She stood up and gave him her hand, smiling back. There wasn't going to be any trouble tonight.

She hadn't counted on the drinking. Harrison kept to a schedule. One whiskey every fifteen minutes. For everybody, including the girl. Her name was Anna. She was Polish. She had come from Warsaw four months ago. Her papers were doubtful. She worked as a receptionist because she spoke five languages. She wanted to marry an American, for the passport, so she wouldn't be sent back to Warsaw. Strictly a marriage of convenience, she wanted that understood from the beginning, and a quick divorce and the passport.

Harrison did something in the British Embassy. He smiled benignly at Anna, relieved, Rosemary thought, that Anna would not settle for a British passport. He was on the watch for a likely American.

He ordered another round of whiskeys. They seemed to make no difference to him. He sat straight, his hands did not tremble as he lit cigarettes, his voice remained low and cultured and clublike. The Empire had not crumbled because of the likes of him.

They were in a small dark bar near Rosemary's hotel. Convenient little spot, Harrison had said. There were a thousand convenient little spots in Paris for Harrison, Rosemary was sure. He knew most of the people in the bar. Some other Englishmen, about Harrison's age, in their forties, some young Frenchmen. The whiskey arrived on schedule. The bar became somewhat hazy, although Rosemary felt that her eyes were growing dazzlingly bright. Dinner was for the future. They were to dine with a young American. Rosemary couldn't quite make out just where they were to meet him.

They spoke about Bert. Athens. The Army had just taken over in Athens. Bert would like that. He swam in trouble. "I fear for him," Harrison said. "He is always being beaten up. He likes rough trade. One day, I'm sure they'll find him floating in the harbor of Piraeus, some harbor. A peculiar taste."

Rosemary nodded. "I've felt the same thing. I've talked to him about it." Oh, Love, Bert had said, a boy does what a boy has to do, Love.

Anna smiled over her fifth whiskey. She reminded Rosemary of her own daughter, smiling over the rim of a glass of milk at some secret eleven-year-old joke before bedtime.

"I knew somebody else like that," Rosemary said. "An interior decorator. A small, pleasant man. Over fifty. Quiet. Not blatant, like Bert. American. He was beaten to death by three sailors in a bar in Livorno. Nobody ever could figure out what he was doing in Livorno." What was his name? She knew it. She *knew* she knew it. She had met him dozens of times, had talked to him often at parties. He had invented a chair, she remembered. She was annoyed at not remembering his name. A bad sign. If a man you've talked *hours* to, a man who had done something important like inventing a chair is murdered, the least you can do is remember his name. A very bad sign.

Another round of drinks. Anna smiled. The bar grew appreciably darker. Rosemary wished Bert weren't in Athens. Tanks on the streets, curfew, people being rounded up at the point of a gun, nervous soldiers not likely to understand an English fairy's jokes. Be lugubrious, Love.

They walked across a bridge. The river flowed among monuments. Paris is a Bible in stone. Victor Hugo. A taxi driver nearby ran them down and shouted, "*Sales cons*," at them. The voice of Lutetia.

"*Ta gueule*," Harrison called, out of character.

Anna smiled

"The streets are dangerous." Harrison held her elbow protectively. "Chap I know, Frenchman, got into a tangle with another car on a side street near the Opera, the other driver came raging out, hit him once and killed him on the spot. In front of his wife. Turned out to be a karate expert, something along that line."

Anna smiled. "It's worse in Warsaw," she said.

She had been in prison in Warsaw. Only for forty-eight hours, but in prison. They were in the restaurant by this time, but waiting at the bar, with the whiskeys still coming. The American hadn't shown up yet. The restaurant was a small one off the Champs-Elysées, with men sitting alone reading newspapers. On the front page of one of the newspapers there was a large photograph of two fattish middle-aged gentlemen gingerly poking rapiers at each other. There had been a duel that morning in a garden in Neuilly between two representatives of the Chambre des Députés. A little blood had been spilled. A nick in the arm. Honor had been satisfied. France.

"I am only sixteen at the time," Anna was saying. "I am invited to party. A diplomat from Italy. I am in demand in foreign circles because of my languages." She was a mistress of the present tense, Anna. "I still drink only juices of fruit. All the Poles present are arrested."

"*Encore trois whiskeys, Jean,*," said Harrison to the barman.

"The diplomat is smuggling works of art out of Poland." Anna said. "He is a lover of art. The police talk to me for ten hours in small room in prison. They want me to tell them how I help smuggle out works of art and what I am paid. They say they know I am spy, besides. All I can do is cry. I know nothing. When I am invited to party I go to party. A girl goes to party when she is invited. I want to see my mother, but they say they will lock me up and keep me in prison until I talk, they do not tell nobody I am there. Forever." She smiled. "They put me in cell with two other women. Prostitutes. Very bad talking. They laugh when they see me crying, but I cannot stop. They are in prison three months already, they do not know when they must get out. They are crazy for man. Three months too long to go without man, they say. Out of cloth, twisted around, they make an," she hesitated, searching for the word, "an object," she said modestly, "shaped like sex of man."

"Penis," Harrison said, helpfully British.

"They use it on each other," Anna said. "They want to use it on me. I scream and the guard comes and they laugh. They say in three months I be screaming for them to lend it to me." She sipped her drink, smiling. "The next night, I am set free. I am not to tell anybody where I have been. So now I am in Paris and I would like to marry American and live in America."

On cue, the American entered the restaurant. There was a young blond-and-pink *Journey's End* kind of Englishman with him. The American was called Carroll and had a long, gaunt, sunburnt face. He was wearing a leather jacket and a black turtleneck sweater under it. He was a news photographer working for a big agency and had just come back from Vietnam and he explained he was late because he had been waiting in the office for blowups of some of his shots. They hadn't arrived yet. The Englishman had something to do with the BBC and seemed shy. The American kissed Anna, a brotherly kiss. He was not the type to enter into a marriage of convenience.

More whiskey appeared. Rosemary felt radiant. The young Englishman seemed to blush again and again, whenever she caught him looking at her. How much better this was than sitting brooding alone in the hotel room, with lights too dim to read by.

"Prison is the ultimate experience," Harrison was saying, on his schedule of whiskey. Anna's reminiscence had set him off. He had been in a Japanese prisoner-of-war camp for three years. "It is more of a test of character, it is more essential than combat, even."

They were at table. They were eating hors d'oeuvres. The restaurant was famous for its hors d'oeuvres. There were two large carts loaded with plates of tuna, sardines, little radishes, céleri rémoulade, eggs with mayonnaise, raw mushrooms in oil, ratatouille, a dozen different kinds of sausage and pâté. The armies of the poor could be fed indefinitely on these tidbits of Paris. The young Englishman was sitting next to Rosemary. When his knee touched Rosemary's accidentally under the table, he pulled his leg back frantically, as though her knee were a bayonet. The whiskey had been transmuted to wine. New Beaujolais. The purple bottles came and went.

"The guards had a little game," Harrison was saying. "They would smoke a cigarette, very slowly, in front of us. A hundred men, starving, in rags, who literally would have given their lives for a cigarette. There wouldn't be a sound. Nobody would move. We just stood there, our eyes riveted on a little man with his rifle, looking at us over the smoke, letting the cigarette burn away in his hand. Then when it was half-finished, he'd throw it to the ground and trample it with his boot and walk away a few yards. And a hundred men would fling themselves on their knees, punching, scratching, kicking, cursing, to get at the shreds of the tobacco, while the guards laughed at us.''

"The magical East,'' Carroll said. "Some of the things I've seen in Vietnam. . . .''

Rosemary hoped he wouldn't elaborate. She was enjoying her hors d'oeuvres and given half a chance the wine, after all that whiskey, would make her happy to be in Paris. Luckily, Carroll was a taciturn man and didn't go on. All he did was to reach into his pocket and take out a photograph and put in on the table in front of Rosemary. It was the sort of photograph you were used to seeing these days. A woman who looked about eighty years old, in black, squatting against a wall, her hand held out, begging, with a small, starved, almost naked child seated, puppy-eyed, beside her. A slender Eurasian girl, heavily made up, with a bouffant hairdo and a long slit in her silk dress showing a marvelous leg was walking past the old woman without a glance at her. On the wall that filled the background of the picture somebody had scrawled in large chalk letters, God was here, but He left early.

"I took it for my religious editor,'' Carroll said, pouring himself some more wine.

Anna picked up the photograph. "That girl,'' she said. "If I am man I would never look at white women.'' She handed the photograph to the young Englishman, who studied it for a long time.

"In China,'' he said, "I understand there are no more beggars.'' Then he blushed, as though he had said something dirty and put the picture down quickly.

Eldred Harrison tilted his head, birdlike, to peer at the photograph. "The new art of America,'' he said. "Graffiti. Wall-to-wall communication.'' He smiled deprecatingly at his joke.

Carroll put the picture back into his pocket.

"I didn't see a woman for two and a half years,'' Harrison said, starting on his steak.

Paris, Rosemary thought, the capital of dazzling conversation. Flaubert and his friends. She began to try to think of excuses for leaving before the dessert. The young Englishman poured her some more wine, almost filling the deep glass. "Thank you,'' she said. He turned his head away, uncomfortable. He had a beautiful long English nose, blond eyelashes, drawn-in pink cheeks, and full, girlish lips. *Alice in Wonderland* in his pocket during the barrage, Rosemary remembered vaguely, from a summer revival of *Journey's End*. All this talk of war. She wondered what he'd do if she quietly said, *Does anybody here know of a reliable abortionist?*

"We had a large group of Gurkhas in the camp, maybe two hundred," Harrison said, slicing his steak. We are in the Far East for the night, Rosemary thought. "Wonderful chaps. Enormous soldiers. The Japs kept working on them to come over to their side. Brothers-in-color, exploited by the white imperialists, that sort of thing. Gave them extra rations, cigarettes. The Gurkhas would carefully divide the rations with all the other prisoners. As for the cigarettes. . . ." Harrison shook his head in wonderment, twenty-five years later. "They'd accept the cigarettes, without a word. Then, as one man, they'd tear them deliberately to bits. Right in front of the guards. The guards would laugh and next day they'd give them more cigarettes and the same thing would happen. It went on like that for more than six months. Inhuman discipline. Marvelous troops, they were. In all that mud and dust, with people dropping dead all around them." Harrison sipped at his wine. All this seemed to be aiding his appetite, distant deprivation edging today's pleasure. "Finally," he said, "their colonel called them together and said it had to stop, it was degrading that the Japs could still think they could buy Gurkhas. He said a gesture was needed, a convincing gesture. The next day a Jap had to be killed— publicly. They were on work details and were issued shovels. He wanted one man to sharpen the rim of a shovel and when the work details were formed up next morning brain the nearest guard." Harrison finished his steak and pushed the plate an inch away from him, reflecting on Asia. "The colonel asked for a volunteer. Every man stepped forward in one moment, as if it were a parade. The colonel didn't hesitate. He picked the man directly in front of him. The man worked on sharpening his shovel all night with a big stone. And in the morning, in the sunlight, he moved over to the guard who was assigning the details and brained him. He himself was shot immediately, of course, and fifty others were beheaded. But the Japs stopped handing out cigarettes to Gurkhas."

"I'm glad I was too young for that war," Carroll said.

"Excuse me," Rosemary said, standing. "I'll be right back." The ladies' room was upstairs and she climbed the steps carefully, holding onto the banister, trying not to weave. In the ladies' room she put cold water on her eyelids, small remedy against all that whiskey and all that wine and fifty beheaded soldiers. She put on some lipstick, moving her hand very precisely. Her face in the mirror was surprisingly fresh, a nice American lady tourist enjoying a night out in Paris with some of the people you're likely to pick up in a place like Paris. If there had been another door and she could have slipped out unnoticed, she would have gone home.

"Armstead," she said, "Brian Armstead." That was the name of the interior decorator they had found dead in Livorno. He had done Yoga exercises every day, she remembered, and once when she had met him on the beach at Southampton she had noticed that he had a firm brown delicate body with shapely legs and small sunburned feet with polished toenails.

The lights had been turned off outside the ladies' room and the landing was in darkness. Rosemary made her way cautiously toward the glow coming up the stairwell from the restaurant below. She stepped back with a little cry when she felt a hand touch her wrist.

"Mrs. Maclain," a man's voice whispered. "Don't be frightened. I wanted to talk to you alone." It was the young Englishman. He spoke rapidly, nervously. "I saw you were disturbed."

"Not really," she said. She wished she could remember his name. Robert? Ralph? No. She was having trouble with names tonight. "I've been around ex-soldiers before."

"He shouldn't really talk like that," the young man said (Rodney, that was it, Rodney). "Eldred. It's because you're Americans. You and the photographer. He's obsessed with what you're doing in Vietnam, his rooms're cluttered with the most dreadful photographs, he collects them. That's how he got so friendly with Carroll. He's a most peaceful man, Eldred, and he can't bear the thought. But he's too polite to argue with you openly, he's very fond of Americans, so he keeps on about all those other horrors he went through. It's his way of saying, Please stop, no more horror, please."

"Vietnam?" Rosemary said stupidly. She felt foolish talking about things like this in the dark outside the ladies' room with a nervous breathy young man who seemed frightened of her. "I'm not doing anything in Vietnam."

"Of course not," Rodney said hurriedly. "It's just that—well, being American, you see. . . . He really is an extraordinary man, Eldred, it's really worthwhile to get to know him and understand him, you see."

Fags, she thought cruelly. Is that it? But then Rodney said, "May I see you home safely, Mrs. Maclain? That is, whenever you're ready to go home, of course."

"I'm not that drunk," Rosemary said with dignity.

"Of course not," Rodney said. "I do apologize if that's the

impression I . . . I think you're a splendidly beautiful woman, Mrs. Maclain."

He wouldn't have been able to say that if the light were on and she could see his face. *Splendidly*. Right out of Trollope.

"That's very kind of you, Rodney," she said. Neither a yes nor a no. "Now I think we'd better get back to our table."

"Of course," Rodney said. He took her arm and guided her toward the stairwell. His hand was trembling. English education, she thought.

"There was this sergeant we called Brother Three-Iron," Harrison was saying as they came to the table. He stood up as Rosemary sat down. Carroll made a symbolic American move in his chair, theoretically rising. "He was tall for a Jap," Harrison went on, seating himself, "with bulging arms and shoulders and a cigarette dangling all the time from his lips. We called him Brother Three-Iron because he had got himself a golf club somewhere and was never seen without it. When he was displeased, which was often, he beat our people with it. Brother Three-Iron." Harrison spoke fondly, as if the Japanese sergeant and he had many warm memories to share between them. "He was displeased with me more than anyone else in the camp, it seemed, although he had killed several men with the club from time to time. But more or less impersonally. In the rounds of his duty, as it were. But with me, it was a . . . a particular impatience with my existence. When he saw me he would smile and say, 'Are you still alive?' He spoke some English, in that peculiar harmless way Japanese speak the language. I think he must have overheard something I said about him before I knew he could understand. Perhaps I smiled once inadvertently. I lost count of the number of times he beat me senseless. But he was always careful not to finish me off. I believe he was waiting for me to kill myself. That would have satisfied him. It helped keep me alive, the thought of not satisfying him. But if the war had lasted another month or two I doubt that I would have lasted. One last bottle of wine, wouldn't you say?" Harrison gestured toward the only waiter left in the empty restaurant.

"Policemen," Anna said. "They are the same everywhere." She pronounced it "ahveryverhere." She seemed younger than earlier in the evening, much younger. Her eyes were like the eyes of the child in the photograph.

"What happened to the sonofabitch?" Carroll asked. He was slumped in his chair, his chin resting on his chest in ruffles of dark wool from the turtleneck collar, his own bust in thin bronze. "Do you know?"

689

"I know," Harrison said offhandedly. "But it's of no importance. Mrs. Maclain, you must be terribly bored with these sorry reminiscences. I must really have had one too many to drink. I'm sure you didn't come to Paris to hear about a war that took place so far away, when you were just a little girl learning how to read. If Bert hears about this evening he'll be furious with me."

*If you knew what I came to Paris for, brother*, Rosemary thought. She was conscious of Rodney looking at her almost imploringly. "I would like to know what happened," she said.

She could hear Rodney exhale. Relief, she thought. I have passed a test.

"The Japanese have an admirable stoicism about death," Harrison said, pouring the last bottle of wine. His voice was light-timbred, unemphatic. "When the war was over teams came in from our Army to try to round up war criminals. There was a section among the guards that was composed of people very much like the German SS. They were the systematic torturers and interrogators and ex-terminators. There were about twenty of them still in the camp and when the British team came to their quarters they were all lined up at attention in their best uniforms. Before anybody could say a word to them, they went down on their knees and bowed their heads and their commanding officer said, in passable English, to the British major in charge of the party, 'Sir, we are war criminals. Kindly execute us immediately.' " Harrison shook his head, almost amused, almost admiring.

"Did you ever see the sergeant again?" Carroll asked.

"Brother Three-Iron? Oh, yes. Only a few days after the camp was liberated. When they let me out of hospital, I was down to ninety-eight pounds. I weighed a hundred and sixty at the beginning of the war. I was a young man then. I was called to the Camp Commandant's office. The major in charge of the war-crimes team was there. Ellsworth, his name was. A sturdy no-nonsense type. He'd been sent out from North Africa when they closed up shop there. Seen all kinds of fighting. I never saw him smile. Brother Three-Iron was standing in front of his desk. And behind Ellsworth's desk there was the golf club."

Rosemary began to feel very warm. She could sense the sweat breaking out on her throat.

"Brother Three-Iron looked the same as usual. Except that there was no cigarette hanging from his lip. It made a different man of him. It deprived him of authority. After our first glance we didn't look at each other. He gave no sign of recognition and I . . . well, to tell the truth, and I can't really understand it, I felt slightly . . .

embarrassed. After all those years, the situation seemed . . . well, irregular. Wrong. One falls into patterns of behavior and when they are suddenly upset . . .'' Harrison shrugged. ''Ellsworth didn't waste any words. 'I've heard about this fellow,' he said, 'and the way he went for you with that club.' He picked up the club and laid it on his desk, right in front of Brother Three-Iron. Brother Three-Iron looked at it once and something went on behind his eyes, though I couldn't say even to this day what it was. 'Well,'' Ellsworth said, 'the club's yours now.' He pushed it a little way toward me. '*He*'s yours.' But I didn't pick it up. 'What're you waiting for, man?' Ellsworth said. 'I'm afraid I don't understand, sir,' I said. I was telling the truth. I actually didn't. Then Ellsworth began to curse. I've never seen a man so angry. 'Ah, get out of my sight. There're too many like you. You went under. If I had my way you'd never get back to Britain. You'll always be prisoners. You've got the balls of prisoners.' Forgive me, Mrs. Maclain.'' Harrison turned apologetically toward Rosemary. ''I've never told this part of the story before and my memory has remained uncensored.''

''What finally happened?'' Rosemary asked, disregarding the apology.

''I got out of Ellsworth's sight. Never saw him again, either. Luckily for me. His contempt was unendurable. I imagine Brother Three-Iron was eventually executed.'' He looked at his watch. ''It *is* getting late,''  He waved for the bill.

Carroll hunched forward on the wine-stained tablecloth. ''I wish I could be sure that I would have acted the same way as you did,'' he said to Harrison.

''Really?'' Harrison sounded mildly surprised. ''I keep wondering if Ellsworth wasn't right. I might be an entirely different man today.'' He made a failure's gesture.

''I wouldn't want you to be different man,'' Anna said softly.

Harrison patted her hand on the table. ''You're a dear young girl, my Anna,'' he said. ''Oh, perhaps it didn't really matter. In the state I was in it would have taken me weeks to kill him.'' Harrison paid the check and they stood up. ''May I suggest a nightcap? I told some friends I'd meet them in St.-Germain-des-Près.''

''I have to go back to the office,'' Carroll said. ''They promised the blowups'd be in before midnight.''

''It's late for me,'' Rosemary said. ''I have a big day tomorrow.''

The lights went out in the restaurant as they closed the door behind them. There was a wind blowing and the street was dark.

"Well, then," Harrison said, "we'll take Mrs. Maclain home."

"There's no need," Rosemary said.

"I've offered to accompany Mrs. Maclain, Eldred," Rodney said. His voice was tentative.

"Ah, then," said Harrison, "you're in safe hands." He kissed Rosemary's hand. He had been in France for years. "I *have* enjoyed this evening. Mrs Maclain, I hope I may call you again. I must write to Bert and thank him."

They said their good nights. Rosemary said she wanted to walk a bit, to clear her head, and Carroll and Harrison and Anna got into a taxi together, since Carroll's office was on Harrison's way. The taxi dieseled down the dark street into silence. Rosemary allowed Rodney to take her arm and they walked toward the Champs-Elysées without talking.

The cold air hit Rosemary hard and there was an elliptical spin that started at the base of her neck and widened to include the city of Paris. She leaned harder on Rodney's arm.

"I say," he began, "I think a taxi might . . ."

"Shhh," she said. She stopped and kissed him in the last ten yards of darkness before the lights of the boulevard. To create a fixed point. To keep the spin within reasonable limits. His mouth tasted like fresh grapes. He trembled as he kissed her. His face was very warm in the cold spring night wind.

She pulled away, without haste. "Shhh," she said again, although he hadn't said anything.

They walked up the Champs-Elysées. People were coming out of a movie theater. On a giant poster above the entrance, a gigantic girl in a nightgown pointed a pistol the size of a cannon at a thirty-foot-tall man in a dinner jacket. Whores cruised slowly in pairs in sports cars, searching trade. If she were a man, she would try that. At least once. The flesh of Paris spinning against the flesh of Paris. Man and Woman, created He them. At this moment, in the whirling, secret beds of the city, how many were clasped, the world forgot . . . ? Harrison, prisoners' balls, forgetting Asia on the warm young chubby body of the girl from the Warsaw jail? Carroll, with one of those superb fashion models he photographed when he wasn't taking pictures of wars? God was here but He left early, propped against the mantelpiece, to oversee the exercise?

Jean-Jacques, with his hard, expert body, entwined in legitimate abandon with the wide-eyed wife who didn't like to ski, in the great *lit matrimonial* off the Avenue Foch, and a girl in Strasbourg in reserve and another for the weekend of spring skiing, before he stopped off in Zurich to find an obliging psychiatrist?

The various uses and manifestations of the flesh. To caress, to mangle, to behead, to kill with a karate stroke on a city street, to prepare out of cloth a derisive simulacrum of the instrument of sex in a Polish prison. To cherish and despise. To protect and destroy. To clamor in the womb to become flesh. (A boy does what he has to do, Love.) To lie like Armstead, dead in the Livorno alley, with the polished toenails and shapely Yoga brown legs. To turn into Bert with a Greek sailor in besieged Athens, the window open and a view of the Parthenon. Or floating face-down in the oily waters of the harbor of Piraeus. The grapey young kiss of the young Englishman.

Two stout, decorously dressed middle-aged men came out of the café. They were discussing interest rates. Tomorrow would they cross swords gingerly in a garden and claim blood's honor while the photographers clicked away?

A man with a turban passed them. A Gurkha with a shovel, honing it down to a knife edge to avenge the insult of the cigarettes. Violence, costumed, pursues us. Rosemary shivered.

"You're cold," Rodney said and they got into a taxi. She huddled against him, as close as she could get. She unbuttoned his shirt and put her hand on his chest. The skin was soft and hairless; the flesh, unscarred, had never known the harshness of uniforms, the death of prisons. Gentle, that fair English skin, gentle the soft hands.

"I don't want to be alone tonight," she whispered in the dark taxi.

Gentle the uncertain, unfamiliar, undemanding kiss. The winy desires of the Paris night, the torment of the past, the imperious clamor of tomorrow, were made cozy, manageable. Even if she hadn't remembered his name it would have been all right.

They went up to her room together. The night clerk didn't even look up when he handed her the key. They didn't put on the light when they undressed. But then, in bed, it turned out he didn't want to make love to her. He merely wanted to spank her. She repressed the desire to laugh. She allowed him to do whatever he wanted to do. Who was she to be spared?

When he left, toward dawn, he kissed her, gently as ever, and asked if they could meet for lunch. When he had gone through the door she put on the light, went into the bathroom and took off her makeup. Looking into the mirror, she began to laugh, coarse, unstoppable laughter.

# Love on a Dark Street

The night is the time for calls across the ocean. Alone in the hours past midnight in a foreign city, a man's thoughts center on another continent, he remembers loved voices far away, he calculates differences in time zones *(it is eight o'clock in New York, the taxis are bumper to bumper, all the lights are lit)*, he promises himself that there will be a general saving on such things as cigarettes, liquor, and restaurants to make up for the sweet extravagance of several moments of conversation across the three thousand miles of space.

In his apartment on the narrow street behind the Boulevard Montparnasse, Nicholas Tibbell sat, holding a book in his hand, but not reading. He was too restless to sleep, and although he was thirsty and would have liked a beer, he was not resolute enough to go out once more and find a bar that was still open. There was no beer on ice in the apartment because he had neglected to buy any. The apartment, which he had rented from a German photographer for six months, was an ugly, small place, with only two badly furnished rooms, the walls of which were covered by blown-up photographs of emaciated nude women whom the German had posed in what Tibbell considered rather extreme positions. Tibbell spent as little time and thought on the apartment as possible. At the end of six months, the company for which he worked, a large organization which dealt in chemicals on both sides of the Atlantic, would decide whether he was to be kept in Paris or sent somewhere else. If his base was to be permanently in Paris, he would have to find more comfortable quarters for himself. In the meantime, he used the apartment merely for sleeping and for changing his clothes, and tried to keep down the waves of self-pity and home-sickness which assailed him at moments like this, late at night, trapped among the unfleshed contortionists of the German's living room.

From the stories he had heard from other young Americans in Paris, it had never occurred to Tibbell that he would have to face so many nights of loneliness and vague, unformed yearning once he had established himself in the city. But he was shy with girls and clumsy with men and he saw now that shyness and clumsiness were exportable articles that passed from country to country without tax or quota restrictions and that a solitary man was as likely to find himself alone and unremarked in Paris as in New York. Each night, after a silent dinner with only a book for companion, Tibbell, with his neat American haircut, his uncreased, neat Dacron suit, his naïve, questing, blue, polite American eyes, would go from one crowded *terrasse* of St. Germain des Près to another, drinking as little as he dared, waiting for the one brilliant night when he would be noticed by some glorious, laughing band of young people who, with the legendary freedom of the capital, would seize upon him, appreciate him, sweep him along with them in their expeditions among the joyous tables of the Flore, the Epi Club, the Brasserie Lipp and out to the gay and slightly sinful inns in the smiling green countryside beyond Paris.

But the one brilliant night never arrived. The summer was nearly over and he was as alone as ever, trying to read a book, near the open window, through which the warm night breeze carried an erratic distant hum from the traffic of the surrounding city and a thin fragrance of river water and dusty September foliage. The thought of sleep, even though it was after midnight, was intolerable.

Tibbell put down the book (it was *Madame Bovary*, to improve his French) and went over to the window and looked out. He found himself looking out the window a good deal of the time when he was in the apartment. There wasn't much to see. The apartment was one floor up, confronted by tightly locked shutters and flaky soot-grey stone walls. The street was narrow and looked as though it was waiting to be bombed or torn down to make way for a modern prison and at the busiest of times carried very little traffic. Tonight it was silent, and deserted except for two lovers who made a single, unmoving shadow in a doorway diagonally across from him.

Tibbell peered at the lovers with envy and admiration. What a thing it was to be French, he thought, and experience no shame in the face of desire and be able to display it so honestly, on a public thoroughfare. If only he had gone to Paris during his formative years instead of to Exeter!

Tibbell turned away from the window. The lovers kissing in the arch of the doorway across the street disturbed him.

He tried to read, but he kept going over the same lines again and again—"Une exhalaison s'échappait de ce grand amour embaumé et qui, passant à travers tout, parfumait de tendresse l'atmosphère d'immaculation où elle voulait vivre."

He put the book down. He felt much sorrier for himself than for Emma Bovary. He would have to improve his French some other night.

"The hell with it," he said aloud, making a decision, and picked up the phone from its cradle on the bookcase full of German books. He dialed the overseas operator and asked for Betty's number in New York, in his careful, accurate, though unimproved French, which he had learned in two years in Exeter and four at Swarthmore. The operator told him to hold on, saying that there was a possibility that she could put the call through immediately. He began to sweat a little, pleasurably, at the thought of talking to Betty within the next two minutes. He had a premonition that he was likely to say something original and historic tonight and he turned out the light because he felt he could express himself more freely in the dark.

But then the operator came on the line again to say that the call would take some time to put through. Tibbell looked at the radium dial of his watch and told her to try anyway. He pushed the phone to one side and leaned back in his chair with his eyes half-closed, and thought of what Betty's voice would sound like from the other side of the ocean, and how she would look, curled on the sofa of her tiny apartment, twelve stories above the streets of New York, as she spoke into the telephone. He smiled as he remembered the familiar, lovely, small image. He had only known Betty eight months and if the Paris trip hadn't come up two months before, he was sure that a propitious moment would have presented itself in which to ask her to marry him. He was nearly thirty and if he was ever going to get married it would have to be soon.

Leaving Betty behind had been a sorrowful experience and it had only been by the exercise of the stoniest self-control that he had managed to get through their last evening together without risking everything then and there and asking her to follow him on the next plane. But he prided himself on being a sensible man and arriving to take up a new and perhaps temporary job in a new country with a new wife at his side was not his idea of how a sensible man should act. Still, the combination of pleasure and longing with which, hour after hour, he thought of her, was something he had never experienced before and tonight he wanted to make powerful and naked statements to her that until now he had been too timid to voice. Up to now Tibbell had contented himself with writing a letter a day, plus a call on Betty's birthday. But tonight he was irresistibly moved to indulge himself in the sound of her voice and in his own avowal of love.

He waited, impatiently, for the phone to ring, trying to make the time seem shorter by imagining what it would be like if Betty were beside him now, and what they would be saying to each other if they were hand in hand in the same room instead of divided by three thousand miles of humming wire. He had closed his eyes, his head leaning back against the chair, a little smile on his lips as he remembered old whispers of conversation and imagined new exchanges, when he heard voices, harsh and excited, coming through the open window. The voices were passionate, insistent. Tibbell stood up and went to the window and looked down.

Below him, outlined in the light of the street lamp stood three people, tensely together, arguing, their voices sometimes hushed, as though they were trying to keep their quarrel to themselves, and sometimes in bursts of anger, carelessly loud and brutal. There was a man of about sixty, with gray hair and a bald spot, clearly visible from Tibbell's post at the window, and a young woman who was sobbing into a handkerchief, and a young man in a windjacket. The young woman had on a gay, flowered-cotton dress and her hair was blond and piled high on her head in the inevitable Brigitte Bardot style of the season, the ensemble making her look like a stuffed, cleansed little piglet. The old man looked like a respectable engineer or government official, robust and vaguely intellectual at the same time. They were grouped around a Vespa that was parked in front of the building. During the most heated exchanges the young man kept stroking the machine, as though reassuring himself that *in extremis* a means of escape was still available to him.

"I repeat, *Monsieur*," the old man was saying loudly, "you are a *salaud*." His speech had a rotund, self-important ring to it, almost oratorical, as if he were accustomed to addressing large audiences.

"I repeat once more to you, Monsieur Banary-Cointal," the young man said, equally loudly, "I am not a *salaud*." His speech was street-Parisian, rasping, rough, formed by twenty-five years of constant argument with the fellow citizens of his city, but his overall air suggested the student or laboratory assistant or pharmacist's clerk.

The young woman wept, her hands trembling on a large patent-leather purse she was carrying.

"But you are," the old man said, his face close to the other

697

man's face. "The worst kind. Do you wish proof?" It was an oratorical question. "I will give you proof. My daughter is pregnant. Due to your attentions. And what do you do now that she is in this condition? You abandon her. Like a serpent. And to add to the injury, you propose to get married tomorrow. To another woman."

Undoubtedly, the conversation would have had a different ring to it for a Frenchman who happened to overhear it, but to Tibbell's Exeter-cum-Swarthmore ear all spoken French was translated automatically into English that was constructed like a schoolboy's version of excerpts from Racine and Cicero. To Tibbell, all Frenchmen seemed to have a slightly archaic and elevated vocabulary and they always sounded to him as though they were making a speech to a group of senators in the forum or exhorting the Athenians to kill Socrates. Far from annoying Tibbell, it gave an added, mysterious charm to his contacts with the inhabitants of the country, and on the rare occasions when he understood accurately a few words of argot it supplied a piquancy to his relations with the language, as though he had discovered a phrase of Damon Runyon's in Act Three of *Le Cid*.

"I will leave it to the opinion of the most neutral observer," M. Banary-Cointal was saying, "if that is not the action of a man who deserves to be termed a *salaud*."

The young woman, standing stiffly upright, not yet looking pregnant, wept more loudly.

In the shadow of their doorway, the lovers shifted a little; a bare arm moved, a kiss was planted on an ear rather than on lips, a muscular arm took a new hold—but whether that was due to the commotion around the Vespa or to the natural fatigue and need for variation of prolonged *amour* Tibbell could not tell.

Farther down the street a car approached, with bright lights and an Italian roar of motor, but it stopped near the corner, swinging in to park in front of a closed laundry shop, and the lights were extinguished. The street was left to the disputants.

"If I'm getting married tomorrow," the young man said, "it's her fault." He pointed accusingly at the girl.

"I forbid you to go on," said M. Banary-Cointal with dignity.

"I tried," the young man shouted. "I did everything I could. I lived with her for a year, didn't I?" He said this righteously, with pride and self-pity, as if he expected congratulations all around for his sacrifice. "At the end of the year it became clear to me— if I ever wanted a worthy home for any children I might have, I would never get it from your daughter. It is time to speak frankly,

Monsieur. Your daughter conducts herself in an impossible manner. Impossible. In addition, her character is abominable.''

"Be careful in your choice of words, young man," the father said.

"Abominable," the young man repeated. He waved his arms in emphasis and his long black hair fell over his forehead into his eyes, adding to the effect of blind and uncontrollable rage. "As her father, I will spare you the details, but I will permit myself to say that never has a man had to bear such treatment from a woman who in theory shared his home for twelve months. Even the phrase makes me laugh," he said, without laughing. "When you say 'share a home,' you imagine that it means that a woman is occasionally physically present in the foyer—for example, when a man comes home to lunch or when he returns for an evening of peace and relaxation after a hard day's work. But if you imagine that in the case of your daughter, M. Banary-Cointal, you are sadly mistaken. In the last year, M. Banary-Cointal, I assure you I have seen more of my mother, of my maiden aunt in Toulouse, of the woman who sells newspapers opposite the Madeleine, than I have seen of your daughter. Ask for her at any hour of the day or night—winter or summer—and where was she? Absent!''

"Raoul," the girl sobbed, "how can you talk like that? I was faithful from the first day to the last.''

"Faithful!" Raoul snorted contemptuously. "What difference does that make? A woman says she is faithful and believes that excuses everything from arson to matricide. What good did your fidelity do me? You were never home. At the hairdresser, at the cinema, at the Galéries Lafayette, at the Zoo, at the tennis matches, at the swimming pool, at the dressmaker, at the Deux Magots, on the Champs-Elysées, at the home of a girl friend in St.Cloud— but never home. Monsieur''—Raoul turned to the father—"I do not know what it was in her childhood that formed your daughter's character, but I speak only of the results. Your daughter is a woman who has only the most lively detestation of a home.''

"A home is one thing, Monsieur," the old man said, his voice trembling with parental emotion, "and a clandestine and illicit ménage is another. It is the difference between a church and a . . . a . . .'' The old man hesitated, searching for the proper crushing comparison. "The difference between a church and a racecourse.'' He permitted himself a wild smile at the brilliance of his rhetoric.

"I swear to you, Raoul," the girl said, "if you marry me I will not *budge* from the kitchen.''

"A woman will promise anything," Raoul said, "on the night

before a man is due to marry somebody else." He turned brutally to the father. "I will give you my final judgment on your daughter. I pity the man who marries her, and if I were a good citizen and a good Christian, I would send such a man an anonymous letter of warning before he took the fatal step."

The young woman cried out as though she had been struck and threw herself against her father heartbrokenly, to sob against his shoulder. Her father patted her distractedly, saying, "There, there, Moumou," while the girl brokenly repeated, "I love him, I love him, I can't live without him. If he leaves me I'm going to throw myself in the river."

"You see," the father said accusingly, over his daughter's bent, tragic head, "you serpent of ingratitude, she can't live without you."

"That's just too bad," Raoul said, his voice high with exasperation. "Because I can't live *with* her."

"I warn you," the father said, speaking loudly, to be heard above the thunder of his daughter's sobs, "I hold you personally responsible if she throws herself in the river. I, her father, am saying this. Solemnly."

"The river!" Raoul laughed in harsh disbelief. "Call me when it happens. I will personally accompany her. Anyway, she swims like a fish. I'm surprised that a man your age can be innocent enough to be taken in by female guff like that."

Somehow, this last statement enraged Moumou more than anything else Raoul had said. With a sound that was a kind of mixture of growl and air-raid siren, Moumou leapt from the shelter of her father's arms and flung herself on Raoul, hurling him out into the middle of the street, whacking him ferociously with the huge leather bag, holding it by the handle, swinging it again and again like an Olympic hammer-thrower. From the noise it made as it smashed against Raoul's head and shoulders Tibbell calculated that it weighed about ten pounds and was filled with glass and metalware. Raoul raised his arms to protect himself, shouting, dancing backwards, "Moumou, Moumou, you're losing control of yourself!"

To halt the brutal, arching blows of the bag, which were coming in at all angles, he lunged forward and grappled with Moumou, but she continued her attack with her sharply pointed shoes, kicking him pitilessly in the shins and grinding her high, needle-sharp heels into the soft suede of his moccasins. To Tibbell, watching bemused from his window, the couple seemed to be performing some eccentric tribal dance, with their shadows, thrown by the nearby lamppost, whirling around them and up and down the face of the buildings opposite in an elongated African pattern.

"Moumou, Moumou," Raoul shouted hoarsely, as he clutched her and at the same time kept up his painful, jigging dance, to try to avoid the cruel pert heels that dug into his toes. "What good does this do? It solves none of our problems. Moumou, stop it!"

But Moumou, now that she had started, had no mind to stop it. All the indignities, deceptions, and false hopes of her life were welling up in her, finding ecstatic expression in the blows and kicks with which she was belaboring her defaulting partner. The grunts and muffled growls that accompanied her efforts had a note of triumph and wild, orgiastic release in them, hardly fitting, Tibbell thought, for a public performance on a public street. Foreign and American as he was, he was uneasy at the thought of intervention. In New York City, if he had been the witness of a fight between a man and a woman, he would have rushed to part the combatants. But here, in the strange land of France, where the code of behavior between the sexes was at best a titillating mystery to him, he could only wait and hope for the best. Besides, by any system of scoring, the woman was clearly winning by a large margin, delivering all the blows, gaining many points for what is approvingly called aggressiveness in the prize ring and only suffering such incidental damage as came her way when Raoul's head bumped her forehead as she tried to bite him.

The father, who might have been expected to be disturbed by the spectacle of his pregnant daughter locked in hand-to-hand combat with her faithless lover at this odd hour of the morning, never made a move to stop the action. He merely moved along the street with the struggle, circling it warily, keeping a keen eye on the principals, like a referee who is loath to interfere in a good fight so long as the clinching is not too obvious and the low blows unintentional.

The noise, however, had awakened sleepers, and here and there along the street, shutters opened a crack on dark windows and heads appeared briefly, with that French combination of impartiality, curiosity and caution which would lock the shutters fast on the scene of violence with the approach of the first gendarme.

By this time, Moumou had stamped and hammered Raoul some fifteen yards away from the point of the original attack and they were swaying and panting in front of the lovers who had been tranquilly kissing all this time in the shadow of the doorway on the other side of the street. But now, with the noise of battle on their very doorstep, as it were, and the contestants threatening

701

invasion at any moment, the lovers separated, and the man stepped out protectively in front of the figure of the girl he had been crushing so cosily and for so long against the stone doorway. Tibbell saw that the man was short and burly and dressed in a sports jacket and an open-necked shirt. "Here, here," the man in the sports jacket said authoritatively, seizing Raoul by the shoulders and pulling at him, "that's enough of that. Go home and go to sleep."

His appearance distracted Moumou for an instant. "Go back to your doorway fornication, Monsieur!" she said. "We don't need your advice." At that moment, Raoul slid away from her and pounded up the street. "Coward," Moumou shouted, and took off after him, swinging her bag menacingly, running with surprising speed and agility in her high-heeled, pointed shoes. She seemed actually to be gaining on Raoul when he came to the corner and ducked around it, closely followed by Moumou.

The street seemed strangely quiet now and Tibbell could hear the discreet clicking of shutters being closed, now that the principals had departed the scene.

But the father was still there, staring with melancholy, weary eyes at the corner around which he had last seen his daughter disappear, brandishing the patent-leather handbag. He turned his glance on the young man in the sports jacket, who was saying to his girl, "Well, there's a pair for you. Barbarians."

"Monsieur," the father said gravely, "who asked you to meddle in other peoples' affairs? It is the same all over this poor country. Nobody minds his own business any more. Privacy is a thing of the past. No wonder we are on the edge of anarchy. They were on the point of agreement when you destroyed everything."

"Listen, Monsieur," the man in the sports jacket said belligerently, "I am by nature a simple, honorable man. I do not stand by idly while a man and a woman beat each other in my presence. It was my duty to separate them and, if you were not old enough to be my grandfather, I would say that you should be ashamed of yourself for not having separated them sooner."

M. Banary-Cointal examined the simple, honorable man with scientific detachment, as though he were weighing the last statement judiciously, without prejudice. But instead of answering, he turned to the girl, still discreetly in shadow and arranging her ruffled hair with little pats of her hand. "Young woman," the old man said loudly, "you see what's ahead of you? The same thing will happen to you as happened to my daughter. Mark my words, you'll find yourself pregnant and that one"—the old man pointed like a prosecuting attorney at the sports coat—"that one will disappear like a hare in a cornfield."

"Simone," the man in the sports coat said, before the girl had a chance to reply, "we have better ways of spending our time than listening to this old windbag." He pushed a button on the wall next to him and the door against which he and the girl had been leaning opened with an electric buzzing. With dignity, he took the girl's arm and escorted her into the deeper shadow of the inner court. The old man shrugged, his duty done, his warning to a careless generation delivered, as the huge wooden door clicked shut behind the interrupted lovers. Now the old man seemed to be looking around for another audience for his views on life, but the street was deserted, and Tibbell pulled back a bit from the window, fearful of being harangued.

Deprived of further targets for his wisdom, M. Banary-Cointal sighed, then walked slowly toward the corner around which his daughter had vanished in pursuit of Raoul. Tibbell could see him standing there, caught in the dark stone geometry of the city crossroads, a solitary and baffled figure, peering off in the distance, searching the lonely street for survivors.

Now there was the click of shutters again below Tibbell and old women's voices, seeming to rise from some underground of the night, made themselves heard, from window to window.

"Ah," one voice said, "this city is becoming unbearable. People will do anything on the street at any hour. Did you hear what I heard, Madame Harrahs?"

"Every word," a second old voice said in a loud, hoarse, accusing, concierge's whisper. "He was a thief. He tried to snatch her purse. Since de Gaulle a woman isn't safe after dark any more in Paris. And the police have the nerve to demand a rise in pay."

"Not at all, Madame," the first voice said irritably. "I saw with my own eyes. She hit him. With her bag. Thirty or forty of the best. He was bleeding like a pig. He's lucky to be alive. Though he only got what's coming to him. She's pregnant."

"Ah," said Madame Harrahs, "the *salaud*."

"Though to tell the truth," said the first voice, "she didn't seem any better than she should be. Never at home, flitting around, only thinking about marriage when it was too late, after the rabbit test."

"Young girls these days," said Madame Harrahs. "They deserve what they get."

"You can say that again," said the first concierge. "If I told you some of the things that go on in this very house."

703

"You don't have to tell me," said Madame Harrahs. "It's the same on both sides of the street. When I think of some of the people I have to open the door to and say Monsieur Blanchard lives on the third, to the right, it's a wonder I still have the courage to go to Mass at Easter."

"The one I feel sorry for is the old man," said the first concierge. "The father."

"Don't waste your pity," said Madame Harrahs. "It's probably all his fault. He is obviously lacking in authority. And if a man hasn't authority, he has to expect the worst from his children. Besides, I wouldn't be a bit surprised if he didn't have a little thing on the side himself, a little *poupette* in the Sixteenth, like that disgusting lawyer in Geneva. I got a good look at him. I know the type."

"Ah, the dirty old man," the first voice said.

Now Tibbell heard footsteps approaching from the corner and he turned to see the dirty old man approaching. The shutters clicked tight again and the old ladies subsided after their choric irruption, leaving the street to the weary sound of the old man's shoes on the uneven concrete and the asthmatic sighs he emitted with every other step. He stopped below Tibbell's window, looking sorrowfully at the Vespa, shaking his head, then sat down uncomfortably on the curb, his feet in the gutter, his hands dangling loose and helpless between his knees. Tibbell would have liked to go down and comfort him, but was uncertain whether M. Banary-Cointal was in any condition that night to be consoled by foreigners.

Tibbell was on the verge of closing his own shutters, like the two concierges, and leaving the old man to his problems on the street below, when he saw Moumou appear at the corner, sobbing exhaustedly, walking unsteadily on her high heels, the bag with which she had so vigorously attacked Raoul now hanging like a dead weight from her hand. The father saw her too and stood up, with a rheumatic effort, to greet her. When she saw the old man, Moumou sobbed more loudly. The old man opened his arms and she plunged onto his shoulder, weeping and clutching him, while he patted her back clumsily.

"He got away," Moumou wept. "I'll never see him again."

"Perhaps it is for the best," the old man said. "He is far from dependable, that fellow."

"I love him, I love him," the girl said wetly. "I'm going to kill him."

"Now, now, Moumou . . . ." The father looked around him uneasily, conscious of witnesses behind the shuttered windows.

"I'll show him," the girl said wildly. She broke away from her father and stood accusingly in front of the parked Vespa, glaring at it. "He took me out to the Marne on this the first time we went out together," she said in a throbbing voice, meant to carry the memory of ancient tenderness, betrayed promises, to unseen and guilty ears. "I'll show him." With a swift movement, before her father could do anything to stop her, she took off her right shoe. Violently, holding the shoe by the pointed toe, she smashed the sharp heel into the headlight of the scooter. There was the crash of breaking glass and a tinkling on the pavement, closely followed by a shriek of pain from Moumou.

"What is it? What is it?" The old man asked anxiously.

"I cut myself. I opened a vein." Moumou held out her hands, like Lady Macbeth. Tibbell could see blood spurting from several cuts on her hand and wrist.

"Oh, my poor child," the old man said distractedly. "Hold your hand still. Let me see . . ."

But Moumou pulled her hand away and danced unevenly on her one shoe around the Vespa, waving her arm over the machine, spattering the wheels, the handle bars, the saddle, the black pillion, with the blood that sprayed from her wounds. "There!" she shouted. "You wanted my blood, take it! I hope it brings you good luck!"

"Moumou, don't be so impetuous," the old man implored her. "You will do yourself a permanent harm." Finally he managed to grab his daughter's arm and inspect the cuts. "Oh, oh," he said. "This is dolorous. Stand still." He took out a handkerchief and bound her wrist tight. "Now," he said, "I will take you home and you will get a good night's sleep and you will forget about that serpent."

"No," Moumou said. She backed against the wall of the building on the opposite side of the street and stood there stubbornly. "He will come back for his Vespa. Then I will kill him. And after that I will kill myself."

"Moumou . . ." the old man wailed.

"Go home, Papa."

"How can I go home and leave you like this?"

"I will wait for him if I have to stand here in this place all night." Moumou said her words awash with tears. She gripped the wall behind her with her hands, as if to keep her father from taking her away by force. "He has to come here sometime before the church. He won't get married without his scooter. You go home. I will handle him myself."

705

"I can't leave you here alone in this condition," the old man said, sighing. Beaten, he sat down again on the curb to rest.

"I want to die," Moumou said.

The street was quiet again, but not for long. The door behind which the two lovers had taken refuge opened and the man in the sports jacket came out, his arm around his girl. They passed slowly beneath Tibbell's window, ostentatiously ignoring Moumou and her father. The old man looked balefully up at the linked couple. "Young lady," he said, "remember my warning. Profit by the events you have witnessed tonight. If it is not too late already. Reenter into your home, I speak as a friend."

"See here, old man," the man in the sports jacket pulled away from his companion and stood threateningly in front of Moumou's father, "that's enough out of you. I do not permit anybody to speak like that in front of . . ."

"Come on, Edouard," the girl said, pulling the man in the sports jacket away. "It is too late at night to become enraged."

"I ignore you, Monsieur," Edouard said, then let the girl lead him away.

"Permit, permit. . . ." M. Banary-Cointal said loudly, getting in the last word, as the couple rounded the corner and disappeared.

Tibbell watched the old man and his daughter for another moment, wishing that the two of them would move away from their stations of affliction on his doorstep. It would be difficult to sleep, Tibbell felt, knowing that those two grieving, dissatisfied, vengeful figures were still outside his window, waiting for some horrid, violent last act of their drama.

He was just about to turn away when he heard a car door slam far down the street. He looked and saw a woman in a green dress striding swiftly toward him, away from the car that he had earlier noticed being parked near the far corner. Now the car lights switched on, very bright, and the car followed the woman as she half-walked, half-ran, in the direction of Moumou and her father. She was obviously in flight. Her dress shone a violent, electric lime color in the headlights of the pursuing car. The car, which was a bright red, new Alfa Romeo Giulietta, stopped abruptly just before it reached the old man, who was still sitting on the curb, but with his head turned suspiciously in the direction of the woman bearing swiftly down on him, as though he feared that she was bringing with her, stranger though she was, a new burden of trouble to load onto his bowed and tortured shoulders. The woman darted toward a doorway, but before she could press the button for entry, a man in a black suit leaped out of the car and seized her wrist.

Tibbell watched without surprise. By now he felt that the street below him was a preordained scene of conflict, like Agincourt or the pass of Thermopylae, and that clash would follow clash there continually, like the performances in a twenty-four-hour-a-day movie house.

"No, you don't!" the man in the black suit was saying, pulling the woman away from the door. "You don't get away that easily."

"Let me go," the woman said, trying to escape. She was breathless and she sounded frightened and Tibbell wondered if now, finally, was the time for him to run down the stairs and enter into the night life of the street in front of his window, a tardy Spartan, a belated recruit for Henry's army.

"I'll let you go when you give me my three hundred francs," the man in the black suit said loudly. He was young and slender and Tibbell could see, by the light of the automobile headlights, that he had a small mustache and long, carefully brushed hair that fell over the back of his high, white collar. He reminded Tibbell of certain young men he had seen lounging in various bars in the neighborhood of Pigalle, and he had the kind of face which looks fitting in newspaper photographs that accompany the stories of the arrest of suspects after particularly well-planned jewel robberies and pay-roll thefts.

"I don't owe you any three hundred francs," the woman said. Now Tibbell heard that she had an accent in French, probably Spanish. She looked Spanish, too, with luxuriant black hair swooping down over her exposed shoulders, and a wide, shiny black leather belt around a very narrow waist. Her skirt was short and showed her knees every time she moved.

"Don't lie to me," the man in the dark suit said, still holding the woman's wrist and shaking her arm angrily. "It was never my intention to buy them."

"And it was never my intention to let you follow me to my home," the woman snapped back at him, trying to pull away. "Let me go, you've annoyed me enough tonight!"

"Not until I get my three hundred francs," the man said, gripping her more firmly.

"Unless you let me go," the woman said, "I'll call for the police."

The man glared at her and dropped her wrist. Then he slapped her hard across the face.

"Here, here!" said Moumou's father, who had been watching the affair with mournful interest. He stood up. Moumou, lost in

707

the egotism of her own unhappiness, took no notice of what was happening.

The man in the dark suit and the Spanish woman stood close to each other, breathing heavily, looking curiously undecided, as though the slap had brought some new and unexpected problem into their relationship which for the moment confused them and made them uncertain about further action. Then the young man, his white teeth gleaming under his mustache, slowly raised his hand again.

"Once is enough," the woman said and ran over to Moumou's father for protection. "Monsieur," she said, "you have seen him strike me."

"The light is bad," the old man said, even in his sorrow instinctively extricating himself from possible formal involvement with the police. "And at the moment, I happened to be looking the other way. Still," he said to the young man, who was advancing menacingly on the Spanish woman, "let me remind you that striking a woman is considered in certain quarters to be a most serious offense."

"I throw myself on your protection, Monsieur," the woman said, stepping behind M. Banary-Cointal.

"Don't worry," the man with the mustache said contemptuously. "I won't hit her again. She is not worth the emotion. All I want is my three hundred francs."

"What do you think of a man," the woman said, from the shelter of the old man's bulk, "who buys a lady flowers and then demands to be reimbursed?"

"To keep the record clear," the man with the mustache said, "let me say once and for all that I never bought her any flowers. When I went to the toilet she took the violets from the basket and when I came back the woman asked me for three hundred francs and rather than make a scene I . . ."

"Please," the old man said, interested now despite himself, "this is all very confusing. If you would be good enough to start from the beginning, perhaps I can be of service."

Tibbell was grateful to the old man for this request for clarification, since without it he was sure he would be kept awake most of the night trying to figure out just what the sequence of events had been which had resulted in this midnight chase and punishment. Tibbell had never hit a woman in his life and could not imagine ever doing so, and certainly never for three hundred francs which was, after all, worth just about sixty cents.

"Let me reconstruct," the man in the dark suit said immediately, presenting his side quickly, before the Spanish woman could roil the crystal waters of truth. "I saw her sitting at a bar, waiting to be picked up."

"I was not waiting to be picked up," the woman said hotly. "I was on my way home from the cinema and I stopped in to have a glass of beer, before going to bed."

"*Enfin,*" the man in the dark suit said impatiently, "you allowed yourself to be picked up. If we are going to quibble about terms, we will be here all night."

"I allowed you to pay for one glass of beer," the woman said. "I am not responsible for any sordid interpretation you choose to put on it."

"You also allowed me to pay for three hundred francs' worth of violets," the man in the dark suit said.

"I allowed it as a small gesture of gallantry," the woman said haughtily. "In Spain one is used to gentlemen."

"You also allowed yourself to get into my car," the man in the dark suit said, "and you furthermore allowed yourself to inflame the emotions by kissing on the lips."

"That, now," the woman said dramatically to Moumou's father, "is a superb lie."

"If it's a lie," said the man in the dark suit, "what about this?" Violently, he seized the point of his white collar and pulled it away from his neck to show M. Banary-Cointal.

The old man peered at it nearsightedly, bending close to the man in the dark suit. "What is it?" the old man asked. "It's awfully dark here. I can't see anything."

"Lipstick," said the man in the dark suit. "Look." He took the old man's arm and pulled him over in front of the headlights. Both men leaned over low so that the old man could inspect the collar. M. Banary-Cointal stood up. "There's no doubt about it," he said. "Lipstick."

"Aha," said the man in the dark suit, casting a look of angry triumph at the Spanish woman.

"It is not mine," she said coldly. "Who knows where this gentleman has been spending his time and who knows how many times a week he changes his shirt?"

"I warn you," said the man in the dark suit, his voice thick with rage, "I regard that as insulting."

"What difference does it make whose lipstick it is?" the woman said. "You do not please me. All I want is to be allowed to go home alone."

"Ah," said Moumou, her attention finally caught, "if that were only possible—to go home alone."

Everybody, including Moumou's father, looked puzzledly for a moment at the somber figure against the wall, as though it had been a statue that had given cryptic utterance.

"My dear man," said M. Banary-Cointal reasonably, addressing the man in the dark suit, "certainly this lady has made herself very clear." He made a slight bow in the direction of the Spanish woman, who nodded politely in answer. "She doesn't demand very much. Just to go to her own home in peace. Surely, this is not too much to ask."

"She can go wherever she damn pleases," said the man in the dark suit, "as soon as she gives me my three hundred francs."

A look of censure creased the old man's face. "Monsieur," he said, with some asperity, "I am a little surprised that a man like you, the possessor of an automobile of this quality and price"— he touched the gleaming hood of the little Italian car—"could really need three hundred francs enough to make such a . . ."

"It is not a question of three hundred francs," said the man in the dark suit, his voice beginning to be edged, too, at this imputation of miserliness. "It would not even be a question if the sum were fifty thousand francs. It is a question of principle. I have been led on, I have been inflamed, as I mentioned before, I have been induced to spend my money—the amount has nothing to do with the matter, I assure you, Monsieur—all corruptly and under false pretenses. I am a generous and reasonable man but I do not like to be cynically made a fool of by a *putain!*"

"Here, now," the old man said sternly.

"What's more, look at her hand!" The man in the dark suit seized the woman's hand and held it in front of M. Banary-Cointal's eyes. "Do you see that? The wedding ring? By a *putain*, who, on top of everything else, is married!"

Tibbell, listening, fascinated, could not discover why the girl's marital condition added so powerfully to the rage of the man in the dark suit, and concluded that perhaps it was something in the man's past, some painful disappointment with some other married woman that had left him tender on the subject and which now served to pour fuel on the fire of his wrath.

"There is nothing more disgraceful than a Spanish whore with a wedding band," the man in the dark suit shouted.

"Here, that's enough of that," M. Banary-Cointal said with authority, as the woman unexpectedly began to sob. The old man had had enough of women's tears for the night, and this new flood made him testy. "I will not allow you to talk in such terms in front of ladies, one of whom happens to be my daughter," he said to the man in the dark suit. "I suggest you leave immediately."

"I will leave when I get my three hundred francs," the man said stubbornly, crossing his arms.

"Here!" M. Banary-Cointal dug angrily in his pocket and pulled out some coins. "Here are your three hundred francs!" He threw them at the man in the dark suit. They bounced off his chest and onto the pavement. With great agility, the man in the dark suit bent and scooped up the coins and threw them back into M. Banary-Cointal's face. "If you're not careful, Monsieur," the old man said with dignity, "you are going to get a punch in the nose."

The man in the dark suit raised his fists and stood there, in the pose of a bare-knuckle English fighter of the early part of the eighteenth century. "I await your attack, Monsieur," he said formally.

Both women now wept more loudly.

"I warn you, Monsieur," M. Banary-Cointal said, taking a step backwards, "that I am sixty-three years of age, with a faulty heart, and besides, I wear glasses, as you can see. The police will be inclined to ask you some very searching questions in the event of an accident."

"The police!" said the man in the dark suit. "Good. It is the first sensible suggestion of the evening. I invite you all to get into my car and accompany me to the commissariat."

"I am not getting into that car again," said the Spanish woman.

"I am not budging from here," Moumou said, "until Raoul gets back."

There was a ringing behind Tibbell, and he suddenly became conscious that it had been going on for some time, and that it was the telephone. He stumbled across the dark room and picked up the instrument, the voices outside his window becoming a blurred buzzing on the night air. He wondered who could be calling him at this time of the night.

"Hello," he said, into the mouthpiece.

"Is this Littré 2576?" an impatient female voice crackled through the receiver.

"Yes," Tibbell said.

"On your call to New York," the operator said, "we are ready now."

"Oh, yes," Tibbell said. He had forgotten completely that he had put the call in for Betty. He tried to compose himself and put himself back into the tender and rosy mood that had swept over him an hour before, when he had decided to call her. "I'm waiting."

"Just a minute, please." There were some Atlantic, electric howls on the wire and Tibbell pulled the telephone away from his ear. He tried to hear what was being said outside, but all he could distinguish was the noise of a car starting up and surging down the street.

He stood next to the German's bookcase, the telephone held loosely along his cheek, remembering that he had wanted to tell Betty how much he loved her and missed her, and perhaps, if the conversation turned irrevocably in that direction, as indeed it might in the three allotted minutes, to tell her that he wanted to marry her. He found himself breathing heavily, and the ideas churned confusedly in his head, and when he tried to think of a proper opening phrase, all he could think of was, "There is nothing more disgraceful than a Spanish whore with a wedding band."

"Just a moment, please," said an American voice. "We are ringing."

There was some more electrical scratching and Tibbell switched the phone to his other ear and tried to make out what was being said downstairs and at the same time to push from his mind the remark about the wedding band.

"Miss Thompson is not home," the American voice said, with great crispness and authority. "She has left word she will come back in an hour. Do you wish us to put the call in then?"

"I . . . I . . . ." Tibbell hesitated. He remembered the old man's admonition to the girl who had been kissing in the doorway— "Profit by the events you have witnessed tonight."

"Can you hear me, sir?" the crisp New World voice was saying. "Miss Thompson will be back within an hour. Do you wish to place the call then?"

"I . . . no," Tibbell said. "Cancel the call, please. I'll make it some other time."

"Thank you." America clicked off.

Tibbell put the phone down slowly. After a moment, he walked across to the window, and looked down. The street was empty and silent. Thermopylae had been cleared of corpses. Agincourt lay waiting for the plow. Unfinished, unfinishable, unresolved, unresolvable, the conflict, the inextricable opponents, had moved off into the darkness, and now there were only fleeting admonitory echoes, ghosts with warning fingers raised to vanishing lips.

Then Tibbell saw a figure stealing furtively down the other side of the street, keeping close to the walls. It was Raoul. He came out into the light of the lamppost to inspect the scooter. He kicked once at the broken glass on the pavement. Then he waved at the corner. A girl came running out toward him, her white dress gay and dancing and bridal on the dark street. As she sat on the pillion behind Raoul and put her arms lovingly around his waist, she laughed softly. Her laughter rose lightly and provocatively to Tibbell's window. Raoul started the Vespa, with the usual loud, underpowered, falsely important snarl. The Vespa, without headlight, sped down the street, the white dress dancing in the wind, slanting out of sight at the far corner. Tibbell sighed and silently wished the bride luck.

Downstairs, there was the creak of a shutter.

"Spaniards," the night voice said, "what can you expect from Spaniards?"

The shutter creaked again and the voice ceased.

Tibbell closed his own shutters. As he stepped back into the dark room he was thankful for the first time that he had gone to Exeter and Swarthmore for his education.

# Small Saturday

His sleep had been troubled for weeks. Girls came in and out of the misty edges of dreams to smile at him, beckon him, leer at him, invite him, almost embrace him. He was on city streets, on the decks of great ships, in satiny bedrooms, on high bridges, accompanied and not quite accompanied by the phantom figures whom he always seemed on the verge of recognizing and never recognized, as they slipped away beyond the confines of dream, to leave him lying awake in his single bed, disturbed, sleepless, knowing only that the figures that haunted him were sisters in a single respect—they were all much taller than he—and that when they vanished, it was upward, toward unreachable heights.

Christopher Bagshot woke up remembering that just a moment before he opened his eyes, he had heard a voice saying, "You must make love to a woman at least five feet, eight inches tall tonight." It was the first time in weeks of dreaming that a voice had spoken. He recognized a breakthrough.

He looked at the clock on the bedside table. Twelve minutes to eight. The alarm would go off on the hour. He stared at the ceiling, searching for significance. He remembered it was Saturday.

He got out of bed and took off the top of his pajamas and did his exercises. Fifteen push-ups, twenty-five sit-ups. He was a small man, five feet, six, but fit. He had beautiful dark eyes, like a Moroccan burro's, with long lashes. His hair was straight and black and girls liked to muss it. Small girls. In another age, before everybody looked as though he or she had been brought up in Texas or California, his size would not have bothered him. He could have fitted into *Henri Quatre*'s armor. And *Henri Quatre* was large enough to say that Paris was worth a Mass. How the centuries slide by.

"I had this dream," he said. They were standing on the corner, waiting for the 79th Street crosstown bus. Stanley Hovington, five

714

feet, ten inches tall, neighbor and friend, was waiting for the bus with him. It was a cool, sunny, New York October. Two boys, aged no more than fifteen, one of them carrying a football, slouched into Central Park. Each of them was nearly six feet tall. Autumn Saturday. All over the country, long-legged girls wearing chrysanthemums, cheering for Princeton, Ohio State, Southern California. Large, fearsome men, swift on green turf.

"I had a dream last night, too," Stanley said. "I was caught in an ambush in the jungle. It's the damned television."

"In my dream . . ." Christopher said, uninterested in Stanley's nighttime problems. Stanley, too, had to work on Saturdays. He had a big job at Bloomingdale's, but the thing was, he had to work on Saturdays. "In my dream," Christopher persisted, "a voice said to me, 'You must make love to a woman at least five feet, eight inches tall tonight.' "

"Did you recognize the voice?"

"No. Anyway, that isn't the point."

"It would seem to me," Stanley said, "that's just the point. Who said it, I mean. And why." He was a good friend, Stanley, but argumentative. "Five feet, eight inches. There might be a clue there."

"What I think it means," Christopher said, "is that my subconscious was telling me it had a message for me."

The bus came along and they mounted and found seats at the rear, because it was Saturday.

"What sort of message?" Stanley asked.

"It was telling me that deep in my soul I feel deprived," Christopher said.

"Of a five-foot-eight girl?"

"It stands to reason," Christopher said earnestly in the rocking bus. "All my life"—he was twenty-five—"all my life, I've been short. But I'm proud, so to speak. I can't bear the thought of looking foolish."

"Stalin wasn't any taller than you," Stanley said. "He wasn't worried about looking foolish."

"That's the other danger," Christopher said, "the Napoleonic complex. Even worse."

"What are you deprived of?" Stanley asked. "What's her name—that girl—she's crazy about you."

"June," Christopher said.

"That's it, June. Damn nice girl."

"I'm not saying anything against June," Christopher said. "Far from it. But do you know how tall she is?"

"I think you're obsessive on the subject," Stanley said, "to tell the truth."

"Five feet, three. And she's the *tallest* girl I ever had."

"So what? You don't play basketball with her." Stanley laughed, appreciating himself.

"It's no laughing matter," Christopher said gravely, disappointed in Stanley. "Look—you have to figure it this way—in this day and age in America for some goddamn reason, almost all the *great* girls, I mean the *really* great ones, the ones you see in the movies, in the fashion magazines, with their pictures in the papers at all the parties, almost all of them are suddenly *big*."

"Maybe you've got something there," Stanley said thoughtfully. "I hadn't correlated before."

"It's like a new natural resource of America," Christopher said. "A new discovery or a new invention or something. It's part of our patrimony, if you want to talk fancy. Only I'm not getting any of it. I'm being *gypped*. It's like the blacks. They see all these terrific things on television and in the magazines, sports cars, hi-fis, cruises to the Caribbean, only they can't get in on them. I tell you, it teaches you sympathy."

"They're pretty tall," Stanley said. "I mean, look at Wilt Chamberlain."

Christopher made an impatient gesture. "You don't get my point."

"Yeah, yeah," Stanley said, "actually, I do. Though maybe it's more in your imagination than anything else. After all, it doesn't go by *volume*, for God's sake. I mean, I've had girls all sizes; and once it comes down to the crunch, in bed, I mean, size is no criterion."

"You can say that, Stanley," Christopher said, "you have a choice. And I'm not only talking about in bed. It's the whole attitude. It stands to reason. They're the darlings of our time, the big ones, I mean the marvelous big ones, and they know it, and it gives them something extra, something a lot extra. They feel they're superior and they have to live up to it. If they're naturally funny, they're funnier. If they're sexy, they're sexier. If they're sad, they're sadder. If there're two parties that night, they get invited to the better one. If there're two guys who want to take them to dinner, they go out with the handsomer, richer one. And it's bound to rub off on the guy. *He* feels superior. He knows every other man in the place envies him, he's way up there with the privileged classes. But if a small guy walks somewhere with one of the big beautiful ones, he knows that every cat in the place who's two inches taller than he is is thinking to himself, 'I can take that big mother away from that shrimp any time,' and they're just waiting for the small guy to go to the john or turn his head to talk to the headwaiter, to give his date the signal.''

"Jesus," Stanley said, "you've got it bad."

"Have I ever," Christopher said.

Stanley brightened. "I have an idea," he said. "I know some pretty smashing tall girls—"

"I bet you do," Christopher said, loathing his friend momentarily.

"What the hell," Stanley said. "I'll give a party. Just you and me and maybe two or three fellers even shorter than you and four or five girls, five feet, eight and over. . . . A quiet party, where everybody is just sitting or lying around, no dancing or charades or anything embarrassing like that.''

"What're you doing tonight?" Christopher asked eagerly.

"The thing is," Stanley said, "tonight I'm busy. But for next Saturday—"

"The voice said tonight," Christopher said.

They sat in silence, listening to the echo of that ghostly imperative in the back of the cross-town bus.

"Well," Stanley began, his tone dubious, "maybe I could fix you up with a blind date.''

"It's Saturday," Christopher reminded him. "What sort of a girl five feet, eight or over would be available to go out on a blind date on a Saturday night in New York in October?''

"You can never tell," Stanley said, but without conviction.

"I can just see it," Christopher said bitterly, "I'm sitting in a bar waiting, and this big girl comes in, looking around for me, and I get off the stool and I say, 'You must be Jane' or Matilda or whatever, and she takes one look and that expression comes over her face.''

"What expression?"

"That 'What the hell did I let myself in for tonight?' expression," Christopher said. "That 'I should've worn flat heels' expression.''

"Maybe you're too sensitive, Chris.''

"Maybe I am. Only I'll never know until I've tried. Look, I want to get married, it's about time. I want to marry some great girl and be happy with her and have kids, the whole deal. But I don't want to be nagged all my life by the feeling that I did my shopping only in the bargain basement, in a manner of speaking.'' Christopher felt that this was an apt and convincing phrase, considering that Stanley worked in Bloomingdale's. "I want to feel I had a pick from every goddamn floor in the place. And I don't want my kids to look at me when they're nineteen and they're five feet, six, and say, 'Is this as high as I go?' the way I look at my father and mother.'' Christopher's father was even shorter than he was and there was just no use in measuring his mother.

"Do you *know* any big girls?" Stanley asked as Christopher stood up, because they were approaching Madison Avenue. "At least to talk to?"

"Sure," Christopher said. "Plenty of them come into the store." He was the manager of a book-and-record store, one of a chain his father owned. There was a section devoted to greeting cards. Christopher found this demeaning, but his father was profit-minded. When his father retired, Christopher would wipe out the greeting-card section the first week. His father had no complexes about being small. If he had been running the Soviet Union, he would have run it very much along the same lines as Joseph Stalin, only more drastically. Still, Christopher couldn't complain. He was more or less his own boss and he liked being around books and his father was so busy with the more important shops in the chain that he made only flying, unexpected visits to the comparatively minor enterprise over which Christopher presided.

"I *know* plenty of tall girls," he said. "I encourage charge accounts, so I have plenty of addresses." When a tall girl came into the shop, Christopher tried to be on a library ladder, reaching for a book on an upper shelf. "And telephone numbers. That's no problem."

"Have you tried any yet?"

"No."

"Try," Stanley said. "My advice is, try. Today."

"Yeah," Christopher said dully.

The bus stopped and the door opened and Christopher stepped down onto the curb, with a wintry wave of his hand.

Might as well start with the A's, he thought. He was alone in the store. It was impossible to get a decent clerk who would work on Saturdays. He had tried college boys and girls for the one-day-a-week stint, but they stole more than they sold and they mixed up the stock so that it took three days to get it straight again after they had gone. For once, he did not pity himself for working on Saturday and being alone. God knew how many calls he would have to put in and it would have been embarrassing to have someone listening in, male or female. There was no danger of his father's dropping in, because he played golf all day Saturday and Sunday in Westchester County.

*Anderson, Paulette\*\**, he read in his pocket address book. He had a system of drawing stars next to the names of girls. One star meant that she was tall and pretty or even beautiful and that, for one reason or another, she seemed to be a girl who might be free with her favors.

*Anderson, Paulette\*\**, had large and excellently shaped breasts, which she took no pains to hide. June had once told Christopher that in her experience, girls with voluptuous bosoms were always jumping into bed with men, out of vanity and exhibitionism. Treacherously, after his conversation with June, Christopher had added a second star to *Anderson, Paulette\**.

He didn't have her home address or telephone number, because she worked as an assistant to a dentist in the neighborhood and came around at lunch hour and after work. She wore a womanly chignon and was at least five feet, ten inches tall. Although usually provocatively dressed in cashmere sweaters, she was a serious girl, interested in psychology and politics and prison reform. She bought the works of Erich Fromm and copies of *The Lonely Crowd* as birthday presents for her friends. She and Christopher engaged in deep discussions over the appropriate counters. She sometimes worked on Saturdays, she had told Christopher, because the dentist remade mouths for movie actors and television performers and people like that, who were always pressed for time and had to have their mouths remade on weekends, when they were free.

*Anderson, Paulette\*\** wasn't really one of those *marvelous* girls— she wasn't a model and she didn't get her picture in the paper or anything like that—but if she were to do her hair differently and take off her glasses, and didn't tell anybody she was a dental assistant, you certainly would look at her more than once when she came into a room. For the first one, Christopher thought, might as well start modestly. Get the feel.

He sat down at the desk next to the cash register toward the rear of the shop and dialed the number of *Anderson, Paulette\*\**.

Omar Gadsden sat in the chair, his mouth open, the chromium tube for saliva bubbling away under his tongue. Occasionally, Paulette, comely in white, would reach over and wipe away the drool from his chin. Gadsden was a news commentator on Educational Television, and even before he had started to come to Dr. Levinson's office to have his upper jaw remade, Paulette had watched him faithfully, impressed by his silvering hair, his well-bred baritone, his weary contempt for the fools in Washington, his trick of curling the corners of his thin lips to one side to express more than the network's policy would otherwise have permitted him.

Right now, with the saliva tube gurgling over his lower lip and all his upper teeth mere little pointed stumps, waiting for the carefully sculpted bridge that Dr. Levinson was preparing to put permanently into place, Omar Gadsden did not resemble the assured and eloquent early-evening father figure of Educational Television. He had suffered almost every day for weeks while Dr. Levinson meticulously ground down his teeth and his dark, noble eyes reflected the protracted pain of his ordeal. He watched Dr. Levinson fearfully as the dentist scraped away with a hooked instrument at the gleaming arc of caps that lay on a mold on the marble top of the high chest of drawers against the wall of the small office.

He was a sight for his enemies' eyes at that moment, Paulette thought; the Vice-President would enjoy seeing him now, and she felt a motherly twinge of pity, although she was only twenty-four. She had become very friendly with the commentator during the last month of preparing hypodermics of Novocain for him and adjusting the rubber apron around his neck and watching him spit blood into the basin at the side of the chair. Before and after the sessions, in which he had shown exemplary courage, they had had short but informative conversations about affairs of the day and he had let drop various hints about scandals among the mighty and prophecies of disaster, political, financial and ecological, that lay ahead for America. She had gained a new respect from her friends in retelling, in the most guarded terms, of course, some of the more dire items that Omar Gadsden vouchsafed her.

She was sure that Mr. Gadsden liked her. He addressed her by her first name and when he telephoned to postpone an appointment, he always asked her how she was doing and called her his Angel of Hygeia. One day, after a grueling two hours, after Dr. Levinson had put in his temporary upper bridge, he had said, "Paulette, when this is over, I'm going to treat you to the best lunch in town."

Today it was all going to be over and Paulette was wondering if Mr. Gadsden was going to remember his promise, when the telephone rang.

"Excuse me," she said and went out of the office, in a starchy, bosomy white bustle, to her desk in the small reception room, where the telephone was.

"Dr. Levinson's office," she said. "Good morning." She had a high, babyish voice, incongruous for her size and womanly dimensions. She knew it, but there was nothing she could do about it. When she tried to pitch it lower, she sounded like a female impersonator.

"Miss Anderson?"

"Yes." She had the feeling she had heard the voice before, but she couldn't quite place it.

"This is Christopher Bagshot."

"Yes?" She waited. The name meant something, but, like the voice, it was just beyond the boundaries of recognition.

"From the Browsing Corner."

"Oh, yes, of course," Paulette said. She began to riffle through Dr. Levinson's appointment book, looking for open half hours on the schedule for the next week. Dr. Levinson was very busy and sometimes patients had to wait for months. She remembered Bagshot now and was mildly surprised he had called. He had perfect white teeth, with canines that were curiously just a little longer than ordinary, which gave him a slightly and not unpleasantly wild appearance. But, of course, you never could tell about teeth.

"What I called about"—he seemed to have some difficulty in speaking—"is, well, there's a lecture at the Y.M.H.A. tonight. It's a professor from Columbia. 'You and Your Environment.' I thought maybe if you weren't busy. We could have a bite to eat first and . . ." He dribbled off.

Paulette frowned. Dr. Levinson didn't like personal calls while there were patients in the office. She had been with him for three years and he was satisfied with her work and all that, but he was elderly and had old-fashioned notions about employees' private lives.

She thought quickly. She had been invited to a party that night at the home of an economics instructor at NYU, down in the Village, and she hated going into a room full of people alone and Bagshot was a good-looking serious young man who could talk about books and the latest problems very sensibly and would make a welcome escort. But there was Mr. Gadsden in the chair, and his promise. Of course, it had only been for lunch, but she knew his wife was visiting her family in Cleveland this week. She knew because he had come into the office on Monday and made a joke about it. "Doc," he'd said, "this is one week I'm glad to see you. You may tear my jaw apart, but it's nothing to what my father-in-law does to my brain. Without instruments." He had a wry way of putting things, Mr. Gadsden, when he wanted to. If he was alone, she thought, and remembered about lunch, and had nothing to do for the evening . . . It would be OK going to the party at the instructor's apartment with the bookstore boy, but it would be dazzling to walk in and say, "I guess I don't have to introduce Omar Gadsden."

"Miss Anderson," Dr. Levinson was calling testily from the office.

"Yes, doctor," Paulette said, then into the phone: "I'm terribly busy now. I'll tell you what—I'll come by after work this afternoon and let you know."

"But—" Bagshot said.

"Have to run," she whispered, making her voice intimate to give him enough hope to last till five o'clock. "Goodbye."

She hung up and went back to the office, where Dr. Levinson was standing with the new shining set of teeth held aloft above the gaping mouth of Omar Gadsden and Mr. Gadsden looking as though he were going to be guillotined within the next two seconds.

Christopher hung up the phone. Strike one, he thought. The last whisper over the phone had left him tingling weirdly, but he had to face facts. Strike one. Who knew what would happen to a girl like that before five o'clock of a Saturday afternoon? He tried to be philosophical. What could you expect the very first number you called? Still, he had nothing really to reproach himself for. He had not just jumped in blindly. The invitation to the lecture at the Y.M.H.A. had been calculatingly and cunningly chosen as bait for a girl who was interested in the kind of books *Anderson, Paulette*\*\* was interested in. He had carefully perused the "Entertainment Events" section in the *Times* before dialing Dr. Levinson's office and had studied *Cue* magazine and had rejected the pleasures of the movies and the theater as lures for the dental assistant. And she *had* said that she would come by at five o'clock. She wouldn't have said that if she'd felt it was ridiculous for a girl her size to be seen with a man his size. The more he thought about it, the better he felt. It hadn't been a blazing success, of course, but nobody could say it had been a total failure.

Two college students, a boy and a girl, who made a habit of Saturday-morning visits, came in. They were unkempt and unprincipled and they rarely bought anything, at the most a paperback, and he kept a sharp eye on them, because they had a nasty habit of separating and wandering uninnocently around the shop and they both wore loose coats that could hide any number of books. It was fifteen minutes before they left and he could get back to the telephone.

He decided to forget about alphabetical order. It was an unscientific way of going about the problem, dependent upon a false conception of the arrangement of modern society. Now was the time for a judicious weighing of possibilities. As he thumbed through his address book, he thought hard and long over each starred name, remembering height, weight, coloring, general amiability, signs of flirtatiousness and/or sensuality, indications of loneliness and popularity, tastes and aversions.

*Stickney, Beulah*\*\*. He lingered over the page. Under *Stickney, Beulah*\*\*, in parentheses, was *Fleischer, Rebecca*, also double-starred. The two girls lived together, on East 74th Street. *Stickney, Beulah*\*\* was actually and honestly a model and often had her photograph in *Vogue* and *Harper's Bazaar*. She had long dark hair that she wore down loose over her shoulders and a long bony sensational body and a big model's mouth and a model's arrogant look, as though no man alive was good enough for her. But the look was just part of her professional equipment. Whenever she came into the shop, she was friendly as could be with Christopher and squatted unceremoniously on the floor or loped up the ladder when she was looking for books that were in out-of-the way places. She was a great one for travel books. She had worked in Paris and Rome and London and while she bought books about distant places by writers like H. V. Morton and James Morris and Mary McCarthy, when she talked about the cities she had visited, her vocabulary was hardly literary, to say the least. "You've got to get to Paris before the Germans come in again, luv," she would say. "It's a gas." Or, "You'd go ape over Rome, luv." Or, "Marrakesh, luv! Stoned! Absolutely stoned!" She had picked up the habit of calling people luv in London. Christopher knew it was just a habit, but it was friendly and encouraging, all the same.

*Fleischer, Rebecca*\*\* was just about as tall and pretty as *Stickney Beulah*\*\*, with short dark red hair and a pale freckled complexion to go with it and tapering musician's fingers and willowy hips. She was a receptionist for a company that made cassettes and she wore slacks on Saturdays that didn't hide anything. She was a Jewish girl from Brooklyn and made no bones about it, larding her conversation with words like shmeer and schmuck and nebbish. She didn't buy books by the reviews nor by their subject matter, she bought them after looking at the pictures of the authors on the back covers. If the authors were handsome, she would put down her $6.95. She bought the books of Saul Bellow, John Cheever and John Hersey. It wasn't a scientific system, but it worked and she put an awful lot of good writing on her shelf that way. At least it worked in America. Christopher wasn't so sure it would work with foreign authors. She had endeared herself to Christopher by buying *Portnoy's Complaint* and having him gift-wrap it and send it to her mother in Flatbush. "The old bag'll sit shiva for six months when she reads it," Rebecca had said, smiling happily.

Christopher wouldn't have dared send anything more advanced than the works of G. A. Henty to *his* mother and he appreciated the freedom of spirit in Miss Fleischer's gesture. He had never gone out with a Jewish girl, not that he was anti-Semitic or anything like that but because somehow the occasion hadn't arisen. Listening to a Jewish girl in skintight slacks who was five inches taller than he talk the way Miss Fleischer talked was intriguing, if not more. June said that Jewish girls were voracious in bed. June came from Pasadena and her father still believed *The Protocols of the Elders of Zion*, so her opinions on the subject could not be called scientific; but even so, whenever Miss Fleischer came into the shop, Christopher looked carefully for pleasing signs of voracity.

He hesitated over the two names. Then he decided. *Stickney, Beulah*\*\*. A redheaded giantess who was also Jewish would be too much for the first go. He dialed the Rhinelander number.

Beulah sat under the drier in the living room of the three-room flat, with kitchen, that she shared with Rebecca. Rebecca was painting Beulah's nails a luminous pearly pink. The ironing board on which Rebecca had ironed out Beulah's hair into a straight shining sheet of living satin was still in place. Beulah kept looking nervously over Rebecca's bent head at the clock on the mantelpiece of the false fireplace, although the plane wasn't due in at Kennedy until 3:15 and it was only 10:40 now. The girls did each other's hair and nails every Saturday morning, if other amusements didn't intervene. But this was a special Saturday morning, at least for Beulah, and she'd said she was too nervous to work on Rebecca and Rebecca had said that was OK, there was nobody she had to look good for this weekend, anyway.

Rebecca had broken with her boyfriend the week before. He worked in Wall Street and even with the way things were going down there, he had an income that was designed to please any young girl with marriage on her mind. Her boyfriend's family had a seat on the stock exchange, a *big* seat, and unless Wall Street vanished completely, which was a possibility, of course, he had nothing to worry about. And, from all indications, he was approaching marriage, like a squirrel approaching a peanut, apprehensive but hungry. But the week before, he had tried to take Rebecca to an orgy on East 63rd Street. That is, he *had* taken Rebecca to an orgy without telling her that was what it was going to be. It had seemed like a superior party to Rebecca, with well-dressed guests and champagne and pot, until people began to take off their clothes.

Then Rebecca had said, "George, you have brought me to an orgy."

And George had said, "That's what it looks like, honey."

And Rebecca had said, "Take me home. This is no place for a nice Jewish girl from Brooklyn."

And George had said, "Oh, for Christ's sake, when are you going to stop being a nice Jewish girl from Brooklyn?" He was taking off his Countess Mara tie as she went out the front door. So she had nobody this Saturday to look good for and she was putting in some extra time on Beulah's nails, because Beulah had somebody to look good for, at precisely 3:15 that afternoon, to be exact, if the goddamn air-traffic controllers didn't keep the plane from Zurich in a holding pattern between Nantucket and Allentown, Pennsylvania, for five hours, as they sometimes did.

The picture of the man who was arriving at Kennedy that afternoon was in a silver frame on an end table in the living room and another picture of him, in a leather frame, was on the dresser in Beulah's bedroom. In both pictures he was in ski clothes, because he was a ski instructor by the name of Jirg in St. Anton, where Beulah had spent a month the previous winter. In the picture in the living room he was in motion, skis beautifully clamped together, giving it that old Austrian reverse shoulder, a spray of snow pluming behind him. He was at rest in the bedroom, brown, smiling, long hair blowing boyishly in the wind, like Jean-Claude Killy, all strong white teeth and Tyrolean charm. Even Rebecca had to admit he was luscious, Beulah's word for Jirg, although Rebecca had said when Beulah had first reported on him, "John Osborne says in some play or other that having an affair with a ski instructor is vulgar."

"Englishmen," Beulah had said, hurt, "'re jealous of everybody. They'll say anything that comes into their heads, because they zilched the Empire." It hadn't been vulgar at all. On the contrary. It hadn't been like getting involved with a man in the city, worrying about finding a taxi in the rain to get there on time and waking up at seven o'clock in the morning to go to work and eating lunch alone in Hamburger Heaven and worrying if the man's stuffy friends would think your clothes were extreme and listening to him complain about the other men in the office. In the mountains everybody lived in ski pants and it was all snow like diamonds and frosty starlight and huge country feather beds and rosy complexions and being together day and night and incredibly graceful young men doing dangerous, beautiful things to show off for you and eating in cute mountain huts with hot wine and people singing jolly Austrian songs at the next table and all the other girls trying to get your ski teacher away from you both on the slopes and off, and not managing it, because, as he said in his darling Austrian accent, wrinkling that dear tanned face in an effort to speak English correctly. "It is neffer come my way before, a girl so much like you."

Beulah hadn't seen him since St. Anton, but his influence had lingered on. She hadn't been pleased with any man she'd gone out with since she'd come back to America and she'd been saving her money so that she could spend three months at least this winter in the Tirol. Then the letter had come from Jirg, telling her that he'd been offered a job at Stowe starting in December and would she be glad to see him? Beulah had written back the same day. December was too far off, she wrote, and why didn't he come to New York immediately? As her guest. (The poor boys were paid a pitiful pittance in Austria, despite their great skills, and you always had to show practically inhuman delicacy about paying when you went anywhere with them, so as not to embarrass them. In the month in St. Anton she had become one of the most unobtrusive bill payers the Alps had ever seen.) She could afford it, she told herself, because this winter she wasn't going on an expensive jaunt to Europe but would be skiing at Stowe.

"You're crazy," Rebecca had said when she learned about the invitation. "I wouldn't pay for a man to lead me out of a burning building." Sometimes Rebecca's mother showed through a little in her daughter's attitudes.

"I'm giving myself a birthday gift, luv," Beulah had said. Her birthday was in November. "One beautiful brown, energetic young Austrian who doesn't know what's hit him. It's my money, luv, and I couldn't spend it better."

Jirg had written that he liked the idea and as soon as he was finished with his summer job, he would be happy to accept his old pupil's invitation. He had underlined pupil roguishly. He had some clean outdoor job on a farm in the summer. He had sent another picture, to keep his memory green. It was of himself, winning a ski teachers' race at the end of the season. He was wearing goggles and a helmet and was going so fast that the picture was a little blurred, but Beulah was certain she would have recognized him anyway. She had pasted the picture in a big scrapbook that contained photographs of all the men she had had affairs with.

There was one thing really worrying Beulah as she sat in her robe in the living room, watching Rebecca buff her nails. She hadn't yet decided where to put Jirg. Ideally, the best place would be the apartment. She and Rebecca had separate rooms and the bed in her room was a double one and it wasn't as though she and Rebecca were shy about bringing men home with them. And stashing Jirg away in a hotel would cost money and he wouldn't always be on hand when she wanted him. But Rebecca had had an unsettling effect on some of her boyfriends, with her red hair and white skin and that brazen (that was the only word for it, Beulah thought), that brazen Brooklyn camaraderie with men. And let's face it, Beulah thought, she's a wonderful girl and I'd trust her with my life, but when it comes to men, there isn't a loyal bone in her body. And a poor gullible ski teacher who'd never been off the mountain in his life and used to avid girls coming and going in rapacious batches all winter long. . . . And sometimes Beulah had to work nights or go out of town for several days at a time on a job. . . .

She had been puzzling over the problem ever since she got the letter from Jirg and she still hadn't made up her mind. Play it by ear, she decided. See what the odds are on the morning line.

"There you are," Rebecca said, pushing her hand away. "The anointed bride."

"Thanks, luv," Beulah said, admiring her nails. "I'll buy you lunch at P.J.'s" There were always a lot of extra men who ate lunch at P.J.'s on Saturday, with nothing to do for the weekend and an eye out for companionship or whatever, and maybe she could make a connection for Rebecca and get her out of the apartment at least for the afternoon and evening. With luck, for the whole night.

"Naah," Rebecca said, standing and yawning. "I don't feel like going out. I'm going to stay home and watch the game of the week on the tube."

*Shit*, Beulah said to herself.

Then the phone rang.

"Miss Stickney's residence," Beulah said into the phone. She always answered that way, as though she were a maid or the answering service, so that if it was some pest, she could say, "Miss Stickney's not at home. Can I take a message?"

"May I speak to Miss Stickney, please?"

"Who's calling?"

"Mr. Bagshot."

"Who?"

727

"From the Browsing—"

"Hi, luv," Beulah said. "My book on Sicily come in yet, you know the one?"

"It's on order," Christopher said. He was disappointed with this commercial prelude, even though she called him luv. "What I'm phoning for, beautiful," he said daringly, suddenly deciding to be racy and familiar, put himself right up there on her level, so to speak, "what I'm phoning for is what do you say you and me hit the town tonight?"

"Hit what?" Beulah asked, puzzled.

"Well, I thought I just happen to be free and maybe you're hanging loose yourself and we could go to some joint for dinner and then split off downtown to the Electric—"

"Oh, shit, luv," Beulah said, "I'm prostrate with grief. This is Drearsville Day for me. I've got an aunt coming into Kennedy from Denver this P.M. and God knows when I can get rid of her." It was standard policy on her part never to admit that she even *knew* another man when asked for a date.

"Oh, that's all right. . . ."

"Wait a minute, luv," she said. "There's a buzz at the door. Hold fast, like a dear." She put her hand over the phone. "Hey, Becky," she said to Rebecca, who was screwing the top on the nail-polish bottle, "how'd you like to hit the town with a divine—"

"Hit *what*?"

"That beautiful boy from the bookstore is on the phone. He's invited me to dinner. But—"

"That *dwarf*?" Rebecca said.

"He's not so small, actually," Beulah said, "He's very well proportioned."

"I don't go in for comedy acts," Rebecca said. "He'd have to use his ladder even to get into scoring territory."

"There's no need to be vulgar about my friends," Beulah said frigidly, realizing finally that the whole Sixth Fleet wouldn't be able to get her roommate out of the house today. "And I do think it shows a surprisingly ugly side to your character. Prejudice is the word, luv. It's a kind of anti-Semitism, if you want to know what I think."

"Tell him to pick on somebody his own size," Rebecca said, taking the nail polish into the bathroom.

Beulah lifted her hand from the phone. "It was the super with the mail, luv," she said. "Bills and more bills."

"Yeah," said Christopher dispiritedly, "I know how it is." He remembered that Beulah Stickney owed him $47 since July, but of course this was not the time to bring it up. "Well, have a nice time. . . ." He prepared to hang up.

"Hold on, Chris. . . ." That was his name, Christopher. "Maybe something can be salvaged from Be Kind to Aunts Day, after all. Maybe I can get her drunk at the airport or she'll turn out to be suffering from some dreadful female disease and will have to plunge into bed. . . ." The plane was due at 3:15, but you never could tell, it might be held up for engine trouble or darling Jirg, who had never been out of the hills before, might be confused by the wild traffic of the city of Zurich and miss the connection or go to the wrong gate and wind up in Tehran. Or even, the way things were going with airlines these days, the plane could be hijacked or bombed by Arabs or just fall down into a lake in Labrador. One thing she couldn't bear and that was having dinner alone. "I'll tell you what, you just sit there among all those lovely books like a good boy and I'll get on the horn this afternoon and tell you if Auntie looks like conking out or not. What time do you stay open to?"

"Seven o'clock," Christopher said.

"You poor overworked boy," Beulah said. "Stay near the phone, luv."

"Yeah," Christopher said.

"It *was* dear of you to call," Beulah said and hung up. She always concluded on the telephone with "It was dear of you to call" and without saying goodbye. It was original and it spread good will.

She looked at the clock and then went into the bathroom to experiment with her hair.

Christopher put the phone down slowly, the palms of his hands damp. The store felt very warm and he went to the front door and opened it. He stared out at Madison Avenue. People were passing by in the sunlight. Perhaps it was his imagination, but it looked to him as though the tall people on the avenue were strolling and the short ones were, well *burrowing*. He closed the door and went back into the shop, reflecting on his conversation with *Stickney, Beulah\*\**. If luck had been with him, if he'd had a premonition or extrasensory perception or something, he'd have asked to speak to Rebecca Fleischer, instead of Beulah Stickney. The chances were that no aunt of Rebecca Fleischer's was coming in from Denver that afternoon. Now, after having tried to make it with Beulah, he could not call back and ask Rebecca. There were limits.

The girl would be mortally offended, being tapped to go into the game as a substitute, as it were, and he wouldn't blame her.

He didn't trust Beulah's ability to get rid of her aunt before seven o'clock. He had aunts of his own and once they got hold of you, they stuck.

Back to the address book. It was nearly twelve o'clock and people would be going out to lunch and then matinees or linen showers or whatever it was girls went to on Saturday afternoons.

Caroline Trowbridge was in bed with Scotty Powalter. At one time, Caroline Trowbridge had been Caroline Powalter, but Scotty Powalter had found her in bed with his ex-roommate from Yale, Giuliano Ascione, and had divorced her for adultery. It hadn't been a completely friendly divorce. It had been all over the New York *Daily News* and Caroline had been dropped from the social register the next year, but she and Scotty had what they both agreed was a Big Physical Thing for each other and every once in a while they spent a night or a week together until something happened to remind Scotty of his ex-roommate at Yale.

The truth was that Caroline had a Big Physical Thing with almost every man she met. She was a tall, sturdy, inbred, healthy social-register kind of girl who was crazy about boats and horses and Italians and if she had had to swear to it under oath, she wouldn't have been able to say what was more fun—leaping a ditch on an Irish hunter or crewing a Dragon in a force-six gale or going on a weekend to a sinful little inn in the country with one of her husband's best friends.

Despite her catholic approval of the entire male sex, she often regretted not being married to Scotty anymore. He was six feet, four inches tall and built accordingly and the way he behaved in bed, you'd never suspect he came from one of the oldest families along the Main Line in Philadelphia. His family had a place up in Maine with horses and he had a sixty-foot ketch at Center Island and he didn't have to bother with anything boring like working. As she sometimes said to her lovers, if he hadn't been so insanely and irrationally possessive, it would have been the marriage of the century.

He had called her the evening before from the Racquet Club, where he had been playing backgammon. When she recognized his voice on the telephone and he said he was calling from the Racquet Club, she knew he had been losing, because he always got horny when he lost at backgammon, especially on weekends. She'd canceled the man she was supposed to go to Southampton with—after all, husbands, even ex-husbands, came first—and Scotty had come over and she'd opened two cans of turtle soup and they'd been in bed ever since 9:30 the night before. It had been such a complete night that sometime around dawn, he'd even mentioned something about getting remarried. It was almost noon now and they were hungry and she got out of bed and put on a pink terry-cloth robe and went into the kitchen to make some bloody marys, for nourishment. She was always strict with herself about no drinks before 11 o'clock, because she had seen too many of her friends go that route. She was dashing in the Worcestershire sauce when the phone rang.

What Christopher liked about her, he thought, as his hand hovered over the phone, preparing to dial, was that she was wholesome. In the polluted city, she was a breath of fresh country air. If you didn't know about her and her family's steel mills and her divorce and her expulsion from the social register, you'd think she was a girl just in from the farm, milking cows. She came into the shop often, breezing in with a big childish smile, hanging onto a man's arm, a different one each time, and buying large, expensive, color-plate books about boats or horses. She had an account at the shop, but usually the man with her would pay for the books and then she would throw her strong firm arms around her escort and kiss him enthusiastically in gratitude, no matter who was looking.

She had kissed Christopher once, too. Although not in the shop. He had gone to the opening of a one-man show at an art gallery four doors down on Madison Avenue and she was there, too, squinting over the heads of the other connoisseurs at the geometric forms in clashing colors that represented the painter's reaction to being alive in America. Extraordinarily, she was unaccompanied, and when she spotted Christopher, she bulled her way through the crowd, smiling sexily, and said, "My deliverer," and put her arm through his and stroked his forearm. There was something unnatural about her being alone, like a free-floating abalone. Her predestined form was the couple. Knowing this, Christopher was not particularly flattered by her attention, since it was no more personal than a swan's being attracted to a pond or a wildcat to a pine tree. Still, the touch of her capable ex-social-register fingers on his arm was cordial.

"I suppose," she said, "clever man that you are, that you know what all this is about."

"Well . . ." Christopher began.

"They remind me of my trigonometry class at Chatham Hall. That distressing pi sign. Don't they make you thirsty, Mr. —uh?"

"Bagshot."

"Of course. Why don't you and I just sidle out of here like true art lovers and go out into the night and snap on one or two martinis?"

They were nearly at the door by now, anyway, so Christopher said, as brightly as he could, "Right on." The owner of the gallery, who was a business friend of his, was near the door, too, looking at him with a betrayed expression for leaving so quickly. Christopher tried to show, by a grimace and a twitch of his shoulders, that he was under the sway of powers stronger than he and that he would come back soon, but he doubted that he communicated.

They went to the Westbury Polo Bar and sat in one of the booths and ordered martinis and Caroline Trowbridge sat very close to him and rubbed her knee against his and told him how lucky he was to have a vocation in life, especially one as rewarding as his, involved in the fascinating world of books. She had no vocation, she said sadly, unless you could consider horses and sailing a vocation, and she had to admit to herself that with the way the world was going—just look at the front page of any newspaper— horses and boats were revoltingly frivolous, and didn't he think they ought to call a waiter and order two more martinis?

By the time they had finished the second martini, she had his head between her two strong hands and was looking down into his eyes. She had a long torso as well as long legs and she loomed over him in the semiobscurity of the Polo Bar. "Your eyes," she was saying, "are dark, lambent pools." Perhaps she hadn't paid much attention in the trigonometry class at Chatham Hall, but she certainly had listened in freshman English.

Emboldened by alcohol and lambency, Christopher said, "Caroline"—they were on a first-name basis by now—"Caroline, have dinner with me?"

"Oh, Christopher," she said, "what a dear thoughtful thing to say," and kissed him. On the lips. She had a big mouth, that went with the rest of her, and she was pleasantly damp.

"Well," he said when she unstuck, "shall we?"

"Oh, my poor, dear, beautiful little mannikin," she said, "nothing would give me greater joy. But I'm occupied until a week from next Thursday." She looked at her watch and jumped up, pulling her coat around her. "Rum dum dum," she cried. "I'm hideously tardy right this very moment and everybody will be cross with me all the wretched night and say nasty things to me and tweak my ear and suspect the worst and never believe I was in an art gallery, you naughty boy." She leaned over and pecked the top of his head. "What bliss," she said and was gone.

He ordered another martini and had dinner alone, remembering her kiss and the curious way she had of expressing herself. One day, when she was a little less busy, he knew he was going to see her again. And not in the shop.

Oh, damn, she thought as she reached for the phone hanging on the kitchen wall, I forgot to switch it to the answering service. When she expected Scotty over, she made a practice of instructing the service to pick up all calls on the first ring, because nothing infuriated Scotty more than hearing her talk to another man. She loved him, divorce or no divorce, but she had to admit that he was a neurotically suspicious creature.

"Hello," she said.

"Caroline," the male voice said, "this is Christopher—"

"Sorry, Christopher," she said, "you have the wrong number," and hung up. Then she unhooked the phone, so that if he called again, he'd get a busy signal. She still had the bottle of Worcestershire sauce in her hand and she shook a few more spurts into the tomato juice. She added a double shot of vodka, to calm Scotty down, if by any chance he didn't believe that it was a wrong number.

Scotty was lying with his eyes closed, all the covers thrown off, when she came into the bedroom with the bloody marys. He really filled a bed, Scotty; you got your money's worth of man with her ex-husband. His expression was peaceful, almost as if he had gone back to sleep. The phone on the table next to the bed didn't look as though it had been moved, she noted with relief.

"All up on deck for grog," she said cheerily.

He sat up, monumentally, muscles rippling, and swung his legs over the side of the bed. He reached out his hand and took the glass from her, looked at it consideringly, then hurled it against the opposite wall. A good part of the room turned red.

"Oh, Scotty," she said reproachfully, "don't tell me you're being seized by one of your unreasonable moods again." She backed off a little, being careful to avoid broken glass, and took two swift swallows of bloody mary for her nerves.

He stood up. It was an awful sight when he stood up naked like that in a comparatively small bedroom. It was like seeing the whole front line of the Dallas Cowboys wrapped into one moving in on you. The funny scar on his forehead that he had had since his brother had hit him with a baseball bat when they were boys, and

733

which stood out when he was angry, was turning a frightening bright pink.

"Scotty Powalter," she said, "I absolutely forbid you to touch me."

Thank God he only slapped me with an open hand, she thought as she reeled back into a chair, still miraculously holding on to her drink.

"You're unjust," she said from the depths of the chair. "You're a fundamentally unjust man. Hitting a girl for a little old wrong number."

"Some wrong number," he said. "Who's Christopher?"

"How should I know who Christopher is? This voice said, 'Hello, this is Christopher,' and I said—"

"This voice said, 'Caroline,'" Scotty said.

"Sneak," she said. "Listening in on other people's conversations. Is that what they taught you at Yale?" Scotty wasn't really unintelligent, but his thought processes were cumbersome and sometimes you could fuddle him and make him forget his dreadful intentions by attacking him.

"I suppose he was calling up to remind you you had a date to screw him this afternoon," Scotty said. "Knowing how dizzy you are about little matters like that."

"You're fully aware of what I think about your vocabulary, Scotty," Caroline said with dignity.

"Fuck my vocabulary," Scotty said.

"If you must know, and I don't see where it's any business of yours, anyway, considering the nature of our relationship," she said, "I haven't had a date with anybody since a week ago last Tuesday. And if your poor little brain isn't drowned in the mists of alcohol, you'll recall that a week ago last Tuesday, you didn't get out of this very bed until six P.M. Wednesday." As she spoke, she began to believe herself and tears of self-pity formed in her eyes. It was almost like being married again.

"Who's Christopher?" Scotty said. He began to prowl dangerously, like a berserk elephant, and she feared for the lamps and other glassware in the room.

"I'm perfectly willing to tell you," she said, "if you'll stop marauding around like some mad beast in the jungle. You know I've never hid anything *significant* from you."

"Hah," he said, but he stopped prowling.

"He's just a poor little table-model clerk in a bookstore on Madison Avenue," Caroline said. "He's just a little Shetland pony of a man, you'd be ashamed of yourself being jealous of him if you ever saw him.''

"He called you, no matter what size he is," Scotty said stubbornly.

"Sometimes he calls me when he gets in a book he thinks I'd like.''

"*The Child's Manual of Sex*," Scotty said. "*A Thousand and Three Indian Positions.* I can guess what kind of bookstore he runs.''

"That's hardly the way to talk to a woman who's been your wife," Caroline said fastidiously. "If you want to see with your own eyes and convince yourself once and for all, just you get yourself dressed and I'll take you over to Madison Avenue and I'll bet you'll take one look and get down right then and there on your bended knee and beg my forgiveness for the bestial way you've treated me this morning.''

"I don't want to get dressed," Scotty said. "I want a bloody mary and I want to go back to bed. In that order. Make it snappy.''

He was like that. Anger aroused other emotions in him.

He was stretching himself on the bed like some huge beached vessel as she went out of the bedroom toward the kitchen to make another batch of bloody marys. Her head was ringing a little from that Yale-sized slap along the side of her jaw, but she was pleased with her over-all handling of what could very easily have developed into a crisis. As she shook the bloody marys, she hummed to herself. She might, later on, at the proper moment, remind Scotty that along about dawn he had mentioned the possibility of getting remarried. And she was damn well going to get him to write a check to have the bedroom repapered. And if he turned ugly again this afternoon, as he was likely to do, there was always that dear little man waiting patiently on Madison Avenue.

Wrong number, Christopher thought, staring at the dead phone in his hand. Who is she kidding? That was no wrong number. He had an annoyed impulse to dial her again, just to show her that he wasn't being fooled, but decided against it, out of tact. He could imagine all too well why she had said it was a wrong number.

Luckily, a spate of customers entered the store and he was too busy wrapping books and ringing up cash to brood about it.

By the time the store emptied in the lunchtime lull, he had almost convinced himself that it didn't matter at all to him what Caroline Trowbridge did with her Saturday afternoon.

He sat down at the desk by the cash register and took out his address book.

*Toye, Dorothea*\*\*. He would never have given her two stars on his own, although she was pretty enough and if she wasn't exactly five feet, eight inches tall, she was certainly in the neighborhood of five feet, seven and a half. She was not a flashy woman. She was shapely, but in a polite way, and wore simple, sober-colored, almost college-girl clothes, or at least the kind of clothes that girls used to wear in college, and although he guessed she was twenty-eight or twenty-nine, her appearance was demure, her voice low and hesitant, her smile rare. The first two or three times she came into the shop, he had hardly remarked her. But then he had noticed that if there were other men in the shop, even old men or men who at other times seemed to lose themselves in the books, they would slowly begin following her with their eyes and then somehow drift helplessly in her direction. He regarded Dorothea Toye more carefully to see what it was that acted so magnetically on his male customers. He decided that it was probably her complexion. She was always a light tan, with a glow, like a touch of the sun, on her silken skin. She was brilliantly clean. If Caroline Trowbridge looked like a girl just in from a farm, Dorothea Toye looked like a child who had just splashed out of the sea to be dried with a rough towel by her mother. He had been surprised when she had ordered a book of prints by Aubrey Beardsley.

He had been even more surprised when one of his old customers, Mr. O'Malley, who to the best of his knowledge had never spoken a word to the lady, had followed her out of the shop one afternoon at three o'clock and gotten into a cab with her. It was then that he had awarded her her second star. Seeing her get into a cab with Mr. O'Malley heightened his interest in her.

She didn't buy many books, but concentrated for the most part on the small record library against the rear wall, buying albums of every new Broadway musical. At the cut-rate music stores and discount houses farther downtown, she could have gotten the same albums much more cheaply, but as she once told Christopher while he was wrapping the album of *Hair* for her, "I don't go downtown much. I'm really a homebody."

She was an outside chance, Dorothea Toye, but the day was passing swiftly.

He dialed her number. The phone rang and rang and he was just about to give up when it was answered.

"Yes?" The voice was businesslike, but it was Dorothea Toye's.

"This is Christopher Bagshot. . . ."

"Who?" Now the voice was cold and suspicious.

It was a dream of Christopher's that the day would come on

736

which people would not say, "Who?" when he said, "This is Christopher Bagshot."

"From the bookstore, Miss Toye."

"Oh, yes." The voice was warmer but had a hint of puzzlement in it.

"I hope I'm not disturbing you," Christopher said.

"Oh, no, I'm just making myself a bit of breakfast." Christopher looked at his watch. It was nearly one o'clock, and he realized he was hungry. He wondered briefly where Miss Toye could have been the night before to be having breakfast now at one P.M.

"I guess you're surprised, my calling you up like this, I mean," Christopher said, "but I thought—"

"Oh, I get a lot of calls," Miss Toye said. She sounded husky and not demure over the phone.

"I'm sure you do," Christopher said gallantly. "What I am calling about is— I mean, what are you doing tonight?"

Miss Toye laughed peculiarly.

"I could see if I could get some tickets to a show," he said hurriedly, "unless, of course, you've seen them all."

"I'm booked from eight on tonight, honey," Miss Toye said, "but if you want, you could come over right now."

"I can't leave the store," Christopher said, confused by the bluntness of the invitation. "And I don't close till around seven and. . . ."

"Well," Miss Toye said, "I can handle it at seven, if you don't waste any time getting over here. Fifty dollars."

"What was that, Miss Toye?" Christopher said faintly.

"I said my price was fifty dollars." She sounded annoyed at something.

At that moment, the front door of the shop opened and June came in, wearing a raincoat, although there wasn't a cloud in the sky. She waved gaily. Christopher tried to frown in a businesslike way as he cupped the telephone in both hands. He felt himself getting very rosy. "I'm afraid that isn't exactly what I had in mind, madam," he said.

"Look, Mr. Bagshot," Miss Toye said crisply, "you don't give *books* away free, do you?"

June was approaching him swiftly.

"I'll talk it over with my father," Christopher said loudly as June came into earshot, "and perhaps we can come to an arrangement."

Miss Toye's second laugh was even more peculiar than the first one had been. Christopher put the telephone down decisively as June kissed him on the cheek.

"My idea," June said, "is that you close the shop and take me to lunch."

"You know I can't do that." He walked away quickly from the phone and June followed him.

"You have to eat," she said.

"I call the deli and they deliver," he said. He wondered what he could say, without actually hurting her feelings, to discourage her from these raids at all hours.

"You look like someone in the final stages of *mal de mer*," June said. She was studying French at Berlitz in case she ever had the occasion to go to France. "What's the matter?"

"Nothing's the matter. Nothing."

"My God, we're emphatic today," June said. "OK, nothing. You glad I came?"

"As always," he said. His conversation with Miss Toye had done something cramping to his throat and he had difficulty in pronouncing words correctly. Ordinarily, he would have been happy to see June come into the shop, she was a sweet girl, darling, even, at certain times, but her coming in just when Miss Toye was laughing that bruising laugh on the telephone showed an unfortunate, even if unconscious, sense of timing on June's part.

His nose began to run. It was a familiar symptom. Whenever he was under tension, his nose leaked. In school, he always went to exams with three large handkerchiefs in his pockets. He pulled out a handkerchief and blew vigorously.

"Are you catching a cold or something?" June asked.

"Not that I know of." He sneezed. He wondered if any other of Miss Toye's potential clients were affected the same way after a telephone call.

"I know an absolutely fabulous pill that—"

"I am not catching a cold," he said. He blew again.

"You don't have to snap my head off just because I show a normal human interest in your health," June said.

"June," he said, "I'm having a rough day. All alone here in the store and—"

"I'm sorry," June said, instantly contrite. "That's why I came. I thought I might cheer you up. Maybe even help you a little this afternoon. . . ."

"That's awfully sweet of you," he said, aghast at the thought of having June there with Miss Anderson coming in around five o'clock and maybe even Beulah Stickney, too, if she got rid of her aunt. "But it's too complicated with someone who isn't familiar with the stock and all."

"Anyway," June said, "I'm going to have lunch with you. No protests." She certainly was a bossy girl. "I'll go to the delicatessen myself and buy us both a perfectly scrumptious lunch and we'll have a picnic in the office."

There was no getting out of it, so he pulled out his wallet and took a five-dollar bill from it. But June waved it away. "This lunch is on me," she said. "I've had a big week." She worked out of an office that supplied temporary secretarial help and some weeks she made as much as $150. She wouldn't take a permanent job, because she had come all the way East from Pasadena to become a singer. She studied with a man who said he had been responsible for Petula Clark.

Christopher put the five-dollar bill back into his wallet.

"Aren't you insanely happy now I came by?" she asked.

"Insanely," he said.

"Then smile," she said, "and say something nice."

"I love you," he said. That's what she meant when she said say something nice.

"That's better," she said. She kissed him briefly and went out, blonde and small, lovable and intent on marriage, in her raincoat. She always wore a raincoat to protect her throat, just in case.

He thought of Miss Toye and had to blow his nose again.


"Isn't this cozy?" June asked as they ate their roastbeef sandwiches and pickles and drank their milk at the table in the little back office. June was against alcohol because of her throat.

"Uh-huh," Christopher said, chewing hard on a piece of gristle.

"Sometimes, when I'm alone," June said, "and I happen to think of this little room, I'm almost tempted to cry."

The reason she was tempted to cry was that the first time they had kissed, it had been in the little back office. If you wanted to look at it that way, it had all started there. The kiss had been wonderful and it had led to other and better things and there was no denying they had had a lot of fun together and she was a pretty and lively girl, nubile and often gay; but still the dark little office was hardly a shrine, for heaven's sake.

He tried to make himself think unkindly about her. When he was exposed to her for any length of time, he felt himself melting in her direction and once or twice he had been perilously close to asking her to marry him. Maybe if before he had met her he'd known a lot of tall girls intimately and had a standard of comparison, they'd be married already.

Sitting there in the cluttered little office watching her lick mayonnaise off her finger with delicious unself-consciousness, he was tempted to forget his whole damn crusade and ask her to have dinner with him that night, even though he'd lied to her successfully and told her he had to have dinner with his mother and father in Westchester that night—they were getting uptight about never seeing him anymore, now that he'd found a girl. But the front doorbell rang just as he was about to speak and he had to go out into the store and stand around for almost a half hour while an elderly couple shuffled around the poetry counter denouncing Allen Ginsberg and finally buying a play in verse by Christopher Fry that must have been on the shelves since the year one.

While the old couple were still fussing around the store, June had come out of the back office, putting on her raincoat, and had whispered, "I have to go now." She had a date with a girlfriend in front of the Museum of Modern Art and then, since he was busy tonight, maybe they'd go to a concert at Town Hall. "Call me tomorrow. And have a nice evening with your family," she said, and kissed him quickly, at a moment when the old couple had their backs to them.

He had a severe twinge of guilt as he watched the brave little raincoated figure vanish through the doorway. Perfidy did not come easily to him. He even took a step toward the door, to tell her to come back, but at that moment the old lady called, "Young man, I believe we'll take this one," waving the Christopher Fry about like a captured bird.

When he escorted the old couple to the door and opened it for them, he looked across the street and could have sworn that he saw Paulette Anderson walking uptown, holding the arm of a man with wavy gray hair. They seemed to be in earnest conversation.

One more shot, he decided, and then the hell with it.

He went through his address book with the utmost care. He didn't want to have any more Dorothea Toyes sprung on him.

He stopped at the Ms. *Marsh, Susan*\*\*. She wasn't preternaturally tall, but she was a good size and you could be sure she wouldn't ever ask a man $50 for the pleasure of her company. She was a dark girl with green eyes who was politically advanced, although in a quiet, unpushy way. The reason Christopher knew she was politically advanced was that the only books she ever showed an interest in were written by people like Fanon and Marcuse and Cleaver and LeRoi Jones and Marshall McLuhan. She had beautiful legs. It was unsettling to sell books of that nature to a girl with legs as beautiful as that.

She had once told Christopher that he had a good mind. It was then that he had put her name in his address book and given her two stars. She had been caught in the shop by a rainstorm and they had got to talking. It turned out she was from a wealthy family in Grosse Pointe that she despised. She had been one of the youngest girls ever to graduate from Radcliffe and had intended to take her master's in philosophy when she had seen the irrelevance of it all. She expressed disapproval of every book Christopher was displaying at the moment in the window and he said, "Actually, the whole world would be better off if they didn't print another book for the next fifty years."

That's when she said he had a good mind. "Books are dividers," she said. "They form a false elite. To immerse ourselves in the masses, we need song, ritual and bloodshed." She had invited him to a meeting that night she said might interest him, but he had a date with June and he had to decline.

Now, seeing her name in his book, he remembered the rainy afternoon and the quiet beauty of her green eyes and her sensational legs. A girl with legs like that, he thought, doesn't use them just for walking, no matter what her politics are.

He reached for the phone. But just as he was about to pick it up, the front door opened and a huge young man without a hat entered the shop, took three steps into the room and stopped, staring the length of the shop at him with a pensive but at the same time somehow threatening expression on his heavy, handsome face. Six feet, four, Christopher thought automatically. At least.

Christopher moved away from the phone to the new customer, who remained planted and silent in the aisle in a tentlike raglan tweed coat, his face ruddy and athletic, with an old diagonal scar pinkish on his forehead, running down almost into one eye.

"May I help you, sir?" Christopher said.

"No," the man said, continuing to stare fixedly at him. "I'm browsing. This is The Browsing Corner, isn't it?"

"Yes."

"Well, I'm browsing." But the man never looked at a book, just at Christopher, as though he were measuring Christopher for some unpleasant uniform or deciding whether he could use him for some unpleasant purpose.

Christopher turned away to fuss with a display of books on a table. The man didn't move and the only sound from him was a rather hoarse breathing. He was too well dressed to be a stick-up man and he didn't have the look of somebody who was interested in books. Naturally, Christopher couldn't call Susan Marsh with a customer like that in the shop.

Christopher was pleased when a young couple came into the shop and negotiated their way around the huge man in the middle of the aisle and asked if he had a copy of *The Red Badge of Courage*. Christopher knew he didn't have a copy, but he told the young couple to wait while he looked in back. He stayed in back as long as he dared. By that time, the young couple were gone, but the man was still there, still with that fixed, pensive, animal-like stare.

"Have you found anything you like?" Christopher ventured.

"I'm still browsing," the man said. He had the gift of immobility. While Christopher moved nervously from Popular Fiction to Drama to Biography to Greeting Cards, the man stood there, still, mountainlike, only unblinking his eyes flicking in their sockets, to follow Christopher's movements.

This is the worst Saturday afternoon I have lived through in my life, Christopher thought, after it had gone on for what must have been at least half an hour.

Finally, the man said, "Hah!" and shrugged. He smiled slowly. "Thank you," he said, "it's been a nice browse, Christopher." Massively, he departed.

Christopher looked after him, confounded. Christopher! How did the man know his name? He could have sworn he had never seen him before in his life. The city is full of nuts, he said to himself. And it's getting worse.

For some reason, he was trembling and he sat down to calm his nerves. Then he remembered he had had his hand on the phone to call Susan Marsh when the tall stranger had come into the shop. It was a lucky thing he wasn't in the middle of an intimate conversation when the door had opened.

He strode over to the phone, determined not to let himself be shaken. His hand was almost steady as he dialed Susan Marsh's number.

Sue watched closely as Harry Argonaut put the machine together on the carpet in her living room. The time might come when she would have to do it herself and there was no room for error. Harry Argonaut wasn't his real name. It was his nom de plume or, more accurately, his *nom de guerre*. He was a small, pudgy, slow-moving man. Although he was only twenty-four, he was already bald. Fred Drabner, who had brought over the detonating device after lunch, was seated in an Eames armchair, watching Harry

Argonaut attach the last two wires. The machine was to be used that night in Newark. Newark had been picked for the demonstration because it was one of the most explosive communities in America and the bombing of a bank in the heart of the city would create maximum confusion and with luck provoke some shooting by the police and perhaps a few spectacular arrests of innocent passers-by.

The room was quiet as Harry worked. It was a nice room, luxuriously furnished, because Sue got a whopping allowance from her family in Grosse Pointe. Now she gave almost all her money to the movement, but she had leased the apartment and furnished it before she had seen the light. Since it was on a very good block just off Park Avenue, in a converted town house with high-rent apartments and no doorman, it was a perfect place for making bombs.

Harry Argonaut, whose accent could have come from any part of the country, hadn't told them yet who was going to take the machine to Newark. He gave out information sparingly and at the latest possible moment.

He was caressing the little machine lightly when the telephone rang.

Sue looked inquiringly at Harry, waiting for orders.

"Answer it," he said.

She went over to the leather-topped English mahogany desk in front of the windows and picked up the phone. She was conscious of Harry Argonaut and Fred Drabner watching her intently in the lamplight. All the curtains were drawn and the room looked like evening.

"May I speak to Miss Marsh?" the man said on the phone.

"This is Miss Marsh."

"This is Christopher Bagshot, Miss Marsh."

"Who?"

"From the bookstore."

"Oh, yes." Her tone was noncommittal and she watched Harry Argonaut for signs.

"I was wondering if you'd like to have dinner with me tonight, Miss Marsh."

She thought the man sounded strange, as though the simple sentence was for some reason costing him a great deal of effort to get out.

Harry Argonaut was moving his lips elaborately, silently mouthing the question, "Who is it?"

"Hold on for a moment, please, Mr. Bagshot," Sue said. "A

743

friend of mine is just leaving and I have to say goodbye." She put her hand over the phone. "It's a man called Bagshot," she said to Harry. "He works in the bookstore on Madison Avenue."

"What does he want?" Harry asked.

"He wants to take me to dinner tonight."

"Let me think," Harry said. That was one reliable thing about Harry—he always took time to size up every situation and figure out what advantage might be drawn from it. "Do you know him well?" he asked.

"I've spoken to him four or five times, that's all."

"Do you think he suspects anything?"

"Oh, no. He's a harmless little man." She regretted the little. Harry was no taller than Mr. Bagshot.

"Why is he calling at this hour on Saturday to ask you for dinner?"

Sue shrugged. "Maybe his girl stood him up and he's lonely."

"How did he get your telephone number?"

"It's in the book, for one thing," Sue said. She was used to Harry's intense questioning by now. "And I have a charge account with him besides."

"Get an unlisted number first thing Monday," Harry said.

Sue nodded. She wondered if Bagshot was still on the phone.

Harry thought for thirty seconds, kneeling on the carpet, his eyes closed in concentration.

"Tell him you can't give him an answer now," he said, "but that you have to pass by his shop in a half hour or so and you'll drop in and tell him then. Go ahead."

Sue nodded. She didn't know what was in Harry's mind, but whatever it was, it was part of a greater plan.

"Mr. Bagshot," she said, "are you still there?"

"Yes." His voice was eager.

"I'm sorry to have kept you waiting so long, but—"

"Oh, that's perfectly all right, Miss Marsh," he said.

"I'm a little up in the air right now," Sue said, "and I'm late for an appointment. But I'll be passing by your shop in a half hour or so. I ought to be sorted out by then; and if I can possibly make it, I'd adore having dinner with you." Being in the movement was a lot like being in the theater. The better you were as an actress, the more effective you were as a revolutionary.

"That's fine, Miss Marsh," Bagshot said. The way he said it, you could tell his life was full of postponements, if not worse. "I'll be waiting."

She hung up.

"Well done," Harry Argonaut said.

She flushed with pleasure. Coming from him, that was high praise, indeed.

Without speaking, Harry got up off his knees and went to the hall closet and took out the blue tennis bag that a small boy had delivered to her apartment three days before. She had asked the boy no questions and had put the bag in the closet, hiding it behind a leather-and-canvas valise from Mark Cross that her father had given her as a Christmas present.

Harry brought the tennis bag into the living room and opened it. It was jammed with crumpled sheets of the *Newark Evening News* and the *Newark Star-Ledger*. While Sue and Fred Drabner watched him silently, he took out some of the newspapers and made a nest of those that remained and lovingly fitted the machine into the nest. Then he zipped up the bag and snapped a small padlock through the two overlapping eyelets in the brass zipper tags.

"Now," he said to Sue, "you're going to put on your nicest, most respectable dress and you're going to walk over to Madison Avenue carrying the tennis bag. You'll go into the shop and tell this fellow Bagshot that you haven't been able to get hold of this man you have a tentative date with, but you'll know definitely by six o'clock. You have some shopping to do, meanwhile, you say, and can you leave the bag there until you come back. You've got all that now?"

"Yes," Sue said and repeated word for word what he had told her.

"It's always safer policy," Harry said, "to store material in a place other than the one where the material is assembled. That way, if one cover is broken, all the others remain intact."

Sue wished Harry would let her take notes when he delivered his rare instructive generalities, but she knew it was out of the question.

"After you deposit the bag," Harry Argonaut said, "you come back here. I will not be here and neither will Fred. At a quarter to six, your phone will ring. A voice you will not recognize will say, 'I'll meet you at a certain corner.' If the person adds, 'At the southwest corner of Twenty-third Street and Eighth Avenue, at six-thirty,' you will do the following. You will add ten to twenty-three, that makes Thirty-third Street, subtract one from eight, that makes Seventh Avenue, you will add one hour to the time, that makes seven-thirty, and you will reverse the compass points, that makes northeast corner. Got it?"

"Repeat, please," Sue said.

Harry repeated his instructions patiently. Then he made her repeat them back to him twice, until he was satisfied there would be no mistake. When he was certain that she knew what she was to do, he went on, "At six o'clock, you will go to the bookshop. You will tell the man that you'd be delighted to have dinner with him, but you have to go to a cocktail party, but that you'll meet him at a restaurant at eight-fifteen. Choose the restaurant yourself. Make sure that it is a crowded one, where you are well known. After you have made the contact and delivered the bag, take a taxi downtown to the Village. Get out in front of a restaurant there. When the taxi has gone, hail another taxi and go to the restaurant where you're going to meet the man from the bookstore."

"All clear," Sue said.

"Keep him out as late as possible. If he suggests going to his place, by all means do so. Just be back here at four A.M., for possible further instructions."

Sue nodded, then frowned.

"What is it?" Harry asked. He was terribly alert, even for the smallest signs.

"I have no money for all those taxis," Sue said. "I gave Fred my last ten dollars yesterday. And my allowance doesn't come in before the first."

Harry thought patiently about the absence of money. "Cash a check," he said.

"It's Saturday afternoon," she said, "the bank is closed. Anyway, I'm overdrawn this month."

Harry thought patiently again. "Cash a check in the bookstore. Is he good for a hundred, do you think?"

"I can try."

"Do the best you can," Harry said. "Now go get dressed." He was stuffing the extra newspapers from the tennis bag into the fireplace and once again Sue had to admire him for his foresight. If anything went wrong and the tennis bag were found, with the Newark newspapers in it, there would be nothing in her apartment that even by the wildest chance could connect her with the event. As she was pulling on a soft brown wool dress with a midiskirt, she could hear the crackling from the fireplace in the living room as the papers went up in flames.

She went back into the living room and put on a tweed coat over the brown dress and picked up the tennis bag. How invariably clever Harry was, she thought. Who would suspect that a well-dressed, aristocratic-looking girl carrying a tennis bag had destruction at her fingertips; saw, in her mind's eye, Park Avenue in ruins, Madison Avenue smoldering in the cleansing fire of revolution? She wanted to ask Harry when she was going to see him again. But she knew better and all she said was goodbye.

One hundred dollars, Christopher thought as he watched the door close behind Miss Marsh. I wonder if I wasn't a little excessive. He took the check out of the cash-register drawer and examined it once more, interested in the handwriting. It was bold but controlled, generous but intellectual. He put the check back into the cash-register drawer and picked up the blue tennis bag and carried it into the back office for safekeeping. He tried to keep his excitement down. The bag was a hostage, a guarantee that she would return. And she had said that she was almost one hundred percent sure that she would be free to have dinner with him tonight. And she hadn't been political at all during her brief visit, but sort of twinkly and almost coquettish, especially when he had been enterprising enough to say that it was a shame a girl like her, with legs like that, thought she had to wear a midiskirt, to be in fashion.

It was the most hopeful thing that had happened to him all day, he thought.

When Sue opened the door to her apartment with her key, she didn't have the time to be surprised that Harry and Fred were still there. There were four other men in the living room and they immediately turned out to be detectives.

Harry had handcuffs on his beautiful slender wrists, and he spoke to her quickly in a loud clear voice, "Don't say anything until we get a lawyer."

At exactly the moment that Sue Marsh was arrested, Beulah Stickney was in the glassed-in visitors' gallery at Kennedy peering down at the floor where the passengers from Zurich were waiting for their baggage before going through Customs. Quite a few miles away to the west, in a one-room apartment on East 87th Street that Omar Gadsden used, he said, when he was kept in town too late to go to his home in Mount Kisco, Paulette Anderson was fighting weakly to keep the silvery-haired commentator from tearing off her cashmere sweater.

"Please," she said plaintively, struggling to sit up on the day bed on which she somehow had been trapped. "Please. . . ." He had gotten one hook of her brassiere undone. It was like wrestling with a man with ten arms. It was obscene for a man with that much gray hair to be so strong. "You mustn't, Mr. Gadsden," Paulette said, half smothered by a shoulder that butted into her mouth. "Really, you mustn't."

"Come on, treasure," Mr. Gadsden said hoarsely, all his ten arms working at once.

It was nice being called Treasure, even nicer than Angel of Hygeia, but she would have preferred it at a distance.

His behavior had come as a complete surprise. He had been fatherly and wise at lunch, suggesting delicious dishes and talking authoritatively about campus disorders and the ABM and Nixon's Southern strategy and integration and the relation of the G.N.P. to ecological decay in America. She didn't remember ever having a more informative lunch. He hadn't even tried to touch her hand in the restaurant. It had been so friendly and he seemed to be enjoying her company so much that she had ventured to say that she was invited down to a party in the Village that evening where he would meet some young people who would be wildly interested to hear his views. And he had said yes, he'd like to go, he knew a nice little place on Ninth Street where they could have dinner first. She had hoped that he would take her to a movie to fill in the time between lunch and dinner, but he said he was exhausted from the morning session with Dr. Levinson, as well he might be, poor man, and why didn't they go to this place of his that he kept for emergencies and play some music on the hi-fi and just relax until it was time to go downtown. Although she was disappointed about the movie, she told herself that she could go to a movie any time and when would she ever get the chance again to have Omar Gadsden for an entire afternoon, with the knowledge that when the evening came, she was going to give her friends something to talk about for months to come.

But in the meantime, Mr. Gadsden was working powerfully on her stockings. There was a fiendish ingenuity to his attack. When she defended one place, the assault shifted, with demonic energy, to another. If this was the way he was when exhausted, he must be perfectly shocking when fresh. If his public were to see him now, she thought, they might take his pronouncements on public morality with a grain of salt.

Suddenly, he stopped. He didn't move away, but he stopped. He looked at her, wrinkling his lovely gray eyebrows inquiringly. His hair was tousled and he looked sad and disturbed. As long as he didn't move, she liked him very much. If you had to do it with an old man, she thought, he wouldn't be a bad one to start with. She lay on the couch, disheveled, skin showing here and there.

"What is it?" he asked. "Are you a Lesbian?"

She began to cry. Nothing as bad as that had ever been said to her before, she said. What she didn't tell him was that she was something even stranger. She was a virgin. She felt that she would die of shame if Mr. Gadsden found out that she was a virgin.

She sobbed bitterly, not knowing whether it was because Mr. Gadsden had asked her if she was a Lesbian or because she was a virgin. He took her in his arms and stroked her hair and kissed her tears away and said, "There, there, treasure," and in eight minutes she was lying naked on top of the day bed and Mr. Gadsden was taking off his shirt. She kept her eyes averted from him and looked at the photographs on the walls, of Mr. Gadsden with President Kennedy and Mr. Gadsden with Mayor Lindsay and Mr. Gadsden with John Kenneth Galbraith. When the moment comes, she thought, I'll close my eyes. I can't bear the thought of doing it in front of all those important people.

Mr. Gadsden seemed to be taking a long time and she looked over at him out of the corner of her eye. He was putting his shirt on.

"I'm sorry," he said. "You'd better get dressed. I can't go through with it."

She closed her eyes to shut out the sight of Mr. Gadsden, President Kennedy, Mayor Lindsay, John Kenneth Galbraith.

But she couldn't shut her ears. "I looked down at you, lying there, so young and perfect," Mr. Gadsden was saying, "and I thought of you in your white uniform performing those humble necessary tasks in Dr. Levinson's office, peering in at my bleeding jaws with all those weird little stumps of teeth, the ugly maw of age, and I thought, Omar Gadsden, you are trading on innocence and pity, you despicable old lecher; it is unbecoming and disgusting."

It was too bad that she was in no condition to appreciate him at that moment, because later on she realized he had never been as eloquent or convincing on any of the programs on which she had seen him.

"Get dressed, Paulette," he said gently, living up to his image. "I'll go into the bathroom until you're ready."

He left the room and she dressed slowly, half hoping he would come out and say he'd changed his mind. She didn't know how she'd ever be able to get this far with a man again.

But he didn't come out until she was fully dressed and had put up her hair, which had fallen loose in the scuffling.

He poured stiff whiskeys and they sat in elegiac silence in the dying light of the late October afternoon. When she reminded him

749

timidly that he'd wanted to go to the party downtown, he said his jaws were hurting him and he was going to stay home and nurse them.

They had another drink and it was dark when she left his apartment, leaving him sunk in a chair, swishing whiskey around his wounded gums.

She remembered that she had told the boy in the bookstore that she'd come in around five. She didn't really make a decision, but she started across toward Madison. She had to go downtown tonight anyway, she told herself.

People came crowding into the baggage and Customs area from Immigration in clotted lumps of tourism and there was so much milling around that it would have been hard to pick out your own mother from the visitors' gallery, let alone a man you had only seen for thirty days in your whole life nine months before. Beulah peered through the plate glass anxiously, trying to spot Jirg, with people all around her waving spastically to relatives on the floor below and holding up babies and waving the babies' hands for them.

Finally, she saw him and she took a deep breath. He was wearing a long black-leather coat, down to his ankles, like an SS officer, and a green Tyrolean hat, with a feather. He was warm and he opened his coat and took off his hat to fan his face. Under the coat, he was wearing a bright-green tweed suit. Even from where she was standing, the bumps on the tweed looked like an outbreak of green boils. And when he took his hat off, she saw that he had gotten a haircut for his trip. A good economical haircut that would last a long time, probably until next spring. A wide pale expanse showed under the high, sharp hairline on the back of his neck, and his ears, she noticed for the first time, stuck out alarmingly from the bare pink scalp. Out of a sense of style, he was wearing long pointed Italian blue-suede shoes and fawn-colored suede gloves.

She regretted that she was farsighted.

Before he could see her, she shrank back away from the window to think. She wheeled and ran down a corridor and went into the ladies' room. She looked around her wildly. There was a Tampax vending machine on the wall. "Thank God," she said. She pushed past a square little Puerto Rican lady with three little girls and fumbled for a coin and put it into the machine.

When she came out of the ladies' room, she didn't bother to go back to the visitors' gallery, but went directly to the exit where the passengers came out after clearing Customs. She fixed a wan smile on her lips and waited.

When he finally came out of Customs, he was thriftily carrying his own bags and sweating. He had put on weight since the end of the skiing season and his face was curiously round. He was short, she noticed, almost as short as the bookstore boy. Was it possible that he could have shrunk since last winter? When he saw her, he dropped his bags, making an old lady behind him stumble, and roared "*Schatzl*" at her and nearly knocked down a child of three running over to embrace her.

The leather coat smelled as though it had been improperly cured, she noted as he kissed her, and he had doused himself with airline lavatory perfume. If I have a friend at this airport who recognizes me, she thought as she permitted herself to be chucked under the chin, I shall sink through the floor.

"Here," she said, "we'd better get your bags out of the way. I'll help you."

"Finally in your country I come," Jirg said as they gathered up the bags and started toward the taxis. "Where is the nearest bed?"

"Sssh," Beulah said. "They understand English here." Her eyes swiveled around uneasily. The people on both sides of her looked very thoughtful.

"They giff me a big party for farewell, the boys," Jirg said. For the first time she realized his voice had been trained for shouting instructions to people caught in distant avalanches. "They know you wait for me. You should hear some of the jokes they make. You would laughing die."

"I bet," Beulah said.

They got into a taxi, Jirg holding onto the little air travel bag he was carrying.

"Where to, lady?" the driver asked.

Oy, she thought. "I'll tell you when you cross the bridge to Manhattan," she said.

The driver gave her a look. "Games," he said. He was one of those insufferable New York taxi drivers. He started his car with a neck-snapping jerk.

Jirg put his hand on her knee and looked conqueringly into her eyes. He had his hat on again.

"And what was the weather like?" she asked lovingly. "In Austria this summer, I mean."

"Always rain," he said. "Sometimes hail." He stroked her knee. In Austria it would have sent her through the ceiling with desire. His hands were horny with callus and she could hear him making snags in her stocking.

"Did you enjoy your trip?"

"Filthy," he said. "The plane was all *Amerikaners*. Maybe they are all right in their own country, but they haff no *Kultur* when they voyage. Except for one *Amerikanerin* I know." He leered seductively at her. He had had his teeth fixed since she had seen him last and one molar and one front tooth were pure gold. His hand went up her thigh, snagging thread.

"How was the food on the plane?" she asked, grabbing the other hand fondly, to immobilize it. She regretted not having worn culottes that day. They didn't offer much protection, but they offered some.

"Swiss food," he said. "For cows. And they make you pay for drinks. The Swiss love one thing. Money."

"All airlines charge for drinks in tourist class," she said, sweetly reasonable.

"Drink," he said. "Oh, that reminds me." He smiled benevolently. "I brought my *Amerikanisches Schatzl* a gift."

In the rearview mirror, she saw the taxi driver grimace, as though he had a gas pain. Jirg took his hand off her leg and dug in the air travel bag on the seat beside him and took out a small squarish unlabeled bottle. She recognized the shape of the bottle and felt her duodenum contract.

Jirg proudly held up the bottle. "See," he said, "I remembered."

It was a drink she loathed, a Tyrolean home product made up of odds and ends of herbs and poisonous weeds that grew in dank spots near precipices in the Alps. Jirg imbibed it in huge quantities, like a giant intake valve. She had pretended to be one of the boys in Austria and had expressed her enthusiasm for the foul stuff. He twisted the cork and offered her the bottle. A smell came out of the neck of the bottle like old and ill-cared-for animals.

She took a ladylike sip, managing not to gag.

He took a huge swig. "Ach," he said, nostalgically, "the nights we drank together."

"Hey, lady," the taxi-driver half turned his head, scowling. "No drinking allowed in this cab."

"You'll have to put the bottle away, luv," Beulah said. "He says it's against the law."

"It is not believable," Jirg said. "Drinking against the law. He is making fun of me. I believe he is a Jew." Jirg's face turned a sudden Master Race purple. "I haff heard about New York."

"He isn't a Jew, luv, he's an Irishman." She looked at the

752

driver's ticket, stuck in its frame at the back of the front seat. The man's name was Meyer Schwartz. "Put the bottle away, luv. We'll drink it later."

Muttering in German, Jirg put the bottle back in the air travel bag. The driver swerved the taxi in front of a truck, missing it by seven inches.

By the time they reached the cutoff to Shea Stadium, Jirg's hand was all the way under her skirt, sliding under her panties. She was surprised it had taken that long. Luckily, she was in the right hand corner of the back seat and the driver couldn't see what was happening in his mirror.

Jirg panted convincingly in the region of her neck, while his hand worked expertly between her thighs, his middle finger amorously exploring. She lay back, tense but waiting. Suddenly, the middle finger stopped moving. Then it moved again, two or three sharp scientific probes. Jirg took his hand away abruptly and sat up.

"*Scheisse*," he said, "*vas ist das?*"

"That's fate, luv." Beulah sat up, too.

"Fate? I do not know that word."

"It means what will be will be."

"Speak slowly."

"It means I have the curse, luv."

"Who cursed?" he said. "So, I said *Scheisse*."

"It's a word American girls use when they are temporarily out of commission. Not in working order. Not ready for visitors."

"Four thousand miles I flew," Jirg said piteously.

"Mother nature, luv," Beulah said. "Take heart. It only lasts a few days. For most girls." She was preparing him for the moment when she would tell him it sometimes went on with her for months, especially in the autumn.

"Vat vill I do for a few days?" Jirg whined.

"Sight-see," Beulah said. "I think the boat that goes all around Manhattan Island is still running."

"I did not come to New York to go boat riding," Jirg said. He looked bleakly out the window at the passing architecture. "New York is a pigsty," he said.

He sat in silence, disapproving of New York, until they had crossed the Triborough Bridge.

"We are in Fun City, lady," the taxi driver said. "Where to?"

"That motel on Ninth Avenue," Beulah said. "I forget the name." She had never been inside it, but it looked clean, efficient and inexpensive from the outside. It had the added charm of being distant from her flat. She was sure there would be ice water for Jirg, probably running out of the taps, which would entertain him for a day or two.

"We are not to your apartment going?" Jirg asked.

"I was going to explain about that, luv," Beulah said nervously. "You see, I have a roommate."

"Does she ski?"

"That isn't the point, luv. She . . . she is neurotically puritanical. Religious."

"So?" Jirg said. "I am also religious. Nobody is more religious than Austria. I will talk religion with your roommate."

"She believes it is immoral for unmarried girls to sleep with men." Beulah was briefly thankful that Rebecca was not there to overhear this comment.

"I did not come to New York to be married," Jirg said warily.

"Of course not, luv. But just to keep peace in the apartment, it would be better if you stayed in a hotel for the first few days. Until she gets used to you."

"In Austria," Jirg said, "I haff slept in the same room with two girls. In the same *bed*."

"I'm sure you have, luv," Beulah said soothingly. "But we have different customs here. You'll catch on in no time."

"I do not like New York," Jirg said gloomily. "I do not like New York at all."

At the motel, which was not as inexpensive as it looked, Beulah got Jirg a single room with a shower. He wanted her to go up with him, but she said she was poorly, because of her malady; he could see how pale she was, she wouldn't even have stirred from her bed that day if he hadn't been arriving from Zurich; and if she didn't go home and lie down with a cold compress, she probably would faint right there in the lobby. She gave him $30 in American money, because all he had with him was Austrian shillings and Swiss francs, and told him to eat in the hotel so he wouldn't get lost. If she was strong enough that evening, she said, she would call him.

She watched him follow the bellboy with his bags to the elevator. When the elevator doors slid shut behind him, she sprinted for the main entrance.

She walked blindly cross-town. By Eighth Avenue, she had decided she was going skiing in Sun Valley this winter. By Seventh Avenue, she had decided to take an offer for a modeling job in Brazil that meant leaving by Tuesday. By Sixth Avenue, she decided she wasn't going home before midnight, because she wasn't going to give Rebecca the satisfaction. By Fifth Avenue, she realized that that meant having dinner alone. By Madison Avenue, she remembered Christopher Bagshot. She went into a bar and sat alone over a white lady, trying to decide which was worse.

It was past six o'clock, 6:15, to be exact, and Sue Marsh hadn't shown up at the bookstore for her tennis bag. Christopher was beginning to worry. He could not keep open, waiting for her. He was disappointed in her. He hadn't thought of her as a flighty girl who made idle promises. And Miss Anderson hadn't come into the store at five o'clock, either, as she had said she would. He knew he should be angry at the type of girl who treated a man with so little consideration, but what he really felt was desolation.

Then the door opened from the comparative darkness of Madison Avenue and a tall girl with straight blonde hair came into the store. She was wearing a miniskirt that showed a great length of leg, and a hip-length fun fur, more or less electric-blue in color. He had never seen her before and from the uncertain way she moved around the shop, it looked as though she had never been in a bookstore before. He moved briskly toward her. "Is there anything I can do for you, miss?" he said.

She had big gray eyes that seemed to be imploring him. She was beautiful, in a strange, haunted way, like some of those movie actresses in Swedish pictures who have affairs with their brothers or sisters. An incoherent, unreasonable hope stirred in his breast. "Do you have any cookbooks?" she said.

"We have a selection. This way, please."

"Thank you very much," she said, in a near whisper. Her voice trembled. He wondered if she was a young wife who had a fancy dinner to prepare that evening for her husband's boss or somebody and who had met disaster in the kitchen an hour or so before the guests were to arrive. Saturday evening at 6:15 was a queer time to buy a cookbook. He didn't catch sight of a wedding ring, though.

He hovered near. "Just what sort of cooking are you interested in? French, Italian, American . . . ?"

"Oh, any kind."

"There's an amusing one that has come out fairly recently," he said. Because it was getting so late, he resolved to be daring. "*The Myra Breckinridge Cook Book*, by a friend of the author, Gore Vidal. It's quite risqué." He chuckled, to show that she could take his risqué or leave it alone. "Here, let me get it down for you." He reached for the shelf. It wasn't there. He had seen it when he closed the shop the night before and he knew he hadn't sold it since. Somebody had stolen it during the day. "I'm afraid I've sold the last copy," he said lamely. "If you'll give me your name and address, I'll order one and—"

"Oh, there's no need to bother, thank you," she said softly. Just from the tone of her voice, you knew she wasn't the sort of girl who would say she'd come by at five o'clock and never show up, or the kind of girl who deposited a tennis bag and then irresponsibly left it with you while she consorted with New Left agitators who made love in public parks.

The girl took down a huge illustrated book on French cooking and opened it at random to a page on which there was a color photograph of *poularde de Bresse en cocotte*. She stroked the page absently. "Chicken," she said.

"You like chicken?" It was awfully pedestrian, but he had to keep the conversation going. If she had been at the literary-criticism counter, the dialog would have been more inspiring.

"I love it," the girl said. "Chicken. My mother used to kill two every Sunday. Whenever I have chicken, it's like a day I don't have to work."

"What do you work at?" The conversation was getting more intimate in long leaps and heady bounds. Although the picture of the girl's mother wringing the heads of two chickens every Sunday was a little disquieting.

"An actress. A dancer. A little bit of both," the girl said.

A dancer. That explained the legs. "Where are you working now?"

"No place for the moment." She kept stroking the picture of *poularde de Bresse en cocotte*. "I'm up for a part off-off-Broadway. One of those naked plays." She kept looking down at the cookbook and her voice was so low he wasn't sure that he'd heard correctly.

But whether he had heard correctly or not, it was making an effervescent impression on him. To have a beautiful girl, with pretty nearly the longest legs in the world, who had been walking around in the nude all day before dozens of people, just wander in off the street like that. And just before closing time!

"If you like chicken," he said, putting everything on the one throw, "I know a place on Sixty-first Street where they do it better than anyplace in New York. A French place."

"I wouldn't mind a good chicken dinner," the girl said.

"By a lucky accident," he said, "I'm free tonight."

"By a lucky accident," she said, "so am I."

He looked at his watch. "I close up here in about forty minutes. There's a nice bar around the corner on Lexington. Smiley's. Why don't you have a drink there and I'll be right along and then we can go on to dinner at this great place?''

"You're sure you won't forget and leave me there?" she said, sounding dubious.

"You just don't know me, Miss—"

"My name is Anna. Anna Bukowski. I'm going to change it if I get the part."

"My name is Christopher Bagshot."

"It's a good name," the girl said, "for a man who works in a bookshop. What time did you say you'd be there?"

She was eager, to top it all. "No later than seven-fifteen. Are you hungry?"

"I can eat," she said. She gave him the Swedish-actress incest smile and went out of the shop in her miniskirt and electric-blue fun fur.

He raced catatonically around the store, getting things in order before closing up and speeding over to Smiley's Bar. Now he knew that voice in his dream hadn't spoken for nothing.

Anna Bukowski walked slowly and deliberately over toward Lexington Avenue. She had to walk slowly to conserve her energy. She hadn't eaten for two whole days now and she was dizzy from lack of food, and every step she took was like dragging through hot tar. She wasn't on a diet or anything like that. She was just flat broke. She was just in from Cleveland and she had had no idea New York was so expensive. She had spent her last money on subway fare downtown for the tryouts that morning and she had walked all the way up from St. Mark's Place after parading around naked all day, which was also fatiguing, even though it didn't seem like much. But people didn't count the nervous strain.

The reason she had gone into the bookstore was to see if she could steal a book and sell it to a corrupt little man in a basement. Somewhere, she had heard that was a thriving industry. But then that young man had stood so close to her she wouldn't have had a chance to steal a rubber band. And she had asked to see cookbooks because she had been thinking of food all day.

Her landlord had thrown her out that morning, too, and kept her bag, and she was standing in all the clothes she possessed in this world, in a miniskirt that was two centuries out of style. If that man in the bookstore was as wild to get laid as he seemed and if she didn't ruin things at dinner, she might be able to swing getting him to ask her to spend the night with him in his place. If he didn't live with his dying mother or something. And that would mean at least breakfast, too, the next morning. As an old dancer had once told her in Cleveland, "I was in Buenos Aires and I was living off coffee and rolls. My stomach was shrinking to the size of a pistachio nut and I had to make a decision, and I made it. I sold one part of me to support another."

When she got to Lexington Avenue, she had forgotten which way the man had told her to turn, uptown or downtown, for Smiley's Bar. Hunger wasn't good for the memory. Well, there were only two ways to go. She chose uptown. She stepped down off the curb without looking which way the lights were on and a taxi made a wild swing, with a loud screeching of tires, to avoid hitting her. She jumped back, but fell down. She was safe, but the day had been so awful and she had come so near to being killed that she just sat there on the cold pavement of the city of New York and began to weep.

A man who had been waiting for the lights to change came across the street and said, "Please, let me help you."

She didn't say anything but, still sobbing, allowed the man to pull her to her feet.

"You really have to watch the lights," the man said gently. "All things combine in an attempt to destroy you in this town."

She sobbed uncontrollably. She was in no mood to hear lectures on safety precautions at the moment.

"What you need is a drink, young lady." She looked at him, conscious of rivulets on her cheeks. He was about forty and wore a nice dark topcoat and a hat.

She nodded. Her tears stopped. If the nice man took her to a bar, maybe it would be Smiley's; it was in the neighborhood. And even if it wasn't, there would probably be potato chips there and olives and salted peanuts and she could put down a little foundation so she wouldn't disgust the man from the bookstore with her gluttony at dinner and ruin her chances for a bed for the night and Sunday breakfast.

"It's very good of you, sir," she said.

The bar he took her to wasn't Smiley's. It was a dark, elegant small place, with candles on the restaurant tables in the rear. There were plenty of potato chips and olives and salted peanuts and she just couldn't help from tearing into them as she drank a bull shot, which was good for dulling the appetite, too, because of the bouillon. Bull shot, Bagshot. It was funny having a bull shot before going to dinner with a Bagshot. She giggled, the liquor getting to her swiftly in her condition. The nice man watched her with a smile on his face as she ravaged three plates of potato chips and two of salted peanuts.

"Have you been on a diet?" he asked.

"Sort of," she said.

"But you're off it now?"

"Thank God."

"Do you know," he said, "I think the best thing I could do would be to march you to a table and order us dinner."

"I'm expected in a half hour or so," she said, although it took a great effort to say no.

"We'll just have one dish," the man said, taking her down off the bar stool. "And then you can flitter off."

She couldn't refuse an offer like that, so she allowed the man to lead her to a table. She asked the bartender where Smiley's was and he said it was just down Lexington Avenue two blocks, so there was plenty of time.

The menu looked so tempting that with a little coaxing from the nice forty-year-old man, now without his hat and topcoat, she ordered the whole thing. Hors d'oeuvres, cream-of-tomato soup, steak with broccoli with hollandaise sauce and French fried potatoes, salad, cheese, and strawberry tart for dessert. It seemed like a lot to cram into a half hour before going out to dinner, but the waiter assured her he would hurry.

Christopher was just about to lock the front door and go into the little lavatory next to the back office and shave. He would be cheating his father of about five minutes' worth of service, but he felt he really had to shave. He had shaved in the morning, but although he was small he was manly and he needed to shave twice a day. But just as he was about to turn the handle of the lock, through the glass of the door he saw Beulah Stickney striding toward him, like a model advertising health food. He stepped back and she entered briskly.

"Hi, luv," she said, morning-fresh, vital and friendly. "Auntie folded like last year's violets. Aren't you the lucky boy tonight? Let's celebrate. The night is young and you are beautiful. Where're you taking your friend Beulah to dinner? I hear there's a new place over on First that's—"

"I'm afraid tonight is out," Christopher said, with a delicious sense of power. "I've made other arrangements. Perhaps if I'm free some night next week. . . ."

"You mean you're feeding another bird, luv?" Beulah asked,

a slight edge of what he thought was sharpness in her tone, and what she knew as hysteria.

"If you mean do I have an engagement for dinner with another lady," Christopher said, liking his language round tonight, "you're correct."

"Pah, luv," Beulah said airily, "let's make it à trois. It can be a load of laughs. May the best woman win." She didn't ordinarily descend to lures like that, but it was Saturday night and seven o'clock.

"Well. . . ." He hadn't thought about that possibility and it intrigued him. He hesitated, thinking hard. But then the door opened and Paulette Anderson came into the shop.

All I need now, Christopher thought, is for Sue Marsh finally to show up for her bag and Caroline Trowbridge to come in to apologize for saying it was a wrong number and Dorothea Toye to pass by, offering to cut her price.

"Why, Beulah," Paulette cried, "what on earth are you doing here?"

"This is my friendly neighborhood think tank, luv," Beulah said. "I was just passing by on the way home to change and I saw the beckoning light of literature and I came in to see if he had the new *Harper's Bazaar* or the latest Mailer to read in the tub." Her eyes flashed a clear signal to Christopher, and with a sudden maturity and understanding of women that he had never had before, he knew that she was warning him not to let Paulette Anderson know that she had come in to get him to take her to dinner. And certainly not to let her know that she had been turned down. "What brings you to these parts at this hour yourself, luv?" Beulah asked, her voice rising infinitesimally.

"I was going to invite Mr. Bagshot to a party," Paulette said.

Dental assistants, Christopher realized, did not observe the same rules of feint and parry as models. Paulette looked as though she had had a wearing day and her clothes didn't seem to be on just right, but she had taken her glasses off and there was a winsome fluster to her hair.

"I see you ladies know each other," Christopher said. He hoped they didn't know each other too well.

"We're cap-and-crown sisters, luv," Beulah Stickney said. "I patronize the sainted Dr. Levinson and Paulette holds my hand to keep me from screaming while he wreaks his will on me. I have also taken her shopping in the rag bazaar on Seventh Avenue at wholesale rates so that she can be beautiful enough to invite popular young men like you to parties."

760

Bitch, Christopher thought. It gave him great pleasure to say this in his mind. "Oh," he said, "so that's how you know each other."

"Well, I must be toddling along," Beulah said. "I'm late as it is." She picked up a copy of the French *Vogue*. "Put it on my bill, luv. The next time I have a toothache, Paulette, you can tell me how the party turned out."

She left, smiling, the air perfumed and polar behind her.

"I'm always a little in awe of her," Paulette said. "Aren't you?"

"Not really," Christopher said.

"Well, I suppose men are different," Paulette said. She breathed loudly. "I hope I'm not too late. But the afternoon was just one thing after another and I just took a chance that you might still be open and. . . . Well, anyway, I'm invited to a party and if you still want to. . . ." She ran down and stopped. The way he was looking at her, with this new light in his eyes, she was sure he knew that she had been lying naked on the day bed of Mr. Gadsden's emergency apartment as late as 4:30 that afternoon.

He just remained silent, silent and powerful, looking at her.

"Of course," she said. She was nervous, even if she did tower over him and she had thought of him as a last resort until this very minute. "Of course, if you don't want to go to a party, I'll understand. . . ."

"I'd love to go, Paulette," he said easily. "It's just that I'm taken for the evening."

"Naturally," Paulette said. "At this hour. Well, maybe another time. Good night."

"*Ciao*," he said. He had never said *ciao* before to anyone. "Good of you to drop by."

He opened the door for her. She heard it locking behind her.

As she walked heavily down Madison Avenue, she was overcome with the awful certainty that she was going to be a virgin for the rest of her life.

Humming, Christopher shaved. He felt marvelous. He didn't remember feeling this marvelous since the day he got his 4-F classification in the draft. Before going in to shave, he had tripped over the blue tennis bag and put it out of the way under the table. Looking at it, he decided he'd have it delivered on Monday by messenger to Miss Marsh's apartment, with a big bunch of forget-me-nots from that florist on Fifth Avenue. That would be ironic.

He shaved slowly because he didn't want to bleed. Even if he were late, that girl in the miniskirt with the great legs, what was her name, Anna, would wait. Tonight women waited for Bagshot.

It would have been all right if the steak hadn't been so good. But it was more than an inch thick and so tender you hardly needed the knife to cut it and it tasted the way steaks look in advertisements. It had just disappeared from her plate while the nice forty-year-old man was barely beginning on his and he had said, "My dear girl, I haven't seen anything like this since I played football in college." And he had insisted, it was the only word you could use, insisted, that she have another one, and what with the wine and all, and three kinds of cheese that she had never tasted before and the strawberry tart and the Cointreau with the coffee, well, it was 10:30 before she looked at her watch again and there was no use searching up and down Lexington Avenue at that hour like a lost soul for Smiley's Bar. And when she got out of the nice forty-year-old man's apartment at five o'clock the next day, which was Sunday, after a pancake and bacon-and-eggs brunch, served by a butler, there would have been even less use, wouldn't there, to look for Smiley's Bar?

She got the job in the off-off-Broadway naked show and two good reviews, mostly for her figure, if you wanted to be honest, and the nice forty-year-old man was as generous as nice forty-year-old men are supposed to be to tall young naked actresses, and all she had to worry about that autumn was her weight.

Lying idly in bed right before Christmas, reading the "Society" section of the Sunday *Times*, she saw an announcement that Mr. Christopher Bagshot, son of Mr. Bernard Bagshot, the owner of the well-known chain of bookstores, had been married the day before at St. Thomas's, in Mamaroneck, to a girl by the name of June Leonard.

So it had turned out well for everybody. It gave her a nice feeling.

# Pattern of Love

"I'll go into a nunnery," Katherine said, holding her books rigidly at her side, as they walked down the street toward Harold's house. "I'll retire from the world."

Harold peered uneasily at her through his glasses. "You can't do that," he said. "They won't let you do that."

"Oh, yes, they will." Katherine walked stiffly, looking squarely in front of her, wishing that Harold's house was ten blocks farther on. "I'm a Catholic and I can go into a nunnery."

"There's no need to do that," said Harold.

"Do you think I'm pretty?" Katherine asked. "I'm not looking for compliments. I want to know for a private reason."

"I think you're pretty," Harold said. "I think you're about the prettiest girl in school."

"Everybody says so," Katherine said, worrying over the "about," but not showing it in her face. "Of course I don't really think so, but that's what everybody says. You don't seem to think so, either."

"Oh, yes," said Harold. "Oh, yes."

"From the way you act," Katherine said.

"It's hard to tell things sometimes," Harold said, "by the way people act."

"I love you," Katherine said coldly.

Harold took off his glasses and rubbed them nervously with his handkerchief. "What about Charley Lynch?" he asked, working on his glasses, not looking at Katherine. "Everybody knows you and Charley Lynch . . ."

"Don't you even like me?" Katherine asked stonily.

"Sure. I like you very much. But Charley Lynch . . ."

"I'm through with him." Katherine's teeth snapped as she said it. "I've had enough of him."

"He's a very nice fellow," Harold said, putting his glasses on.

763

"He's the captain of the baseball team and he's the president of the eighth grade and . . ."

"He doesn't interest me," Katherine said, "any more."

They walked silently. Harold subtly increased his speed as they neared his house.

"I have two tickets to Loew's for tonight," Katherine said.

"Thanks," said Harold. "I've got to study."

"Eleanor Greenberg is giving a party on Saturday night." Katherine subtly slowed down as she saw Harold's house getting nearer. "I can bring anyone I want. Would you be interested?"

"My grandmother's," Harold said. "We're going to my grandmother's on Saturday. She lives in Doylestown, Pennsylvania. She has seven cows. I go there in the summertime. I know how to milk the cows and they . . ."

"Thursday night," Katherine said, speaking quickly. "My mother and father go out on Thursday night to play bridge and they don't come home till one o'clock in the morning. I'm all alone, me and the baby, and the baby sleeps in her own room. I'm all alone," she said in harsh invitation. "Would you like to come up and keep me company?"

Harold swallowed unhappily. He felt the blush come up over his collar, surge under his glasses. He coughed loudly, so that if Katherine noticed the blush, she'd think it came from the violence of his coughing.

"Should I slap you on the back?" Katherine asked eagerly.

"No, thank you," Harold said clearly, his coughing gone.

"Do you want to come up Thursday night?"

"I would like to very much," Harold said, "but my mother doesn't let me out at night yet. She says when I'm fifteen . . ."

Katherine's face set in grim lines. "I saw you in the library at eight o'clock at night, Wednesday."

"The library's different," Harold said weakly. "My mother makes an exception."

"You could tell her you were going to the library," Katherine said. "What's to stop you?"

Harold took a deep, miserable breath. "Every time I lie my mother knows it," he said. "Anyway, you shouldn't lie to your mother."

Katherine's lip curled with cold amusement. "You make me laugh," she said.

They came to the entrance to the apartment house in which Harold lived, and halted.

"In the afternoons," Katherine said, "a lot of times nobody's home in the afternoons but me. On your way home from school you could whistle when you pass my window, my room's in front, and I could open the window and whistle back."

"I'm awful busy," Harold said, noticing uneasily that Johnson, the doorman, was watching him. "I've got baseball practice with the Montauk A.C. every afternoon and I got to practice the violin a hour a day and I'm behind in history, there's a lot of chapters I got to read before next month and . . ."

"I'll walk home every afternoon with you," Katherine said. "From school. You have to walk home from school, don't you?"

Harold sighed. "We practice in the school orchestra almost every afternoon." He stared unhappily at Johnson, who was watching him with the knowing, cynical expression of doormen who see everyone leave and everyone enter and have their own opinions of all entrances and exits. "We're working on 'Poet and Peasant' and it's very hard on the first violins and I never know what time we'll finish and . . ."

"I'll wait for you," Katherine said, looking straight into his eyes, bitterly, not hiding anything. "I'll sit at the girls' entrance and I'll wait for you."

"Sometimes," said Harold, "we don't get through till five o'clock."

"I'll wait for you."

Harold looked longingly at the doorway to the apartment house, heavy gilt iron and cold glass. "I'll admit something," he said. "I don't like girls very much. I got a lot of other things on my mind."

"You walk home from school with Elaine," Katherine said. "I've seen you."

"O.K.," Harold shouted, wishing he could punch the rosy, soft face, the large, coldly accusing blue eyes, the red, quivering lips. "O.K.!" he shouted, "I walk home with Elaine! What's it to you? I like to walk home with Elaine! Leave me alone! You've got Charley Lynch. He's a big hero, he pitches for the baseball team. I couldn't even play right field. Leave me alone!"

"I don't want him!" Katherine shouted. "I'm not interested in Charley Lynch! I hate you!" she cried, "I hate you! I'm going to retire to a nunnery!"

"Good!" Harold said. "Very good!" He opened the door of the apartment house. Johnson watched him coldly, unmoving, knowing everything.

"Harold," Katherine said softly, touching his arm sorrowfully, "Harold—if you happen to pass my house, whistle 'Begin the

Beguine.' Then I'll know it's you. 'Begin the Beguine,' Harold . . .''

He shook her hand off, went inside. She watched him walk without looking back at her, open the elevator door, go in, press a button. The door closed finally and irrevocably behind him. The tears nearly came, but she fought them down. She looked miserably up at the fourth-story window behind which he slept.

She turned and dragged slowly down the block toward her own house. As she reached the corner, her eyes on the pavement before her, a boy spurted out and bumped her.

"Oh, excuse me," said the boy. She looked up.

"What do you want, Charley?" she asked coldly.

Charley Lynch smiled at her, forcing it. "Isn't it funny, my bumping into you? Actually bumping into you. I wasn't watching where I was going, I was thinking of something else and . . .''

"Yeah," said Katherine, starting briskly toward home. "Yeah."

"You want to know what I was thinking about?" Charley asked softly, falling in beside her.

"Excuse me," Katherine said, throwing her head back, all tears gone, looking at a point thirty feet up in the evening sky. "I'm in a hurry."

"I was thinking of that night two months ago," Charley said quickly. "That party Norah O'Brien gave. That night I took you home and I kissed your neck. Remember that?"

"No," she said. She walked at top speed across the street corner, down the row of two-story houses, all alike, with the children playing potsy and skating and leaping out from behind stoops and going, "A-a-a-a-a-a-h," pointing pistols and machine guns at each other. "Pardon me, I've got to get home and mind the baby; my mother has to go out."

"You weren't in a hurry with Harold," Charley said, his eyes hot and dry, as he matched her step for step. "You walked slow enough with him."

Katherine looked briefly and witheringly at Charley Lynch. "I don't know why you think that's your business," she said. "It's my own affair."

"Last month," Charley said, "you used to walk home with me."

"That was last month," Katherine said loudly.

"What've I done?" Pain sat clearly on Charley Lynch's face, plain over the freckles and the child's nose with the bump on it where a baseball bat had once hit it. "Please tell me what I've done, Katie."

766

"Nothing," said Katherine, her voice bored and businesslike. "Absolutely nothing."

Charley Lynch avoided three small children who were dueling seriously with wooden swords that clanged on the garbage-pail cover shields with which they protected themselves. "I must have done something," he said sorrowfully.

"Nothing!" Katherine's tones were clipped and final.

"Put 'em up, Stranger!" a seven-year-old boy said right in front of Charley. He had a pistol and was pointing it at a boy who had another pistol. "This town ain't big enough for you and me, Stranger," said the first little boy as Charley went around him, keeping his eyes on Katherine. "I'll give you twenty-four hours and then come out shooting."

"Oh, yeah?" said the second little boy with the pistol.

"Do you want to go to the movies tonight?" Charley asked eagerly, rejoining Katherine, safely past the Westerners. "Cary Grant. Everybody says it's a very funny picture."

"I would love to go," said Katherine, "but I've got to catch up on my reading tonight."

Charley walked silently among the dueling, wrestling, gunfighting children. Katherine walked slightly ahead of him, head up, pink and round and rosy-kneed, and Charley looked at the spot on her neck where he had kissed her for the first time and felt his soul drop out of his body.

He laughed suddenly, falsely. Katherine didn't even look at him. "I was thinking about that feller," Charley said. "That Harold. What a name—Harold! He went out for the baseball team and the coach threw him out the first day. The coach hit three balls at him and they went right through his legs. Then he hit another one at him and it bounced and smacked him right in the nose. You should've seen the look on that Harold's face." Charley chuckled shrilly. "We all nearly died laughing. Right square in the nose. You know what all the boys call him? 'Four-eyed Oscar.' He can't see first base from home plate. 'Four-eyed Oscar.' Isn't that funny?" Charley asked miserably.

"He's very nice about you," Katherine turned into the vestibule of her own house. "He tells me he admires you very much; he thinks you're a nice boy."

The last trace of the manufactured smile left Charley's face. "None of the other girls can stand him," Charley said flatly. "They laugh at him."

Katherine smiled secretly, remembering the little girls' conversations in the wardrobes and at recess.

"You think I'm lying!" Charley shouted. "Just ask."

Katherine shrugged coolly, her hand on the inner door leading to her house. Charley moved close to her in the vestibule gloom.

"Come to the movies with me," he whispered. "Please, Katie, please . . ."

"As I told you," she said, "I'm busy."

He put his hand out gropingly, touched hers. "Katie," he begged.

She pulled her hand away sharply, opened the door. "I haven't the time," she said loudly.

"Please, please . . ." he whispered.

Katherine shook her head.

Charley spread his arms slowly, lunged for Katherine, hugged her, tried to kiss her. She pulled her head savagely to the side, kicked him sharply in the shins. "Please . . ." Charley wept.

"Get out of here!" Katherine slapped his chest with her hands.

Charley backed up. "You used to let me kiss you," he said. "Why not now?"

"I can't be bothered," Katherine pulled down her dress with sharp, decisive, warning movements.

"I'll tell your mother," Charley shouted desperately. "You're going around with a Methodist! With a Protestant!"

Katherine's eyes grew large with fury, her cheeks flooded with blood, her mouth tightened. "Now get out of here!" she said. "I'm through with you! I don't want to talk to you. I don't want you to follow me around!"

"I'll walk wherever I goddamn please!" Charley yelled.

"I heard what you said," Katherine said. "I heard the word you used."

"I'll follow whoever I goddamn please!" Charley yelled even louder. "This is a free country."

"I'll never talk to you as long as I live," Katherine stamped for emphasis, and her voice rang off the mailboxes and doorknobs of the vestibule. "You bore me! I'm not interested in you. You're stupid! I don't like you. You're a big idiot! Go home!"

"I'll break his neck for him!" Charley shouted, his eyes clouded, his hands waving wildly in front of Katherine's face. "I'll show him! A violin player! When I get through with him you won't be so anxious to be seen with him. Do you kiss him?"

"Yes!" Katherine's voice clanged triumphantly. "I kiss him all the time. And he really knows how to kiss! He doesn't slobber all over a girl, like you!"

"Please," Charley whimpered, "please . . ." Hands out gropingly, he went toward Katherine. She drew back her arm coldly, and with all her round, solid, well-nourished eighty-five pounds, caught him across the face, turned, and fled up the stairs.

"I'll kill him!" Charley roared up the stairwell. "I'll kill that violinist with my bare hands!"

The door slammed in answer.

"Please tell Mr. Harold Pursell," Charley said soberly to Johnson, the doorman, "that a certain friend of his is waiting downstairs; he would like to see him, if it's convenient."

Johnson went up in the elevator and Charley looked with grim satisfaction around the circle of faces of his eight friends, who had come with him to see that everything was carried out in proper order.

Harold stepped out of the elevator, walked toward the boys grouped at the doorway. He peered curiously and short-sightedly at them, as he approached, neat, clean, white-fingered, with his glasses.

"Hello," Charley stepped out and faced Harold. "I would like to talk to you in private."

Harold looked around at the silent ring of faces, drained of pity, brimming with punishment. He sighed, realizing what he was in for.

"All right," he said, and opened the door, holding it while all the boys filed out.

The walk to the vacant lot in the next block was performed in silence, broken only by the purposeful tramp of Charley Lynch's seconds.

"Take off your glasses," Charley said when they reached the exact center of the lot.

Harold took off his glasses, looked hesitantly for a place to put them.

"I'll hold them," Sam Rosenberg, Charley's lieutenant, said politely.

"Thanks," Harold said, giving him the glasses. He turned and faced Charley, blinking slowly. He put up his hands. "O.K." he said.

Charley stood there, breathing deeply, his enemy, blinking, thin-armed, pale, twenty pounds lighter than Charley, before him. A deep wave of exultation rolled through Charley's blood. He put up his hands carefully, stepped in and hit Harold square on the eye with his right hand.

The fight did not take long, although it took longer than Charley had expected. Harold kept punching, advancing into the deadly fire of Charley's fists, the most potent and sharp and brutal in the whole school. Harold's face smeared immediately with blood, and his eye closed, and his shirt tore and the blood soaked in down his clothes. Charley walked in flat-footed, not seeking to dodge or block Harold's weak punches. Charley felt his knuckles smashing against skin and bone and eye, and running with blood, half-delirious with pleasure, as Harold reeled and fell into the cruel, unpitying fists. Even the knuckles on his hands, and the tendons in Charley's fists, carrying the shock of the battle up to his shoulders, seemed to enjoy the pitiless administration of punishment.

From time to time Harold grunted, when Charley took time off from hitting him in the head to hit him, hooking upward from his ankles, in the belly. Except for that, the battle was conducted in complete quiet. The eight friends of Charley watched soberly, professionally, making no comment, finally watching Harold sink to the ground, not unconscious, but too exhausted to move a finger, and lie, spread out, his bloody face pressed harshly, but gratefully, into the dust and rubble of the vacant lot.

Charley stood over the fallen enemy, breathing heavily, his fists tingling joyfully, happy to see the weak, hated, frail figure face down and helpless on the ground, sorry that the pleasure of beating that figure was over. He watched in silence for a minute until Harold moved.

"All right," Harold said, his face still in the dirt. "That's enough." He lifted his head, slowly sat up, then, with a trembling hand, pulled himself to his feet. He wavered, his arms out from his sides and shaking uncontrollably, but he held his feet. "May I have my glasses?" he asked.

Silently, Sam Rosenberg, Charley's lieutenant, gave Harold his glasses. Harold fumblingly, with shaking hands, put them on. Charley watched him, the incongruously undamaged glasses on the damaged face. Suddenly Charley realized that he was crying. He, Charley Lynch, victor in fifty more desperate battles, who had shed no tear since the time he was spanked at the age of four, was weeping uncontrollably, his body shaken with sobs, his eyes hot and smarting. As he wept, he realized that he had been sobbing all through the fight, from the first right-hand to the eye until the final sinking, face-first, of the enemy into the dirt. Charley looked at Harold, eye closed, nose swollen and to one side, hair sweated and muddy, mouth all gore and mud, but the face, the spirit behind it, calm, unmoved. Harold wasn't crying then, Charley knew, as he sobbed bitterly, and he wouldn't cry later, and nothing he, Charley Lynch, could ever do would make him cry.

Harold took a deep breath and slowly walked off, without a word.

Charley watched him, the narrow, unheroic, torn and bedraggled back, dragging off. The tears swelled up in a blind flood and Harold disappeared from view behind them.

# Whispers in Bedlam

He was a typical 235-pound married American boy, rosy-cheeked, broken-nosed, with an excellent five-tooth bridge across the front of his mouth and a sixty-three-stitch scar on his right knee, where the doctors had done some remarkable things with floating cartilage. His father-in-law had a thriving insurance agency and there was a place open in it for him, the sooner, his father-in-law said, the better. He was growing progressively deafer in the left ear, due to something that had happened to him during the course of his work the year before on a cold Sunday afternoon out in Green Bay, Wisconsin. He was a professional football player. He played middle linebacker on defense and a certain amount of physical wear and tear was to be expected, especially in Green Bay.

His name was Hugo Pleiss. He was not famous. He had played on three teams, the sort of teams that are always around the bottom of their division. When coaches said they were going to rebuild their clubs for next year, the first thing they did was to trade Hugo or declare him a free agent. But with all the new teams coming into the leagues, and the consequent demand for experienced players, Hugo always managed to be on somebody's roster when a new season started. He was large and eager to learn and he liked to play football and he had what coaches called "desire" when talking to sportswriters. While intelligent enough in real life (he had been a B student in college), on the field he was all too easily fooled. Perhaps, fundamentally, he was too honest and trusting of his fellow man. Fake hand-offs sent him crashing to the left when the play went to the right. He covered decoys with religious devotion while receivers whistled past him into the clear. He had an unenviable record of tackling blockers while allowing ball carriers to run over him. He hadn't intercepted a single pass in his entire career. He was doing well enough, though, until the incident of his ear at Green Bay. The man who played left corner back with him, Johnny Smathers, had a quick instinct for reading plays and, as the offense

772

shaped up, would shout to Hugo and warn him where the play was going. Smathers was small, distrustful and crafty, with a strong instinct for self-preservation and more often than not turned out to be right. So Hugo was having a pretty fair season until he began to go deaf in the ear on Smathers' side and could no longer hear the corner back's instructions.

After two games in which Smathers had correctly diagnosed and called dozens of plays, only to see Hugo go hurtling off in the opposite direction, Smathers had stopped talking to Hugo at all, on or off the field. This hurt Hugo, who was a friendly soul. He liked Smathers and was grateful for his help and he wished he could explain about his left ear; but once the word got around that he was deaf, he was sure he'd be dropped from the squad. He wasn't yet ready to sell insurance for his father-in-law.

Luckily, the injury to Hugo's ear came near the end of the season and his ordinary level of play was not so high that the drop in his efficiency had any spectacular effect on the coaches or the public. But Hugo, locked in his auditory half-world, fearful of silent enemies on his left and oblivious to the cheers and jeers of half the stadium, brooded.

Off the field, despite occasional little mishaps, he could do well enough. He learned to sit on the left of the coach at all meetings and convinced his wife that he slept better on the opposite side of the bed than on the one he had always occupied in the three years of their marriage. His wife, Sibyl, was a girl who liked to talk, anyway, mostly in protracted monologues, and an occasional nod of the head satisfied most of her demands for conversational responses. And a slight and almost unnoticeable twist of the head at most gatherings put Hugo's right ear into receiving position and enabled him to get a serviceable fix on the speaker.

With the approach of summer and the imminence of the pre-season training sessions, Hugo brooded more than ever. He was not given to introspection or fanciful similes about himself, but he began to think about the left side of his head as a tightly corked carbonated cider bottle. He poked at his eardrum with pencil points, toothpicks and a nail clipper, to let the fizz out; but aside from starting a slight infection that suppurated for a week, there was no result.

Finally, he made hesitant inquiries, like a man trying to find the address of an abortionist, and found the name of an ear specialist on the other side of town. He waited for Sibyl to go on her annual two-week visit to her parents in Oregon and made an appointment for the next day.

Dr. G. W. Sebastian was a small oval Hungarian who was enthusiastic about his work. He had clean, plump little busy hands and keen, merry eyes. Affliction, especially in his chosen field, pleased him and the prospect of long, complicated and possibly dangerous operations filled him with joy. "Lovely," he kept saying, as he stood on a leather stool to examine Hugo's ear, "Oh, absolutely lovely." He didn't seem to have many patients. "Nobody takes ears seriously enough," he explained, as he poked with lights and curiously shaped instruments into Hugo's ear. "People always think they hear well enough or that other people have suddenly all begun to mumble. Or, if they do realize they're not getting everything, that there's nothing to be done about it. You're a wise young man, very wise, to have come to me in time. What is it you told Miss Cattavi your profession was?"

Miss Cattavi was the nurse. She was a six-foot, 165-pounder who looked as though she shaved twice a day. She had immigrated from northern Italy and was convinced that Hugo played soccer for a living. "That Pelé," she had said. "The money he makes!"

Dr. Sebastian had never seen a football game in his life, either, and an impatient look came over his face as Hugo tried to explain what he did on Sundays and about Johnny Smathers and not being able to hear cleats pounding perilously on his left side when he went in to stop a draw over center. Dr. Sebastian also looked a little puzzled when Hugo tried to explain just exactly what had happened at Green Bay. "People do things like that?" he had said incredulously. "Just for money? In America?"

He probed away industriously, clucking to himself and smelling of peppermint and newly invented antiseptics, orating in little bursts that Hugo couldn't quite hear. "We are far behind the animals," was one thing Hugo *did* hear. "A dog responds to a whistle on a wave length that is silence for a human being. He hears a footfall on grass fifty yards away and growls in the darkness of the night. A fish hears the splash of a sardine in the water a mile away from him, and we have not yet begun to understand the aural genius of owls and bats."

Hugo had no desire to hear whistles on dogs' wave lengths or footfalls on grass. He was uninterested in the splash of distant sardines and he was not an admirer of the genius of owls and bats. All he wanted to be able to hear was Johnny Smathers ten yards to his left in a football stadium. But he listened patiently. After what doctors had done for his knee, he had a childlike faith in them; and if Dr. Sebastian, in the course of restoring his hearing, wanted to praise the beasts of the field and the birds of the air,

Hugo was prepared to be polite and nod agreement from time to time, just as he did when Sibyl spoke about politics or miniskirts or why she was sure Johnny Smathers' wife was no better than she should be when the team was on the road.

"We have allowed our senses to atrophy." Hugo winced as Dr. Sebastian rose on his toes for leverage and went rather deep with a blunt instrument. "We have lost our animal magic. We are only one third in communication, even the best of us. Whole new fields of understanding are waiting to be explored. When Beethoven's last quartets are played in a concert hall, a thousand people should fall out of their seats and writhe in unbearable ecstasy on the floor. Instead, what do they do? They look at their programs and wonder if there will be time for a beer before catching the last train home."

Hugo nodded. He had never heard any of Beethoven's last quartets and the floor of a concert hall didn't seem like the place a nice, well-brought-up married American boy should choose to writhe in ecstasy; but now that he had taken the step of going to a doctor, he was going to see it through. Still, with talk like that, about dogs and owls and sardines, he could see why there were no patients waiting in Dr. Sebastian's outer office.

"A crusade," Dr. Sebastian was saying, his eye glued to a lighted chromium funnel whose narrow end seemed to be embedded deep in Hugo's brain. Dr. Sebastian's breath pepperminted warmly on Hugo's bare neck. "A crusade is called for. You have a most unusually arranged collection of bones, Mr. Pleiss. A crusade to lift the curtain of sound, to unmuffle, to recapture our animal heritage, to distinguish whispers in bedlam, to hear the rustle of roses opening in the morning sun, to catch threats before they are really spoken, to recognize promises that are hardly formulated. I never did see a bone structure like this, Mr. Pleiss."

"Well, that feller in Green Bay weighed nearly three hundred pounds and his elbow—"

"Never mind, never mind." Dr. Sebastian finally pulled various bits of machinery out of his ear. "We will operate tomorrow morning, Miss Cattavi."

"OK," Miss Cattavi said. She had been sitting on a bench, looking as though she were ready to go in as soon as her team got the ball. "I'll make the arrangements."

"But—" Hugo began.

"I'll have everything ready," Dr. Sebastian said. "You've got nothing to worry about. Merely present yourself at the Lubenhorn Eye, Ear and Nose Clinic at three P.M. this afternoon."

"But there're one or two things I'd like to—"

"I'm afraid I'm terribly busy, Mr. Pleiss," Dr. Sebastian said. He whisked out of the office, peppermint receding on the aseptic air.

"He'll fix you," Miss Cattavi said, as she showed him to the door.

"I'm sure he will," said Hugo, "but—"

"I wouldn't be surprised," Miss Cattavi said, "if you came back to have the other ear done."

When Hugo woke up after the operation, Dr. Sebastian was standing next to his bed, smiling merrily. "Naturally," Dr. Sebastian said, "there is a certain slight discomfort."

The left side of Hugo's head felt as though it were inside the turret of a tank that was firing sixty rounds a minute. It also still felt like a corked cider bottle.

"You have an extraordinary bone structure, Mr. Pleiss." The doctor raised himself on tiptoe, so as to be able to smile approvingly down into Hugo's face. He spent a lot of time on his toes, Dr. Sebastian. In one way, it would have been more sensible if he had specialized in things like knees and ankles, instead of ears. "So extraordinary that I hated to finish the operation. It was like discovering a new continent. What a morning you have given me, Mr. Pleiss! I am even tempted not to charge you a penny."

It turned out later that Dr. Sebastian resisted this temptation. He sent a bill for $500. By the time Hugo received the bill, on the same day that Sibyl came back from Oregon, he was happy to pay it. The hearing in his left ear was restored. Now, if only Johnny Smathers wasn't traded away and if their relationship could be patched up, Hugo was sure he'd be in there at middle linebacker for the whole season.

There was a red scar behind his ear, but Sibyl didn't notice it for four days. She wasn't a very observant girl, Sibyl, except when she was looking at other girls' clothes and hair. When Sibyl finally did notice the scar, Hugo told her he'd cut himself shaving. He'd have had to use a saw-toothed bread knife to shave with to give himself a scar like that, but Sibyl accepted his explanation. He was rock-bottom honest, Hugo, and this was the first time he'd ever lied to his wife. The first lie is easy to get away with.

When he reported in to training camp, Hugo immediately patched up his friendship with Johnny Smathers. Johnny was a little cool at first, remembering how many times at the end of last season he had been made to look bad, all alone out there with two and three blockers trampling over him as Hugo was dashing away to the other side of the field, where nothing was happening. But when Hugo went as far as to confide in him that he'd had a little ringing in his left ear after the Green Bay game, a condition that had subsided since, Smathers had been understanding, and they even wound up as roommates.

Pre-season practice was satisfactory. The coach understood about the special relationship between Hugo and Smathers and always played them together and Hugo's performance was respectable, even though nobody was confusing him with Sam Huff or Dick Butkus or people like that.

The exhibition games didn't go badly and while Hugo didn't distinguish himself particularly, he made his fair share of tackles and batted down a few passes, listening carefully to Johnny Smathers' instructions and not being caught out of position too many times. It was a more-or-less normal September for Hugo, like so many Septembers of his life—sweaty, full of aches and bruises and abuse from coaches, not making love on Friday and Saturday, so as not to lose his edge for Sunday, feeling frightened for his life on Sunday morning and delighted to be able to walk out of the stadium on his own two feet in the dusk on Sunday afternoon. For want of a better word, what Hugo felt was happiness.

Then, just a minute before the end of the first regular league game of the season, something peculiar happened. Hugo's team was ahead twenty-one to eighteen, and the other team had the ball on his team's eight-yard line. It was third down and four to go and the crowd was yelling so much, the opposing quarterback, Brabbledoff, kept holding up his arms to get them to quiet down enough so that he could be heard in the huddle. The crowd hushed a bit; but, even so, Hugo was afraid he wouldn't be able to hear Smathers when the play started. He shook his head to clear the sweat from the inside of his helmet and, for a moment, his left ear was parallel to the opposing huddle. Then the peculiar thing happened. He heard what Brabbledoff was saying, just as if he were right there next to him in the huddle. And the huddle was a good fifteen yards away from Hugo, at least, and the crowd was roaring. "I'm going to bootleg it to the weak side," Brabbledoff was saying. "And, for Christ's sake, make it look real!"

The opposing team lined up and just before the snap, Hugo heard Smathers yell, "Around end to the strong side, around end to the strong side, Hugo!"

The two lines leaped into action; the guards pulled out to lead the run to the strong side. Hugo could have sworn he saw Brabbledoff

777

hand off to Frenzdich, the halfback, who churned after the screen of interference, while Brabbledoff sauntered back, as though out of the play. Everybody on Hugo's team scrambled to stop the strong-side thrust. Everybody but Hugo. It was as though a button had been pushed somewhere in his back, making his moves mechanical. Struggling against the tide of traffic, he trailed Brabbledoff, who suddenly, in the clear, with no one near him, began to run like a frightened deer toward the weak-side corner, the ball now pulled out from behind the hip that had been hiding it. Hugo was there on the line of scrimmage, all alone, and he hurled himself at Brabbledoff. Brabbledoff said something unsportsmanlike as he went down with Hugo on top of him, then fumbled the ball. Hugo kneeled on Brabbledoff's face and recovered the ball.

Hugo's teammates pummeled him in congratulation and they ran out the clock with two line bucks and the game was over, with the score twenty-one to eighteen.

The team voted Hugo the game ball in the locker room and the coach said, "It's about time you read a play correctly, Pleiss," which was high praise, indeed, from that particular coach.

In the shower, Johnny Smathers came over to him. "Man," Johnny said, "I could have killed you when I saw you drifting over to the weak side after I yelled at you. What tipped you off?"

"Nothing," Hugo said, after a moment's hesitation.

"It was a hell of a play," said Smathers.

"It was just a hunch," Hugo said modestly.

He was quieter than usual that Sunday night, especially after a win. He kept thinking about Dr. Sebastian and the sound of roses opening.


The next Sunday, Hugo went out onto the field just like every Sunday. He hadn't heard anything all week that a man wouldn't ordinarily hear and he was sure that it had been an acoustical freak that had carried Brabbledoff's voice to him from the huddle. Nothing unusual happened in the first half of the game. Smathers guessed right about half of the time and while there was no danger that Hugo was going to be elected defensive player of the week by the newspapers, he served creditably for the first thirty minutes.

It was a rough game and in the third quarter, he was shaken breaking into a screen and got up a little groggy. Moving around to clear his head while the other team was in the huddle, he happened to turn his left side toward the line of scrimmage. Then it happened again. Just as though he were right there, in the middle of the opposing huddle, he heard the quarterback say, in a hoarse whisper, "Red right! Flood left! Wing square in! R down and out . . . on five!"

Hugo looked around to see if any of his teammates had heard, too. But they looked just the way they always looked—muddy, desperate, edgy, overweight, underpaid and uninformed. As the opposing team came out of the huddle, up to the line of scrimmage, Hugo moved automatically into the defensive formation that had been called by Krkanius, who played in the front four and ran the defense positions. "Red right! Flood left! Wing square in! R down and out . . . on five!" he repeated silently to himself. Since he didn't know the other team's signals, that didn't help much, except that "on five" almost certainly meant that the ball was going to be snapped on the fifth count.

Smathers yelled, "Pass. On the flank!" and, again, Hugo felt as though a button had been pushed in his back. He was moving on the four count and was across the line of scrimmage, untouched, a fraction of a second after the ball was snapped, and laid the quarterback low before he could take a half step back into the pocket.

"Have you got a brother on this team, you son of a bitch?" the quarterback asked Hugo as Hugo lay on the quarterback's chest.

After that, for most of the rest of the afternoon, by turning to his right, Hugo heard everything that was said in the opposing huddle. Aside from an occasional commonplace remark, like "Where were you on that play, fat ass, waving to your girl?" or "If that Hunsworth puts his fingers into my eye once more, I'm going to kick him in the balls," the only operational intelligence that came across to Hugo was in the quarterback's coded signals, so there wasn't much advantage to be gained from Hugo's keenness of hearing. He knew *when* the ball was going to be snapped and could move a step sooner than otherwise, but he didn't know where it was going and still had to depend upon Smathers in that department.

Going into the last two minutes of the game, they were ahead, fourteen to ten. The Studs were one of the strongest teams in the league and Hugo's team was a twenty-point underdog on the Las Vegas line and a win would be a major upset. But the Studs were on his team's thirty-eight-yard line, first down and ten to go, and moving. Hugo's teammates were getting up more and more slowly from the pileups, like losers, and they all avoided looking over toward the bench, where the coach was giving an imitation of General George S. Patton on a bad day along the Rhine.

The Studs went briskly into their huddle, keyed up and confident. Hugo had been blocked out of the last three plays ("wiped out like my three-year-old daughter'' had been the phrase the coach had used) and he was preparing his excuses if he was pulled out of the game. The Studs were talking it up in the huddle, a confused babel of sound, when suddenly Hugo heard one voice, very clearly. It was Dusering, the leading pass catcher in the league. Hugo knew his voice well. Dusering had expressed himself to Hugo with some eloquence after Hugo had pushed him out of bounds in what Dusering considered an ungentlemanly manner after a thirty-yard gain on a pass to the side line.

"Listen," Dusering was saying in the huddle fifteen yards away, "I got Smathers all set up. I can beat him on a buttonhook on the inside."

"OK," Hugo heard the quarterback say, and then the signal.

The Studs trotted up to the line of scrimmage. Hugo glanced around at Smathers. Smathers was pulling back deep, worried about Dusering's getting behind him, too busy protecting his area to bother about calling anything to Hugo. Hugo looked at Dusering. He was wide, on the left, looking innocent, giving nothing away.

The ball was snapped and Dusering went straight down the side line, as though for the bomb. A half-back came charging out in front of Hugo, yelling, his arms up, but Hugo ignored him. He cut back to his left, waited for a step, saw Dusering stop, then buttonhook back inside, leaving Smathers hopelessly fooled. The ball came floating out. Just as Dusering set himself to get it at waist height, Hugo flung himself across the trajectory of the pass and gathered it in. He didn't get far with it, as Dusering had him on the first step, but it didn't matter. The game was, to all intents and purposes, over, a stunning victory. It was the first pass Hugo had ever intercepted.

He was voted the game ball that Sunday, too.

In the locker room, the coach came over to Hugo while he was taking off his jockstrap. The coach looked at him curiously. "I really ought to fine you," the coach said. "You left the middle as open as a whore's legs on Saturday night."

"Yes, Coach," Hugo said, modestly wrapping a towel around him. He didn't like rough language.

"What made you cover the buttonhook?" the coach asked.

"I . . ." Hugo looked guiltily down at his bare toes. They were bleeding profusely and one nail looked as though he was going to lose it. "Dusering tipped it off. He does something funny with his head before the buttonhook."

The coach nodded, a new light of respect in his eyes.

It was Hugo's second lie. He didn't like to lie, but if he told the coach he could hear what people were whispering in a huddle fifteen yards away, with 60,000 people screaming in the stands like wild Indians, the coach would send him right over to the doctor to be treated for concussion of the brain.

During the week, for the first time, he was interviewed by a sportswriter. The article came out on Friday and there was a picture of him crouching with his hands spread out, looking ferocious. The headline over the article said, "MR. BIG PLAY MAN."

Sibyl cut the article out and sent it to her father, who always kept saying that Hugo would never amount to anything as a football player and ought to quit and start selling insurance before he got his brains knocked out, after which it would be too late to sell anything, even insurance.

Practice that week was no different from any other week, except that Hugo was limping because of his crushed toes. He tested himself, to see if he could hear what people were saying outside of normal range, but even in the comparative silence of the practice field, he didn't hear any better or any worse than he had before his ear was hurt. He didn't sleep as well as he usually did, as he kept thinking about the next Sunday, and Sibyl complained, saying he was making an insomniac out of her, thrashing around like a beached whale. On Thursday and Friday nights, he slept on the couch in the living room. The clock in the living room sounded like Big Ben to him, but he attributed it to his nerves. On Saturday, the whole team went to a hotel for the night, so Sibyl had nothing to complain about. Hugo shared a room with Smathers. Smathers smoked, drank and chased girls. At two in the morning, still awake, Hugo looked over at Johnny, sleeping beatifically, and wondered if perhaps he was making a mistake somewhere in the way he led his life.

Even limping from his crushed toes, Sunday was a remarkable day for Hugo. In the middle of the first quarter, after the opposing tackle had given him the knee to the head on a block, Hugo discovered that he not only could hear the signals in the other team's huddle but *knew what they meant*, just as though he had been studying their playbook for months. "Brown right! Draw fifty-five . . . on two!" came through in the quarterback's voice to his left ear, as though on a clear telephone connection, and was somehow instantly translated in Hugo's brain to "Flanker to the right, fake to the fullback over right guard, hand-off to right halfback and cutback inside left end."

Hugo still lined up obediently in the defensive formations called by Krkanius; but once the plays got under way, he disregarded his regular assignments and went where he knew the plays were going. He intercepted two passes, knocked down three more and made more tackles than the rest of the team put together. It was with somber satisfaction mixed with a curious sense of guilt that he heard Gates, the opposing quarterback, snarl in the huddle. "Who let that fish face Pleiss in there again?" It was the first time that he had heard any quarterback in the league mention him by name.

It was only as he was leaving the field that Hugo realized that Smathers hadn't called a play to him once during the whole game. He tried to catch Smathers' eye in the locker room, but Smathers always seemed to be looking the other way.

On Monday morning, when they ran the game films, the coach kept stopping the film on plays in which Hugo figured and rerunning those bits in slow motion over and over again. Hugo began to feel even more uncomfortable than he usually felt at these Monday-morning entertainments. The coach didn't say anything, except, "Let's look at that once more"; but seeing himself over and over again, in the center of plays so many times, embarrassed Hugo, as though he were showboating in front of his teammates. It was also embarrassing to see how often, even though he was right there, he allowed himself to be knocked down by blockers who were primarily going for another man, and how many tackles he had made that should have been clean but that developed into dogged, drag-me-along-with-you-Nellie yard-eating affairs. It was a stern rule with the coach that no comments were allowed by the players at the showings, so Hugo had no notion of what his team-mates' estimate of his performance might be.

When the film was finally over, Hugo tried to be the first man out the door, but the coach signaled to him and pointed with his thumb to the office. Leaning heavily on his cane, Hugo hobbled into the office, prepared for the worst. The cane was not merely window dressing. The toes on Hugo's right foot looked like a plate of hamburger and, while he waited for the coach, Hugo thought of ways to introduce his infirmity as an excuse for some of the less glorious moments of his performance as revealed by the movies of the game.

The coach came in, opening the collar of his size-nineteen shirt so that he could express himself freely. He shut the door firmly, sat down and grunted. The grunt meant that Hugo could sit down, too. Hugo seated himself on a straight wooden chair, placing his cane prominently in front of him.

Behind the coach, on the wall, there was a blown-up photograph of a player in a 1940ish uniform. The player's name was Jojo Baines and he had once been voted the dirtiest lineman ever to play in the National Football League. The only time Hugo had ever heard a note of tenderness creep into the coach's voice was when he mentioned Jojo Baines.

"Ever since you joined this club, Pleiss," said the coach, "I have been appalled when I looked down at the starting line-up and seen your name on it—in my own handwriting."

Hugo smiled weakly, hoping to recognize a pleasantry.

"I won't keep it a secret from you, Pleiss," the coach went on. "For two years, I've been trying to get rid of you. I have made the circuit of every city in this league with my hat in hand, eating the bread of humiliation, trying to beg, borrow or steal another middle linebacker. To no avail." The coach had an ear for rhetoric, when he was so inclined. "No avail," he repeated. "They all knew that as long as I had to start you every Sunday, we were never a threat to anybody. I am going to give you an impersonal estimate of your abilities, Pleiss. You're slow, you have a miserable pair of hands, you don't hit hard enough to drive my grandmother out of a rocking chair, you close your eyes on contact, you run like a duck with gout, you wouldn't get angry if a man hit you over the head with an automobile jack and raped your wife in front of your eyes, and you get fooled on plays that would have made a high school cheerleader roar with laughter in 1910. Have I left out anything?"

"Not that I can think of, sir," Hugo said.

"With all that," the coach went on, "you have saved three games in a row for us. You make a mockery out of the holy sport of football, but you have saved three games in a row for us and I am hereby increasing your salary by one thousand dollars for the season. If you tell this to anyone else on the team, I will personally nail you by the hands to the locker-room wall."

"Yes, sir," said Hugo.

"Now, get out of here," the coach said.

"Yes, sir," Hugo said. He stood up.

"Give me that cane," the coach said.

Hugo gave him the cane. The coach broke it in two, without rising from his chair. "I can't stand the sight of cripples," he said.

"Yes, sir," Hugo said. He tried not to limp as he walked out of the office.

The next Sunday was unsettling.

It started on an audible.

When the opposing team lined up after the huddle, Hugo knew that the play that had been called in the huddle was a short pass to the right flank. But when the quarterback took his position behind the center, Hugo saw him scanning the defensive setup and frowning. The quarterback's lips didn't move, but Hugo heard, just as though the man were talking directly to him, the word "No." There was a little pause and then, "It won't work, they're overshifting on us."

Hugo didn't have time to wonder at this new extension of his powers, as the quarterback began to call a set of signals aloud, changing the play he'd picked in the huddle. Everybody could hear the signals, of course, but Hugo was the only one on his team who knew that the quarterback was calling for an end around, from left to right. Just before the snap, when it was too late for the quarterback to call any changes, Hugo broke for the left side. He knew, without thinking about why he knew it, that the end would take two steps to his left, hesitate for one beat, then whirl around and streak for the quarterback and the ball on the way around the opposite end. As the ball was snapped, Hugo was knifing in between the end and the tackle, and when the end, after his two steps, came around, Hugo flattened him with a block. The quarterback was left all alone, holding the ball, like a postman delivering a package to the wrong door, and was downed for a five-yard loss.

But it was an expensive exploit for Hugo. The end's knee caught him in the head as they went down together and he was stretched out unconscious when the whistle blew.

When he woke up some minutes later, he was lying behind the bench, with the doctor kneeling over him, prodding the back of his neck, for broken vertebrae, and the trainer jamming spirits of ammonia under his nostrils. The jolt had been so severe that when the coach asked him at half time how he had been able to nip the end-around play in the bud, Hugo had to confess that he didn't remember anything about the play. In fact, he didn't remember leaving the hotel that morning, and it took him a good ten minutes after the coach had spoken to him to remember the coach's name.

The doctor wouldn't let him go back into the game and his value to the team was neatly demonstrated to the coach by the fact that they lost by three touchdowns and a field goal.

The plane was quiet on the flight home. The coach did not appreciate a show of youthful high spirits or resilience in adversity by teams of his when they had lost by three touchdowns and a field goal. And, as usual on such occasions, he had forbidden any drinks to be served, since he didn't believe the fine, full flavor of defeat should be adulterated by alcohol. So the plane sped through the night sky in a long funereal hush.

Hugo himself was feeling better, although he still didn't remember anything about the game that afternoon. He had a nagging sensation that something peculiar and fundamentally unwholesome had occurred *before* his injury, but he couldn't bring it up to the level of consciousness. There was a small poker game going on up front in low whispers and Hugo decided to sit in, to stop himself from profitless probing into the afternoon's events. He usually lost in these games, since one glance at his open face by any normally acquisitive poker player showed whether Hugo had a pair, two pairs or was buying to a straight.

Either because it was too dark in the plane for the other players to get a clear look at Hugo's face or because the head injury had hurt some nerve and rendered him expressionless, Hugo kept winning a fair proportion of the pots. He was a careless player and didn't keep track of his winnings and merely felt that it was about time that luck was turning his way.

After about an hour of play, he had a sizable stack of chips in front of him. He was sitting with three aces in his hand, having gotten two of them on a four-card draw, and he was about to raise the man on his left, Krkanius, who had drawn three cards, when somehow, just as though Krkanius had nudged him and whispered the news into his ear, he knew that Krkanius had a full house, jacks and fours. He didn't raise Krkanius but threw his cards in. Someone else saw Krkanius and Krkanius put his cards down. Full house. Jacks and fours.

"I'm not feeling so well," Hugo said. "I'm cashing in."

He stood up and went back to his seat.

It was a miserable night and the plane was bucking through thick cloud and Hugo sat at the window, looking out and feeling horrible. He was a cheat. He could make all sorts of excuses to himself, he could say he had acted out of surprise, without thinking, that it was the first time anything like that had ever happened to him, but he knew that if that weird message hadn't come through to him from Krkanius, on his left, he'd have raised Krkanius $10 and Krkanius would have raised him and Krkanius would be at least $20 or $30 richer right now. No matter how he tried to wriggle out of it, his conscience told him he was just as guilty as if he had taken $30 out of Krkanius' wallet.

Then, in a flash, he remembered the afternoon—the moment on the field when he was sure that he knew what the quarterback was thinking on the end-around play and his automatic reaction to it and his blotting out the end. It was another form of cheating, but he didn't know what to do about it. He could keep from playing poker, but he made his living out of playing football.

He groaned. He came from a deeply religious family, with a stern sense of morality. He didn't smoke or drink and he believed in hell.

After the plane landed, Hugo didn't go right home. Sibyl was away in Chicago, attending the wedding of one of her sisters, and he didn't feel like rattling around in an empty house. Krkanius, who had emerged from the poker game the big winner, invited him and a couple of the other boys to join him for a drink and, while Hugo didn't drink, he went along for the company.

The bar Krkanius took them to was crowded and noisy. There was a group of men with some girls at the bar, and as Hugo followed Krkanius to the back room, he heard a woman's voice say, "Uh-huh. That's for me. That big innocent-looking one."

Hugo looked around. A round blonde at the bar was staring directly at him, a sweet small smile on her full lips. If you didn't know what went on in her head, she looked like somebody's pure young daughter. "I'm going to teach you a few things tonight, baby," Hugo heard, staring, frozen, at the girl. The girl's mouth had never shown the slightest tremor of movement.

Hugo wheeled and hurried into the back room. When the waiter asked him what he wanted to drink, he ordered bourbon.

"Man," Krkanius said, surprised, "you really must've got shaken up today." Nobody had ever seen Hugo drink anything stronger than ginger ale before.

Hugo drank his bourbon quickly. He didn't like the taste, but it seemed to help his nerves. The blonde girl came into the back room and leaned over a table nearby to talk to somebody she knew. Remembering what she had been thinking as he passed her on the way in, Hugo ordered another bourbon. She glanced, as though by accident, at the table of football players. The way her sweater fit around her bosom made a peculiar ache come up in Hugo's throat.

"What're you waiting for, sweets?" he heard her think as her glance swept over him. "The night's not getting any younger."

He drank the second bourbon even more quickly than the first. "Oh, God," he thought, "I'm becoming a drunkard." The bourbon didn't seem to do anything for his nerves this time.

"It's time to go home," he said, standing up. His voice didn't sound like his. "I'm not feeling so well."

"Get a good night's sleep," Krkanius said.

"Yeah." If Krkanius knew that he'd had $30 stolen from him that evening, he wouldn't have been so solicitous.

Hugo walked quickly past the bar, making sure not to look at the girl. It was raining outside now and all the taxis were taken. He was just about to start walking when he heard the door open behind him. He couldn't help but turn. The girl was standing there, alone, with her coat on. She was scanning the street for a taxi, too. Then she looked at him. "Your move, baby," he heard, in a voice that was surprisingly harsh for a girl so young.

Hugo felt himself blush. Just then, a taxi drove up. Both he and the girl started for it.

"Can I give you a lift?" Hugo heard himself saying.

"How kind of you," the girl said, demurely.

On the way home, in the dawn, many hours later, Hugo wished for the first time in his life that he had been born a Catholic. Then he could have gone directly to a priest, confessed, accepted penance and been absolved of sin.

Sibyl called in the morning to tell him that her parents, who had come East for the wedding, were taking a trip to New York and wanted her to go along with them. Ordinarily, he wouldn't have been able to keep the disappointment at news like that out of his voice. He loved Sibyl dearly and usually felt lost without her. But now a wave of relief swept over him. The moment of confrontation, the moment when he would have to tell his innocent and trusting young wife about his appalling lapse from grace or, even worse, lie to her, was postponed.

"That's all right, honey," he said, "you just go along with your mother and dad and have a good time. You deserve a holiday. Stay as long as you like."

"Hugo," Sibyl said, "I just could break down and cry, you're so good to me."

There was the sound of a kiss over the telephone and Hugo kissed back. When he hung up, he leaned his head against the wall and closed his eyes in pain. One thing he was sure of, he wasn't going to see that girl, that Sylvia, again. Sylvia. Almost the same name as Sibyl. How rotten could a man be?

Passion spent for the moment, he lay in the largest double bed he had ever seen, next to the dazzling body that had opened

787

undreamed-of utopias of pleasure for him. Ashamed of himself even for thinking about it, he was sure that if Sibyl lived to the age of ninety, she wouldn't know one tenth as much as Sylvia must have known the day she was born.

In the soft glow of a distant lamp, he looked at the bedside clock. It was past four o'clock. He had to report for practice, dressed, at ten o'clock. After a losing game, the coach gave them wind sprints for forty-five minutes every day for a week. He groaned inwardly as he thought of what he was going to feel like at 10:45 that morning. Still, for some reason, he was loath to go.

An hour later, he was finally dressed. He leaned over Sylvia to kiss her good-bye. She lay there, fresh as the morning, smiling, breathing placidly. He wished he were in as good condition as she was. "G'night, sweets," she said, an arm around his neck. "Don't let those rough boys hurt you today. And bring Baby a little giftie tonight. Try Myer's, on Sanford Street. They're full of goodies."

Walking home along the dark streets, Hugo thought, "Of course. Girls like little tokens of affection. Flowers, candy. Sentimental creatures." He didn't remember any store called Myer's on Sanford Street, but he supposed it was a confectionery shop that had some specialties that Sylvia had a taste for. He resolved to get her the best five-pound box of candy money could buy.

That afternoon, feeling a little light-headed from lack of sleep and the wind sprints, he walked along Sanford Street, searching for a shop called Myer's. He stopped short. MYER, the thin lettering read on the window. But instead of boxes of candy displayed behind the glass, there was a blaze of gold and diamonds. Myer's sold jewelry. Expensive jewelry.

Hugo did not go in. Thrift was another of the virtues his excellent family had instilled in him as a boy. He walked along Sanford Street until he found a candyshop and bought a five-pound box of chocolates. It cost $15 and Hugo felt a twinge at his extravagance as the clerk wrapped the box in festive paper.

That night, he didn't stay more than ten minutes in Sylvia's apartment. She had a headache, she said. She didn't bother to unwrap the candy.

The next night, he stayed longer. He had visited Myer's during the afternoon and bought a gold bracelet for $300. "I like a generous man," Sylvia said.

The pain Hugo had felt in handing over the $300 to the clerk in Myer's was considerably mitigated by the fact that the night before, when he had left Sylvia with her headache, he had re-membered that every Tuesday there was a poker game at Krkanius' apartment. Hugo had sat in for three hours and won $416, the record for a single night's winnings since the inception of the game. During the course of the evening, by twisting his head a little now and then to get a fix with his left ear, he had been warned of lurking straights, one flush and several full houses. He had discarded a nine-high full house himself because Croker, of the taxi squad, was sitting in the hole with a jack-high full house; and Hugo had won with a pair of sevens after Krkanius had bluffed wildly through a hand with a pair of fives. Somehow, he told himself piously, as he stuffed bills and checks into his wallet when the game broke up, he would make it up to his teammates. But not just now. Just now, he couldn't bear the thought of Sylvia having any more headaches.

Luckily, Sibyl didn't return until Friday. On Friday nights during the season, Hugo slept on the living-room couch, so as not to be tempted to impair his energies for Sunday's games, so *that* problem was postponed. He was afraid that Sibyl's woman's intuition would lead her to discover a fateful change in her husband, but Sibyl was so grateful for her holiday that her intuition lay dormant. She merely tucked him in and kissed him chastely on the forehead and said, "Get a good night's sleep, honey."

When she appeared with his breakfast on a tray the next morning, his conscience stirred uneasily; and after the light Saturday-morning practice, he went into Myer's and bought Sibyl a string of cultured pearls for $85.

Sunday was triumphal. Before the game, suiting up, Hugo decided that the best way he could make up to his teammates for taking $416 away from them was by doing everything he could to win the game for them. His conscience clear, obeying the voices within his head, he was in on half the tackles. When he intercepted a pass in the last quarter and ran for a touchdown, the first of his life, to put the game on ice, the entire stadium stood and cheered him. The coach even shook his hand when he came off the field. He felt dainty footed and powerful and as though he could play forever without fatigue. The blood coursing through his veins felt like a new and exhilarating liquid, full of dancing bubbles.

After the game, he was dragged off to a television interview in a little makeshift studio under the stands. He had never been on television before, but he got through it all right and later that night, somebody told him he was photogenic.

His life entered a new phase. It was as definite as opening and going through a door and closing it behind him, like leaving a small, shabby corridor and with one step emerging into a brilliantly lit ballroom.

His photograph was in the papers every week, with laudatory articles. Newspapermen sought him out and quoted him faithfully when he said, "The trick is to study your opponents. The National Football League is no place for guesswork."

He posed for advertising stills, his hair combed with greaseless products. He modeled sweaters and flowered bathing trunks and was amazed at how simple it was to earn large sums of money in America merely by smiling.

His picture was on the cover of *Sports Illustrated* and small boys waited for him at the players' entrance after practice. He autographed footballs, and taxi drivers recognized him and sometimes refused to take payment for their fares. He took to eating out in restaurants with Sibyl, because the managers more often than not tore up the check when he asked for it. He learned to eat caviar and developed a taste for champagne.

He was invited to parties at the home of Bruce Fallon, the quarterback, who had been paid $200,000 to sign and who was called a superstar by the sportswriters. Until then, Fallon, who only went around with the famous old-timers and the upper-bracket players on the club, had never even said hello to him when they passed on the street. "Do you play bridge, Hugo?" Fallon asked.

They played bridge, Fallon and Fallon's wife, Nora, and Hugo and Sibyl, in the huge living room of the Fallons' apartment, which had been decorated by an imported Norwegian. "Isn't this cozy?" Nora Fallon said, as the four of them sat around the pale wood table before the fire, playing for ten cents a point. Hugo's left ear worked for bridge as well as poker and Hugo wound up the first evening with an $800 profit, and Fallon said, "I've heard about your poker from the boys, Hugo. I've never met anybody with a card sense like yours."

Fallon discussed the coach with him. "If Bert would really let me call my own game," Fallon said, pouring whiskeys for himself and Hugo, "we'd be twenty points better a Sunday."

"He's a little primitive, Bert, that's true," Hugo said, "but he's not a bad guy at heart." He had never heard anybody criticize the coach before and had never even thought of him by his first name. Even now, with the coach a good seven miles away across town and safely in bed, Hugo felt a curious little tickling in the small of his back as he realized that he had actually said "Bert."

When they left that night, with Fallon's check for $800 in his pocket, Nora Fallon put up her cheek to be kissed. She had gone to school in Lausanne. She said, "We have to make this a weekly affair," as Hugo kissed her, and he knew she was thinking, "Wouldn't it be nice if we could have a little quiet tête-à-tête, you and I, sometime soon?"

That night, when Hugo got home, he wrote the Fallon telephone number in his little pocket address book. He wondered what it could be like, making love to a woman who thought in French.

The trainer took a fussy interest in him now and, when he came up with a small bruise on his knee, insisted on giving him whirlpool baths for six days. The coach let him off a half hour early one day to make a speech at a local high school. Brenatskis, the publicity man, rewrote his biography for the programs and said that he had made Phi Beta Kappa in college. When Hugo protested, mildly, Brenatskis said, "Who'll know?" and, "It's good for your image." He also arranged for a national magazine to have Hugo photographed at home for a feature article. Sibyl insisted on buying a pair of gold-lamé pajamas if she was going to be photographed for a national magazine, and on having new curtains in the living room and new slipcovers made. When the article came out, there was only one picture accompanying it—Hugo in an apron, cooking in the kitchen. He was supposed to be making a complicated French dish. He never actually even made coffee for himself.

He bought three loud checked sports jackets for himself and a $400 brooch for Sylvia, who was still subject to headaches. He couldn't tear himself away from Sylvia, although he was beginning to find her rather common, especially compared with Nora Fallon. He bought a $100 pair of earrings for Sibyl.

On Sundays, he raged over all the fields in the league, and at the end of home games, he had to get to the locker room fast to keep from being mobbed by fans. He began to receive love letters from girls, who sometimes included photographs taken in surprising positions. He knew that these letters disturbed Sibyl, but the mails were free, after all. By now, everybody agreed that he was photogenic.

Sibyl one day announced that she was pregnant. Until then, although Hugo had wanted children from the beginning of their marriage, she had insisted that she was too young. Now, for some reason, she had decided that she was no longer too young. Hugo was very happy, but he was so occupied with other things that he didn't have quite the time to show it completely. Still, he bought her a turquoise necklace.

Fallon, who was a born gambler, said that it was a shame to

waste Hugo's card sense on penny-ante poker games and ten-cent-a point family bridge. There was a big poker game in town that Fallon played in once a week. In the game, there was a stockbroker, a newspaper publisher, the president of an agricultural-machinery firm, an automobile distributor and a man who owned, among other things, a string of race horses. When Fallon brought Hugo into the hotel suite where the game was held, there was a haze of money in the room as palpable as the cigar smoke that eddied over the green table and against the drawn curtains. Hugo and Fallon had made a private deal that they would split their winnings and their losses. Hugo wasn't sure about the morality of this, since they weren't letting the others know that they were up against a partnership, but Fallon said, "What the hell, Huge, they're only civilians." Anybody who wasn't in some way involved in professional football was a civilian in Fallon's eyes. "Huge" was Fallon's friendly corruption of Hugo's name and it had caught on with the other men on the team and with the newspapermen who followed the club. When the offensive team trotted off the field, passing the defensive team coming in, Fallon had taken to calling out, "Get the ball back for me, Huge." A sportswriter had picked it up and had written a piece on Hugo using that as the title, and now, whenever the defensive team went in, the home crowd chanted "Get the ball back for me, Huge." Sometimes, listening to all that love and faith come roaring through the autumn air at him, Hugo felt like crying for joy out there.

The men around the green table all stood up when Fallon and Hugo came into the room. The game hadn't started yet and they were still making up the piles of chips. They were all big men, with hearty, authoritative faces. They shook hands with the two football players as Fallon introduced Hugo. One of them said, "It's an honor," and another man said, "Get the ball back for me, Huge," as he shook Hugo's hand and they all roared with kindly laughter. Hugo smiled boyishly. Because of the five-tooth bridge in the front of his mouth, Hugo for years had smiled as little as possible: but in the past few weeks, since he had become photogenic, he smiled readily. He practiced grinning boyishly from time to time in front of the mirror at home. People, he knew, were pleased to be able to say about him, "Huge? He looks rough, but when he smiles, he's just a nice big kid." Civilians.

They played until two o'clock in the morning. Hugo had won $6020 and Fallon had won $1175. "You two fellers are just as tough off the field as on," said the automobile distributor admiringly as he signed a check, and the other men laughed jovially. Losing money seemed to please them.

"Beginner's luck," Hugo said. Later on, the automobile distributor would tell his wife that Huge didn't look it, but he was witty.

They hailed a taxi outside the hotel. Fallon hadn't brought his Lincoln Continental, because there was no sense in taking a chance that somebody would spot it parked outside the hotel and tell the coach his quarterback stayed out till two o'clock in the morning. In the taxi, Fallon asked, "You got a safe-deposit box, Huge?"

"No," Hugo said.

"Get one tomorrow."

"Why?"

"Income tax," Fallon said. In the light of a street lamp, he saw that Hugo looked puzzled. "What Uncle Sam doesn't know," Fallon said lightly, "won't hurt him. We'll cash these checks tomorrow, divvy up and stash the loot away in nice dark little boxes. Don't use your regular bank, either."

"I see," Hugo said. There was no doubt about it; Fallon was a brainy man. For a moment, he felt a pang of regret that he had taken Nora Fallon to a motel the week before. He hadn't regretted it at the time, though. Quite the contrary. He had just thought that if the child Sibyl was carrying turned out to be a girl, he wouldn't send her to school in Lausanne.

Sibyl awoke when he came into the bedroom. "You win, honey?" she asked sleepily.

"A couple of bucks," Hugo said.

"That's nice," she said.


By now, Hugo was free of doubt. If God gave you a special gift, He obviously meant you to use it. A man who could run the hundred in nine flat would be a fool to allow himself to be beaten by a man who could do only nine, five. If it was God's will that Hugo should have the good things of life—fame, success, wealth, beautiful women—well, that was God's will. Hugo was a devout man, even though, in the season, he was busy on Sunday and couldn't go to church.

During next week's poker game, Hugo saw to it that he didn't win too much. He let himself get caught bluffing several times and deliberately bet into hands that he knew were stronger than his. There was no sense in being greedy and killing the goose that laid the golden eggs. Even so, he came out almost $2000 ahead. Fallon lost nearly $500, so nobody had reason for complaint.

When the game broke up, Connors, the automobile distributor, told Hugo he'd like to talk to him for a minute. They went downstairs and sat in a deserted corner of the lobby. Connors was opening a sports-car agency and he wanted Hugo to lend his name to it. "There's nothing to it," Connors said. "Hang around the showroom a couple of afternoons a week and have your picture taken sitting in a Porsche once in a while. I'll give you ten thousand a year for it."

Hugo scratched his head boyishly, turning his left ear slightly toward Connors. The figure $25,000 came through loud and clear. "I'll take twenty-five thousand dollars and ten percent of the profits," Hugo said.

Connors laughed, delighted with his new employee's astuteness. "You must have read my mind," he said. They shook on the deal. Hugo was to go on the payroll the next day.

"He's got a head on his shoulders, old Huge," Connors told his wife. "He'll sell cars."

Another of the poker players, Hartwright, the racehorse owner, called Hugo and, after swearing him to secrecy, told him that he and what he called "a few of the boys" were buying up land for a supermarket in a suburb of the city. There was inside information that a superhighway was being built out that way by the city. "It'll be a gold mine," Hartwright said. "I've talked it over with the boys and they think it'd be a nice idea to let you in on it. If you don't have the cash, we can swing a loan. . . ."

Hugo got a loan for $50,000. He was learning that nothing pleases people more than helping a success. Even his father-in-law, who had until then never been guilty of wild feats of generosity, was moved enough by the combination of Hugo's new-found fame and the announcement that he was soon to be a grandfather to buy Hugo and Sibyl an eight-room house with a swimming pool in a good suburb of the city.

So the season went on, weeks during which Hugo heard nothing, spoken or unspoken, that was not for his pleasure or profit, the golden autumn coming to a rhythmic climax once every seven days in two hours of Sunday violence and huzzas.

The newspapers were even beginning to talk about the possibility of "The Cinderella Boys," as Fallon and Hugo and their teammates were called, going all the way to the showdown with Green Bay for the championship. But on the same day, both Fallon and Hugo were hurt—Fallon with a cleverly dislocated elbow and Hugo with a head injury that gave him a severe attack of vertigo that made it seem to him that the whole world was built on a slant.

They lost that game and they were out of the running for the championship of their division and the dream was over.

Before being injured, Hugo had had a good day; and in the plane flying home, even though it seemed to Hugo that it was flying standing on its right wing, he did not feel too bad. All that money in the bank had made him philosophic about communal misfortunes. The team doctor, a hearty fellow who would have been full of cheer at the fall of the Alamo, had assured him that he would be fine in a couple of days and had regaled him with stories of men who had been in a coma for days and had gained more than 100 yards on the ground the following Sunday.

An arctic hush of defeat filled the plane, broken only by the soft complaints of the wounded, of which there were many. Amidships sat the coach, with the owner, forming glaciers of pessimism that flowed inexorably down the aisle. The weather was bad and the plane bumped uncomfortably through soupy black cloud and Hugo, seated next to Johnny Smathers, who was groaning like a dying stag from what the doctor had diagnosed as a superficial contusion of the ribs, was impatient for the trip to end, so that he could be freed from this atmosphere of Waterloo and return to his abundant private world. He remembered that next Sunday was an open date and he was grateful for it. The season had been rewarding, but the tensions had been building up. He could stand a week off.

Then something happened that made him forget about football.

There was a crackling in his left ear, like static. Then he heard a man's voice saying, "VHF one is out." Immediately afterward he heard another man's voice saying, "VHF two is out, too. We've lost radio contact." Hugo looked around, sure that everybody else must have heard it, too, that it had come over the public-address system. But everybody was doing just what he had been doing before, talking in low voices, reading, napping.

"That's a hell of a note." Hugo recognized the captain's voice. "There's forty thousand feet of soup from here to Newfoundland."

Hugo looked out the window. It was black and thick out there. The red light on the tip of the wing was a minute blood-colored blur that seemed to wink out for seconds at a time in the darkness. Hugo closed the curtain and put on his seat belt.

"Well, kiddies," the captain's voice said in Hugo's ear, "happy news. We're lost. If anybody sees the United States down below, tap me on the shoulder."

Nothing unusual happened in the passenger section.

The door to the cockpit opened and the stewardess came out. She had a funny smile on her face that looked as though it had been painted on sideways. She walked down the aisle, not changing her expression, and went to the tail of the plane and sat down there. When she was sure nobody was looking, she hooked the seat belt around her.

The plane bucked a bit and people began to look at their watches. They were due to land in about ten minutes and they weren't losing any altitude. There was a warning squawk from the public-address system and the captain said, "This is your captain speaking. I'm afraid we're going to be a little late. We're running into head winds. I suggest you attach your seat belts."

There was the click of metal all over the plane. It was the last sound Hugo heard for a long time, because he fainted.

He was awakened by a sharp pain in one ear. The right one. The plane was coming down for a landing. Hugo pulled the curtain back and looked out. They were under the cloud now, perhaps 400 feet off the ground and there were lights below. He looked at his watch. They were nearly three hours late.

"You better make it a good one," he heard a man's voice say, and he knew the voice came from the cockpit. "We don't have enough gas for another thousand yards."

Hugo tried to clear his throat. Something dry and furry seemed to be lodged there. Everybody else had already gathered up his belongings, placidly waiting to disembark. They don't know how lucky they are, Hugo thought bitterly as he peered out the window, hungry for the ground.

The plane came in nicely and as it taxied to a halt, the captain said cheerily, "I hope you enjoyed your trip, folks. Sorry about the little delay. See you soon."

The ground hit his feet at a peculiar angle when he debarked from the plane, but he had told Sylvia he would look in at her place when he got back to town. Sibyl was away in Florida with her parents for the week, visiting relatives.

Going over in the taxi, fleeing the harsh world of bruised and defeated men and the memory of his brush with death in the fogbound plane, he thought yearningly of the warm bed awaiting him and the expert, expensive girl.

Sylvia took a long time answering the bell and when she appeared, she was in a bathrobe and had her headache face on. She didn't let Hugo in, but opened the door only enough to speak to him. "I'm in bed, I took two pills," she said, "I have a splitting—"

"Ah, honey," Hugo pleaded. There was a delicious odor coming from her nightgown and robe. He leaned gently against the door.

"It's late," she said sharply. "You look awful. Go home and

get some sleep." She clicked the door shut decisively. He heard her putting the chain in place.

On the way back down the dimly lit staircase from Sylvia's apartment, Hugo resolved always to have a small emergency piece of jewelry in his pocket for moments like this. Outside in the street, he looked up longingly at Sylvia's window. It was on the fourth floor and a crack of light, cozy and tantalizing, came through the curtains. Then, on the cold night air, he heard a laugh. It was warm and sensual in his left ear and he remembered, with a pang that took his breath away, the other occasions when he had heard that laugh. He staggered down the street under the pale lampposts, carrying his valise, feeling like Willy Loman coming toward the end of his career in *Death of a Salesman*. He had the impression that he was being followed slowly by a black car, but he was too distracted to pay it much attention.

When he got home, he took out a pencil and paper and noted down every piece of jewelry he had bought Sylvia that fall, with its price. The total came to $3468.30, tax included. He tore up the piece of paper and went to bed. He slept badly, hearing in his sleep the sound of faltering airplane engines mingled with a woman's laughter four stories above his head.

It rained during practice the next day and as he slid miserably around in the icy, tilted mud, Hugo wondered why he had ever chosen football as a profession. In the showers later, wearily scraping mud off his beard, Hugo became conscious that he was being stared at. Croker, the taxi-squad fullback, was in the next shower, soaping his hair and looking at Hugo with a peculiar small smile on his face. Then, coming from Croker's direction, Hugo heard the long, low, disturbing laugh he had heard the night before. It was as though Croker had it on tape inside his head and was playing it over and over again, like a favorite piece of music. Croker, Hugo thought murderously, Croker! A taxi-squadder! Didn't even get to make the trips with the team. Off every Sunday, treacherously making every minute count while his teammates were fighting for their lives.

Hugo heard the laugh again over the sound of splashing water. The next time there was an intra-squad scrimmage, he was going to maim the son of a bitch.

He wanted to get away from the locker room fast, but when he was dressed and almost out the door, the trainer called to him.

"The coach wants to see you, Pleiss," the trainer said, "Pronto."

Hugo didn't like the "pronto." The trainer had a disagreeable habit of editorializing.

The coach was sitting with his back to the door, looking up at the photograph of Jojo Baines. "Close the door, Pleiss," the coach said, without turning around.

Hugo closed the door.

"Sit down," the coach said, still with his back to Hugo, still staring at the photograph of what the coach had once said was the only 100 percent football player he had ever seen.

Hugo sat down.

The coach said, "I'm fining you two hundred and fifty dollars Pleiss."

"Yes, sir," Hugo said.

The coach finally swung around. He loosened his collar. "Pleiss," he said, "what in the name of Knute Rockne are you up to?"

"I don't know, sir," Hugo said.

"What the hell are you doing staying up until dawn night after night?"

Staying up was not quite an accurate description of what Hugo had been doing, but he didn't challenge the coach's choice of words.

"Don't you know you've been followed, you dummy?" the coach bellowed.

The black car on the empty street. Hugo hung his head. He was disappointed in Sibyl. How could she be so suspicious? And where did she get the money to pay for detectives?

The coach's large hands twitched on the desk. "What are you, a sex maniac?"

"No, sir," Hugo said.

"Shut up!" the coach said.

"Yes, sir," said Hugo.

"And don't think it was me that put a tail on you," the coach said. "It's a lot worse than that. The tail came from the commissioner's office."

Hugo let out his breath, relieved. It wasn't Sibyl. How could he have misjudged her?

"I'll lay my cards on the table, Pleiss," the coach said. "The commissioner's office has been interested in you for a long time now. It's their job to keep this game clean, Pleiss, and I'm with them all the way on that, and make no mistake about it. If there's one thing I won't stand for on my club, it's a crooked ballplayer."

Hugo knew that there were at least 100 things that the coach had from time to time declared he wouldn't stand for on his club, but he didn't think it was the moment to refresh the coach's memory.

"Coach," Hugo began.

"Shut up! When a ballplayer as stupid as you suddenly begins to act as though he has a ouija board under his helmet and is in the middle of one goddamn play after another, naturally they begin to suspect something." The coach opened a drawer in his desk and took out a dark-blue folder from which he extracted several closely typewritten sheets of paper. He put on his glasses to read. "This is the report from the commissioner's office." He ran his eyes over some of the items and shook his head in wonder. "Modesty forbids me from reading to you the account of your sexual exploits, Pleiss," the coach said, "but I must remark that your ability even to trot out onto the field on Sunday after some of the weeks you've spent leaves me openmouthed in awe."

There was nothing Hugo could say to this, so he said nothing.

"So far, you've been lucky," the coach said. "The papers haven't latched onto it yet. But if one word of this comes out, I'll throw you to the wolves so fast you'll pull out of your cleats as you go through the door. Have you heard me?"

"I've heard you, Coach," Hugo said.

The coach fingered the papers on his desk and squinted through his bifocals. "In your sudden career as a lady's man, you also seem to have developed a sense of largess in the bestowal of jewelry. In one shop in this town alone, you have spent well over three thousand dollars in less than two months. At the same time, you buy an eight-room house with a swimming pool, you send your wife on expensive vacations all over the country, you invest fifty thousand dollars in a real-estate deal that is barely legal, you are known to be playing cards for high stakes with the biggest gamblers in the city and you rent a safe-deposit box and are observed stuffing unknown sums of cash into it every week. I know what your salary is, Pleiss. Is it unmannerly of me to inquire whether or not you have fallen upon some large outside source of income recently?"

The coach closed the folder and took off his glasses and sat back. Hugo would have liked to explain, but the words strangled in his throat. All the things that had seemed to him like the smiling gifts of fate now, in that cold blue folder, were arranged against him as the criminal profits of corruption. Hugo liked everyone to like him and he had become used to everyone wishing him well. Now the realization that there were men, the coach among them, who were ready to believe the worst of him and ruin him forever because of it, left him speechless. He waved his hands helplessly.

"Pleiss," the coach said, "I want you to answer one question, and if I ever find out you're lying. . . ." He stopped, significantly.

He didn't add the usual coda, "I'll personally nail you by the hands to the locker-room wall." This omission terrified Hugo as he waited numbly for the question.

"Pleiss," the coach said, "are you getting information from gamblers?"

A wave of shame engulfed Hugo. He couldn't remember ever having felt so awful. He began to sob, all 235 pounds of him.

The coach looked at him, appalled. "Use your handkerchief, man," he said.

Hugo used his handkerchief. Damply he said, "Coach, I swear on the head of my mother, I never talked to a gambler in my life."

"I don't want the head of your mother," the coach snarled. But he seemed reassured. He waited for Hugo's sobs to subside. "All right. Get out of here. And be careful. Remember, you're being watched at all times."

Drying his eyes, Hugo dragged himself out of the office. The public-relations man, Brenatskis, was having a beer in the locker room with a small, gray-haired man with cigarette ash on his vest. Hugo recognized the man. It was Vincent Haley, the sports columnist. Hugo tried to get out without being seen. This was no day to be interviewed by a writer. But Brenatskis spotted him and called, "Hey, Hugo, come over here for a minute."

Flight would be damning. Hugo was sure that the whole world knew by now that he was a man under suspicion. So he tried to compose his face as he went over to the two men. He even managed an innocent, deceitful, country boy's smile.

"Hello, Mr. Haley," he said.

"Glad to see you, Pleiss," said Haley. "How's your head?"

"Fine, fine," Hugo said hurriedly.

"You're having quite a season, Pleiss," Haley said. His voice was hoarse and whiskeyish and full of contempt for athletes, and his pale eyes were like laser beams. "Yeah, quite a season. I don't think I've ever seen a linebacker improve so much from one game to another."

Hugo began to sweat. "Some years you're lucky," he said. "Things fall into place." He waited, cowering inwardly, for the next doomful inquiry. But Haley merely asked him some routine questions, like who was the toughest man in the league going down the middle and what he thought about the comparative abilities of various passers he had played against. "Thanks, Pleiss," Haley said, "that's about all. Good luck with your head." He held out his hand and Hugo shook it gratefully, glad that in another moment he was going to be out of range of those bone-dissolving eyes.

With his hand still in the writer's hand, Hugo heard the whiskeyish voice, but different, as though in some distant echo chamber, saying, in his left ear, "Look at him—two hundred and thirty-five pounds of bone and muscle, twenty-five years old, and he's back here raking in the dough, while my kid, nineteen years old, a hundred and thirty pounds dripping wet, is lying out in the mud and jungle in Vietnam, getting his head shot off. Who did *he* pay off?"

Haley gave Hugo's hand another shake. He even smiled, showing jagged, cynical, tar-stained teeth. "Nice talking to you, Pleiss," he said. "Keep up the good work."

"Thanks, Mr. Haley," Hugo said earnestly. "I'll try."

He went out of the stadium, not watching or caring where he was going, surrounded by enemies.

He kept hearing that rasping, disdainful "Who did *he* pay off?" over and over again as he walked blindly through the streets. At one moment, he stopped, on the verge of going back to the stadium and explaining to the writer about the sixty-three stitches in his knee and what the Army doctor had said about them. But Haley hadn't said anything aloud and it would be a plunge into the abyss if Hugo had to acknowledge that there were certain moments when he could read minds.

So he continued to walk toward the center of the city, trying to forget the coach and the gamblers, trying to forget Vincent Haley and Haley's nineteen-year-old son, weight 130 pounds, getting his head shot off in the jungle. Hugo didn't bother much about politics. He had enough to think about trying to keep from being killed every Sunday without worrying about disturbances 10,000 miles away in small Oriental countries. If the United States Army had felt that he wasn't fit for service, that was their business.

But he couldn't help thinking about that kid out there, with the mortars bursting around him or stepping on poisoned bamboo stakes or being surrounded by grinning little yellow men with machine guns in their hands.

Hugo groaned in complicated agony. He had walked a long way and he was in the middle of the city, with the bustle of the business section all around him, but he couldn't walk away from that picture of Haley's kid lying torn apart under the burned trees whose names he would never know.

Slowly, he became aware that the activity around him was not just the ordinary traffic of the weekday city. He seemed to be in a parade of some kind and he realized, coming out of his private torment, that people were yelling loudly all around him. They also seemed to be carrying signs. He listened attentively now. "Hell, no, we won't go," they were yelling, and, "U.S. go home," and other short phrases of the same general import. And, reading the signs, he saw BURN YOUR DRAFT CARDS and DOWN WITH AMERICAN FASCISM. Interested, he looked carefully at the hundreds of people who were carrying him along with them. There were quite a few young men with long hair and beards, barefooted in sandals, and rather soiled young girls in blue jeans, carrying large flowers, all intermingled with determined-looking suburban matrons and middle-aged, grim-looking men with glasses, who might have been college professors. My, he thought, this is worse than a football crowd.

Then he was suddenly on the steps of the city hall and there were a lot of police, and one boy burned his draft card and a loud cheer went up from the crowd, and Hugo was sorry he didn't have his draft card on him, because he would have liked to burn it, too, as a sort of blind gesture of friendship to Haley's soldier son. He was too shy to shout anything, but he didn't try to get away from the city-hall steps; and when the police started to use their clubs, naturally, he was one of the first to get hit, because he stood head and shoulders above everybody else and was a target that no self-respecting cop would dream of missing.

Standing in front of the magistrate's bench a good many hours later, with a bloody bandage around his head, Hugo was grateful for Brenatskis' presence beside him, although he didn't know how Brenatskis had heard about the little run-in with the police so soon. But if Brenatskis hadn't come, Hugo would have had to spend the night in jail, where there was no bed large enough to accommodate him.

When his name was called, Hugo looked up at the magistrate. The American flag seemed to be waving vigorously on the wall behind the magistrate's head, although it was tacked to the plaster. Everything had a bad habit of waving after the policeman's club.

The magistrate had a small, scooping kind of face that made him look as though he would be useful in going into small holes to search for vermin. The magistrate looked at him with distaste. In his left ear, Hugo heard the magistrate's voice—"What are you, a fag or a Jew or something?" This seemed to Hugo like a clear invasion of his rights, and he raised his hand as if to say something, but Brenatskis knocked it down, just in time.

"Case dismissed," the magistrate said, sounding like a ferret who could talk. "Next."

A lady who looked like somebody's grandmother stepped up belligerently.

Five minutes later, Hugo was going down the night-court steps with Brenatskis. "Holy man," Brenatskis said, "what came over you? It's a lucky thing they got hold of me or you'd be all over the front page tomorrow. And it cost plenty, I don't mind telling you."

Bribery, too, Hugo recorded in his book of sorrows. Corruption of the press and the judiciary.

"And the coach—" Brenatskis waved his arm hopelessly, as though describing the state of the coach's psyche at this juncture were beyond the powers of literature. "He wants to see you. Right now."

"Can't he wait till morning?" Hugo wanted to go home and lie down. It had been an exhausting day.

"He can't wait until morning. He was very definite. The minute you got out, he said, and he didn't care what time it was."

"Doesn't he ever sleep?" Hugo asked forlornly.

"Not tonight, he's not sleeping," said Brenatskis. "He's waiting in his office."

A stalactite formed in the region of Hugo's liver as he thought of facing the coach, the two of them alone at midnight in naked confrontation in a stadium that could accommodate 60,000 people. "Don't you want to come along with me?" he asked Brenatskis.

"No," said Brenatskis. He got into his car and drove off. Hugo thought of moving immediately to Canada. But he hailed a cab and said "The stadium" to the driver. Perhaps there would be a fatal accident on the way.

There was one 40-watt bulb burning over the player's entrance and the shadows thrown by its feeble glare made it look as though a good part of the stadium had disappeared centuries before, like the ruins of a Roman amphitheater. Hugo wished it *were* the ruins of a Roman amphitheater as he pushed the door open. The night watchman, awakened from his doze on a chair tilted back against the wall, looked up at him. "They don't give a man no rest, none of them," Hugo heard the watchman think as he passed him. "Goddamned prima donnas. I hope they all break their fat necks."

"Evenin', Mr. Pleiss. Nice evenin'," the watchman said.

"Yeah," said Hugo. He walked through the shadows under the stands toward the locker room. The ghosts of hundreds of poor, aching, wounded, lame, contract-haunted football players seemed to accompany him, and the wind sighing through the gangways carried on it the echoes of a billion boos. Hugo wondered how he had ever thought a stadium was a place in which you enjoyed yourself.

His hand on the locker-room door, Hugo hesitated. He had never discussed politics with the coach, but he knew that the coach cried on the field every time the band played *The Star-Spangled Banner* and had refused to vote for Barry Goldwater because he thought Goldwater was a Communist.

Resolutely, Hugo pushed the door open and went into the deserted locker room. He passed his locker. His name was still on it. He didn't know whether it was a good or a bad sign.

The door to the coach's office was closed. After one last look around him at the locker room, Hugo rapped on it.

"Come in," the coach said.

Hugo opened the door and went in. The coach was dressed in a dark suit and his collar was closed and he had a black tie on, as though he were en route to a funeral. His face was ravaged by his vigil, his cheeks sunk, his eyes peered out of purplish caverns. He looked worse than Hugo had ever seen him, even worse than the time they lost 45 to 0 to a first-year expansion club.

"My boy," the coach said in a small, racked voice, "I am glad you came late. It has given me time to think, to take a proper perspective. An hour ago, I was ready to destroy you in righteous anger with my bare hands. But I am happy to say that the light of understanding has been vouchsafed me in the watches of this painful night." The coach was in one of his Biblical periods. "Luckily," he said, "after Brenatskis called me to tell me that he had managed to persuade the judge to dismiss the case against you for a hundred dollars—naturally, your pay will be docked— and that the story would be kept out of the papers for another hundred and fifty—that will make two hundred and fifty, in all— I had time to consider. After all, the millions of small boys throughout America who look up to you and your fellows as the noblest expression of clean, aggressive American spirit, who model themselves with innocent hero worship after you and your teammates, are now going to be spared the shock and disillusionment of learning that a player of mine so far forgot himself as to be publicly associated with the enemies of his country—Are you following me, Pleiss?"

"Perfectly, Coach," said Hugo. He felt himself inching back toward the door. This new, gentle-voiced, understanding aspect of the coach was infinitely disturbing, like seeing water suddenly start running uphill, or watching the lights of a great city go out all at once.

"As I was saying, as long as no harm has been done to this

multitude of undeveloped souls who are, in a manner of speaking, our responsibility, I can search within me for Christian forbearance.'' The coach came around the desk and put his hand on Hugo's shoulder. ''Pleiss, you're not a bad boy—you're a stupid boy, but not a bad boy. It was my fault that you got involved in that sordid exhibition. Yes, my fault. You received a terrible blow on the head on Sunday—I should have spotted the symptoms. Instead of brutally making you do wind sprints and hit the dummy for two hours, I should have said, 'Hugo, my boy, go home and lie down and stay in bed for a week, until your poor head has recovered.' Yes, that's what I should have done. I ask your forgiveness, Hugo, for my shortness of vision.''

''Sure, Coach,'' Hugo said.

''And now,'' said the coach, ''before you go home to your loving wife and a good long rest, I want you to do one thing for me.''

''Anything you say, Coach.''

''I want you to join me in singing one verse—just one small verse—of The Star-Spangled Banner. Will you do that for me?''

''Yes, sir,'' Hugo said, sure that he was going to forget what came after ''the rockets' red glare.''

The coach gripped his shoulder hard, then said, ''One two, three. . . .''

They sang The Star-Spangled Banner together. The coach was weeping after the first line.

When they had finished and the echoes had died down under the grandstand, the coach said, ''Good. Now go home. I'd drive you home myself, but I'm working on some new plays I want to give the boys tomorrow. Don't you worry. You won't miss them. I'll send them along to you by messenger and you can glance at them when you feel like it. And don't worry about missing practice. When you feel ready, just drop around. God bless you, my boy.'' The coach patted Hugo a last time on the shoulder and turned to gaze at Jojo Baines, his eyes still wet from the anthem.

Hugo went out softly.

He stayed close to home all the rest of the week, living off canned goods and watching television. Nothing much could happen to him, he figured, in the privacy of his own apartment. But even there, he had his moments of distress.

He was sitting watching a quiz show for housewives at nine o'clock in the morning when he heard the key in the door and the cleaning woman, Mrs. Fitzgerald, came in. Mrs. Fitzgerald was a gray-haired lady who smelled of other people's dust. "I hope you're not feeling poorly, Mr. Pleiss," she said solicitously. "It's a beautiful day. It's a shame to spend it indoors."

"I'm going out later," Hugo lied.

Behind his back, he heard Mrs. Fitzgerald think. "Lazy, hulking slob. Never did an honest day's work in his life. Comes the revolution, they'll take care of the likes of him. He'll find himself with a pick in his hands, on the roads. I hope I live to see the day."

Hugo wondered if he shouldn't report Mrs. Fitzgerald to the FBI, but then decided against it. He certainly didn't want to get involved with *them*.

He listened to a speech by the President and was favorably impressed by the President's command of the situation, both at home and abroad. The President explained that although things at the moment did not seem 100 percent perfect, vigorous steps were being taken, at home and abroad, to eliminate poverty, ill health, misguided criticism by irresponsible demagogues, disturbances in the streets and the unfavorable balance of payments. Hugo was also pleased, as he touched the bump on his head caused by the policeman's club, when he heard the President explain how well the war was going and why we could expect the imminent collapse of the enemy. The President peered out of the television set, masterly, persuasive, confident, including all the citizens of the country in his friendly, fatherly smile. Then, while the President was silent for a moment before going on to other matters, Hugo heard the President's voice, though in quite a different tone, saying, "Ladies and gentlemen, if you really knew what was going on here, you'd *piss*."

Hugo turned the television off.

Then the next day, the television set broke down, and as he watched the repairman fiddle with it, humming mournfully down in his chest somewhere, Hugo heard the television repairman think, "Stupid jerk. All he had to do was take a look and he'd see the only thing wrong is this loose wire. Slap it into the jack and turn a screw and the job's done." But when the television man turned around, he was shaking his head sadly. "I'm afraid you got trouble, mister," the television repairman said. "There's danger of implosion. I'll have to take the set with me. And there's the expense of a new tube."

"What's it going to cost?" Hugo asked.

"Thirty, thirty-five dollars, if we're lucky," said the television repairman.

Hugo let him take the set. Now he knew he was a moral coward, along with everything else.

He was cheered up, though, when his mother and father telephoned, collect, from Maine, to see how he was. They had a nice chat. "And how's my darling Sibyl?" Hugo's mother said. "Can I say hello to her?"

"She's not here," Hugo said. He explained about the trip to Florida with her parents.

"Fine people, fine people," Hugo's mother said. She had met Sibyl's parents once, at the wedding. "I do hope they're all enjoying themselves down South. Well, take care of yourself, Hooey. . . ." Hooey was a family pet name for him. "Don't let them hit you in the face with the ball." His mother's grasp of the game was fairly primitive. "And give my love to Sibyl when she gets home."

Hugo hung up. Then very clearly, he heard his mother say to his father, 1000 miles away in northern Maine, "With her parents. I bet."

Hugo didn't answer the phone the rest of the week.

Sibyl arrived from Florida late Saturday afternoon. She looked beautiful as she got off the plane and she had a new fur coat that her father had bought her. Hugo had bought a hat to keep Sibyl from noticing the scalp wound inflicted by the policeman's club, at least at the airport, with people around. He had never owned a hat and he hoped Sibyl wouldn't notice this abrupt change in his style of dressing. She didn't notice it. And back in their apartment, she didn't notice the wound, although it was nearly four inches long and could be seen quite clearly through his hair, if you looked at all closely. She chattered gaily on about Florida, the beaches, the color of the water, the flamingos at the race track. Hugo told her how glad he was that she had had such a good time and admired her new coat.

Sibyl said she was tired from the trip and wanted to have a simple dinner at home and get to bed early. Hugo said he thought that was a good idea. He didn't want to see anybody he knew, or anybody he didn't know.

By nine o'clock, Sibyl was yawning and went in to get undressed. Hugo had had three bourbons to keep Sibyl from worrying about his seeming a bit distracted. He started to make up a bed on the living-room couch. From time to time during the week, he had remembered the sound of the low laugh from Sylvia's window and it had made the thought of sex distasteful to him. He had even noticed a certain deadness in his lower regions and he doubted whether he ever could make love to a woman again. "I bet," he thought, "I'm the first man in the history of the world to be castrated by a laugh."

Sibyl came out of the bedroom just as he was fluffing up a pillow. She was wearing a black nightgown that concealed nothing. "Sweetie," Sibyl said reproachfully.

"It's Saturday night," Hugo said, giving a final extra jab at the pillow.

"So?" You'd never guess that she was pregnant as she stood there at the doorway in her nightgown.

"Well, Saturday night, during the season," Hugo said. "I guess I've gotten into the rhythm, you might say, of sleeping alone."

"But there's no game tomorrow, Hugo." There was a tone of impatience in Sibyl's voice.

The logic was unassailable. "That's true," Hugo said. He followed Sibyl into the bedroom. If he was impotent, Sibyl might just as well find it out now as later.

It turned out that his fears were groundless. The three bourbons, perhaps.

As they approached the climax of their lovemaking, Hugo was afraid Sibyl was going to have a heart attack, she was breathing so fast. Then, through the turbulence, he heard what she was thinking. "I should have bought that green dress at Bonwit's," Sibyl's thoughtful, calm voice echoed just below his eardrum. "I could do without the belt, though. And then I just might try cutting up that old mink hat of mine and using it for cuffs on that dingy old brown rag I got last Christmas. Maybe my wrists wouldn't look so skinny with fur around them."

Hugo finished his task and Sibyl said "Ah" happily and kissed him and went to sleep, snoring a little. Hugo stayed awake for a long time, occasionally glancing over at his wife's wrists and then staring at the ceiling and thinking about married life.

Sibyl was still asleep when he woke up. He didn't waken her. A church bell was ringing in the distance, inviting, uncomplicated and pure, promising peace to tormented souls. Hugo got out of bed and dressed swiftly but carefully and hurried to the comforts of religion. He sat in the rear, on the aisle, soothed by the organ and the prayers and the upright Sunday-morning atmosphere of belief and remittance from sin.

The sermon was on sex and violence in the modern world and Hugo appreciated it. After what he had gone through, a holy examination of those aspects of today's society was just what he needed.

The minister was a big red-faced man, forthright and vigorous.

Violence actually got only a fleeting and rather cursory condemnation. The Supreme Court was admonished to mend its ways and to refrain from turning loose on a Christian society a horde of pornographers, rioters, dope addicts and other sinners because of the present atheistic conception of what the minister scornfully called civil rights, and that was about it.

But when it came to sex, the minister hit his stride. The church resounded to his denunciation of naked and leering girls on magazine stands, of sex education for children, of an unhealthy interest in birth control, of dating and premarital lasciviousness, of Swedish and French moving pictures, of mixed bathing in revealing swimsuits, of petting in parked cars, of all novels that had been written since 1910, of coeducational schools, of the new math, which the minister explained, was a subtle means of undermining the moral code. Unchaperoned picnics were mentioned, miniskirts got a full two minutes, and even the wearing of wigs, designed to lure the all-too-susceptible American male into lewd and unsocial behavior, came in for its share of condemnation. The way the minister was going on, it would not have surprised some members of the congregation if he finished up with an edict against cross-pollination.

Hugo sat at the rear of the church, feeling chastened. It was a good feeling. That was what he had come to church for, and he almost said "Amen" aloud after one or two of the more spiritedly presented items on the minister's list.

Then, gradually, he became aware of a curious cooing voice in his left ear. "Ah, you, fourth seat to the left in the third row," he heard, "you with that little pink cleft just peeping out, why don't you come around late one weekday afternoon for a little spiritual consolation, ha-ha." Aghast, Hugo realized it was the minister's voice he was hearing.

Aloud, the minister was moving on to a rather unconvincing endorsement of the advantages of celibacy. "And you, the plump one in the fifth row, with the tight brassiere, Mrs. What's-your-name, looking down at your hymnbook as though you were planning to go into a nunnery," Hugo heard, mixed with loud advice on holy thoughts and vigorous, innocent exercise, "I can guess what you're up to when your husband goes out of town. I wouldn't mind if you had *my* private telephone number in your little black book, ha-ha."

Hugo sat rigid in his pew. This was going just a little bit too far.

The minister had swung into chastity. He wanted to end on a note of uplift. His head was tilted back, heavenward, but through slitted eyes, he scanned his Sunday-best parishioners. The minister had a vested interest in chastity and his voice took on a special solemn intonation as he described how particularly pleasing this virtue was in the eyes of God and His angels. "And little Miss Crewes, with your white gloves and white socks," Hugo heard, "ripening away like a tasty little Georgia persimmon, trembling on the luscious brink of womanhood, nobody has to tell me what you do behind the stands on the way home from school. The rectory is only two blocks from school, baby, and it's on your way home. Just one timid knock on the door will suffice, ha-ha. There's always tea and little cakes for little girls like you at the rectory, ha-ha."

If Hugo hadn't been afraid of making a scene, he would have got up and run out of the church. Instead, he rapped himself sharply across the left ear. The consequent ringing kept him from hearing anything else. Several people turned around at the sound of the blow and stared disapprovingly at Hugo, but he didn't care. By the time the ringing stopped, the sermon was over and the minister was announcing the number of the hymn.

It was *Rock of Ages*. Hugo wasn't sure of the words, but he hummed, so as not to draw any more attention to himself.

The organ swelled, the sopranos, altos, tenors and bassos joined in, musical and faithful.

> "Rock of Ages, cleft for me,
> Let me hide myself in Thee.
> Let the water and the blood,
> From Thy side, a healing flood,
> Be of sin the double cure . . ."

Hugo was swept along on the tide of sound. He didn't have much of an ear for music and the only things he played on the phonograph at home were some old 78-rpm Wayne King records that his mother had collected when she was a girl and had given him as a wedding present. But now the diapason of the organ, the pure flutelike tones of the women and young girls addressing God, the deep cello support of the men, combined to give him a feeling of lightness, of floating on spring airs, of being lost in endless fragrant gardens. Virgins caressed his forehead with petaled fingers, waters sang in mountain streams, strong men embraced him in everlasting brotherhood. By the time the congregation reached "Thou must save, and Thou alone," Hugo was out of his pew and writhing in ecstasy on the floor.

It was lucky he was in the last row, and on the aisle.

The hymn was never finished. It started to falter at "While I draw this fleeting breath," as people turned around to see what was happening and came to a final stop on "When I rise to worlds unknown." By that time, everybody in the church was standing up and looking at Hugo, trembling, sprawled on his back, in the middle of the aisle.

The last notes of the organ came to a halt discordantly, at a signal from the minister. Hugo lay still for an instant, conscious of 300 pairs of eyes on him. Then he leaped up and fled.

He rang the bell a long time, but it was only when he roared, "I know you're in there. Open up or I'll break it down," and began to buck at the door with his shoulder that it opened.

"What's going on here?" Miss Cattavi asked, blocking his way. "There are no visiting hours on Sunday."

"There will be this Sunday," Hugo said hoarsely. He pushed roughly past Miss Cattavi. She was all muscle. It was the first time he had ever been rude to a lady.

"He's in Romania," Miss Cattavi said, trying to hold on to him.

"I'll show him Romania," Hugo cried, throwing open doors and dragging Miss Cattavi after him like a junior high school guard.

Dr. Sebastian was behind the fourth door, in a room like a library, practicing dry-fly casting. He was wearing hip-length rubber boots.

"Oh, Mr. Pleiss," Dr. Sebastian said merrily, "you came back."

"I sure did come back," Hugo said. He had difficulty talking.

"You want your other ear done, I wager," said Dr. Sebastian, reeling in delicately.

Hugo grabbed Dr. Sebastian by the lapels and lifted him off the floor so that they were eye to eye. Dr. Sebastian weighed only 140 pounds, although he was quite fat. "I don't want the other ear done," Hugo said loudly.

"Should I call the police?" Miss Cattavi had her hand on the phone.

Hugo dropped Dr. Sebastian, who went down on one knee but made a creditable recovery. Hugo ripped the phone out of the wall. He had always been very careful of other people's property. It was something his father had taught him as a boy.

"Don't tell me," Dr. Sebastian said solicitously, "that the ear has filled up again. It's unusual, but not unheard of. Don't worry about it. The treatment is simple. A little twirl of an instrument and—"

Hugo grabbed the doctor's throat with one hand and kept Miss Cattavi off with the other. "Now, listen to this," Hugo said, "listen to what you did to me."

"Cawlsnhnd on my goddamn windpipe," the doctor said.

Hugo let him go.

"Now, my dear young man," Dr. Sebastian said, "if you'll only tell me what little thing is bothering you. . . ."

"Get her out of the room." Hugo gestured toward Miss Cattavi. The things he had to tell Dr. Sebastian could not be said in front of a woman.

"Miss Cattavi, please . . ." Dr. Sebastian said.

"Animal," Miss Cattavi said, but she went out of the room and closed the door behind her.

Moving out of range, Dr. Sebastian went behind a desk. He remained standing. "I could have sworn that your ear was in superb condition," he said.

"Superb!" Hugo was sorry he had taken his hand off the doctor's throat.

"Well, you can hear your team's signals now, can't you?" Dr. Sebastian said.

"If that's all I could hear," Hugo moaned.

"Ah." Dr. Sebastian brightened. "Your hearing is better than normal. I told you you had an extraordinary aural arrangement. It only took a little cutting, a bold clearing away of certain extraneous matter. . . . You must be having a very good season."

"I am having a season in hell," Hugo said, unconscious that he was now paying tribute to a French poet.

"I'm terribly confused," the doctor said petulantly. "I do better for you than you ever hoped for and what is my reward—you come in here and try to strangle me. I do think you owe me an explanation, Mr. Pleiss."

"I owe you a lot more than that," Hugo said. "Where did you learn your medicine—in the Congo?"

Dr. Sebastian drew himself to his full height. "Cornell Medical School," he said with quiet pride. "Now, if you'll only tell me—"

"I'll tell you, all right," Hugo said. He paced up and down the room. It was an old house and the timbers creaked. The sound was like a thousand sea gulls in Hugo's ear.

"First," said Dr. Sebastian, "just what is it that you want me to do for you?"

"I want you to put my ear back the way it was when I came to you," Hugo said.

"You want to be deaf again?" the doctor asked incredulously.

"Exactly."

Dr. Sebastian shook his head. "My dear fellow," he said, "I can't do that. It's against all medical ethics. If it ever got out, I'd be barred forever from practicing medicine anyplace in the United States. A graduate of Cornell—"

"I don't care where you graduated from. You're going to do it."

"You're overwrought, Mr. Pleiss," the doctor said. He sat down at his desk and drew a piece of paper to him and took out a pen. "Now, if you'll only attempt, in a calm and orderly way, to describe the symptoms. . . ."

Hugo paced up and down some more, trying to be calm and orderly. Deep down, he still had a great respect for doctors. "It started," he began, "with hearing the other team's signals."

Dr. Sebastian nodded approvingly and jotted something down.

"In the huddle," Hugo said.

"What's a huddle?"

Hugo explained, as best he could, what a huddle was. "And it's fifteen yards away and they whisper and sixty thousand people are yelling at the top of their lungs all around you."

"I knew it was a successful operation," Dr. Sebastian said, beaming in self-appreciation, "but I had no idea it was *that* successful. It must be very helpful in your profession. Congratulations. It will make a most interesting paper for the next congress of—"

"Shut up," Hugo said. He then went on to describe how he began understanding what the signals meant. Dr. Sebastian's face got a little graver as he asked Hugo to kindly repeat what he had just said and to explain exactly what was the significance of "Brown right! Draw fifty-five . . . on two!" When he finally got it straight and noted that it was a secret code, different for each team, and that the codes were as jealously guarded from opposing teams as the crown jewels, he stopped jotting anything down. And when Hugo went on to the moment when he knew that the opposing quarterback was thinking, "No. . . . It won't work, they're over-shifting on us," in just those words, Dr. Sebastian put his pen down altogether and a look of concern came into his eyes.

The description of the poker game only made the doctor shrug. "These days," he said, "we are just beginning to catch a glimmer of the powers of extrasensory perception, my dear fellow. Why, down at Duke University—"

"Keep quiet," Hugo said, and described, with a reminiscent

thrill of terror, the radio breakdown in the cockpit of the airplane and hearing the conversation between the pilots.

"I'm sure that could be explained," the doctor said. "A freak electronic phenomenon that—"

Hugo cut in. "I want you to hear what happened to me with a girl," Hugo said. "There was nothing electronic about that."

Dr. Sebastian listened with interest as Hugo relived the experience with Sylvia. Dr. Sebastian licked his lips from time to time but said nothing. He clucked sympathetically, though, when Hugo described the laughter four stories up and Croker's replay in the shower.

Hugo didn't say anything about his conversations with the coach. There were certain things too painfull to recall.

In a rush, Hugo let all the rest of it out—Vietnam, the clubbing by the policeman, the interior sneer of the magistrate, Mrs. Fitzgerald's dangerous radical leanings, the President's speech, the television repairman's chicanery, his mother's judgment of his wife.

Dr. Sebastian sat there without saying a word, shaking his head pityingly from time to time.

Hugo went on, without mercy for himself, about the green dress and mink cuffs at a time when you'd bet for sure a woman would be thinking about other things. "Well," he demanded, "what've you got to say about that?"

"Unfortunately," Dr. Sebastian said, "I've never been married. A man my size." He shrugged regretfully. "But there are well-documented cases on record of loving couples who have spent long years together, who are very close together, who have a telepathic sympathy with each other's thoughts. . . ."

"Let me tell you what happened in church this morning," Hugo said desperately. The doctor's scientific ammunition was beginning to take its toll. The fearful thought occurred to him that he wasn't going to shake the doctor and that he was going to walk out of that door no different from the way he had entered.

"It is nice to hear that a big, famous, attractive young man like you still goes to church on Sunday morning," the doctor murmured.

"I've gone to my last church," Hugo said and gave him the gist of what he had heard the minister think while he was delivering his sermon on sex and violence.

The doctor smiled tolerantly. "The men of the cloth are just like us other poor mortals," he said. "It's very probable that it was merely the transference of your own desires and—"

"Then the last thing," Hugo said, knowing he *had* to convince the doctor somehow. He told him about writhing on the floor of the church, the spring breezes, the smell of flowers, the unutterable ecstasy during *Rock of Ages*.

The doctor made an amused little *moue*. "A common experience," he said, "for simple and susceptible religious natures. It does no harm."

"Three hundred people watching a two-hundred-and-thirty-five-pound man jerking around on the floor like a hooked tuna!" Hugo shouted. "That does no harm? And you yourself told me that if people could *really* hear, they'd writhe on the floor in ecstasy when they listened to Beethoven."

"Beethoven, yes," the doctor said. "But *Rock of Ages*?" He was a musical snob, Dr. Sebastian. "Tum-tum-tah-dee, tum-tum-dah," he sang contemptuously. Then he became professional. He leaned across the desk and patted Hugo's hand and spoke quietly. "My dear young man, I believe every word you say. You undoubtedly think you have gone through these experiences. The incidents on the playing field can easily be explained. You are highly trained in the intricacies of a certain game, you are coming into your full powers, your understanding of your profession leads you into certain instantaneous practical insights. Be grateful for them. I've already explained the cards, the minister, your wife. The passage with the lady you call Sylvia is a concretization of your sense of guilt, combined with a certain natural young man's sexual appetite. Everything else, I'm afraid, is hallucination. I suggest you see a psychiatrist. I have the name of a good man and I'll give him a call and—"

Hugo growled.

"What did you say?" the doctor asked.

Hugo growled again and went over to the window. The doctor followed him, worried now, and looked out the window. Fifty yards away, on the soft, leaf-covered lawn, a five-year-old boy in sneakers was crossing over toward the garage-way of the next house.

The two men stood in silence for a moment.

The doctor sighed. "If you'll come into my operating room," he said.

When he left the doctor's house an hour later, Hugo had a small bandage behind his left ear, but he was happy. The left side of his head felt like a corked-up cider bottle.

Hugo didn't intercept another pass all the rest of the season. He was fooled by the simplest hand-offs and dashed to the left when the play went to the right, and he couldn't hear Johnny Smathers' shouts of warning as the other teams lined up. Johnny Smathers stopped talking to him after two games and moved in with another roommate on road trips. At the end of the season, Hugo's contract was not renewed. The official reason the coach gave to the newspapers was that Hugo's head injury had turned out to be so severe that he would be risking permanent disablement if he ever got hit again.

Dr. Sebastian charged him $500 for the operation and, what with the fine and making up the bribes to the magistrate and the newspapers, that took care of the $1000 raise the coach had promised him. But Hugo was glad to pay for it.

By January tenth, he was contentedly and monogamously selling insurance for his father-in-law, although he had to make sure to sit on the left side of prospects to be able to hear what they were saying.

# Where All Things Wise and Fair Descend

He woke up feeling good. There was no reason for him to wake up feeling anything else.

He was an only child. He was twenty years old. He was over six feet tall and weighed 180 pounds and had never been sick in his whole life. He was number two on the tennis team and back home in his father's study there was a whole shelf of cups he had won in tournaments since he was eleven years old. He had a lean, sharply cut face, straight black hair that he wore just a little long, which prevented him from looking merely like an athlete. A girl had once said he looked like Shelley. Another, like Laurence Olivier. He had smiled noncommittally at both girls.

He had a retentive memory and classes were easy for him. He had just been put on the dean's list. His father, who was doing well up North in an electronics business, had sent him a check for $100 as a reward. The check had been in his box the night before.

He had a gift for mathematics and probably could get a job teaching in the department if he wanted it upon graduation, but he planned to go into his father's business.

He was not one of the single-minded educational wizards who roamed the science departments. He got A's in English and history and had memorized most of Shakespeare's sonnets and read Roethke and Eliot and Ginsberg. He had tried marijuana. He was invited to all the parties. When he went home, mothers made obvious efforts to throw their daughters at him.

His own mother was beautiful and young and funny. There were no unbroken silver cords in the family. He was having an affair with one of the prettiest girls on the campus and she said she loved him. From time to time he said he loved her. When he said it he meant it. At that moment, anyway.

Nobody he had ever cared for had as yet died and everybody in his family had come home safe from all the wars.

The world saluted him.

He maintained his cool.

No wonder he woke up feeling good.

It was nearly December, but the California sun made a summer morning of the season and the girls and boys in corduroys and T-shirts and bright-colored sweaters on their way to their ten-o'clock classes walked over green lawns and in and out of the shadows of trees that had not yet lost their leaves.

He passed the sorority house where Adele lived and waved as she came out. His first class every Tuesday was at ten o'clock and the sorority house was on his route to the arts buildings in which the classroom was situated.

Adele was a tall girl, her dark, combed head coming well above his shoulder. She had a triangular, blooming, still-childish face. Her walk, even with the books she was carrying in her arms, wasn't childish, though, and he was amused at the envious looks directed at him by some of the other students as Adele paced at his side down the graveled path.

"'She walks in beauty,'" Steve said, "'like the night/Of cloudless climes and starry skies;/And all that's best of dark and bright/Meet in her aspect and her eyes.'"

"What a nice thing to hear at ten o'clock in the morning," Adele said. "Did you bone up on that for me?"

"No," he said. "We're having a test on Byron today."

"Animal," she said.

He laughed.

"Are you taking me to the dance Saturday night?" she asked.

He grimaced. He didn't like to dance. He didn't like the kind of music that was played and he thought the way people danced these days was devoid of grace. "I'll tell you later," he said.

"I have to know today," Adele said. "Two other boys've asked me."

"I'll tell you at lunch," he said.

"What time?"

"One. Can the other aspirants hold back their frenzy to dance until then?"

"Barely," she said. He knew that with or without him, Adele would be at the dance on Saturday night. She loved to dance and he had to admit that a girl had every right to expect the boy she was seeing almost every night in the week to take her dancing at least once on the weekend. He felt very mature, almost fatherly, as he resigned himself to four hours of heat and noise on Saturday night. But he didn't tell Adele that he'd take her. It wouldn't do her any harm to wait until lunch.

He squeezed her hand as they parted and watched for a moment as she swung down the path, conscious of the provocative way she was walking, conscious of the eyes on her. He smiled and continued on his way, waving at people who greeted him.

It was early and Mollison, the English professor, had not yet put in an appearance. The room was only half full as Steve entered it, but there wasn't the usual soprano-tenor turning-up sound of conversation from the students who were already there. They sat in their chairs quietly, not talking, most of them ostentatiously arranging their books or going through their notes. Occasionally, almost furtively, one or another of them would look up toward the front of the room and the blackboard, where a thin boy with wispy reddish hair was writing swiftly and neatly behind the teacher's desk.

"Oh, weep for Adonais—he is dead!" the red-haired boy had written. "Wake, melancholy Mother, wake and weep!"

> Yet wherefore? Quench within their burning
>   bed
> Thy fiery tears, and let thy loud heart keep
> Like his a mute and uncomplaining sleep;
> For he is gone where all things wise and fair
> Descend. Oh, dream not that the amorous
>   Deep
> Will yet restore him to the vital air;
> Death feeds on his mute voice, and laughs
>   at our despair.

Then, on a second blackboard, where the boy was finishing the last lines of another stanza, was written:

> He has outsoared the shadow of our night;
> Envy and calumny and hate and pain,
> And that unrest which men miscall delight;
> Can touch him not and torture not again;
> From the contagion of the world's slow stain
> He is secure, and now can never mourn
> A heart grown cold, a head grown grey in vain;

Professor Mollison came bustling in with the half-apologetic smile of an absent-minded man who is afraid he is always late.

He stopped at the door, sensing by the quiet that this was no ordinary Tuesday morning in his classroom. He peered nearsightedly at Crane writing swiftly in rounded chalk letters on the blackboard.

Mollison took out his glasses and read for a moment, then went over to the window without a word and stood there looking out, a graying, soft-faced, rosy-cheeked old man, the soberness of his expression intensified by the bright sunlight at the window.

"Nor," Crane was writing, the chalk making a dry sound in the silence,

> *when the spirit's self has ceased to burn,*
> *With sparkless ashes load an unlamented urn.*

When Crane had finished, he put the chalk down neatly and stepped back to look at what he had written. A girl's laugh came in on the fragrance of cut grass through the open window and there was a curious hushing little intake of breath all through the room.

The bell rang, abrasively, for the beginning of classes. When the bell stopped, Crane turned around and faced the students seated in rows before him. He was a lanky, skinny boy, only nineteen, and he was already going bald. He hardly ever spoke in class and when he spoke, it was in a low, harsh whisper.

He didn't seem to have any friends and he never was seen with girls and the time he didn't spend in class he seemed to spend in the library. Crane's brother had played fullback on the football team, but the brothers had rarely been seen together, and the fact that the huge, graceful athlete and the scarecrow bookworm were members of the same family seemed like a freak of eugenics to the students who knew them both.

Steve knew why Crane had come early to write the two verses of Shelley's lament on the clean morning blackboard. The Saturday night before, Crane's brother had been killed in an automobile accident on the way back from the game, which had been played in San Francisco. The funeral had taken place yesterday, Monday. Now it was Tuesday morning and Crane's first class since the death of his brother.

Crane stood there, narrow shoulders hunched in a bright tweed jacket that was too large for him, surveying the class without emotion. He glanced once more at what he had written, as though to make sure the problem he had placed on the board had been correctly solved, then turned again to the group of gigantic, blossoming, rosy California boys and girls, unnaturally serious and a little embarrassed by this unexpected prologue to their class, and began to recite.

He recited flatly, without any emotion in his voice, moving casually back and forth in front of the blackboards, occasionally turning to the text to flick off a little chalk dust, to touch the end of a word with his thumb, to hesitate at a line, as though he had suddenly perceived a new meaning in it.

Mollison, who had long ago given up any hope of making any impression on the sun-washed young California brain with the fragile hammer of nineteenth-century Romantic poetry, stood at the window, looking out over the campus, nodding in rhythm from time to time and occasionally whispering a line, almost silently, in unison with Crane.

" '. . . an unlamented urn,' " Crane said, still as flat and unemphatic as ever, as though he had merely gone through the two verses as a feat of memory. The last echo of his voice quiet now in the still room, he looked out at the class through his thick glasses, demanding nothing. Then he went to the back of the room and sat down in his chair and began putting his books together.

Mollison, finally awakened from his absorption with the sunny lawn, the whirling sprinklers, the shadows of the trees speckling in the heat and the wind, turned away from the window and walked slowly to his desk. He peered nearsightedly for a moment at the script crammed on the blackboards, then said, absently, "On the death of Keats. The class is excused."

For once, the students filed out silently, making a point, with youthful good manners, of not looking at Crane, bent over at his chair, pulling books together.

Steve was nearly the last one to leave the room and he waited outside the door for Crane. *Somebody* had to say something, do something, whisper "I'm sorry," shake the boy's hand. Steve didn't want to be the one, but there was nobody else left. When Crane came out, Steve fell into place beside him and they went out of the building together.

"My name is Dennicott," Steve said.

"I know," said Crane.

"Can I ask you a question?"

"Sure." There was no trace of grief in Crane's voice or manner. He blinked through his glasses at the sunshine, but that was all.

"Why did you do that?"

"Did you object?" The question was sharp but the tone was mild, offhand, careless.

"Hell, no," Steve said. "I just want to know why you did it."

"My brother was killed Saturday night," Crane said.

"I know."

"'The death of Keats. The class is excused.'" Crane chuckled softly but without malice. "He's a nice old man, Mollison. Did you ever read the book he wrote about Marvell?"

"No," Steve said.

"Terrible book," Crane said. "You really want to know?" He peered with sudden sharpness at Steve.

"Yes," Steve said.

"Yes," Crane said absently, brushing at his forehead, "you would be the one who would ask. Out of the whole class. Did you know my brother?"

"Just barely," Steve said. He thought about Crane's brother, the fullback. A gold helmet far below on a green field, a number (what number?), a doll brought out every Saturday to do skillful and violent maneuvers in a great wash of sound, a photograph in a program, a young, brutal face looking out a little scornfully from the page. Scornful of what? Of whom? The inept photographer? The idea that anyone would really be interested in knowing what face was on that numbered doll? The notion that what he was doing was important enough to warrant this attempt to memorialize him, so that somewhere, in somebody's attic fifty years from now, that young face would still be there, in the debris, part of some old man's false memory of his youth?

"He didn't seem much like John Keats to you, did he?" Crane stopped under a tree, in the shade, to rearrange the books under his arm. He seemed oppressed by sunshine and he held his books clumsily and they were always on the verge of falling to the ground.

"To be honest," Steve said, "no, he didn't seem much like John Keats to me."

Crane nodded gently. "But I knew him," he said. "I knew him. And nobody who made those goddamned speeches at the funeral yesterday knew him. And he didn't believe in God or in funerals or those goddamned speeches. He needed a proper ceremony of farewell," Crane said, "and I tried to give it to him. All it took was a little chalk, and a poet, and none of those liars in black suits. Do you want to take a ride today?"

"Yes," Steve said without hesitation.

"I'll meet you at the library at eleven," Crane said. He waved stiffly and hunched off, gangling, awkward, ill-nourished, thin-haired, laden with books, a discredit to the golden Coastal legend.

822

They drove north in silence. Crane had an old Ford without a top and it rattled so much and the wind made so much noise as they bumped along that conversation would have been almost impossible, even if they had wished to talk. Crane bent over the wheel, driving nervously, with an excess of care, his long pale hands gripping the wheel tightly. Steve hadn't asked where they were going and Crane hadn't told him. Steve hadn't been able to get hold of Adele to tell her he probably wouldn't be back in time to have lunch with her, but there was nothing to be done about that now. He sat back, enjoying the sun and the yellow, burnt-out hills and the long, grayish-blue swells of the Pacific beating lazily into the beaches and against the cliffs of the coast. Without being told, he knew that this ride somehow was a continuation of the ceremony in honor of Crane's brother.

They passed several restaurants alongside the road. Steve was hungry, but he didn't suggest stopping. This was Crane's expedition and Steve had no intention of interfering with whatever ritual Crane was following.

They rocked along between groves of lemon and orange and the air was heavy with the perfume of the fruit, mingled with the smell of salt from the sea.

They went through the flecked shade of avenues of eucalyptus that the Spanish monks had planted in another century to make their journeys from mission to mission bearable in the California summers. Rattling along in the noisy car, squinting a little when the car spurted out into bare sunlight, Steve thought of what the road must have looked like with an old man in a cassock nodding along it on a sleepy mule, to the sound of distant Spanish bells, welcoming travelers. There were no bells ringing today. California, Steve thought, sniffing the diesel oil of a truck in front of them, has not improved.

The car swerved around a turn, Crane put on the brakes and they stopped. Then Steve saw what they had stopped for.

There was a huge tree leaning over a bend of the highway and all the bark at road level on one side of the tree had been ripped off. The wood beneath, whitish, splintered, showed in a raw wound.

"This is the place," Crane said, in his harsh whisper. He stopped the engine and got out of the car. Steve followed him and stood to one side as Crane peered nearsightedly through his glasses at the tree. Crane touched the tree, just at the edge of the wound.

"Eucalyptus," he said. "From the Greek, meaning well covered; the flower, before it opens having a sort of cap. A genus of plants of the N. O. Myrtaceae. If I had been a true brother," he said, "I would have come here Saturday morning and cut this tree down. My brother would be alive today." He ran his hand casually over the torn and splintered wood, and Steve remembered how he had touched the blackboard and flicked chalk dust off the ends of words that morning, unemphatically, in contrast with the feel of things, the slate, the chalk mark at the end of the last "s" in Adonais, the gummy, drying wood. "You'd think," Crane said, "that if you loved a brother enough you'd have sense enough to come and cut a tree down, wouldn't you? The Egyptians, I read somewhere," he said, "were believed to have used the oil of the eucalyptus leaf in the embalming process." His long hand flicked once more at the torn bark. "Well, I didn't cut the tree down. Let's go."

He strode back to the car, without looking back at the tree. He got into the car behind the wheel and sat slumped there, squinting through his glasses at the road ahead of him, waiting for Steve to settle himself beside him. "It's terrible for my mother and father," Crane said, after Steve had closed the door behind him. A truck filled with oranges passed them in a thunderous whoosh and a swirl of dust, leaving a fragrance of a hundred weddings on the air. "We live at home, you know. My brother and I were the only children they had, and they look at me and they can't help feeling, If it had to be one of them, why couldn't it have been *him?* and it shows in their eyes and they know it shows in their eyes and they know I agree with them and they feel guilty and I can't help them." He started the engine with a succession of nervous, uncertain gestures, like a man who was just learning how to drive. He turned the car around in the direction of Los Angeles and they started south. Steve looked once more at the tree, but Crane kept his eyes on the road ahead of him.

"I'm hungry," he said. "I know a place where we can get abalone about ten miles from here."

They were sitting in the weather-beaten shack with the windows open on the ocean, eating their abalone and drinking beer. The jukebox was playing *Downtown*. It was the third time they were listening to *Downtown*. Crane kept putting dimes into the machine and choosing the same song over and over again.

"I'm crazy about that song," he said. "Saturday night in America. Budweiser Bacchanalia."

"Everything all right, boys?" The waitress, a fat little dyed blonde of about thirty, smiled down at them from the end of the table.

"Everything is perfectly splendid," Crane said in a clear, ringing voice.

The waitress giggled. "Why, that sure is nice to hear," she said.

Crane examined her closely. "What do you do when it storms?" he asked.

"What's that?" She frowned uncertainly at him.

"When it storms," Crane said. "When the winds blow. When the sea heaves. Then the young sailors drown in the bottomless deeps."

"My," the waitress said, "and I thought you boys only had one beer."

"I advise anchors," Crane said. "You are badly placed. A turn of the wind, a twist of the tide, and you will be afloat, past the reef, on the way to Japan."

"I'll tell the boss," the waitress said, grinning. "You advise anchors."

"You are in peril, lady," Crane said seriously. "Don't think you're not. Nobody speaks candidly. Nobody tells you the one-hundred-percent honest-to-God truth." He pushed a dime from a pile at his elbow, across the table to the waitress. "Would you be good enough to put this in the box, my dear?" he said formally.

"What do you want to hear?" the waitress asked.

"*Downtown*," Crane said.

"Again?" The waitress grimaced. "It's coming out of my ears."

"I understand it's all the rage," Crane said.

The waitress took the dime and put it in the box and *Downtown* started over again.

"She'll remember me," Crane said, eating fried potatoes covered with ketchup. "Everytime it blows and the sea comes up. You must not go through life unremembered."

"You're a queer duck all right," Steve said, smiling a little, to take the sting out of it, but surprised into saying it.

"Ah, I'm not so queer," Crane said, wiping ketchup off his chin. "I don't behave like this ordinarily. This is the first time I ever flirted with a waitress in my life."

Steve laughed. "Do you call that flirting?"

"Isn't it?" Crane looked annoyed. "What the hell is it if it isn't flirting?" He surveyed Steve appraisingly. "Let me ask you a question," he said. "Do you screw that girl I always see you with around the campus?"

Steve put down his fork. "Now, wait a minute," he said.

"I don't like the way she walks," Crane said. "She walks like a coquette. I prefer whores."

"Let's leave it at that," Steve said.

"Ah, Christ," Crane said, "I thought you wanted to be my friend. You did a friendly, sensitive thing this morning. In the California desert, in the Los Angeles Gobi, in the Camargue of Culture. You put out a hand. You offered the cup."

"I want to be your friend, all right," Steve said, "but there're limits . . ."

"The word friend has no limits," Crane said harshly. He poured some of his beer over the fried potatoes, already covered with ketchup. He forked a potato, put it in his mouth, chewed judiciously. "I've invented a taste thrill," he said. "Let me tell you something, Dennicott, friendship is limitless communication. Ask me anything and I'll answer. The more fundamental the matter, the fuller the answer. What's your idea of friendship? The truth about trivia— and silence and hypocrisy about everything else? God, you could have used a dose of my brother." He poured some more beer over the gobs of ketchup on the fried potatoes. "You want to know why I can say Keats and name my brother in the same breath?" he asked challengingly, hunched over the table. "I'll tell you why. Because he had a sense of elation and a sense of purity." Crane squinted thoughtfully at Steve. "You, too," he said, "that's why I said you would be the one to ask, out of the whole class. You have it, too—the sense of elation. I could tell—listening to you laugh, watching you walk down the library steps holding your girl's elbow. I, too," he said gravely, "am capable of elation. But I reserve it for other things." He made a mysterious inward grimace. "But the purity—" he said. "I don't know. Maybe you don't know yourself. The jury is still out on you. But I knew about my brother. You want to know what I mean by purity?" He was talking compulsively. Silence would have made memory unbearable. "It's having a private set of standards and never compromising them," he said. "Even when it hurts, even when nobody else knows, even when it's just a tiny, formal gesture, that ninety-nine out of a hundred people would make without thinking about it."

Crane cocked his head and listened with pleasure to the chorus of *Downtown*, and he had to speak loudly to be heard over the jukebox. "You know why my brother wasn't elected captain of the football team? He was all set for it, he was the logical choice, everybody expected it. I'll tell you why he wasn't, though. He wouldn't shake the hand of last year's captain, at the end of the season, and last year's captain had a lot of votes he could influence any way he wanted. And do you know why my brother wouldn't shake his hand? Because he thought the man was a coward. He saw him tackle high when a low tackle would've been punishing, and he saw him not go all the way on blocks when they looked too rough. Maybe nobody else saw what my brother saw or maybe they gave the man the benefit of the doubt. Not my brother. So he didn't shake his hand, because he didn't shake cowards' hands, see, and somebody else was elected captain. That's what I mean by purity," Crane said, sipping at his beer and looking out at the deserted beach and the ocean. For the first time, it occurred to Steve that it was perhaps just as well that he had never known Crane's brother, never been measured against that Cromwellian certitude of conduct.

"As for girls," Crane said. "The homeland of compromise, the womb of the second best—" Crane shook his head emphatically. "Not for my brother. Do you know what he did with his first girl? And he thought he was in love with her, too, at the time, but it still didn't make any difference. They only made love in the dark. The girl insisted. That's the way some girls are, you know, darkness excuses all. Well, my brother was crazy about her, and he didn't mind the darkness if it pleased her. But one night he saw her sitting up in bed and the curtains on the window moved in the wind and her silhouette was outlined against the moonlight, and he saw that when she sat like that she had a fat, loose belly. The silhouette, my brother said, was slack and self-indulgent. Of course, when she was lying down it sank in, and when she was dressed she wore a girdle that would've tucked in a beer barrel. And when he saw her silhouette against the curtain, he said to himself, This is the last time, this is not for me. Because it wasn't perfect, and he wouldn't settle for less. Love or no love, desire or not. He, himself, had a body like Michelangelo's David and he knew it and he was proud of it and he kept it that way, why should he settle for imperfection? Are you laughing, Dennicott?"

"Well," Steve said, trying to control his mouth, "the truth is, I'm smiling a little." He was amused, but he couldn't help thinking that it was possible that Crane had loved his brother for all the wrong reasons. And he couldn't help feeling sorry for the unknown girl, deserted, without knowing it, in the dark room, by the implacable athlete who had just made love to her.

"Don't you think I ought to talk about my brother this way?" Crane said.

"Of course," Steve said. "If I were dead, I hope my brother could talk like this about me the day after the funeral."

"It's just those goddamned speeches everybody makes," Crane whispered. "If you're not careful, they can take the whole idea of your brother away from you."

He wiped his glasses. His hands were shaking. "My goddamned hands," he said. He put his glasses back on his head and pressed his hands hard on the table, so they wouldn't shake.

"How about you, Dennicott?" Crane said. "Have you ever done anything in your whole life that was unprofitable, damaging, maybe even ruinous, because it was the pure thing to do, the uncompromising thing, because if you acted otherwise, for the rest of your life you would remember it and feel shame?"

Steve hesitated. He did not have the habit of self-examination and had the feeling that it was vanity that made people speak about their virtues. And their faults. But there was Crane, waiting, himself open, naked. "Well, yes . . ." Steve said.

"What?"

"Well, it was never anything very grandiose . . ." Steve said, embarrassed, but feeling that Crane needed it, that in some way this exchange of intimacies helped relieve the boy's burden of sorrow. And he was intrigued by Crane, by the violence of his views, by the almost comic flood of his reminiscence about his brother, by the importance that Crane assigned to the slightest gesture, by his searching for meaning in trivialities, which gave the dignity of examination to every breath of life. "There was the time on the beach at Santa Monica," Steve said, "I got myself beaten up and I knew I was going to be beaten up . . ."

"That's good," Crane nodded approvingly. "That's always a good beginning."

"Oh, hell," Steve said, "it's too picayune."

"Nothing is picayune," said Crane. "Come on."

"Well, there was a huge guy there who always hung around and made a pest of himself," Steve said. "A physical-culture idiot, with muscles like basketballs. I made fun of him in front of some girls and he said I'd insulted him, and I had, and he said if I didn't apologize, I would have to fight him. And I was wrong, I'd been snotty and superior, and I realized it, and I knew that if I apologized, he'd be disappointed and the girls'd still be laughing at him—so I said I wouldn't apologize and I fought him there on the beach and he must have knocked me down a dozen times and he nearly killed me."

"Right." Crane nodded again, delivering a favorable judgment. "Excellent."

"Then there was this girl I wanted . . ." Steve stopped.

"Well?" Crane said.

"Nothing," Steve said. "I haven't figured it out yet." Until now he had thought that the episode with the girl reflected honorably on him. He had behaved, as his mother would have put it, in a gentlemanly manner. He wasn't sure now that Crane and his mother would see eye to eye. Crane confused him. "Some other time," he said.

"You promise?" Crane said.

"I promise."

"You won't disappoint me, now?"

"No."

"OK." Crane said. "Let's get out of here."

They split the check.

"Come back again sometime, boys," the blond waitress said. "I'll play that record for you." She laughed, her breasts shaking. She had liked having them there. One of them was very good-looking, and the other one, the queer one with the glasses, she had decided, after thinking about it, was a great joker. It helped pass the long afternoon.

On the way home, Crane no longer drove like a nervous old maid on her third driving lesson. He drove very fast, with one hand, humming *Downtown*, as though he didn't care whether he lived or died.

Then, abruptly, Crane stopped humming and began to drive carefully, timidly, again. "Dennicott," he said, "what are you going to do with your life?"

"Who knows?" Steve said, taken aback by the way Crane's conversation jumped from one enormous question to another. "Go to sea, maybe, build electronic equipment, teach, marry a rich wife . . ."

"What's that about electronics?" Crane asked.

"My father's factory," Steve said. "The ancestral business. No sophisticated missile is complete without a Dennicott supersecret what-do-you-call-it."

"Nah," Crane said, shaking his head, "you won't do that. And you won't teach school, either. You don't have the soul of a didact. I have the feeling something adventurous is going to happen to you."

"Do you?" Steve said. "Thanks. What're you going to do with *your* life?"

"I have it all planned out," Crane said. "I'm going to join the forestry service. I'm going to live in a hut on the top of a mountain and watch out for fires and fight to preserve the wilderness of America."

That's a hell of an ambition, Steve thought, but he didn't say it. "You're going to be awfully lonesome," he said.

"Good," Crane said. "I expect to get a lot of reading done. I'm not so enthusiastic about my fellow man, anyway, I prefer trees."

"What about women?" Steve asked, "A wife?"

"What sort of woman would choose me?" Crane said harshly. "I look like something left over after a New Year's party on skid row. And I would only take the best, the most beautiful, the most intelligent, the most loving. I'm not going to settle for some poor, drab Saturday-night castaway."

"Well, now," Steve said, "you're not so awful." Although, it was true, you'd be shocked if you saw Crane out with a pretty girl.

"Don't lie to your friends," Crane said. He began to drive recklessly again, as some new wave of feeling, some new conception of himself, took hold of him. Steve sat tight on his side of the car, holding on to the door, wondering if a whole generation of Cranes was going to meet death on the roads of California within a week.

They drove in silence until they reached the university library. Crane stopped the car and slouched back from the wheel as Steve got out. Steve saw Adele on the library steps, surrounded by three young men none of whom he knew. Adele saw him as he got out of the car and started coming over to him. Even at that distance Steve could tell she was angry. He wanted to get rid of Crane before Adele reached him. "Well, so long," Steve said, watching Adele approach. Her walk *was* distasteful, self-conscious, teasing.

Crane sat there, playing with the keys to the ignition, like a man who is always uncertain that the last important word has been said when the time has come to make an exit.

"Dennicott," he began, then stopped, because Adele was standing there, confronting Steve, her face set. She didn't look at Crane.

"Thanks," she said to Steve. "Thanks for the lunch."

"I couldn't help it," Steve said. "I had to go someplace."

"I'm not in the habit of being stood up," Adele said.

"I'll explain later," Steve said, wanting her to get out of there, away from him, away from Crane, watching soberly from behind the wheel.

"You don't have to explain anything," Adele said. She walked away. Steve gave her the benefit of the doubt. Probably she didn't know who Crane was and that it was Crane's brother who had been killed Saturday night. Still . . .

"I'm sorry I made you miss your date," Crane said.

"Forget it," Steve said. "She'll get over it."

For a moment he saw Crane looking after Adele, his face cold, severe, judging. Then Crane shrugged, dismissed the girl.

"Thanks, Dennicott," Crane said. "Thanks for coming to the tree. You did a good thing this afternoon. You did a friendly thing. You don't know how much you helped me. I have no friends. My brother was the only friend. If you hadn't come with me and let me talk, I don't know how I could've lived through today. Forgive me if I talked too much."

"You didn't talk too much," Steve said.

"Will I see you again?" Crane asked.

"Sure," said Steve. "We have to go back to that restaurant to listen to *Downtown* real soon."

Crane sat up straight, suddenly, smiling shyly, looking pleased, like a child who has just been given a present. If it had been possible, Steve would have put his arms around Crane and embraced him. And with all Crane's anguish and all the loneliness that he knew so clearly was waiting for him, Steve envied him. Crane had the capacity for sorrow and now, after the day Steve had spent with the bereaved boy, he understood that the capacity for sorrow was also the capacity for living.

"*Downtown*," Crane said. He started the motor and drove off, waving gaily, to go toward his parents' house, where his mother and father were waiting, with the guilty look in their eyes, because they felt that if one of the sons had to die, they would have preferred it to be him.

Steve saw Adele coming back toward him from the library steps. He could see that her anger had cooled and that she probably would apologize for her outburst. Seeing Adele suddenly with Crane's eyes, he made a move to turn away. He didn't want to talk to her. He had to think about her. He had to think about everything. Then he remembered the twinge of pity he had felt when he had heard about the fat girl erased from her lover's life by the movement of a curtain on a moonlit night. He turned back and smiled in greeting as Adele came up to him. Crane had taught him a good deal that afternoon, but perhaps not the things Crane had thought he was teaching.

"Hello," Steve said, looking not quite candidly into the young blue eyes on a level with his own. "I was hoping you'd come back."

But he wasn't going to wake up, automatically feeling good, ever again.

# Full Many a Flower

You have no doubt heard of me. My name is Carlos Romanovici. I am a gypsy, suffering from a deep psychic wound and unutterably rich.

Among my other credentials is the fact that I am the first and only gypsy to be admitted to the Maidstone Club in East Hampton, Long Island. I am married and have four children. All daughters and all Episcopalians. I believe I am the only gypsy to have played three full seasons as a defensive tackle for a major American university. I am a graduate of the Harvard School of Business, a teaching establishment that led me to ignore all accepted theories of economics, currency, finance and management; to fear experts in whatever field and to reject informed statistical advice. As a result of my skeptical years in Cambridge, I own, to all intents and purposes, the entire state of Vermont, am the president and controlling stockholder of a large chain of television and gasoline stations, among other holdings too numerous to mention, and am, as I repeat, unutterably rich.

About Vermont. By playing hunches and ignoring trends, I had already done remarkably well in the stock and commodities markets when a geologist friend of mine, who was no longer in a state of grace with his peers because he had to be put away in a mental clinic for years at a time, came to me with a map of North America that he had drawn himself on which he had traced lines that suggested to him that Vermont had been linked since paleolithic times by profound tropical forests and marshes with the newly discovered oil fields in Alaska. Vermont, known until recently as fit only for the habitation of inbred Puritans and exiled French Canadians, as a stony waste hostile to agriculture and inimical, because of its uncertain climate, even to skiers, concealed under its rock-strewn fields, said my geologist friend in his daft way, a vast pool of high-grade petroleum.

His insistence upon this so-called discovery of his was received by the officers of the oil companies to whom he divulged it in much the same manner as the account of Saint Joan's visions was received by her judges in Rouen and contributed, I'm afraid, to the geologist's later visits to the mental clinic. Unfortunately, although later events proved that he was saner than any of the vice-presidents he harangued at Shell or Exxon, the strain of the struggle against educated disbelief overcame him once and for all and he is at present weaving baskets under guard in Connecticut. At my expense.

Knowing nothing about the oil business and open to all seminal ideas as a bonus of my straightforward unorthodoxy, I listened carefully to the poor man and studied his map. Since no one had ever suggested that anybody could extract any wealth from the state of Vermont except by such marginally lucrative enterprises as tapping maple trees, quarrying for marble, building ski lifts or renting rooms to travelers on the way to Montreal, leases for the right to drill for oil cost no more, as my wife jokingly put it, than the price of a meal at La Grenouille, a French restaurant in New York that she favors.

Now the inconspicuous squat pumps that cap the wells of my company can be seen dotting the landscape from Manchester and Pawlet in the south to Burlington and Winooski in the north, nodding like steel hens pecking in a barnyard, bringing enough oil to the surface each day to give pause to any Arab potentate.

Wealth to the very rich becomes a toy, an adult version of building blocks, Erector sets and miniature electric trains, a diversion to fill the hours of the day, a game of one old cat for idle boys on a vacant lot. My own diversions are limited. I do not drink or smoke, I am bored by travel, repelled by art galleries, safaris, philanthropy and the competition for political office, the ordinary playthings of men who do not have to worry where their next dividend is coming from. Athletics, except for football, are of no interest to me, and I am well past the age when stopping a fullback at the line of scrimmage could be considered a possible form of amusement. I am happily married and would not stoop to running after women. But I am not built merely to sit back and watch money roll in. Since my wound, and conscious of my racial heritage, my pleasure has always been to demonstrate to the world that I am right and it is wrong and it remains so to this moment. In my heart, I knew that there were other Vermonts to conquer. One day, I was sure, in a random overheard phrase, a fragment of a dream, what I was searching for would be revealed to me.

Now to the wound to which I referred earlier.

In my last year at the university, I had an excellent season on the football field. I attracted national attention by gathering in a forward pass that had been tipped as it left the hand of the opposing quarterback and running with the ball for 70 yards for a touchdown. I was mentioned for all-American in several polls and almost automatically picked as the 14th draft choice by a National Football League team whose name I do not wish to divulge, as I have no desire to embarrass men who are still making a living from the game by holding them up to possible ridicule. In short, I reported to the team's training camp along with over 100 other players, confidently prepared for a career of autumn Sundays full of glory and terror in the stadiums of the country. After one week, in which I knew that I had performed with honor and occasional spurts of brilliance and had clearly, I thought, outshone all the other candidates for the defensive-line positions, I, along with some 30 other aspirants, was cut from the squad and sent home and later—luckily, in my case—to the Harvard School of Business. Though things in the long run turned out well, I have never gotten over the damage to my self-esteem, which was compounded some years later when I met an assistant coach under other circumstances (he was looking for a job in one of my companies) and I questioned him about my summary dismissal. "Well, you know," he said, "by league rules we can only finally carry forty-three men and we had to cut *some-where*. When your name came up at the meeting, the coach said, 'Isn't he a gypsy? I have enough trouble as it is. What the hell do I need a gypsy for?' "

I gave the man the job he was looking for (he turned out to be absolutely incompetent and is still working for me at $43,000 a year, a figure whose significance I am sure he has never wondered at) and went back to old newspapers and game programs and studied the records of all the players who had been cut on the same day as myself and then the records of the players who had been cut in similar depletions from the other teams in the league. Almost invariably, I discovered that they had been stars in high school and college, had been the captains of their teams, had been cheered by hundreds of thousands of spectators, had trophy rooms lined with game footballs given to them by grateful teammates for outstanding performances, yards gained, tackles made, crucial blocks thrown. Surely, I thought, a team that could go all the way, to use the language of the sports page, could have been formed without the benefit of computers, reports and the cold-blooded estimates of dozens of assistant coaches from any 43 of the men who had desolately packed their bags and departed from their locker rooms on the same day as myself.

My new Vermont slowly began to take shape within my head.

At first, I thought of buying a franchise to test my theory. I found that it would not be difficult. My millions and the possession of a nationwide television network, it was intimated to me, would make me most welcome to join the fraternity of club owners. But after consideration, I decided that putting together a single team of 43 players chosen from one season's culls would prove nothing or almost nothing. Even the most obstinate of the believers in the present system could admit that by the law of averages, a mere handful of deserving athletes had for one reason or another been passed over in the early days of practice sessions. Even if the team I chose went on to win the Super Bowl in its first year, I might be at best praised for my acumen as an architect of victory, which would leave matters more or less where they stood before and bring the bitter taste of ashes to my mouth. I did not wish to be congratulated for gypsy luck or gypsy guile—what I wanted was a gigantic demonstration that the entire system of choice in the modern world was founded on illusion and the frivolity and towering egos of theory-bound gurus and false messiahs in all theaters of endeavor. The reputation of the *class* of men who had dismissed me and scores of other players after one week on a hot practice field would have to be shattered and the mindless belief in their powers held by their countless followers dissolved into dust.

I would have to create not one team but a confederation of teams, a league of rejects who would play a full, scheduled season of games, under the pitiless eye of the television camera and in the full glare of publicity, to choose a winner among them that could then challenge, successfully, the victor in the pompously named Super Bowl.

In the middle of the summer, when the dejected athletes were beginning to stream back to their homes from the training camps, I had my staff prepare lists of positions, addresses, phone numbers. All this was done quietly, without fanfare. Equally quietly, I made the round of cities that had what I considered suitable or at least tolerable stadiums. The major cities were, of course, already taken, but if Tampa could support a major-league football team, what forbade Tallahassee, Toledo, Trenton from also enjoying the pleasures of first-class sport? Out of decent respect for luck, I included Montpelier, the capital of Vermont, among my choices. My guarantees were in cash, the advantages of my having a television network at my disposal were mentioned, old favors were invoked. When necessary, politicians were bribed. In every case, I signed firm contracts for five-year leases. Actually, no risk was involved. From the point of view of my complicated relations with the Internal Revenue Service, a loss of venture capital over that period would prove more profitable than not.

The same reckoning applied to the contracts I offered the players. As I had anticipated, almost every one of them responded eagerly to my explanatory telegrams. They felt, as I knew they would, as *I* had on that fateful day when I was turned away, that they had been denied their fair chance at fame and fortune and were ready to jump at this unexpected second opportunity to prove themselves. There was to be no bargaining for terms—each man was to be offered the same sum, $30,000 a year for two years, with a no-cut clause and a no-limit insurance policy in case or injury.

The selected players themselves, their names taken at random out of a hat, were to elect their own head coaches, assistant coaches, club managers and staff. I promised in no way to interfere with the running of any of the clubs after the offensive and defensive lls, the special teams and the taxi squads had been picked by lot in my office and assigned, again by lot, to the various cities with which I had contracted.

Many of the replies I received to my telegrams to the players I had rescued from lifelong obscurity were embarrassing in their expression of gratitude. One letter from a player who had probably majored in English literature contained a quotation from the works of Thomas Gray:

> *Full many a gem of purest ray serene*
> *The dark unfathom'd caves of*
> *ocean bear:*
> *Full many a flower is born to blush*
> *unseen,*
> *And waste its sweetness on the*
> *desert air.*

"Dear Mr. Romanovici," the scholar-athlete wrote, "I guarantee I will not blush unseen. Thanks to you."

I welcomed him among the chosen in a letter written in my own hand.

Naturally, my activities did not go long unnoticed. Howls of pain rose from the owners of the established clubs, suits were filed in the courts—to no avail—the newspapers, those guardians of the public welfare, poured abuse on my head, as I had expected. One eminent syndicated sports columnist, who also was in much demand as a commentator for special events such as the Olympics and championship prize fights, reached a new low in competitive prose by writing, "The gypsy has raided the henhouse." He was a peculiarly distasteful man, but I hired him at twice his yearly income to serve as chief commentator at the games of the new league. His attitude suffered a not surprising sea change in his new position and the authority of his famous voice made instant stars out of a good many of the players in my employ.

I refused to compete head on with the National Football League. Our games were played on Wednesday and Friday evenings, when the viewing public had recovered from the weekend satiety with the sport. At first, I refused all advertising sponsors, contenting myself with a modest announcement before the start of play at each half that the spectacle was being presented (tax-free for me) on behalf of one or another of my national companies. Because of this, I did away with the endless time outs and tasteless promotions of beer, razor blades, laxatives and armpit protection that made the viewer pay a high negative emotional price for his pleasure. This simple improvement met such a huge response with the public that before the first season was half over, I was besieged with offers from advertisers for the same minimum, low-key and now demonstrably effective exposure.

Another innovation that met with instant acclaim was the elimination of the singing of *The Star-Spangled Banner* before the start of each game. I had never seen the connection between watching an exercise in professional brutality and patriotism and the polls I had taken among the spectators on the spot and the television audience in their homes confirmed my belief that the usual roar that arose as the anthem came to its last notes was not a demonstration of allegiance to the nation but a sign of relief that the game was finally going to begin.

Indulging myself in a long-standing prejudice, I forbade the marching and foolish tootling of high school bands between halves. If my clients liked parades and martial music, they could join the Army. Instead, I picked rock combinations at random, merely by placing small advertisements in the specialized journals devoted to what has always seemed to me to be mindless noisemaking, but which I recognized as a part of our current culture, and had the groups that flocked to my office perform when the athletes were off the field. The change was greeted with screams of joy, especially among the younger element, as the pathetically underpaid musicians in outlandish costumes who answered my invitation blared away under the lights in the autumn evenings.

I even went so far as to improve the quality of the frankfurters and rolls to be hawked in the stands and the high percentage of sales per spectator was satisfactory evidence to me that the national palate had not been permanently ruined by the years of munching on plaster-of-Paris rolls and the sweepings of the abattoirs of America.

With all this, the experiment would have been a failure if the play itself had not been up to standard. By constant exposure, the public had become a body of sophisticated critics and they responded gratifyingly to the reckless ferocity shown by the athletes who had nothing to lose and everything to gain by giving their utmost efforts at every moment of the game. Professional football has been compared all too often to the gladiatorial combats of Rome, but here, at last, the simile almost achieved the status of actual fact rather than remaining another example of rhetoric born in the feverish minds of bemused journalists.

In short, in the first season, the Players' League, as I named it, turned out to be a huge success, but I made no claims and carefully refrained from issuing any challenges to the older league.

But the next year, when one of the less successful teams in the new confederation happened to be conducting pre-season practice in the same area in which one of the N.F.L. teams was preparing for the upcoming campaign, I innocently suggested to the owner of the club, who was a friend of mine and owed me a favor, that it might be useful to stage an informal scrimmage between the two teams. With no spectators or newspapermen present, of course. My friend did not leap at the opportunity and was not encouraged by the reactions of the other owners when the idea was presented to them. I reminded him, gently, of the favor he owed me, which was no less than keeping him out of Federal prison for at least three years, and he consented, with the worst grace possible.

The scrimmage was duly held, with ambulances coming and going. No scores were kept and no official word was vouchsafed to the newspapers, but the rumors were delightful. Two weeks later, my friend called me to say, bitterly, that it would have been better for him if he had spent the three years in prison.

Confident now of the future (wrongly, as it developed), I suggested no further relations between the leagues and through the season allowed the sportswriters to do their work. By December, the clamor for the meeting between the two champions was irresistible. I pretended to be loath to risk my inexperienced young men against the triumphant veterans of the N.F.L., and the clamor swelled into an uproar. There was even a speech on the subject on the floor of the Senate in which the doctrine of free enterprise was invoked and fair competition under the democratic rules of the game was mentioned. My hesitation paid off in my dealings with the N.F.L. and was reflected in certain concessions that were finally included in the contract, chiefly concerned with the percentages assigned to the two parties involved. But try as I would, I could not persuade the opposing lawyers to agree to the sale of the improved frankfurters and rolls I preferred. I am not a stubborn man and at the end gave in gracefully on this point.

We were lucky, or so it seemed at the time, that the race in our league was undecided until the last Sunday in December, which kept the attention of the public, especially the bettors among them, riveted to our games, while the championship in the N.F.L. had become a foregone conclusion early in October, with the Dallas team monotonously running up lopsided scores against all opposition and finishing the season undefeated, with the absurd combined total of 620 points gained to 34 points scored against them. At their own Super Bowl, they won 56 to 17 and there were empty seats in the stands.

By a happy coincidence (for me), Montpelier was the victor in our league and grimly went about its preparations for the test ahead of it.


The Sunday of the big game dawned clear and balmy. The Las Vegas line indicated a Dallas victory by 24 points. I had avoided Texas almost successfully during my career and was not prepared for the delirium, inflamed by drink, with which the natives of the Panhandle celebrated, well in advance, the massacre of the invaders from the North. One would have thought that Davy Crockett, smiling and in perfect health, had strode forth from the Alamo on Saturday evening.

The stadium was a bedlam of sound, even before the game and the warming-up period of the two teams and during the marching of the massed high school bands, a ceremony I had been unable to prohibit.

We won the toss and Montpelier received the kickoff. I was sitting with my wife in one of the ornate boxes, high above the field, in which a family could live comfortably for months. At the beginning, I watched with composure as Montpelier ground out yardage and advanced steadily toward the Dallas goal. But even as the crowd groaned with each new first down, I began to feel uneasy. There was something methodical, craftily planned in the manner in which the Dallas defense yielded territory. It seemed to me, if not to the other spectators, that they were *permitting* Montpelier to gain, allowing plays to form and surge forward so as to be able to study, with disturbing serenity, the separate moves that constituted the Montpelier offense. Even before Montpelier scored within the first six minutes, I suspected ambush.

By the middle of the second quarter, my suspicions proved to have been all too well justified. After the first score, Montpelier hadn't managed another first down. The Dallas defense was subtly rearranged and handled our best runners and pass receivers with ridiculous ease. Meanwhile, the Dallas offense moved the ball smoothly through huge gaps in the Montpelier line and their receivers were more often than not completely in the open for long receptions, short receptions and bruising and ground-devouring screen plays.

By that time, I was down on the field, on the bench, which now resembled an encampment of soldiery in full retreat, all hope gone, waiting only for the final blow that would sweep them all from the face of the earth. The coach, Bo McGill, who had led a Kansas high school team to a state championship, seemed to have fallen into a numb reverie as the score mounted against us, and even our spotters in their booth above the stands had drifted into dejected silence.

The crowd, wild at the beginning, was now delirious and amused itself by cheering us when we managed to gain inches on a play or when our quarterback, exceptionally, managed to get a pass off without being knocked off his feet, even if the pass harmlessly dribbled a few yards into territory where not a single Montpelier jersey could be seen.

On the bench, all thought seemed to have come to a complete and dreadful halt, as though every mind in what had been a group of intelligent and resourceful men had been subjected to a new and much improved industrial deep-freezing process. Needless to say, *my* mind was racing. In the heat of the moment, I felt, melodramatically, that everything I believed in, everything I had accomplished was faced with failure and doomed forever to mockery.

At the half, we were behind 27 to 7 and all indications pointed to a final score for Dallas of between 50 and 60 points. As we walked off the field to the accompaniment of loud, ironic applause, I had finished my calculations. I had figured out, or imagined I had figured out, why the disaster had overcome us. A team that had started out as inspired amateurs had through the trials of two seasons turned into experienced professionals. In other words, experts. Predictable, playing just the sort of game that Dallas had feasted on since August. The Dallas team was composed of experts, too, but superexperts, with long years of experience behind them. If we were to have any chance against them, we would have to play unpredictably, inexpertly, at random, ignoring completely the percentages and statistics that by now were burned into McGill's consciousness as they were into the consciousness of every other professional coach.

The poor man was near tears as we reached the locker room, which resembled a forward medical station during the battle in the Ardennes rather than a football locker room. "Mr. Romanovici," McGill said brokenly, as he pulled me aside to a corner of the room, "I hereby tender my resignation. I would like to remain indoors for the second half. Give out any story you wish—tell the papers I've had a heart attack or that I slipped and broke my leg—anything. . . ."

"Nonsense, man," I said, putting a soothing hand on his arm. "You'll do nothing of the kind. You'll go out on the field with the team and you'll look cunning and confident. You may even smile if you catch a camera pointed in your direction."

"Smile, man," McGill said. "I'm not going to smile again for the rest of my life. What is there to smile at?"

"We're going to change our tactics," I said.

"Change tactics!" McGill was spluttering now. "What do you think I've been doing? I've tried every trick in the book."

"In the book," I said. "There's the trouble. You're now going to throw out the book."

"What do you propose?" McGill asked, with just the merest hint of curiosity.

"First of all, we are now going to encourage the boys to block and tackle," After our first touchdown, the power and deception of Dallas had thoroughly intimidated the Montpelier team and the blocking and tackling had gone from being tentative in the first quarter to a demonstration of the gentlest courtesy in the second.

"Block and tackle," McGill groaned. "How do you expect to arrange that?"

"In a minute, I'm going to ask for silence in the locker room," I said, "and I'm going to make a little speech."

McGill hit his head in despair. "Mr. Romanovici," he said, "these men are professionals. This isn't a high school team that you fire up with a pep talk between halves. You could read them a new Sermon on the Mount and they'd still lose by forty points."

"Listen to my speech," I said and climbed onto a rubbing table and called for quiet. The room had not been noisy. There had been only a small whispering, like the fall of rain on a newly dug grave, until now, and that stopped abruptly at the sound of my voice. "Gentlemen," I said loudly, "there is no need to dwell on our performance in the first half."

A small sigh, like a vagrant wind, swept the room.

"We are now going to forget it and get on with the business of winning a ball game." As I said this, two of the players sat down on the floor and turned their faces to the wall. "We are going to be a different team in this half. For one thing, as of this moment, there are no regulars on this squad. We are going to put in the suicide squad and they are going to stay in there, on both offense and defense, as long as it seems wise."

"Mr. Romanovici," McGill wailed, "they never even ran the ball once in practice all season."

"I understand," I said. "But they all have their playbooks, which I believe they are charged with memorizing."

"Memorize," McGill said. "You don't beat Dallas out of memory."

"I don't like to bring it up, Coach," I said, "but we don't seem to be beating Dallas with the team that's been running the ball ever since August, do we?" I turned back to the men. "In going over our roster," I went on, "I see that most of you at one time or another in your careers in high school and college have played various positions. We have twelve ex-fullbacks on the club, who now back up the line or fill in at guard or go down under punts. In this half, you may very well find yourselves carrying the ball three times in a row. Let me ask you gentlemen a question. How many of you have ever thrown a forward pass in a game? A show of hands, please."

Ten hands went up.

"Some of you or maybe even all of you," I said, "may be called on, when the occasion seems propitious, to throw a pass or pretend to throw a pass and run with the ball when that seems advisable to you. Any member of the team may also discover that he is playing a position, on either the defense or the offense, that he has never played before. For the next thirty minutes out on that field, there are no set offensive and defensive units. There are forty-three football players and that is all."

"I am going back to Kansas," McGill said, "by the first plane." But he said it in a whisper, for my ears only.

"There is an excellent play by a distinguished Italian author, unfortunately now dead," I went on. "The title of the play, translated into English, is *Tonight We Improvise*. The writer of the play, if my memory is correct, won the Nobel Prize. I am asking you to take heart from his title and do as much this afternoon to win a mere football game."

Here and there on several faces I could see a fugitive gleam of hope, but the general mood was still one of abject surrender. So far, McGill's warning that professional athletes could not be moved by locker-room appeals was an accurate appraisal of the situation. "One more detail," I said, holding up my hand as some of the athletes, looking like men on the way to their own execution, prepared to leave the room. "If you win today," I said flatly, without emotion, "each member of this club, including coaches and trainers, will have his winning share doubled by me."

The men who were moving toward the door stopped dead in their tracks. "What's more," I said, "again, if you win, each and every player, coach and trainer in our confederation, the men you will be facing for the rest of your careers, will receive a bonus of ten thousand dollars." I did not feel I had to add that what they would be faced with in the following seasons would be either lifelong gratitude or murderous fury.

A curious sound could now be heard in one corner of the room, like the growling of wild animals some distance off. The growling grew to a roar, frightening and inhuman, and filled the locker room, and the athletes were jostling one another in their eagerness to race out onto the field.

McGill helped me down from the rubbing table. His face was white. "Shades of Knute Rockne," he said. "One for the Gipper. Two for the bank. Permit me to shake your hand, man."

We shook hands gravely and went out, walking slowly and in a dignified manner, to the bench.

On the kickoff, the team swept down the field like an assault of dervishes inflamed by visions of heaven, impervious to wounds or death. The kicker, who had not made a tackle since his sophomore year in high school, brought the runner down on Dallas' 21-yard line. He hit the man so hard that the ball spurted out of the melee and was scooped up by a lumbering tackle who fled across the goal line with the speed of an Olympic 100-yard-dash man. The kick for the point was good and the score after just a few seconds of the half was now Dallas 27, Montpelier 14.

From then on, the ambulances came and went. The ferocity of play was so great that I told myself that if I were in a position of political power, I would abolish football except in prisons and commando camps.

"It's like nothing anybody has ever seen before," McGill kept whispering hoarsely beside me, as safety men dropped quarterbacks behind the line of scrimmage, ends threw passes, tackles drifted, guards changed positions with halfbacks and plunged for first downs or ran lonely weird pass patterns into the end zone. Our kicker, because of his new enthusiasm for going down under his own kicks, was hurt, but a substitute center fell back and *dropkicked* a crucial field goal from 33 yards out. Barefooted. Blockers appeared in places that reason told they could never reach, tackles split wedges like walnuts, men whose names had hardly ever made the line-ups called signals, ran away from their interference, instead of behind it, and galloped toward the Dallas goal, broken plays were the rule rather than the exception as the heat of battle made men forget their playbooks entirely and scramble savagely through pile-ups. I had the firm impression that none of our players knew what he was going to do or actually did on either the offense or the defense and the spotters were screaming helplessly over the telephone lines to the bench.

With all order gone and confusion rampant, Dallas began to disintegrate. Since our men usually had no notion of where they were going, there was no way in which Dallas, a highly trained, logical group of athletes, could foresee any development, and the poor Dallas fullback was heard to say, as he was thrown out of bounds by four tacklers. "Why the fuck don't you guys play football?"

Still, with only seconds remaining in the game, Dallas led 34 to 30. On the side lines, McGill stood with his back to the field, staring desolately up to heaven. The ball was on the Dallas 30-yard line, but even if we had had a place kicker we could depend upon, three points would still leave us on the short end of the score. We used our last time out and the last substitutes trotted onto the field, one of them with instructions from me to call for an end-around play. A halfback who had been out of the line-up for the last four games with a concussion of the brain started toward the bench, moving in a peculiar manner. Suddenly, I realized that he thought he had been pulled from the game and was heading for the bench, which would have left us with only ten men on the field, making whatever play we ran invalid. I shouted at him to stand still and he came to a halt two feet from the side line, a puzzled look on his face.

The ball was snapped, the quarterback scampered to his rear and turned to hand the ball off to the right end. Just as the end reached the quarterback, he and the quarterback were hit simultaneously by the *left* end, who, he told me later, had thought he had been designated to run the play. The three men dropped to the ground as though they had been felled by sledge hammers and the ball spurted out of the melee and back to the 50-yard line, with what seemed like dozens of players racing for it and bodies dropping on all sides.

Our left guard, who had thought it was a pass play and had come back to protect the quarterback, managed to grab the ball and run backward. Meanwhile, the halfback who had thought he had been removed from the game was walking pensively, all alone, his head down, toward the Dallas goal.

"Throw it! Throw it!" I yelled.

Surrounded by Dallas players, his eyes blank with fear, the guard, who in eight years of football had never thrown a single pass, leaped above the menacing hands all around him and threw a wobbly, end-over-end high pass that moved so slowly you could count the lace holes on the ball. The halfback, walking all alone toward the Dallas goal, turned, as though he had just remembered he had left something behind him, and was hit in the chest by the ball. It bounced off him and above his head. He put his hands up as it came down and he had it. He was only ten feet from the goal line and he limped across it, put the ball down in the end zone and dropped on it.

Final score, Montpelier 36, Dallas 34. The silence of the crowd was funereal as our players ran hysterically off the field. McGill was so exhausted he had to be carried to the locker room by two trainers.

The official celebration of our victory came in March, after the checks had been mailed out to all the teams in the confederation. I hired the large ballroom in the Waldorf-Astoria for a banquet for over 2000 of my guests, who included all the personnel of the eight clubs and whatever family and lovers of either sex they wished to invite.

I made the only speech. I thanked them one and all, announced that I was retiring, because of reasons of health, from all connection with the sport, though I would, of course, keep a strong sentimental attachment to those once-scorned athletes who had needed only a fair second chance to show their worth. Bo McGill would succeed me as president of the confederation. I didn't say so, but I feared that another game on the bench would endanger his life. In farewell, I announced that I was turning over the ownership of the teams to the men themselves, though naturally I would expect to be paid back through the years for my original investment. I did not bring up my strongly held belief that wanton charity is counterproductive. The announcement gave rise to a wild demonstration, in which 1000 glasses were broken and half that number of chairs were destroyed in various ways. The next day, the newspapers hailed my gesture as a landmark in creative capitalism.

I left the Waldorf before the celebration reached its peak and later, without hesitation, paid the quite impressive bill for damage done to the premises.


On my next visit to my poor demented friend, the geologist, in the clinic in Connecticut, I explained to him over a bottle of Jack Daniel's, his one remaining interest in the world outside the walls, something of what had happened. As he drank, he nodded politely, but I could see his mind, such as it was, was on other things. "There's a fellow here," he said, "I believe he's something of a chemist, worked for Dupont, the rumor goes, who claims he's discovered a new process—I think it's a cheap way of producing hydrogen for fuel. Dupont laughed at him. I told him about you and Vermont and he said he'd like to meet you. Should I call him in?"

"By all means," I said.

Since then, I have visited the clinic 20 times in two months.

# Circle of Light

There was mist lying low along the ground and the headlights made a milky thin soup in every dip of the road. It was nearly one o'clock in the morning and they didn't pass any other cars as they wound along the narrow road up the hill toward the house. There were only four other houses between the main highway and the Willards' house, and they were all dark.

They were sitting in the front seat, Martin and his sister and her husband. Linda had the radio on and was singing softly, accompanying the orchestra, singing, "It's the wrong time, and the wrong place . . ."

John Willard sat comfortably at the wheel, driving fast, smiling when Linda leaned over and sang into his ear, burlesquing passion in the style of a nightclub singer, "Though it's such a pretty fa-aaace . . ."

"Be careful," Willard said. "You're tickling the ear of the driver."

"There were more fatalities on the roads last year," Martin said, "from tickling the ear of the driver than from drunkenness, national holidays, and faulty brakes."

"Who said that?" Linda asked aggressively.

"It's a well-known statistic," Martin said.

"I don't care," Linda said. "I'm crazy about the ear of the driver."

Willard chuckled.

"Wipe that complacent grin off your face, soldier," Linda said.

Willard chuckled again and Linda went back to finishing the song, her head leaning against Martin's arm, her face lit dimly by the dashboard glow, looking gay and young, framed by her loose dark hair.

Ten years after *I* get married, Martin thought, glancing sideways at his sister, I hope my wife and I feel like that on the way home after a night in the city.

Martin had arrived from California late that afternoon, after sending a telegram that he was giving up his job and was on his way to Europe and could he count on a bed and meal enroute. Linda had met him at the airport, looking the same, he thought, after the two years of separation, and they had picked up Willard at his office and had had a couple of drinks and a good dinner and an extravagant bottle of wine to celebrate Martin's arrival. It was Friday and Willard didn't have to work the next day, so they had gone to a nightclub and listened to a girl in a white dress singing French songs. Martin and Willard had taken turns dancing with Linda, and Linda had said, "Isn't this nice? If you had given me more warning I'd have felt I'd have had to find a girl for you for the evening and there would've been four of us and the whole thing would've been ruined. Don't you hate the number four?"

Martin was seven years younger than Linda, and her favorite brother. When he was still in college he had spent his summers with Linda and Willard, acting as spare man at parties, playing tennis with Willard, and endangering the lives of their two small sons, as Linda put it, teaching them how to swim and dive and ride bicycles and catch a baseball and fall out of trees.

"Oh, God," Linda said as the car swung through an overgrown stone gate, "two years are too long, Martin. What're we going to do without you when you're in Europe?"

"Come and visit me," Martin said.

"Listen to that," Linda said.

"It's only overnight by plane."

"You know anybody wants to give us a free ride?" She waved her hand at the dark woods outside the car window. "It'll take ten years before we get through paying off Gruesome Acres."

"It looks very nice." Martin peered through the misted window at the dripping black woods. "Very rural."

"It's rural all right," Linda said. "Seventeen acres of impenetrable underbrush."

"Can't you clear part of it," Martin asked, "and grow something on it?"

"Taxes," Willard said briefly, swinging out of the woods and into the circular driveway in front of a large brick house with white pillars, rising dimly out of the mist.

There were no lights showing downstairs, only a pale glimmer coming from a curtained window on the upper storey, and the house bulked impressively in the darkness.

"There ought to be at least one light left on at the entrance, Linda," Willard said.

"It's the new maid," Linda said. "I tell her all the time, but she's a demon for economy."

Willard stopped the car and they all got out, Martin taking his bag off the back seat.

"Notice the exquisite architecture," Linda said, as they climbed the steps and went between the pillars to the front door. "Spectral Greek."

"Wait till you see the inside, though," Willard said, opening the door and turning on the light. "It makes up for the whole thing. And the land around it is great for the kids."

"It has one other glorious advantage," Linda said, taking off her coat and throwing it across a chair in the wall-papered front hall. "The television reception is horrible."

They went into the living room and Linda switched on the lamps and Willard poured them some whiskeys for Martin to admire the house on. The living room was big and airy and pleasant, with a clutter of paintings on the walls and a lot of books and magazines and small semiuseful objects not quite in place. Martin smiled, looking at it and recognizing his sister's undisciplined, cheerful touch in the bright choice of colors, the profusion of vases, flowers, antique odds and ends, and in the air of comfortable disorder that the room presented now, at one o'clock in the morning, after it had been empty and unused all evening.

Linda took her shoes off and sat with her legs up in the corner of the big couch, holding her whiskey glass in two hands and the two men sat facing her, sleepy, but reluctant to end the night of reunion. "Now, really, Martin," Linda said, "you can't possibly mean it when you say you're not going to stay at least a week."

"I have to go up to Boston on Monday," Martin said. "And I'm taking the plane for Paris from there on Wednesday."

"The boys're going to be black with disappointment," Linda said. "Maybe you'll meet somebody over the weekend here and you'll change your mind. We're invited to three parties."

Martin laughed. "It's a lucky thing I have to go to Boston," he said. "I can recover in Boston."

Linda swished the whiskey around in her glass. "John," she said, "don't you think this is as good a time as any to give him the lecture?"

"It's awfully late, you know, Linda," Willard said, a little uncomfortably.

"What lecture?" Martin asked suspiciously, beginning to feel, in advance, like a younger brother.

"Well," Willard began, "Linda and I were talking on the phone after you sent the telegram, and we began to add up—What's this, the third job you've given up since you left college?''

"Fourth," Martin said.

"First in New York," Willard said, doing his duty as a brother-in-law and as a friend and as a solid citizen who was still with the same firm he had joined when he finished law school fifteen years before. "Then in Chicago. Then California. Now Europe. You're not a kid any more and maybe a little stability would . . . .''

"Don't lay it on too thick, now," Linda said, worried by the way Martin's face was closing up as he sat there, listening, playing with his glass. "I mean, don't make it sound like a commencement address at M.I.T. or General Patton addressing the troops, John. What we were talking about to each other," she said, addressing Martin, "was that all of a sudden one day you're liable to find out you're thirty and your life is sliding away. . . .''

Willard grinned at her. "Have you found out you're thirty and your life is sliding away?''

"Like sand through the fingers," Linda said. Then she giggled, and Martin's face began to open up again.

"But it *is* important," Linda said, grave once more. "It's so easy for the good-looking ones to wind up bums. Especially in France.''

"I don't know enough French to wind up as a bum," Martin said cheerfully. He got up and touched the top of his sister's hair and then went over to the low table in front of the window which they used as a bar, to put some ice into his drink.

"The idea was, Martin," Linda said, "just to give you a carefully modulated warning. We don't want to . . .''

"Say," Martin said, staring out the window, "are you expecting guests?''

"Guests?" Willard asked, surprised. "At this hour?''

"There's a man out there, looking in," Martin said. He twisted his neck to look toward the corner of the house. "And there's a ladder up against the balcony. . . . Now he's gone. . . .''

"A ladder!" Linda sprang up. "The children!" She ran out of the room and up the staircase, with the two men racing after her.

There was a lamp in the hall outside the children's bedroom and by its light Martin could see the two small boys sleeping quietly in their beds, ranged against the walls on opposite sides of the room. Through the half-opened door which led into the next room came the steady snoring of the maid. While Linda and Willard reassured themselves about the children, Martin went to the windows. They were open, but the room was closed off from the balcony by full-length shutters, still hooked in place. Martin undid the shutters and stepped out onto the balcony, which ran along the front of the floor of the house, supported by the porch columns. The night was raw and dark and the mist had grown thicker and the light from the downstairs windows reflected back confusingly. Martin went to the edge of the balcony and peered down. He heard a sound to his left, off to the side of the house, and looked in that direction. He got a glimpse of a patch of white moving swiftly against the dark background of tree trunks and he turned and ran back through the boys' room, whispering to Willard, "He's down there. On that side."

Willard came after him as he took the steps four at a time and flung open the front door and ran across the driveway gravel, and around the side of the house, past the ladder. Willard had picked up a flashlight in the front hall, but it wasn't a strong one, and its beam flickered meaninglessly across the sloping, overgrown wet lawn and the tangled mass of shrubs and trees into which the intruder had disappeared.

Without much hope of success, Martin and Willard pushed their way some distance through the woods, scratching themselves on bushes and ploughing through drifts of soaked dead leaves, flickering the searchlight beam around them in sudden, prying movements. They were silent and angry and if they had found the man he would have had to be armed and ready to use his weapon to get away from them. But they saw nothing, heard nothing.

After five minutes, Willard gave up. "Ah, it's no use," he said. "Let's get back."

They walked back to the house in silence. When they reached the edge of the lawn they saw Linda out on the corner of the balcony with the light from the now opened shutters of the children's room outlining her form in the darkness. She was leaning over and pushing at the ladder and finally it teetered and fell to the ground.

"Did you find him?" she called to Martin and Willard.

"No," Willard said.

"Nothing's been touched in any of the rooms," Linda said. "He never got in. It's our ladder. The gardener was using it this afternoon and he must have left it out."

"Get inside," Willard called to her. "You'll freeze up there."

Martin and Willard took one last look at the dark lawn and the looming black wall of the woods. They waited until Linda had stepped back into the children's room and locked the shutters. Then they went into the house. Martin stayed downstairs while

Willard went up to look at the children once more. The living room didn't look as gay and pleasant to Martin as it had before.

When Willard and Linda came down again Martin was standing at the window from which he had seen the man on the lawn outside, and the ladder.

"What an idiot," he said. " 'Are you expecting guests?' " He shook his head ruefully. "At this hour of the morning."

"Well, remember," Linda said, "you've just come from California."

They laughed then and everybody felt better and Willard poured them some more whiskey.

"What I should've done," Martin said, "was pretend I hadn't seen him and just acted natural and gone out a side door. . . ."

"People are only as clever as that in the movies," Willard said. "In real life they say, 'Are you expecting guests?' "

"You know something," Martin said, remembering, "I think I'd recognize that fellow if I saw him again. After all, he was only five feet away from me and the light from the window was right on him."

"Did he look like a criminal?" Linda asked.

"Everybody looks like a criminal at one o'clock in the morning," Martin said.

"I'm going to call the police and report this," Willard said and got up and started toward the telephone, which was in the hall.

"Oh, Johnny," Linda said, putting out her hand and stopping him. "Wait till morning. If you call, they'll just come over and keep us up all night."

"Well, you can't let people climb all over your house and try to break in and do nothing about it, can you?" Willard said.

"It won't do any good. They'll never find him out there tonight," Linda said.

"That's true enough," said Martin.

"And they'll want to go up and look at the children's room and they'll wake them up and scare them. . . ." Linda was talking rapidly and nervously. She had been calm enough before but the reaction had set in and she didn't seem to be able to sit still or talk at a normal speed now. "What's the sense in it? Don't be pig-headed."

"Who's being pig-headed?" Willard asked, surprised. "All I said was that I thought we ought to call the police. Did I sound pig-headed to you, Martin?"

"Well," Martin began judicially, wanting to placate his sister. "I think . . ."

But Linda interrupted. "He didn't do anything, anyway, did he? After all, he just looked in the window. There's no sense in losing a night's sleep just because a man happened to look in the window. I bet he wasn't a robber, at all. . . ."

"What do you mean?" Willard asked sharply.

"Well, what've we got to rob here? I don't have any jewels and the one fur coat I own is seven years old and any thief in his right mind . . ."

"Then what was he doing here with his damn ladder?" Willard asked.

"Maybe he was just a peeping Tom," Linda said.

"Just!" Willard gulped down his drink. "If you wouldn't walk around naked with all the blinds up all the time . . ."

"Oh, don't be such a prude," Linda said. "Who's going to see me in this house? The chipmunks?"

"Not only this house," Willard said. "Wherever we live. Women these days." He turned bitterly toward Martin. "When you get married you'll find you're spending half your time pulling down blinds to keep the American public from admiring your wife dressing and undressing."

"Don't be stuffy, John," Linda said, her voice rising. "Who'd ever think in the middle of the woods like this . . ."

"I'd think," Willard said. "And that guy with the ladder obviously thought, didn't he?"

"Who knows what he thought?" Linda said. "All right, you win. From now on, I'll pull every blind in the house. But it's so awful. To have to live like that in your own house. All closed in."

"It's not being all closed in to put on a bathrobe once in a while," Willard said.

"John," Linda said, her voice sharp, "you have a terrible tendency to turn stuffy in a crisis."

"Boys, boys," Martin said. "I'm here on a holiday."

"Sorry," Willard said shortly, and Linda laughed, strainedly.

"You ought to buy a dog," Martin said.

"He hates dogs," said Linda, starting to turn the lamps out. "He prefers to live in a vault."

They left it at that and went up to bed, leaving an extra light on in the downstairs hall, for security, although it was certain that the prowler, whoever he was, and for whatever reason he had come, would not come back that night, at least.

Willard called the police in the morning and they promised to come over. Linda had to invent an elaborate reason to take the children away until lunchtime, because she didn't want them to see the policemen and ask questions and begin to feel insecure in their own house. It was difficult to get the children out of the house because they wanted to spend the morning with their uncle and they couldn't understand why Martin wouldn't come with them and he couldn't tell them that he had to stay and try to give the police a description of a man who had prowled outside their window while they slept.

The children were out of the way when the police car drove up. The two policemen walked soberly over the grounds, looking professionally at the ladder and the balcony and the woods and taking notes. When they asked Martin what the man looked like he was a little embarrassed by the vagueness of the description he could offer and had the feeling that the policemen were disappointed in him.

"I'm pretty sure I could recognize him, if I saw him again," Martin said, "but there wasn't anything particularly special about him to latch onto. I mean, he didn't have a big scar or a patch over one eye or a broken nose or anything like that."

"How old was he?" Madden, the older of the policemen, asked.

"Sort of middle-aged, Sergeant," Martin said. "Somewhere between thirty and forty-five, I guess."

Willard smiled and Martin saw that Madden was trying not to smile.

"You know what I mean," Martin said. "In between."

"What kind of complexion did he have, Mr. Brackett?" Madden asked.

"Well, in that light, in the mist . . ." Martin hesitated, digging into his memory. "He looked pale."

"Was he bald?" Madden made an entry in his book. "Did he have a lot of hair?"

Again Martin hesitated. "I guess he was wearing a kind of hat," he said.

"What kind of hat?"

Martin shrugged. "A hat."

"A cap, would you say?" Madden suggested.

"No, I guess not. Just a hat."

"What sort of shape was he, would you say?" Madden went on methodically, putting everything down. "Tall, stocky, what?"

Martin shook his head embarrassedly. "I'm afraid I'm not much help," he said. "He was standing there with the light just hitting his head, below the window, and I . . . I really couldn't say. He looked . . . well, if I had to make up my mind about it . . . solid."

"Have you any notions about who it might be, Sergeant?" Willard asked.

The two policemen looked at each other judiciously. "Well, Mr. Willard," Madden said, "there're bound to be two or three cases of people walking around at night in any town. We'll check. They're building that new shopping center near the bank and there're a lot of workmen in from New Haven. All sorts of people," he said, making a heavy judgment on foreigners from New Haven. He closed his book and put it in his pocket. "We'll let you know if anything comes up."

"I'm pretty sure I'd know him if I saw him," Martin repeated, trying to reestablish himself with the policemen.

"If we get any ideas," said Madden, "maybe we'll ask you to come with us and look over a suspect or two."

"I'm leaving tomorrow night," Martin said. "For France."

The two policemen exchanged glances again, bleakly eloquent about the civic attitude of Americans who witnessed crimes and then fled to France.

"Well," Madden said heavily, without optimism, "we'll see what we can do."

Martin and Willard watched the police car drive off. "Isn't it funny," Willard said, "how easy it is for a policeman to make you feel guilty?"

Then they went into the house and Willard used the telephone to call Linda and tell her it was all right to bring the children home, the police had gone.

They had been invited to a friend's house for cocktails that evening and after that to another friend's for dinner and at first Linda said she wouldn't go, she couldn't dream of leaving the children alone in the house after what had happened. But Willard asked her what she intended to do—stay home every night until the children were twenty years old? Anyway, Willard said, whoever it was had had a real scare and would keep as far away from the house as possible. Then Linda decided that he was right, but now she'd have to tell the maid. It wouldn't be moral, she said, to go out and leave the maid in ignorance. But, she warned her husband, there was a good chance that the maid would pack her bags and leave. The maid had only been with them for six weeks and was getting on in years and was not a calm type. So Linda went into the kitchen while Willard paced the living room jumpily, saying to Martin, "One thing I couldn't stand is going through finding a new maid. We've had five since we moved in here."

But Linda came out of the kitchen smiling and saying the maid was a calmer type than she appeared and was taking the news placidly. "She's too old to be raped," Linda said, "and she loves the children, so she'll stay."

Willard put the ladder in the garage and locked the garage and made sure the shutters were hooked from the inside in the children's room and in Linda's bedroom and in his own bedroom and in the bathroom in between, because all those rooms gave on the balcony against which the ladder had been propped the night before.

At the cocktail party, which was a replica of a thousand other cocktail parties being given on that particular Saturday night within a radius of one hundred miles from New York City, Willard and Linda told about the prowler and Martin had to describe what he looked like, feeling once more, as he had with the policemen, that it was a sign of low intelligence on his part that he couldn't be more accurate. "He had this hat over his eyes and he didn't have any expression on his face and he was rather pale, as I told the sergeant, and intense-looking. . . ." Even as he spoke, Martin realized that he was adding to the portrait of the man on the other side of the window in the misty night, that the intensity of the man's expression was a new discovery, dredged from his memory, that the remembered face was being simplified, intensified, becoming heraldic, symbolic, a racial, dangerous apparition staring out of dark and dripping forests at the frail safety of the sheltered circle of light.

The Willards' visitor started everyone off on their own stories of burglars, prowlers, kidnappers.

". . . so there was this fellow suddenly staring down the skylight, it was summer and the skylight was open, on West 23rd Street, and my friend ran up to the roof and chased him across the roofs and cornered him and the fellow whipped out a knife and it took five transfusions before he was out of danger. Of course, the police never found him."

". . . a loaded .45. Right next to my bed, at all times. These days, with all these crazy kids. Anybody who tries anything in my house is in for a hot welcome. And don't think I wouldn't shoot to kill."

". . . the chain on the door and everything from every single drawer and cupboard piled in a heap on the rug. And I can't tell

857

you what else they did, in mixed company, but you can imagine. The police told them it was quite common. especially when they were disappointed in their haul. But of course, they were asking for it, living surrounded by all those Puerto Ricans.''

''. . . this was a long time ago, of course, when he had this Great Dane kennel, but the day after the Lindbergh kidnapping he sold every single dog he had in the place. At three times what he'd been asking before.''

Glass in hand, Martin listened politely, realizing with some surprise that all these solid, comfortable people, in their cosy and orderly community, shared a general fear, a widespread uneasiness, and that the face outside the Willard window had made them all remember that there were obscure and unpredictable forces always ready to descend upon them in their warm homes and that, with all their locked doors and all their police and all their loaded .45's, they were exposed and vulnerable to attack.

''You've sent a delicious shiver down every spine,'' Linda said, coming over to Martin.

''Not so delicious,'' he said thoughtfully, looking around him at the serious home-owning faces. Linda, he saw, had made up her mind to take the whole thing lightly, after the rattled nerves of the night before and the fuss about the police. He admired her for it, but it worried him, and he didn't like the idea of leaving her out there in that pillared, echoing house surrounded by acres of wilderness, especially since Willard worked late in the city several times a week and didn't get home until midnight. After all, uncaught and unsuspected, there was nothing to stop the man from coming back a week from now, a month, two months. . . . On another rainy night, with no moon.

''We'd better be going now,'' Linda said. ''We're expected for dinner at eight-thirty.'' She glanced slyly around the room. ''Anybody you want to take? The Charles's said if you wanted to bring anybody, it's only a buffet supper, really. . . .''

''No, thanks,'' Martin said, smiling. ''They're all very nice, but . . .'' Then he stopped. A tall, blond woman in a blue dress had just come into the room and was making her excuses to the hostess for being late. Her hair was done in a low bun on the back of her neck, making her look stately and old-fashioned. Her voice, as she made her explanations to the hostess, was murmuring and melodious, and she was by far the prettiest woman in the place. ''Well,'' Martin said to Linda, grinning, ''maybe that one. Give me ten minutes.''

Linda shook her head. ''No go, Brother,'' she said. ''Her name is Anne Bowman, and she's married. And there's her husband at the door.''

Linda gestured with her glass toward the door and Martin saw a tall man in a well-tailored dark suit, with his back to him, talking to Willard and the host.

"In that case," Martin said, taking a last look at the beautiful Mrs. Bowman, "we might as well leave now."

"You'll see her tomorrow," Linda said, as they made their way to the door. "I think Willard arranged a tennis game at their house tomorrow morning."

They pushed unobtrusively toward the door to pick up Willard, who was still talking to their host. Bowman had moved off several steps and was talking to a group nearby.

"We're going?" Willard said, when Linda and Martin came up to him. "Good, it's about time." He reached over and tapped Bowman on the shoulder. "Harry," he said, "I want you to meet my brother-in-law. He's coming over with me tomorrow to play tennis."

Bowman had his back to them, finishing a story, and it was a moment before he turned around, on a burst of laughter that the story had provoked from his listeners. He had a smile on his pale, well-kept face and he put out his hand to Martin. "This is a pleasure," he said, "I've heard so much about you. Your sister tells me all. Is it true, as she says, that you once nearly took a set from Herb Flam?"

"We were both twelve years old at the time," Martin said, keeping his face straight and trying to act naturally, like anybody else leaving a cocktail party and responding in the ordinary way to an ordinary and casual introduction. It wasn't easy, because after ten seconds of looking at the candid, healthy, successful face in front of him, he was sure that Bowman was the man he had seen outside the window the night before.

"Get a good night's sleep," Bowman was saying to Willard. "We'll have a hot doubles." He leaned over and kissed Linda goodbye, familiarly, on the cheek. "You can bring your boys," he said to her. "They can play with our kids. They won't be in the way." He waved and turned back to the people he had been talking to, mannerly, well-dressed, at home, surrounded by friends, the sort of man, pushing a robust forty, you might see at the reunions of a good college or behind a vice-president's desk of one of those polite businesses where everybody has a deep rug on the floor and where money is only mentioned in quiet tones and behind closed doors.

859

Martin walked silently out of the house behind Willard and his sister, not responding when Willard said, "He plays a damn good game, especially doubles. He doesn't like to run too much any more." And he was still silent in the car going over to the dinner party, trying to piece everything together and wanting solitude and reflection for it, remembering Bowman's open and untouched smile as he shook hands, remembering the hard feel of Bowman's dry, tennis-player's hand, remembering the familiar, habitual way Bowman had kissed Linda good night.

"Linda," Willard was saying, at the wheel of the car, as they bumped along the narrow country road toward the dinner party, "you must promise me one thing."

"What's that?" Linda asked.

"You must promise to announce, each time we set out for a cocktail party, 'Willard, you are too old for gin.' "

At the dinner party Martin had to repeat, for the benefit of the guests who had not been at the Slocum's for cocktails, his description of the man he had seen outside the window. This time he made it as vague as possible. It was not easy. Bowman's face and figure (aged nearly forty, blue eyes, sandy hair cut close, wide, smiling mouth, white, even teeth, height nearly six feet, weight probably about one seventy-five, complexion fair, shoulders broad, general impression—good citizen, father of family, responsible businessman) kept crowding in, the statistics, recognizable, damaging, on the tip of his tongue, making it difficult to recall the hazy generalities by which he had described the man until then. But there was no sense, Martin decided, in damning the man so soon and it would only lead to trouble if even a random word of his cast suspicion on Bowman before he made absolutely certain that Bowman was the man he had seen.

On the way home with Linda and Willard, and over a nightcap before going up to bed, he decided not to say anything to them yet, either. Staring at his sister, he remembered how anxious she had been not to call the police, how she had fought Willard about it and won, how she had leaned over to be kissed by Bowman at the door as they were leaving the cocktail party. She and Willard slept in separate rooms, he remembered, both giving on the balcony, and Willard stayed in town late two or three times a week. . . . Martin was ashamed of himself for the speculation, but he couldn't help it. Linda was his sister and he loved her, but how well did he know her, after all these years? He remembered his own sensuality and the regrettable things he had done, himself, because of it. She was his sister, however innocent and wifely and delightful she seemed, and the same blood ran in both of them. No, he thought, wait.

They were on the tennis court at eleven o'clock the next morning, Willard and Martin playing against Bowman and a man called Spencer, who had a big service but nothing much beyond that. Bowman turned out to be agile and crafty and played with a good-humored enjoyment of the game, whether he was winning or losing.

Martin and Willard had brought over the two boys and they played at the edge of the court with the Bowman's three children, two boys and a girl, ranging in age from six to eleven, all three of them rather pale and subdued, too polite and reserved, Martin thought, for children their age.

After the second set, Mrs. Bowman, looking surprisingly formal in a dark cotton dress with a white collar under her heavy bun of rich, dark blond hair, came out of the house with a tray with orangeade in a pitcher and some glasses. She stayed for some time, watching the game, and while she was there Martin made more errors than usual, because he kept glancing over at her, studying her, trying, almost unconsciously, to catch an exchange of looks between her and her husband, a sign, an indication. . . . But she sat there quietly, not saying anything, not applauding the good shots or commenting on the bad ones. She seemed to pay no attention, either, to the five children playing around her, and after a while, she got up, in the middle of a point, and wandered back toward the house, tall, curiously elegant, unattached, a silent and decorative figure on the sweeping green lawn which led up to the big, white, pleasant house.

The wind sprang up during the third set and made lobbing and overheads difficult and they decided to quit. They all shook hands and went over to the side of the court and drank their orangeade. The two Willard boys climbed all over their father, clamoring for a drink, but the Bowman children stood off at a little distance, silently, watching their father, and only coming over when he had poured a glass of the orangeade for each of them and called to them to come and drink it. They said, ''Thank you,'' in hushed voices and retired again to sip their drinks.

''It's too bad you won't be here all summer,'' Bowman said to Martin, as they sat at the edge of the court with their drinks. ''You'd raise the level of the tennis around here considerably. You might even get your poor old brother-in-law up to the net

861

once in a while." He chuckled good-naturedly, winking at Martin and wiping the sweat off his forehead with a towel.

"I have to be in Paris by the end of the week," Martin said, watching Bowman's face for a change of expression, a flicker of relief.

But Bowman merely kept wiping his face with the towel, placidly, smiling. "We'll miss you," he said, "especially on weekends. But, anyway, you're coming to dinner this evening, aren't you?"

"He's set on catching the six o'clock to New York," Willard said.

"Oh, that's silly," said Bowman. "We're having a barbecue in the garden. If it doesn't rain. Stay another night. New York is dead on Sunday, anyway." He sounded friendly, hospitable.

"Well," said Martin, deciding suddenly, "maybe I will."

"That's the boy," Bowman said heartily, as Willard looked at Martin, mildly surprised. "We'll try to make it worth your while. I'll warn the dull country folk they have to put their best foot forward. All right, children," he called. "Ready for lunch."

On the way home, Willard looked over from the wheel. "What made you change your mind, Martin?" he asked. "Mrs. Bowman?"

"She is beautiful, isn't she?" Martin said, going along with his brother-in-law.

"Every one of the local Don Juan's has tried his luck," Willard said, grinning. "Zero."

"Daddy," asked the older boy from the back seat, "what's a Don Juan?"

"He was a man who lived a long time ago," Willard said briskly.


During the afternoon, Martin asked as many questions as he dared about the Bowmans. He found out that they had been married fourteen years, that they were rich (Mrs. Bowman's family owned cotton mills and Bowman himself ran the New York office), that they gave many parties, that they were liked by everybody, that the Willards saw them two or three times a week, that Bowman, unlike some of the other husbands of the community, never seemed the least bit interested in other women.

While he was dressing for the evening, Martin felt himself growing more and more baffled. When he had first seen Bowman at the party the night before, Martin had been sure Bowman was the man who had stared up at him from outside the living-room window, and when he had first seen him that morning on the tennis court the certainty had grown. But the house, the wife, the children, the things that Willard and Linda had said about Bowman, above all, the candid and relaxed manner in which Bowman had greeted him and pressed him to come to dinner, the transparent good humor, with no hint of any shadow beneath it, all conspired to shake Martin. If it really had been Bowman, he must surely have recognized Martin and been almost certain that Martin had recognized him. After all, they had stared at each other, both of them in a strong light, for a full ten seconds, at a distance of five feet. And if it had been Bowman, it would have been so easy for him to have called off the tennis game, to have telephoned and said he had a hangover, or there was too much wind, or with a dozen other excuses.

"Oh, hell," Martin said to himself, knotting his tie in front of the mirror, knowing he had to do something and do it that night, but feeling rushed, isolated, unsure of himself, on the verge of acts which might have grotesque, perhaps tragic consequences. When he went downstairs, Willard was alone in the living room reading the Sunday papers and Martin was tempted to tell him everything and get some of the load of responsibility off his own shoulders. But just as he was about to talk, Linda came in, ready for the party, and he had to keep quiet. He went out to the car with them, still carrying the whole thing himself, wishing he had two weeks more, a month, to observe, to move carefully, to act discreetly and with decision. But he didn't have two weeks. He had one night. For the first time since he had decided to quit his job in California he bitterly regretted that he was going to France.

The party was a big one, with more than twenty people. The night was warm enough and they were all outside on the lawn, which was set with tables and hurricane lamps in which candles burned, throwing a soft, generous light on the guests grouped around them, while two waiters the Bowmans had hired for the occasion hurried back and forth from the big barbecue at the end of the garden at which Bowman, dressed in a chef's apron and pink with the heat of the fire, was broiling steaks.

Martin sat at the same table with Mrs. Bowman, between her and a pretty young woman by the name of Winters who kept flirting with a man at the next table. In the middle of the meal, Martin was surprised to learn that the man Mrs. Winters was flirting with was her own husband. Mrs. Bowman talked to Martin about France, where she had been, as a girl, before the war, and once again, some five years before. It turned out that she was interested in tapestries and told Martin he must go to Bayeux to see the great ones in the cathedral there and to the Museum of Modern Art in Paris, where there were examples of some of the work that contemporary artists had done in the same field. Her voice was soft, gentle, rather flat and uninflected and you felt that even on other, more intimate subjects, she probably would speak in the same melodious, murmuring, impersonal, changeless tone, like a song in a minor key, restricted arbitrarily to one low octave.

"Do you plan to go to France again, soon?" Martin asked.

"No," she said. "I don't travel any more."

She turned to the neighbor on her right and Martin didn't get a chance to ask her why she didn't travel any more, and the sentence stood like that, flat, definite, a statement of policy. For the rest of the meal the conversation was general at the table and Martin joined in it sporadically, his eyes from time to time straying over to the table at which Bowman presided, in his white apron, flushed, speaking a little loudly, busy with the wine bottle, laughing easily at his guests' jokes, never looking in the direction of the table at which his wife sat, next to Martin.

It was nearly midnight and some of the guests had already left when Martin finally got a chance to talk to Bowman alone. Bowman was standing at a table that had been put alongside the wall of the house to serve as a bar and was pouring himself a brandy. He had taken his apron off and after he had poured the brandy he stood there staring down at it, his face pale once more and suddenly fatigued and remote, as though for the moment he had forgotten the party, his role as host, his departing guests. Martin came up to him, ready to use the opening he had been planning for the last half-hour.

"Mr. Bowman," he said.

For a second or two Bowman didn't seem to hear him. Then he shook himself, almost imperceptibly, and raised his head and put on the easy, friendly smile he had been using all evening.

"Harry, boy," Bowman said, "Harry."

"Harry," Martin said dutifully.

"Your glass is empty, boy," Bowman said, reaching for the brandy bottle.

"No, thank you," Martin said. "I've had enough."

"You're right," said Bowman. "Brandy keeps you from sleeping at night."

"I've been thinking," Martin said, "about your problem,"

"Uh . . . what's that?" Bowman squinted at him.

"About your tennis court," Martin said quickly. "I mean about

864

the fact that it's on a rise and as soon as a wind comes up, like today . . ."

"Oh, yes," Bowman said. "It's a nuisance, isn't it? I guess we put it in the wrong place, exposed to the north, but the builder insisted. I don't know, something about drainage. . . ." He waved his hand vaguely, then sipped his brandy.

"You know," Martin said, "I think I could show you how to fix it."

"Oh, you could? Good. Very kind of you." Bowman was speaking a little thickly now. "You must come over some day and we'll . . ."

"Well," Martin said, "I'm leaving tomorrow and . . ."

"Oh, yes, of course." Bowman shook his head as though irritated with himself for his lapse of memory. "France. The city of light. I forgot. Lucky boy. At your age."

"I thought," Martin said, "if you wanted to come with me now, it would only take a minute or two. . . ."

Bowman put his glass down thoughtfully, then peered into Martin's face, blinking a little.

"Of course," he said. "Very good of you."

They started through the garden, among the tables, in the direction of the tennis court, whose fence made a distant, spikey tracery of iron poles and wire against the starlit sky some hundred yards away.

"Martin," Linda called, "where're you two off to? It's time to go home."

"I'll be back in a minute," Martin said.

He and Bowman walked up the gentle slope toward the tennis court, their footsteps silent in the dewy grass.

"I hope it wasn't too boring for you," Bowman said. "The party. I'm afraid there weren't enough young people. There're never enough young people. . . ."

"It wasn't boring at all," Martin said. "It was a wonderful party."

"Was it?" Bowman shrugged. "Well, you have to do something," he said, obscurely.

They were at the tennis court now, and the quarter moon made a shadowy pattern of the base lines. There was no wind and it was very still up there and the sounds of the dying party among the candles a hundred yards away were small but clear in the distance.

"A friend of mine had the same problem," Martin said, watching Bowman closely, "on a court he built outside Santa Barbara and he put up a row of box-hedge along the north side. You don't get a shadow on the court that way. In a couple of years it was about eight feet high, and except for lobs, you could play a normal game, even when the wind was really bad. And you put it back about two feet from the fence, so it doesn't stick through and the balls don't get lost in it. Right about there, I'd say," Martin said, pointing.

"Ah, yes. Good idea," Bowman said. "I'll talk to the gardener this week." He was fiddling with his trouser zipper. "Join me?" he said. "One of the most satisfactory of pleasures. Adding to the dew in the moonlight in this overmechanized age."

Martin waited silently until Bowman had zipped up his trousers again and said, brightly, "There we are," like a child after a small praiseworthy achievement. "Now, I'd better get back to my guests."

Martin put out his hand and held Bowman's arm. "Bowman," he said.

"Huh?" Bowman stopped, sounding surprised.

"What were you doing outside my sister's window Friday night?"

Bowman pulled away a little and turned and faced Martin, his head to one side, looking puzzledly at Martin. "What's that?" He laughed. "Oh, it's a joke. Your sister never told me you were a joker. In fact, I got the impression from her that you were rather a solemn young man. It worried her, she told me once, now I remember. . . ."

"What were you doing outside the window?" Martin repeated.

"Boy, I'm afraid you'd better go home now," Bowman said.

"All right," said Martin. "I'll go home. But I'll tell my sister and Willard it was you, and I'll call the police and I'll tell them."

"You're becoming something of a pest, boy," Bowman said lightly, smiling in the moonlight. "You'll just embarrass everybody. Yourself, most of all. Nobody'll believe you, you know."

"My sister'll believe me. And Willard." Martin started back toward the candlelit garden. "We'll see about the rest." He heard Bowman's steps behind him.

"Wait a minute," Bowman said.

Martin stopped and the two men faced each other in silence.

Then Bowman chuckled drily. "Is that why you decided to stay another night, boy?"

"Yes."

Bowman nodded. "I thought so." He rubbed his face with the back of his hand, making a little dry, unshaven sound. "All right," he said in a flat voice. "Supposing it was me. What do you want?"

"I want to know what you were doing there," Martin said.

"What's the difference?" Bowman said. Now he sounded like

a stubborn and unreasonable child and his voice had taken on a whining, high tone. "Was anything stolen? Was anything broken? Let's put it this way—I was paying a visit."

"With a ladder?" Martin said. "That's a hell of a visit."

"People shouldn't leave ladders lying around." Bowman said wearily. "Why don't you leave me alone? Why don't you go to France and leave me alone?"

"What were you doing there?" Martin persisted.

Bowman waved both his hands, clumsily, in a broken gesture. "I was on my rounds," he said.

"For the last time," Martin said, "I tell you I'm going to go to the police."

Bowman sighed. "All I ever do is watch," he said, whispering. "I never hurt anyone. Why don't you leave me alone, boy?"

"What do you mean, watch?"

Bowman chuckled, almost soundlessly. "I watch the happy ones," he said. Now he sounded coquettish, like a young girl, and Martin, for the first time, began to wonder about the sanity of the man standing beside him on the moonlit dewy grass. "You'd be surprised," Bowman said, as though imparting a secret, "how many happy people there seem to be around here. All ages, all sizes, all religions. . . . They go around with big smiles on their faces, they shake each other's hands, they go to work in the morning and kiss their wives at the station when they come home, they sing at parties, they put money in the collection box at church, they make speeches at the parent-teachers' association meetings about how to bring up the younger generation, they go off together on vacations, they invite their friends in, they make love, they deposit money in the bank and buy insurance, they make deals, they tell each other how successful they are, they buy new houses, they greet their in-laws and baptize their children, they get checked for cancer every twelve months, they all seem to know what they're doing, what they want, where they're going. . . . Like me." He chuckled again, the same rasping chuckle. "The major question is, who're they fooling? Who am I fooling? Look at me." He came close to Martin, his breath, freighted with gin and wine and brandy, hot in Martin's face. "The biggest house in the neighborhood, the prettiest wife. I'm proud to say ten men around here've made passes at her and she's never as much as blinked an eye. Three children who say 'Yes sir, no sir,' and recite their prayers at night, if I die before I wake, and remember Mommy and Daddy. And it's all a show. Don't believe a minute of it. Sometimes I make love to my wife and it doesn't mean anything.

One animal falling on another animal in the jungle. One driven, the other—what shall I say—resigned. No more than that. I get up from her bed and I go to my bed and I'm ashamed of myself, I don't feel like a human being. Can you understand that? I'm drunk, I'm drunk, but if I ever was honest when I was sober, I'd say the same thing. And what does it mean to my wife? She's more interested in whether she's going to buy green curtains next year for the dining room than whether I live or die. I have the feeling when I go to work in the morning, she has to stop and think hard three times a day to remember my name. And my children—they're a separate state, behind frontiers, waiting for the appropriate time to declare war. Surprise—drop the bomb and kill Daddy. It's normal. Read the papers. Children kill their fathers every day. To say nothing of abandoning them and letting them die. Look at the populations of the old peoples' homes. The incurable wards. I sit in an office all day, I hire people and fire them, I make important, businesslike gestures, and right behind me all the time, what is there—a blank, a big blank.''

Martin stepped back a little, feeling smothered by the alcoholic breath, by the sudden, racing spill-over of language from this man who until that moment had sounded more or less like everyone else Martin had met during the weekend. "Still," he said, wondering if Bowman was cunningly sidetracking him with this incoherent, rambling, pitiable confession, "what's that got to do with climbing balconies and looking in at windows?''

"I'm looking for an answer." Bowman grinned slyly. "I'm an explorer, looking for an oasis in the middle of the great American desert. I'm an optimist. I believe there's an answer. I believe that some people aren't fooling. They seem happy and they *are* happy. Only you have to catch them by surprise, boy, when they don't know you're watching them, to find out the secret. Anybody puts a smile on his face when he knows you're watching him, like getting your picture taken in front of a monument on vacation. The beast in his natural habitat. Preferably at a significant moment, as the photographers say, when the secret is laid bare. Sitting having a cup of coffee late at night in the kitchen talking over what his life is like with his wife. Is there love on his face, hate, boredom? Is he thinking of going off to Florida with another woman? Helping his ten-year-old son with his homework. What does his face reveal? Does he have any hope? Making love. Do they show the tenderness of human beings, do they touch each other with benevolence and gratitude, or is it one animal falling on another animal, like my wife and myself?''

"You mean to say," Martin asked incredulously, "that you try to watch at times like that?"

"Of course," Bowman said calmly.

"You're crazy," Martin said.

"Well, if you're going to talk like that . . ." Bowman shrugged, sounding aggrieved and misunderstood. "There's no sense in trying to explain to you. What's crazier—living the way I do, year after year, not feeling anything, thinking, Somebody has the secret, it's there, I just have to find out, and doing something about it. Or just giving up, surrendering. . . . What is it? Is the whole thing a blank? For everybody? Do you know? Maybe you ought to watch outside a couple of windows yourself sometime," Bowman said contemptuously. "With that honest, eager California face of yours. Stay here—I'll take you around with me. *You*'ll get the inside dope on some of the people right there now—" He gestured toward the candlelit garden. "That pretty one who was on your right during dinner. Mrs. Winters. The one that's hanging all over her husband all the time and laughing at his jokes as though he made a million dollars a year on television and holding his hands at parties as though they're going to be married three days later. I've been there, I've been there. . . . You know what they do when they get home at night?"

"I don't want to hear," Martin said. He had liked Mrs. Winters.

"That's all right," Bowman said mockingly. "It won't offend your ristine sense of modesty. They never say a word. She goes upstairs and takes a handful of pills and greases her face and puts a mask over her face to sleep and he sits downstairs by himself, with one light on, drinking whiskey straight. And after he's knocked off half a bottle he lies down on the couch with his shoes on and sleeps. I've been there four times and it's been the same each time. Pills, whiskey, silence. The public lovebirds. God, it makes me laugh. And the others . . . even when they're alone. You don't know our minister, do you, the Right Reverend Fenwick?"

"No," Martin said.

"No, of course not. We played tennis today instead of worshipping." Bowman chuckled. "I made a call on the man of God a few Sundays ago. His bedroom is on the ground floor. He's a marvelous-looking gray-haired gentleman. If you were casting somebody to play the Pope in a movie, he'd get the job in five minutes. Always with a soft humble smile on his face, and divine forgiveness radiating out from him all over the state of Connecticut. And what do you think he was doing when I looked in on him? He was standing in front of a full-length mirror with only his shorts on, pulling his gut in, looking at himself critically and approvingly in profile. You'd've been surprised what good condition he's in, he must do fifty pushups a day. Standing there, pushing his hair forward in little dabs, like a woman making up, to get that effect of other-worldly carelessness he's famous for. He always looks as though he's too busy communicating with God to pay attention to mundane things like combing his hair. And he was making faces at himself and raising his hands in holy benediction, practicing for next Sunday's performance, just about naked in his shorts, with legs like an old fullback. The old faker. I don't know what I hoped for. Maybe to find him on his knees, praying, in communion with God, with some secret happiness showing on his face that never is quite there in church. For the joys of the flesh,'' Bowman said, switching abruptly, speaking in a confidential whisper, leaning toward Martin in the darkness, ''I tried our African cousins. . . .''

''What're you talking about?'' Martin asked, puzzled.

''Our colored population,'' Bowman said. ''Closer to the primeval push. Simpler, I thought, less inhibited. The Slocums have a colored couple. You saw them passing drinks last night. About thirty-five years old, both of them. The man's huge, he looks as though he could move walls with his bare hands. And the woman's beautiful. Oversized, black, with great big breasts and a fantastic behind. I've sat behind them in the movies and when they laugh it's like cannon going off in a twenty-one-gun salute. You'd think that if you saw them in bed together you'd shrivel with shame at your own white, niggling, sin-haunted, worn-out, puritanical gropings. Well, I saw them once. They have a room back of the kitchen at the Slocums and you can get up real close. I saw them, and they were in bed together all right, only all they were doing was reading. And do you know what she was reading?'' Bowman laughed breathlessly. ''She was reading *The Second Sex*. That's that French book about how badly women have been treated since the Pleistocene Age. And he was reading the Bible. The first page. Genesis. In the beginning, there was the Word.'' Bowman laughed again, sounding delighted with his story. ''I went back a couple of times, but they had the curtains drawn, so I don't know what they're reading these days. . . .''

''Harry! Harry!'' It was Mrs. Bowman's voice, calling. She was standing, a white blur in the moonlight, about thirty yards from them. ''What're you doing out there? People're going home.''

''Yes, dear,'' Bowman called. ''We're coming right away. I'm just coming to the tag line of a joke with young Martin, here. I'll be right along.''

"Well, hurry. It's late." Mrs. Bowman turned and walked through the moonlight back toward the house. Bowman watched his wife silently, his eyes brooding and puzzled.

"What did you want from my sister and Willard?" Martin asked, shaken by everything he had heard, no more certain now about what he should do than when he had arrived that evening.

"They were my last hope," Bowman said in a low voice. "We'd better get back to the party." He started across the lawn, Martin walking at his side.

"If ever two people seemed"—Bowman hesitated—"*connected*—dear to each other, *pleasurable* to each other . . . I've come home on the same train with Willard in the evening and the wives're waiting, and your sister always seems to be a little apart, preparing herself, almost, and something happens to her face when she sees him. . . . They're not all over each other, of course, like the Winterses, but once in a while they touch each other with their fingertips. And with their boys . . . They know something, they've found something, that I don't know and I haven't found. When I see them, I have the feeling that I'm on the verge. It's almost there, I almost have it. That's why you nearly caught me the other night. God, I've been doing this for years and nobody's ever come close. I'm careful as a cat. But that night, watching all three of you in the living room, late at night, I forgot where I was. When you came to the window, I . . . I wanted to smile, to say . . . to say, yes, good for you . . . Ah, maybe I'm wrong about them, too."

"No," Martin said, thoughtfully, "you're not wrong."

They were close to the candlelit tables by now and somebody had turned on the radio inside the house and from a loudspeaker on the terrace music was playing and several couples were dancing. Willard and Linda were dancing together, lightly, not close to each other, barely holding each other. Martin stopped and put his hand on Bowman's arm to halt him. Bowman was trembling and Martin could feel the little shudders, as though the man were freezing, through the cloth of his sleeve.

"Listen," Martin said, watching his sister and her husband dance, "I ought to tell them. And I ought to tell the police. Even if nobody could prove anything, you know what that would mean to you around here, don't you?"

"Yes," Bowman said, his eyes on the Willards, longing, baffled, despairing. "Ah, do whatever you want," he said flatly. "It doesn't make any difference to me."

"I'm not going to say anything now," Martin said, sounding

harsher than he felt, trying, for Bowman's sake, to keep the pity out of his voice. "But my sister writes me every week. If I hear that anybody has seen a man outside a window—once—just once . . ."

Bowman shrugged, still watching the dancers. "You won't hear anything," he said. "I'll stay home at night. I'm never going to learn anything. Why'm I kidding myself?"

He walked away from Martin, robust and demented, a spy lost in a dark country, his pocket crammed with confused intelligence, impossible to decipher. He walked slowly among the dancers, and a moment later, Martin heard his laughter, loud, genial, from the table that was being used as a bar and around which three or four of the guests were standing, including Mr. and Mrs. Winters, who had their arms around each other's waists.

Martin turned from the group at the bar and looked at his sister and her husband, dancing together on the flagstone terrace to the soft, late-at-night music, that sounded faraway and uninsistent in the open garden. Looking at them with new understanding, he had the feeling that Willard did not feel the need of leading, or Linda of following, that they moved gently and irresistibly together, mysteriously enclosed, beyond danger.

Poor Harry, he thought. But even so, he thought, starting over to Linda to tell her he was ready to go home, even so, tomorrow I'm buying them a dog.

# ᴛHE LAUREL DRAMA SERIES

☐ **FAMOUS AMERICAN PLAYS OF THE 1920s**
Selected and introduced by Kenneth MacGowan.
Six plays including *The Moon of the Caribbees*, Eugene O'Neill; *Porgy*,
DuBose and Dorothy Heyward; and *Street Scene*, Elmer Rice.
$2.50 (32466-1)

☐ **FAMOUS AMERICAN PLAYS OF THE 1930s**
Selected and introduced by Harold Clurman.
Five plays including *Of Mice and Men*, John Steinbeck; and *The Time of
Your Life*, William Saroyan. $3.95 (32478-5)

☐ **FAMOUS AMERICAN PLAYS OF THE 1940s**
Selected and introduced by Henry Hewes.
Five plays including *The Skin of Our Teeth*, Thornton Wilder; *All My Sons*,
Arthur Miller; and *The Member of the Wedding*, Carson McCullers.
$2.95 (32490-4)

☐ **FAMOUS AMERICAN PLAYS OF THE 1950s**
Selected and introduced by Lee Strasberg.
Five plays including *The Autumn Garden*, Lillian Hellman; *Camino Real*,
Tennessee Williams; *Tea and Sympathy*, Robert Anderson; and *The Zoo
Story*, Edward Albee. $3.50 (32491-2)

☐ **FAMOUS AMERICAN PLAYS OF THE 1960s**
Selected and introduced by Harold Clurman.
Five plays including *We Bombed in New Haven*, Joseph Heller, and *The
Boys in the Band*, Mart Crowley. $2.75 (32609-5)

☐ **FAMOUS AMERICAN PLAYS OF THE 1970s**
Selected and introduced by Ted Hoffman.
Six plays including *The Basic Training of Pavlo Hummel*, David Rabe; *Same
Time, New Year*, Bernard Slade; and *Buried Child*, Sam Shepard.
$3.50 (32537-4)

---

At your local bookstore or use this handy coupon for ordering:

**Dell** | **DELL BOOKS**
P.O. BOX 1000, PINE BROOK, N.J. 07058-1000

Please send me the books I have checked above. I am enclosing $ _____ (please add 75c per copy to
cover postage and handling). Send check or money order—no cash or C.O.D.'s. Please allow up to 8 weeks for
shipment.

Name _____

Address _____

City _____ State/Zip _____

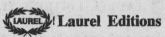

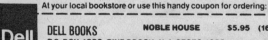

# American Heritage Dictionary

The Dell paperback edition of THE AMERICAN HERITAGE DICTIONARY is exciting, inviting, and easy to read and use. It combines modern usage, American tradition, and a healthy insistence on accuracy and scholarship. Its many features include:

- Pronunciation Key
- Examples of Word Usage
- Capsule Biographies
- Scientific Terms
- Illustrations
- Word Derivations
- Geographic Facts
- Literary Quotations
- Current Usage Indicators
- Maps and Geographic Facts

**THE ONLY TRULY 20TH CENTURY DICTIONARY!**
A DELL BOOK $3.95(10207-3)